SONOVAWITCH!

and other tales of
Supernatural Law

Batton Lash

SAN DIEGO, CALIFORNIA

Acknowledgments

"The Death and Times of 'Dr. Life,'" "Nosferatu: Special Report," and "A Case for Ygor" originally appeared in *Wolff & Byrd, Counselors of the Macabre* issue 17; "Sonovawitch" originally appeared in *Wolff & Byrd, Counselors of the Macabre* issues 18–20; "Mavis, World's Greatest Secretary" originally appeared in *Mavis* issue 1; "Gormagon" originally appeared in *Wolff & Byrd, Counselors of the Macabre* issue 21; "The Human Within Me" originally appeared in *Wolff & Byrd, Counselors of the Macabre* issue 22. All art is by Batton Lash with the exceptions of pages 125–129 by Derek Ozawa and pages 131–135 by Melissa Uran. Nghia Lam assisted with the art on "The Death and Times of 'Dr. Life.'" All lettering is by Jackie Estrada and Batton Lash with the exception of "The Death and Times of 'Dr. Life,'" lettered by Steve Smith.

Dedicated to all those individuals who served as models for the characters in this collection, including: Jim P., Sandy H., Samantha S., Tom F., Cheryl H., the real-life Goth Girls (Betsy, Erica, and Lori), Derek O., Melissa U., Charles B., Denis C., and Gary H.

Writer/artist: Batton Lash
Editor: Jackie Estrada
Technical consultant: Mitch Berger, Esq.
Art assists: Derek Ozawa, Melissa Uran
Cover colors: Michael McAuliffe
Staff 'n stuff: S. Derma

First printing, August 2000.

Printed in the United States of America

ISBN #0-9633954-6-7

Contents

Introduction

Several Introductory Remarks

The funniest legal fictions ever created[1] are A. P Herbert's *Misleading Cases*. I found the two volumes of fictitious suits and torts[2] as a small boy and, reading Herbert's strange court cases, which established, amongst other things, whether or not slugs were wild animals and whether the law of the road or the law of the sea applied on a flooded road, I felt a mighty yearning to become a barrister[3], to wear a wig and gown[4], to address a fusty and doddering Judge as "Me lud." I felt the lure of the law. I knew, instinctively, that of all the fictions mankind has come up with, the law was the funniest, the strangest, and the weirdest.

So, aged about 14, I volunteered for paralegal work, and a local legal body, more fool they, took me up on it. It only took a couple of days of gathering papers (on, if memory serves, and I'm sure it does, the SOLAS Convention[5]) for me to decide that if, as Mr Bumble had suggested, the law was an ass[6], the primary function of that ass was not that of entertaining 14-year-old boys. It was not, I reluctantly admitted to myself as I threw in the towel, funny. And that was the end of my infatuation with The Law.

Or it was for many years, at any rate. As I grew older, I learned to think of the law as a wearisome expensive thing, a sour-faced, mean-spirited crap shoot of a game. With one shining exception, a volume of which you are holding in your hand.

Opening Argument

Batton Lash's delicious Wolff and Byrd tales—*Supernatural Law*—are the second funniest legal fictions ever created. On the other hand they are the finest funny supernatural fictions ever created, and (as you will see as the tales in this book unfold) one of the best legal soap operas out there.

Mr Lash's[7] primary genius is in creating people one cares about and making the humour comes second to the people. His secondary genius is in larding his confections with rare delights, gags and moments you'll only notice on the second or third reading. There are puns aplenty, in-jokes (it doesn't matter if you don't know who the Friends of Lulu[8] are, though, nor need you have heard of Northampton cartoonist Jill deRais and her deconstructive strip cartoon *Maxwell the Magic Cat.*[9] It's still funny—it's pretty much always funny). There are artistic tributes galore here, moments to take pleasure in (the first few Ditkoesque[10] pages of the Mavis chapter are a particular delight) but again, they all come in second. The most important thing is the story and the people (and monsters) who people (and monster) it.

---

[1] After the thing about corporations really being people who never die.
[2] Nothing to do with clothing or cakes.
[3] An English lawyer who can plead in court. Although these days solicitors can plead in courts too.
[4] It's an English thing, like flagellation and rhubarb crumble.
[5] It's short for Safety of Lives At Sea. See? You're actually learning things from these footnotes.
[6] A donkey. Mr Bumble was not swearing, although nobody would have blamed him if he had.
[7] When I'm chatting to him I call him Bat.
[8] It's an organization to help promote the standing and work of women in the field of comics.
[9] Nope. You're on your own. These aren't really helpful footnotes. These are the other kind.
[10] *In re: Ditko v. The Hoary Hosts of Hoggoth.* 722 MBRE. Misc. 2D139.

Summing Up: Some Frequently Asked Questions

I am a lawyer. Will I find Sonovawitch! *funny?*
Many lawyers have quite finely developed senses of humor, at least until it comes to the matter of their fees.

I am a monster. Will I find Sonovawitch! *funny?*
While many monsters do find it difficult to laugh at themselves, they can, along with the rest of the human race, and many lawyers, find enormous and hearty amusement in the suffering of others.

I am a general reader of books who knows nothing of comics and frankly I find the whole thing pretty suspicious. Will I find Sonovawitch! *funny?*
You read comics left to right, from up to down. Other than that, you're on your own.

And yes, it's funny.

Neil Gaiman
June 2000

SONOVAWITCH!

and other tales of
Supernatural Law

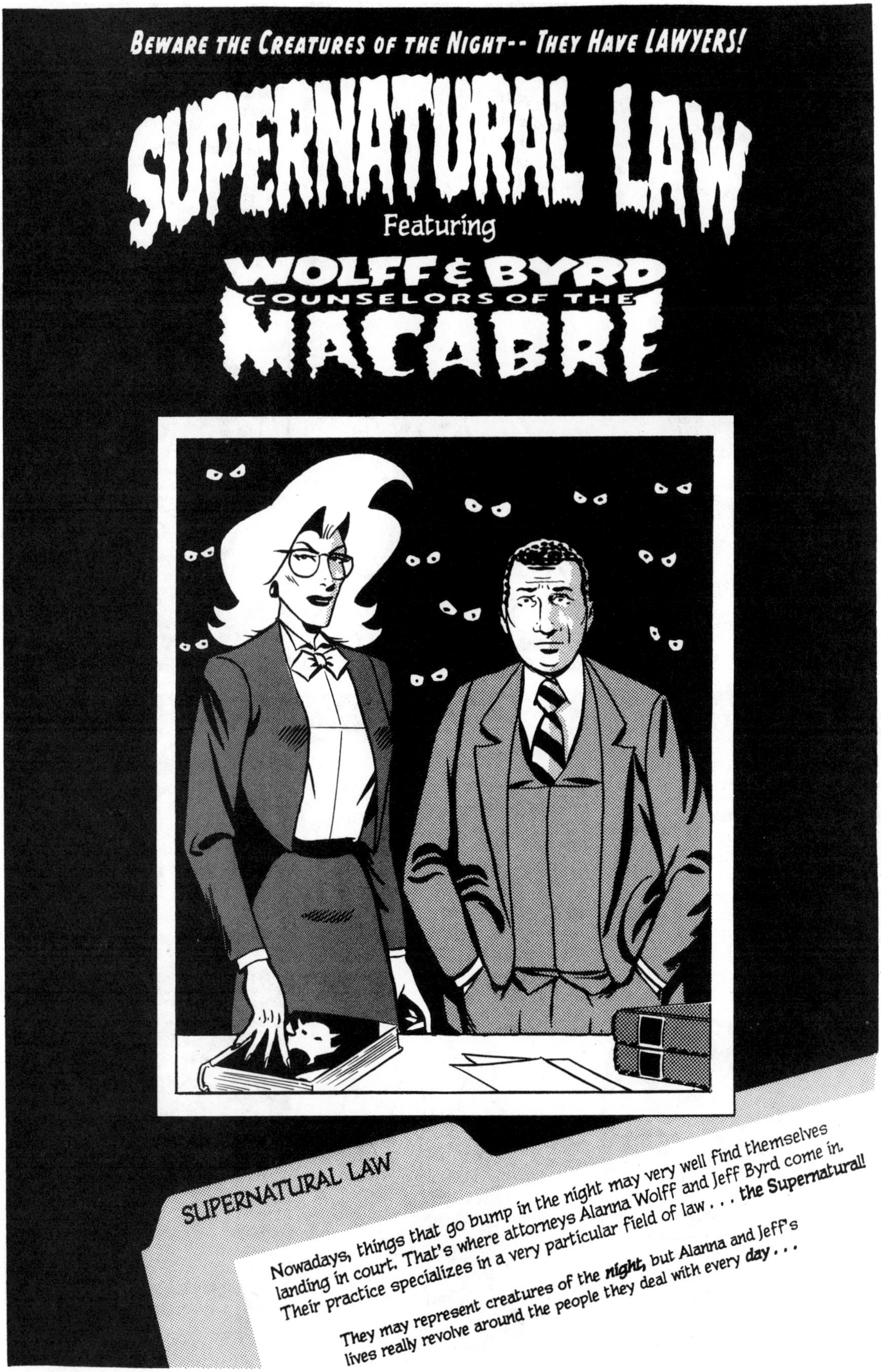
Beware the Creatures of the Night-- They Have LAWYERS!
SUPERNATURAL LAW
Featuring
WOLFF & BYRD
COUNSELORS OF THE
MACABRE
SUPERNATURAL LAW
Nowadays, things that go bump in the night may very well find themselves landing in court. That's where attorneys Alanna Wolff and Jeff Byrd come in. Their practice specializes in a very particular field of law . . . the Supernatural!
They may represent creatures of the night, but Alanna and Jeff's lives really revolve around the people they deal with every day . . .

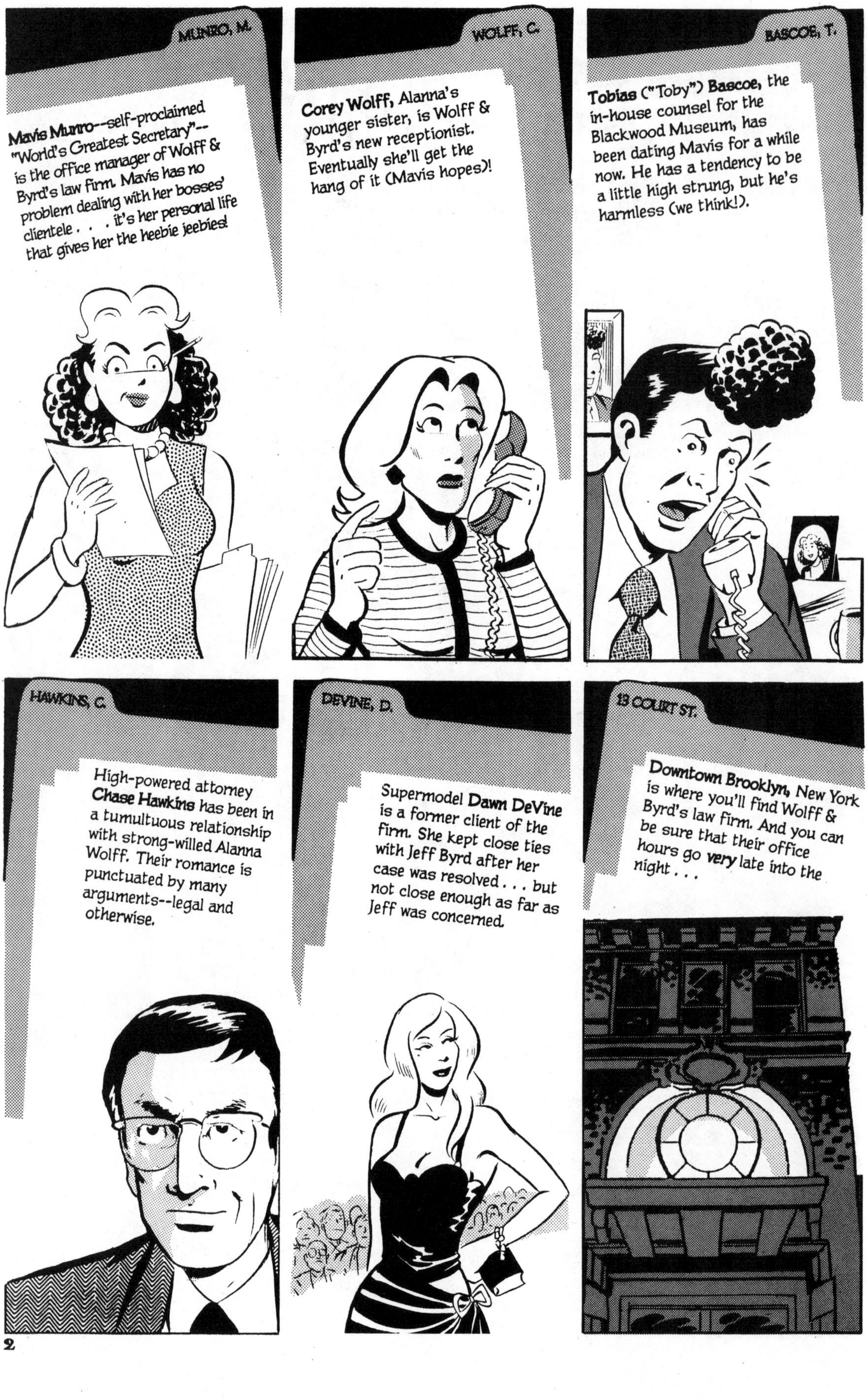
MUNRO, M.
Mavis Munro--self-proclaimed "World's Greatest Secretary"--is the office manager of Wolff & Byrd's law firm. Mavis has no problem dealing with her bosses' clientele . . . it's her personal life that gives her the heebie jeebies!
WOLFF, C.
Corey Wolff, Alanna's younger sister, is Wolff & Byrd's new receptionist. Eventually she'll get the hang of it (Mavis hopes)!
BASCOE, T.
Tobias ("Toby") Bascoe, the in-house counsel for the Blackwood Museum, has been dating Mavis for a while now. He has a tendency to be a little high strung, but he's harmless (we think!).
HAWKINS, C.
High-powered attorney Chase Hawkins has been in a tumultuous relationship with strong-willed Alanna Wolff. Their romance is punctuated by many arguments--legal and otherwise.
DEVINE, D.
Supermodel Dawn DeVine is a former client of the firm. She kept close ties with Jeff Byrd after her case was resolved . . . but not close enough as far as Jeff was concerned.
13 COURT ST.
Downtown Brooklyn, New York is where you'll find Wolff & Byrd's law firm. And you can be sure that their office hours go very late into the night . . .

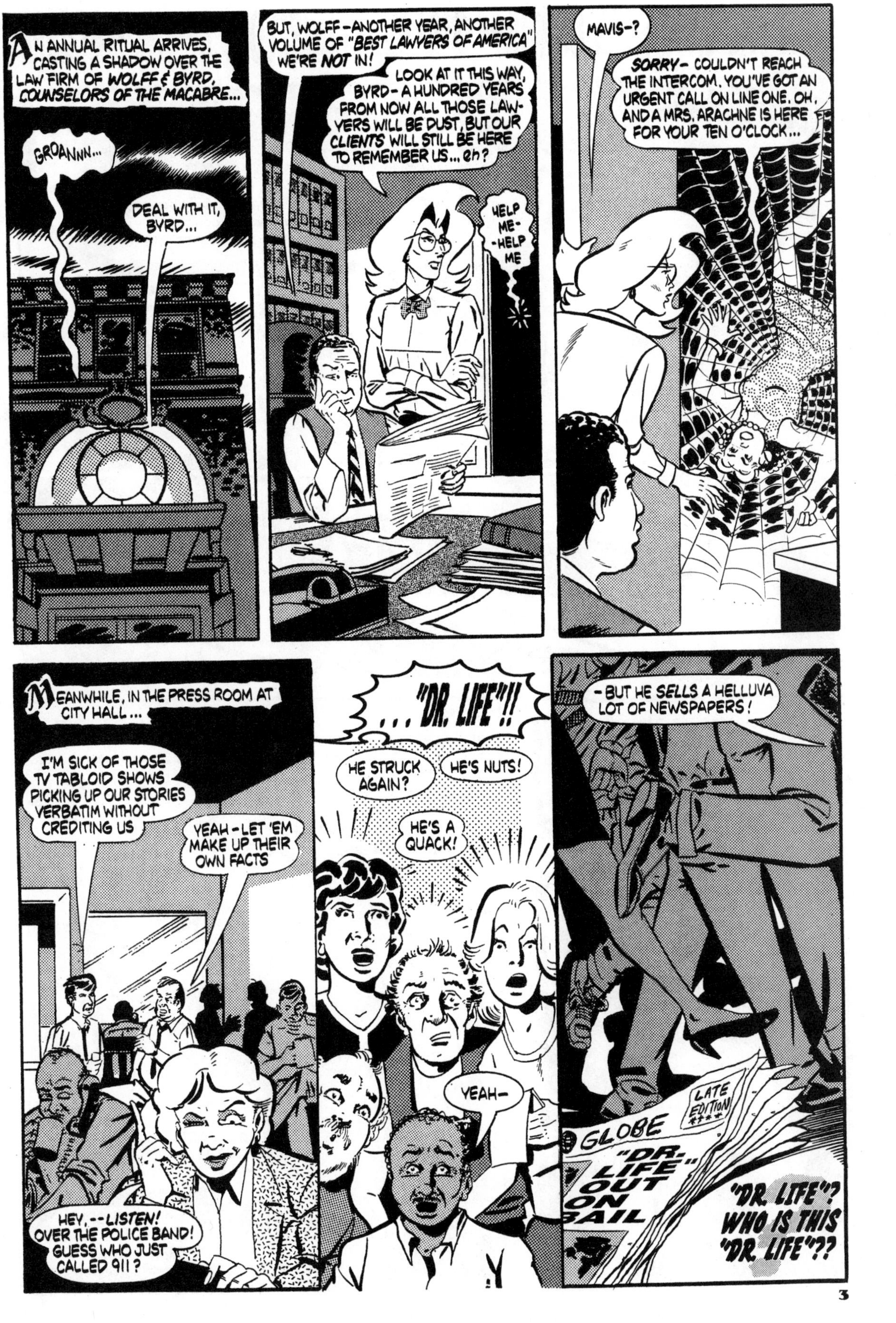
AN ANNUAL RITUAL ARRIVES, CASTING A SHADOW OVER THE LAW FIRM OF WOLFF & BYRD, COUNSELORS OF THE MACABRE...
GROANNN...
DEAL WITH IT, BYRD...
BUT, WOLFF - ANOTHER YEAR, ANOTHER VOLUME OF "BEST LAWYERS OF AMERICA" WE'RE NOT IN!
LOOK AT IT THIS WAY, BYRD - A HUNDRED YEARS FROM NOW ALL THOSE LAWYERS WILL BE DUST, BUT OUR CLIENTS WILL STILL BE HERE TO REMEMBER US... eh?
HELP ME- -HELP ME
MAVIS-?
SORRY - COULDN'T REACH THE INTERCOM. YOU'VE GOT AN URGENT CALL ON LINE ONE. OH, AND A MRS. ARACHNE IS HERE FOR YOUR TEN O'CLOCK...
MEANWHILE, IN THE PRESS ROOM AT CITY HALL...
I'M SICK OF THOSE TV TABLOID SHOWS PICKING UP OUR STORIES VERBATIM WITHOUT CREDITING US
YEAH - LET 'EM MAKE UP THEIR OWN FACTS
HEY, --LISTEN! OVER THE POLICE BAND! GUESS WHO JUST CALLED 911?
..."DR. LIFE"!!
HE STRUCK AGAIN?
HE'S NUTS!
HE'S A QUACK!
YEAH-
- BUT HE SELLS A HELLUVA LOT OF NEWSPAPERS!
GLOBE
LATE EDITION
"DR. LIFE" OUT ON BAIL
"DR. LIFE"? WHO IS THIS "DR. LIFE"??

FROM THE CASE FILES OF WOLFF & BYRD, COUNSELORS OF THE MACABRE

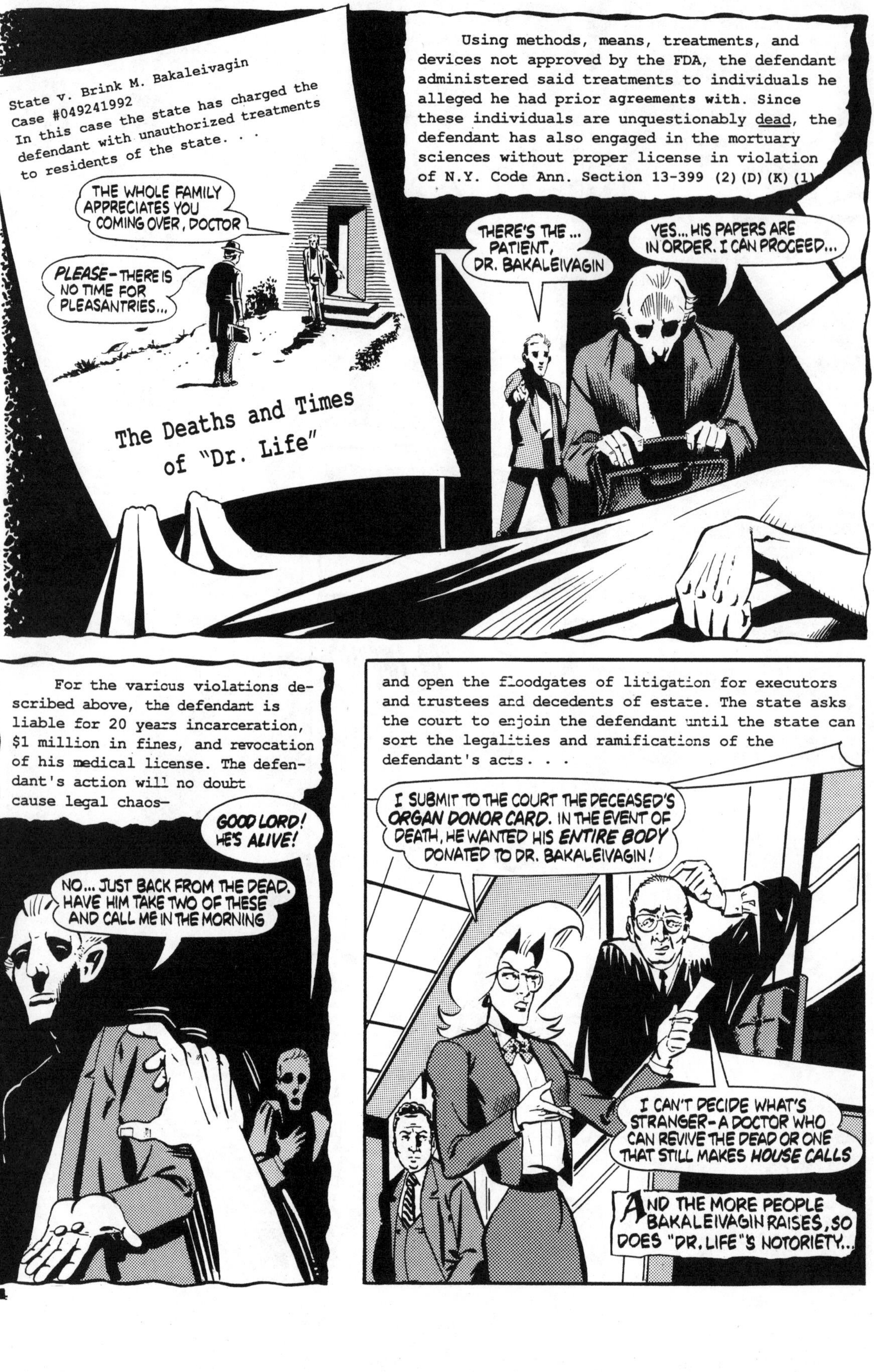

State v. Brink M. Bakaleivagin
Case #049241992
In this case the state has charged the defendant with unauthorized treatments to residents of the state. . .
THE WHOLE FAMILY APPRECIATES YOU COMING OVER, DOCTOR
PLEASE- THERE IS NO TIME FOR PLEASANTRIES...
The Deaths and Times of "Dr. Life"
Using methods, means, treatments, and devices not approved by the FDA, the defendant administered said treatments to individuals he alleged he had prior agreements with. Since these individuals are unquestionably dead, the defendant has also engaged in the mortuary sciences without proper license in violation of N.Y. Code Ann. Section 13-399 (2)(D)(K)(1)
THERE'S THE ... PATIENT, DR. BAKALEIVAGIN
YES... HIS PAPERS ARE IN ORDER. I CAN PROCEED...
For the various violations described above, the defendant is liable for 20 years incarceration, $1 million in fines, and revocation of his medical license. The defendant's action will no doubt cause legal chaos-
GOOD LORD! HE'S ALIVE!
NO... JUST BACK FROM THE DEAD. HAVE HIM TAKE TWO OF THESE AND CALL ME IN THE MORNING
and open the floodgates of litigation for executors and trustees and decedents of estate. The state asks the court to enjoin the defendant until the state can sort the legalities and ramifications of the defendant's acts . . .
I SUBMIT TO THE COURT THE DECEASED'S ORGAN DONOR CARD. IN THE EVENT OF DEATH, HE WANTED HIS ENTIRE BODY DONATED TO DR. BAKALEIVAGIN!
I CAN'T DECIDE WHAT'S STRANGER- A DOCTOR WHO CAN REVIVE THE DEAD OR ONE THAT STILL MAKES HOUSE CALLS
AND THE MORE PEOPLE BAKALEIVAGIN RAISES, SO DOES "DR. LIFE"'S NOTORIETY...

MALPRACTICE

Dr. Bakaleivagin's Afterlife Styles

"Dr. Life" plans to carry on despite the law having him dead to rights

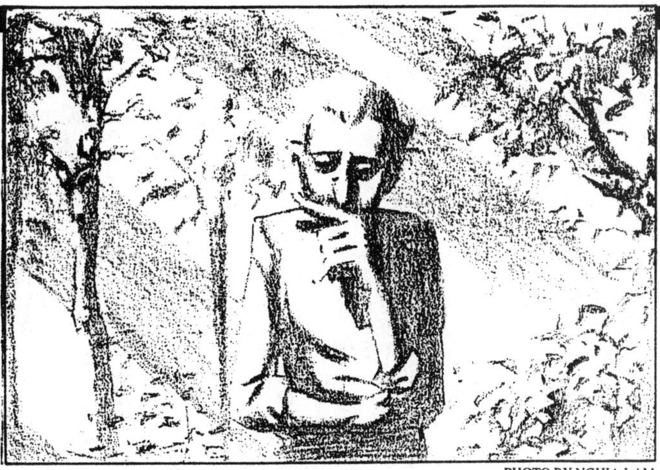

PHOTO BY NGHIA LAM

There are only two givens in life, death and taxes, right? That may have been the case up until a few months ago. But last week, while millions were filing their tax returns, Dr. Brink M. Bakaleivagin was proving that death is not that final, as he returned his eighth recently deceased patient to life. The gaunt, terse Bakaleivagin, 40, spoke with *New Urbane*, and although he declined to talk about specific cases, he described what some would call his "graveside" manner.

NEW URBANE: **How do you respond to your critics that what you do is unnatural?**

BAKALEIVAGIN: I consider it a matter of supply and demand. The people I deal with made a choice. And if I'm in the position of offering them an alternative to death, so be it.

NEW URBANE: **Can you discuss your process of reviving the dead?**

BAKALEIVAGIN: I've studied ancient rituals and applied them with contemporary science. This isn't voodoo. My revivifying process is a remedy. Yes, voodoo offers a return, but that usually requires recipients to submit their will to the person who brings them back. I am not interested in turning people into zombies. I'm more concerned with my patients getting past the death thing and getting on with their lives.

NEW URBANE: **In other words, been there, done that?**

BAKALEIVAGIN: Exactly. In fact, I'd rather not think of people being dead. They're suspended in a euphoric state of fugue.

NEW URBANE: **What about your detractors, who are trying to block you in court?**

BAKALEIVAGIN: They're wimps. They're idiots. Let them do their worst. That's what I've hired my lawyers for. . . .

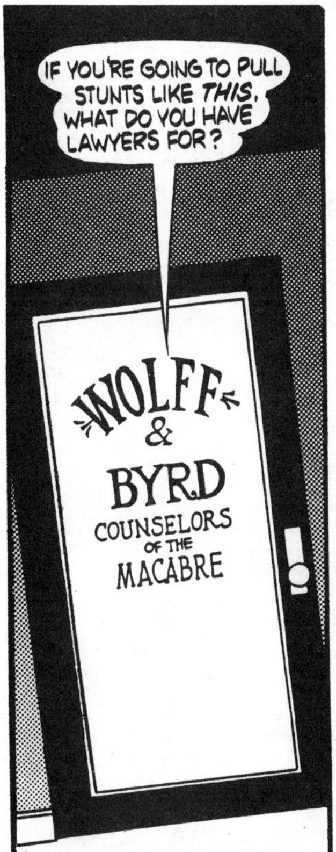
IF YOU'RE GOING TO PULL STUNTS LIKE THIS, WHAT DO YOU HAVE LAWYERS FOR?
WOLFF & BYRD COUNSELORS OF THE MACABRE

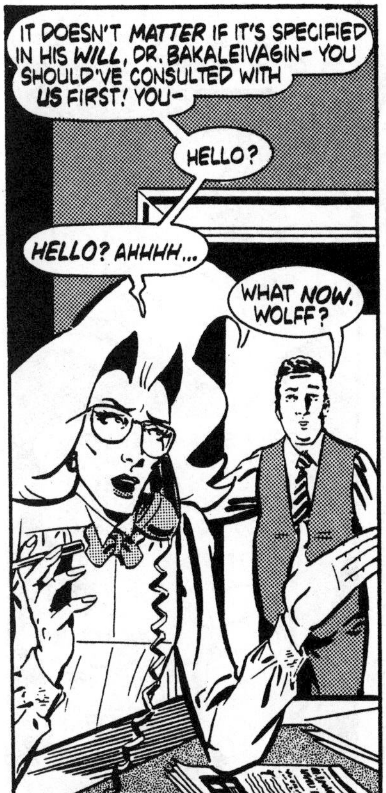
IT DOESN'T MATTER IF IT'S SPECIFIED IN HIS WILL, DR. BAKALEIVAGIN- YOU SHOULD'VE CONSULTED WITH US FIRST! YOU-
HELLO?
HELLO? AHHHH...
WHAT NOW, WOLFF?

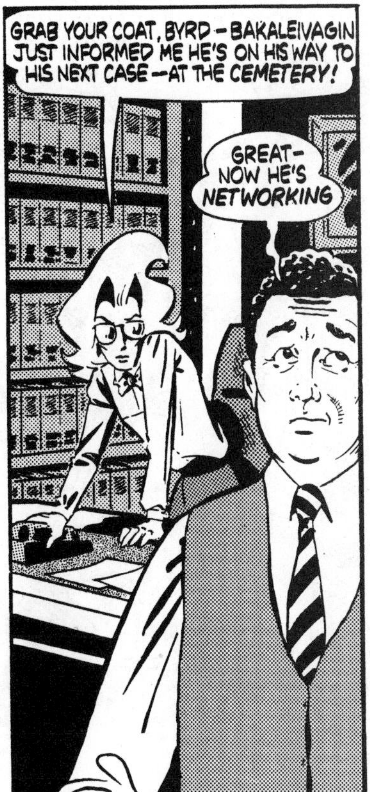
GRAB YOUR COAT, BYRD - BAKALEIVAGIN JUST INFORMED ME HE'S ON HIS WAY TO HIS NEXT CASE -AT THE CEMETERY!
GREAT- NOW HE'S NETWORKING

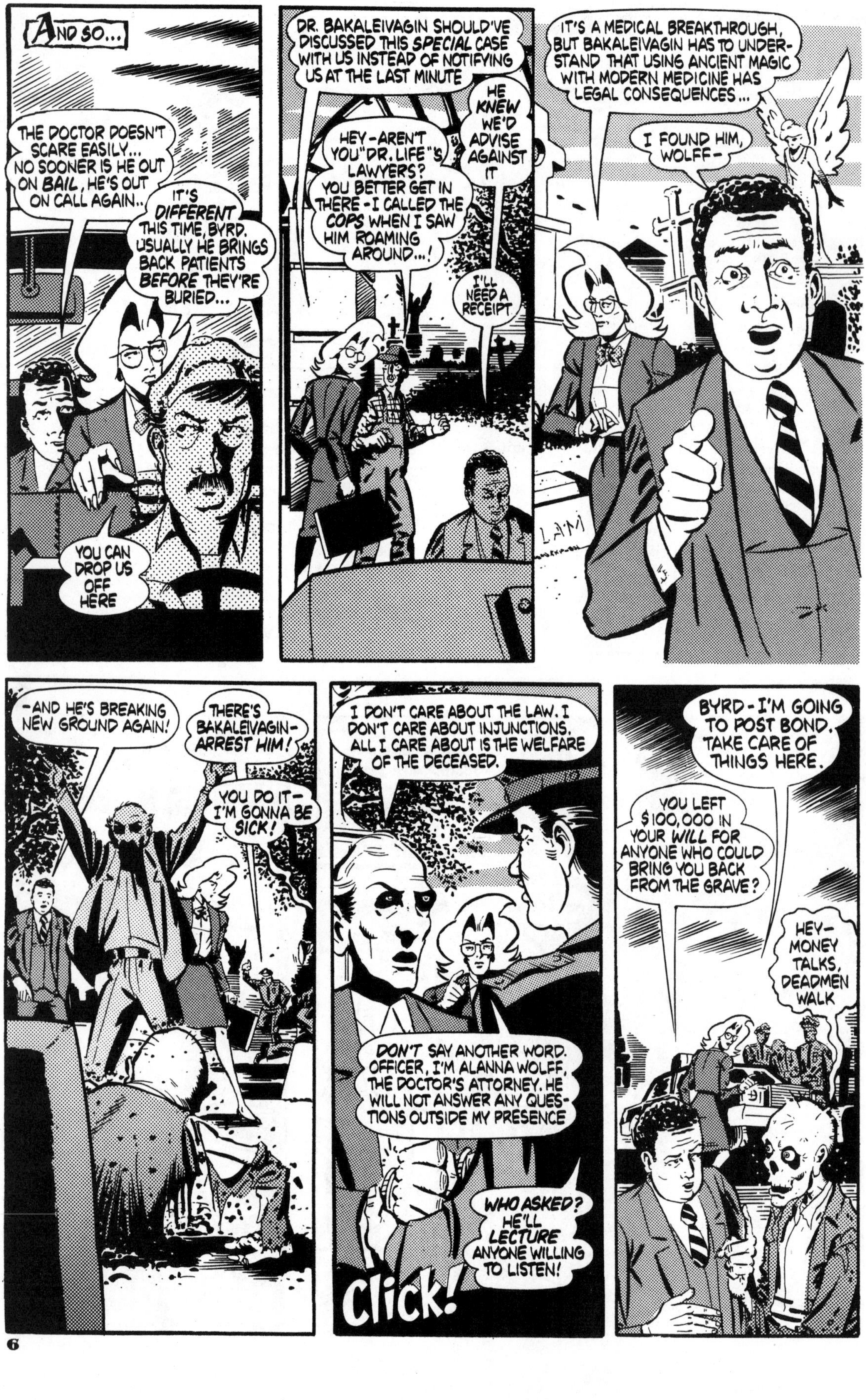
AND SO...
THE DOCTOR DOESN'T SCARE EASILY... NO SOONER IS HE OUT ON BAIL, HE'S OUT ON CALL AGAIN...
IT'S DIFFERENT THIS TIME, BYRD. USUALLY HE BRINGS BACK PATIENTS BEFORE THEY'RE BURIED...
YOU CAN DROP US OFF HERE
DR. BAKALEIVAGIN SHOULD'VE DISCUSSED THIS SPECIAL CASE WITH US INSTEAD OF NOTIFYING US AT THE LAST MINUTE
HE KNEW WE'D ADVISE AGAINST IT
HEY-AREN'T YOU "DR. LIFE"'S LAWYERS? YOU BETTER GET IN THERE - I CALLED THE COPS WHEN I SAW HIM ROAMING AROUND...!
I'LL NEED A RECEIPT.
IT'S A MEDICAL BREAKTHROUGH, BUT BAKALEIVAGIN HAS TO UNDERSTAND THAT USING ANCIENT MAGIC WITH MODERN MEDICINE HAS LEGAL CONSEQUENCES...
I FOUND HIM, WOLFF-
LAM
-AND HE'S BREAKING NEW GROUND AGAIN!
THERE'S BAKALEIVAGIN-ARREST HIM!
YOU DO IT-I'M GONNA BE SICK!
I DON'T CARE ABOUT THE LAW. I DON'T CARE ABOUT INJUNCTIONS. ALL I CARE ABOUT IS THE WELFARE OF THE DECEASED.
DON'T SAY ANOTHER WORD. OFFICER, I'M ALANNA WOLFF, THE DOCTOR'S ATTORNEY. HE WILL NOT ANSWER ANY QUESTIONS OUTSIDE MY PRESENCE
WHO ASKED? HE'LL LECTURE ANYONE WILLING TO LISTEN!
CLICK!
BYRD - I'M GOING TO POST BOND. TAKE CARE OF THINGS HERE.
YOU LEFT $100,000 IN YOUR WILL FOR ANYONE WHO COULD BRING YOU BACK FROM THE GRAVE?
HEY-MONEY TALKS, DEADMEN WALK

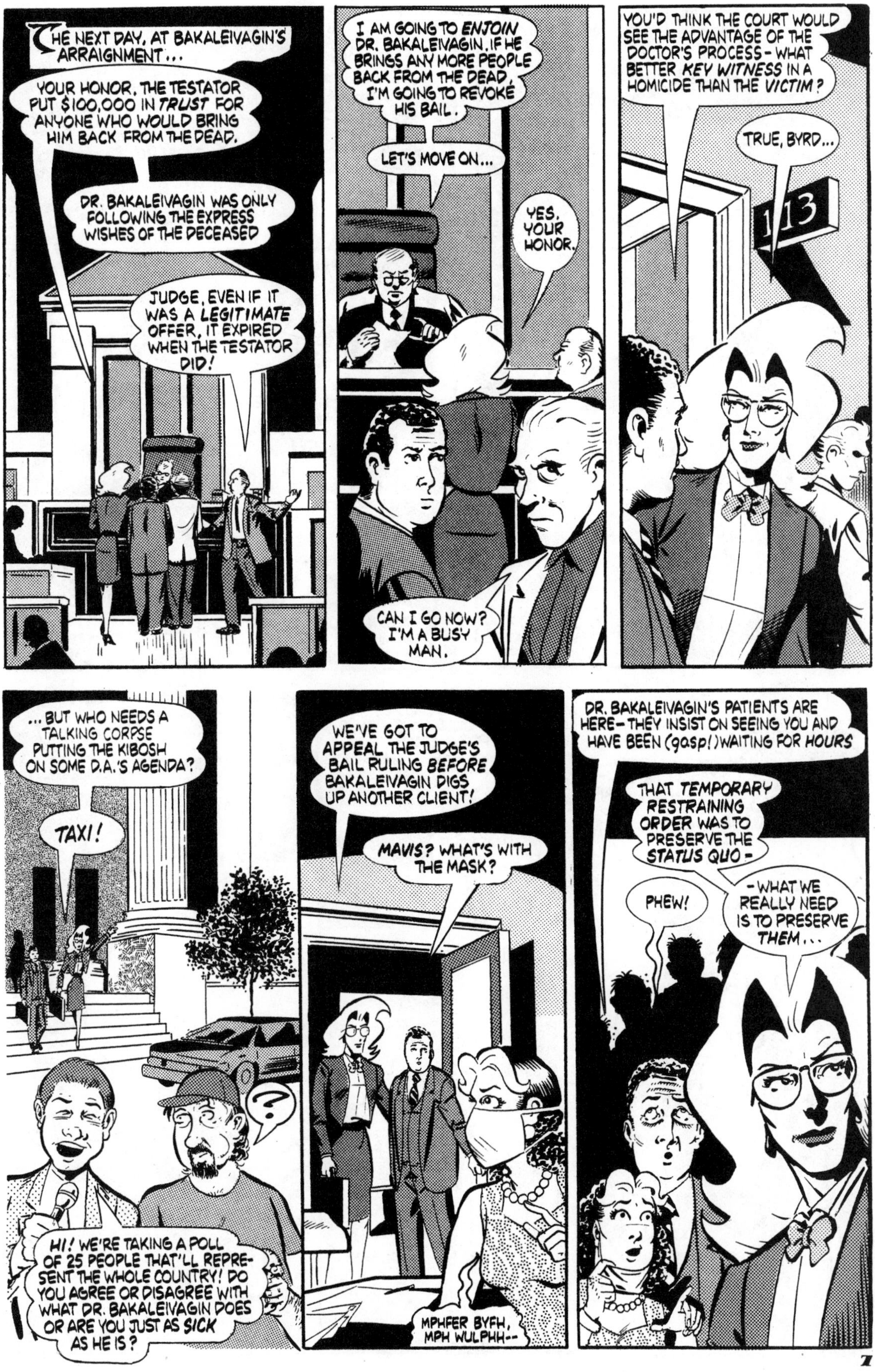
THE NEXT DAY, AT BAKALEIVAGIN'S ARRAIGNMENT...
YOUR HONOR, THE TESTATOR PUT $100,000 IN TRUST FOR ANYONE WHO WOULD BRING HIM BACK FROM THE DEAD.
DR. BAKALEIVAGIN WAS ONLY FOLLOWING THE EXPRESS WISHES OF THE DECEASED
JUDGE, EVEN IF IT WAS A LEGITIMATE OFFER, IT EXPIRED WHEN THE TESTATOR DID!
I AM GOING TO ENJOIN DR. BAKALEIVAGIN. IF HE BRINGS ANY MORE PEOPLE BACK FROM THE DEAD, I'M GOING TO REVOKE HIS BAIL.
LET'S MOVE ON...
YES, YOUR HONOR.
CAN I GO NOW? I'M A BUSY MAN.
YOU'D THINK THE COURT WOULD SEE THE ADVANTAGE OF THE DOCTOR'S PROCESS – WHAT BETTER KEY WITNESS IN A HOMICIDE THAN THE VICTIM?
TRUE, BYRD...
113
...BUT WHO NEEDS A TALKING CORPSE PUTTING THE KIBOSH ON SOME D.A.'S AGENDA?
TAXI!
?
HI! WE'RE TAKING A POLL OF 25 PEOPLE THAT'LL REPRESENT THE WHOLE COUNTRY! DO YOU AGREE OR DISAGREE WITH WHAT DR. BAKALEIVAGIN DOES OR ARE YOU JUST AS SICK AS HE IS?
WE'VE GOT TO APPEAL THE JUDGE'S BAIL RULING BEFORE BAKALEIVAGIN DIGS UP ANOTHER CLIENT!
MAVIS? WHAT'S WITH THE MASK?
MPHFER BYFH, MPH WULPHH--
DR. BAKALEIVAGIN'S PATIENTS ARE HERE – THEY INSIST ON SEEING YOU AND HAVE BEEN (gasp!) WAITING FOR HOURS
THAT TEMPORARY RESTRAINING ORDER WAS TO PRESERVE THE STATUS QUO –
PHEW!
– WHAT WE REALLY NEED IS TO PRESERVE THEM...

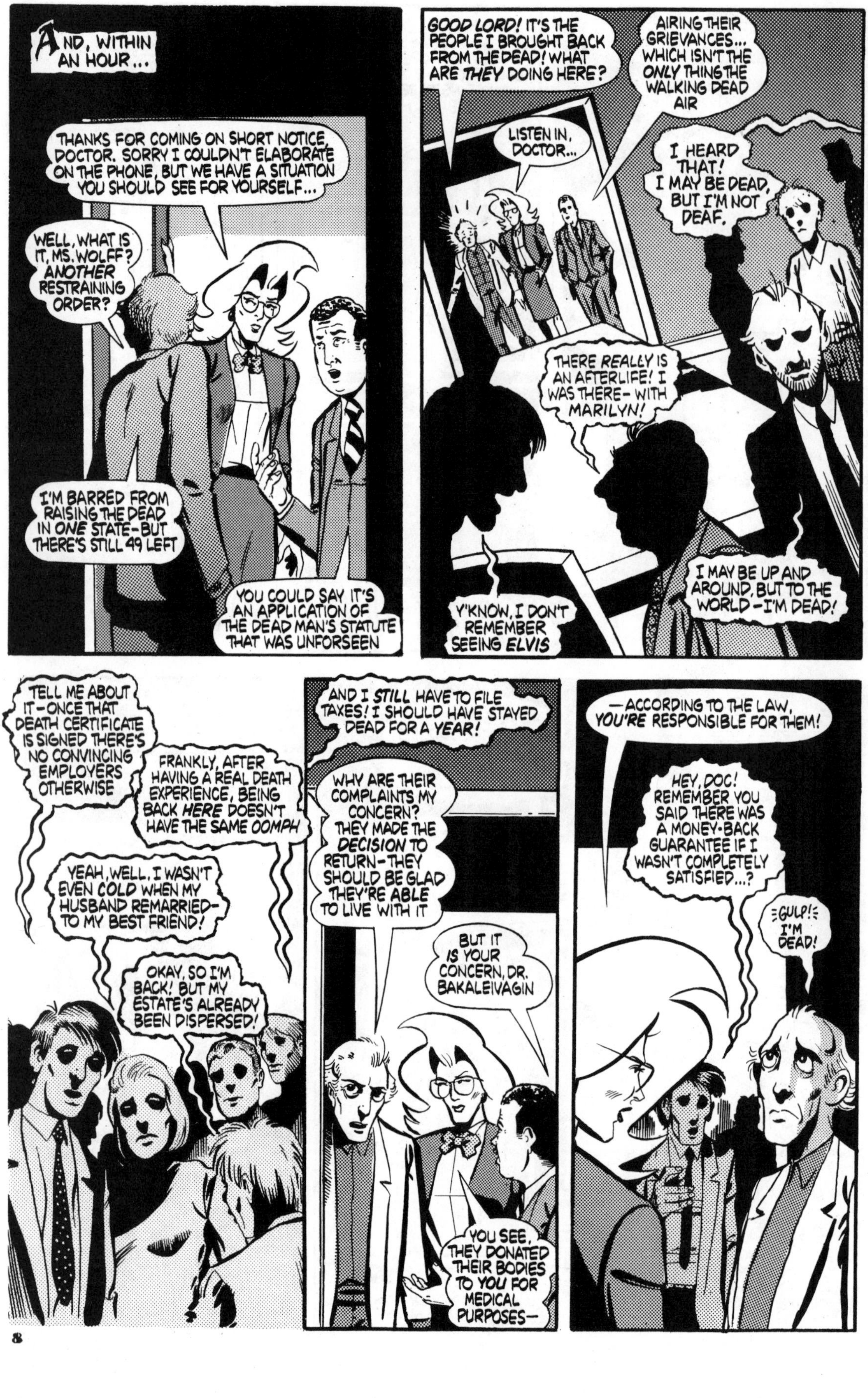
AND, WITHIN AN HOUR...
THANKS FOR COMING ON SHORT NOTICE, DOCTOR. SORRY I COULDN'T ELABORATE ON THE PHONE, BUT WE HAVE A SITUATION YOU SHOULD SEE FOR YOURSELF...
WELL, WHAT IS IT, MS. WOLFF? ANOTHER RESTRAINING ORDER?
I'M BARRED FROM RAISING THE DEAD IN ONE STATE-BUT THERE'S STILL 49 LEFT
YOU COULD SAY IT'S AN APPLICATION OF THE DEAD MAN'S STATUTE THAT WAS UNFORSEEN
GOOD LORD! IT'S THE PEOPLE I BROUGHT BACK FROM THE DEAD! WHAT ARE THEY DOING HERE?
AIRING THEIR GRIEVANCES... WHICH ISN'T THE ONLY THING THE WALKING DEAD AIR
LISTEN IN, DOCTOR...
I HEARD THAT! I MAY BE DEAD, BUT I'M NOT DEAF.
THERE REALLY IS AN AFTERLIFE! I WAS THERE- WITH MARILYN!
Y'KNOW, I DON'T REMEMBER SEEING ELVIS
I MAY BE UP AND AROUND, BUT TO THE WORLD - I'M DEAD!
TELL ME ABOUT IT - ONCE THAT DEATH CERTIFICATE IS SIGNED THERE'S NO CONVINCING EMPLOYERS OTHERWISE
FRANKLY, AFTER HAVING A REAL DEATH EXPERIENCE, BEING BACK HERE DOESN'T HAVE THE SAME OOMPH
YEAH, WELL, I WASN'T EVEN COLD WHEN MY HUSBAND REMARRIED-TO MY BEST FRIEND!
OKAY, SO I'M BACK! BUT MY ESTATE'S ALREADY BEEN DISPERSED!
AND I STILL HAVE TO FILE TAXES! I SHOULD HAVE STAYED DEAD FOR A YEAR!
WHY ARE THEIR COMPLAINTS MY CONCERN? THEY MADE THE DECISION TO RETURN-THEY SHOULD BE GLAD THEY'RE ABLE TO LIVE WITH IT
BUT IT IS YOUR CONCERN, DR. BAKALEIVAGIN
YOU SEE, THEY DONATED THEIR BODIES TO YOU FOR MEDICAL PURPOSES-
—ACCORDING TO THE LAW, YOU'RE RESPONSIBLE FOR THEM!
HEY, DOC! REMEMBER YOU SAID THERE WAS A MONEY-BACK GUARANTEE IF I WASN'T COMPLETELY SATISFIED...?
GULP! I'M DEAD!

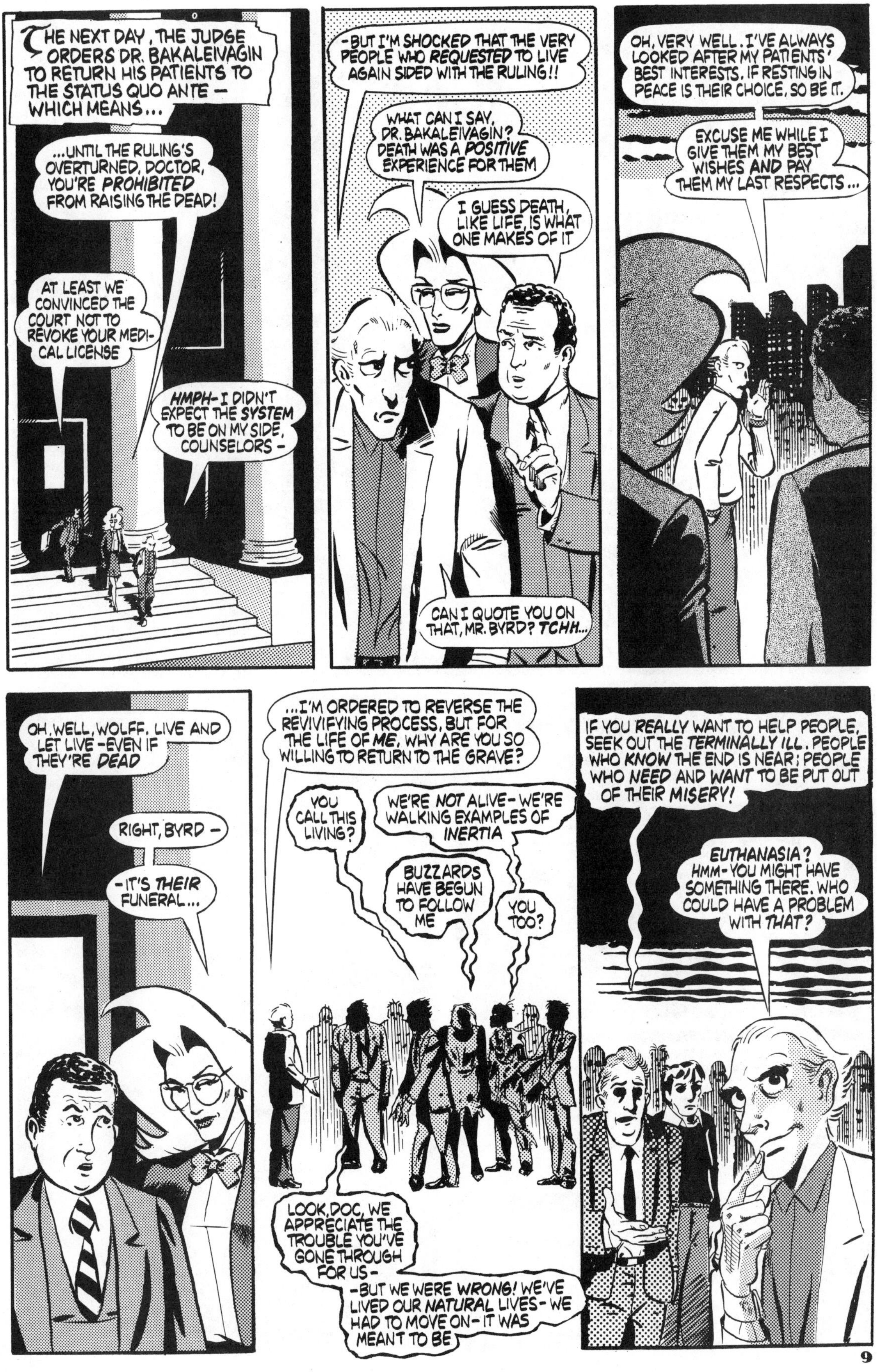
THE NEXT DAY, THE JUDGE ORDERS DR. BAKALEIVAGIN TO RETURN HIS PATIENTS TO THE STATUS QUO ANTE — WHICH MEANS...
...UNTIL THE RULING'S OVERTURNED, DOCTOR, YOU'RE PROHIBITED FROM RAISING THE DEAD!
AT LEAST WE CONVINCED THE COURT NOT TO REVOKE YOUR MEDI-CAL LICENSE
HMPH- I DIDN'T EXPECT THE SYSTEM TO BE ON MY SIDE, COUNSELORS -
-BUT I'M SHOCKED THAT THE VERY PEOPLE WHO REQUESTED TO LIVE AGAIN SIDED WITH THE RULING!!
WHAT CAN I SAY, DR. BAKALEIVAGIN? DEATH WAS A POSITIVE EXPERIENCE FOR THEM
I GUESS DEATH, LIKE LIFE, IS WHAT ONE MAKES OF IT
CAN I QUOTE YOU ON THAT, MR. BYRD? TCHH...
OH, VERY WELL. I'VE ALWAYS LOOKED AFTER MY PATIENTS' BEST INTERESTS. IF RESTING IN PEACE IS THEIR CHOICE, SO BE IT.
EXCUSE ME WHILE I GIVE THEM MY BEST WISHES AND PAY THEM MY LAST RESPECTS...
OH, WELL, WOLFF. LIVE AND LET LIVE -EVEN IF THEY'RE DEAD
RIGHT, BYRD -
-IT'S THEIR FUNERAL...
...I'M ORDERED TO REVERSE THE REVIVIFYING PROCESS, BUT FOR THE LIFE OF ME, WHY ARE YOU SO WILLING TO RETURN TO THE GRAVE?
YOU CALL THIS LIVING?
WE'RE NOT ALIVE- WE'RE WALKING EXAMPLES OF INERTIA
BUZZARDS HAVE BEGUN TO FOLLOW ME
YOU TOO?
LOOK, DOC, WE APPRECIATE THE TROUBLE YOU'VE GONE THROUGH FOR US -
-BUT WE WERE WRONG! WE'VE LIVED OUR NATURAL LIVES- WE HAD TO MOVE ON- IT WAS MEANT TO BE
IF YOU REALLY WANT TO HELP PEOPLE, SEEK OUT THE TERMINALLY ILL. PEOPLE WHO KNOW THE END IS NEAR; PEOPLE WHO NEED AND WANT TO BE PUT OUT OF THEIR MISERY!
EUTHANASIA? HMM- YOU MIGHT HAVE SOMETHING THERE. WHO COULD HAVE A PROBLEM WITH THAT?

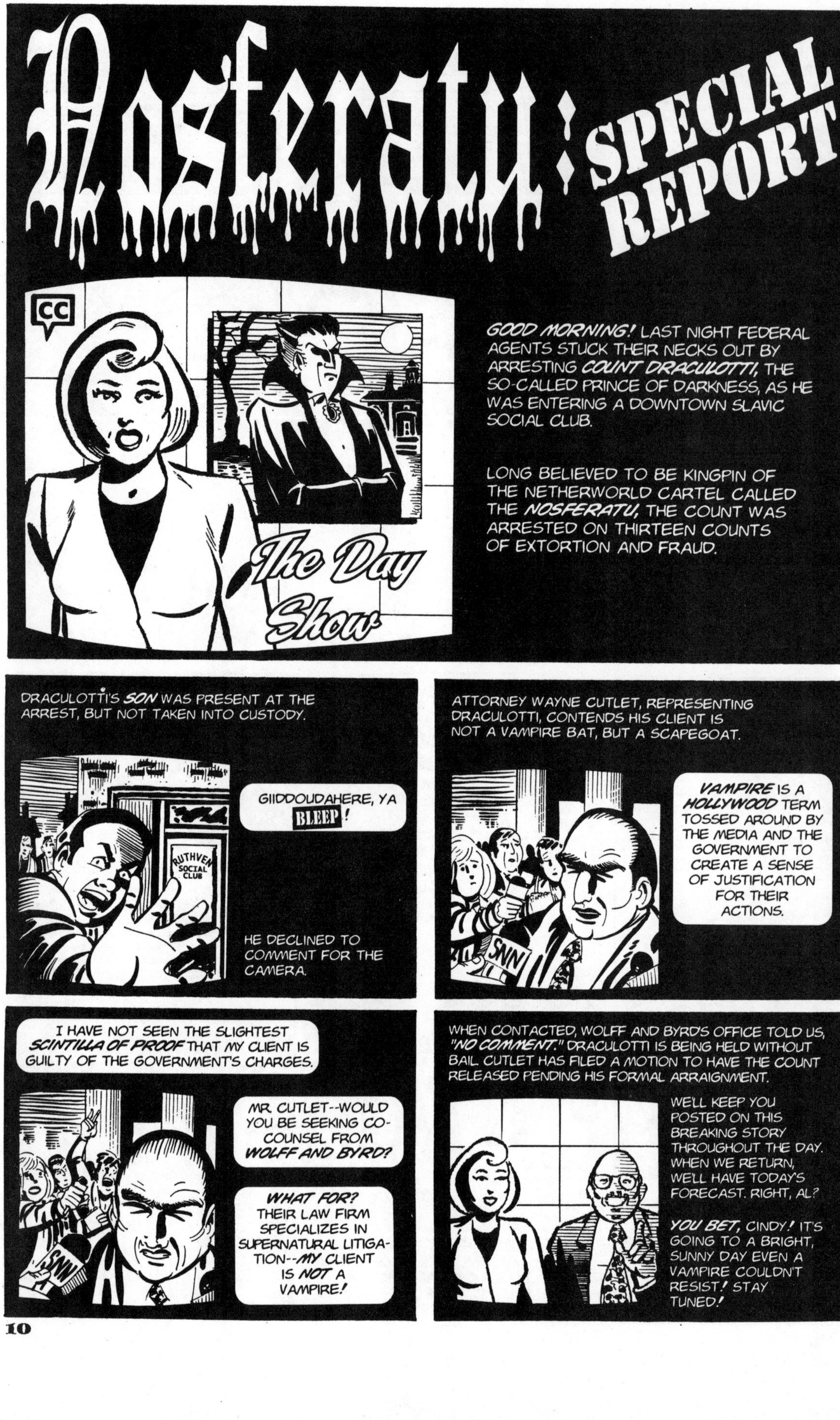
Nosferatu: SPECIAL REPORT
CC
GOOD MORNING! LAST NIGHT FEDERAL AGENTS STUCK THEIR NECKS OUT BY ARRESTING COUNT DRACULOTTI, THE SO-CALLED PRINCE OF DARKNESS, AS HE WAS ENTERING A DOWNTOWN SLAVIC SOCIAL CLUB.
LONG BELIEVED TO BE KINGPIN OF THE NETHERWORLD CARTEL CALLED THE NOSFERATU, THE COUNT WAS ARRESTED ON THIRTEEN COUNTS OF EXTORTION AND FRAUD.
The Day Show
DRACULOTTI'S SON WAS PRESENT AT THE ARREST, BUT NOT TAKEN INTO CUSTODY.
GIIDDOUDAHERE, YA BLEEP!
RUTHVEN SOCIAL CLUB
HE DECLINED TO COMMENT FOR THE CAMERA.
ATTORNEY WAYNE CUTLET, REPRESENTING DRACULOTTI, CONTENDS HIS CLIENT IS NOT A VAMPIRE BAT, BUT A SCAPEGOAT.
VAMPIRE IS A HOLLYWOOD TERM TOSSED AROUND BY THE MEDIA AND THE GOVERNMENT TO CREATE A SENSE OF JUSTIFICATION FOR THEIR ACTIONS.
SNN
I HAVE NOT SEEN THE SLIGHTEST SCINTILLA OF PROOF THAT MY CLIENT IS GUILTY OF THE GOVERNMENT'S CHARGES.
MR. CUTLET--WOULD YOU BE SEEKING CO-COUNSEL FROM WOLFF AND BYRD?
WHAT FOR? THEIR LAW FIRM SPECIALIZES IN SUPERNATURAL LITIGATION--MY CLIENT IS NOT A VAMPIRE!
SNN
WHEN CONTACTED, WOLFF AND BYRD'S OFFICE TOLD US, "NO COMMENT." DRACULOTTI IS BEING HELD WITHOUT BAIL. CUTLET HAS FILED A MOTION TO HAVE THE COUNT RELEASED PENDING HIS FORMAL ARRAIGNMENT.
WE'LL KEEP YOU POSTED ON THIS BREAKING STORY THROUGHOUT THE DAY. WHEN WE RETURN, WE'LL HAVE TODAY'S FORECAST. RIGHT, AL?
YOU BET, CINDY! IT'S GOING TO A BRIGHT, SUNNY DAY EVEN A VAMPIRE COULDN'T RESIST! STAY TUNED!

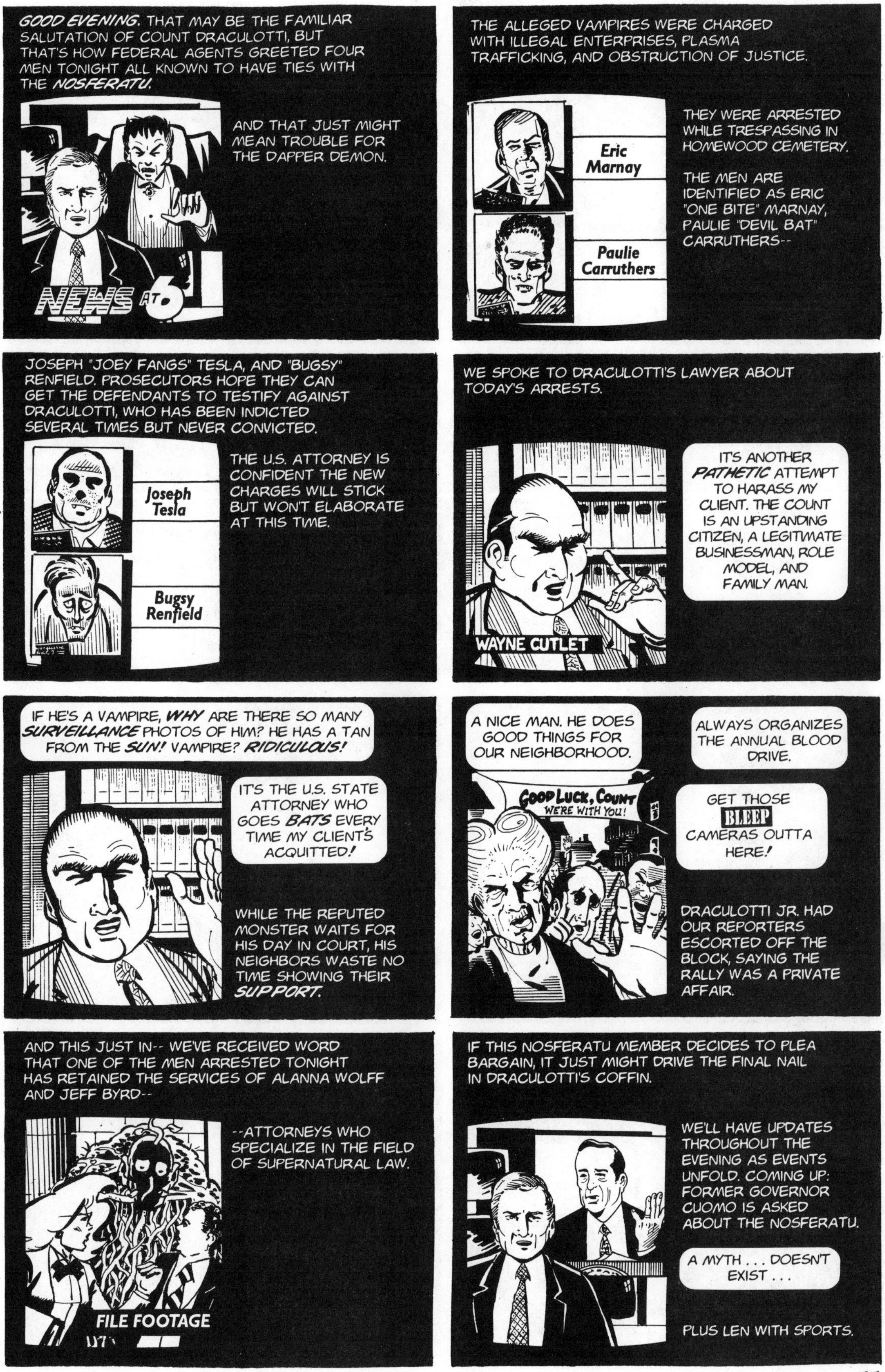
GOOD EVENING. THAT MAY BE THE FAMILIAR SALUTATION OF COUNT DRACULOTTI, BUT THAT'S HOW FEDERAL AGENTS GREETED FOUR MEN TONIGHT ALL KNOWN TO HAVE TIES WITH THE NOSFERATU.
NEWS AT 6
AND THAT JUST MIGHT MEAN TROUBLE FOR THE DAPPER DEMON.
THE ALLEGED VAMPIRES WERE CHARGED WITH ILLEGAL ENTERPRISES, PLASMA TRAFFICKING, AND OBSTRUCTION OF JUSTICE.
Eric Marnay
Paulie Carruthers
THEY WERE ARRESTED WHILE TRESPASSING IN HOMEWOOD CEMETERY.
THE MEN ARE IDENTIFIED AS ERIC "ONE BITE" MARNAY, PAULIE "DEVIL BAT" CARRUTHERS--
JOSEPH "JOEY FANGS" TESLA, AND "BUGSY" RENFIELD. PROSECUTORS HOPE THEY CAN GET THE DEFENDANTS TO TESTIFY AGAINST DRACULOTTI, WHO HAS BEEN INDICTED SEVERAL TIMES BUT NEVER CONVICTED.
Joseph Tesla
Bugsy Renfield
THE U.S. ATTORNEY IS CONFIDENT THE NEW CHARGES WILL STICK BUT WON'T ELABORATE AT THIS TIME.
WE SPOKE TO DRACULOTTI'S LAWYER ABOUT TODAY'S ARRESTS.
IT'S ANOTHER PATHETIC ATTEMPT TO HARASS MY CLIENT. THE COUNT IS AN UPSTANDING CITIZEN, A LEGITIMATE BUSINESSMAN, ROLE MODEL, AND FAMILY MAN.
WAYNE CUTLET
IF HE'S A VAMPIRE, WHY ARE THERE SO MANY SURVEILLANCE PHOTOS OF HIM? HE HAS A TAN FROM THE SUN! VAMPIRE? RIDICULOUS!
IT'S THE U.S. STATE ATTORNEY WHO GOES BATS EVERY TIME MY CLIENT'S ACQUITTED!
WHILE THE REPUTED MONSTER WAITS FOR HIS DAY IN COURT, HIS NEIGHBORS WASTE NO TIME SHOWING THEIR SUPPORT.
A NICE MAN. HE DOES GOOD THINGS FOR OUR NEIGHBORHOOD.
ALWAYS ORGANIZES THE ANNUAL BLOOD DRIVE.
GOOD LUCK, COUNT WE'RE WITH YOU!
GET THOSE BLEEP CAMERAS OUTTA HERE!
DRACULOTTI JR. HAD OUR REPORTERS ESCORTED OFF THE BLOCK, SAYING THE RALLY WAS A PRIVATE AFFAIR.
AND THIS JUST IN-- WE'VE RECEIVED WORD THAT ONE OF THE MEN ARRESTED TONIGHT HAS RETAINED THE SERVICES OF ALANNA WOLFF AND JEFF BYRD--
--ATTORNEYS WHO SPECIALIZE IN THE FIELD OF SUPERNATURAL LAW.
FILE FOOTAGE
IF THIS NOSFERATU MEMBER DECIDES TO PLEA BARGAIN, IT JUST MIGHT DRIVE THE FINAL NAIL IN DRACULOTTI'S COFFIN.
WE'LL HAVE UPDATES THROUGHOUT THE EVENING AS EVENTS UNFOLD. COMING UP: FORMER GOVERNOR CUOMO IS ASKED ABOUT THE NOSFERATU.
A MYTH . . . DOESN'T EXIST . . .
PLUS LEN WITH SPORTS.

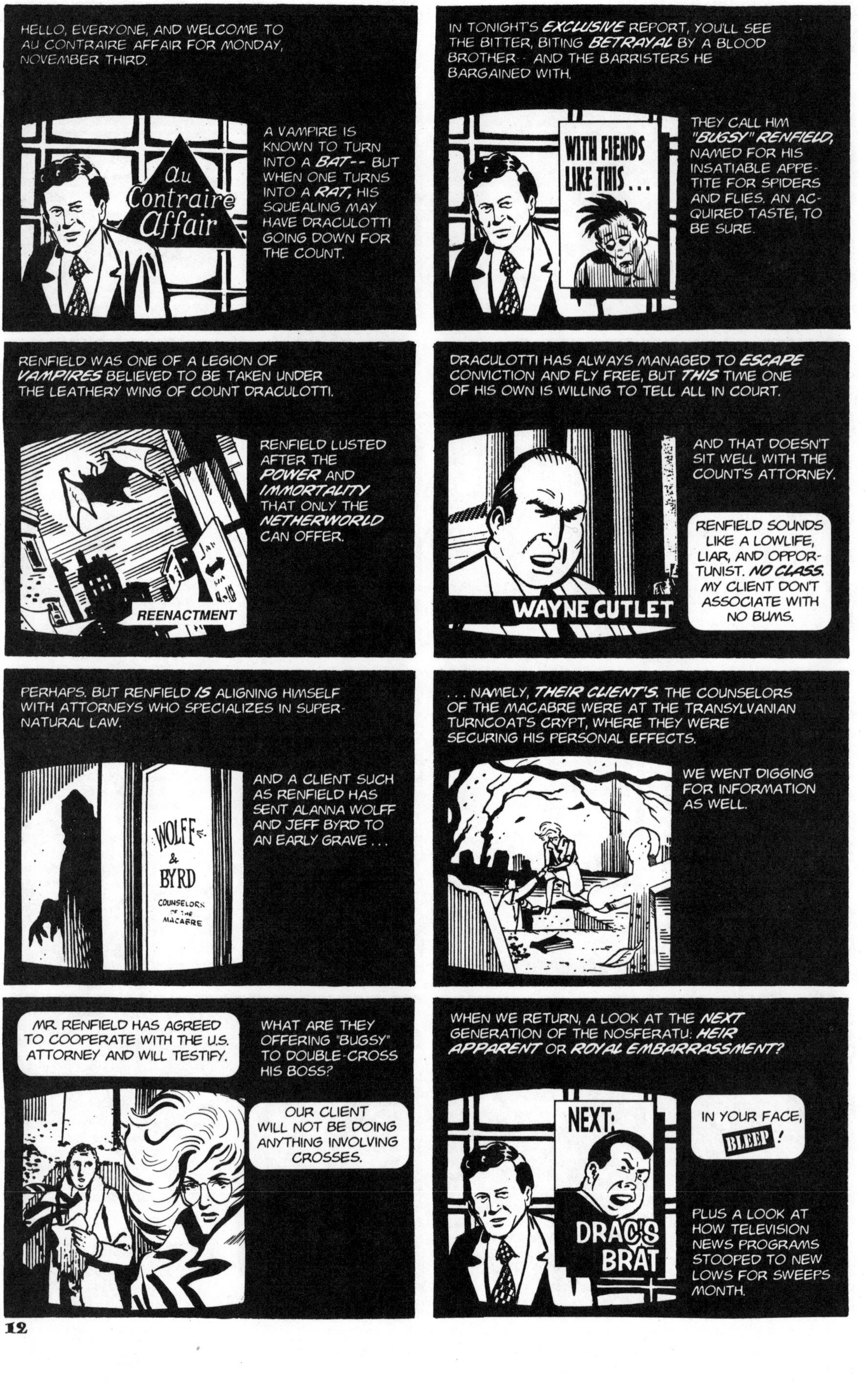
HELLO, EVERYONE, AND WELCOME TO AU CONTRAIRE AFFAIR FOR MONDAY, NOVEMBER THIRD.
Au Contraire Affair
A VAMPIRE IS KNOWN TO TURN INTO A BAT-- BUT WHEN ONE TURNS INTO A RAT, HIS SQUEALING MAY HAVE DRACULOTTI GOING DOWN FOR THE COUNT.
IN TONIGHT'S EXCLUSIVE REPORT, YOU'LL SEE THE BITTER, BITING BETRAYAL BY A BLOOD BROTHER-- AND THE BARRISTERS HE BARGAINED WITH.
WITH FIENDS LIKE THIS . . .
THEY CALL HIM "BUGSY" RENFIELD, NAMED FOR HIS INSATIABLE APPETITE FOR SPIDERS AND FLIES. AN ACQUIRED TASTE, TO BE SURE.
RENFIELD WAS ONE OF A LEGION OF VAMPIRES BELIEVED TO BE TAKEN UNDER THE LEATHERY WING OF COUNT DRACULOTTI.
RENFIELD LUSTED AFTER THE POWER AND IMMORTALITY THAT ONLY THE NETHERWORLD CAN OFFER.
REENACTMENT
DRACULOTTI HAS ALWAYS MANAGED TO ESCAPE CONVICTION AND FLY FREE, BUT THIS TIME ONE OF HIS OWN IS WILLING TO TELL ALL IN COURT.
AND THAT DOESN'T SIT WELL WITH THE COUNT'S ATTORNEY.
WAYNE CUTLET
RENFIELD SOUNDS LIKE A LOWLIFE, LIAR, AND OPPORTUNIST. NO CLASS. MY CLIENT DON'T ASSOCIATE WITH NO BUMS.
PERHAPS. BUT RENFIELD IS ALIGNING HIMSELF WITH ATTORNEYS WHO SPECIALIZES IN SUPERNATURAL LAW.
AND A CLIENT SUCH AS RENFIELD HAS SENT ALANNA WOLFF AND JEFF BYRD TO AN EARLY GRAVE . . .
WOLFF & BYRD
COUNSELORS OF THE MACABRE
. . . NAMELY, THEIR CLIENT'S. THE COUNSELORS OF THE MACABRE WERE AT THE TRANSYLVANIAN TURNCOAT'S CRYPT, WHERE THEY WERE SECURING HIS PERSONAL EFFECTS.
WE WENT DIGGING FOR INFORMATION AS WELL.
MR. RENFIELD HAS AGREED TO COOPERATE WITH THE U.S. ATTORNEY AND WILL TESTIFY.
WHAT ARE THEY OFFERING "BUGSY" TO DOUBLE-CROSS HIS BOSS?
OUR CLIENT WILL NOT BE DOING ANYTHING INVOLVING CROSSES.
WHEN WE RETURN, A LOOK AT THE NEXT GENERATION OF THE NOSFERATU: HEIR APPARENT OR ROYAL EMBARRASSMENT?
NEXT:
DRAC'S BRAT
IN YOUR FACE, BLEEP!
PLUS A LOOK AT HOW TELEVISION NEWS PROGRAMS STOOPED TO NEW LOWS FOR SWEEPS MONTH.

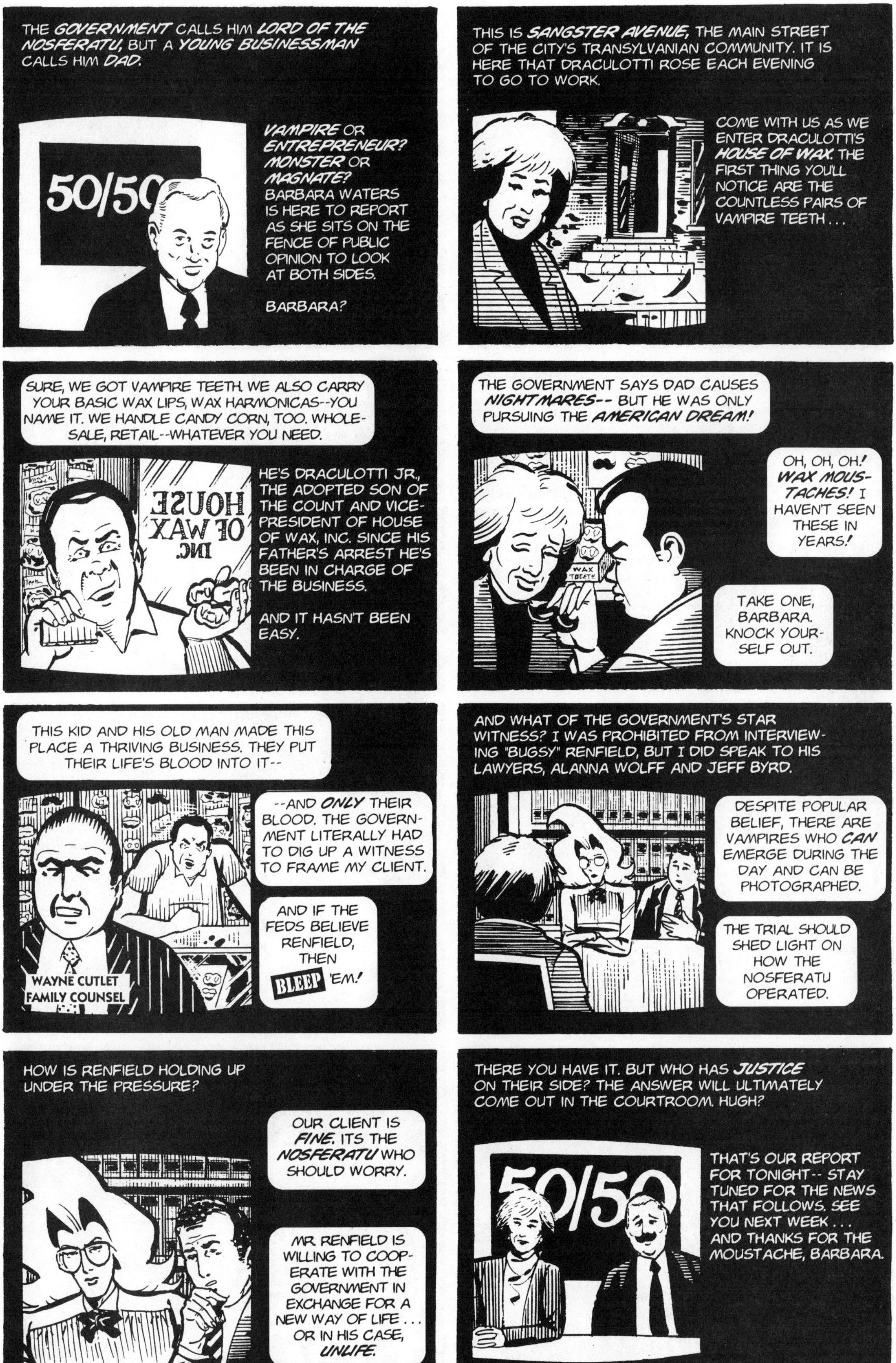
THE *GOVERNMENT* CALLS HIM *LORD OF THE NOSFERATU,* BUT A *YOUNG BUSINESSMAN* CALLS HIM *DAD.*
50/50
VAMPIRE OR *ENTREPRENEUR? MONSTER* OR *MAGNATE?* BARBARA WATERS IS HERE TO REPORT AS SHE SITS ON THE FENCE OF PUBLIC OPINION TO LOOK AT BOTH SIDES.
BARBARA?
THIS IS *SANGSTER AVENUE,* THE MAIN STREET OF THE CITY'S TRANSYLVANIAN COMMUNITY. IT IS HERE THAT DRACULOTTI ROSE EACH EVENING TO GO TO WORK.
COME WITH US AS WE ENTER DRACULOTTI'S *HOUSE OF WAX.* THE FIRST THING YOU'LL NOTICE ARE THE COUNTLESS PAIRS OF VAMPIRE TEETH . . .
SURE, WE GOT VAMPIRE TEETH. WE ALSO CARRY YOUR BASIC WAX LIPS, WAX HARMONICAS--YOU NAME IT. WE HANDLE CANDY CORN, TOO. WHOLE-SALE, RETAIL--WHATEVER YOU NEED.
HE'S DRACULOTTI JR., THE ADOPTED SON OF THE COUNT AND VICE-PRESIDENT OF HOUSE OF WAX, INC. SINCE HIS FATHER'S ARREST HE'S BEEN IN CHARGE OF THE BUSINESS.
AND IT HASN'T BEEN EASY.
THE GOVERNMENT SAYS DAD CAUSES *NIGHTMARES--* BUT HE WAS ONLY PURSUING THE *AMERICAN DREAM!*
OH, OH, OH! *WAX MOUSTACHES!* I HAVEN'T SEEN THESE IN YEARS!
WAX TEETH
TAKE ONE, BARBARA. KNOCK YOURSELF OUT.
THIS KID AND HIS OLD MAN MADE THIS PLACE A THRIVING BUSINESS. THEY PUT THEIR LIFE'S BLOOD INTO IT--
--AND *ONLY* THEIR BLOOD. THE GOVERNMENT LITERALLY HAD TO DIG UP A WITNESS TO FRAME MY CLIENT.
AND IF THE FEDS BELIEVE RENFIELD, THEN BLEEP 'EM!
WAYNE CUTLET
FAMILY COUNSEL
AND WHAT OF THE GOVERNMENT'S STAR WITNESS? I WAS PROHIBITED FROM INTERVIEWING "BUGSY" RENFIELD, BUT I DID SPEAK TO HIS LAWYERS, ALANNA WOLFF AND JEFF BYRD.
DESPITE POPULAR BELIEF, THERE ARE VAMPIRES WHO *CAN* EMERGE DURING THE DAY AND CAN BE PHOTOGRAPHED.
THE TRIAL SHOULD SHED LIGHT ON HOW THE NOSFERATU OPERATED.
HOW IS RENFIELD HOLDING UP UNDER THE PRESSURE?
OUR CLIENT IS *FINE.* ITS THE *NOSFERATU* WHO SHOULD WORRY.
MR RENFIELD IS WILLING TO COOPERATE WITH THE GOVERNMENT IN EXCHANGE FOR A NEW WAY OF LIFE . . . OR IN HIS CASE, *UNLIFE.*
THERE YOU HAVE IT. BUT WHO HAS *JUSTICE* ON THEIR SIDE? THE ANSWER WILL ULTIMATELY COME OUT IN THE COURTROOM. HUGH?
50/50
THAT'S OUR REPORT FOR TONIGHT-- STAY TUNED FOR THE NEWS THAT FOLLOWS. SEE YOU NEXT WEEK . . . AND THANKS FOR THE MOUSTACHE, BARBARA.

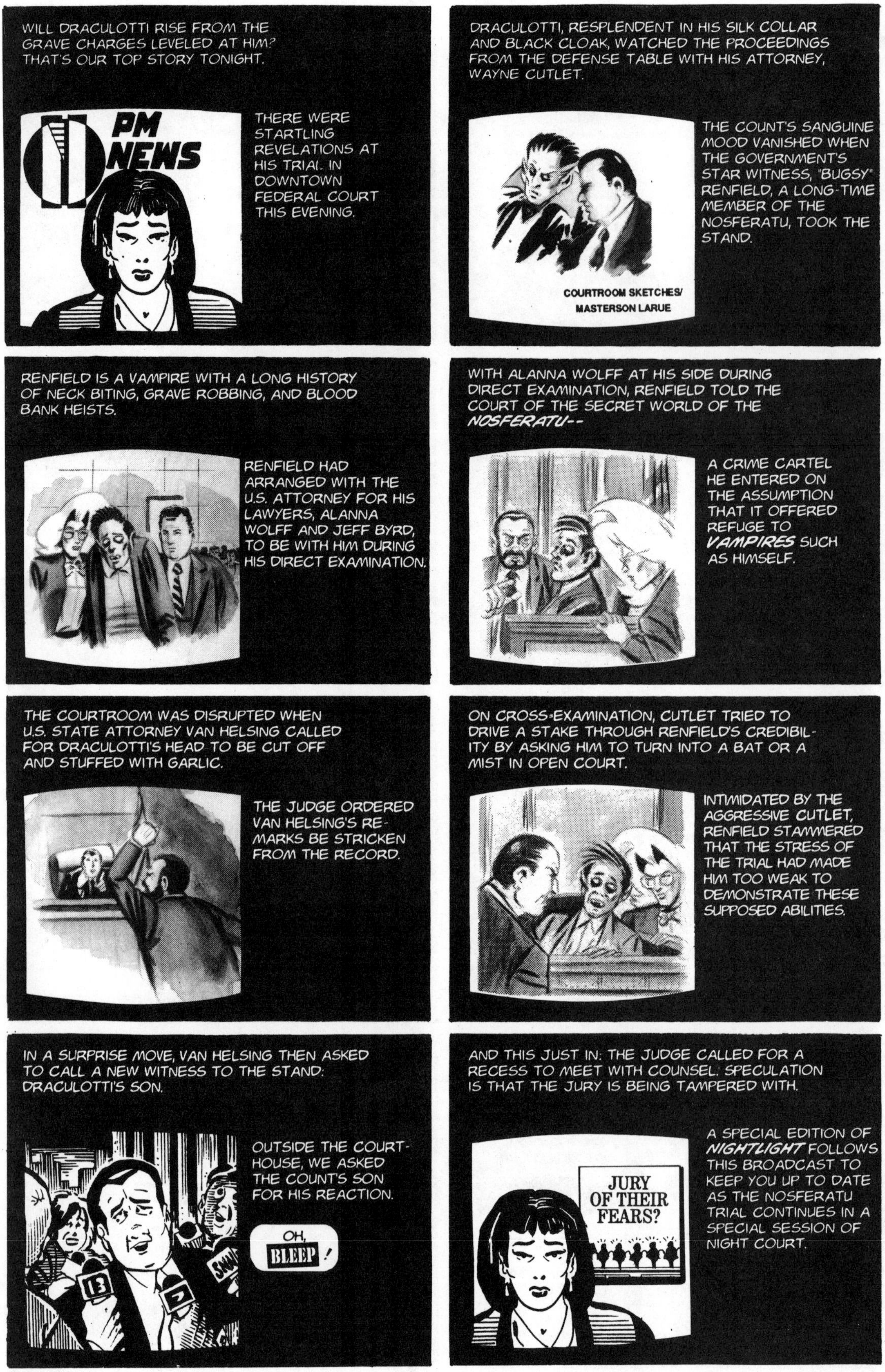
WILL DRACULOTTI RISE FROM THE GRAVE CHARGES LEVELED AT HIM? THAT'S OUR TOP STORY TONIGHT.
PM NEWS
THERE WERE STARTLING REVELATIONS AT HIS TRIAL IN DOWNTOWN FEDERAL COURT THIS EVENING.
DRACULOTTI, RESPLENDENT IN HIS SILK COLLAR AND BLACK CLOAK, WATCHED THE PROCEEDINGS FROM THE DEFENSE TABLE WITH HIS ATTORNEY, WAYNE CUTLET.
THE COUNT'S SANGUINE MOOD VANISHED WHEN THE GOVERNMENT'S STAR WITNESS, "BUGSY" RENFIELD, A LONG-TIME MEMBER OF THE NOSFERATU, TOOK THE STAND.
COURTROOM SKETCHES/ MASTERSON LARUE
RENFIELD IS A VAMPIRE WITH A LONG HISTORY OF NECK BITING, GRAVE ROBBING, AND BLOOD BANK HEISTS.
RENFIELD HAD ARRANGED WITH THE U.S. ATTORNEY FOR HIS LAWYERS, ALANNA WOLFF AND JEFF BYRD, TO BE WITH HIM DURING HIS DIRECT EXAMINATION.
WITH ALANNA WOLFF AT HIS SIDE DURING DIRECT EXAMINATION, RENFIELD TOLD THE COURT OF THE SECRET WORLD OF THE NOSFERATU--
A CRIME CARTEL HE ENTERED ON THE ASSUMPTION THAT IT OFFERED REFUGE TO VAMPIRES SUCH AS HIMSELF.
THE COURTROOM WAS DISRUPTED WHEN U.S. STATE ATTORNEY VAN HELSING CALLED FOR DRACULOTTI'S HEAD TO BE CUT OFF AND STUFFED WITH GARLIC.
THE JUDGE ORDERED VAN HELSING'S RE-MARKS BE STRICKEN FROM THE RECORD.
ON CROSS-EXAMINATION, CUTLET TRIED TO DRIVE A STAKE THROUGH RENFIELD'S CREDIBIL-ITY BY ASKING HIM TO TURN INTO A BAT OR A MIST IN OPEN COURT.
INTIMIDATED BY THE AGGRESSIVE CUTLET, RENFIELD STAMMERED THAT THE STRESS OF THE TRIAL HAD MADE HIM TOO WEAK TO DEMONSTRATE THESE SUPPOSED ABILITIES.
IN A SURPRISE MOVE, VAN HELSING THEN ASKED TO CALL A NEW WITNESS TO THE STAND: DRACULOTTI'S SON.
OUTSIDE THE COURT-HOUSE, WE ASKED THE COUNT'S SON FOR HIS REACTION.
OH, BLEEP!
13
AND THIS JUST IN: THE JUDGE CALLED FOR A RECESS TO MEET WITH COUNSEL. SPECULATION IS THAT THE JURY IS BEING TAMPERED WITH.
JURY OF THEIR FEARS?
A SPECIAL EDITION OF NIGHTLIGHT FOLLOWS THIS BROADCAST TO KEEP YOU UP TO DATE AS THE NOSFERATU TRIAL CONTINUES IN A SPECIAL SESSION OF NIGHT COURT.

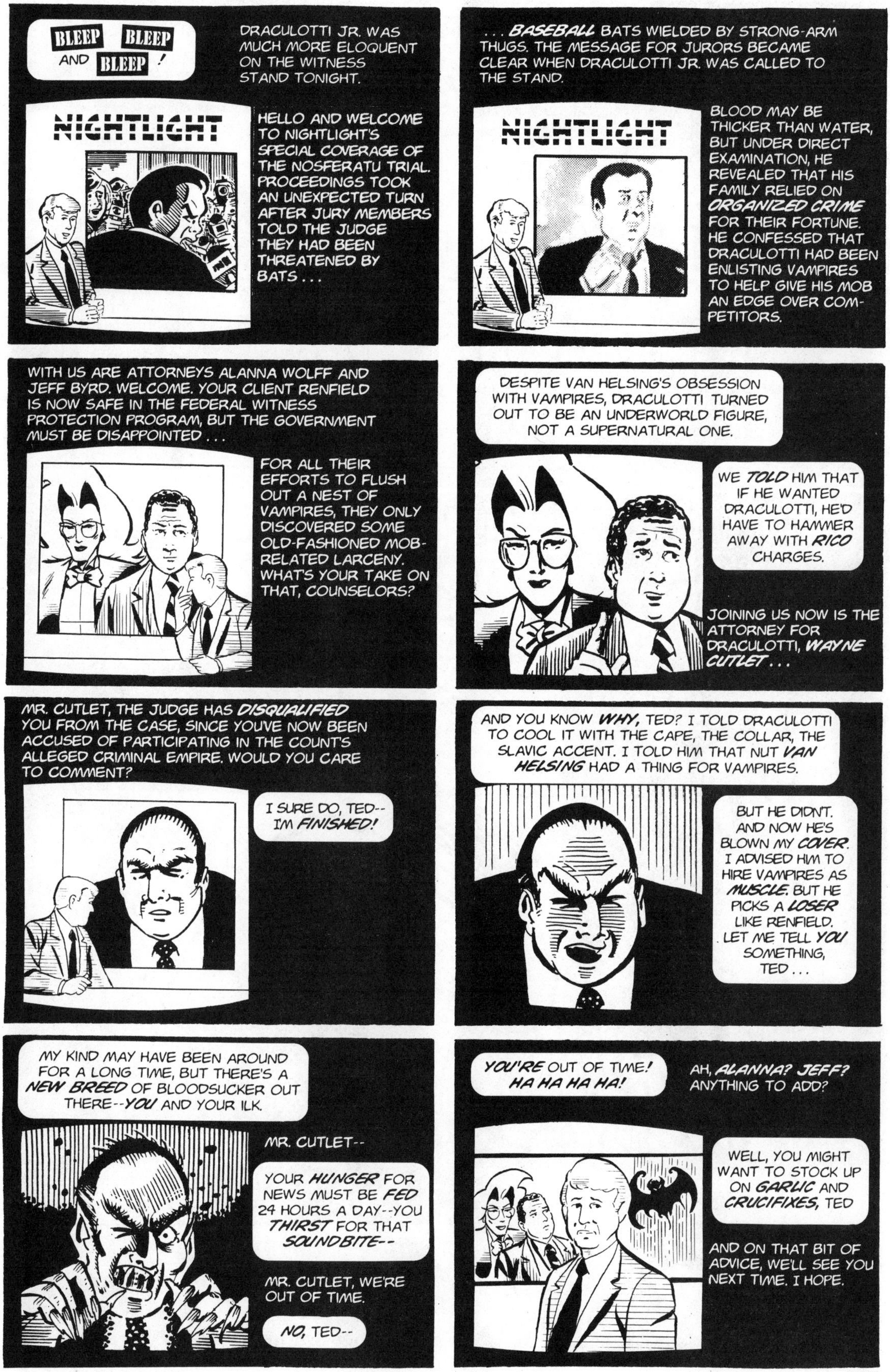
BLEEP BLEEP AND BLEEP!
DRACULOTTI JR. WAS MUCH MORE ELOQUENT ON THE WITNESS STAND TONIGHT.
NIGHTLIGHT
HELLO AND WELCOME TO NIGHTLIGHT'S SPECIAL COVERAGE OF THE NOSFERATU TRIAL. PROCEEDINGS TOOK AN UNEXPECTED TURN AFTER JURY MEMBERS TOLD THE JUDGE THEY HAD BEEN THREATENED BY BATS . . .
. . . BASEBALL BATS WIELDED BY STRONG-ARM THUGS. THE MESSAGE FOR JURORS BECAME CLEAR WHEN DRACULOTTI JR. WAS CALLED TO THE STAND.
NIGHTLIGHT
BLOOD MAY BE THICKER THAN WATER, BUT UNDER DIRECT EXAMINATION, HE REVEALED THAT HIS FAMILY RELIED ON ORGANIZED CRIME FOR THEIR FORTUNE. HE CONFESSED THAT DRACULOTTI HAD BEEN ENLISTING VAMPIRES TO HELP GIVE HIS MOB AN EDGE OVER COMPETITORS.
WITH US ARE ATTORNEYS ALANNA WOLFF AND JEFF BYRD. WELCOME. YOUR CLIENT RENFIELD IS NOW SAFE IN THE FEDERAL WITNESS PROTECTION PROGRAM, BUT THE GOVERNMENT MUST BE DISAPPOINTED . . .
FOR ALL THEIR EFFORTS TO FLUSH OUT A NEST OF VAMPIRES, THEY ONLY DISCOVERED SOME OLD-FASHIONED MOB-RELATED LARCENY. WHAT'S YOUR TAKE ON THAT, COUNSELORS?
DESPITE VAN HELSING'S OBSESSION WITH VAMPIRES, DRACULOTTI TURNED OUT TO BE AN UNDERWORLD FIGURE, NOT A SUPERNATURAL ONE.
WE TOLD HIM THAT IF HE WANTED DRACULOTTI, HE'D HAVE TO HAMMER AWAY WITH RICO CHARGES.
JOINING US NOW IS THE ATTORNEY FOR DRACULOTTI, WAYNE CUTLET . . .
MR. CUTLET, THE JUDGE HAS DISQUALIFIED YOU FROM THE CASE, SINCE YOU'VE NOW BEEN ACCUSED OF PARTICIPATING IN THE COUNT'S ALLEGED CRIMINAL EMPIRE. WOULD YOU CARE TO COMMENT?
I SURE DO, TED-- I'M FINISHED!
AND YOU KNOW WHY, TED? I TOLD DRACULOTTI TO COOL IT WITH THE CAPE, THE COLLAR, THE SLAVIC ACCENT. I TOLD HIM THAT NUT VAN HELSING HAD A THING FOR VAMPIRES.
BUT HE DIDN'T. AND NOW HE'S BLOWN MY COVER. I ADVISED HIM TO HIRE VAMPIRES AS MUSCLE. BUT HE PICKS A LOSER LIKE RENFIELD. LET ME TELL YOU SOMETHING, TED . . .
MY KIND MAY HAVE BEEN AROUND FOR A LONG TIME, BUT THERE'S A NEW BREED OF BLOODSUCKER OUT THERE--YOU AND YOUR ILK.
MR. CUTLET--
YOUR HUNGER FOR NEWS MUST BE FED 24 HOURS A DAY--YOU THIRST FOR THAT SOUNDBITE--
MR. CUTLET, WE'RE OUT OF TIME.
NO, TED--
YOU'RE OUT OF TIME! HA HA HA HA!
AH, ALANNA? JEFF? ANYTHING TO ADD?
WELL, YOU MIGHT WANT TO STOCK UP ON GARLIC AND CRUCIFIXES, TED
AND ON THAT BIT OF ADVICE, WE'LL SEE YOU NEXT TIME. I HOPE.

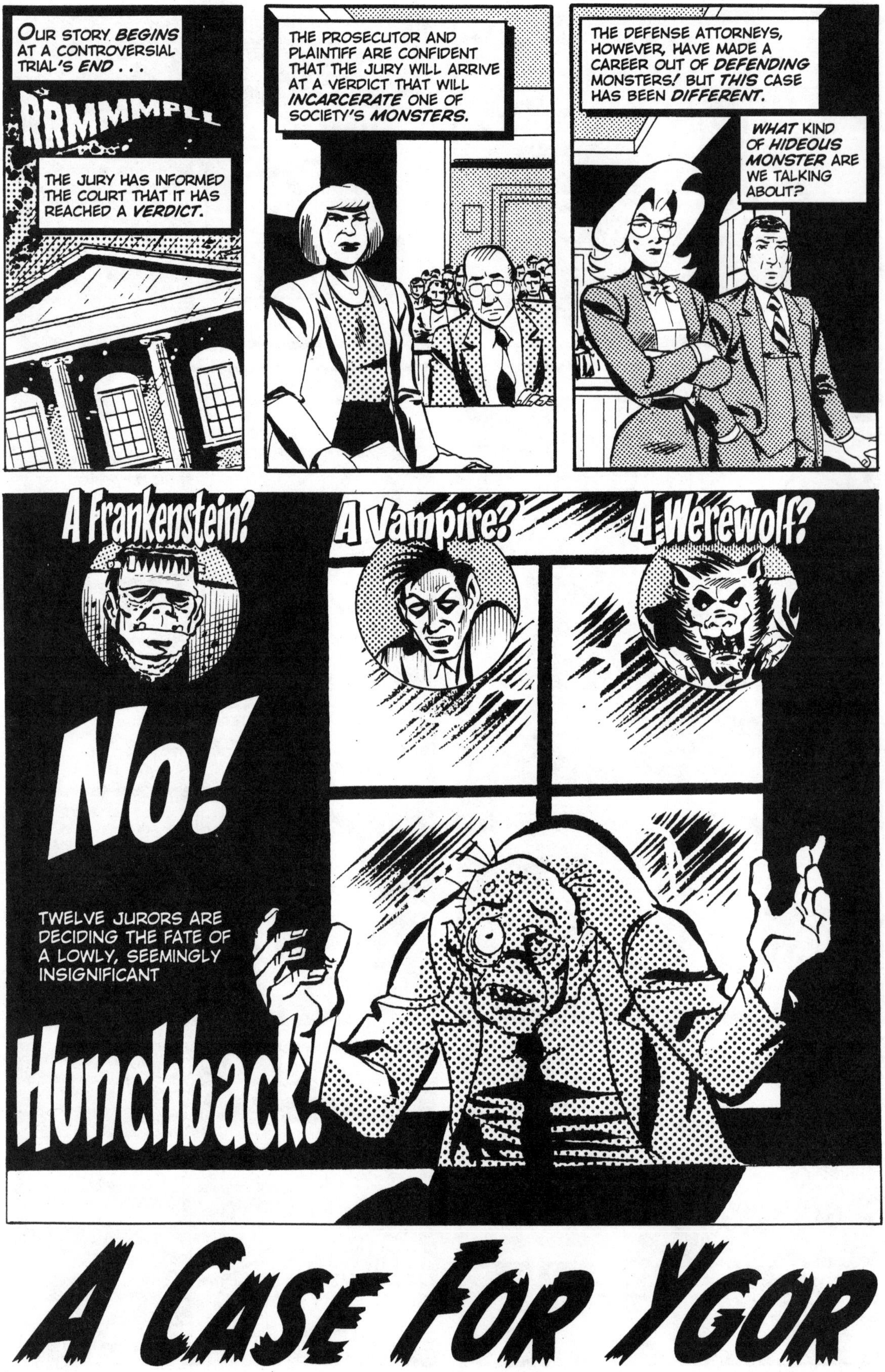
Our story *begins* at a controversial trial's *end* . . .
RRMMMPLL
The jury has informed the court that it has reached a *verdict*.
The prosecutor and plaintiff are confident that the jury will arrive at a verdict that will *incarcerate* one of society's *monsters*.
The defense attorneys, however, have made a career out of *defending* monsters! But *this* case has been *different*.
What kind of *hideous monster* are we talking about?
A Frankenstein?
A Vampire?
A Werewolf?
No!
Twelve jurors are deciding the fate of a lowly, seemingly insignificant
Hunchback!

A Case For Ygor

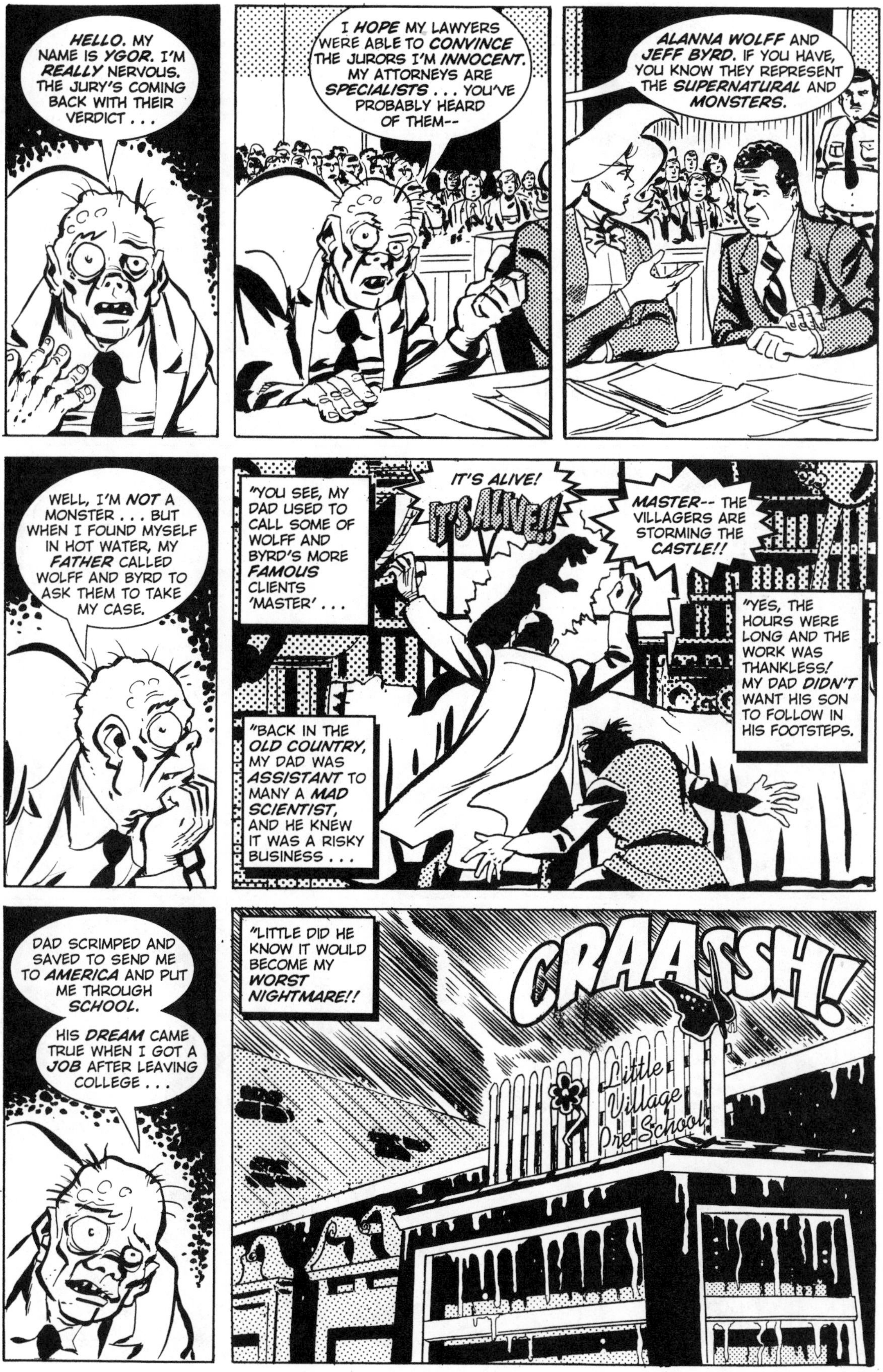

HELLO. MY NAME IS YGOR. I'M REALLY NERVOUS. THE JURY'S COMING BACK WITH THEIR VERDICT . . .
I HOPE MY LAWYERS WERE ABLE TO CONVINCE THE JURORS I'M INNOCENT. MY ATTORNEYS ARE SPECIALISTS . . . YOU'VE PROBABLY HEARD OF THEM--
ALANNA WOLFF AND JEFF BYRD. IF YOU HAVE, YOU KNOW THEY REPRESENT THE SUPERNATURAL AND MONSTERS.
WELL, I'M NOT A MONSTER . . . BUT WHEN I FOUND MYSELF IN HOT WATER, MY FATHER CALLED WOLFF AND BYRD TO ASK THEM TO TAKE MY CASE.
"YOU SEE, MY DAD USED TO CALL SOME OF WOLFF AND BYRD'S MORE FAMOUS CLIENTS 'MASTER' . . .
IT'S ALIVE!
IT'S ALIVE!!
MASTER-- THE VILLAGERS ARE STORMING THE CASTLE!!
"YES, THE HOURS WERE LONG AND THE WORK WAS THANKLESS! MY DAD DIDN'T WANT HIS SON TO FOLLOW IN HIS FOOTSTEPS.
"BACK IN THE OLD COUNTRY, MY DAD WAS ASSISTANT TO MANY A MAD SCIENTIST, AND HE KNEW IT WAS A RISKY BUSINESS . . .
DAD SCRIMPED AND SAVED TO SEND ME TO AMERICA AND PUT ME THROUGH SCHOOL.
HIS DREAM CAME TRUE WHEN I GOT A JOB AFTER LEAVING COLLEGE . . .
"LITTLE DID HE KNOW IT WOULD BECOME MY WORST NIGHTMARE!!
CRAASH!
Little Village Pre-School

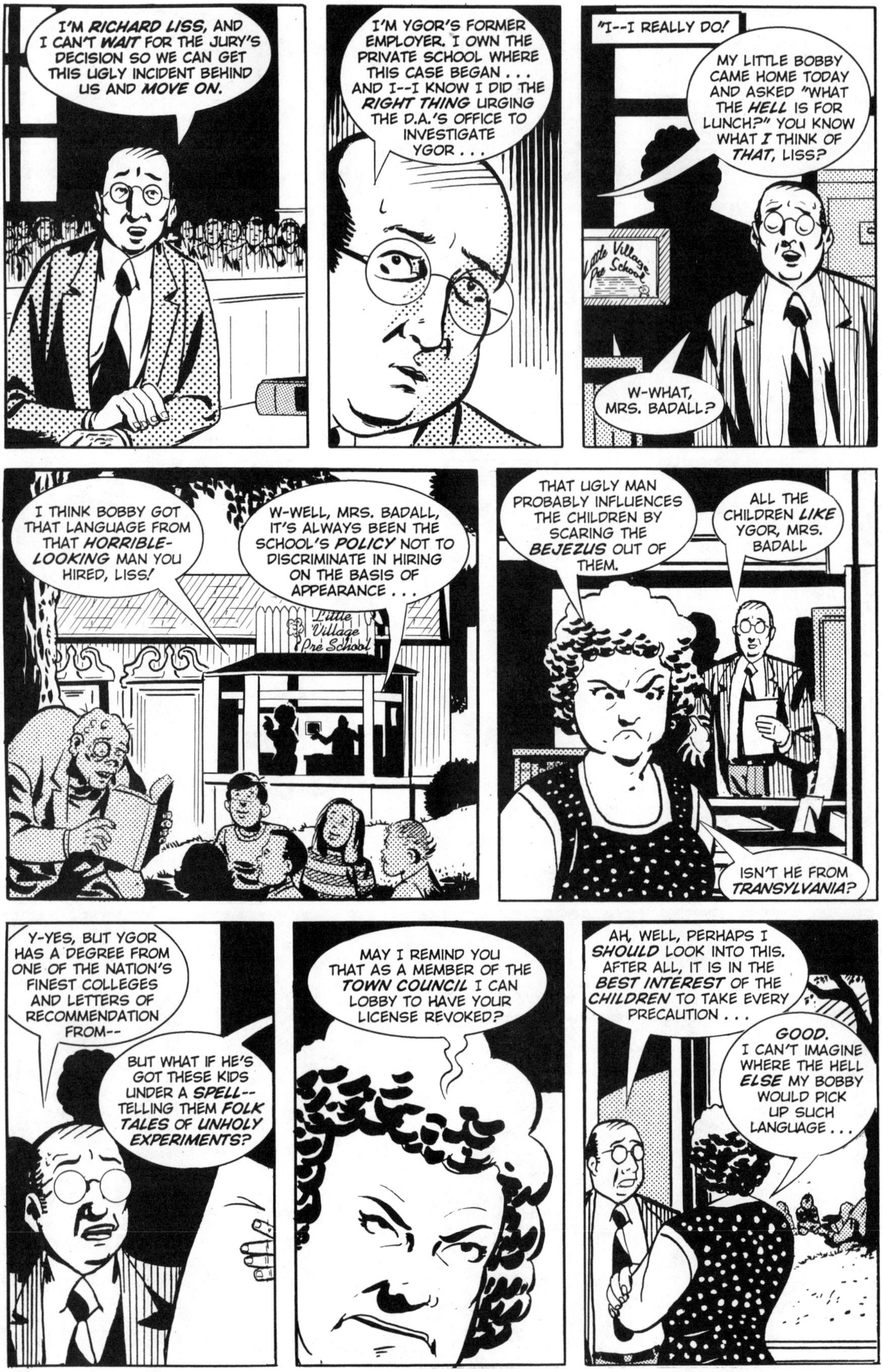
I'M RICHARD LISS, AND I CAN'T WAIT FOR THE JURY'S DECISION SO WE CAN GET THIS UGLY INCIDENT BEHIND US AND MOVE ON.
I'M YGOR'S FORMER EMPLOYER. I OWN THE PRIVATE SCHOOL WHERE THIS CASE BEGAN . . . AND I--I KNOW I DID THE RIGHT THING URGING THE D.A.'S OFFICE TO INVESTIGATE YGOR . . .
"I--I REALLY DO!
MY LITTLE BOBBY CAME HOME TODAY AND ASKED "WHAT THE HELL IS FOR LUNCH?" YOU KNOW WHAT I THINK OF THAT, LISS?
Little Village Pre School
W-WHAT, MRS. BADALL?
I THINK BOBBY GOT THAT LANGUAGE FROM THAT HORRIBLE-LOOKING MAN YOU HIRED, LISS!
W-WELL, MRS. BADALL, IT'S ALWAYS BEEN THE SCHOOL'S POLICY NOT TO DISCRIMINATE IN HIRING ON THE BASIS OF APPEARANCE . . .
Little Village Pre School
THAT UGLY MAN PROBABLY INFLUENCES THE CHILDREN BY SCARING THE BEJEZUS OUT OF THEM.
ALL THE CHILDREN LIKE YGOR, MRS. BADALL
ISN'T HE FROM TRANSYLVANIA?
Y-YES, BUT YGOR HAS A DEGREE FROM ONE OF THE NATION'S FINEST COLLEGES AND LETTERS OF RECOMMENDATION FROM--
BUT WHAT IF HE'S GOT THESE KIDS UNDER A SPELL-- TELLING THEM FOLK TALES OF UNHOLY EXPERIMENTS?
MAY I REMIND YOU THAT AS A MEMBER OF THE TOWN COUNCIL I CAN LOBBY TO HAVE YOUR LICENSE REVOKED?
AH, WELL, PERHAPS I SHOULD LOOK INTO THIS. AFTER ALL, IT IS IN THE BEST INTEREST OF THE CHILDREN TO TAKE EVERY PRECAUTION . . .
GOOD. I CAN'T IMAGINE WHERE THE HELL ELSE MY BOBBY WOULD PICK UP SUCH LANGUAGE . . .

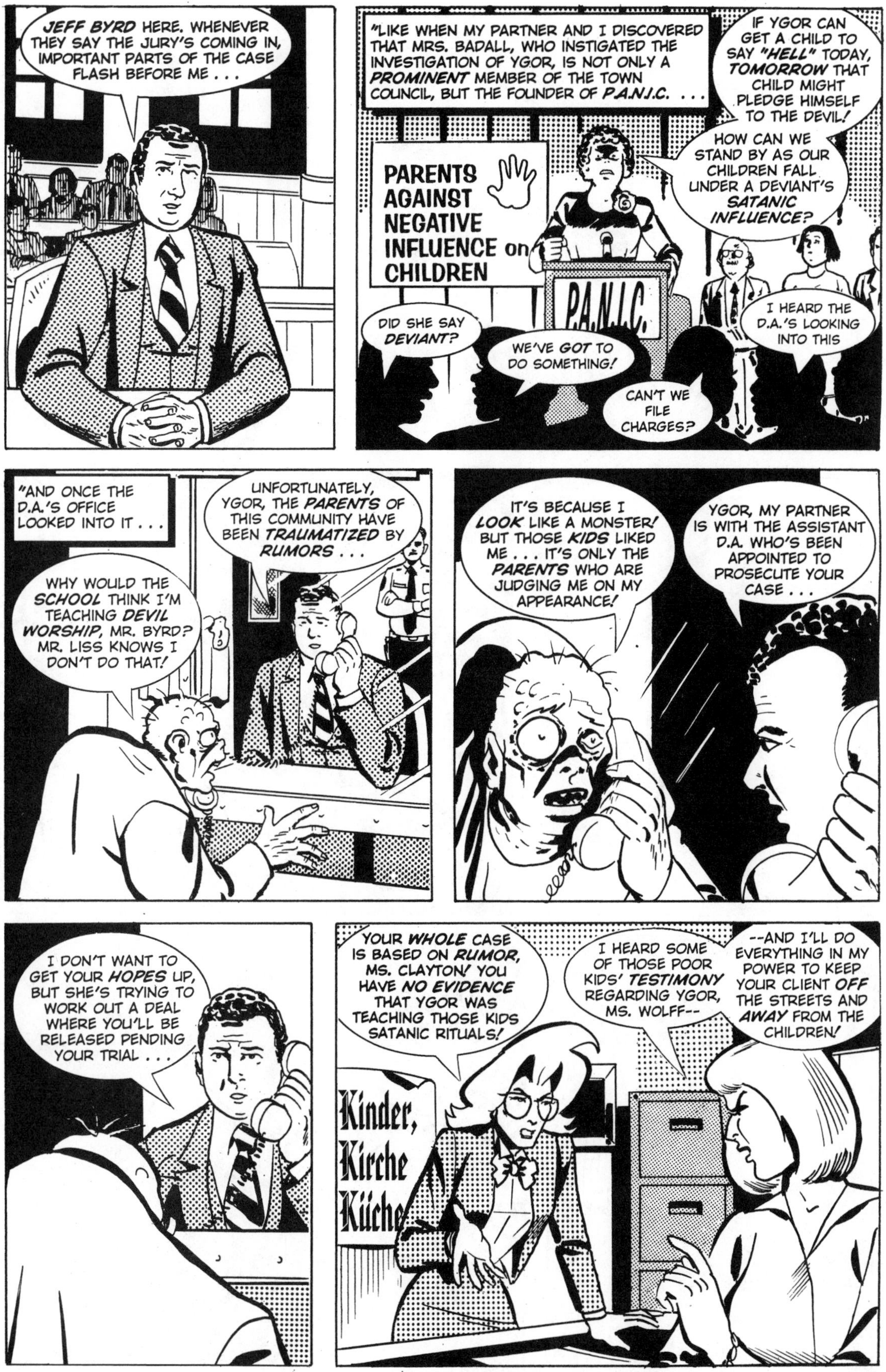
JEFF BYRD HERE. WHENEVER THEY SAY THE JURY'S COMING IN, IMPORTANT PARTS OF THE CASE FLASH BEFORE ME . . .
"LIKE WHEN MY PARTNER AND I DISCOVERED THAT MRS. BADALL, WHO INSTIGATED THE INVESTIGATION OF YGOR, IS NOT ONLY A PROMINENT MEMBER OF THE TOWN COUNCIL, BUT THE FOUNDER OF P.A.N.I.C. . . .
IF YGOR CAN GET A CHILD TO SAY "HELL" TODAY, TOMORROW THAT CHILD MIGHT PLEDGE HIMSELF TO THE DEVIL!
HOW CAN WE STAND BY AS OUR CHILDREN FALL UNDER A DEVIANT'S SATANIC INFLUENCE?
PARENTS AGAINST NEGATIVE INFLUENCE on CHILDREN
P.A.N.I.C.
DID SHE SAY DEVIANT?
WE'VE GOT TO DO SOMETHING!
CAN'T WE FILE CHARGES?
I HEARD THE D.A.'S LOOKING INTO THIS
"AND ONCE THE D.A.'S OFFICE LOOKED INTO IT . . .
UNFORTUNATELY, YGOR, THE PARENTS OF THIS COMMUNITY HAVE BEEN TRAUMATIZED BY RUMORS . . .
WHY WOULD THE SCHOOL THINK I'M TEACHING DEVIL WORSHIP, MR. BYRD? MR. LISS KNOWS I DON'T DO THAT!
IT'S BECAUSE I LOOK LIKE A MONSTER! BUT THOSE KIDS LIKED ME . . . IT'S ONLY THE PARENTS WHO ARE JUDGING ME ON MY APPEARANCE!
YGOR, MY PARTNER IS WITH THE ASSISTANT D.A. WHO'S BEEN APPOINTED TO PROSECUTE YOUR CASE . . .
I DON'T WANT TO GET YOUR HOPES UP, BUT SHE'S TRYING TO WORK OUT A DEAL WHERE YOU'LL BE RELEASED PENDING YOUR TRIAL . . .
YOUR WHOLE CASE IS BASED ON RUMOR, MS. CLAYTON! YOU HAVE NO EVIDENCE THAT YGOR WAS TEACHING THOSE KIDS SATANIC RITUALS!
I HEARD SOME OF THOSE POOR KIDS' TESTIMONY REGARDING YGOR, MS. WOLFF--
--AND I'LL DO EVERYTHING IN MY POWER TO KEEP YOUR CLIENT OFF THE STREETS AND AWAY FROM THE CHILDREN!
Kinder, Kirche Küche

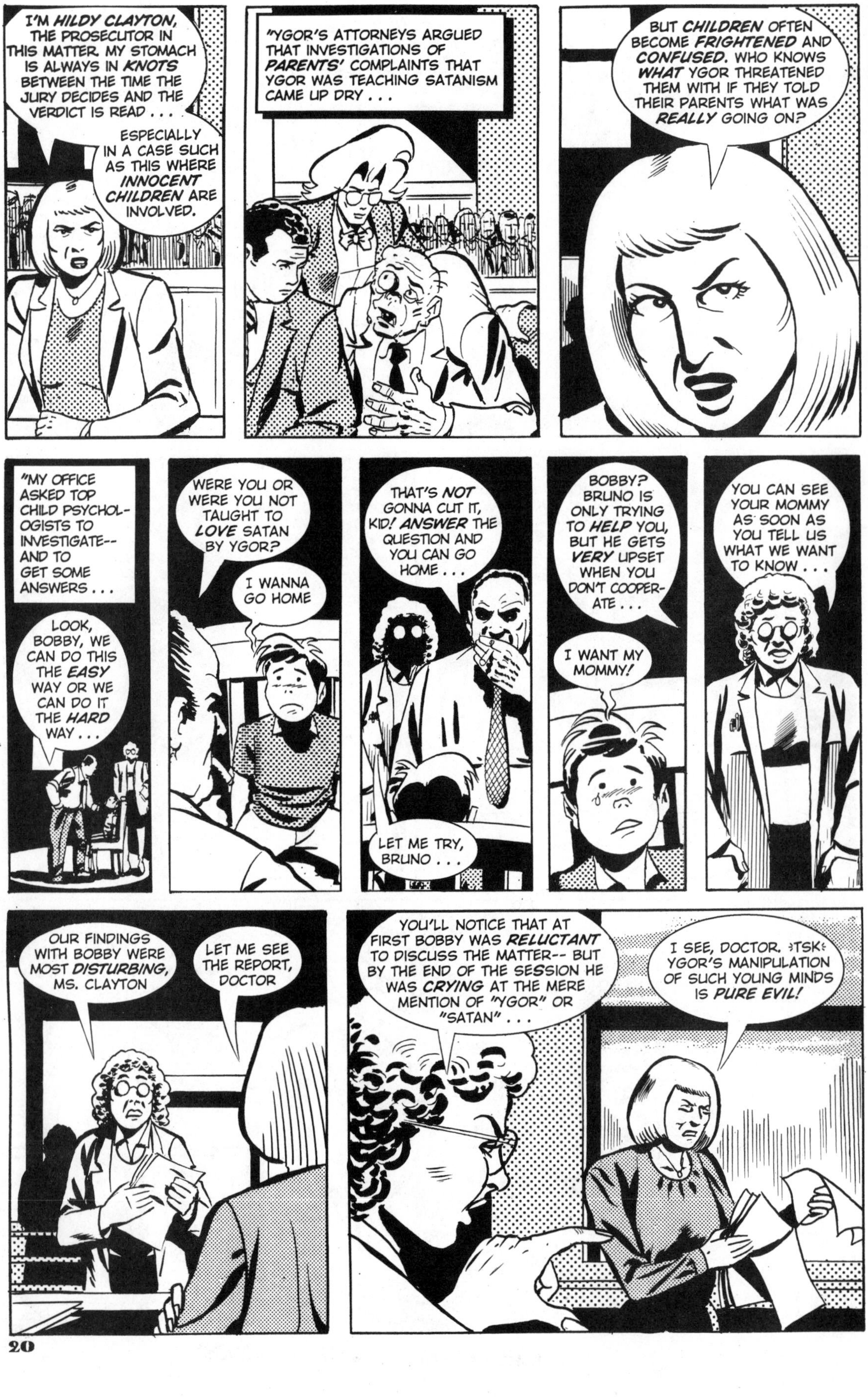
I'M HILDY CLAYTON, THE PROSECUTOR IN THIS MATTER. MY STOMACH IS ALWAYS IN KNOTS BETWEEN THE TIME THE JURY DECIDES AND THE VERDICT IS READ . . .
ESPECIALLY IN A CASE SUCH AS THIS WHERE INNOCENT CHILDREN ARE INVOLVED.
"YGOR'S ATTORNEYS ARGUED THAT INVESTIGATIONS OF PARENTS' COMPLAINTS THAT YGOR WAS TEACHING SATANISM CAME UP DRY . . .
BUT CHILDREN OFTEN BECOME FRIGHTENED AND CONFUSED. WHO KNOWS WHAT YGOR THREATENED THEM WITH IF THEY TOLD THEIR PARENTS WHAT WAS REALLY GOING ON?
"MY OFFICE ASKED TOP CHILD PSYCHOL-OGISTS TO INVESTIGATE-- AND TO GET SOME ANSWERS . . .
LOOK, BOBBY, WE CAN DO THIS THE EASY WAY OR WE CAN DO IT THE HARD WAY . . .
WERE YOU OR WERE YOU NOT TAUGHT TO LOVE SATAN BY YGOR?
I WANNA GO HOME
THAT'S NOT GONNA CUT IT, KID! ANSWER THE QUESTION AND YOU CAN GO HOME . . .
LET ME TRY, BRUNO . . .
BOBBY? BRUNO IS ONLY TRYING TO HELP YOU, BUT HE GETS VERY UPSET WHEN YOU DON'T COOPER-ATE . . .
I WANT MY MOMMY!
YOU CAN SEE YOUR MOMMY AS SOON AS YOU TELL US WHAT WE WANT TO KNOW . . .
OUR FINDINGS WITH BOBBY WERE MOST DISTURBING, MS. CLAYTON
LET ME SEE THE REPORT, DOCTOR
YOU'LL NOTICE THAT AT FIRST BOBBY WAS RELUCTANT TO DISCUSS THE MATTER-- BUT BY THE END OF THE SESSION HE WAS CRYING AT THE MERE MENTION OF "YGOR" OR "SATAN" . . .
I SEE, DOCTOR. ∗TSK∗ YGOR'S MANIPULATION OF SUCH YOUNG MINDS IS PURE EVIL!

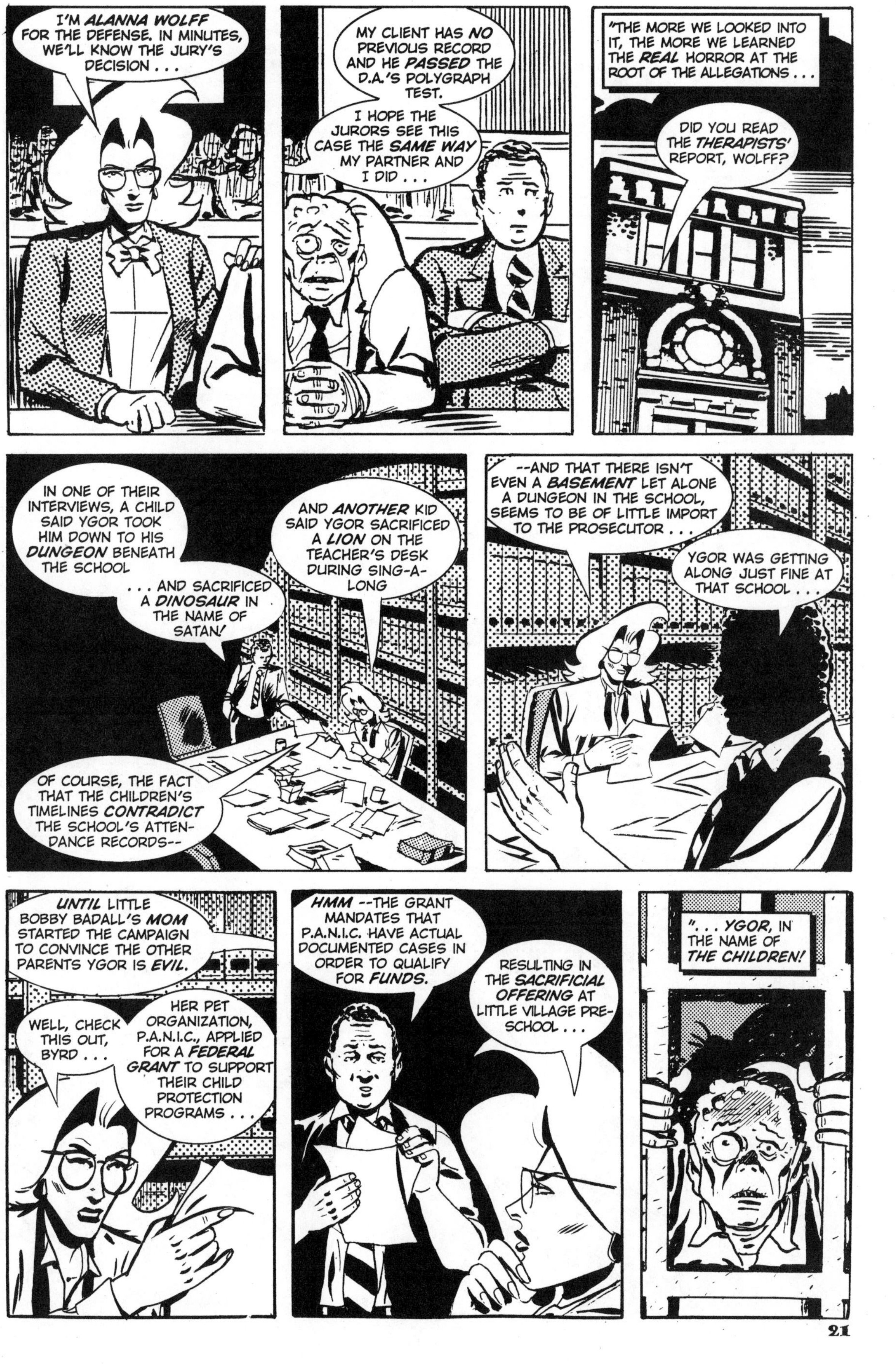

I'M ALANNA WOLFF FOR THE DEFENSE. IN MINUTES, WE'LL KNOW THE JURY'S DECISION . . .
MY CLIENT HAS NO PREVIOUS RECORD AND HE PASSED THE D.A.'S POLYGRAPH TEST.
I HOPE THE JURORS SEE THIS CASE THE SAME WAY MY PARTNER AND I DID . . .
"THE MORE WE LOOKED INTO IT, THE MORE WE LEARNED THE REAL HORROR AT THE ROOT OF THE ALLEGATIONS . . .
DID YOU READ THE THERAPISTS' REPORT, WOLFF?
IN ONE OF THEIR INTERVIEWS, A CHILD SAID YGOR TOOK HIM DOWN TO HIS DUNGEON BENEATH THE SCHOOL
. . . AND SACRIFICED A DINOSAUR IN THE NAME OF SATAN!
AND ANOTHER KID SAID YGOR SACRIFICED A LION ON THE TEACHER'S DESK DURING SING-A-LONG
OF COURSE, THE FACT THAT THE CHILDREN'S TIMELINES CONTRADICT THE SCHOOL'S ATTEN-DANCE RECORDS--
--AND THAT THERE ISN'T EVEN A BASEMENT LET ALONE A DUNGEON IN THE SCHOOL, SEEMS TO BE OF LITTLE IMPORT TO THE PROSECUTOR . . .
YGOR WAS GETTING ALONG JUST FINE AT THAT SCHOOL . . .
UNTIL LITTLE BOBBY BADALL'S MOM STARTED THE CAMPAIGN TO CONVINCE THE OTHER PARENTS YGOR IS EVIL.
WELL, CHECK THIS OUT, BYRD . . .
HER PET ORGANIZATION, P.A.N.I.C., APPLIED FOR A FEDERAL GRANT TO SUPPORT THEIR CHILD PROTECTION PROGRAMS . . .
HMM --THE GRANT MANDATES THAT P.A.N.I.C. HAVE ACTUAL DOCUMENTED CASES IN ORDER TO QUALIFY FOR FUNDS.
RESULTING IN THE SACRIFICIAL OFFERING AT LITTLE VILLAGE PRE-SCHOOL . . .
". . . YGOR, IN THE NAME OF THE CHILDREN!

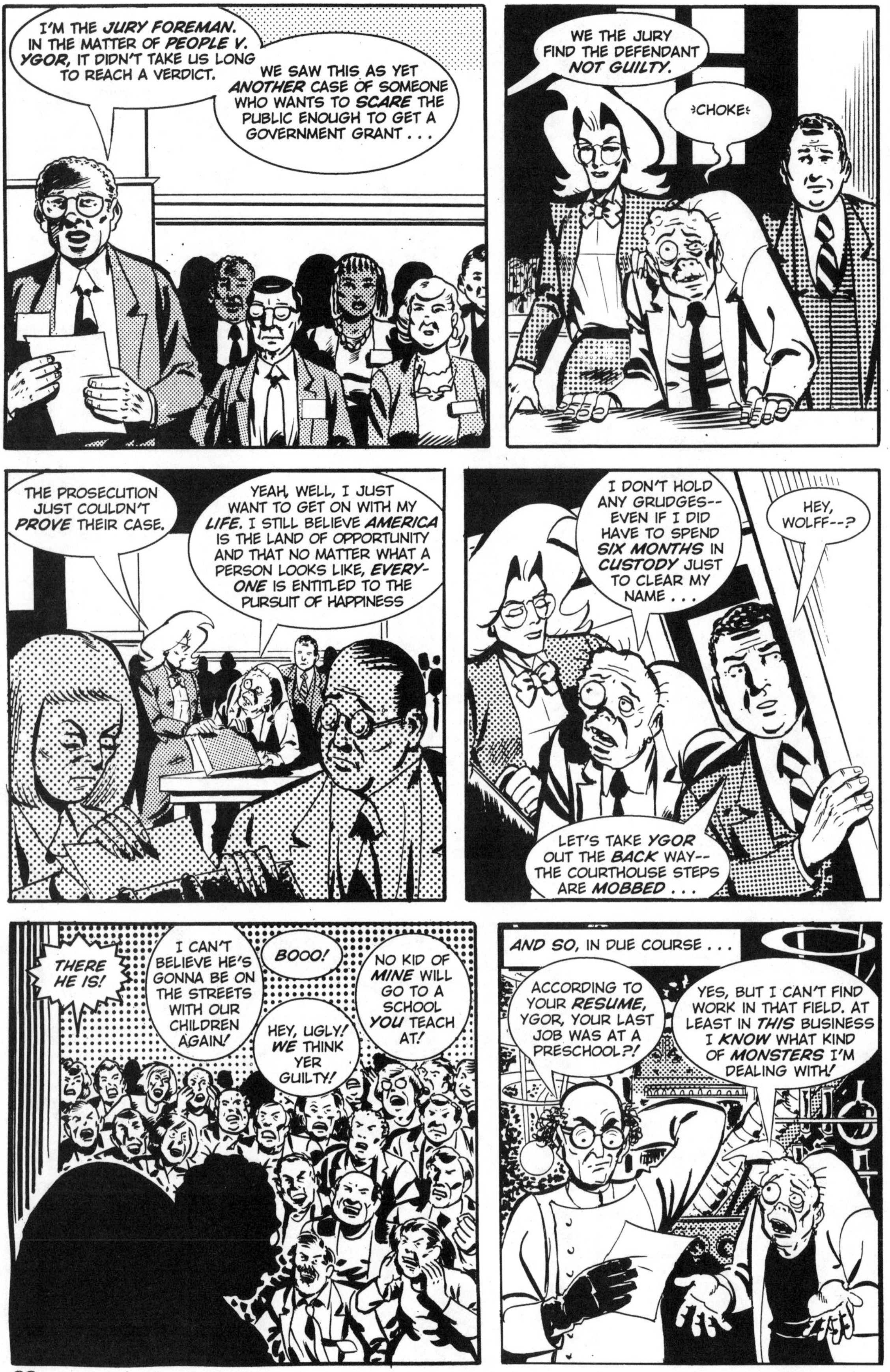
I'M THE JURY FOREMAN. IN THE MATTER OF PEOPLE V. YGOR, IT DIDN'T TAKE US LONG TO REACH A VERDICT.
WE SAW THIS AS YET ANOTHER CASE OF SOMEONE WHO WANTS TO SCARE THE PUBLIC ENOUGH TO GET A GOVERNMENT GRANT . . .
WE THE JURY FIND THE DEFENDANT NOT GUILTY.
CHOKE
THE PROSECUTION JUST COULDN'T PROVE THEIR CASE.
YEAH, WELL, I JUST WANT TO GET ON WITH MY LIFE. I STILL BELIEVE AMERICA IS THE LAND OF OPPORTUNITY AND THAT NO MATTER WHAT A PERSON LOOKS LIKE, EVERY-ONE IS ENTITLED TO THE PURSUIT OF HAPPINESS
I DON'T HOLD ANY GRUDGES-- EVEN IF I DID HAVE TO SPEND SIX MONTHS IN CUSTODY JUST TO CLEAR MY NAME . . .
HEY, WOLFF--?
LET'S TAKE YGOR OUT THE BACK WAY-- THE COURTHOUSE STEPS ARE MOBBED . . .
THERE HE IS!
I CAN'T BELIEVE HE'S GONNA BE ON THE STREETS WITH OUR CHILDREN AGAIN!
BOOO!
NO KID OF MINE WILL GO TO A SCHOOL YOU TEACH AT!
HEY, UGLY! WE THINK YER GUILTY!
AND SO, IN DUE COURSE . . .
ACCORDING TO YOUR RESUME, YGOR, YOUR LAST JOB WAS AT A PRESCHOOL?!
YES, BUT I CAN'T FIND WORK IN THAT FIELD. AT LEAST IN THIS BUSINESS I KNOW WHAT KIND OF MONSTERS I'M DEALING WITH!

Sonovawitch

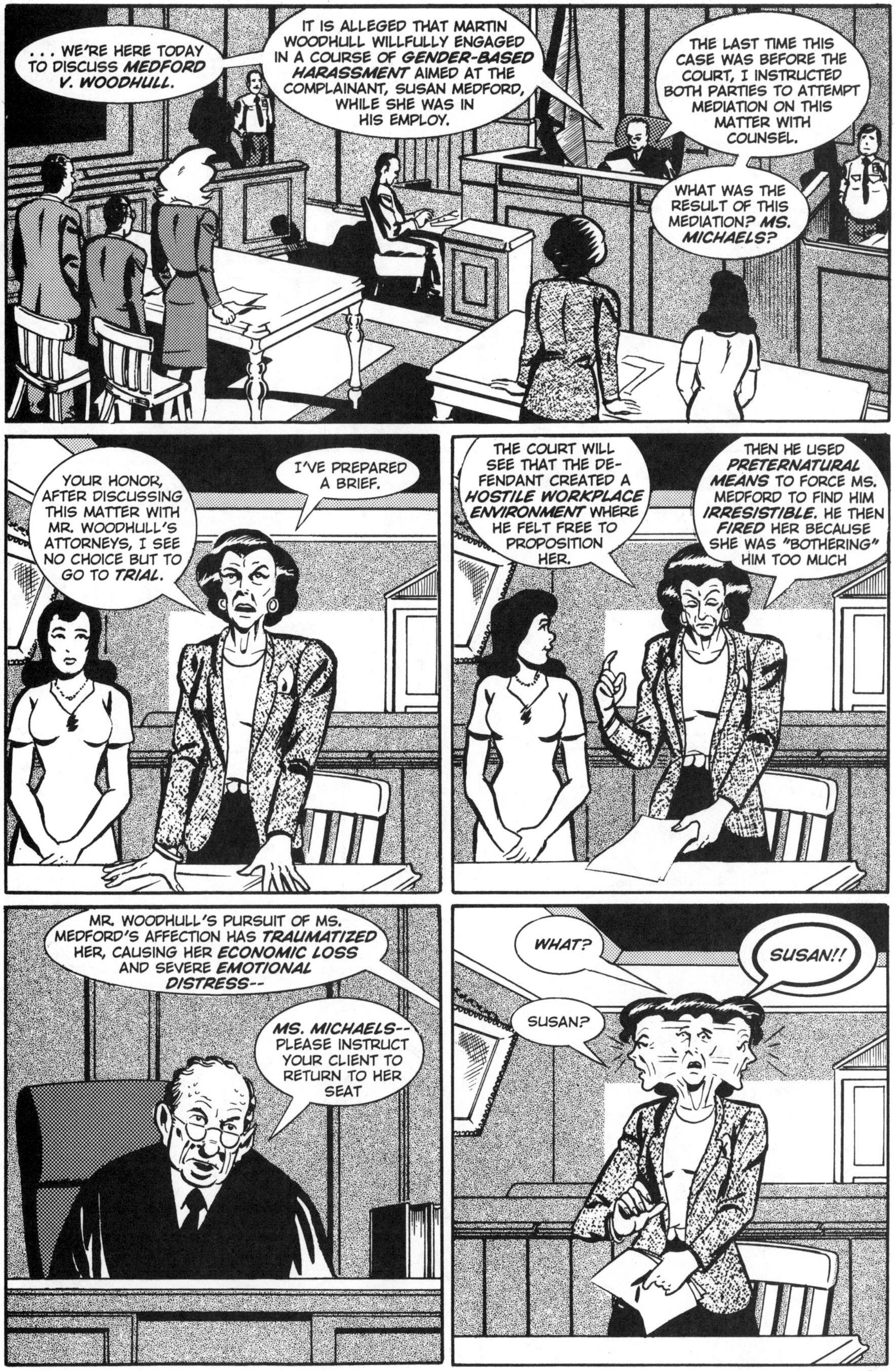
. . . WE'RE HERE TODAY TO DISCUSS MEDFORD V. WOODHULL.
IT IS ALLEGED THAT MARTIN WOODHULL WILLFULLY ENGAGED IN A COURSE OF GENDER-BASED HARASSMENT AIMED AT THE COMPLAINANT, SUSAN MEDFORD, WHILE SHE WAS IN HIS EMPLOY.
THE LAST TIME THIS CASE WAS BEFORE THE COURT, I INSTRUCTED BOTH PARTIES TO ATTEMPT MEDIATION ON THIS MATTER WITH COUNSEL.
WHAT WAS THE RESULT OF THIS MEDIATION? MS. MICHAELS?
YOUR HONOR, AFTER DISCUSSING THIS MATTER WITH MR. WOODHULL'S ATTORNEYS, I SEE NO CHOICE BUT TO GO TO TRIAL.
I'VE PREPARED A BRIEF.
THE COURT WILL SEE THAT THE DE-FENDANT CREATED A HOSTILE WORKPLACE ENVIRONMENT WHERE HE FELT FREE TO PROPOSITION HER.
THEN HE USED PRETERNATURAL MEANS TO FORCE MS. MEDFORD TO FIND HIM IRRESISTIBLE. HE THEN FIRED HER BECAUSE SHE WAS "BOTHERING" HIM TOO MUCH
MR. WOODHULL'S PURSUIT OF MS. MEDFORD'S AFFECTION HAS TRAUMATIZED HER, CAUSING HER ECONOMIC LOSS AND SEVERE EMOTIONAL DISTRESS--
MS. MICHAELS-- PLEASE INSTRUCT YOUR CLIENT TO RETURN TO HER SEAT
WHAT?
SUSAN!!
SUSAN?

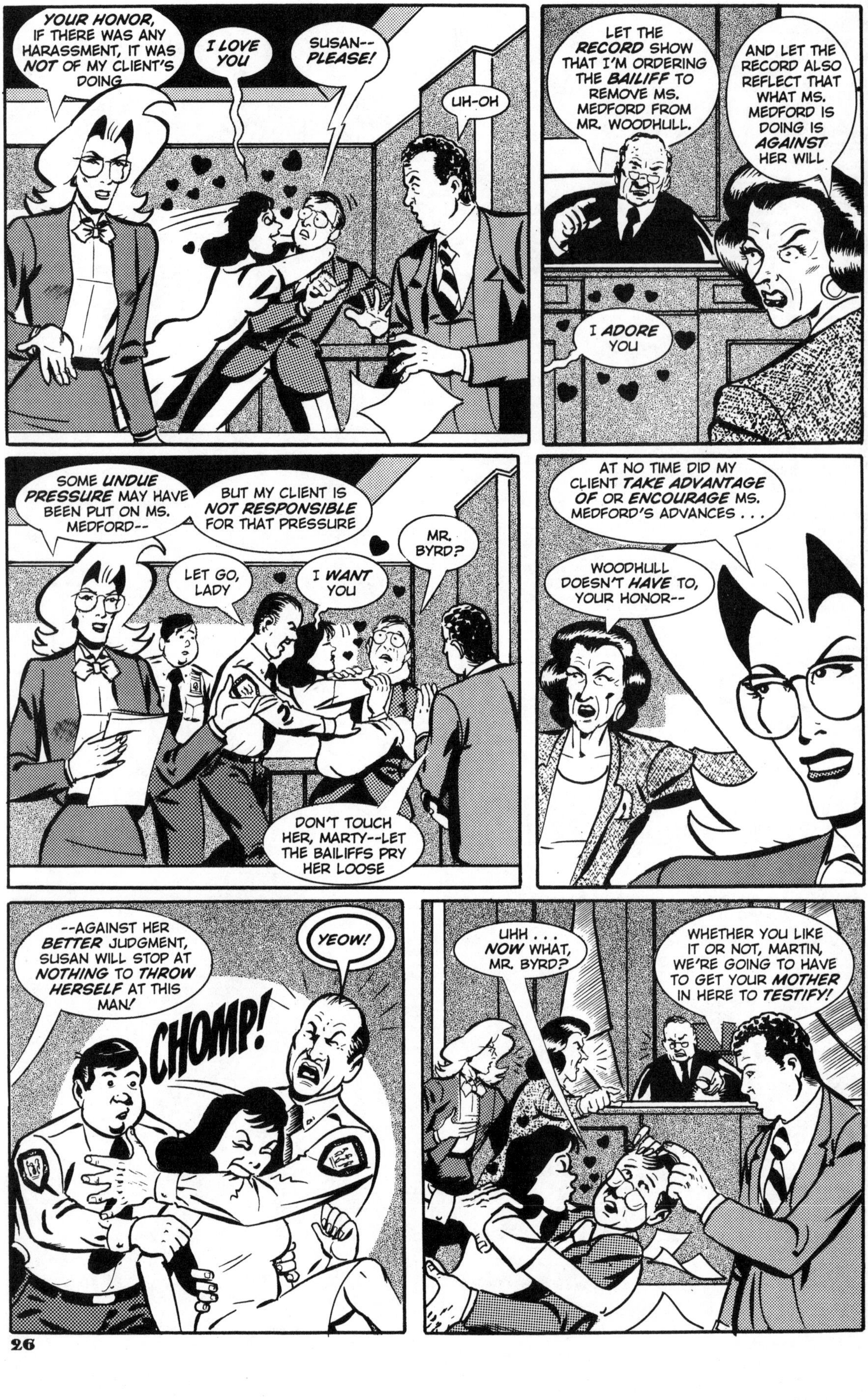

YOUR HONOR, IF THERE WAS ANY HARASSMENT, IT WAS NOT OF MY CLIENT'S DOING
I LOVE YOU
SUSAN-- PLEASE!
UH-OH
LET THE RECORD SHOW THAT I'M ORDERING THE BAILIFF TO REMOVE MS. MEDFORD FROM MR. WOODHULL.
AND LET THE RECORD ALSO REFLECT THAT WHAT MS. MEDFORD IS DOING IS AGAINST HER WILL
I ADORE YOU
SOME UNDUE PRESSURE MAY HAVE BEEN PUT ON MS. MEDFORD--
BUT MY CLIENT IS NOT RESPONSIBLE FOR THAT PRESSURE
LET GO, LADY
I WANT YOU
MR. BYRD?
DON'T TOUCH HER, MARTY--LET THE BAILIFFS PRY HER LOOSE
AT NO TIME DID MY CLIENT TAKE ADVANTAGE OF OR ENCOURAGE MS. MEDFORD'S ADVANCES . . .
WOODHULL DOESN'T HAVE TO, YOUR HONOR--
--AGAINST HER BETTER JUDGMENT, SUSAN WILL STOP AT NOTHING TO THROW HERSELF AT THIS MAN!
YEOW!
CHOMP!
UHH . . . NOW WHAT, MR. BYRD?
WHETHER YOU LIKE IT OR NOT, MARTIN, WE'RE GOING TO HAVE TO GET YOUR MOTHER IN HERE TO TESTIFY!

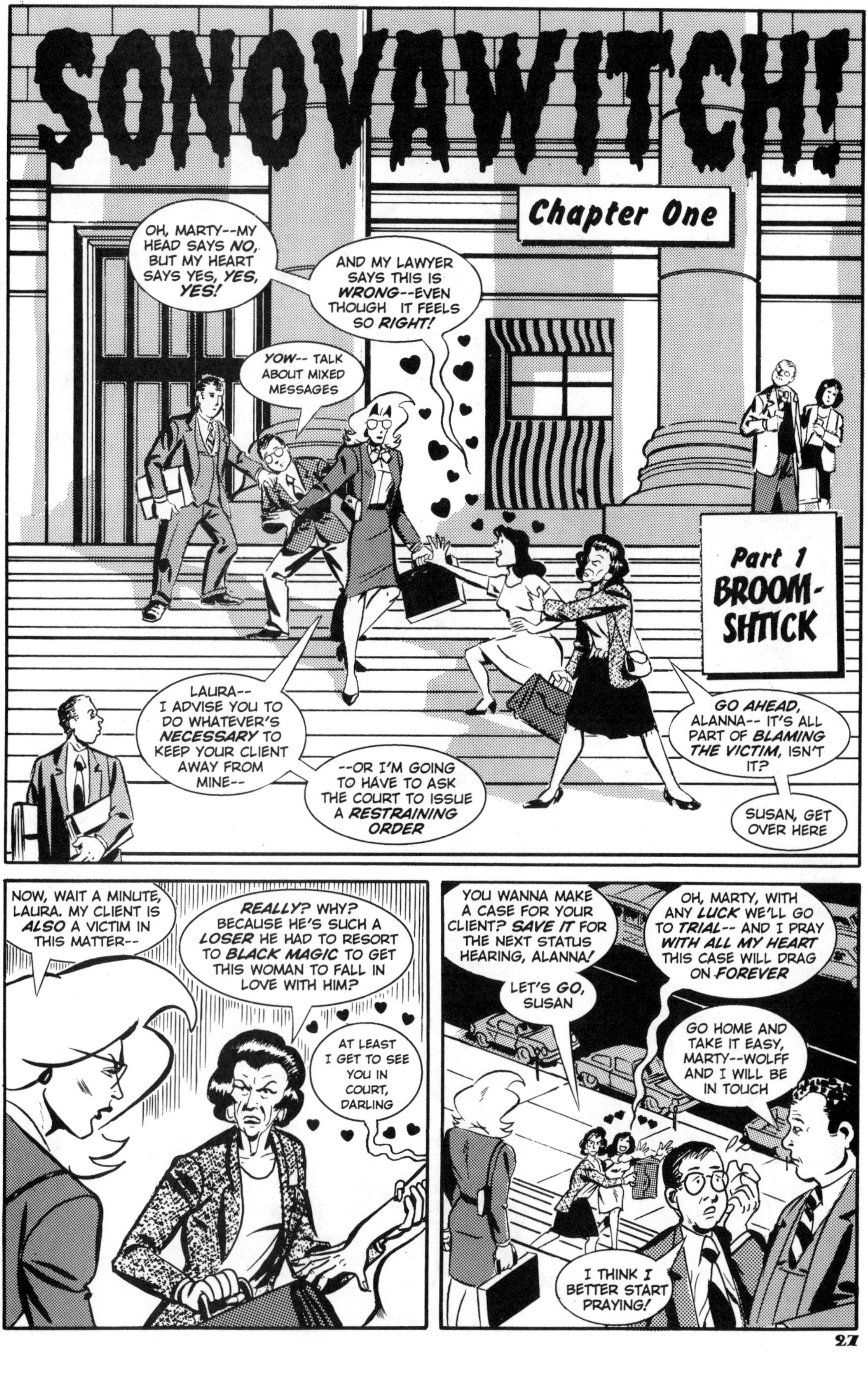
SONOVAWITCH!
Chapter One
OH, MARTY--MY HEAD SAYS NO, BUT MY HEART SAYS YES, YES, YES!
AND MY LAWYER SAYS THIS IS WRONG--EVEN THOUGH IT FEELS SO RIGHT!
YOW-- TALK ABOUT MIXED MESSAGES
Part 1 BROOM-SHTICK
LAURA-- I ADVISE YOU TO DO WHATEVER'S NECESSARY TO KEEP YOUR CLIENT AWAY FROM MINE--
--OR I'M GOING TO HAVE TO ASK THE COURT TO ISSUE A RESTRAINING ORDER
GO AHEAD, ALANNA-- IT'S ALL PART OF BLAMING THE VICTIM, ISN'T IT?
SUSAN, GET OVER HERE
NOW, WAIT A MINUTE, LAURA. MY CLIENT IS ALSO A VICTIM IN THIS MATTER--
REALLY? WHY? BECAUSE HE'S SUCH A LOSER HE HAD TO RESORT TO BLACK MAGIC TO GET THIS WOMAN TO FALL IN LOVE WITH HIM?
AT LEAST I GET TO SEE YOU IN COURT, DARLING
YOU WANNA MAKE A CASE FOR YOUR CLIENT? SAVE IT FOR THE NEXT STATUS HEARING, ALANNA!
LET'S GO, SUSAN
OH, MARTY, WITH ANY LUCK WE'LL GO TO TRIAL-- AND I PRAY WITH ALL MY HEART THIS CASE WILL DRAG ON FOREVER
GO HOME AND TAKE IT EASY, MARTY--WOLFF AND I WILL BE IN TOUCH
I THINK I BETTER START PRAYING!

HOW COULD *MOTHER* DO THIS TO ME? CASTING A *SPELL* ON THAT POOR GIRL . . .

"SHE ALWAYS TOLD ME THAT EVEN FROM THAT DAY SHE FOUND ME *ABANDONED* AS A *BABY* IN PROSPECT PARK, SHE WANTED ME TO GROW UP "NORMAL" . . . SHE KNEW WHAT IT WAS LIKE TO BE AN *OUTSIDER*-- SHE WANTED ME TO *ASSIMILATE* . . .

"WHICH WAS FINE BY ME, BECAUSE I WANTED TO *MAKE IT* IN THE WORLD ON MY OWN, RATHER THAN RELY ON HER *MAGIC* . . .

"I WAS AS 'NORMAL' AS ONE CAN GET-- BUT THAT WASN'T *ENOUGH* FOR MA--

MARTIN WOODHILL VICE PRESIDENT SALES AND MARKETING

"SHE WANTED ME TO *SETTLE DOWN* . . . I SHOULD *NEVER* HAVE TOLD HER THAT I *LIKED* THE BOOKKEEPER AT WORK . . .

UM, AH, SUSAN? ARE YOU BUSY SATURDAY NIGHT?

SORRY, MARTIN-- I HAVE A *BOY-FRIEND!*

"WHEN SUSAN'S ATTITUDE CHANGED *OVERNIGHT*, I JUST THOUGHT SHE HAD *RECONSIDERED*. BUT HER *ENTHUSIASM* JUST DIDN'T SEEM, WELL, *NORMAL* . . .

KISS ME, YOU FOOL!

SUSAN-- WHAT'S GOT-TEN INTO YOU-- *OH, GOD! MOTHER! NO!!*

"I *FIRED* SUSAN FOR HER OWN GOOD. I THOUGHT HER NOT BEING AROUND ME WOULD MAKE THE SPELL *DISSIPATE*. BUT IT ONLY MADE THINGS WORSE . . .

"I'VE HIRED A LAWYER TO *SUE* YOU. I'LL SEE YOU IN COURT. AM COUNTING THE DAYS. SINCERELY, SUSAN MEDFORD. P.S. I WUV YOU!" *GROAN*

NOW I HAVE TO DO WHAT I'VE ALWAYS *DREADED*-- CONVINCE MY MOTHER TO GO PUBLIC THAT SHE'S A *WITCH!*

AT LEAST I FOUND *ATTORNEYS* WHO ARE USED TO DEALING WITH HER *KIND* . . .

AND FOR ALL THE *TROUBLE* MY MOTHER HAS CAUSED ME . . . THIS WHOLE EXPERIENCE MAY BE A *BLESSING* IN DISGUISE . . . !

❷ ❸ Downtown

YOU SHOULD NEVER, *EVER* TELL CLIENTS THEY ARE SURE TO *WIN* THEIR CASES. AND IF YOU *DO* SAY THAT, UNDER NO CIRCUMSTANCES ARE YOU TO *GUARANTEE* THAT WE'LL WIN THE CASE FOR THEM.

WOLFF & BYRD
COUNSELORS OF THE MACABRE

I SHOULDN'T HAVE SAID THAT, HUH MAVIS?

NO, COREY. YOUR JOB IS TO ANSWER THE *PHONES* AND GREET CLIENTS.

IF THERE'S A *LEGAL QUESTION*, ASK YOUR SISTER OR MR. BYRD OR ME.

IF SOMEONE WANTS AN *APPOINTMENT*, CONSULT THE *APPOINTMENT BOOK*.

GOTCHA, MAVIS. I'M REMEMBERING TO *WRITE DOWN* THE APPOINTMENTS, TOO!

GOOD. ANOTHER THING: THERE'S NO TELLING WHEN SOMEONE OR *SOMETHING* WILL COME THROUGH THAT DOOR--OR WALL-- AND SHOCK YOU. *REMEMBER* . . .

WOLFF & BYRD
COUNSELORS OF THE MACABRE

I KNOW: "THIS ISN'T A SIDESHOW, IT'S A LAW OFFICE." DON'T WORRY, MAVIS. MY SISTER HAS TOLD ME ENOUGH ABOUT HER CLIENTS THAT I THINK I'M PREPARED FOR ANYTHING.

THAT'S RIGHT, COREY-- ALWAYS ACT *PROFESSIONAL*.

UH-HUH-- REMEMBER THAT *INVISIBLE* CLIENT THIS MORNING? NOT *ONCE* DID I LOOK AT HIM!

UH, FINE. YOU'RE IMPROVING EVERY DAY . . .

YOU REALLY *THINK* SO, MAVIS?

I'VE NEVER WORKED IN AN OFFICE BEFORE. I BET I'M DRIVING YOU *CRAZY*. YOU MUST THINK I'M A REAL *AIRHEAD*!

OH, NO NO NO . . . I KNOW THIS IS NEW TO YOU . . . WELL, GOTTA GET BACK TO IT-- HANG IN THERE . . .

GAD, THAT *AIRHEAD* IS DRIVING ME *CRAZY*!

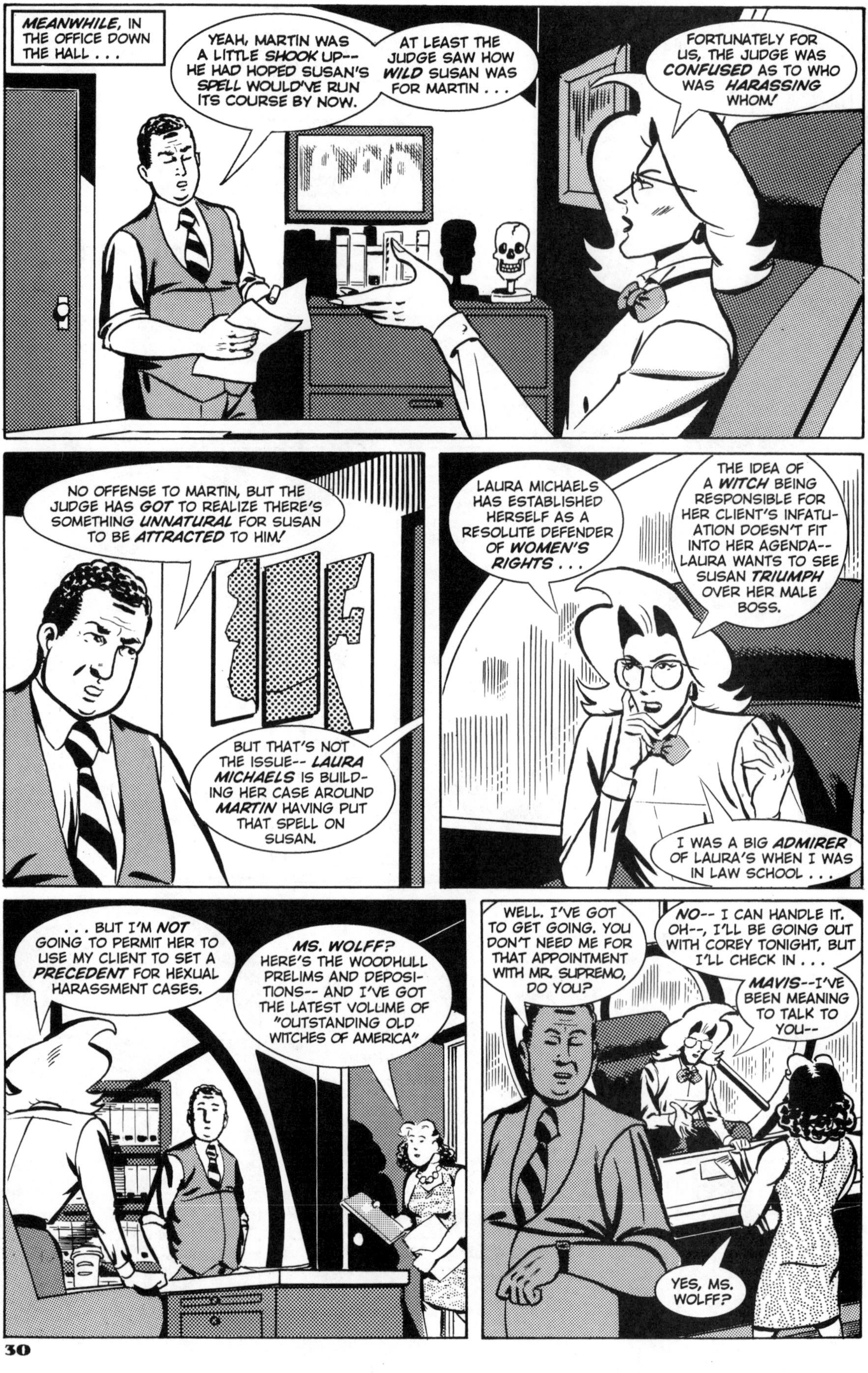

MEANWHILE, IN THE OFFICE DOWN THE HALL . . .
YEAH, MARTIN WAS A LITTLE SHOOK UP-- HE HAD HOPED SUSAN'S SPELL WOULD'VE RUN ITS COURSE BY NOW.
AT LEAST THE JUDGE SAW HOW WILD SUSAN WAS FOR MARTIN . . .
FORTUNATELY FOR US, THE JUDGE WAS CONFUSED AS TO WHO WAS HARASSING WHOM!
NO OFFENSE TO MARTIN, BUT THE JUDGE HAS GOT TO REALIZE THERE'S SOMETHING UNNATURAL FOR SUSAN TO BE ATTRACTED TO HIM!
BUT THAT'S NOT THE ISSUE-- LAURA MICHAELS IS BUILDING HER CASE AROUND MARTIN HAVING PUT THAT SPELL ON SUSAN.
LAURA MICHAELS HAS ESTABLISHED HERSELF AS A RESOLUTE DEFENDER OF WOMEN'S RIGHTS . . .
THE IDEA OF A WITCH BEING RESPONSIBLE FOR HER CLIENT'S INFATUATION DOESN'T FIT INTO HER AGENDA-- LAURA WANTS TO SEE SUSAN TRIUMPH OVER HER MALE BOSS.
I WAS A BIG ADMIRER OF LAURA'S WHEN I WAS IN LAW SCHOOL . . .
. . . BUT I'M NOT GOING TO PERMIT HER TO USE MY CLIENT TO SET A PRECEDENT FOR HEXUAL HARASSMENT CASES.
MS. WOLFF? HERE'S THE WOODHULL PRELIMS AND DEPOSITIONS-- AND I'VE GOT THE LATEST VOLUME OF "OUTSTANDING OLD WITCHES OF AMERICA"
WELL. I'VE GOT TO GET GOING. YOU DON'T NEED ME FOR THAT APPOINTMENT WITH MR. SUPREMO, DO YOU?
NO-- I CAN HANDLE IT. OH--, I'LL BE GOING OUT WITH COREY TONIGHT, BUT I'LL CHECK IN . . .
MAVIS--I'VE BEEN MEANING TO TALK TO YOU--
YES, MS. WOLFF?

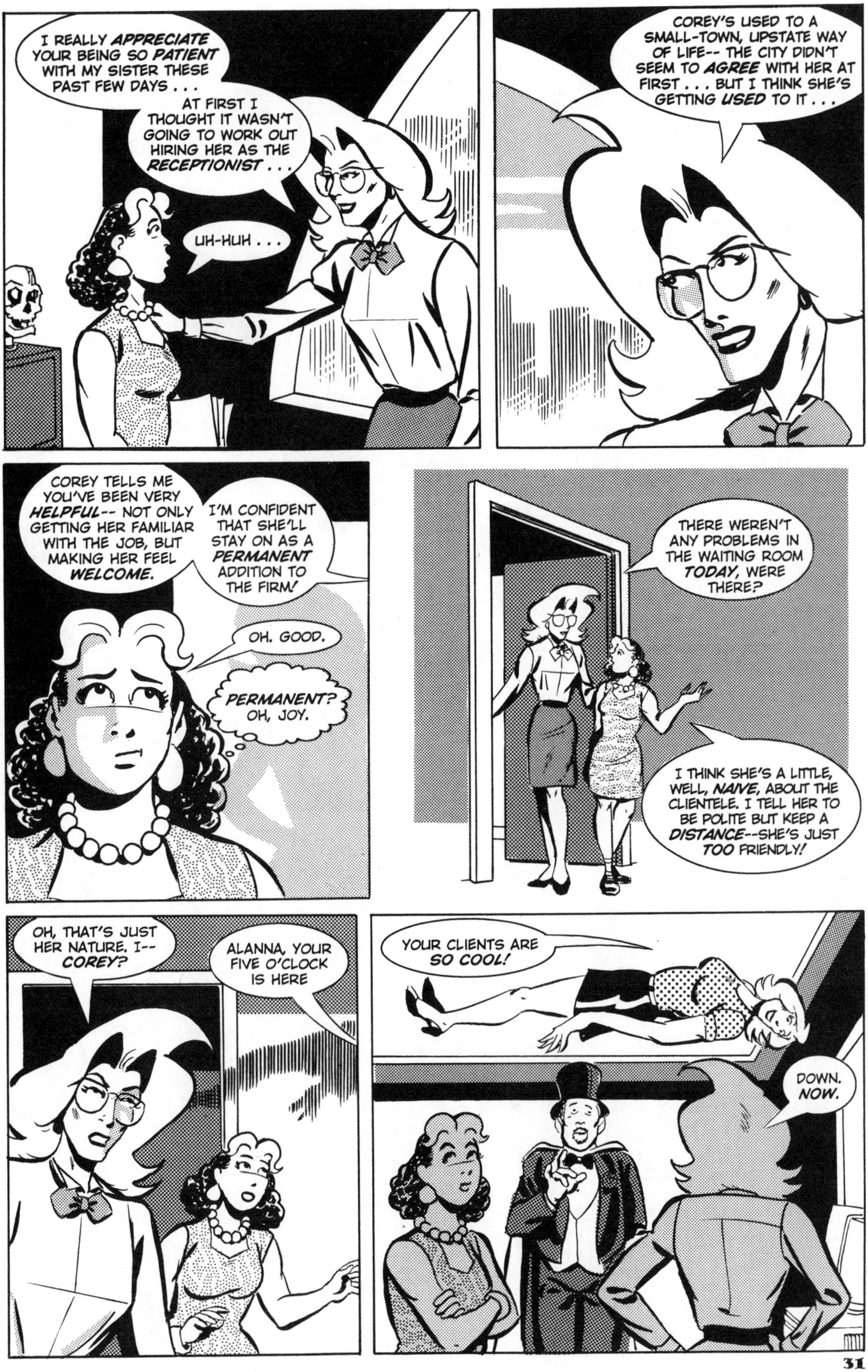
I REALLY APPRECIATE YOUR BEING SO PATIENT WITH MY SISTER THESE PAST FEW DAYS . . .
AT FIRST I THOUGHT IT WASN'T GOING TO WORK OUT HIRING HER AS THE RECEPTIONIST . . .
UH-HUH . . .
COREY'S USED TO A SMALL-TOWN, UPSTATE WAY OF LIFE-- THE CITY DIDN'T SEEM TO AGREE WITH HER AT FIRST . . . BUT I THINK SHE'S GETTING USED TO IT . . .
COREY TELLS ME YOU'VE BEEN VERY HELPFUL-- NOT ONLY GETTING HER FAMILIAR WITH THE JOB, BUT MAKING HER FEEL WELCOME.
I'M CONFIDENT THAT SHE'LL STAY ON AS A PERMANENT ADDITION TO THE FIRM!
OH. GOOD.
PERMANENT? OH, JOY.
THERE WEREN'T ANY PROBLEMS IN THE WAITING ROOM TODAY, WERE THERE?
I THINK SHE'S A LITTLE, WELL, NAIVE, ABOUT THE CLIENTELE. I TELL HER TO BE POLITE BUT KEEP A DISTANCE--SHE'S JUST TOO FRIENDLY!
OH, THAT'S JUST HER NATURE. I-- COREY?
ALANNA, YOUR FIVE O'CLOCK IS HERE
YOUR CLIENTS ARE SO COOL!
DOWN. NOW.

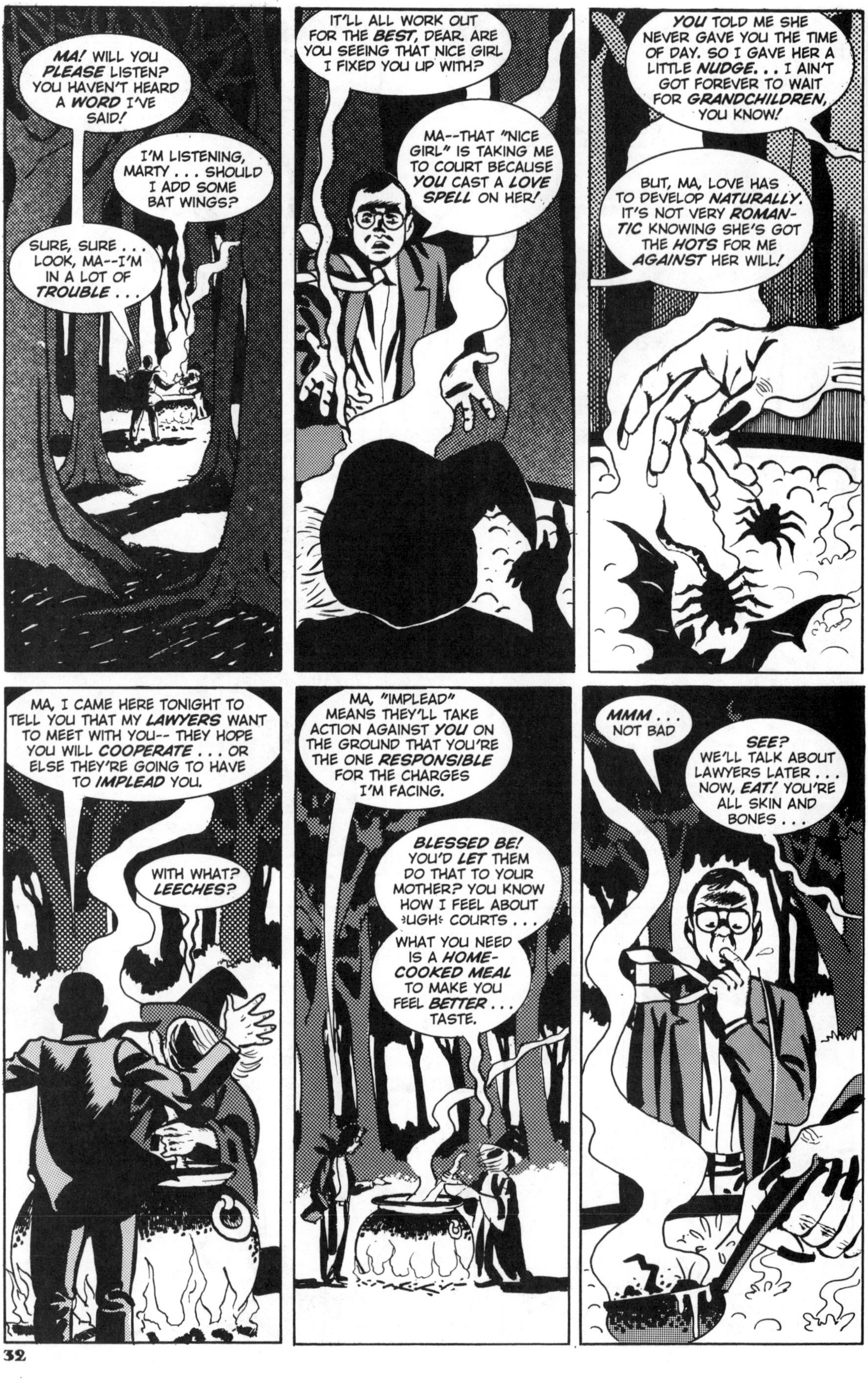
MA! WILL YOU PLEASE LISTEN? YOU HAVEN'T HEARD A WORD I'VE SAID!
I'M LISTENING, MARTY . . . SHOULD I ADD SOME BAT WINGS?
SURE, SURE . . . LOOK, MA--I'M IN A LOT OF TROUBLE . . .
IT'LL ALL WORK OUT FOR THE BEST, DEAR. ARE YOU SEEING THAT NICE GIRL I FIXED YOU UP WITH?
MA--THAT "NICE GIRL" IS TAKING ME TO COURT BECAUSE YOU CAST A LOVE SPELL ON HER!
YOU TOLD ME SHE NEVER GAVE YOU THE TIME OF DAY. SO I GAVE HER A LITTLE NUDGE. . . I AIN'T GOT FOREVER TO WAIT FOR GRANDCHILDREN, YOU KNOW!
BUT, MA, LOVE HAS TO DEVELOP NATURALLY. IT'S NOT VERY ROMANTIC KNOWING SHE'S GOT THE HOTS FOR ME AGAINST HER WILL!
MA, I CAME HERE TONIGHT TO TELL YOU THAT MY LAWYERS WANT TO MEET WITH YOU-- THEY HOPE YOU WILL COOPERATE . . . OR ELSE THEY'RE GOING TO HAVE TO IMPLEAD YOU.
WITH WHAT? LEECHES?
MA, "IMPLEAD" MEANS THEY'LL TAKE ACTION AGAINST YOU ON THE GROUND THAT YOU'RE THE ONE RESPONSIBLE FOR THE CHARGES I'M FACING.
BLESSED BE! YOU'D LET THEM DO THAT TO YOUR MOTHER? YOU KNOW HOW I FEEL ABOUT *UGH* COURTS . . .
WHAT YOU NEED IS A HOME-COOKED MEAL TO MAKE YOU FEEL BETTER . . . TASTE.
MMM . . . NOT BAD
SEE? WE'LL TALK ABOUT LAWYERS LATER . . . NOW, EAT! YOU'RE ALL SKIN AND BONES . . .

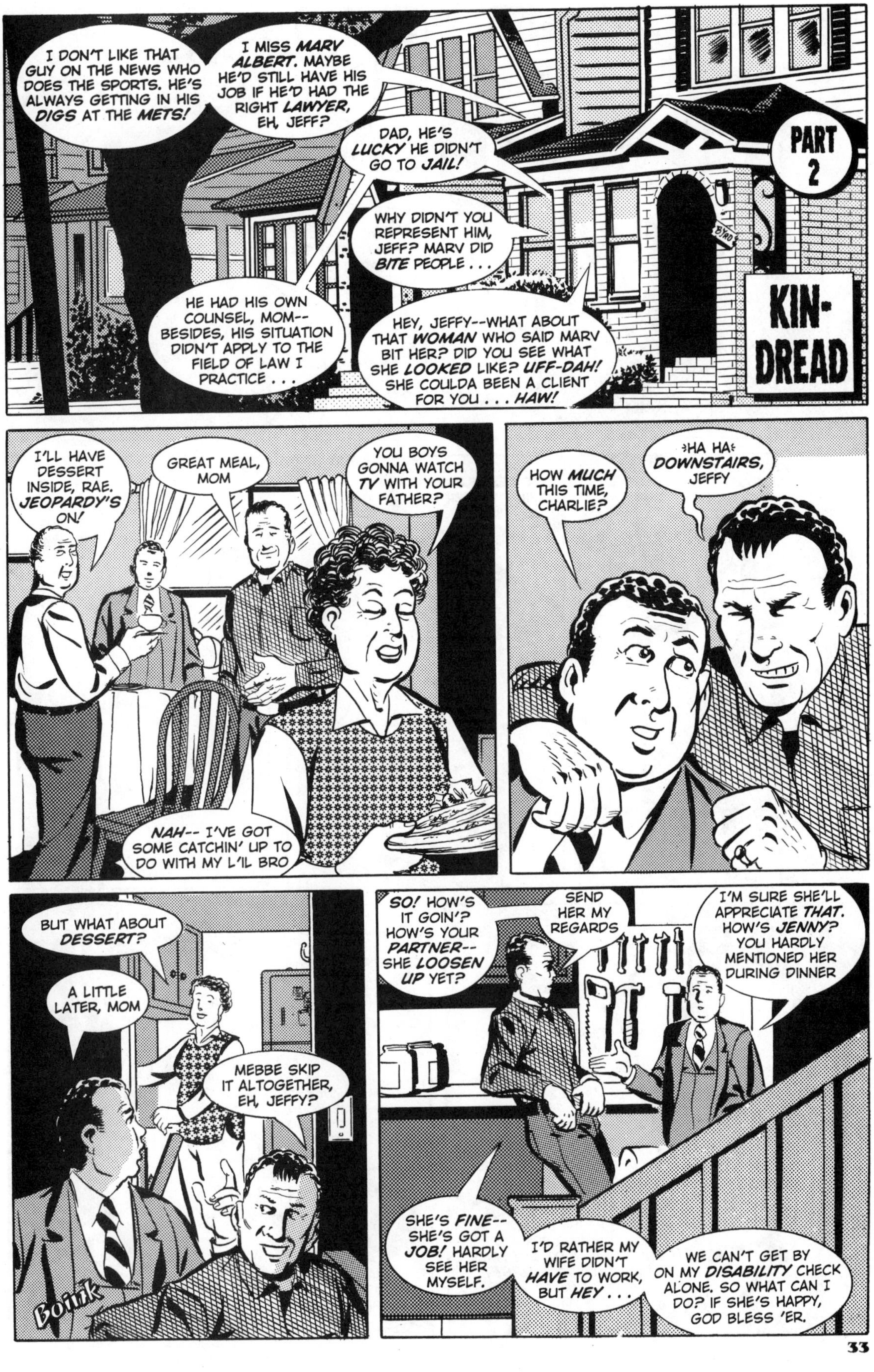
I DON'T LIKE THAT GUY ON THE NEWS WHO DOES THE SPORTS. HE'S ALWAYS GETTING IN HIS *DIGS* AT THE *METS!*
I MISS *MARV ALBERT*. MAYBE HE'D STILL HAVE HIS JOB IF HE'D HAD THE RIGHT *LAWYER*, EH, JEFF?
DAD, HE'S *LUCKY* HE DIDN'T GO TO *JAIL!*
PART 2
WHY DIDN'T YOU REPRESENT HIM, JEFF? MARV DID *BITE* PEOPLE . . .
HE HAD HIS OWN COUNSEL, MOM-- BESIDES, HIS SITUATION DIDN'T APPLY TO THE FIELD OF LAW I PRACTICE . . .
HEY, JEFFY--WHAT ABOUT THAT *WOMAN* WHO SAID MARV BIT HER? DID YOU SEE WHAT SHE *LOOKED* LIKE? *UFF-DAH!* SHE COULDA BEEN A CLIENT FOR YOU . . . *HAW!*
KIN-DREAD
I'LL HAVE DESSERT INSIDE, RAE. *JEOPARDY'S* ON!
GREAT MEAL, MOM
YOU BOYS GONNA WATCH *TV* WITH YOUR FATHER?
NAH-- I'VE GOT SOME CATCHIN' UP TO DO WITH MY L'IL BRO
HOW *MUCH* THIS TIME, CHARLIE?
HA HA *DOWNSTAIRS*, JEFFY
BUT WHAT ABOUT *DESSERT?*
A LITTLE LATER, MOM
MEBBE SKIP IT ALTOGETHER, EH, JEFFY?
Boink
SO! HOW'S IT GOIN'? HOW'S YOUR *PARTNER*-- SHE *LOOSEN UP* YET?
SEND HER MY REGARDS
I'M SURE SHE'LL APPRECIATE *THAT*. HOW'S *JENNY?* YOU HARDLY MENTIONED HER DURING DINNER
SHE'S *FINE*-- SHE'S GOT A *JOB!* HARDLY SEE HER MYSELF.
I'D RATHER MY WIFE DIDN'T *HAVE* TO WORK, BUT *HEY* . . .
WE CAN'T GET BY ON MY *DISABILITY* CHECK ALONE. SO WHAT CAN I DO? IF SHE'S HAPPY, GOD BLESS 'ER.

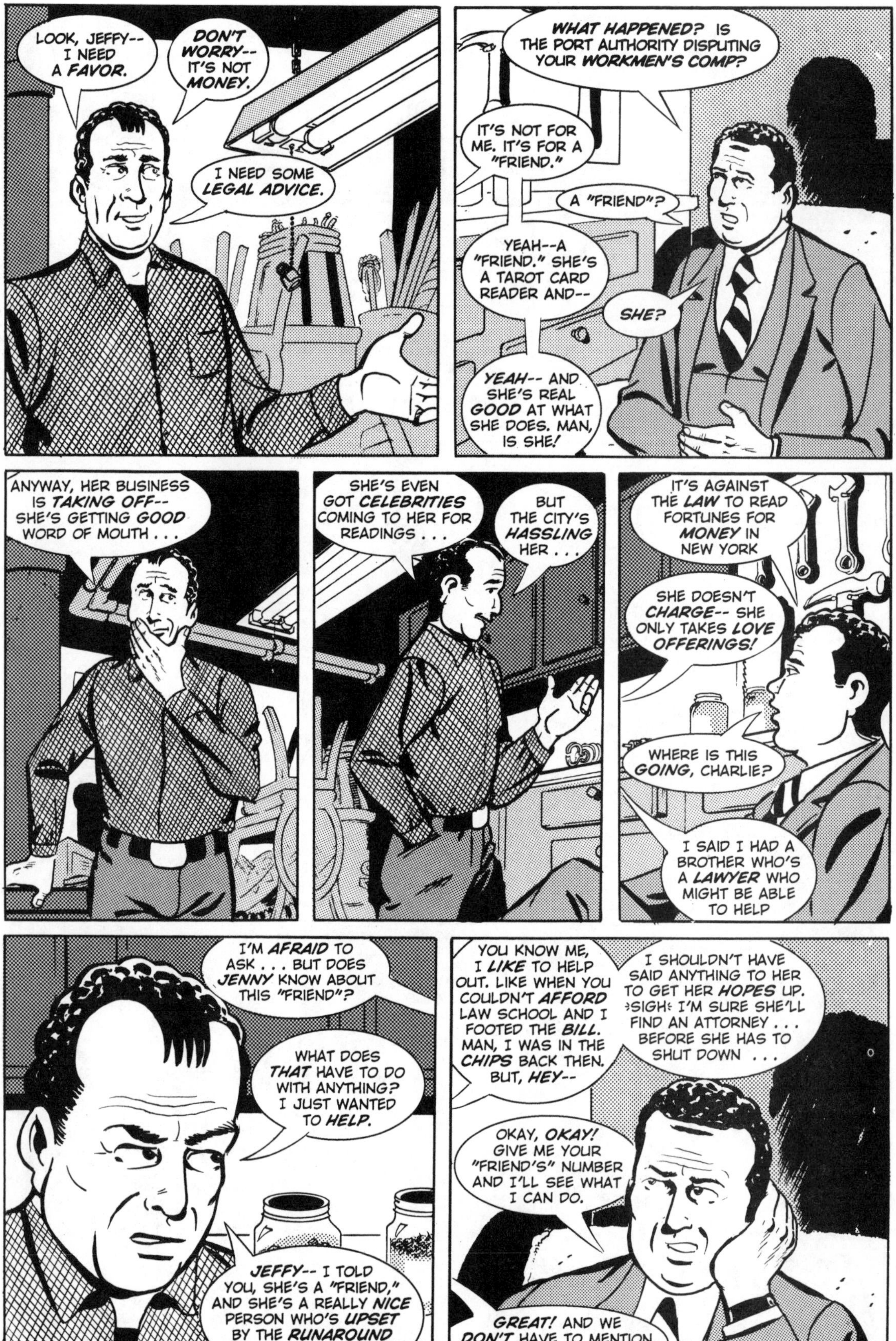
LOOK, JEFFY-- I NEED A FAVOR.
DON'T WORRY-- IT'S NOT MONEY.
I NEED SOME LEGAL ADVICE.
WHAT HAPPENED? IS THE PORT AUTHORITY DISPUTING YOUR WORKMEN'S COMP?
IT'S NOT FOR ME. IT'S FOR A "FRIEND."
A "FRIEND"?
YEAH--A "FRIEND." SHE'S A TAROT CARD READER AND--
SHE?
YEAH-- AND SHE'S REAL GOOD AT WHAT SHE DOES. MAN, IS SHE!
ANYWAY, HER BUSINESS IS TAKING OFF-- SHE'S GETTING GOOD WORD OF MOUTH . . .
SHE'S EVEN GOT CELEBRITIES COMING TO HER FOR READINGS . . .
BUT THE CITY'S HASSLING HER . . .
IT'S AGAINST THE LAW TO READ FORTUNES FOR MONEY IN NEW YORK
SHE DOESN'T CHARGE-- SHE ONLY TAKES LOVE OFFERINGS!
WHERE IS THIS GOING, CHARLIE?
I SAID I HAD A BROTHER WHO'S A LAWYER WHO MIGHT BE ABLE TO HELP
I'M AFRAID TO ASK . . . BUT DOES JENNY KNOW ABOUT THIS "FRIEND"?
WHAT DOES THAT HAVE TO DO WITH ANYTHING? I JUST WANTED TO HELP.
JEFFY-- I TOLD YOU, SHE'S A "FRIEND," AND SHE'S A REALLY NICE PERSON WHO'S UPSET BY THE RUNAROUND SHE'S GETTING FROM THE CITY.
YOU KNOW ME, I LIKE TO HELP OUT. LIKE WHEN YOU COULDN'T AFFORD LAW SCHOOL AND I FOOTED THE BILL. MAN, I WAS IN THE CHIPS BACK THEN. BUT, HEY--
I SHOULDN'T HAVE SAID ANYTHING TO HER TO GET HER HOPES UP. *SIGH* I'M SURE SHE'LL FIND AN ATTORNEY . . . BEFORE SHE HAS TO SHUT DOWN . . .
OKAY, OKAY! GIVE ME YOUR "FRIEND'S" NUMBER AND I'LL SEE WHAT I CAN DO.
GREAT! AND WE DON'T HAVE TO MENTION THIS TO JENNY-- CAPICHE?

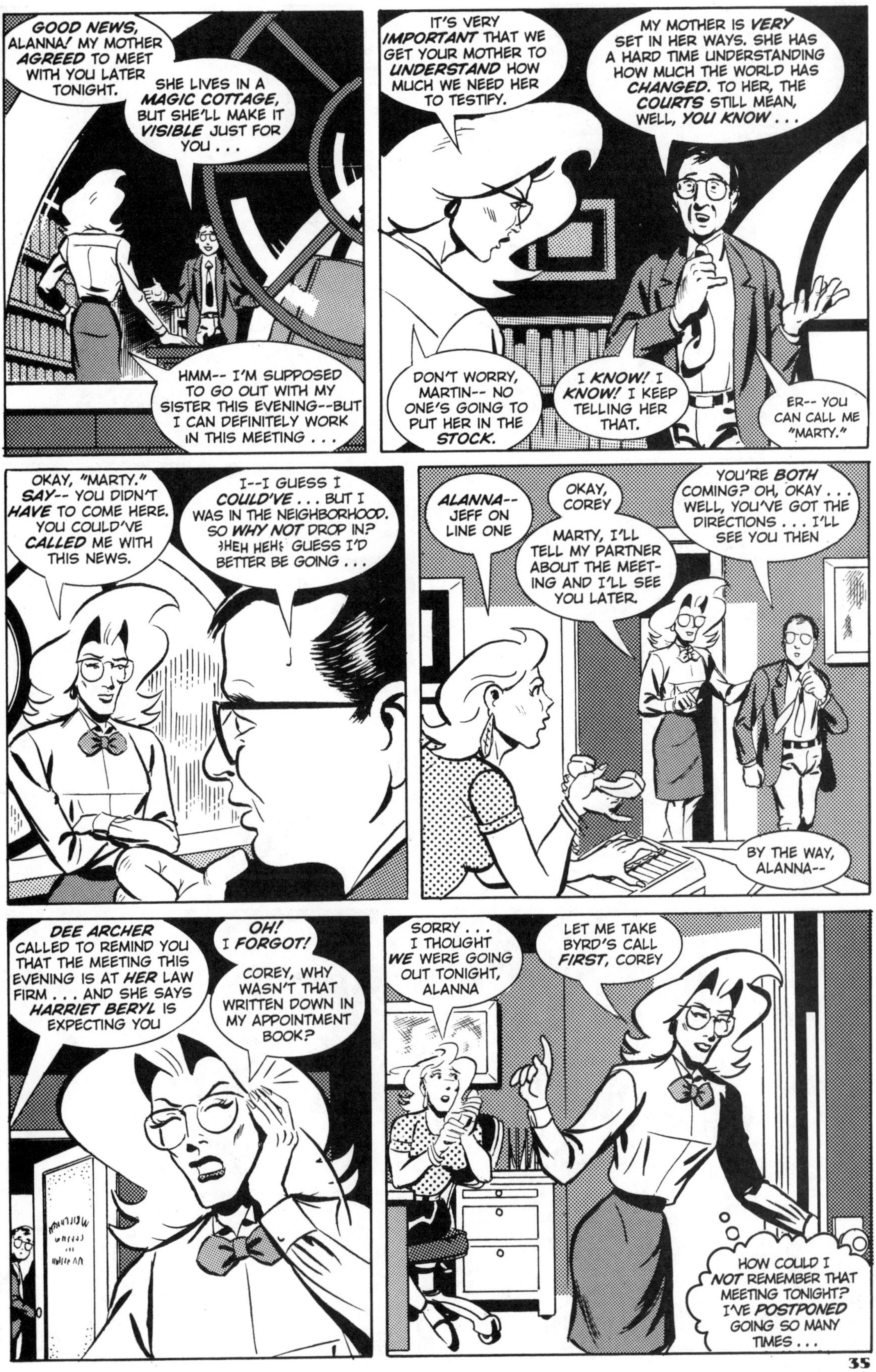
GOOD NEWS, ALANNA! MY MOTHER AGREED TO MEET WITH YOU LATER TONIGHT.
SHE LIVES IN A MAGIC COTTAGE, BUT SHE'LL MAKE IT VISIBLE JUST FOR YOU . . .
HMM-- I'M SUPPOSED TO GO OUT WITH MY SISTER THIS EVENING--BUT I CAN DEFINITELY WORK IN THIS MEETING . . .
IT'S VERY IMPORTANT THAT WE GET YOUR MOTHER TO UNDERSTAND HOW MUCH WE NEED HER TO TESTIFY.
MY MOTHER IS VERY SET IN HER WAYS. SHE HAS A HARD TIME UNDERSTANDING HOW MUCH THE WORLD HAS CHANGED. TO HER, THE COURTS STILL MEAN, WELL, YOU KNOW . . .
DON'T WORRY, MARTIN-- NO ONE'S GOING TO PUT HER IN THE STOCK.
I KNOW! I KNOW! I KEEP TELLING HER THAT.
ER-- YOU CAN CALL ME "MARTY."
OKAY, "MARTY." SAY-- YOU DIDN'T HAVE TO COME HERE. YOU COULD'VE CALLED ME WITH THIS NEWS.
I--I GUESS I COULD'VE . . . BUT I WAS IN THE NEIGHBORHOOD. SO WHY NOT DROP IN? HEH HEH GUESS I'D BETTER BE GOING . . .
ALANNA-- JEFF ON LINE ONE
OKAY, COREY
MARTY, I'LL TELL MY PARTNER ABOUT THE MEETING AND I'LL SEE YOU LATER.
YOU'RE BOTH COMING? OH, OKAY . . . WELL, YOU'VE GOT THE DIRECTIONS . . . I'LL SEE YOU THEN
BY THE WAY, ALANNA--
DEE ARCHER CALLED TO REMIND YOU THAT THE MEETING THIS EVENING IS AT HER LAW FIRM . . . AND SHE SAYS HARRIET BERYL IS EXPECTING YOU
OH! I FORGOT!
COREY, WHY WASN'T THAT WRITTEN DOWN IN MY APPOINTMENT BOOK?
SORRY . . . I THOUGHT WE WERE GOING OUT TONIGHT, ALANNA
LET ME TAKE BYRD'S CALL FIRST, COREY
HOW COULD I NOT REMEMBER THAT MEETING TONIGHT? I'VE POSTPONED GOING SO MANY TIMES . . .

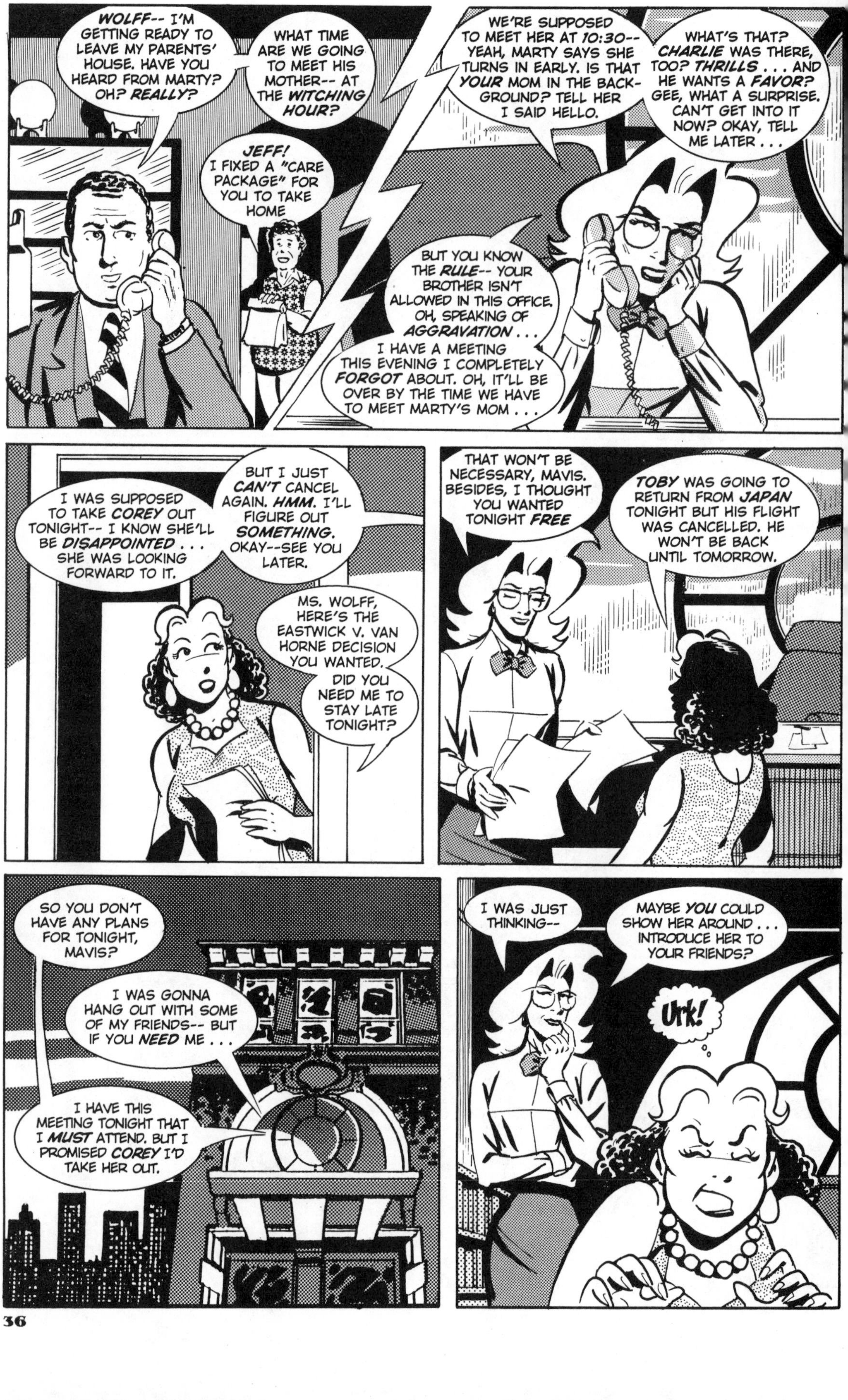
WOLFF-- I'M GETTING READY TO LEAVE MY PARENTS' HOUSE. HAVE YOU HEARD FROM MARTY? OH? REALLY?
WHAT TIME ARE WE GOING TO MEET HIS MOTHER-- AT THE WITCHING HOUR?
JEFF! I FIXED A "CARE PACKAGE" FOR YOU TO TAKE HOME
WE'RE SUPPOSED TO MEET HER AT 10:30-- YEAH, MARTY SAYS SHE TURNS IN EARLY. IS THAT YOUR MOM IN THE BACK-GROUND? TELL HER I SAID HELLO.
WHAT'S THAT? CHARLIE WAS THERE, TOO? THRILLS . . . AND HE WANTS A FAVOR? GEE, WHAT A SURPRISE. CAN'T GET INTO IT NOW? OKAY, TELL ME LATER . . .
BUT YOU KNOW THE RULE-- YOUR BROTHER ISN'T ALLOWED IN THIS OFFICE. OH, SPEAKING OF AGGRAVATION . . .
I HAVE A MEETING THIS EVENING I COMPLETELY FORGOT ABOUT. OH, IT'LL BE OVER BY THE TIME WE HAVE TO MEET MARTY'S MOM . . .
I WAS SUPPOSED TO TAKE COREY OUT TONIGHT-- I KNOW SHE'LL BE DISAPPOINTED . . . SHE WAS LOOKING FORWARD TO IT.
BUT I JUST CAN'T CANCEL AGAIN. HMM. I'LL FIGURE OUT SOMETHING. OKAY--SEE YOU LATER.
MS. WOLFF, HERE'S THE EASTWICK V. VAN HORNE DECISION YOU WANTED.
DID YOU NEED ME TO STAY LATE TONIGHT?
THAT WON'T BE NECESSARY, MAVIS. BESIDES, I THOUGHT YOU WANTED TONIGHT FREE
TOBY WAS GOING TO RETURN FROM JAPAN TONIGHT BUT HIS FLIGHT WAS CANCELLED. HE WON'T BE BACK UNTIL TOMORROW.
SO YOU DON'T HAVE ANY PLANS FOR TONIGHT, MAVIS?
I WAS GONNA HANG OUT WITH SOME OF MY FRIENDS-- BUT IF YOU NEED ME . . .
I HAVE THIS MEETING TONIGHT THAT I MUST ATTEND. BUT I PROMISED COREY I'D TAKE HER OUT.
I WAS JUST THINKING--
MAYBE YOU COULD SHOW HER AROUND . . . INTRODUCE HER TO YOUR FRIENDS?
Urk!

BLESSED BE! I GUESS *AMERICA* WAS MORE *LENIENT* WITH WITCHES THAN *EUROPE* WAS . . .

In 1527, a great number of women were accused of sorcery, through the information of two girls, ~~~ ~~~ years old . . . We are assured by the histo~~~

HERE, THEY *HUNG* 'EM INSTEAD OF *BURNING* THEM AT THE *STAKE* . . .

MARTY HAS *NO IDEA* WHAT KIND OF *HYSTERIA* AND *SUFFERING* THOSE *WITCH TRIALS* CAUSED . . . BUT *I DO*-- AND IT'S *NOT* SOMETHING I WANT TO *RELIVE!*

MEOWRRR?

WHAT'S THAT, ZULEIKA? CALL ON MY *SISTERS?* SUMMON THEM TO *ADVISE* ME?

YEESH! I THINK I'D *RATHER* STAND BEFORE THE COURT!

MEOWRRR

OH, YOU KNOW I DON'T *MEAN* THAT, ZULEIKA. I'LL SEE HOW IT GOES WITH MARTY'S *LAWYERS* BEFORE I DECIDE WHETHER TO CALL ON THE GIRLS . . .

ROWRRR?

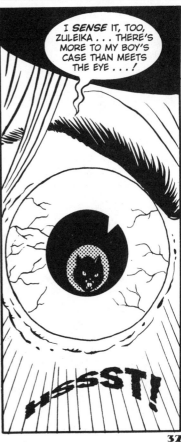

I *SENSE* IT, TOO, ZULEIKA . . . THERE'S MORE TO MY BOY'S CASE THAN MEETS THE EYE . . . !

HSSST!

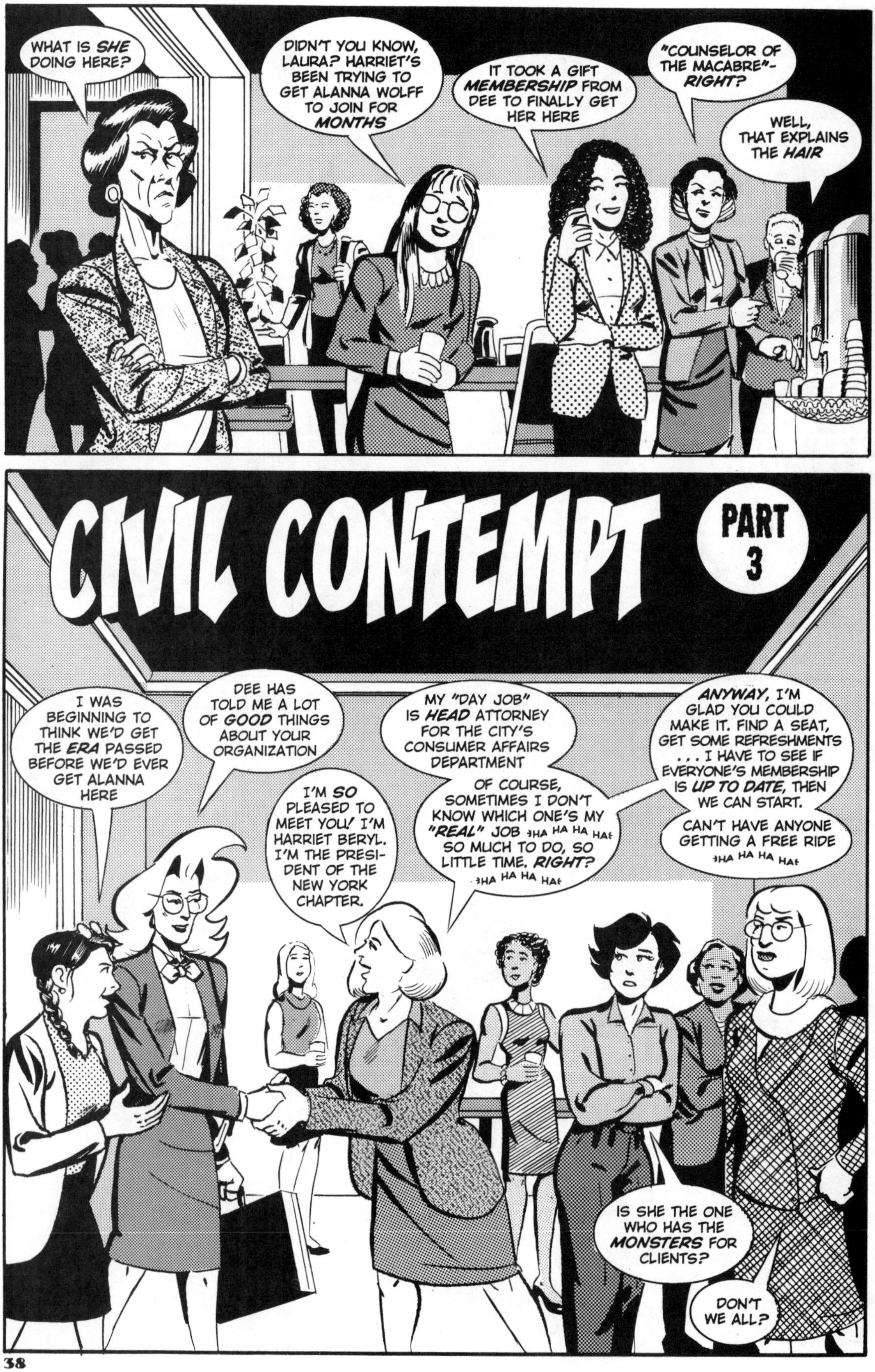
WHAT IS *SHE* DOING HERE?
DIDN'T YOU KNOW, LAURA? HARRIET'S BEEN TRYING TO GET ALANNA WOLFF TO JOIN FOR *MONTHS*
IT TOOK A GIFT *MEMBERSHIP* FROM DEE TO FINALLY GET HER HERE
"COUNSELOR OF THE MACABRE"- *RIGHT?*
WELL, THAT EXPLAINS THE *HAIR*
CIVIL CONTEMPT
PART 3
I WAS BEGINNING TO THINK WE'D GET THE *ERA* PASSED BEFORE WE'D EVER GET ALANNA HERE
DEE HAS TOLD ME A LOT OF *GOOD* THINGS ABOUT YOUR ORGANIZATION
I'M *SO* PLEASED TO MEET YOU! I'M HARRIET BERYL. I'M THE PRESIDENT OF THE NEW YORK CHAPTER.
MY "DAY JOB" IS *HEAD* ATTORNEY FOR THE CITY'S CONSUMER AFFAIRS DEPARTMENT
OF COURSE, SOMETIMES I DON'T KNOW WHICH ONE'S MY *"REAL"* JOB HA HA HA HA! SO MUCH TO DO, SO LITTLE TIME. *RIGHT?* HA HA HA HA!
ANYWAY, I'M GLAD YOU COULD MAKE IT. FIND A SEAT, GET SOME REFRESHMENTS . . . I HAVE TO SEE IF EVERYONE'S MEMBERSHIP IS *UP TO DATE,* THEN WE CAN START.
CAN'T HAVE ANYONE GETTING A FREE RIDE HA HA HA HA!
IS SHE THE ONE WHO HAS THE *MONSTERS* FOR CLIENTS?
DON'T WE ALL?

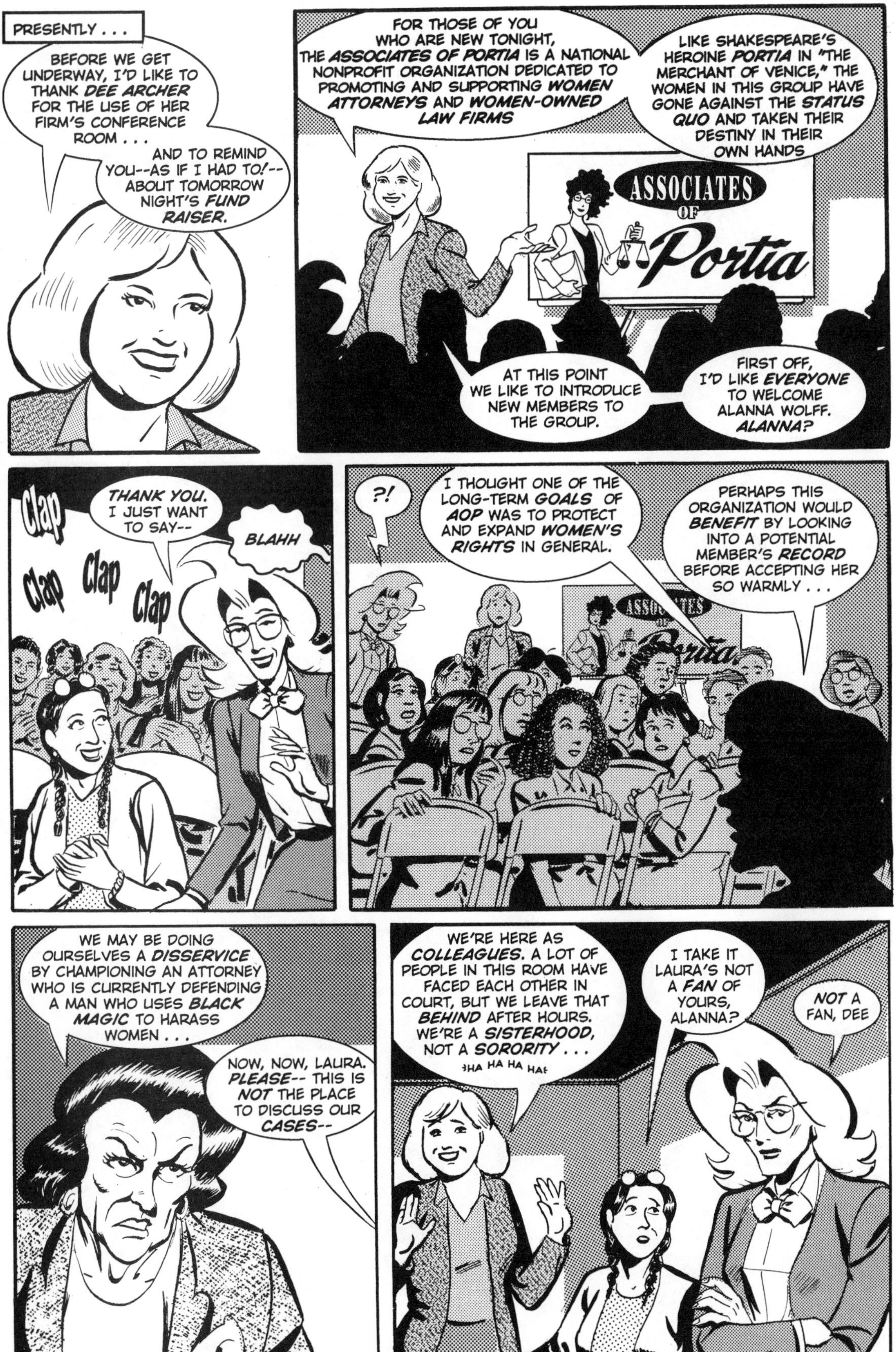
PRESENTLY . . .
BEFORE WE GET UNDERWAY, I'D LIKE TO THANK DEE ARCHER FOR THE USE OF HER FIRM'S CONFERENCE ROOM . . .
AND TO REMIND YOU--AS IF I HAD TO!--ABOUT TOMORROW NIGHT'S FUND RAISER.
FOR THOSE OF YOU WHO ARE NEW TONIGHT, THE ASSOCIATES OF PORTIA IS A NATIONAL NONPROFIT ORGANIZATION DEDICATED TO PROMOTING AND SUPPORTING WOMEN ATTORNEYS AND WOMEN-OWNED LAW FIRMS
LIKE SHAKESPEARE'S HEROINE PORTIA IN "THE MERCHANT OF VENICE," THE WOMEN IN THIS GROUP HAVE GONE AGAINST THE STATUS QUO AND TAKEN THEIR DESTINY IN THEIR OWN HANDS
ASSOCIATES OF Portia
AT THIS POINT WE LIKE TO INTRODUCE NEW MEMBERS TO THE GROUP.
FIRST OFF, I'D LIKE EVERYONE TO WELCOME ALANNA WOLFF. ALANNA?
Clap
THANK YOU. I JUST WANT TO SAY--
BLAHH
Clap Clap Clap
?!
I THOUGHT ONE OF THE LONG-TERM GOALS OF AOP WAS TO PROTECT AND EXPAND WOMEN'S RIGHTS IN GENERAL.
PERHAPS THIS ORGANIZATION WOULD BENEFIT BY LOOKING INTO A POTENTIAL MEMBER'S RECORD BEFORE ACCEPTING HER SO WARMLY . . .
WE MAY BE DOING OURSELVES A DISSERVICE BY CHAMPIONING AN ATTORNEY WHO IS CURRENTLY DEFENDING A MAN WHO USES BLACK MAGIC TO HARASS WOMEN . . .
NOW, NOW, LAURA. PLEASE-- THIS IS NOT THE PLACE TO DISCUSS OUR CASES--
WE'RE HERE AS COLLEAGUES. A LOT OF PEOPLE IN THIS ROOM HAVE FACED EACH OTHER IN COURT, BUT WE LEAVE THAT BEHIND AFTER HOURS. WE'RE A SISTERHOOD, NOT A SORORITY . . .
HA HA HA HA
I TAKE IT LAURA'S NOT A FAN OF YOURS, ALANNA?
NOT A FAN, DEE

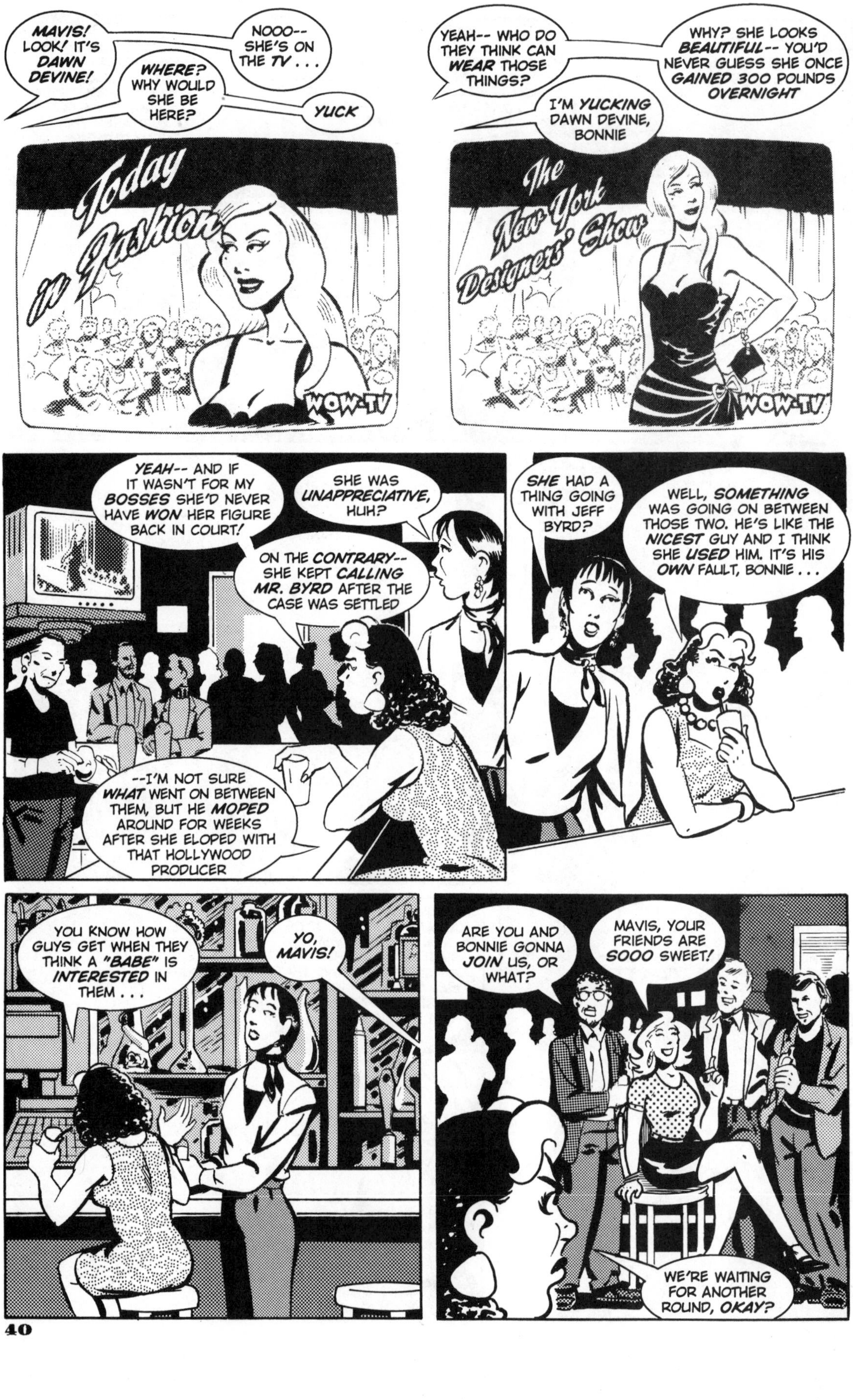
MAVIS! LOOK! IT'S DAWN DEVINE!
NOOO-- SHE'S ON THE TV . . .
WHERE? WHY WOULD SHE BE HERE?
YUCK
Today in Fashion
WOW-TV
YEAH-- WHO DO THEY THINK CAN WEAR THOSE THINGS?
WHY? SHE LOOKS BEAUTIFUL-- YOU'D NEVER GUESS SHE ONCE GAINED 300 POUNDS OVERNIGHT
I'M YUCKING DAWN DEVINE, BONNIE
The New York Designers' Show
WOW-TV
YEAH-- AND IF IT WASN'T FOR MY BOSSES SHE'D NEVER HAVE WON HER FIGURE BACK IN COURT!
SHE WAS UNAPPRECIATIVE, HUH?
ON THE CONTRARY-- SHE KEPT CALLING MR. BYRD AFTER THE CASE WAS SETTLED
--I'M NOT SURE WHAT WENT ON BETWEEN THEM, BUT HE MOPED AROUND FOR WEEKS AFTER SHE ELOPED WITH THAT HOLLYWOOD PRODUCER
SHE HAD A THING GOING WITH JEFF BYRD?
WELL, SOMETHING WAS GOING ON BETWEEN THOSE TWO. HE'S LIKE THE NICEST GUY AND I THINK SHE USED HIM. IT'S HIS OWN FAULT, BONNIE . . .
YOU KNOW HOW GUYS GET WHEN THEY THINK A "BABE" IS INTERESTED IN THEM . . .
YO, MAVIS!
ARE YOU AND BONNIE GONNA JOIN US, OR WHAT?
MAVIS, YOUR FRIENDS ARE SOOO SWEET!
WE'RE WAITING FOR ANOTHER ROUND, OKAY?

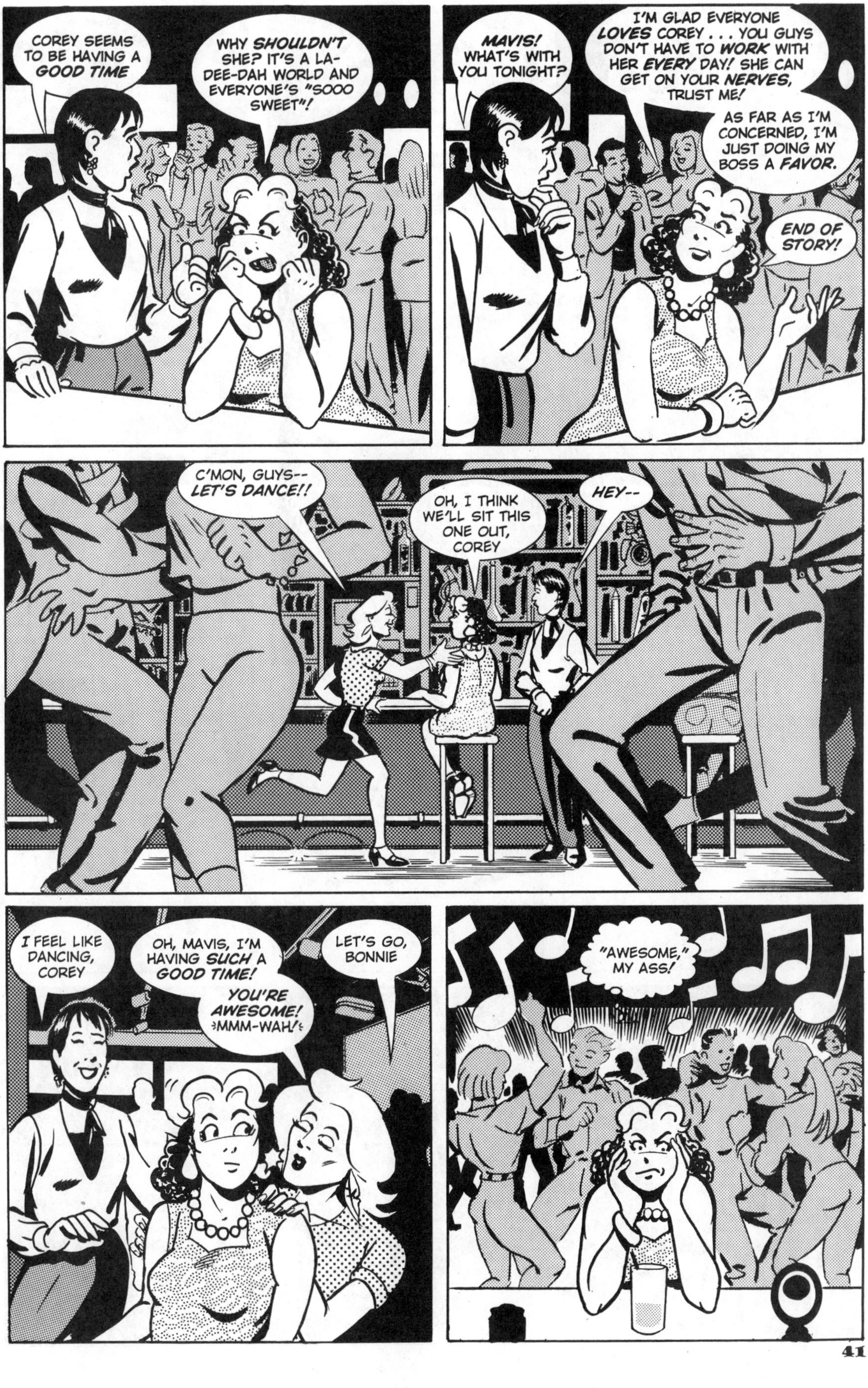
COREY SEEMS TO BE HAVING A GOOD TIME
WHY SHOULDN'T SHE? IT'S A LA-DEE-DAH WORLD AND EVERYONE'S "SOOO SWEET"!
MAVIS! WHAT'S WITH YOU TONIGHT?
I'M GLAD EVERYONE LOVES COREY . . . YOU GUYS DON'T HAVE TO WORK WITH HER EVERY DAY! SHE CAN GET ON YOUR NERVES, TRUST ME!
AS FAR AS I'M CONCERNED, I'M JUST DOING MY BOSS A FAVOR.
END OF STORY!
C'MON, GUYS-- LET'S DANCE!!
OH, I THINK WE'LL SIT THIS ONE OUT, COREY
HEY--
I FEEL LIKE DANCING, COREY
OH, MAVIS, I'M HAVING SUCH A GOOD TIME!
YOU'RE AWESOME! MMM-WAH!
LET'S GO, BONNIE
"AWESOME," MY ASS!

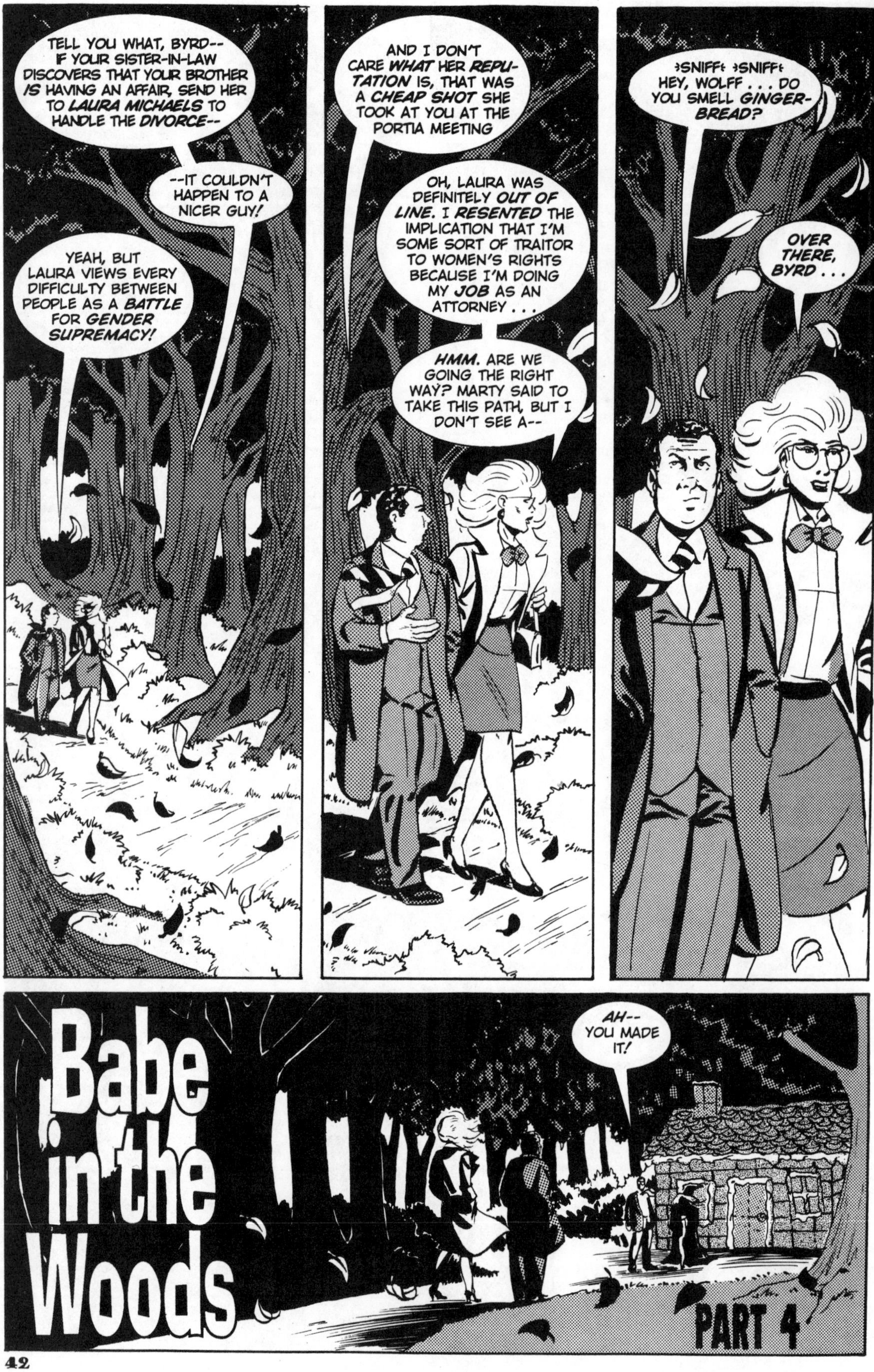
TELL YOU WHAT, BYRD-- IF YOUR SISTER-IN-LAW DISCOVERS THAT YOUR BROTHER IS HAVING AN AFFAIR, SEND HER TO LAURA MICHAELS TO HANDLE THE DIVORCE--
--IT COULDN'T HAPPEN TO A NICER GUY!
YEAH, BUT LAURA VIEWS EVERY DIFFICULTY BETWEEN PEOPLE AS A BATTLE FOR GENDER SUPREMACY!
AND I DON'T CARE WHAT HER REPUTATION IS, THAT WAS A CHEAP SHOT SHE TOOK AT YOU AT THE PORTIA MEETING
OH, LAURA WAS DEFINITELY OUT OF LINE. I RESENTED THE IMPLICATION THAT I'M SOME SORT OF TRAITOR TO WOMEN'S RIGHTS BECAUSE I'M DOING MY JOB AS AN ATTORNEY . . .
HMM. ARE WE GOING THE RIGHT WAY? MARTY SAID TO TAKE THIS PATH, BUT I DON'T SEE A--
SNIFF SNIFF HEY, WOLFF . . . DO YOU SMELL GINGERBREAD?
OVER THERE, BYRD . . .
Babe in the Woods
AH-- YOU MADE IT!
PART 4

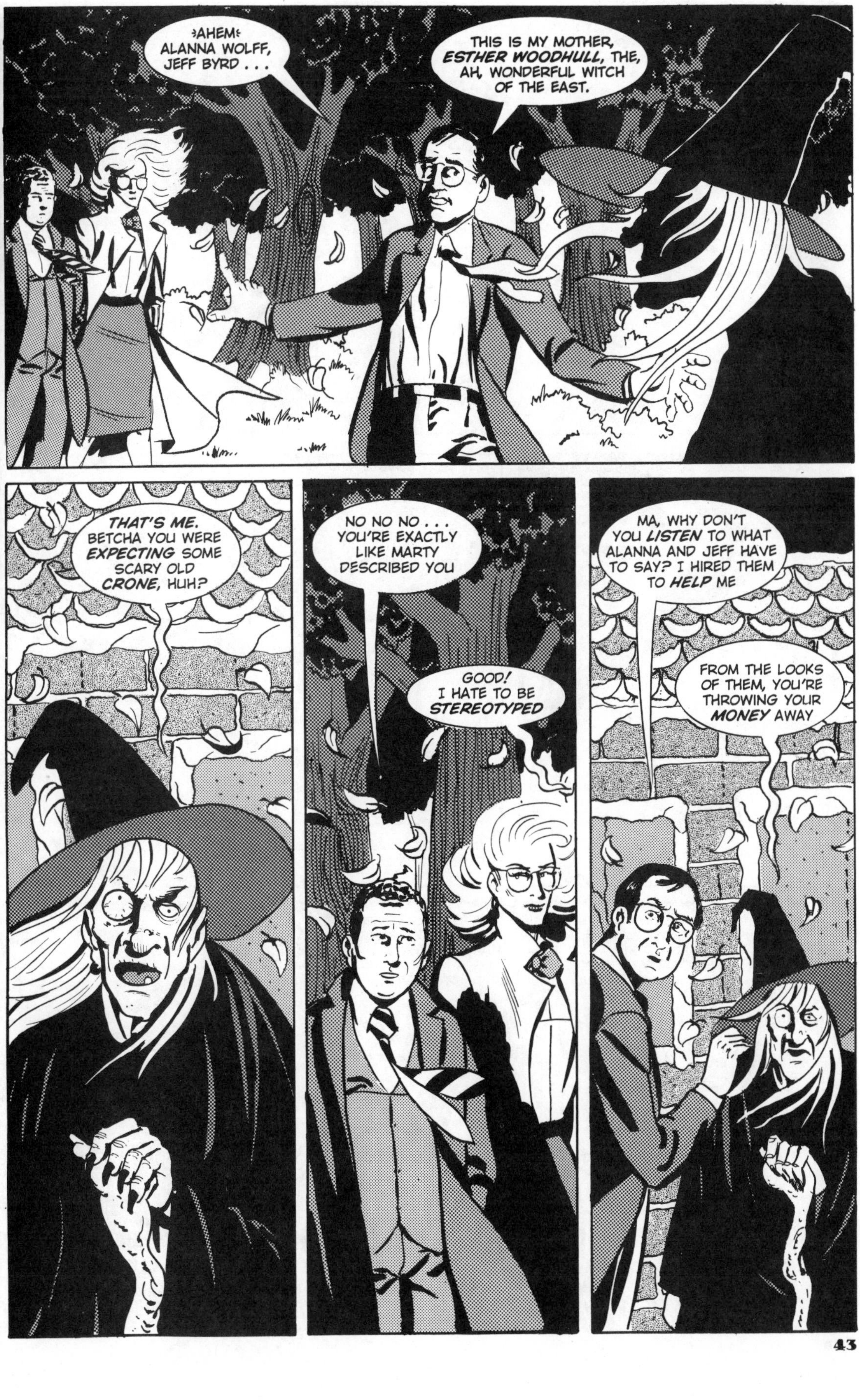

‡AHEM‡ ALANNA WOLFF, JEFF BYRD . . .
THIS IS MY MOTHER, ESTHER WOODHULL, THE, AH, WONDERFUL WITCH OF THE EAST.
THAT'S ME. BETCHA YOU WERE EXPECTING SOME SCARY OLD CRONE, HUH?
NO NO NO . . . YOU'RE EXACTLY LIKE MARTY DESCRIBED YOU
GOOD! I HATE TO BE STEREOTYPED
MA, WHY DON'T YOU LISTEN TO WHAT ALANNA AND JEFF HAVE TO SAY? I HIRED THEM TO HELP ME
FROM THE LOOKS OF THEM, YOU'RE THROWING YOUR MONEY AWAY

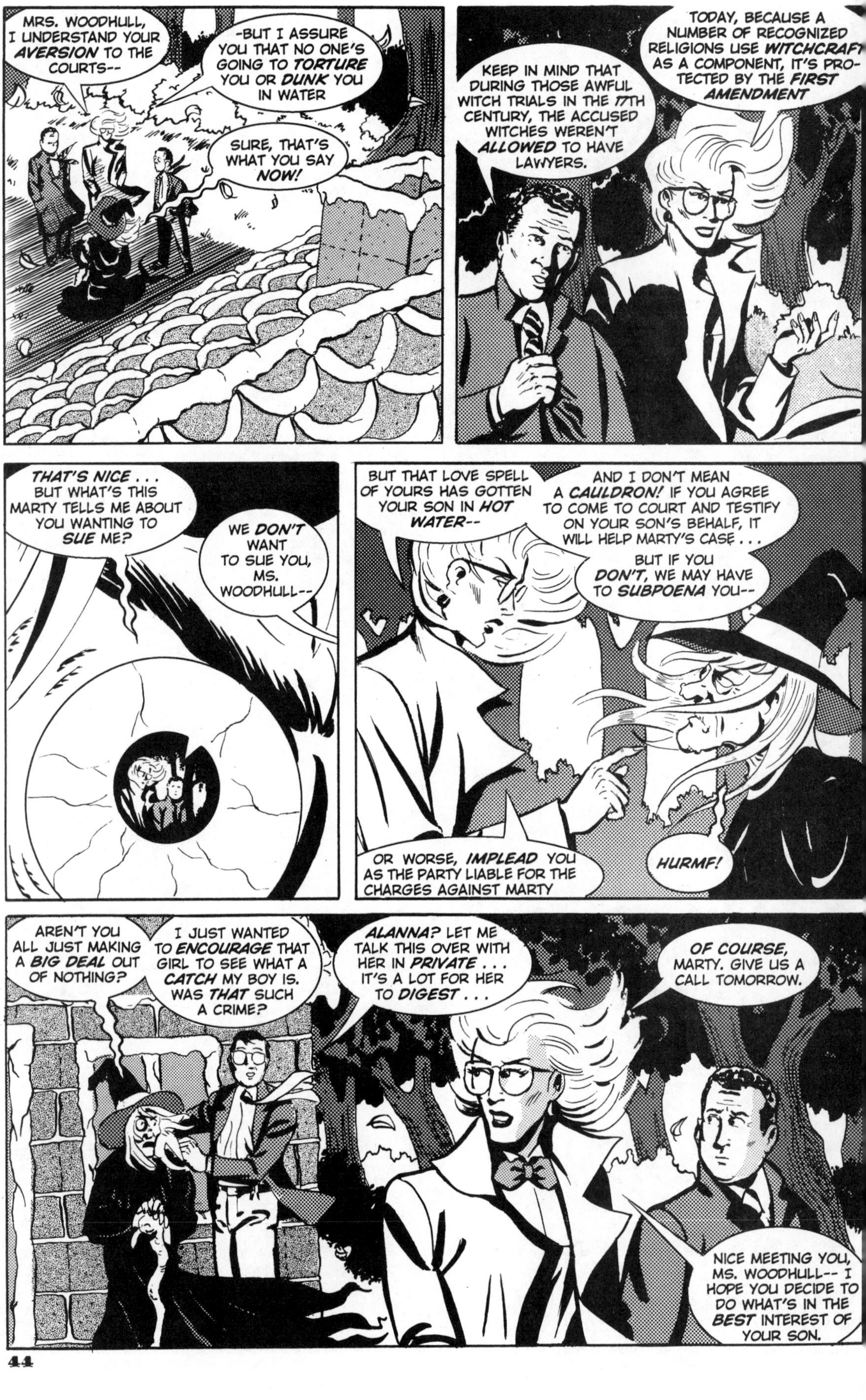

MRS. WOODHULL, I UNDERSTAND YOUR AVERSION TO THE COURTS--
-BUT I ASSURE YOU THAT NO ONE'S GOING TO TORTURE YOU OR DUNK YOU IN WATER
SURE, THAT'S WHAT YOU SAY NOW!
KEEP IN MIND THAT DURING THOSE AWFUL WITCH TRIALS IN THE 17TH CENTURY, THE ACCUSED WITCHES WEREN'T ALLOWED TO HAVE LAWYERS.
TODAY, BECAUSE A NUMBER OF RECOGNIZED RELIGIONS USE WITCHCRAFT AS A COMPONENT, IT'S PROTECTED BY THE FIRST AMENDMENT
THAT'S NICE . . . BUT WHAT'S THIS MARTY TELLS ME ABOUT YOU WANTING TO SUE ME?
WE DON'T WANT TO SUE YOU, MS. WOODHULL--
BUT THAT LOVE SPELL OF YOURS HAS GOTTEN YOUR SON IN HOT WATER--
AND I DON'T MEAN A CAULDRON! IF YOU AGREE TO COME TO COURT AND TESTIFY ON YOUR SON'S BEHALF, IT WILL HELP MARTY'S CASE . . .
BUT IF YOU DON'T, WE MAY HAVE TO SUBPOENA YOU--
OR WORSE, IMPLEAD YOU AS THE PARTY LIABLE FOR THE CHARGES AGAINST MARTY
HURMF!
AREN'T YOU ALL JUST MAKING A BIG DEAL OUT OF NOTHING?
I JUST WANTED TO ENCOURAGE THAT GIRL TO SEE WHAT A CATCH MY BOY IS. WAS THAT SUCH A CRIME?
ALANNA? LET ME TALK THIS OVER WITH HER IN PRIVATE . . . IT'S A LOT FOR HER TO DIGEST . . .
OF COURSE, MARTY. GIVE US A CALL TOMORROW.
NICE MEETING YOU, MS. WOODHULL-- I HOPE YOU DECIDE TO DO WHAT'S IN THE BEST INTEREST OF YOUR SON.

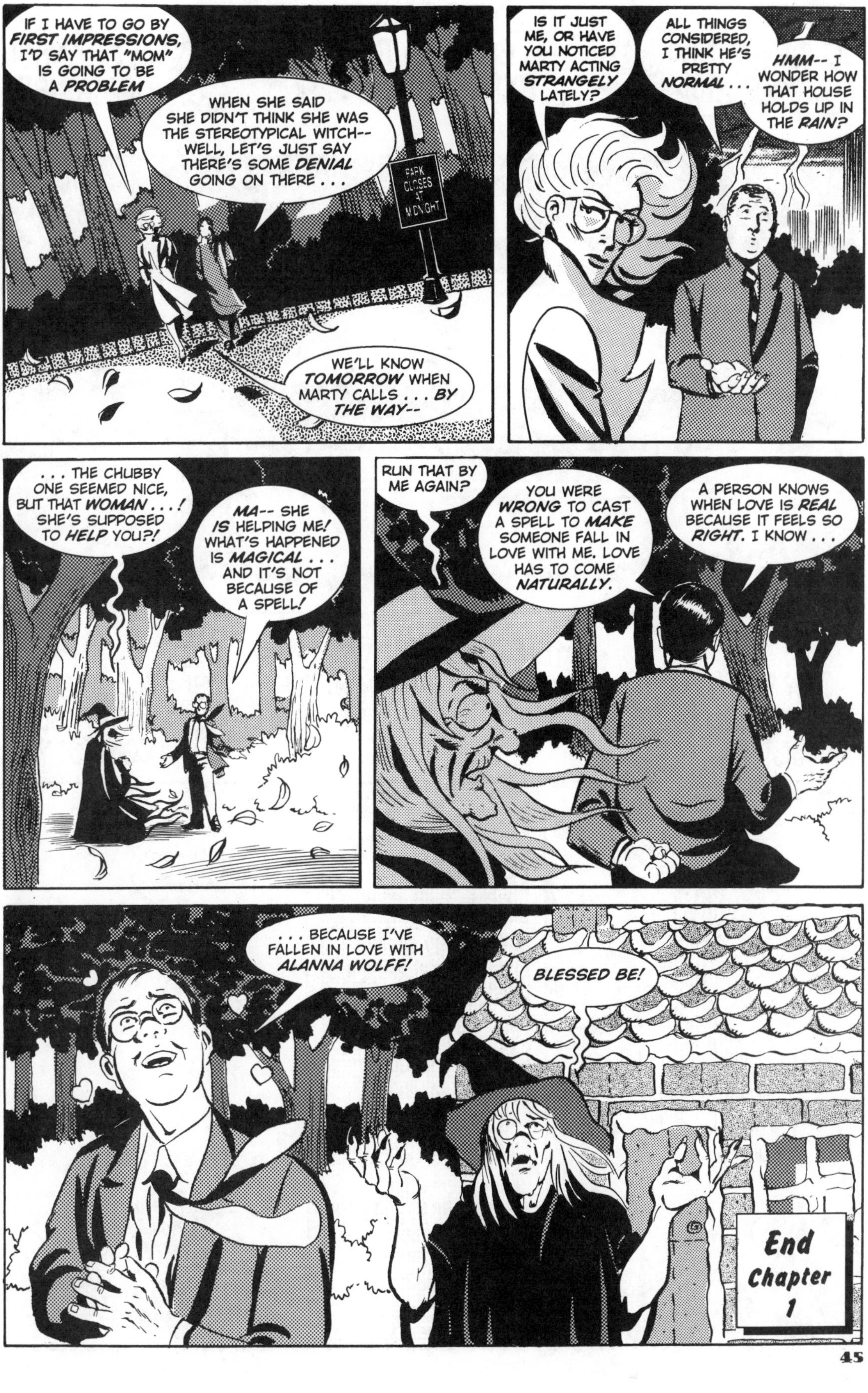
IF I HAVE TO GO BY FIRST IMPRESSIONS, I'D SAY THAT "MOM" IS GOING TO BE A PROBLEM
WHEN SHE SAID SHE DIDN'T THINK SHE WAS THE STEREOTYPICAL WITCH-- WELL, LET'S JUST SAY THERE'S SOME DENIAL GOING ON THERE . . .
PARK CLOSES AT MIDNIGHT
WE'LL KNOW TOMORROW WHEN MARTY CALLS . . . BY THE WAY--
IS IT JUST ME, OR HAVE YOU NOTICED MARTY ACTING STRANGELY LATELY?
ALL THINGS CONSIDERED, I THINK HE'S PRETTY NORMAL . . .
HMM-- I WONDER HOW THAT HOUSE HOLDS UP IN THE RAIN?
. . . THE CHUBBY ONE SEEMED NICE, BUT THAT WOMAN . . . ! SHE'S SUPPOSED TO HELP YOU?!
MA-- SHE IS HELPING ME! WHAT'S HAPPENED IS MAGICAL . . . AND IT'S NOT BECAUSE OF A SPELL!
RUN THAT BY ME AGAIN?
YOU WERE WRONG TO CAST A SPELL TO MAKE SOMEONE FALL IN LOVE WITH ME. LOVE HAS TO COME NATURALLY.
A PERSON KNOWS WHEN LOVE IS REAL BECAUSE IT FEELS SO RIGHT. I KNOW . . .
. . . BECAUSE I'VE FALLEN IN LOVE WITH ALANNA WOLFF!
BLESSED BE!
End Chapter 1

O MY SISTERS, I CALL UPON YOU THREE TO SEEK YOUR COUNSEL
I, YOUR SIBLING OF THE EAST AM IN NEED OF YOUR COMBINED
WISDOM . . . EXPERIENCE . . . AND POWER!!

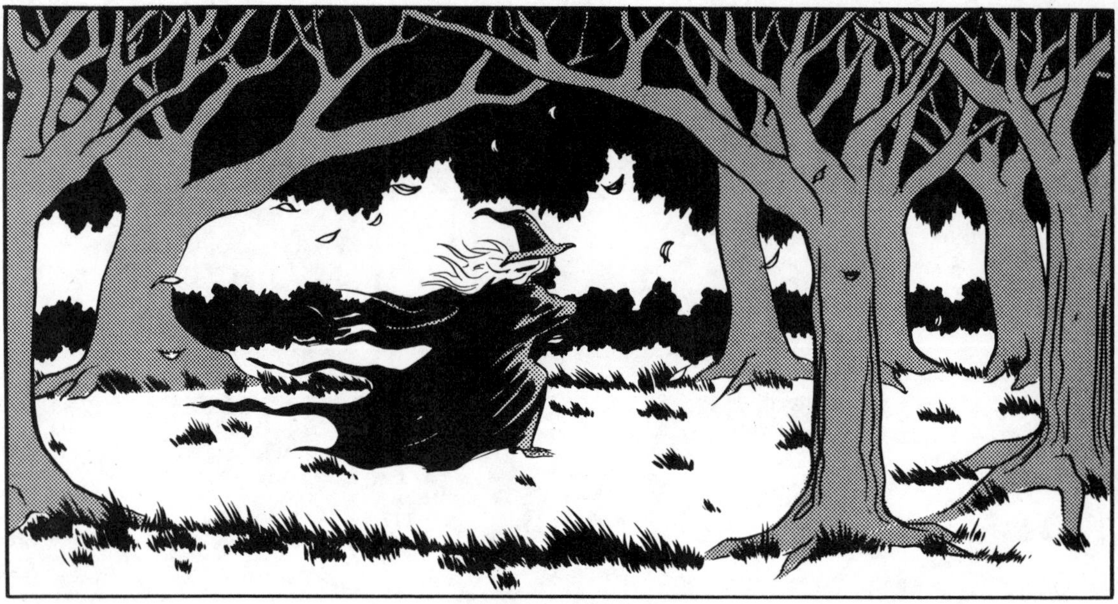

O MY SISTERS OF THE NORTH, OF THE SOUTH AND OF THE WEST, HEED MY CALL!
O MY SISTERS OF THE CRAFT-- NOLA! SOPHIE! WINIFRED! -- ATTEND MY NEED!
O MY SISTERS, BY THE POWERS INVESTED IN ME BY THE ELEMENTS, I CONTACT YOU--

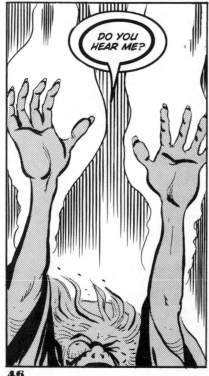

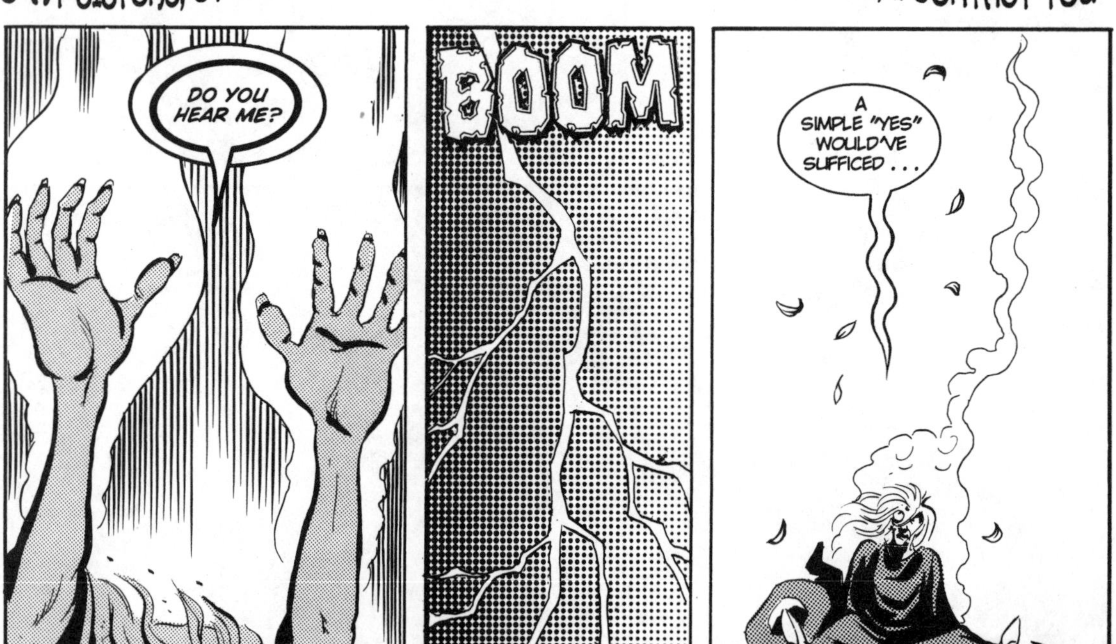
DO YOU HEAR ME?
BOOM
A SIMPLE "YES" WOULD'VE SUFFICED . . .

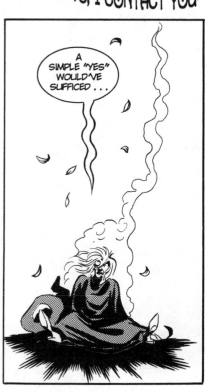

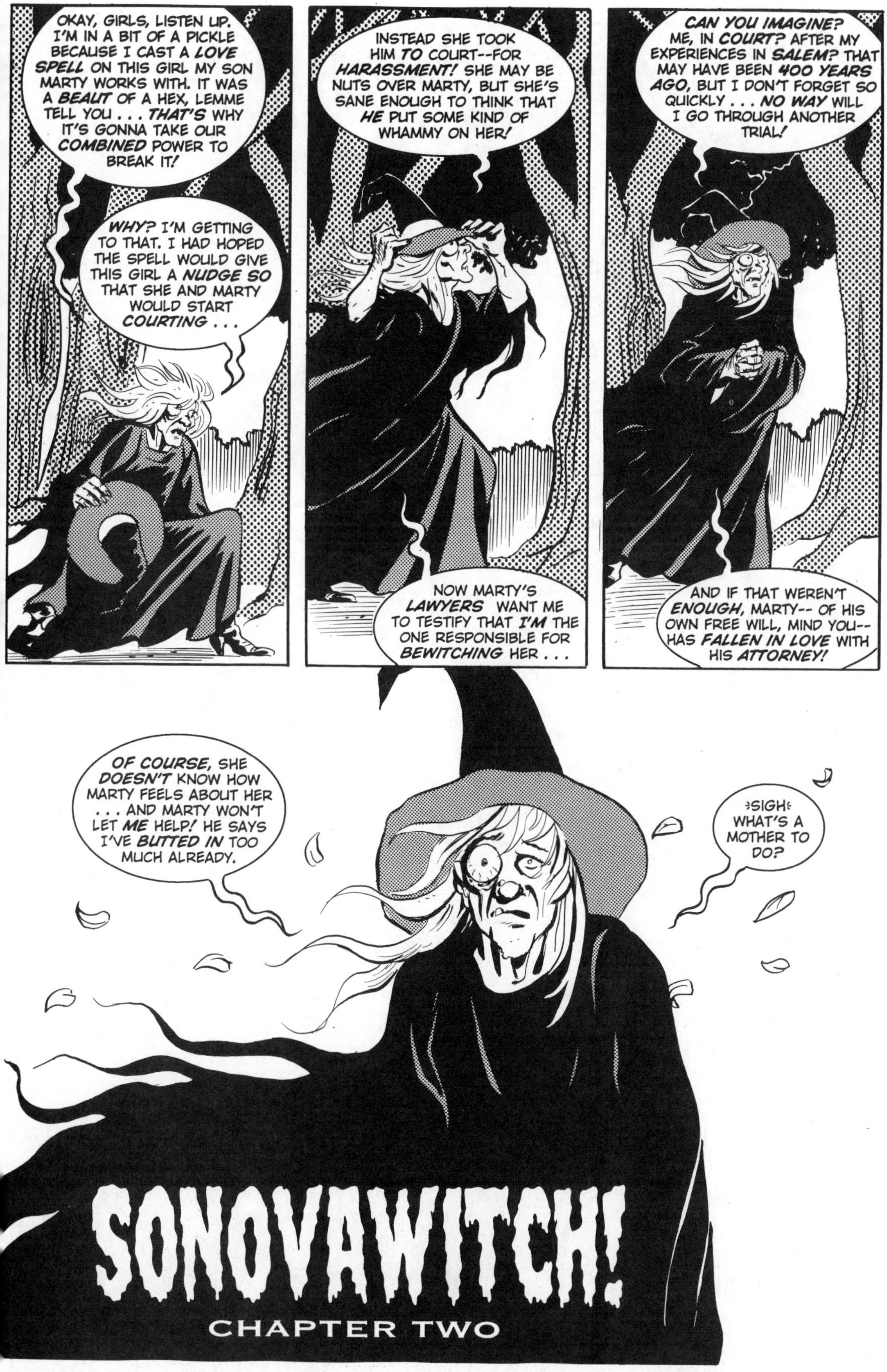
OKAY, GIRLS, LISTEN UP. I'M IN A BIT OF A PICKLE BECAUSE I CAST A LOVE SPELL ON THIS GIRL MY SON MARTY WORKS WITH. IT WAS A BEAUT OF A HEX, LEMME TELL YOU . . . THAT'S WHY IT'S GONNA TAKE OUR COMBINED POWER TO BREAK IT!
WHY? I'M GETTING TO THAT. I HAD HOPED THE SPELL WOULD GIVE THIS GIRL A NUDGE SO THAT SHE AND MARTY WOULD START COURTING . . .
INSTEAD SHE TOOK HIM TO COURT--FOR HARASSMENT! SHE MAY BE NUTS OVER MARTY, BUT SHE'S SANE ENOUGH TO THINK THAT HE PUT SOME KIND OF WHAMMY ON HER!
NOW MARTY'S LAWYERS WANT ME TO TESTIFY THAT I'M THE ONE RESPONSIBLE FOR BEWITCHING HER . . .
CAN YOU IMAGINE? ME, IN COURT? AFTER MY EXPERIENCES IN SALEM? THAT MAY HAVE BEEN 400 YEARS AGO, BUT I DON'T FORGET SO QUICKLY . . . NO WAY WILL I GO THROUGH ANOTHER TRIAL!
AND IF THAT WEREN'T ENOUGH, MARTY-- OF HIS OWN FREE WILL, MIND YOU-- HAS FALLEN IN LOVE WITH HIS ATTORNEY!
OF COURSE, SHE DOESN'T KNOW HOW MARTY FEELS ABOUT HER . . . AND MARTY WON'T LET ME HELP! HE SAYS I'VE BUTTED IN TOO MUCH ALREADY.
SIGH WHAT'S A MOTHER TO DO?
SONOVAWITCH!
CHAPTER TWO

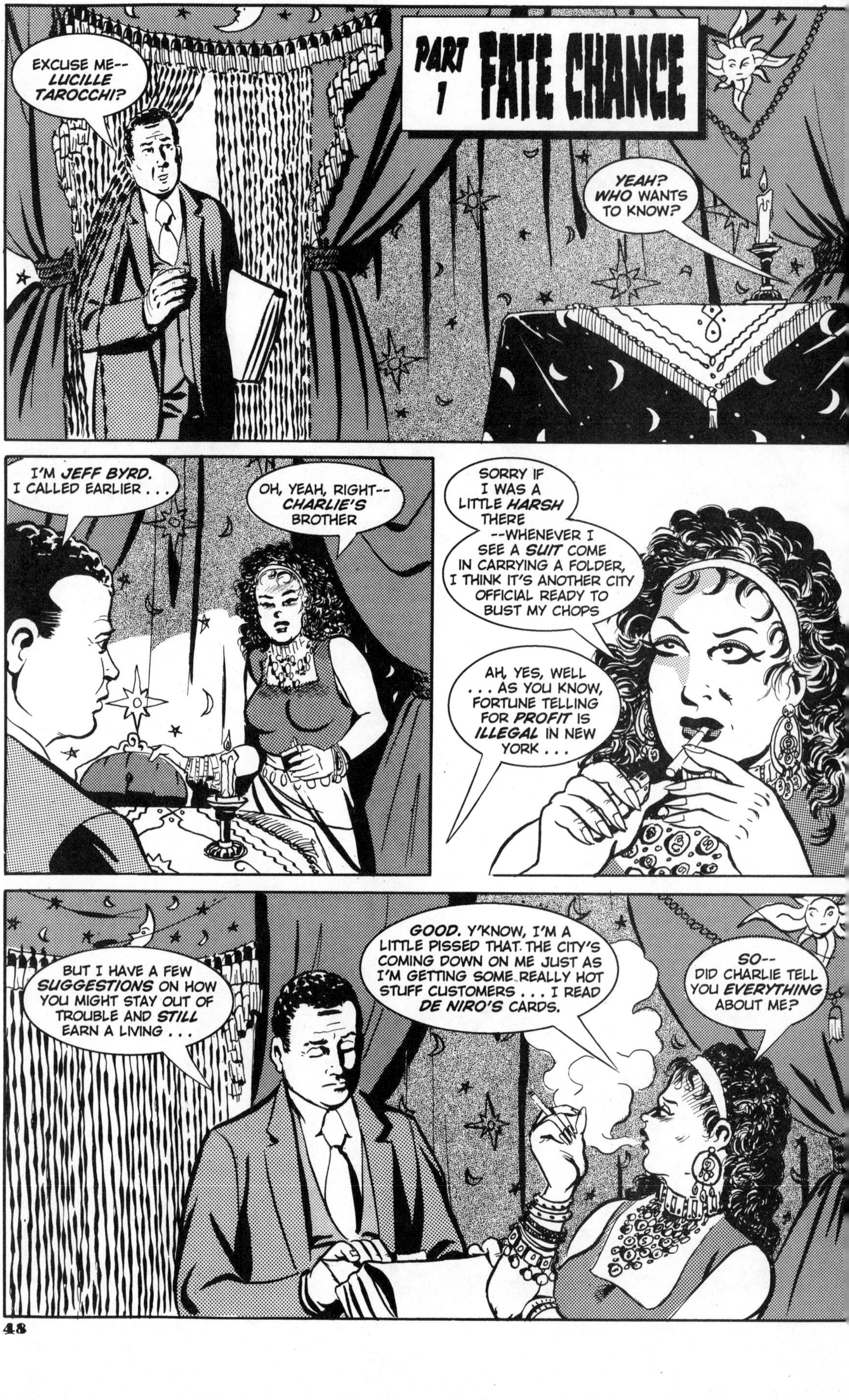
PART 1 FATE CHANCE
EXCUSE ME-- LUCILLE TAROCCHI?
YEAH? WHO WANTS TO KNOW?
I'M JEFF BYRD. I CALLED EARLIER . . .
OH, YEAH, RIGHT-- CHARLIE'S BROTHER
SORRY IF I WAS A LITTLE HARSH THERE --WHENEVER I SEE A SUIT COME IN CARRYING A FOLDER, I THINK IT'S ANOTHER CITY OFFICIAL READY TO BUST MY CHOPS
AH, YES, WELL . . . AS YOU KNOW, FORTUNE TELLING FOR PROFIT IS ILLEGAL IN NEW YORK . . .
BUT I HAVE A FEW SUGGESTIONS ON HOW YOU MIGHT STAY OUT OF TROUBLE AND STILL EARN A LIVING . . .
GOOD. Y'KNOW, I'M A LITTLE PISSED THAT THE CITY'S COMING DOWN ON ME JUST AS I'M GETTING SOME REALLY HOT STUFF CUSTOMERS . . . I READ DE NIRO'S CARDS.
SO-- DID CHARLIE TELL YOU EVERYTHING ABOUT ME?

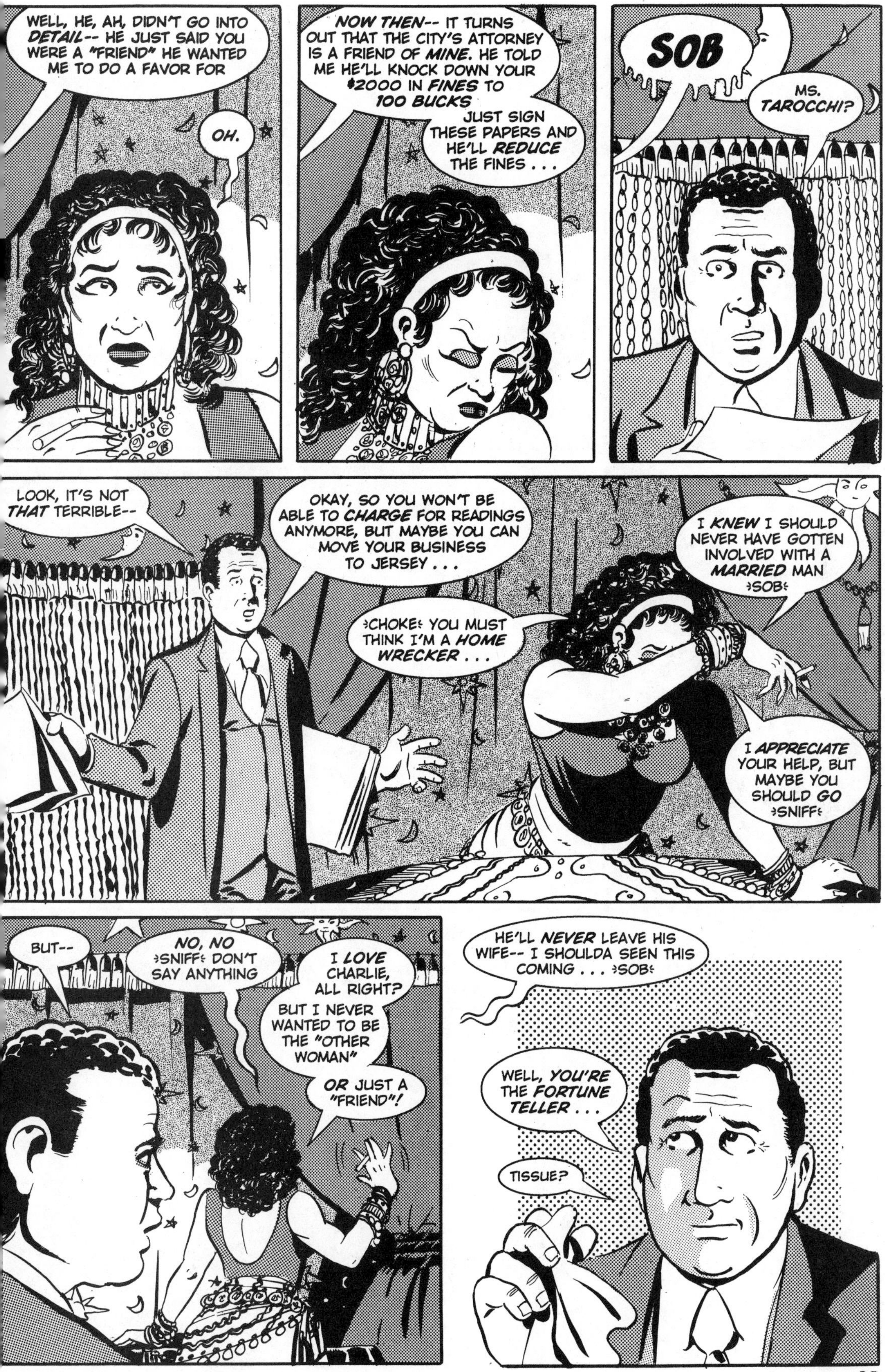
WELL, HE, AH, DIDN'T GO INTO DETAIL-- HE JUST SAID YOU WERE A "FRIEND" HE WANTED ME TO DO A FAVOR FOR
OH.
NOW THEN-- IT TURNS OUT THAT THE CITY'S ATTORNEY IS A FRIEND OF MINE. HE TOLD ME HE'LL KNOCK DOWN YOUR $2000 IN FINES TO 100 BUCKS
JUST SIGN THESE PAPERS AND HE'LL REDUCE THE FINES . . .
SOB
MS. TAROCCHI?
LOOK, IT'S NOT THAT TERRIBLE--
OKAY, SO YOU WON'T BE ABLE TO CHARGE FOR READINGS ANYMORE, BUT MAYBE YOU CAN MOVE YOUR BUSINESS TO JERSEY . . .
I KNEW I SHOULD NEVER HAVE GOTTEN INVOLVED WITH A MARRIED MAN ›SOB‹
›CHOKE‹ YOU MUST THINK I'M A HOME WRECKER . . .
I APPRECIATE YOUR HELP, BUT MAYBE YOU SHOULD GO ›SNIFF‹
BUT--
NO, NO ›SNIFF‹ DON'T SAY ANYTHING
I LOVE CHARLIE, ALL RIGHT?
BUT I NEVER WANTED TO BE THE "OTHER WOMAN"
OR JUST A "FRIEND"!
HE'LL NEVER LEAVE HIS WIFE-- I SHOULDA SEEN THIS COMING . . . ›SOB‹
WELL, YOU'RE THE FORTUNE TELLER . . .
TISSUE?

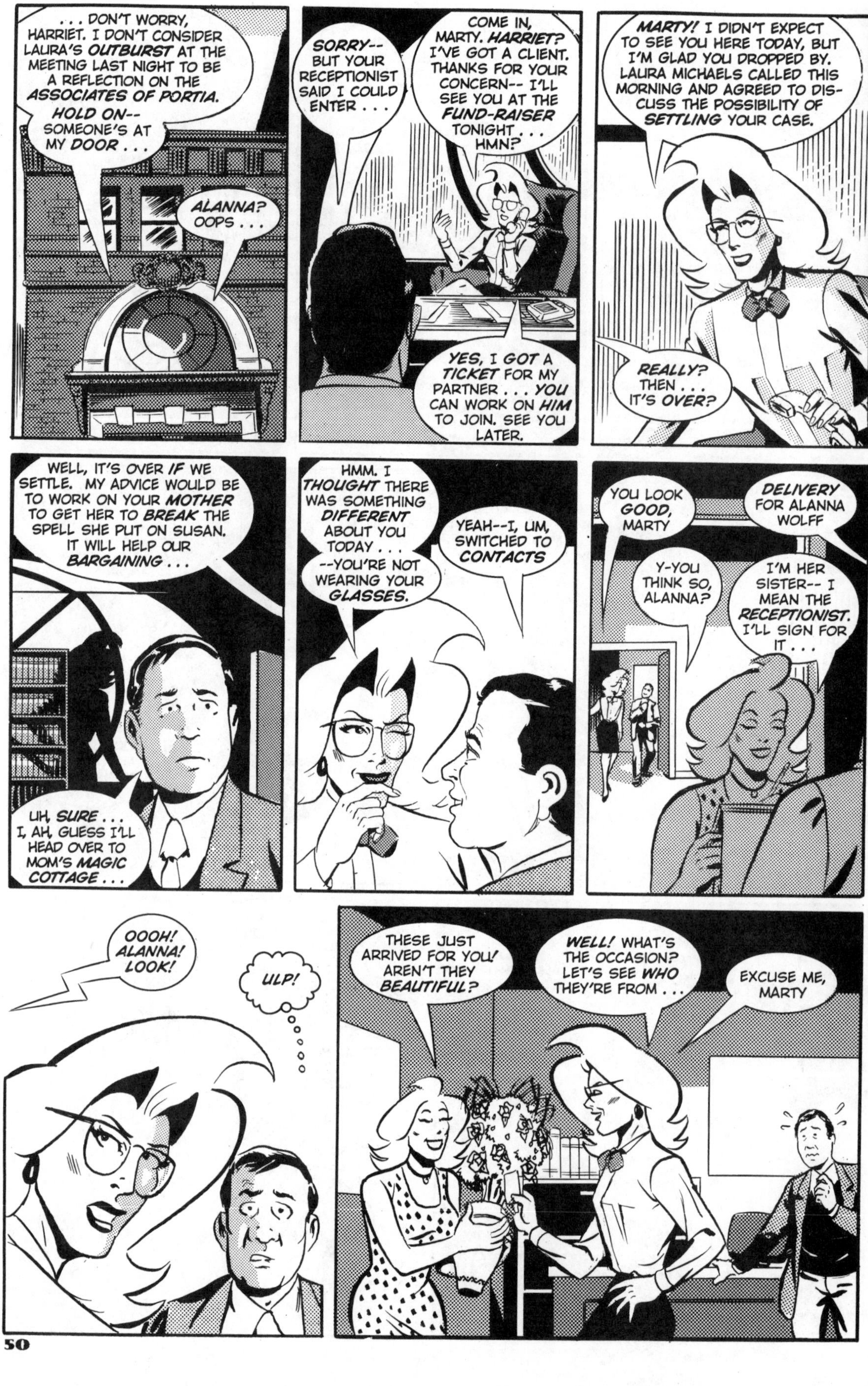

. . . DON'T WORRY, HARRIET. I DON'T CONSIDER LAURA'S OUTBURST AT THE MEETING LAST NIGHT TO BE A REFLECTION ON THE ASSOCIATES OF PORTIA.
HOLD ON-- SOMEONE'S AT MY DOOR . . .
ALANNA? OOPS . . .
SORRY-- BUT YOUR RECEPTIONIST SAID I COULD ENTER . . .
COME IN, MARTY. HARRIET? I'VE GOT A CLIENT. THANKS FOR YOUR CONCERN-- I'LL SEE YOU AT THE FUND-RAISER TONIGHT . . . HMN?
YES, I GOT A TICKET FOR MY PARTNER . . . YOU CAN WORK ON HIM TO JOIN. SEE YOU LATER.
MARTY! I DIDN'T EXPECT TO SEE YOU HERE TODAY, BUT I'M GLAD YOU DROPPED BY. LAURA MICHAELS CALLED THIS MORNING AND AGREED TO DISCUSS THE POSSIBILITY OF SETTLING YOUR CASE.
REALLY? THEN . . . IT'S OVER?
WELL, IT'S OVER IF WE SETTLE. MY ADVICE WOULD BE TO WORK ON YOUR MOTHER TO GET HER TO BREAK THE SPELL SHE PUT ON SUSAN. IT WILL HELP OUR BARGAINING . . .
UH, SURE . . . I, AH, GUESS I'LL HEAD OVER TO MOM'S MAGIC COTTAGE . . .
HMM. I THOUGHT THERE WAS SOMETHING DIFFERENT ABOUT YOU TODAY . . .
--YOU'RE NOT WEARING YOUR GLASSES.
YEAH--I, UM, SWITCHED TO CONTACTS
YOU LOOK GOOD, MARTY
Y-YOU THINK SO, ALANNA?
DELIVERY FOR ALANNA WOLFF
I'M HER SISTER-- I MEAN THE RECEPTIONIST. I'LL SIGN FOR IT . . .
OOOH! ALANNA! LOOK!
ULP!
THESE JUST ARRIVED FOR YOU! AREN'T THEY BEAUTIFUL?
WELL! WHAT'S THE OCCASION? LET'S SEE WHO THEY'RE FROM . . .
EXCUSE ME, MARTY

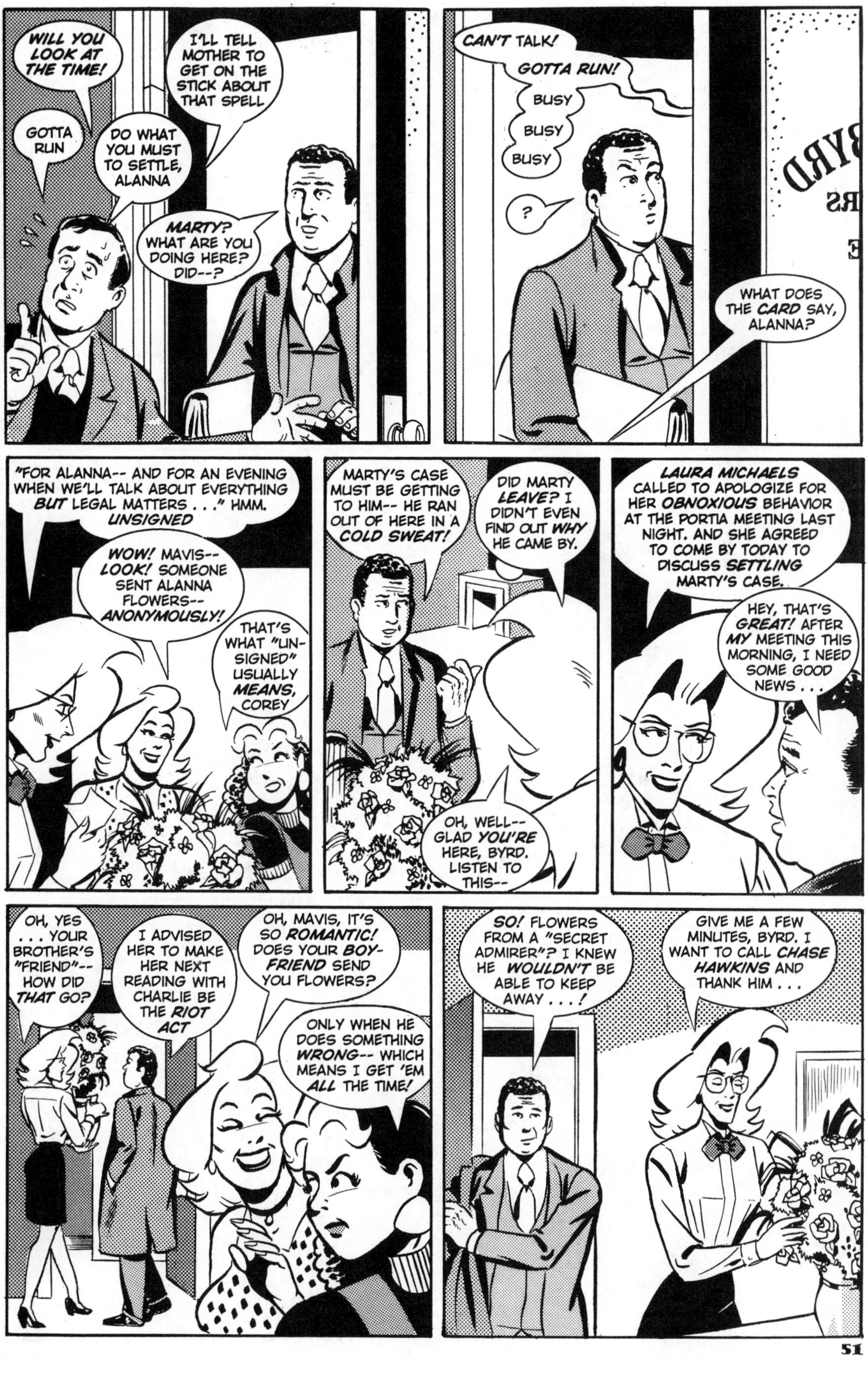

WILL YOU LOOK AT THE TIME!
GOTTA RUN
I'LL TELL MOTHER TO GET ON THE STICK ABOUT THAT SPELL
DO WHAT YOU MUST TO SETTLE, ALANNA
MARTY? WHAT ARE YOU DOING HERE? DID--?
CAN'T TALK!
GOTTA RUN!
BUSY
BUSY
BUSY
?
WHAT DOES THE CARD SAY, ALANNA?
"FOR ALANNA-- AND FOR AN EVENING WHEN WE'LL TALK ABOUT EVERYTHING BUT LEGAL MATTERS . . ." HMM. UNSIGNED
WOW! MAVIS-- LOOK! SOMEONE SENT ALANNA FLOWERS-- ANONYMOUSLY!
THAT'S WHAT "UN-SIGNED" USUALLY MEANS, COREY
MARTY'S CASE MUST BE GETTING TO HIM-- HE RAN OUT OF HERE IN A COLD SWEAT!
DID MARTY LEAVE? I DIDN'T EVEN FIND OUT WHY HE CAME BY.
OH, WELL-- GLAD YOU'RE HERE, BYRD. LISTEN TO THIS--
LAURA MICHAELS CALLED TO APOLOGIZE FOR HER OBNOXIOUS BEHAVIOR AT THE PORTIA MEETING LAST NIGHT. AND SHE AGREED TO COME BY TODAY TO DISCUSS SETTLING MARTY'S CASE.
HEY, THAT'S GREAT! AFTER MY MEETING THIS MORNING, I NEED SOME GOOD NEWS . . .
OH, YES . . . YOUR BROTHER'S "FRIEND"-- HOW DID THAT GO?
I ADVISED HER TO MAKE HER NEXT READING WITH CHARLIE BE THE RIOT ACT
OH, MAVIS, IT'S SO ROMANTIC! DOES YOUR BOY-FRIEND SEND YOU FLOWERS?
ONLY WHEN HE DOES SOMETHING WRONG-- WHICH MEANS I GET 'EM ALL THE TIME!
SO! FLOWERS FROM A "SECRET ADMIRER"? I KNEW HE WOULDN'T BE ABLE TO KEEP AWAY . . .!
GIVE ME A FEW MINUTES, BYRD. I WANT TO CALL CHASE HAWKINS AND THANK HIM . . .

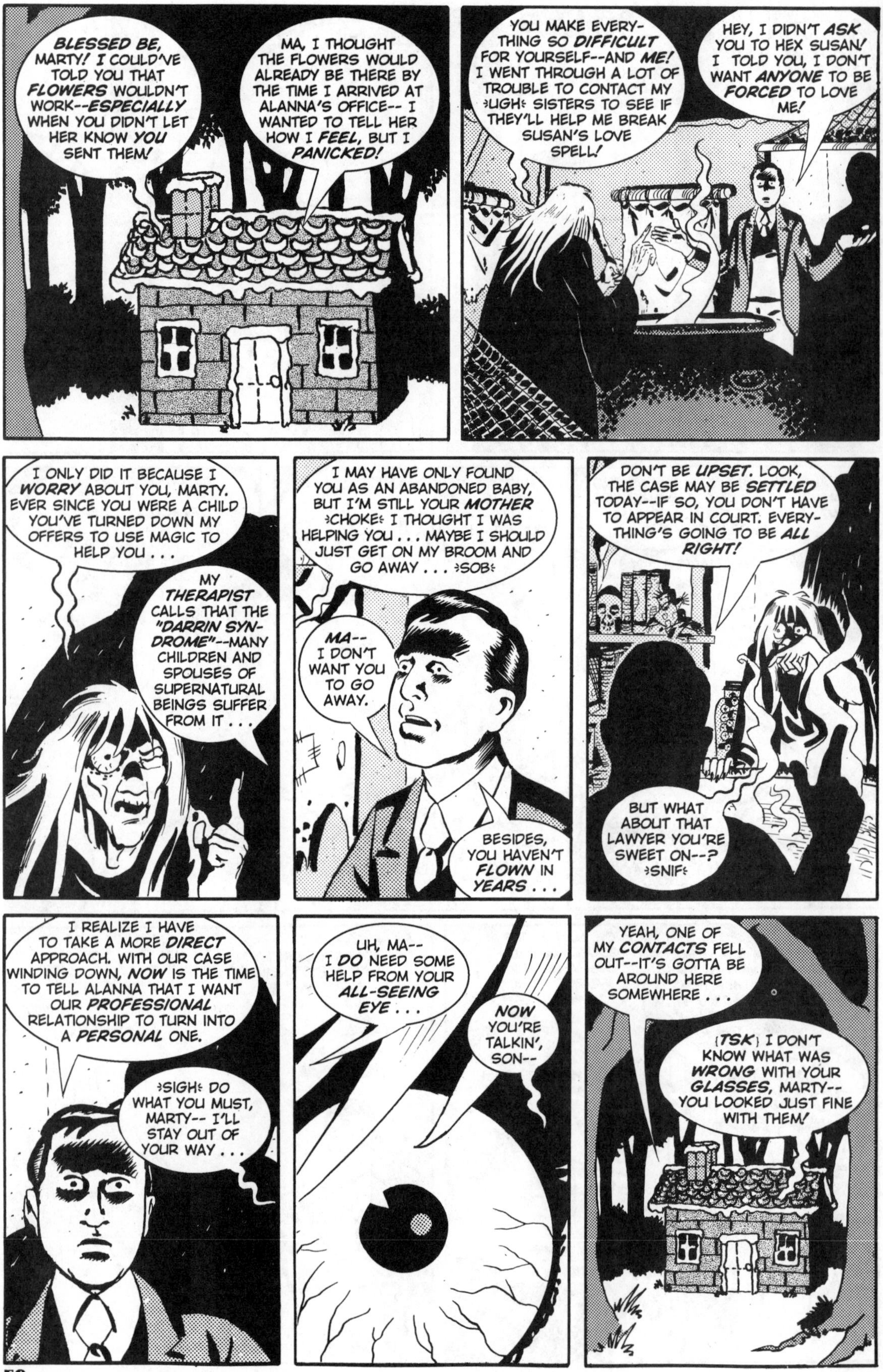
BLESSED BE, MARTY! I COULD'VE TOLD YOU THAT FLOWERS WOULDN'T WORK--ESPECIALLY WHEN YOU DIDN'T LET HER KNOW YOU SENT THEM!
MA, I THOUGHT THE FLOWERS WOULD ALREADY BE THERE BY THE TIME I ARRIVED AT ALANNA'S OFFICE-- I WANTED TO TELL HER HOW I FEEL, BUT I PANICKED!
YOU MAKE EVERY-THING SO DIFFICULT FOR YOURSELF--AND ME! I WENT THROUGH A LOT OF TROUBLE TO CONTACT MY ꞉UGH꞉ SISTERS TO SEE IF THEY'LL HELP ME BREAK SUSAN'S LOVE SPELL!
HEY, I DIDN'T ASK YOU TO HEX SUSAN! I TOLD YOU, I DON'T WANT ANYONE TO BE FORCED TO LOVE ME!
I ONLY DID IT BECAUSE I WORRY ABOUT YOU, MARTY. EVER SINCE YOU WERE A CHILD YOU'VE TURNED DOWN MY OFFERS TO USE MAGIC TO HELP YOU . . .
MY THERAPIST CALLS THAT THE "DARRIN SYN-DROME"--MANY CHILDREN AND SPOUSES OF SUPERNATURAL BEINGS SUFFER FROM IT . . .
I MAY HAVE ONLY FOUND YOU AS AN ABANDONED BABY, BUT I'M STILL YOUR MOTHER ꞉CHOKE꞉ I THOUGHT I WAS HELPING YOU . . . MAYBE I SHOULD JUST GET ON MY BROOM AND GO AWAY . . . ꞉SOB꞉
MA-- I DON'T WANT YOU TO GO AWAY.
BESIDES, YOU HAVEN'T FLOWN IN YEARS . . .
DON'T BE UPSET. LOOK, THE CASE MAY BE SETTLED TODAY--IF SO, YOU DON'T HAVE TO APPEAR IN COURT. EVERY-THING'S GOING TO BE ALL RIGHT!
BUT WHAT ABOUT THAT LAWYER YOU'RE SWEET ON--? ꞉SNIF꞉
I REALIZE I HAVE TO TAKE A MORE DIRECT APPROACH. WITH OUR CASE WINDING DOWN, NOW IS THE TIME TO TELL ALANNA THAT I WANT OUR PROFESSIONAL RELATIONSHIP TO TURN INTO A PERSONAL ONE.
꞉SIGH꞉ DO WHAT YOU MUST, MARTY-- I'LL STAY OUT OF YOUR WAY . . .
UH, MA-- I DO NEED SOME HELP FROM YOUR ALL-SEEING EYE . . .
NOW YOU'RE TALKIN', SON--
YEAH, ONE OF MY CONTACTS FELL OUT--IT'S GOTTA BE AROUND HERE SOMEWHERE . . .
{TSK} I DON'T KNOW WHAT WAS WRONG WITH YOUR GLASSES, MARTY-- YOU LOOKED JUST FINE WITH THEM!

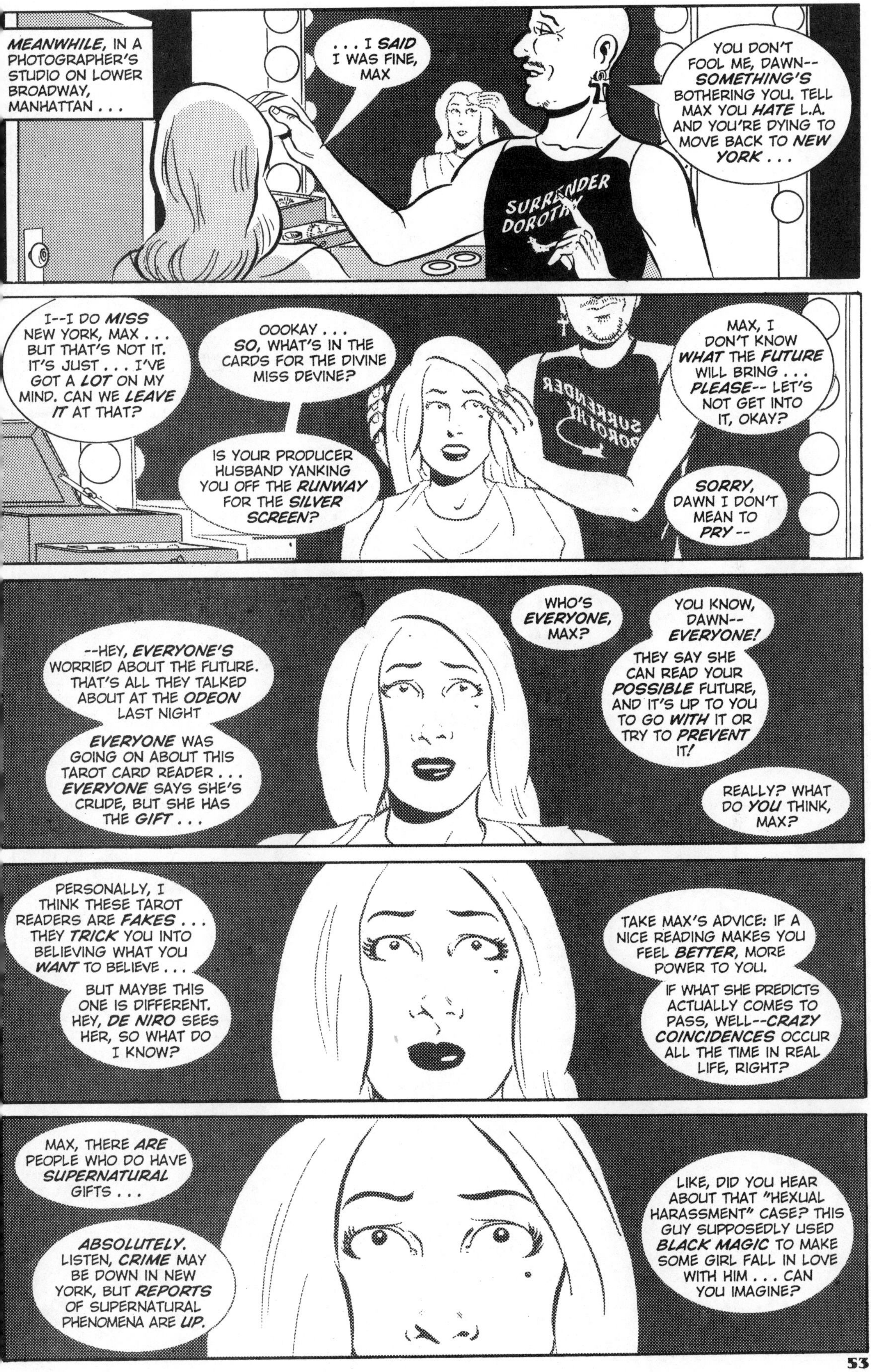
MEANWHILE, IN A PHOTOGRAPHER'S STUDIO ON LOWER BROADWAY, MANHATTAN . . .
. . . I SAID I WAS FINE, MAX
YOU DON'T FOOL ME, DAWN-- SOMETHING'S BOTHERING YOU. TELL MAX YOU HATE L.A. AND YOU'RE DYING TO MOVE BACK TO NEW YORK . . .
SURRENDER DOROTHY
I--I DO MISS NEW YORK, MAX . . . BUT THAT'S NOT IT. IT'S JUST . . . I'VE GOT A LOT ON MY MIND. CAN WE LEAVE IT AT THAT?
OOOKAY . . . SO, WHAT'S IN THE CARDS FOR THE DIVINE MISS DEVINE?
IS YOUR PRODUCER HUSBAND YANKING YOU OFF THE RUNWAY FOR THE SILVER SCREEN?
MAX, I DON'T KNOW WHAT THE FUTURE WILL BRING . . . PLEASE-- LET'S NOT GET INTO IT, OKAY?
SORRY, DAWN I DON'T MEAN TO PRY --
--HEY, EVERYONE'S WORRIED ABOUT THE FUTURE. THAT'S ALL THEY TALKED ABOUT AT THE ODEON LAST NIGHT
EVERYONE WAS GOING ON ABOUT THIS TAROT CARD READER . . . EVERYONE SAYS SHE'S CRUDE, BUT SHE HAS THE GIFT . . .
WHO'S EVERYONE, MAX?
YOU KNOW, DAWN-- EVERYONE!
THEY SAY SHE CAN READ YOUR POSSIBLE FUTURE, AND IT'S UP TO YOU TO GO WITH IT OR TRY TO PREVENT IT!
REALLY? WHAT DO YOU THINK, MAX?
PERSONALLY, I THINK THESE TAROT READERS ARE FAKES . . . THEY TRICK YOU INTO BELIEVING WHAT YOU WANT TO BELIEVE . . .
BUT MAYBE THIS ONE IS DIFFERENT. HEY, DE NIRO SEES HER, SO WHAT DO I KNOW?
TAKE MAX'S ADVICE: IF A NICE READING MAKES YOU FEEL BETTER, MORE POWER TO YOU.
IF WHAT SHE PREDICTS ACTUALLY COMES TO PASS, WELL--CRAZY COINCIDENCES OCCUR ALL THE TIME IN REAL LIFE, RIGHT?
MAX, THERE ARE PEOPLE WHO DO HAVE SUPERNATURAL GIFTS . . .
ABSOLUTELY. LISTEN, CRIME MAY BE DOWN IN NEW YORK, BUT REPORTS OF SUPERNATURAL PHENOMENA ARE UP.
LIKE, DID YOU HEAR ABOUT THAT "HEXUAL HARASSMENT" CASE? THIS GUY SUPPOSEDLY USED BLACK MAGIC TO MAKE SOME GIRL FALL IN LOVE WITH HIM . . . CAN YOU IMAGINE?

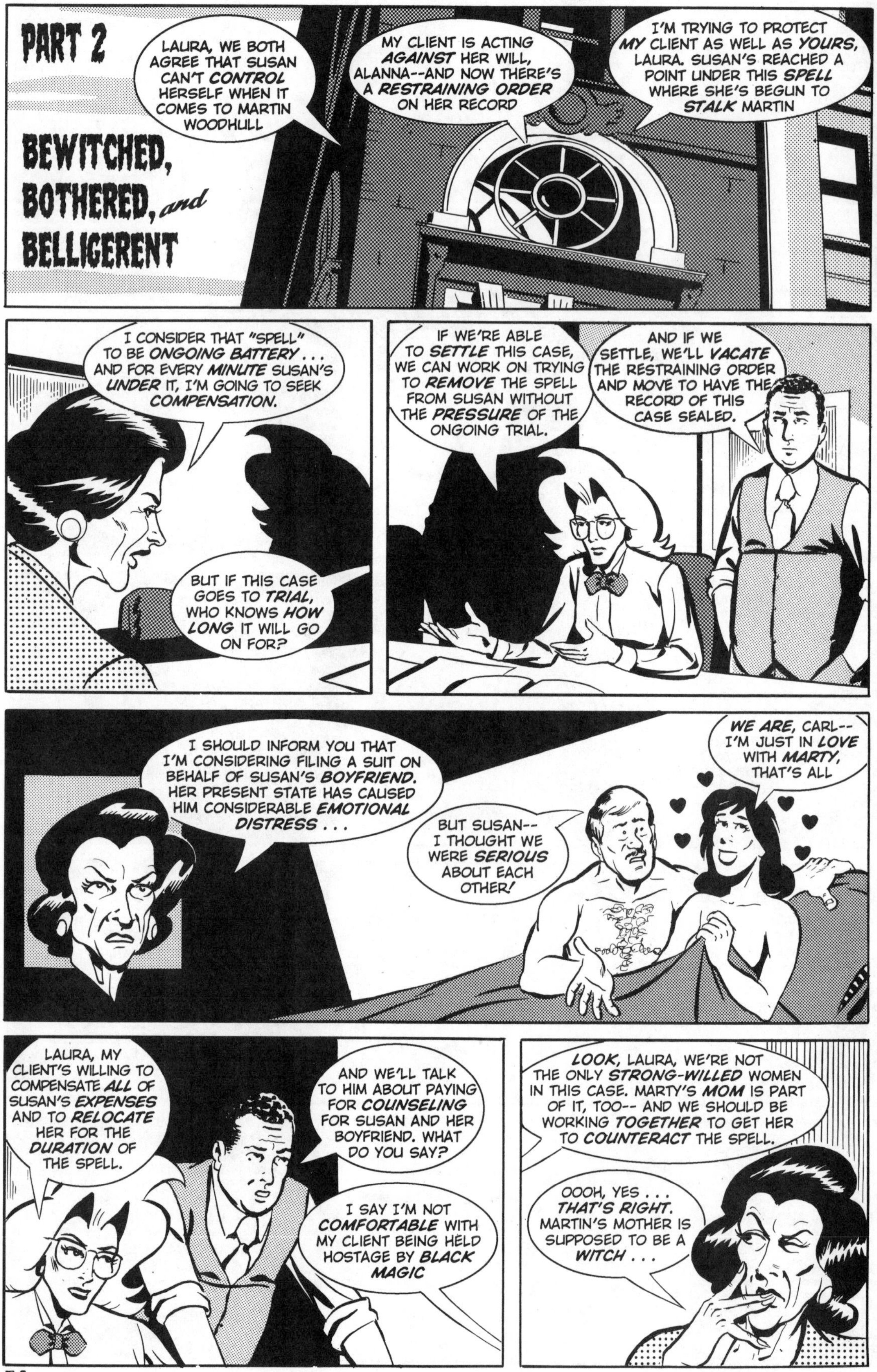
PART 2
BEWITCHED, BOTHERED, and BELLIGERENT
LAURA, WE BOTH AGREE THAT SUSAN CAN'T CONTROL HERSELF WHEN IT COMES TO MARTIN WOODHULL
MY CLIENT IS ACTING AGAINST HER WILL, ALANNA--AND NOW THERE'S A RESTRAINING ORDER ON HER RECORD
I'M TRYING TO PROTECT MY CLIENT AS WELL AS YOURS, LAURA. SUSAN'S REACHED A POINT UNDER THIS SPELL WHERE SHE'S BEGUN TO STALK MARTIN
I CONSIDER THAT "SPELL" TO BE ONGOING BATTERY . . . AND FOR EVERY MINUTE SUSAN'S UNDER IT, I'M GOING TO SEEK COMPENSATION.
BUT IF THIS CASE GOES TO TRIAL, WHO KNOWS HOW LONG IT WILL GO ON FOR?
IF WE'RE ABLE TO SETTLE THIS CASE, WE CAN WORK ON TRYING TO REMOVE THE SPELL FROM SUSAN WITHOUT THE PRESSURE OF THE ONGOING TRIAL.
AND IF WE SETTLE, WE'LL VACATE THE RESTRAINING ORDER AND MOVE TO HAVE THE RECORD OF THIS CASE SEALED.
I SHOULD INFORM YOU THAT I'M CONSIDERING FILING A SUIT ON BEHALF OF SUSAN'S BOYFRIEND. HER PRESENT STATE HAS CAUSED HIM CONSIDERABLE EMOTIONAL DISTRESS . . .
BUT SUSAN-- I THOUGHT WE WERE SERIOUS ABOUT EACH OTHER!
WE ARE, CARL-- I'M JUST IN LOVE WITH MARTY, THAT'S ALL
LAURA, MY CLIENT'S WILLING TO COMPENSATE ALL OF SUSAN'S EXPENSES AND TO RELOCATE HER FOR THE DURATION OF THE SPELL.
AND WE'LL TALK TO HIM ABOUT PAYING FOR COUNSELING FOR SUSAN AND HER BOYFRIEND. WHAT DO YOU SAY?
I SAY I'M NOT COMFORTABLE WITH MY CLIENT BEING HELD HOSTAGE BY BLACK MAGIC
LOOK, LAURA, WE'RE NOT THE ONLY STRONG-WILLED WOMEN IN THIS CASE. MARTY'S MOM IS PART OF IT, TOO-- AND WE SHOULD BE WORKING TOGETHER TO GET HER TO COUNTERACT THE SPELL.
OOOH, YES . . . THAT'S RIGHT. MARTIN'S MOTHER IS SUPPOSED TO BE A WITCH . . .

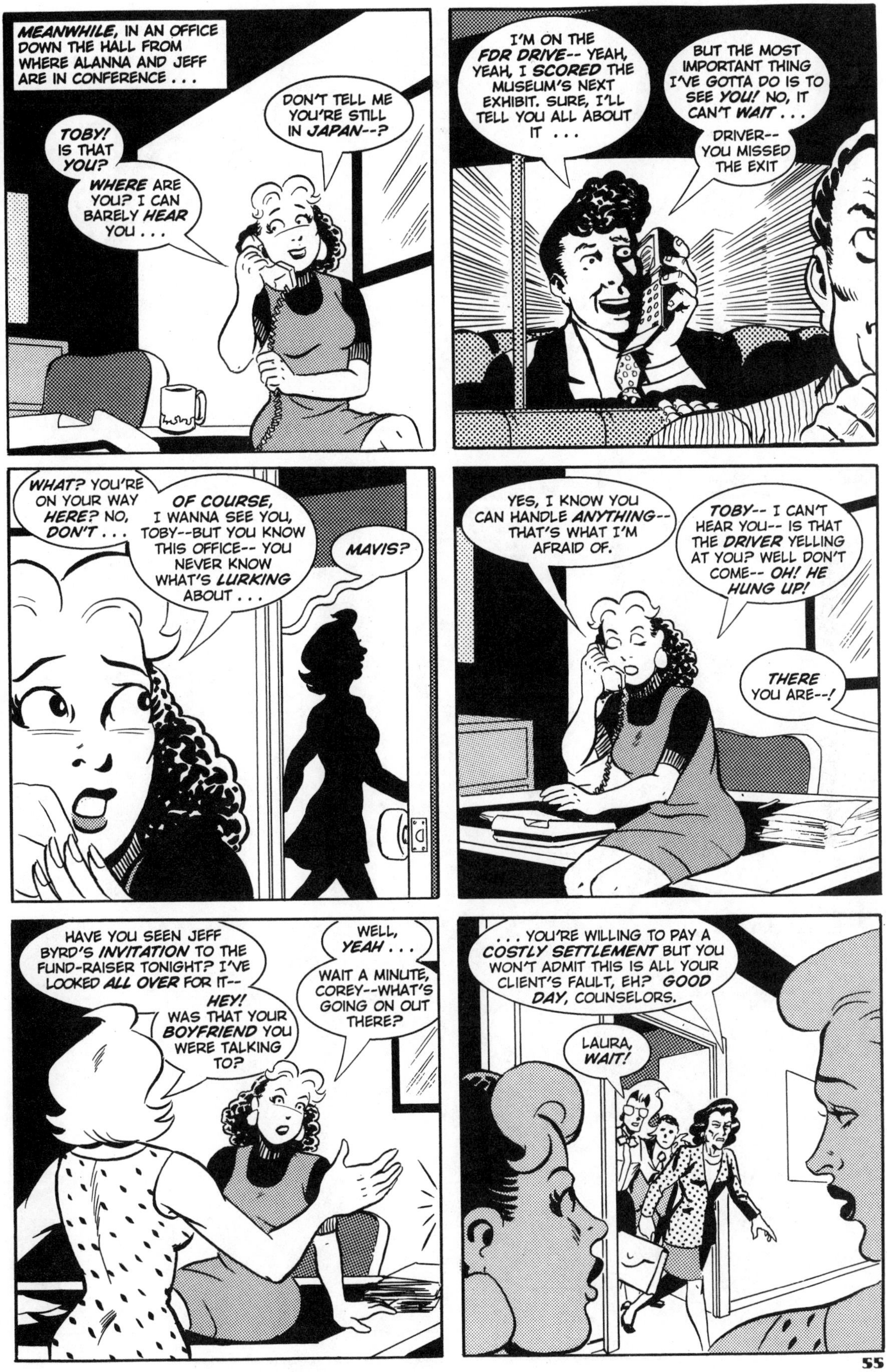
MEANWHILE, IN AN OFFICE DOWN THE HALL FROM WHERE ALANNA AND JEFF ARE IN CONFERENCE . . .
DON'T TELL ME YOU'RE STILL IN JAPAN--?
TOBY! IS THAT YOU?
WHERE ARE YOU? I CAN BARELY HEAR YOU . . .
I'M ON THE FDR DRIVE-- YEAH, YEAH, I SCORED THE MUSEUM'S NEXT EXHIBIT. SURE, I'LL TELL YOU ALL ABOUT IT . . .
BUT THE MOST IMPORTANT THING I'VE GOTTA DO IS TO SEE YOU! NO, IT CAN'T WAIT . . .
DRIVER-- YOU MISSED THE EXIT
WHAT? YOU'RE ON YOUR WAY HERE? NO, DON'T . . .
OF COURSE, I WANNA SEE YOU, TOBY--BUT YOU KNOW THIS OFFICE-- YOU NEVER KNOW WHAT'S LURKING ABOUT . . .
MAVIS?
YES, I KNOW YOU CAN HANDLE ANYTHING-- THAT'S WHAT I'M AFRAID OF.
TOBY-- I CAN'T HEAR YOU-- IS THAT THE DRIVER YELLING AT YOU? WELL DON'T COME-- OH! HE HUNG UP!
THERE YOU ARE--!
HAVE YOU SEEN JEFF BYRD'S INVITATION TO THE FUND-RAISER TONIGHT? I'VE LOOKED ALL OVER FOR IT--
WELL, YEAH . . .
HEY! WAS THAT YOUR BOYFRIEND YOU WERE TALKING TO?
WAIT A MINUTE, COREY--WHAT'S GOING ON OUT THERE?
. . . YOU'RE WILLING TO PAY A COSTLY SETTLEMENT BUT YOU WON'T ADMIT THIS IS ALL YOUR CLIENT'S FAULT, EH? GOOD DAY, COUNSELORS.
LAURA, WAIT!

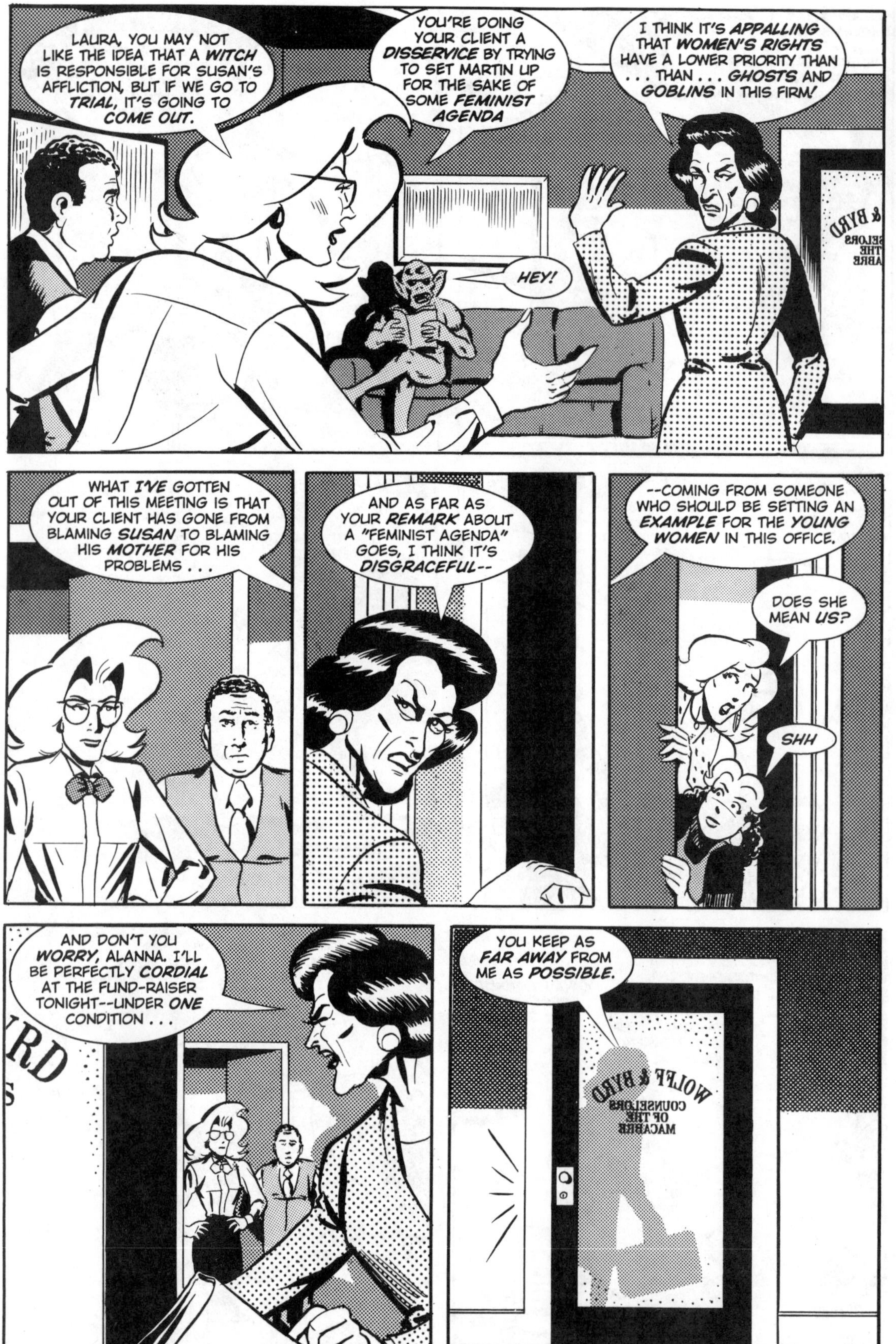
LAURA, YOU MAY NOT LIKE THE IDEA THAT A WITCH IS RESPONSIBLE FOR SUSAN'S AFFLICTION, BUT IF WE GO TO TRIAL, IT'S GOING TO COME OUT.
YOU'RE DOING YOUR CLIENT A DISSERVICE BY TRYING TO SET MARTIN UP FOR THE SAKE OF SOME FEMINIST AGENDA
HEY!
I THINK IT'S APPALLING THAT WOMEN'S RIGHTS HAVE A LOWER PRIORITY THAN . . . THAN . . . GHOSTS AND GOBLINS IN THIS FIRM!
WHAT I'VE GOTTEN OUT OF THIS MEETING IS THAT YOUR CLIENT HAS GONE FROM BLAMING SUSAN TO BLAMING HIS MOTHER FOR HIS PROBLEMS . . .
AND AS FAR AS YOUR REMARK ABOUT A "FEMINIST AGENDA" GOES, I THINK IT'S DISGRACEFUL--
--COMING FROM SOMEONE WHO SHOULD BE SETTING AN EXAMPLE FOR THE YOUNG WOMEN IN THIS OFFICE.
DOES SHE MEAN US?
SHH
AND DON'T YOU WORRY, ALANNA. I'LL BE PERFECTLY CORDIAL AT THE FUND-RAISER TONIGHT--UNDER ONE CONDITION . . .
YOU KEEP AS FAR AWAY FROM ME AS POSSIBLE.
WOLFF & BYRD
COUNSELORS OF THE MACABRE

JUSTICE

GASP!

DON'T WORRY . . . THIS CARD CAN BE INTERPRETED AS A CHANGE IN LIFE-- *OR* AS GIVING UP OLD WAYS AND MOVING ON

GASP!

≈AHEM≈ LET ME *CONTINUE* . . .

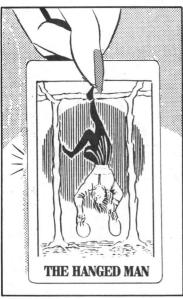

THE HANGED MAN

HMM . . . THERE IS A MATTER LEFT *UNRESOLVED* THAT BOTHERS YOU . . . PERHAPS THE *RESULT* OF A DECISION YOU NOW REGRET?

WHATEVER THAT DECISION WAS, IT HAS LED TO *TWO PATHS* THAT NOW LIE BEFORE YOU . . .

TWO PATHS?

YES. AT THE END OF EACH PATH, YOU WILL FIND *REWARDS* . . .

BUT! YOU MUST CHOOSE *WISELY* . . . FOR IF YOU DECIDE ONE DIRECTION, IT WILL BRING GREAT FEELINGS OF *GUILT,* AND YOU WILL NEVER BE ABLE TO ENJOY THE RICHES THAT AWAIT YOU.

THE OTHER PATH IS FRAUGHT WITH GREAT *UNCERTAINTY* AND *HARDSHIP.* BUT IF YOU ENDURE, YOU WILL BE REWARDED WITH A GREATER SPIRITUALITY AND WISDOM THAN YOU HAVE EVER KNOWN BEFORE

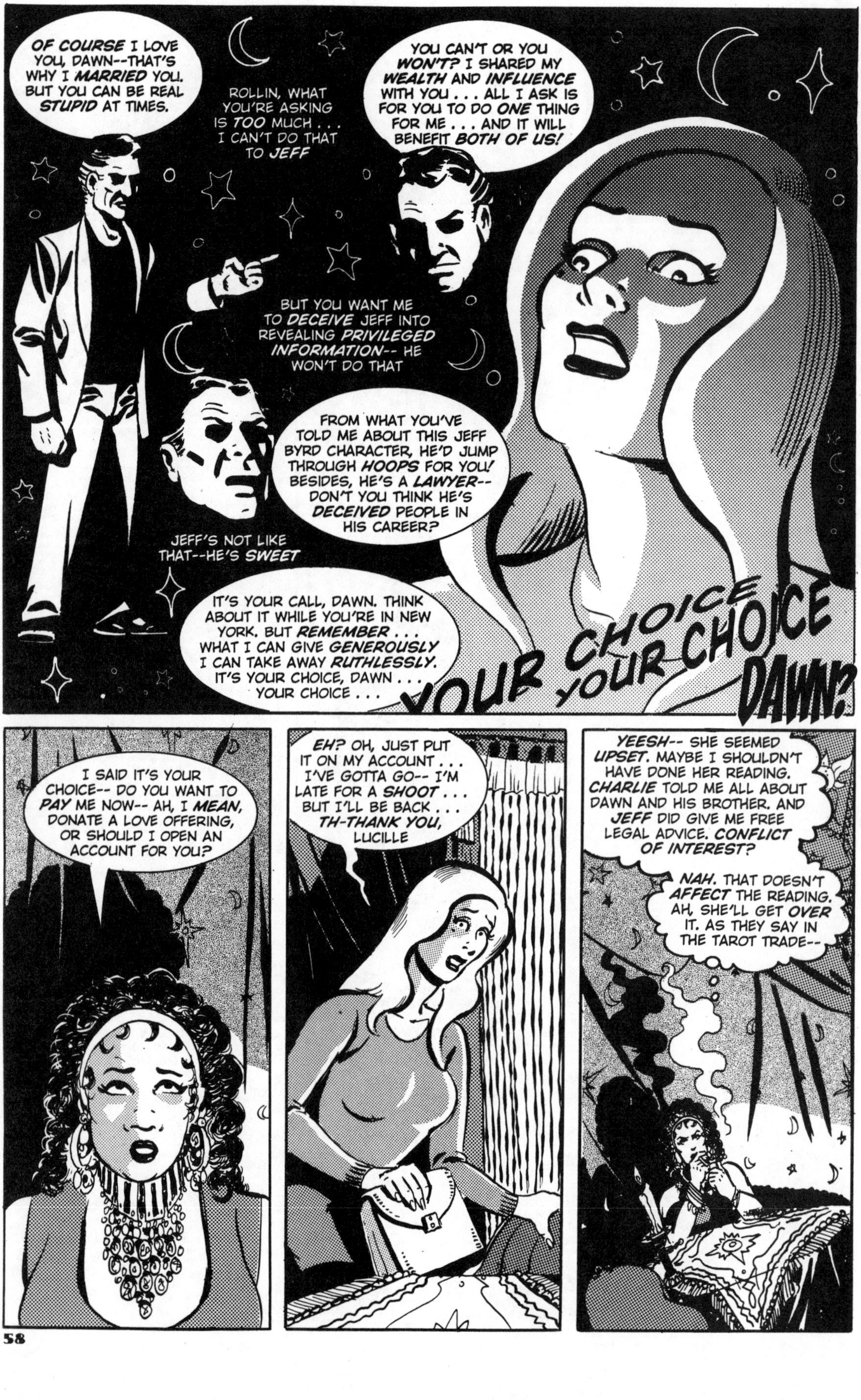

OF COURSE I LOVE YOU, DAWN--THAT'S WHY I MARRIED YOU. BUT YOU CAN BE REAL STUPID AT TIMES.
ROLLIN, WHAT YOU'RE ASKING IS TOO MUCH . . . I CAN'T DO THAT TO JEFF
YOU CAN'T OR YOU WON'T? I SHARED MY WEALTH AND INFLUENCE WITH YOU . . . ALL I ASK IS FOR YOU TO DO ONE THING FOR ME . . . AND IT WILL BENEFIT BOTH OF US!
BUT YOU WANT ME TO DECEIVE JEFF INTO REVEALING PRIVILEGED INFORMATION-- HE WON'T DO THAT
FROM WHAT YOU'VE TOLD ME ABOUT THIS JEFF BYRD CHARACTER, HE'D JUMP THROUGH HOOPS FOR YOU! BESIDES, HE'S A LAWYER-- DON'T YOU THINK HE'S DECEIVED PEOPLE IN HIS CAREER?
JEFF'S NOT LIKE THAT--HE'S SWEET
IT'S YOUR CALL, DAWN. THINK ABOUT IT WHILE YOU'RE IN NEW YORK. BUT REMEMBER . . . WHAT I CAN GIVE GENEROUSLY I CAN TAKE AWAY RUTHLESSLY. IT'S YOUR CHOICE, DAWN . . . YOUR CHOICE . . .
YOUR CHOICE YOUR CHOICE DAWN?
I SAID IT'S YOUR CHOICE-- DO YOU WANT TO PAY ME NOW-- AH, I MEAN, DONATE A LOVE OFFERING, OR SHOULD I OPEN AN ACCOUNT FOR YOU?
EH? OH, JUST PUT IT ON MY ACCOUNT . . . I'VE GOTTA GO-- I'M LATE FOR A SHOOT . . . BUT I'LL BE BACK . . . TH-THANK YOU, LUCILLE
YEESH-- SHE SEEMED UPSET. MAYBE I SHOULDN'T HAVE DONE HER READING. CHARLIE TOLD ME ALL ABOUT DAWN AND HIS BROTHER. AND JEFF DID GIVE ME FREE LEGAL ADVICE. CONFLICT OF INTEREST?
NAH. THAT DOESN'T AFFECT THE READING. AH, SHE'LL GET OVER IT. AS THEY SAY IN THE TAROT TRADE--

"YOU PLAY THE CARDS YOU'RE DEALT . . . !"

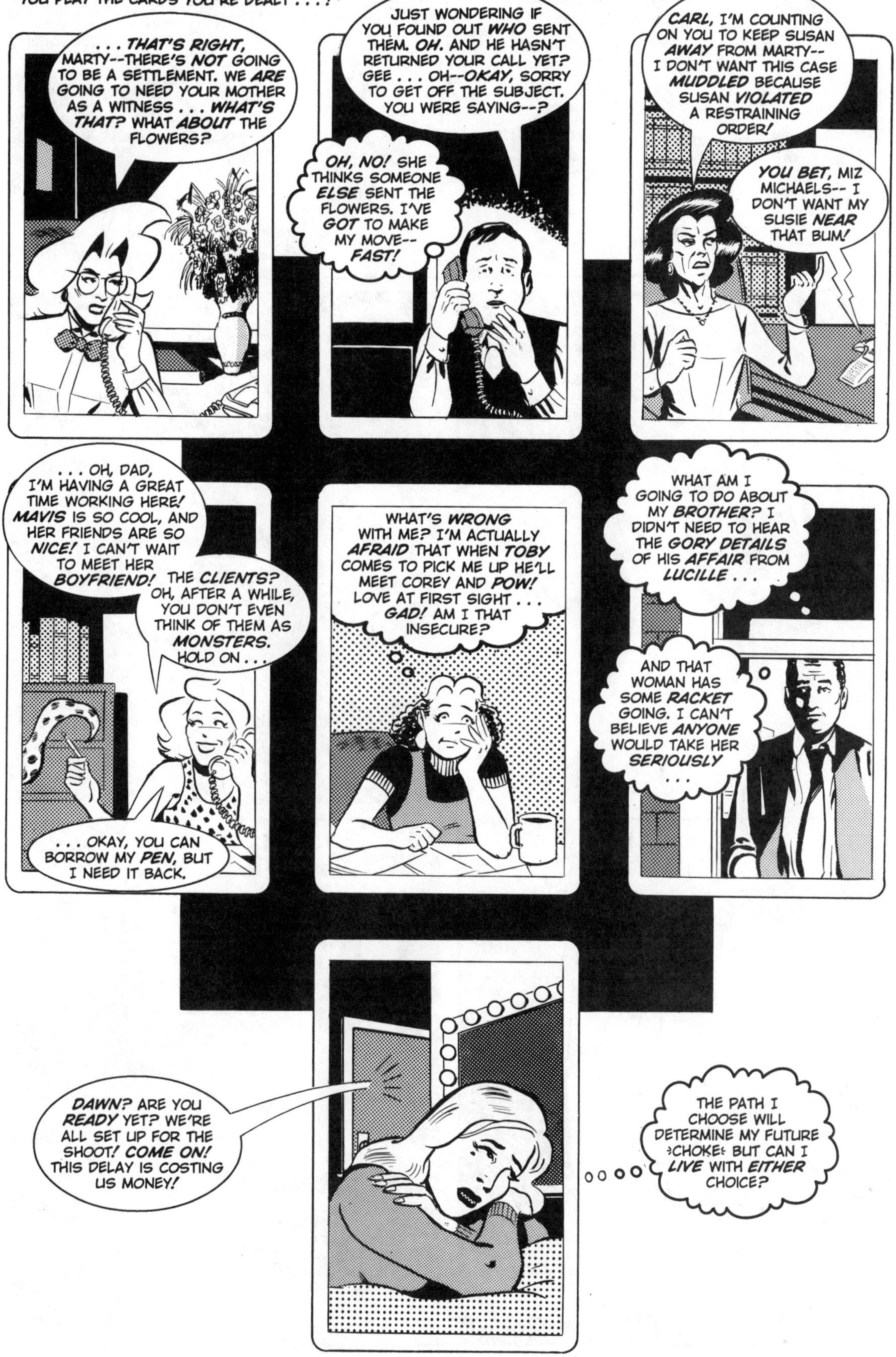

. . . THAT'S RIGHT, MARTY--THERE'S NOT GOING TO BE A SETTLEMENT. WE ARE GOING TO NEED YOUR MOTHER AS A WITNESS . . . WHAT'S THAT? WHAT ABOUT THE FLOWERS?
JUST WONDERING IF YOU FOUND OUT WHO SENT THEM. OH. AND HE HASN'T RETURNED YOUR CALL YET? GEE . . . OH--OKAY, SORRY TO GET OFF THE SUBJECT. YOU WERE SAYING--?
OH, NO! SHE THINKS SOMEONE ELSE SENT THE FLOWERS. I'VE GOT TO MAKE MY MOVE--FAST!
CARL, I'M COUNTING ON YOU TO KEEP SUSAN AWAY FROM MARTY-- I DON'T WANT THIS CASE MUDDLED BECAUSE SUSAN VIOLATED A RESTRAINING ORDER!
YOU BET, MIZ MICHAELS-- I DON'T WANT MY SUSIE NEAR THAT BUM!
. . . OH, DAD, I'M HAVING A GREAT TIME WORKING HERE! MAVIS IS SO COOL, AND HER FRIENDS ARE SO NICE! I CAN'T WAIT TO MEET HER BOYFRIEND!
THE CLIENTS? OH, AFTER A WHILE, YOU DON'T EVEN THINK OF THEM AS MONSTERS. HOLD ON . . .
. . . OKAY, YOU CAN BORROW MY PEN, BUT I NEED IT BACK.
WHAT'S WRONG WITH ME? I'M ACTUALLY AFRAID THAT WHEN TOBY COMES TO PICK ME UP HE'LL MEET COREY AND POW! LOVE AT FIRST SIGHT . . . GAD! AM I THAT INSECURE?
WHAT AM I GOING TO DO ABOUT MY BROTHER? I DIDN'T NEED TO HEAR THE GORY DETAILS OF HIS AFFAIR FROM LUCILLE . . .
AND THAT WOMAN HAS SOME RACKET GOING. I CAN'T BELIEVE ANYONE WOULD TAKE HER SERIOUSLY . . .
DAWN? ARE YOU READY YET? WE'RE ALL SET UP FOR THE SHOOT! COME ON! THIS DELAY IS COSTING US MONEY!
THE PATH I CHOOSE WILL DETERMINE MY FUTURE *CHOKE* BUT CAN I LIVE WITH EITHER CHOICE?

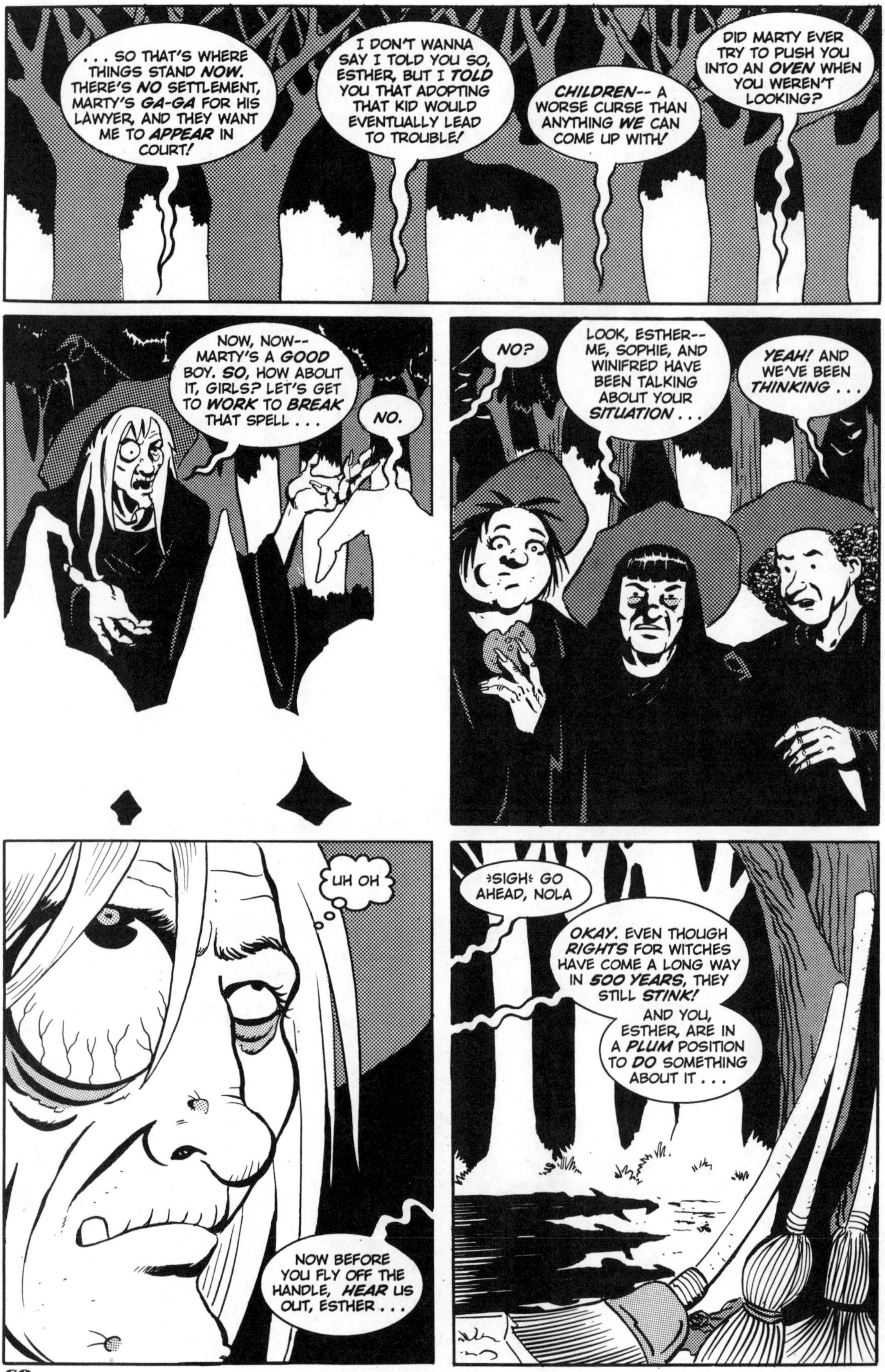
. . . SO THAT'S WHERE THINGS STAND NOW. THERE'S NO SETTLEMENT, MARTY'S GA-GA FOR HIS LAWYER, AND THEY WANT ME TO APPEAR IN COURT!
I DON'T WANNA SAY I TOLD YOU SO, ESTHER, BUT I TOLD YOU THAT ADOPTING THAT KID WOULD EVENTUALLY LEAD TO TROUBLE!
CHILDREN-- A WORSE CURSE THAN ANYTHING WE CAN COME UP WITH!
DID MARTY EVER TRY TO PUSH YOU INTO AN OVEN WHEN YOU WEREN'T LOOKING?
NOW, NOW-- MARTY'S A GOOD BOY. SO, HOW ABOUT IT, GIRLS? LET'S GET TO WORK TO BREAK THAT SPELL . . .
NO.
NO?
LOOK, ESTHER-- ME, SOPHIE, AND WINIFRED HAVE BEEN TALKING ABOUT YOUR SITUATION . . .
YEAH! AND WE'VE BEEN THINKING . . .
UH OH
NOW BEFORE YOU FLY OFF THE HANDLE, HEAR US OUT, ESTHER . . .
SIGH GO AHEAD, NOLA
OKAY. EVEN THOUGH RIGHTS FOR WITCHES HAVE COME A LONG WAY IN 500 YEARS, THEY STILL STINK!
AND YOU, ESTHER, ARE IN A PLUM POSITION TO DO SOMETHING ABOUT IT . . .

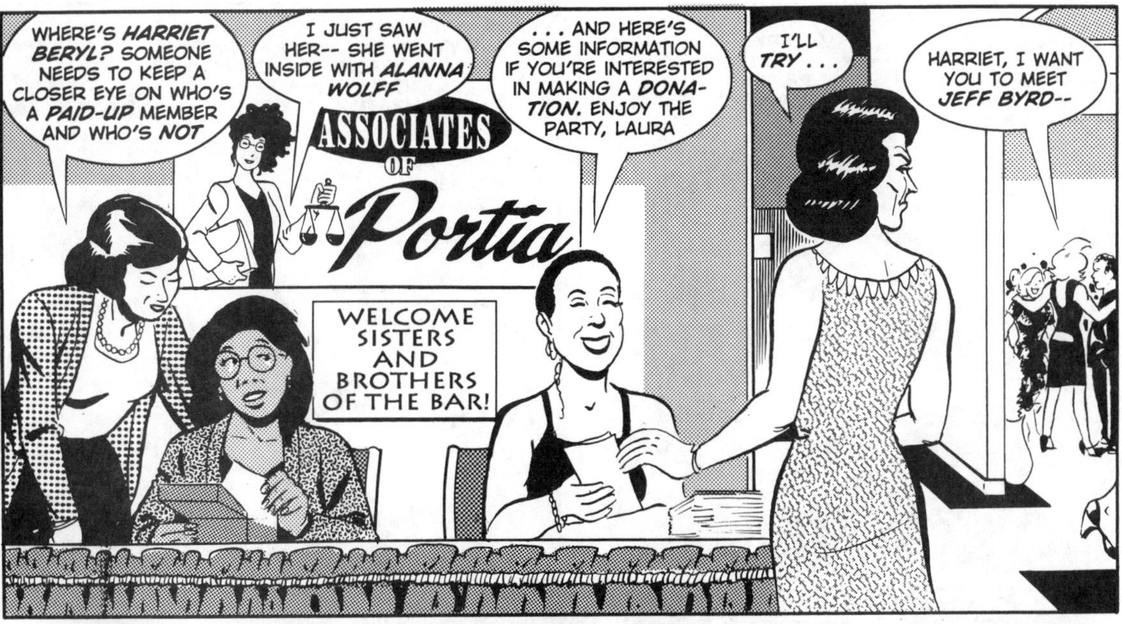
WHERE'S HARRIET BERYL? SOMEONE NEEDS TO KEEP A CLOSER EYE ON WHO'S A PAID-UP MEMBER AND WHO'S NOT
I JUST SAW HER-- SHE WENT INSIDE WITH ALANNA WOLFF
ASSOCIATES OF Portia
WELCOME SISTERS AND BROTHERS OF THE BAR!
. . . AND HERE'S SOME INFORMATION IF YOU'RE INTERESTED IN MAKING A DONATION. ENJOY THE PARTY, LAURA
I'LL TRY . . .
HARRIET, I WANT YOU TO MEET JEFF BYRD--

PART 3 THE STRIFE OF THE PARTY

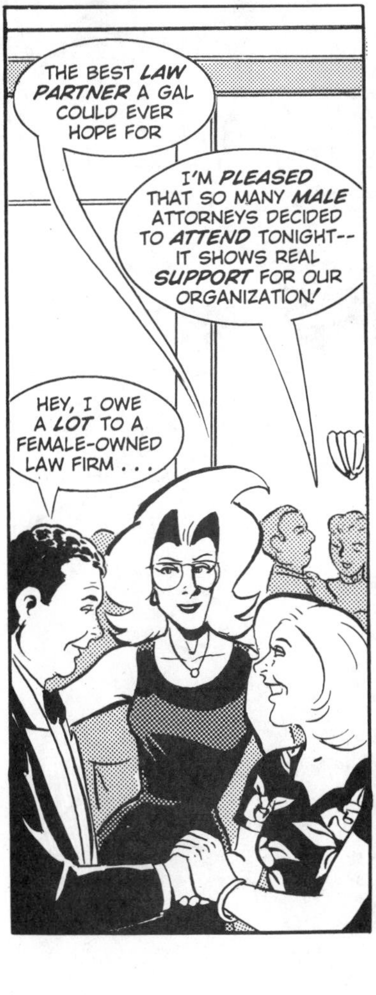
THE BEST LAW PARTNER A GAL COULD EVER HOPE FOR
I'M PLEASED THAT SO MANY MALE ATTORNEYS DECIDED TO ATTEND TONIGHT-- IT SHOWS REAL SUPPORT FOR OUR ORGANIZATION!
HEY, I OWE A LOT TO A FEMALE-OWNED LAW FIRM . . .

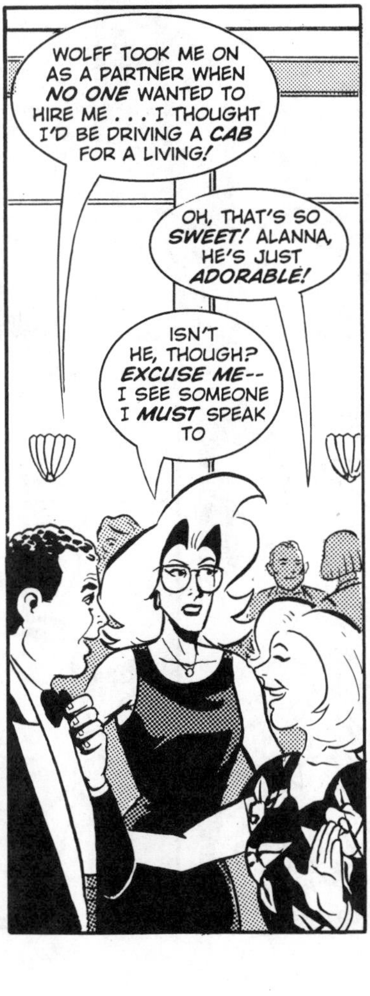
WOLFF TOOK ME ON AS A PARTNER WHEN NO ONE WANTED TO HIRE ME . . . I THOUGHT I'D BE DRIVING A CAB FOR A LIVING!
OH, THAT'S SO SWEET! ALANNA, HE'S JUST ADORABLE!
ISN'T HE, THOUGH? EXCUSE ME-- I SEE SOMEONE I MUST SPEAK TO

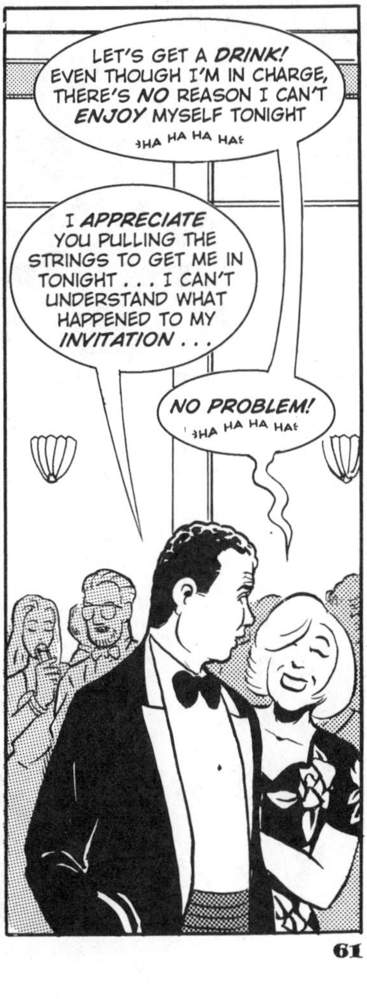
LET'S GET A DRINK! EVEN THOUGH I'M IN CHARGE, THERE'S NO REASON I CAN'T ENJOY MYSELF TONIGHT
HA HA HA HA
I APPRECIATE YOU PULLING THE STRINGS TO GET ME IN TONIGHT . . . I CAN'T UNDERSTAND WHAT HAPPENED TO MY INVITATION . . .
NO PROBLEM!
HA HA HA HA

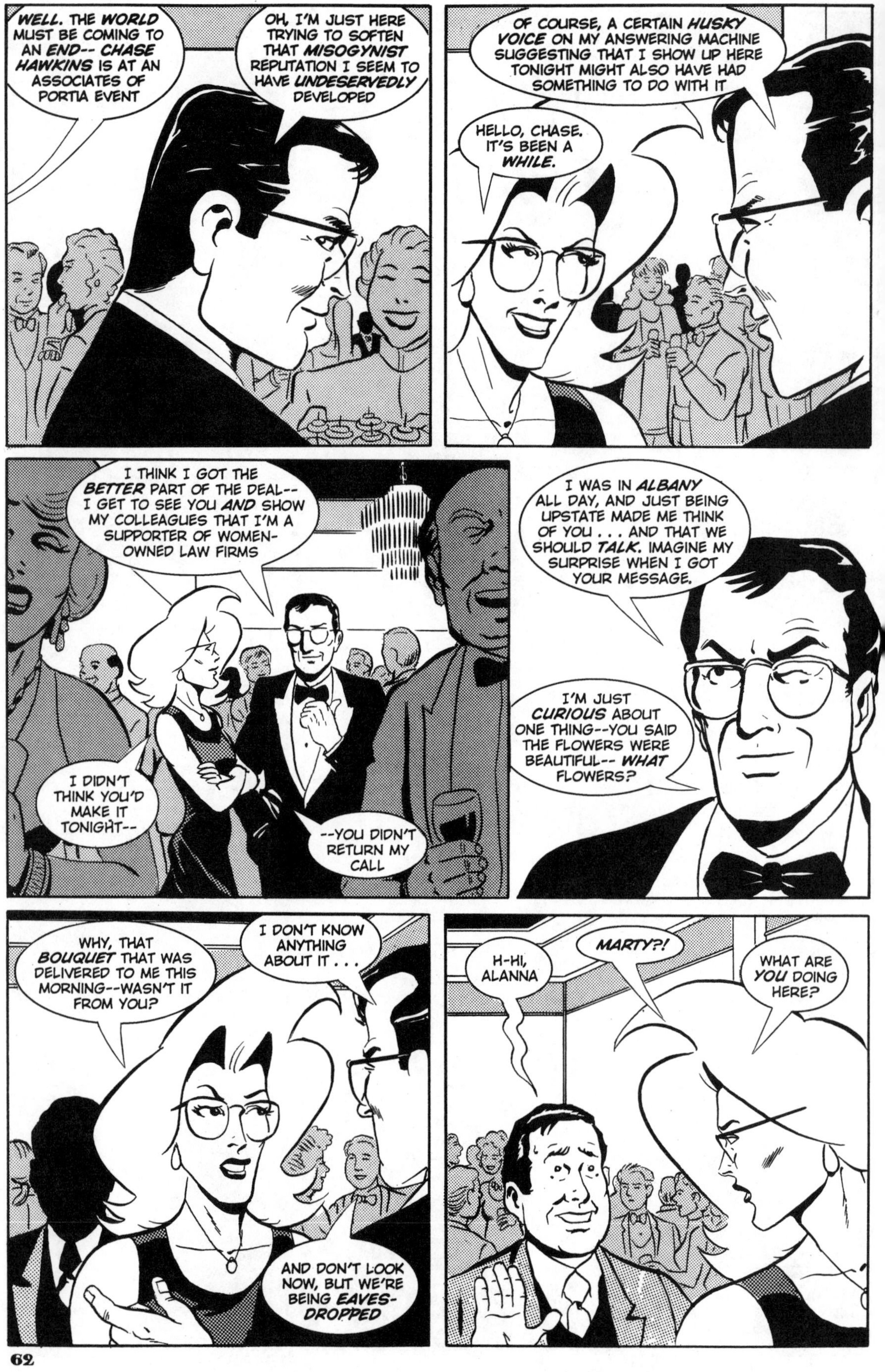
WELL. THE WORLD MUST BE COMING TO AN END-- CHASE HAWKINS IS AT AN ASSOCIATES OF PORTIA EVENT
OH, I'M JUST HERE TRYING TO SOFTEN THAT MISOGYNIST REPUTATION I SEEM TO HAVE UNDESERVEDLY DEVELOPED
OF COURSE, A CERTAIN HUSKY VOICE ON MY ANSWERING MACHINE SUGGESTING THAT I SHOW UP HERE TONIGHT MIGHT ALSO HAVE HAD SOMETHING TO DO WITH IT
HELLO, CHASE. IT'S BEEN A WHILE.
I THINK I GOT THE BETTER PART OF THE DEAL-- I GET TO SEE YOU AND SHOW MY COLLEAGUES THAT I'M A SUPPORTER OF WOMEN-OWNED LAW FIRMS
I DIDN'T THINK YOU'D MAKE IT TONIGHT--
--YOU DIDN'T RETURN MY CALL
I WAS IN ALBANY ALL DAY, AND JUST BEING UPSTATE MADE ME THINK OF YOU . . . AND THAT WE SHOULD TALK. IMAGINE MY SURPRISE WHEN I GOT YOUR MESSAGE.
I'M JUST CURIOUS ABOUT ONE THING--YOU SAID THE FLOWERS WERE BEAUTIFUL-- WHAT FLOWERS?
WHY, THAT BOUQUET THAT WAS DELIVERED TO ME THIS MORNING--WASN'T IT FROM YOU?
I DON'T KNOW ANYTHING ABOUT IT . . .
AND DON'T LOOK NOW, BUT WE'RE BEING EAVES-DROPPED
H-HI, ALANNA
MARTY?!
WHAT ARE YOU DOING HERE?

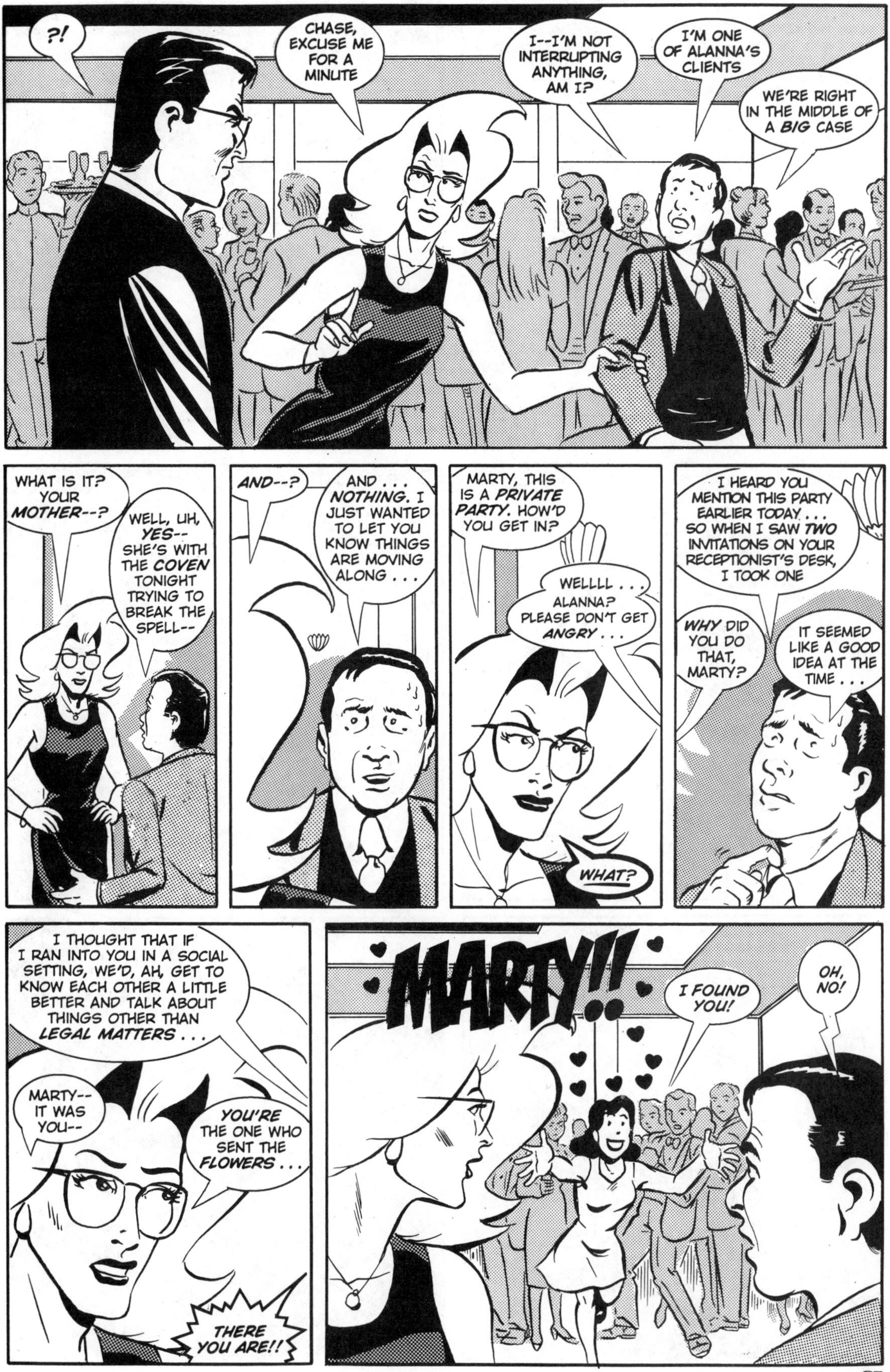
?!
CHASE, EXCUSE ME FOR A MINUTE
I--I'M NOT INTERRUPTING ANYTHING, AM I?
I'M ONE OF ALANNA'S CLIENTS
WE'RE RIGHT IN THE MIDDLE OF A BIG CASE
WHAT IS IT? YOUR MOTHER--?
WELL, UH, YES-- SHE'S WITH THE COVEN TONIGHT TRYING TO BREAK THE SPELL--
AND--?
AND . . . NOTHING. I JUST WANTED TO LET YOU KNOW THINGS ARE MOVING ALONG . . .
MARTY, THIS IS A PRIVATE PARTY. HOW'D YOU GET IN?
WELLLL . . . ALANNA? PLEASE DON'T GET ANGRY . . .
WHAT?
I HEARD YOU MENTION THIS PARTY EARLIER TODAY . . . SO WHEN I SAW TWO INVITATIONS ON YOUR RECEPTIONIST'S DESK, I TOOK ONE
WHY DID YOU DO THAT, MARTY?
IT SEEMED LIKE A GOOD IDEA AT THE TIME . . .
I THOUGHT THAT IF I RAN INTO YOU IN A SOCIAL SETTING, WE'D, AH, GET TO KNOW EACH OTHER A LITTLE BETTER AND TALK ABOUT THINGS OTHER THAN LEGAL MATTERS . . .
MARTY-- IT WAS YOU--
YOU'RE THE ONE WHO SENT THE FLOWERS . . .
THERE YOU ARE!!
MARTY!!
I FOUND YOU!
OH, NO!

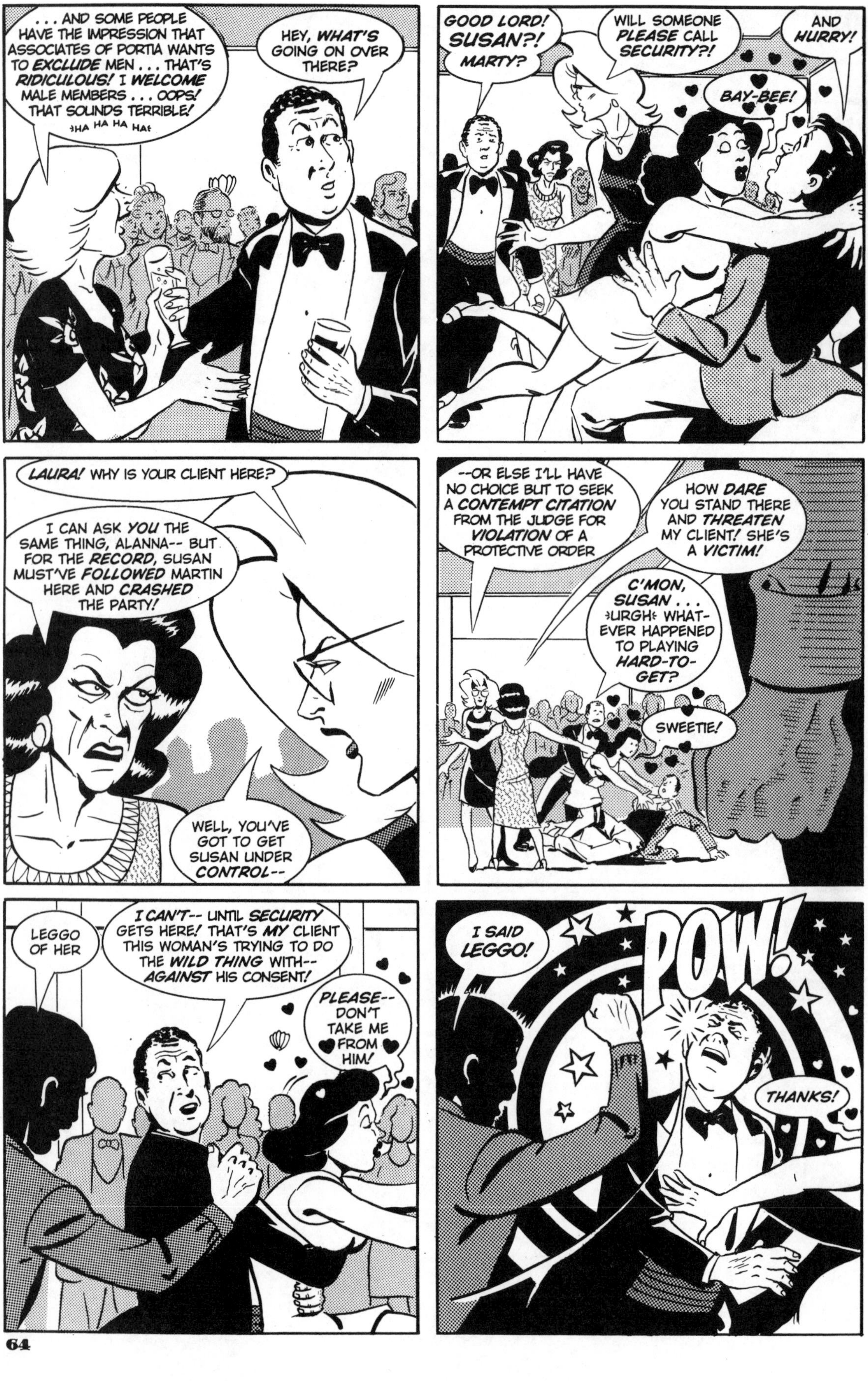

. . . AND SOME PEOPLE HAVE THE IMPRESSION THAT ASSOCIATES OF PORTIA WANTS TO EXCLUDE MEN . . . THAT'S RIDICULOUS! I WELCOME MALE MEMBERS . . . OOPS! THAT SOUNDS TERRIBLE!
HA HA HA HA
HEY, WHAT'S GOING ON OVER THERE?
GOOD LORD! SUSAN?! MARTY?
WILL SOMEONE PLEASE CALL SECURITY?!
AND HURRY!
BAY-BEE!
LAURA! WHY IS YOUR CLIENT HERE?
I CAN ASK YOU THE SAME THING, ALANNA-- BUT FOR THE RECORD, SUSAN MUST'VE FOLLOWED MARTIN HERE AND CRASHED THE PARTY!
WELL, YOU'VE GOT TO GET SUSAN UNDER CONTROL--
--OR ELSE I'LL HAVE NO CHOICE BUT TO SEEK A CONTEMPT CITATION FROM THE JUDGE FOR VIOLATION OF A PROTECTIVE ORDER
HOW DARE YOU STAND THERE AND THREATEN MY CLIENT! SHE'S A VICTIM!
C'MON, SUSAN . . . URGH WHAT-EVER HAPPENED TO PLAYING HARD-TO-GET?
SWEETIE!
LEGGO OF HER
I CAN'T-- UNTIL SECURITY GETS HERE! THAT'S MY CLIENT THIS WOMAN'S TRYING TO DO THE WILD THING WITH-- AGAINST HIS CONSENT!
PLEASE-- DON'T TAKE ME FROM HIM!
I SAID LEGGO!
POW!
THANKS!

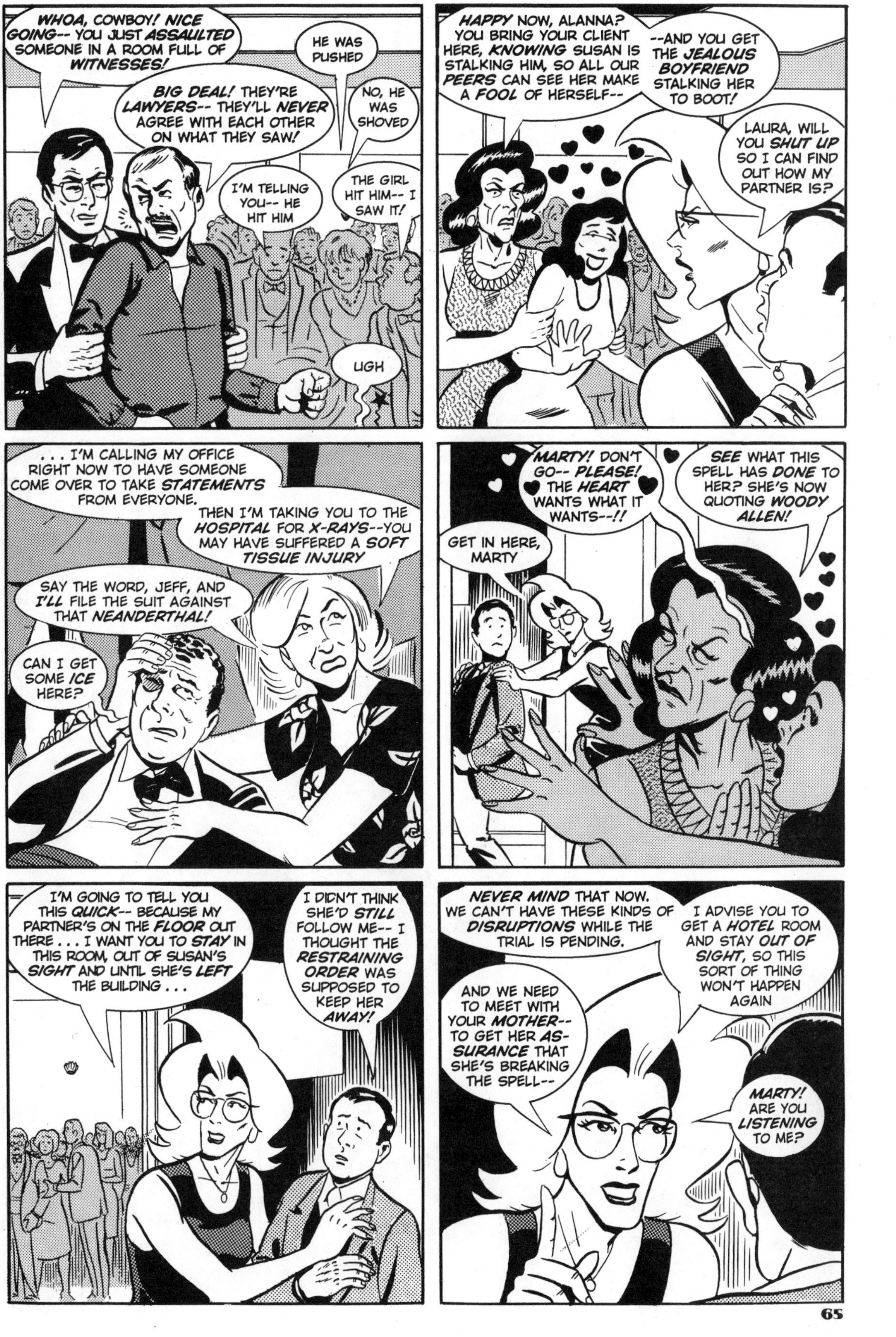
WHOA, COWBOY! NICE GOING-- YOU JUST ASSAULTED SOMEONE IN A ROOM FULL OF WITNESSES!
HE WAS PUSHED
BIG DEAL! THEY'RE LAWYERS-- THEY'LL NEVER AGREE WITH EACH OTHER ON WHAT THEY SAW!
NO, HE WAS SHOVED
I'M TELLING YOU-- HE HIT HIM
THE GIRL HIT HIM-- I SAW IT!
UGH
HAPPY NOW, ALANNA? YOU BRING YOUR CLIENT HERE, KNOWING SUSAN IS STALKING HIM, SO ALL OUR PEERS CAN SEE HER MAKE A FOOL OF HERSELF--
--AND YOU GET THE JEALOUS BOYFRIEND STALKING HER TO BOOT!
LAURA, WILL YOU SHUT UP SO I CAN FIND OUT HOW MY PARTNER IS?
. . . I'M CALLING MY OFFICE RIGHT NOW TO HAVE SOMEONE COME OVER TO TAKE STATEMENTS FROM EVERYONE.
THEN I'M TAKING YOU TO THE HOSPITAL FOR X-RAYS--YOU MAY HAVE SUFFERED A SOFT TISSUE INJURY
SAY THE WORD, JEFF, AND I'LL FILE THE SUIT AGAINST THAT NEANDERTHAL!
CAN I GET SOME ICE HERE?
MARTY! DON'T GO-- PLEASE! THE HEART WANTS WHAT IT WANTS--!!
SEE WHAT THIS SPELL HAS DONE TO HER? SHE'S NOW QUOTING WOODY ALLEN!
GET IN HERE, MARTY
I'M GOING TO TELL YOU THIS QUICK-- BECAUSE MY PARTNER'S ON THE FLOOR OUT THERE . . . I WANT YOU TO STAY IN THIS ROOM, OUT OF SUSAN'S SIGHT AND UNTIL SHE'S LEFT THE BUILDING . . .
I DIDN'T THINK SHE'D STILL FOLLOW ME-- I THOUGHT THE RESTRAINING ORDER WAS SUPPOSED TO KEEP HER AWAY!
NEVER MIND THAT NOW. WE CAN'T HAVE THESE KINDS OF DISRUPTIONS WHILE THE TRIAL IS PENDING.
I ADVISE YOU TO GET A HOTEL ROOM AND STAY OUT OF SIGHT, SO THIS SORT OF THING WON'T HAPPEN AGAIN
AND WE NEED TO MEET WITH YOUR MOTHER-- TO GET HER AS-SURANCE THAT SHE'S BREAKING THE SPELL--
MARTY! ARE YOU LISTENING TO ME?

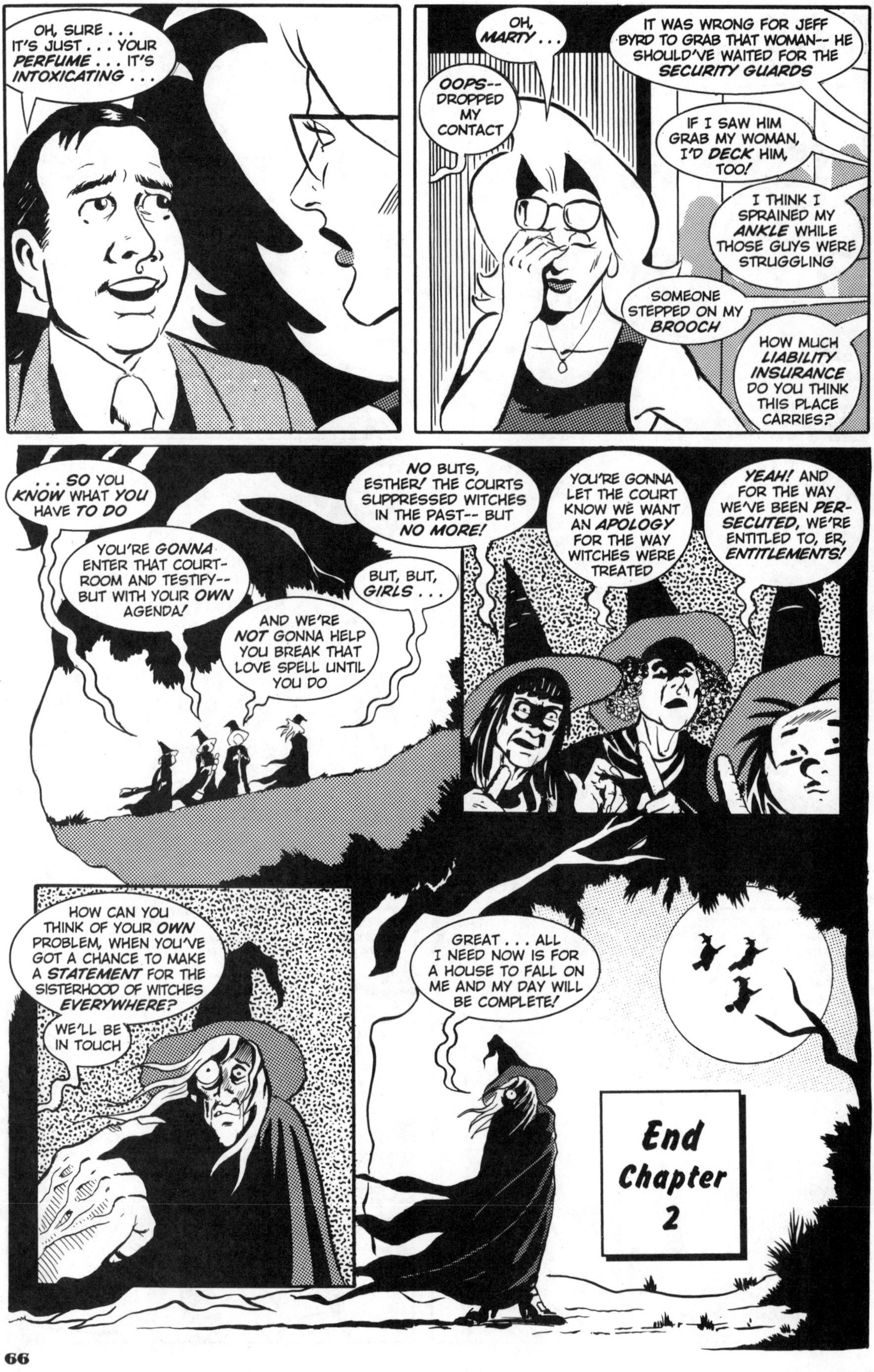
OH, SURE . . . IT'S JUST . . . YOUR PERFUME . . . IT'S INTOXICATING . . .
OH, MARTY . . .
OOPS-- DROPPED MY CONTACT
IT WAS WRONG FOR JEFF BYRD TO GRAB THAT WOMAN-- HE SHOULD'VE WAITED FOR THE SECURITY GUARDS
IF I SAW HIM GRAB MY WOMAN, I'D DECK HIM, TOO!
I THINK I SPRAINED MY ANKLE WHILE THOSE GUYS WERE STRUGGLING
SOMEONE STEPPED ON MY BROOCH
HOW MUCH LIABILITY INSURANCE DO YOU THINK THIS PLACE CARRIES?
. . . SO YOU KNOW WHAT YOU HAVE TO DO
YOU'RE GONNA ENTER THAT COURTROOM AND TESTIFY-- BUT WITH YOUR OWN AGENDA!
AND WE'RE NOT GONNA HELP YOU BREAK THAT LOVE SPELL UNTIL YOU DO
BUT, BUT, GIRLS . . .
NO BUTS, ESTHER! THE COURTS SUPPRESSED WITCHES IN THE PAST-- BUT NO MORE!
YOU'RE GONNA LET THE COURT KNOW WE WANT AN APOLOGY FOR THE WAY WITCHES WERE TREATED
YEAH! AND FOR THE WAY WE'VE BEEN PERSECUTED, WE'RE ENTITLED TO, ER, ENTITLEMENTS!
HOW CAN YOU THINK OF YOUR OWN PROBLEM, WHEN YOU'VE GOT A CHANCE TO MAKE A STATEMENT FOR THE SISTERHOOD OF WITCHES EVERYWHERE?
WE'LL BE IN TOUCH
GREAT . . . ALL I NEED NOW IS FOR A HOUSE TO FALL ON ME AND MY DAY WILL BE COMPLETE!
End Chapter 2

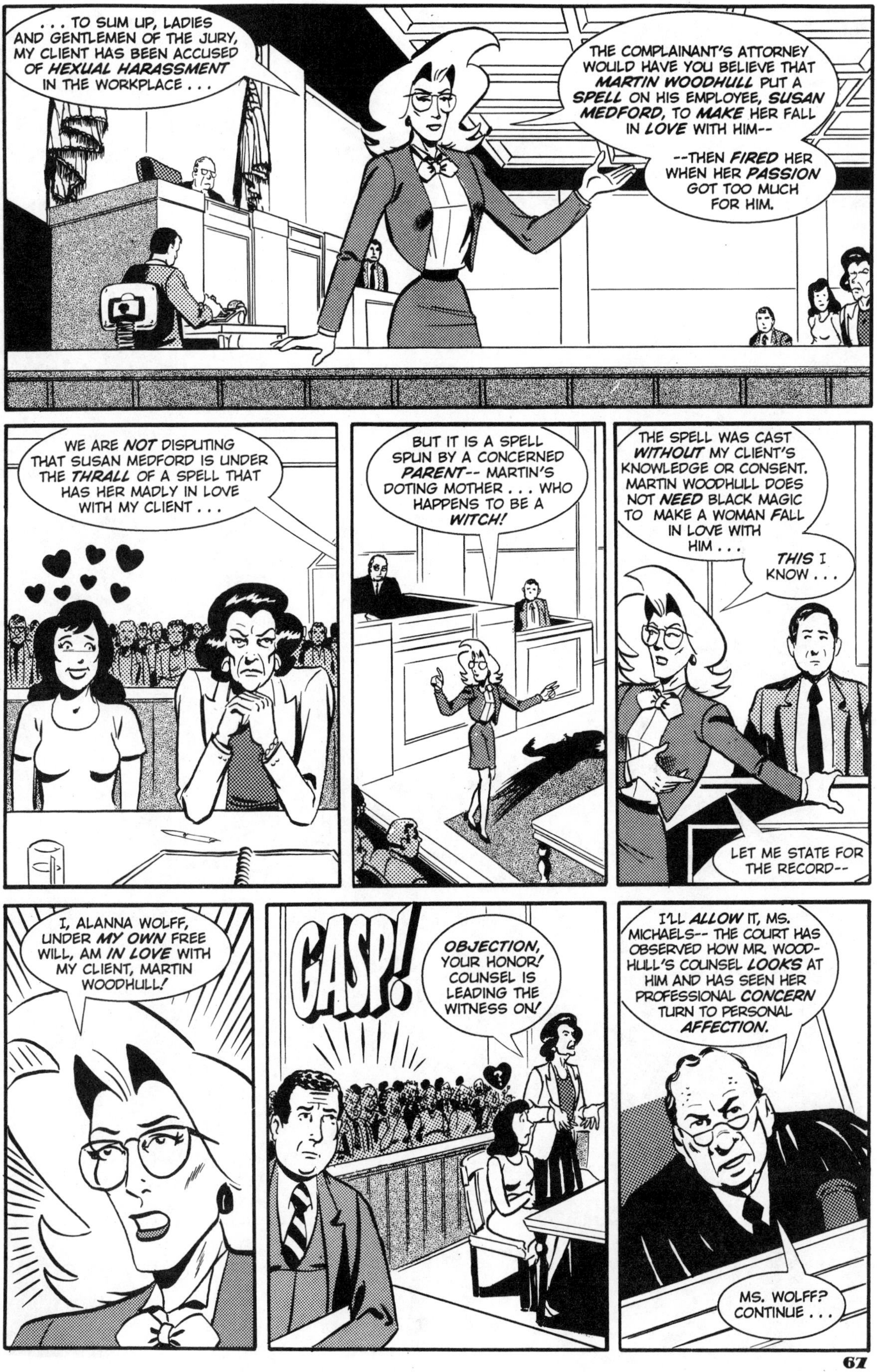
. . . TO SUM UP, LADIES AND GENTLEMEN OF THE JURY, MY CLIENT HAS BEEN ACCUSED OF HEXUAL HARASSMENT IN THE WORKPLACE . . .
THE COMPLAINANT'S ATTORNEY WOULD HAVE YOU BELIEVE THAT MARTIN WOODHULL PUT A SPELL ON HIS EMPLOYEE, SUSAN MEDFORD, TO MAKE HER FALL IN LOVE WITH HIM--
--THEN FIRED HER WHEN HER PASSION GOT TOO MUCH FOR HIM.
WE ARE NOT DISPUTING THAT SUSAN MEDFORD IS UNDER THE THRALL OF A SPELL THAT HAS HER MADLY IN LOVE WITH MY CLIENT . . .
BUT IT IS A SPELL SPUN BY A CONCERNED PARENT-- MARTIN'S DOTING MOTHER . . . WHO HAPPENS TO BE A WITCH!
THE SPELL WAS CAST WITHOUT MY CLIENT'S KNOWLEDGE OR CONSENT. MARTIN WOODHULL DOES NOT NEED BLACK MAGIC TO MAKE A WOMAN FALL IN LOVE WITH HIM . . .
THIS I KNOW . . .
LET ME STATE FOR THE RECORD--
I, ALANNA WOLFF, UNDER MY OWN FREE WILL, AM IN LOVE WITH MY CLIENT, MARTIN WOODHULL!
GASP!
OBJECTION, YOUR HONOR! COUNSEL IS LEADING THE WITNESS ON!
I'LL ALLOW IT, MS. MICHAELS-- THE COURT HAS OBSERVED HOW MR. WOODHULL'S COUNSEL LOOKS AT HIM AND HAS SEEN HER PROFESSIONAL CONCERN TURN TO PERSONAL AFFECTION.
MS. WOLFF? CONTINUE . . .

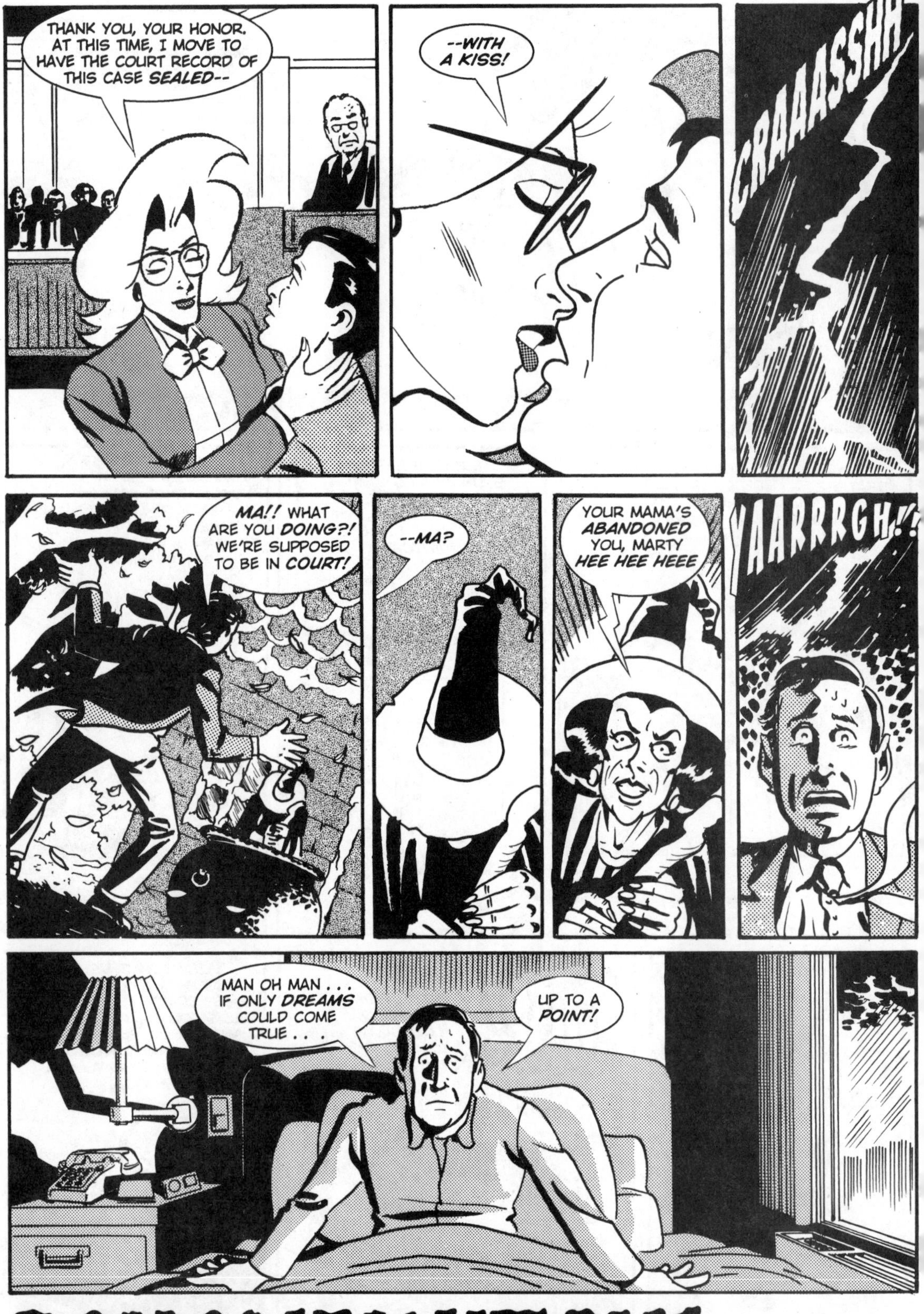
THANK YOU, YOUR HONOR. AT THIS TIME, I MOVE TO HAVE THE COURT RECORD OF THIS CASE SEALED--
--WITH A KISS!
CRAAASSHH
MA!! WHAT ARE YOU DOING?! WE'RE SUPPOSED TO BE IN COURT!
--MA?
YOUR MAMA'S ABANDONED YOU, MARTY HEE HEE HEEE
YAARRRGH!!
MAN OH MAN . . . IF ONLY DREAMS COULD COME TRUE . . .
UP TO A POINT!

SONOVAWITCH! CHAPTER THREE

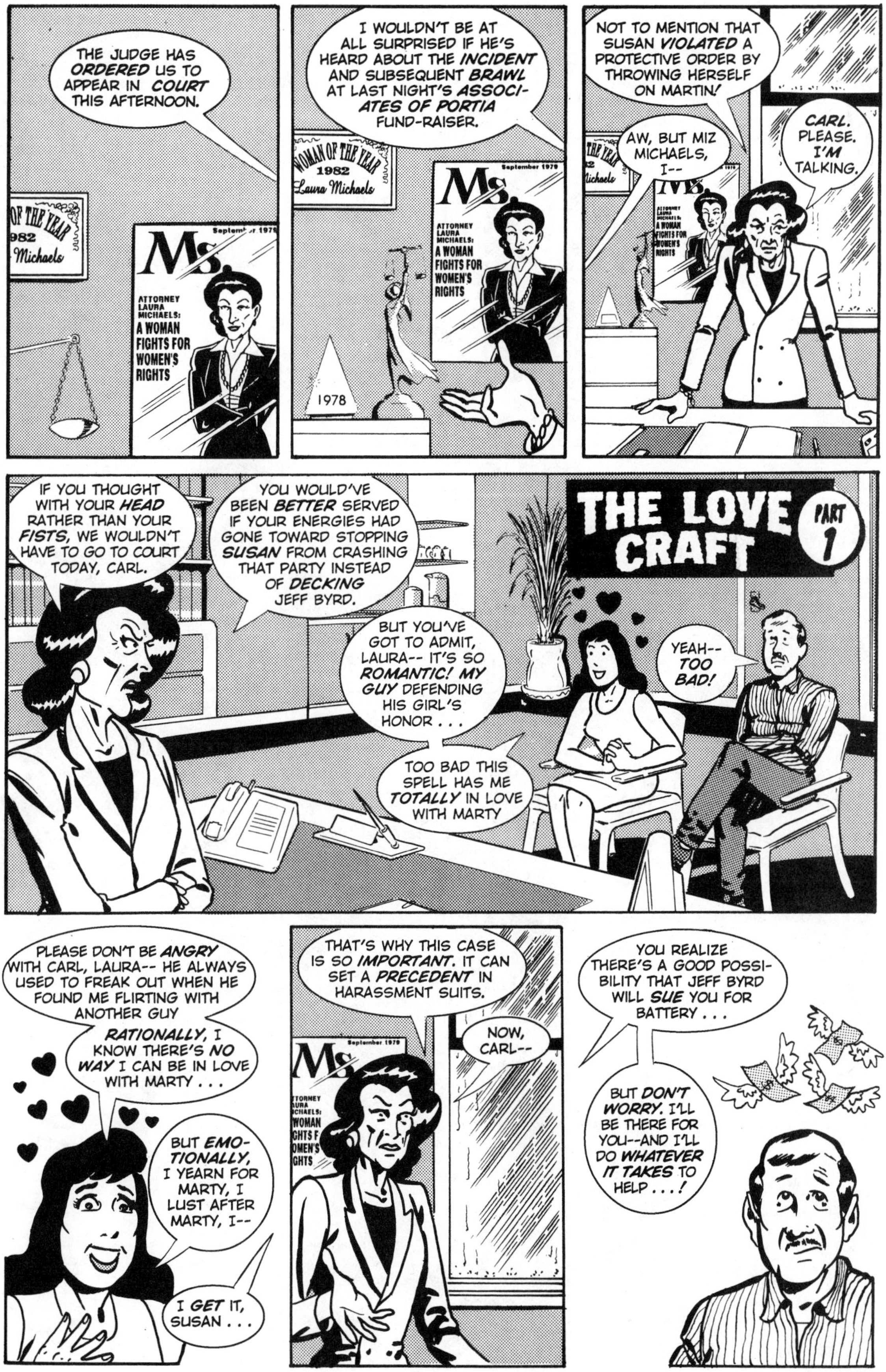
THE JUDGE HAS ORDERED US TO APPEAR IN COURT THIS AFTERNOON.
WOMAN OF THE YEAR 1982 Laura Michaels
Ms September 1979 ATTORNEY LAURA MICHAELS: A WOMAN FIGHTS FOR WOMEN'S RIGHTS
I WOULDN'T BE AT ALL SURPRISED IF HE'S HEARD ABOUT THE INCIDENT AND SUBSEQUENT BRAWL AT LAST NIGHT'S ASSOCIATES OF PORTIA FUND-RAISER.
1978
NOT TO MENTION THAT SUSAN VIOLATED A PROTECTIVE ORDER BY THROWING HERSELF ON MARTIN!
AW, BUT MIZ MICHAELS, I--
CARL. PLEASE. I'M TALKING.
THE LOVE CRAFT PART 1
IF YOU THOUGHT WITH YOUR HEAD RATHER THAN YOUR FISTS, WE WOULDN'T HAVE TO GO TO COURT TODAY, CARL.
YOU WOULD'VE BEEN BETTER SERVED IF YOUR ENERGIES HAD GONE TOWARD STOPPING SUSAN FROM CRASHING THAT PARTY INSTEAD OF DECKING JEFF BYRD.
BUT YOU'VE GOT TO ADMIT, LAURA-- IT'S SO ROMANTIC! MY GUY DEFENDING HIS GIRL'S HONOR . . .
TOO BAD THIS SPELL HAS ME TOTALLY IN LOVE WITH MARTY
YEAH-- TOO BAD!
PLEASE DON'T BE ANGRY WITH CARL, LAURA-- HE ALWAYS USED TO FREAK OUT WHEN HE FOUND ME FLIRTING WITH ANOTHER GUY
RATIONALLY, I KNOW THERE'S NO WAY I CAN BE IN LOVE WITH MARTY . . .
BUT EMOTIONALLY, I YEARN FOR MARTY, I LUST AFTER MARTY, I--
I GET IT, SUSAN . . .
THAT'S WHY THIS CASE IS SO IMPORTANT. IT CAN SET A PRECEDENT IN HARASSMENT SUITS.
NOW, CARL--
YOU REALIZE THERE'S A GOOD POSSIBILITY THAT JEFF BYRD WILL SUE YOU FOR BATTERY . . .
BUT DON'T WORRY. I'LL BE THERE FOR YOU--AND I'LL DO WHATEVER IT TAKES TO HELP . . . !

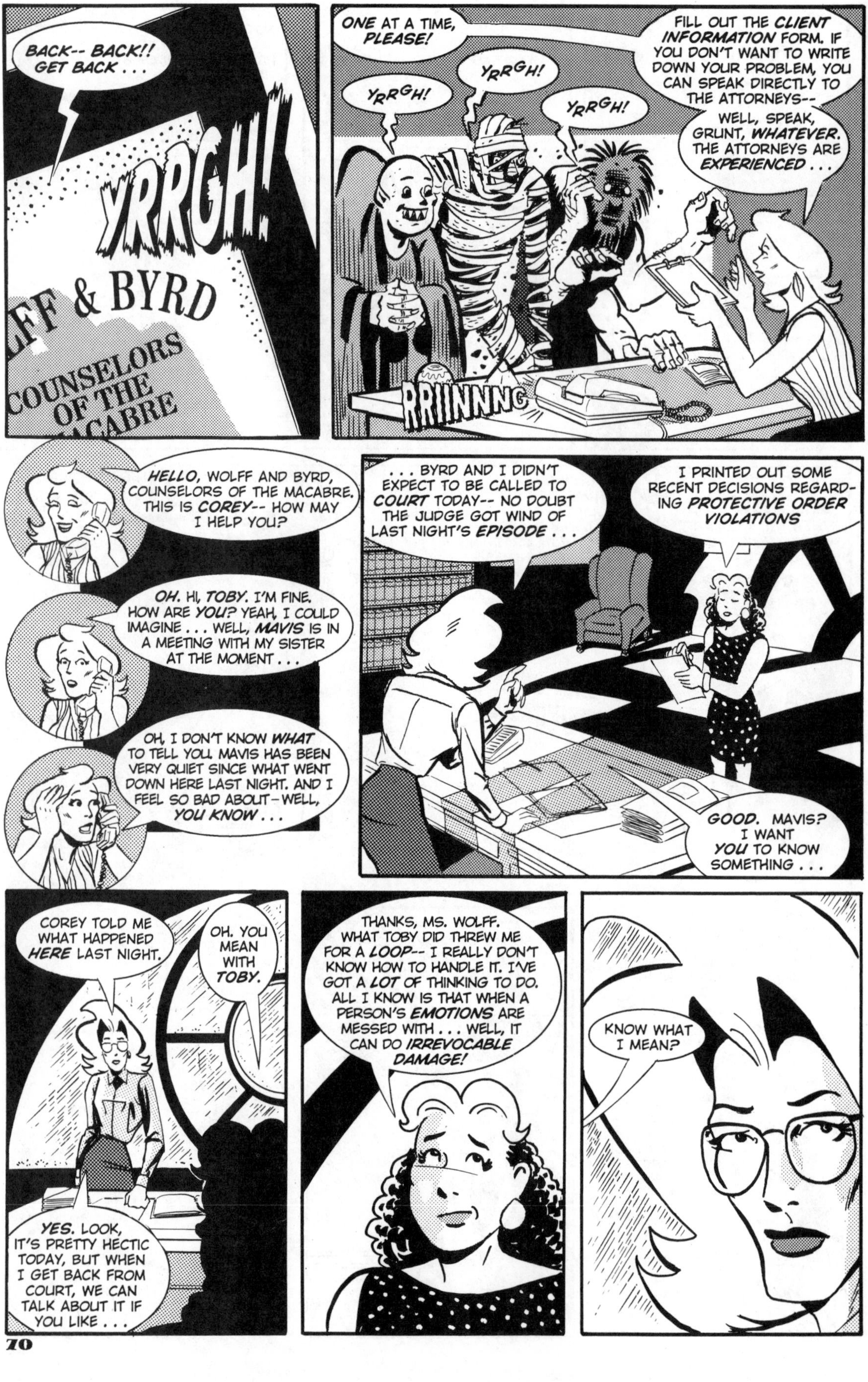

BACK-- BACK!! GET BACK . . .
YRRGH!
LFF & BYRD
COUNSELORS OF THE MACABRE
ONE AT A TIME, PLEASE!
YRRGH!
YRRGH!
YRRGH!
FILL OUT THE CLIENT INFORMATION FORM. IF YOU DON'T WANT TO WRITE DOWN YOUR PROBLEM, YOU CAN SPEAK DIRECTLY TO THE ATTORNEYS--
WELL, SPEAK, GRUNT, WHATEVER. THE ATTORNEYS ARE EXPERIENCED . . .
RRIINNNG
HELLO, WOLFF AND BYRD, COUNSELORS OF THE MACABRE. THIS IS COREY-- HOW MAY I HELP YOU?
OH. HI, TOBY. I'M FINE. HOW ARE YOU? YEAH, I COULD IMAGINE . . . WELL, MAVIS IS IN A MEETING WITH MY SISTER AT THE MOMENT . . .
OH, I DON'T KNOW WHAT TO TELL YOU. MAVIS HAS BEEN VERY QUIET SINCE WHAT WENT DOWN HERE LAST NIGHT. AND I FEEL SO BAD ABOUT-WELL, YOU KNOW . . .
. . . BYRD AND I DIDN'T EXPECT TO BE CALLED TO COURT TODAY-- NO DOUBT THE JUDGE GOT WIND OF LAST NIGHT'S EPISODE . . .
I PRINTED OUT SOME RECENT DECISIONS REGARDING PROTECTIVE ORDER VIOLATIONS
GOOD. MAVIS? I WANT YOU TO KNOW SOMETHING . . .
COREY TOLD ME WHAT HAPPENED HERE LAST NIGHT.
OH. YOU MEAN WITH TOBY.
YES. LOOK, IT'S PRETTY HECTIC TODAY, BUT WHEN I GET BACK FROM COURT, WE CAN TALK ABOUT IT IF YOU LIKE . . .
THANKS, MS. WOLFF. WHAT TOBY DID THREW ME FOR A LOOP-- I REALLY DON'T KNOW HOW TO HANDLE IT. I'VE GOT A LOT OF THINKING TO DO. ALL I KNOW IS THAT WHEN A PERSON'S EMOTIONS ARE MESSED WITH . . . WELL, IT CAN DO IRREVOCABLE DAMAGE!
KNOW WHAT I MEAN?

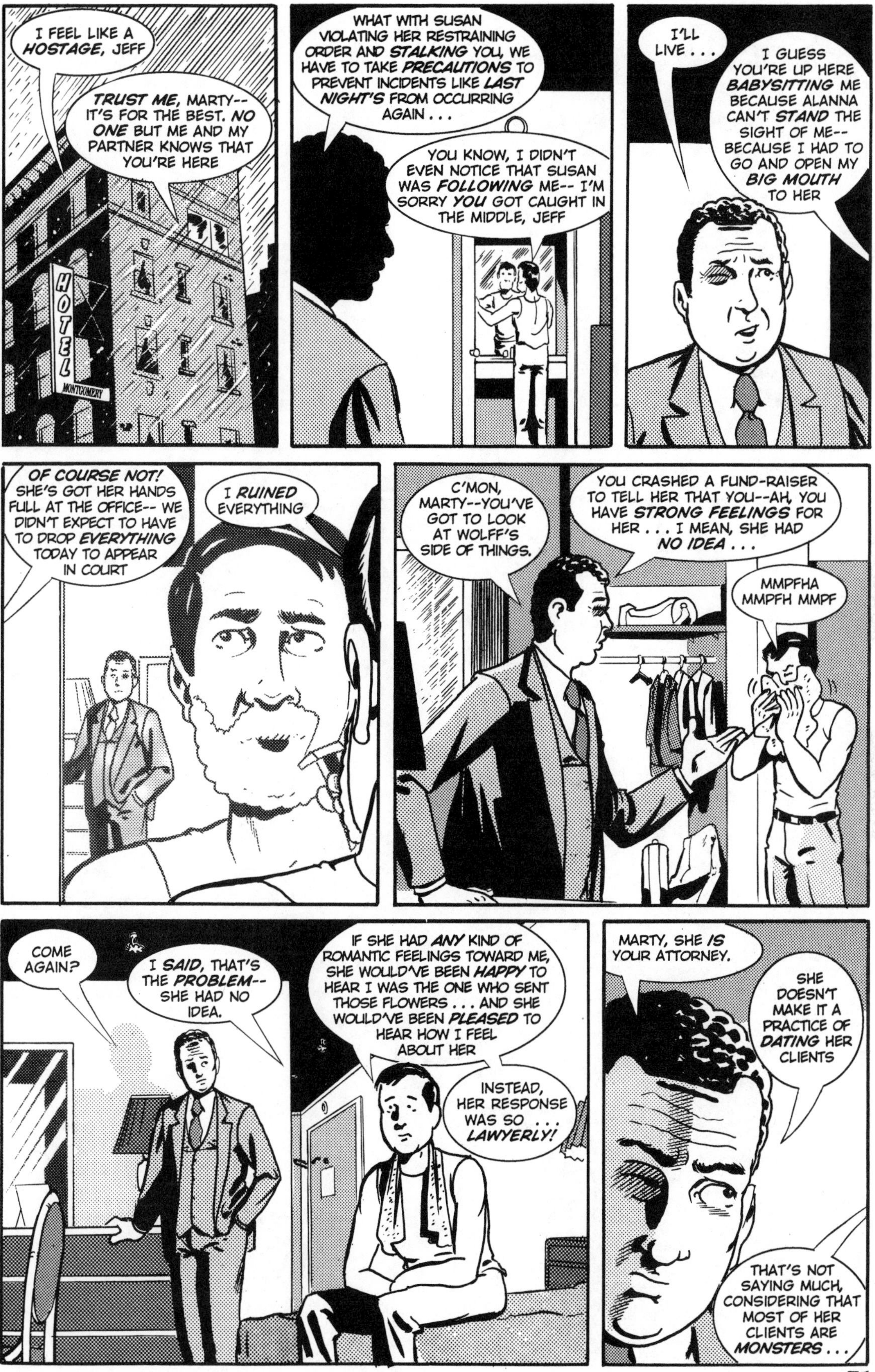
I FEEL LIKE A HOSTAGE, JEFF
TRUST ME, MARTY--IT'S FOR THE BEST. NO ONE BUT ME AND MY PARTNER KNOWS THAT YOU'RE HERE
HOTEL
MONTGOMERY
WHAT WITH SUSAN VIOLATING HER RESTRAINING ORDER AND STALKING YOU, WE HAVE TO TAKE PRECAUTIONS TO PREVENT INCIDENTS LIKE LAST NIGHT'S FROM OCCURRING AGAIN . . .
YOU KNOW, I DIDN'T EVEN NOTICE THAT SUSAN WAS FOLLOWING ME-- I'M SORRY YOU GOT CAUGHT IN THE MIDDLE, JEFF
I'LL LIVE . . .
I GUESS YOU'RE UP HERE BABYSITTING ME BECAUSE ALANNA CAN'T STAND THE SIGHT OF ME--BECAUSE I HAD TO GO AND OPEN MY BIG MOUTH TO HER
OF COURSE NOT! SHE'S GOT HER HANDS FULL AT THE OFFICE-- WE DIDN'T EXPECT TO HAVE TO DROP EVERYTHING TODAY TO APPEAR IN COURT
I RUINED EVERYTHING
C'MON, MARTY--YOU'VE GOT TO LOOK AT WOLFF'S SIDE OF THINGS.
YOU CRASHED A FUND-RAISER TO TELL HER THAT YOU--AH, YOU HAVE STRONG FEELINGS FOR HER . . . I MEAN, SHE HAD NO IDEA . . .
MMPFHA MMPFH MMPF
COME AGAIN?
I SAID, THAT'S THE PROBLEM-- SHE HAD NO IDEA.
IF SHE HAD ANY KIND OF ROMANTIC FEELINGS TOWARD ME, SHE WOULD'VE BEEN HAPPY TO HEAR I WAS THE ONE WHO SENT THOSE FLOWERS . . . AND SHE WOULD'VE BEEN PLEASED TO HEAR HOW I FEEL ABOUT HER
INSTEAD, HER RESPONSE WAS SO . . . LAWYERLY!
MARTY, SHE IS YOUR ATTORNEY.
SHE DOESN'T MAKE IT A PRACTICE OF DATING HER CLIENTS
THAT'S NOT SAYING MUCH, CONSIDERING THAT MOST OF HER CLIENTS ARE MONSTERS . . .

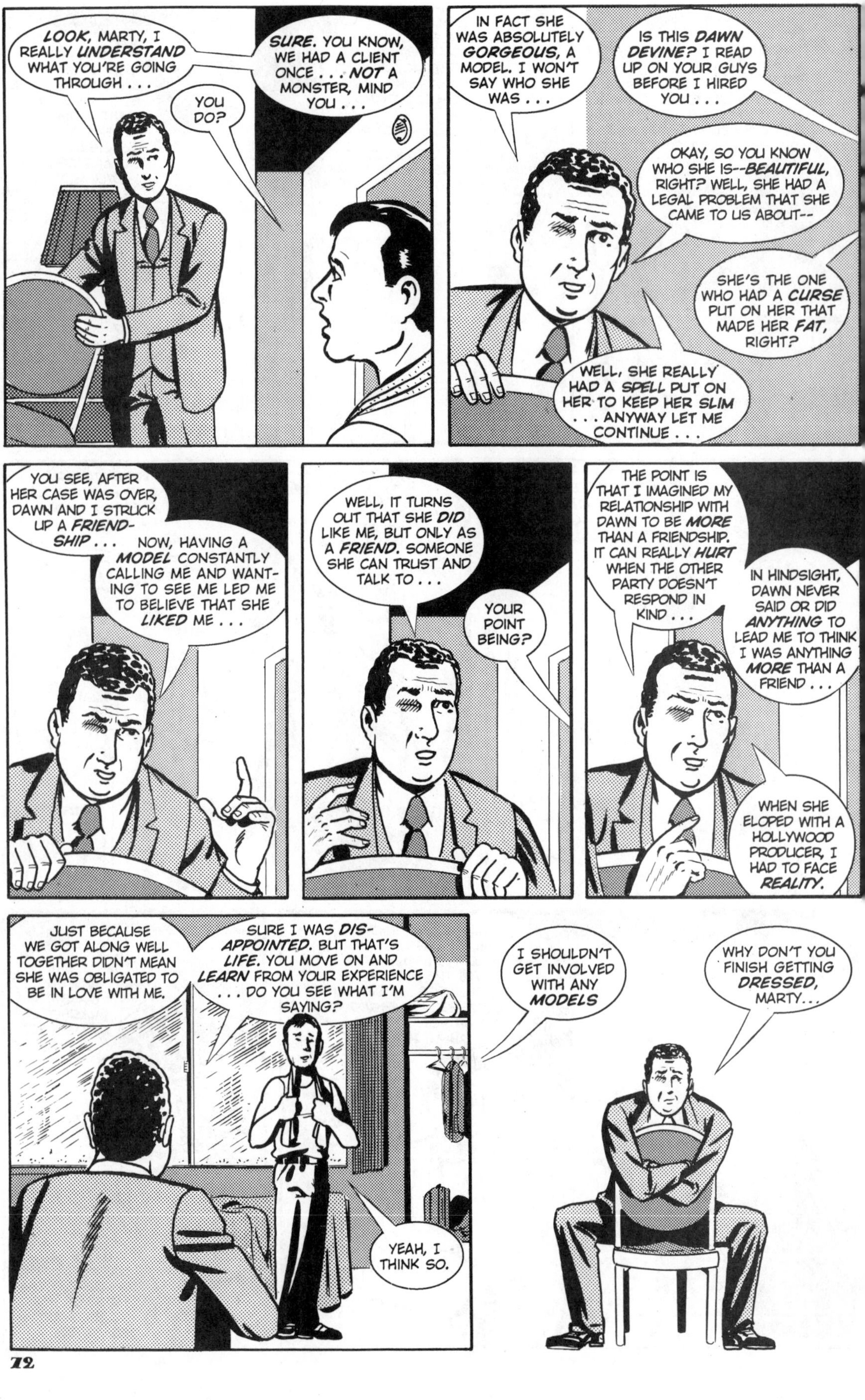
LOOK, MARTY, I REALLY UNDERSTAND WHAT YOU'RE GOING THROUGH . . .
YOU DO?
SURE. YOU KNOW, WE HAD A CLIENT ONCE . . . NOT A MONSTER, MIND YOU . . .
IN FACT SHE WAS ABSOLUTELY GORGEOUS, A MODEL. I WON'T SAY WHO SHE WAS . . .
IS THIS DAWN DEVINE? I READ UP ON YOUR GUYS BEFORE I HIRED YOU . . .
OKAY, SO YOU KNOW WHO SHE IS--BEAUTIFUL, RIGHT? WELL, SHE HAD A LEGAL PROBLEM THAT SHE CAME TO US ABOUT--
SHE'S THE ONE WHO HAD A CURSE PUT ON HER THAT MADE HER FAT, RIGHT?
WELL, SHE REALLY HAD A SPELL PUT ON HER TO KEEP HER SLIM . . . ANYWAY LET ME CONTINUE . . .
YOU SEE, AFTER HER CASE WAS OVER, DAWN AND I STRUCK UP A FRIEND-SHIP . . .
NOW, HAVING A MODEL CONSTANTLY CALLING ME AND WANT-ING TO SEE ME LED ME TO BELIEVE THAT SHE LIKED ME . . .
WELL, IT TURNS OUT THAT SHE DID LIKE ME, BUT ONLY AS A FRIEND. SOMEONE SHE CAN TRUST AND TALK TO . . .
YOUR POINT BEING?
THE POINT IS THAT I IMAGINED MY RELATIONSHIP WITH DAWN TO BE MORE THAN A FRIENDSHIP. IT CAN REALLY HURT WHEN THE OTHER PARTY DOESN'T RESPOND IN KIND . . .
IN HINDSIGHT, DAWN NEVER SAID OR DID ANYTHING TO LEAD ME TO THINK I WAS ANYTHING MORE THAN A FRIEND . . .
WHEN SHE ELOPED WITH A HOLLYWOOD PRODUCER, I HAD TO FACE REALITY.
JUST BECAUSE WE GOT ALONG WELL TOGETHER DIDN'T MEAN SHE WAS OBLIGATED TO BE IN LOVE WITH ME.
SURE I WAS DIS-APPOINTED. BUT THAT'S LIFE. YOU MOVE ON AND LEARN FROM YOUR EXPERIENCE . . . DO YOU SEE WHAT I'M SAYING?
YEAH, I THINK SO.
I SHOULDN'T GET INVOLVED WITH ANY MODELS
WHY DON'T YOU FINISH GETTING DRESSED, MARTY...

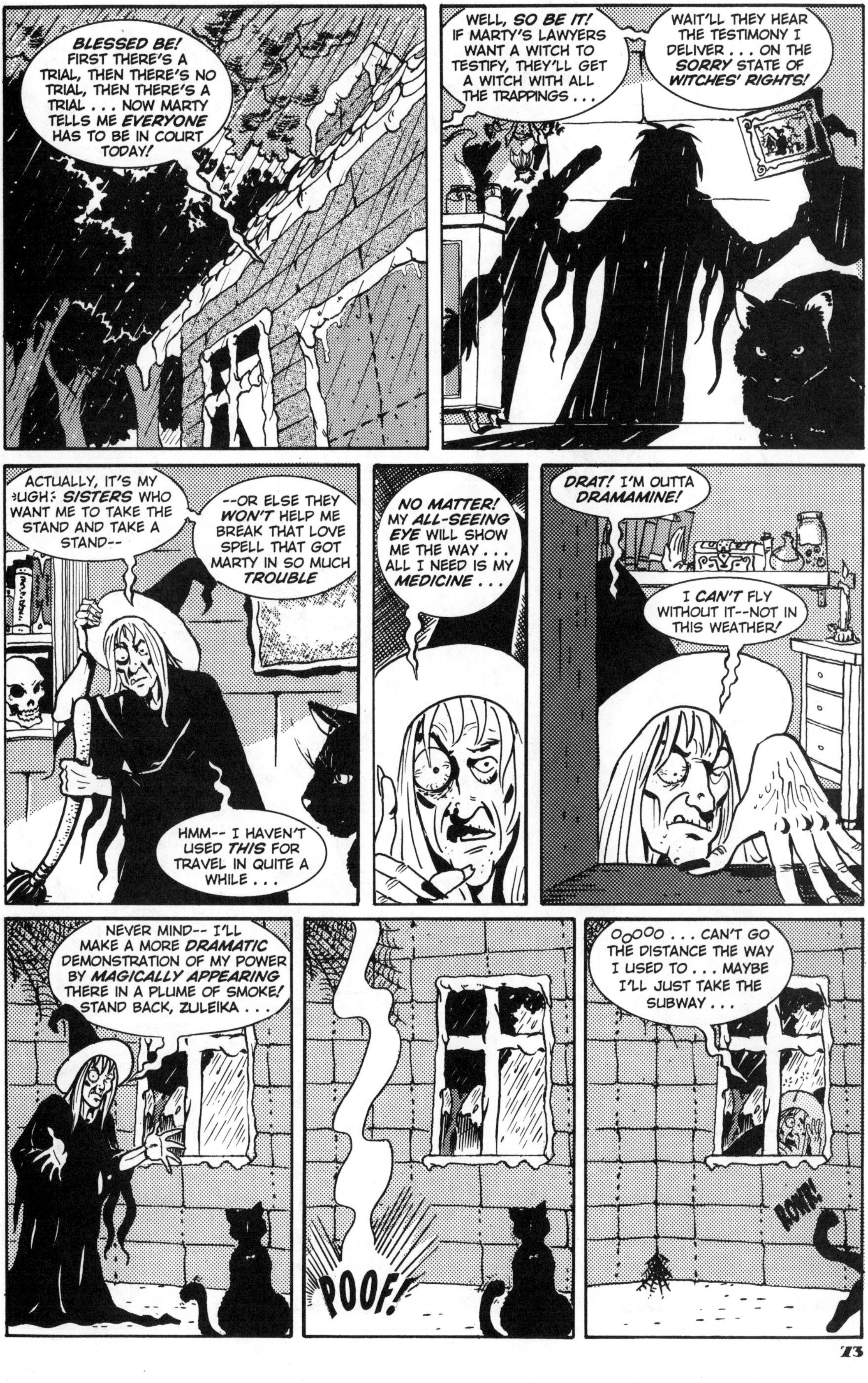
BLESSED BE! FIRST THERE'S A TRIAL, THEN THERE'S NO TRIAL, THEN THERE'S A TRIAL . . . NOW MARTY TELLS ME EVERYONE HAS TO BE IN COURT TODAY!
WELL, SO BE IT! IF MARTY'S LAWYERS WANT A WITCH TO TESTIFY, THEY'LL GET A WITCH WITH ALL THE TRAPPINGS . . .
WAIT'LL THEY HEAR THE TESTIMONY I DELIVER . . . ON THE SORRY STATE OF WITCHES' RIGHTS!
ACTUALLY, IT'S MY ·UGH· SISTERS WHO WANT ME TO TAKE THE STAND AND TAKE A STAND--
--OR ELSE THEY WON'T HELP ME BREAK THAT LOVE SPELL THAT GOT MARTY IN SO MUCH TROUBLE
HMM-- I HAVEN'T USED THIS FOR TRAVEL IN QUITE A WHILE . . .
NO MATTER! MY ALL-SEEING EYE WILL SHOW ME THE WAY . . . ALL I NEED IS MY MEDICINE . . .
DRAT! I'M OUTTA DRAMAMINE!
I CAN'T FLY WITHOUT IT--NOT IN THIS WEATHER!
NEVER MIND-- I'LL MAKE A MORE DRAMATIC DEMONSTRATION OF MY POWER BY MAGICALLY APPEARING THERE IN A PLUME OF SMOKE! STAND BACK, ZULEIKA . . .
POOF!
OOOOO . . . CAN'T GO THE DISTANCE THE WAY I USED TO . . . MAYBE I'LL JUST TAKE THE SUBWAY . . .
BONK!

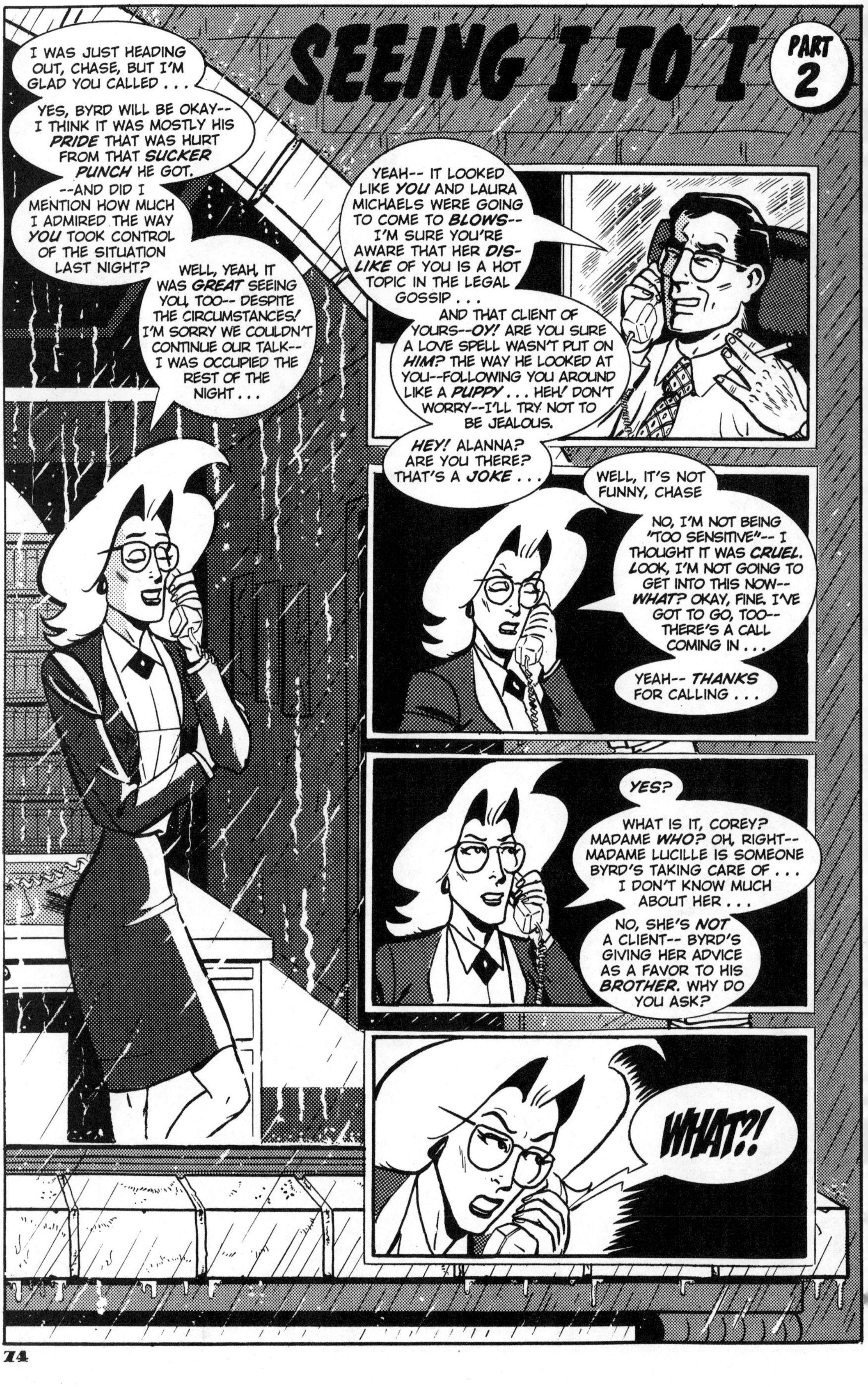
SEEING I TO I PART 2
I WAS JUST HEADING OUT, CHASE, BUT I'M GLAD YOU CALLED . . .
YES, BYRD WILL BE OKAY-- I THINK IT WAS MOSTLY HIS PRIDE THAT WAS HURT FROM THAT SUCKER PUNCH HE GOT.
--AND DID I MENTION HOW MUCH I ADMIRED THE WAY YOU TOOK CONTROL OF THE SITUATION LAST NIGHT?
WELL, YEAH, IT WAS GREAT SEEING YOU, TOO-- DESPITE THE CIRCUMSTANCES! I'M SORRY WE COULDN'T CONTINUE OUR TALK-- I WAS OCCUPIED THE REST OF THE NIGHT . . .
YEAH-- IT LOOKED LIKE YOU AND LAURA MICHAELS WERE GOING TO COME TO BLOWS-- I'M SURE YOU'RE AWARE THAT HER DIS-LIKE OF YOU IS A HOT TOPIC IN THE LEGAL GOSSIP . . .
AND THAT CLIENT OF YOURS--OY! ARE YOU SURE A LOVE SPELL WASN'T PUT ON HIM? THE WAY HE LOOKED AT YOU--FOLLOWING YOU AROUND LIKE A PUPPY . . . HEH! DON'T WORRY--I'LL TRY NOT TO BE JEALOUS.
HEY! ALANNA? ARE YOU THERE? THAT'S A JOKE . . .
WELL, IT'S NOT FUNNY, CHASE
NO, I'M NOT BEING "TOO SENSITIVE"-- I THOUGHT IT WAS CRUEL. LOOK, I'M NOT GOING TO GET INTO THIS NOW-- WHAT? OKAY, FINE. I'VE GOT TO GO, TOO-- THERE'S A CALL COMING IN . . .
YEAH-- THANKS FOR CALLING . . .
YES?
WHAT IS IT, COREY? MADAME WHO? OH, RIGHT-- MADAME LUCILLE IS SOMEONE BYRD'S TAKING CARE OF . . . I DON'T KNOW MUCH ABOUT HER . . .
NO, SHE'S NOT A CLIENT-- BYRD'S GIVING HER ADVICE AS A FAVOR TO HIS BROTHER. WHY DO YOU ASK?
WHAT?!

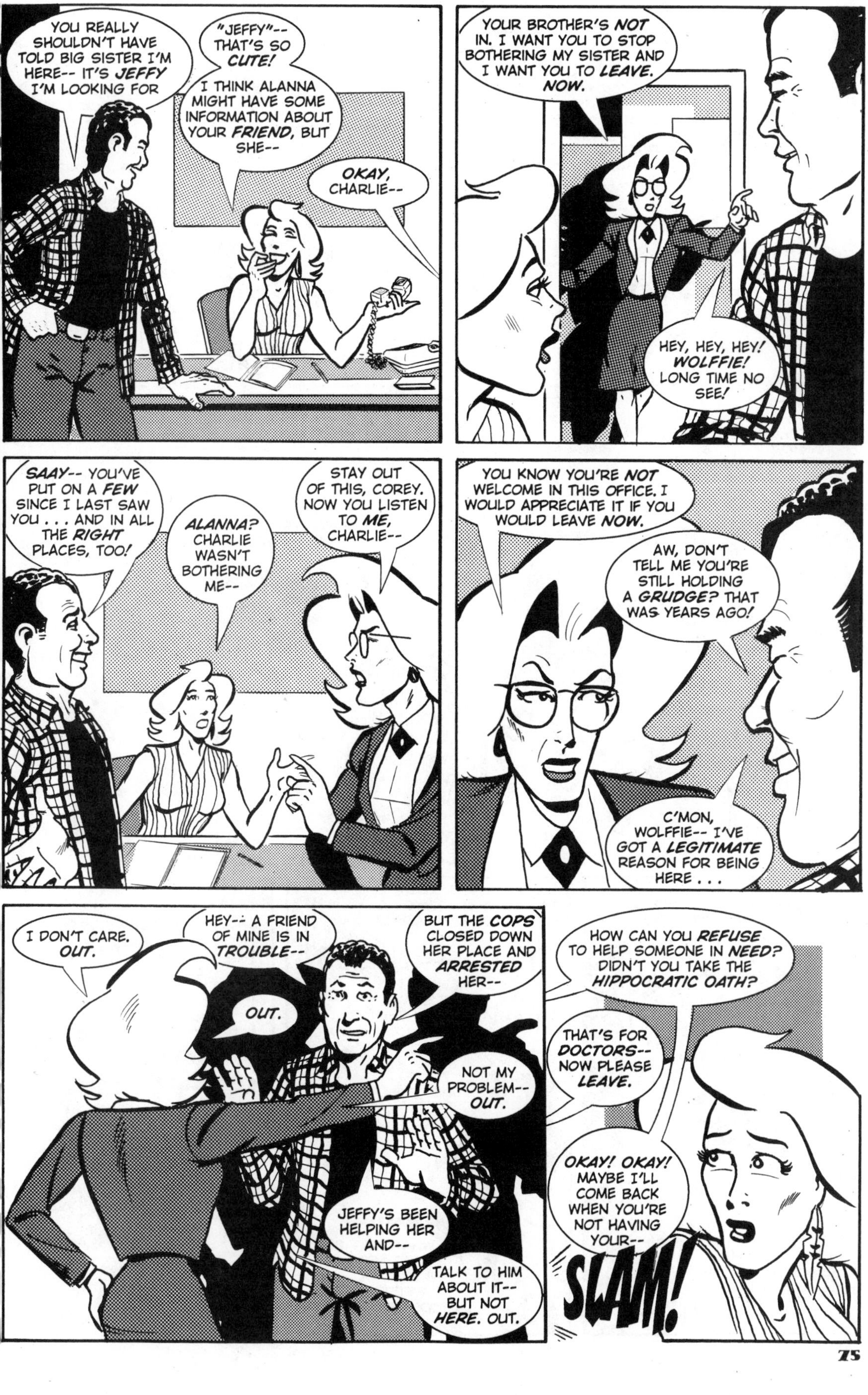
YOU REALLY SHOULDN'T HAVE TOLD BIG SISTER I'M HERE-- IT'S JEFFY I'M LOOKING FOR
"JEFFY"-- THAT'S SO CUTE!
I THINK ALANNA MIGHT HAVE SOME INFORMATION ABOUT YOUR FRIEND, BUT SHE--
OKAY, CHARLIE--
YOUR BROTHER'S NOT IN. I WANT YOU TO STOP BOTHERING MY SISTER AND I WANT YOU TO LEAVE. NOW.
HEY, HEY, HEY! WOLFFIE! LONG TIME NO SEE!
SAAY-- YOU'VE PUT ON A FEW SINCE I LAST SAW YOU . . . AND IN ALL THE RIGHT PLACES, TOO!
ALANNA? CHARLIE WASN'T BOTHERING ME--
STAY OUT OF THIS, COREY. NOW YOU LISTEN TO ME, CHARLIE--
YOU KNOW YOU'RE NOT WELCOME IN THIS OFFICE. I WOULD APPRECIATE IT IF YOU WOULD LEAVE NOW.
AW, DON'T TELL ME YOU'RE STILL HOLDING A GRUDGE? THAT WAS YEARS AGO!
C'MON, WOLFFIE-- I'VE GOT A LEGITIMATE REASON FOR BEING HERE . . .
I DON'T CARE. OUT.
HEY-- A FRIEND OF MINE IS IN TROUBLE--
OUT.
BUT THE COPS CLOSED DOWN HER PLACE AND ARRESTED HER--
NOT MY PROBLEM-- OUT.
JEFFY'S BEEN HELPING HER AND--
TALK TO HIM ABOUT IT-- BUT NOT HERE. OUT.
HOW CAN YOU REFUSE TO HELP SOMEONE IN NEED? DIDN'T YOU TAKE THE HIPPOCRATIC OATH?
THAT'S FOR DOCTORS-- NOW PLEASE LEAVE.
OKAY! OKAY! MAYBE I'LL COME BACK WHEN YOU'RE NOT HAVING YOUR--
SLAM!

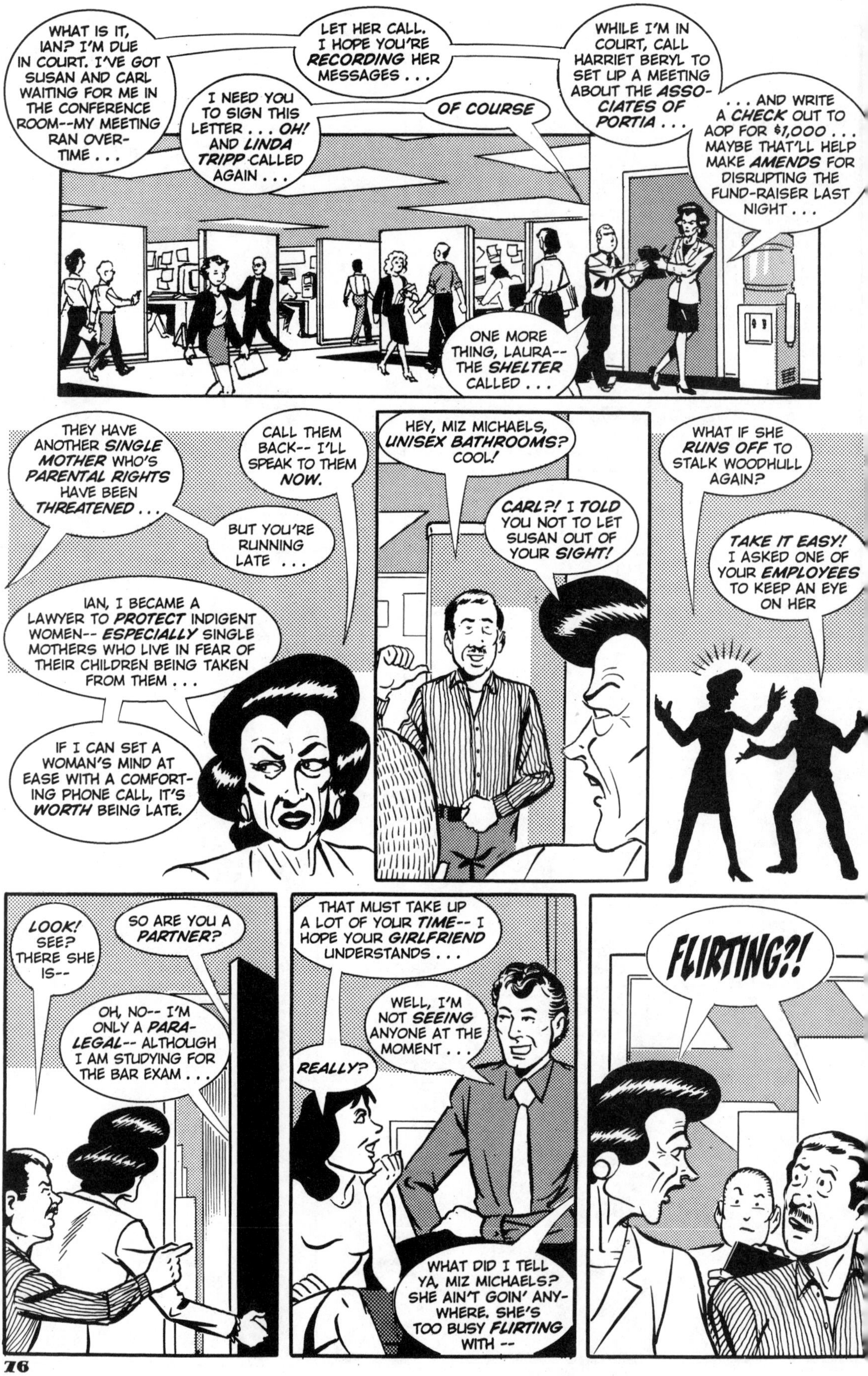
WHAT IS IT, IAN? I'M DUE IN COURT. I'VE GOT SUSAN AND CARL WAITING FOR ME IN THE CONFERENCE ROOM--MY MEETING RAN OVER-TIME . . .
I NEED YOU TO SIGN THIS LETTER . . . OH! AND LINDA TRIPP CALLED AGAIN . . .
LET HER CALL. I HOPE YOU'RE RECORDING HER MESSAGES . . .
OF COURSE
WHILE I'M IN COURT, CALL HARRIET BERYL TO SET UP A MEETING ABOUT THE ASSO-CIATES OF PORTIA . . .
. . . AND WRITE A CHECK OUT TO AOP FOR $1,000 . . . MAYBE THAT'LL HELP MAKE AMENDS FOR DISRUPTING THE FUND-RAISER LAST NIGHT . . .
ONE MORE THING, LAURA-- THE SHELTER CALLED . . .
THEY HAVE ANOTHER SINGLE MOTHER WHO'S PARENTAL RIGHTS HAVE BEEN THREATENED . . .
CALL THEM BACK-- I'LL SPEAK TO THEM NOW.
BUT YOU'RE RUNNING LATE . . .
IAN, I BECAME A LAWYER TO PROTECT INDIGENT WOMEN-- ESPECIALLY SINGLE MOTHERS WHO LIVE IN FEAR OF THEIR CHILDREN BEING TAKEN FROM THEM . . .
IF I CAN SET A WOMAN'S MIND AT EASE WITH A COMFORT-ING PHONE CALL, IT'S WORTH BEING LATE.
HEY, MIZ MICHAELS, UNISEX BATHROOMS? COOL!
CARL?! I TOLD YOU NOT TO LET SUSAN OUT OF YOUR SIGHT!
WHAT IF SHE RUNS OFF TO STALK WOODHULL AGAIN?
TAKE IT EASY! I ASKED ONE OF YOUR EMPLOYEES TO KEEP AN EYE ON HER
LOOK! SEE? THERE SHE IS--
SO ARE YOU A PARTNER?
OH, NO-- I'M ONLY A PARA-LEGAL-- ALTHOUGH I AM STUDYING FOR THE BAR EXAM . . .
THAT MUST TAKE UP A LOT OF YOUR TIME-- I HOPE YOUR GIRLFRIEND UNDERSTANDS . . .
WELL, I'M NOT SEEING ANYONE AT THE MOMENT . . .
REALLY?
WHAT DID I TELL YA, MIZ MICHAELS? SHE AIN'T GOIN' ANY-WHERE. SHE'S TOO BUSY FLIRTING WITH --
FLIRTING?!

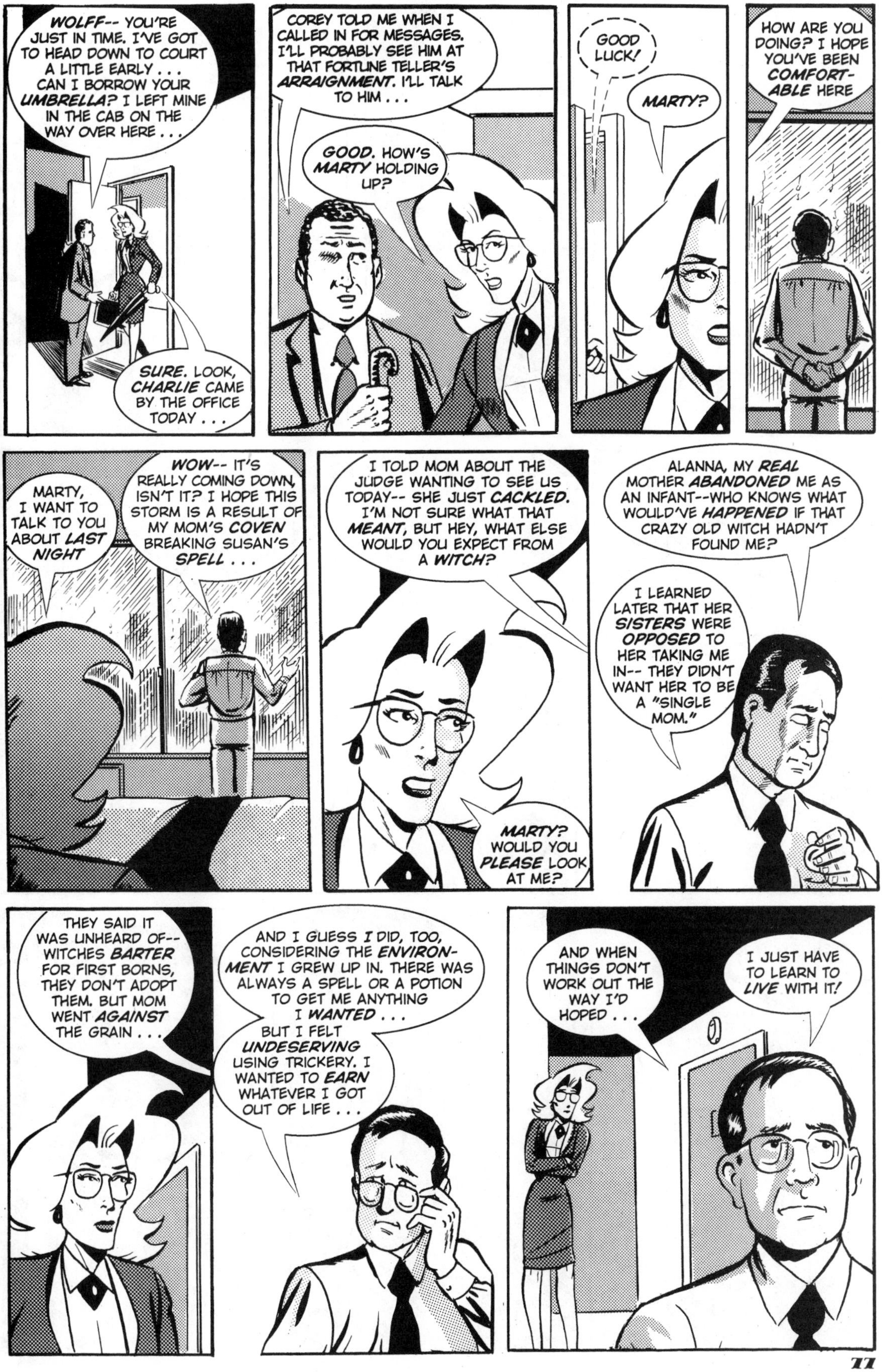

WOLFF-- YOU'RE JUST IN TIME. I'VE GOT TO HEAD DOWN TO COURT A LITTLE EARLY . . . CAN I BORROW YOUR UMBRELLA? I LEFT MINE IN THE CAB ON THE WAY OVER HERE . . .
SURE. LOOK, CHARLIE CAME BY THE OFFICE TODAY . . .
COREY TOLD ME WHEN I CALLED IN FOR MESSAGES. I'LL PROBABLY SEE HIM AT THAT FORTUNE TELLER'S ARRAIGNMENT. I'LL TALK TO HIM . . .
GOOD. HOW'S MARTY HOLDING UP?
GOOD LUCK!
MARTY?
HOW ARE YOU DOING? I HOPE YOU'VE BEEN COMFORTABLE HERE
MARTY, I WANT TO TALK TO YOU ABOUT LAST NIGHT
WOW-- IT'S REALLY COMING DOWN, ISN'T IT? I HOPE THIS STORM IS A RESULT OF MY MOM'S COVEN BREAKING SUSAN'S SPELL . . .
I TOLD MOM ABOUT THE JUDGE WANTING TO SEE US TODAY-- SHE JUST CACKLED. I'M NOT SURE WHAT THAT MEANT, BUT HEY, WHAT ELSE WOULD YOU EXPECT FROM A WITCH?
MARTY? WOULD YOU PLEASE LOOK AT ME?
ALANNA, MY REAL MOTHER ABANDONED ME AS AN INFANT--WHO KNOWS WHAT WOULD'VE HAPPENED IF THAT CRAZY OLD WITCH HADN'T FOUND ME?
I LEARNED LATER THAT HER SISTERS WERE OPPOSED TO HER TAKING ME IN-- THEY DIDN'T WANT HER TO BE A "SINGLE MOM."
THEY SAID IT WAS UNHEARD OF-- WITCHES BARTER FOR FIRST BORNS, THEY DON'T ADOPT THEM. BUT MOM WENT AGAINST THE GRAIN . . .
AND I GUESS I DID, TOO, CONSIDERING THE ENVIRONMENT I GREW UP IN. THERE WAS ALWAYS A SPELL OR A POTION TO GET ME ANYTHING I WANTED . . .
BUT I FELT UNDESERVING USING TRICKERY. I WANTED TO EARN WHATEVER I GOT OUT OF LIFE . . .
AND WHEN THINGS DON'T WORK OUT THE WAY I'D HOPED . . .
I JUST HAVE TO LEARN TO LIVE WITH IT!

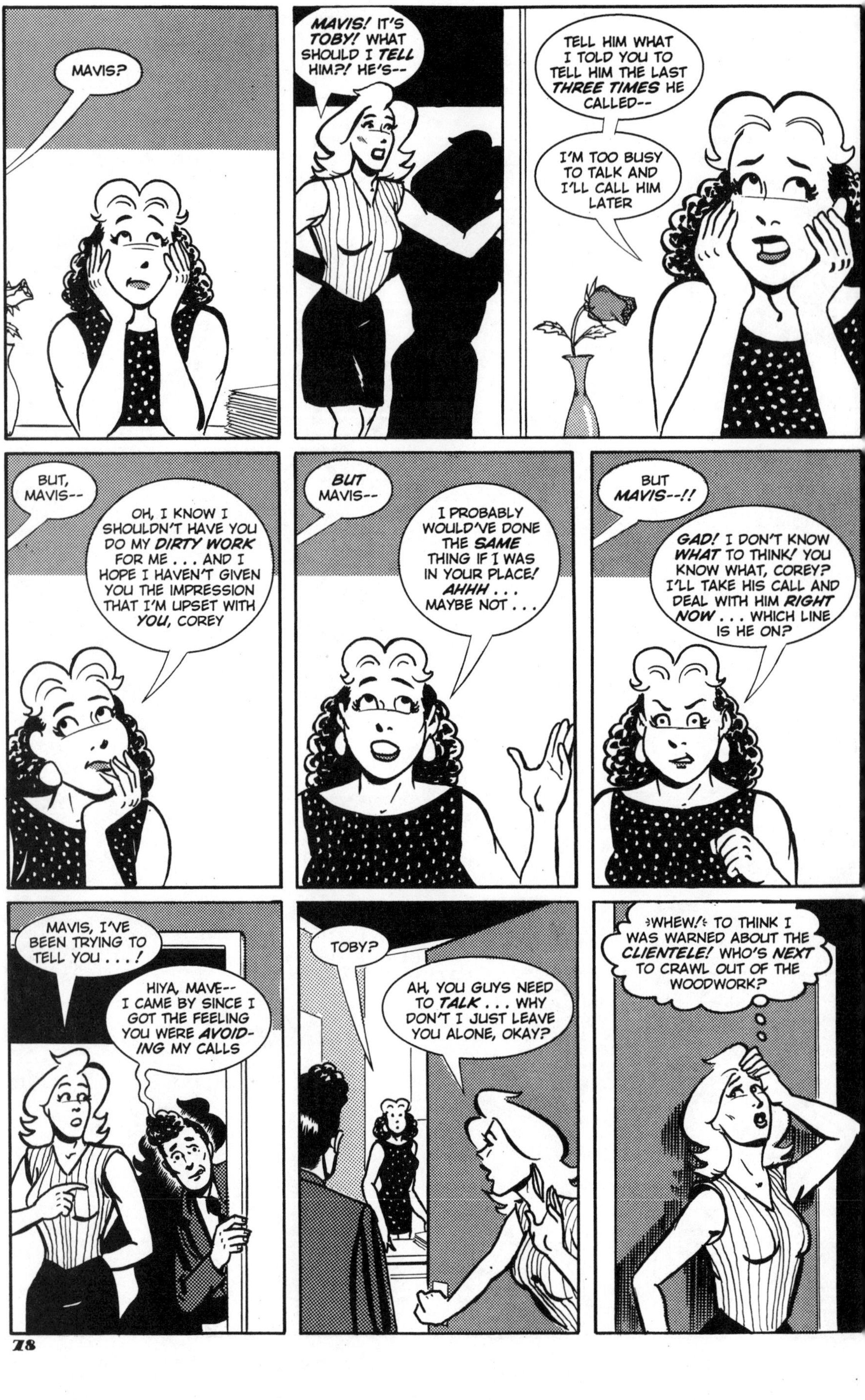
MAVIS?
MAVIS! IT'S TOBY! WHAT SHOULD I TELL HIM?! HE'S--
TELL HIM WHAT I TOLD YOU TO TELL HIM THE LAST THREE TIMES HE CALLED--
I'M TOO BUSY TO TALK AND I'LL CALL HIM LATER
BUT, MAVIS--
OH, I KNOW I SHOULDN'T HAVE YOU DO MY DIRTY WORK FOR ME . . . AND I HOPE I HAVEN'T GIVEN YOU THE IMPRESSION THAT I'M UPSET WITH YOU, COREY
BUT MAVIS--
I PROBABLY WOULD'VE DONE THE SAME THING IF I WAS IN YOUR PLACE! AHHH . . . MAYBE NOT . . .
BUT MAVIS--!!
GAD! I DON'T KNOW WHAT TO THINK! YOU KNOW WHAT, COREY? I'LL TAKE HIS CALL AND DEAL WITH HIM RIGHT NOW . . . WHICH LINE IS HE ON?
MAVIS, I'VE BEEN TRYING TO TELL YOU . . .!
HIYA, MAVE-- I CAME BY SINCE I GOT THE FEELING YOU WERE AVOIDING MY CALLS
TOBY?
AH, YOU GUYS NEED TO TALK . . . WHY DON'T I JUST LEAVE YOU ALONE, OKAY?
WHEW! TO THINK I WAS WARNED ABOUT THE CLIENTELE! WHO'S NEXT TO CRAWL OUT OF THE WOODWORK?

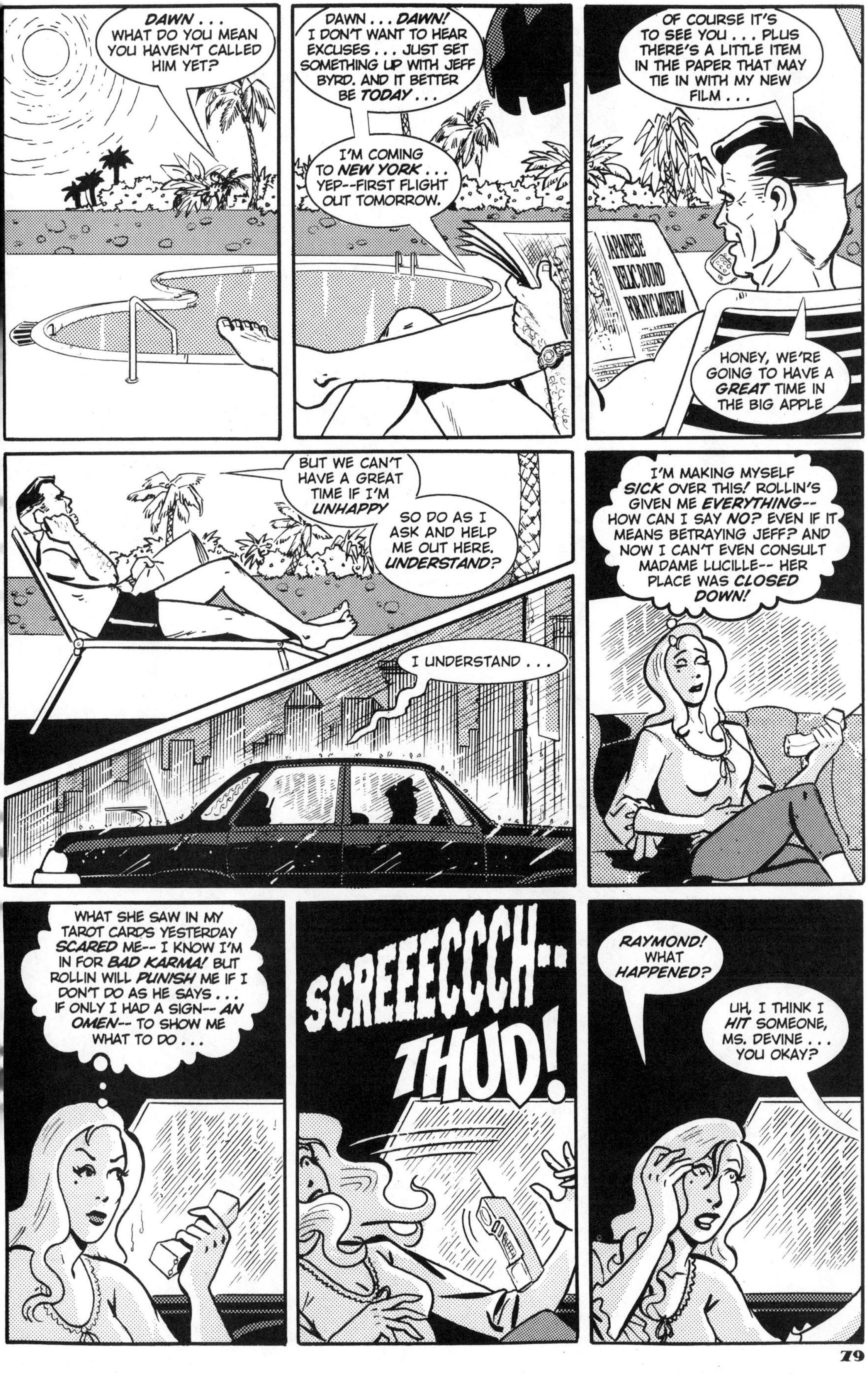
DAWN . . . WHAT DO YOU MEAN YOU HAVEN'T CALLED HIM YET?
DAWN . . . DAWN! I DON'T WANT TO HEAR EXCUSES . . . JUST SET SOMETHING UP WITH JEFF BYRD. AND IT BETTER BE TODAY . . .
I'M COMING TO NEW YORK . . . YEP--FIRST FLIGHT OUT TOMORROW.
OF COURSE IT'S TO SEE YOU . . . PLUS THERE'S A LITTLE ITEM IN THE PAPER THAT MAY TIE IN WITH MY NEW FILM . . .
JAPANESE RELIC BOUND FOR NYC MUSEUM
HONEY, WE'RE GOING TO HAVE A GREAT TIME IN THE BIG APPLE
BUT WE CAN'T HAVE A GREAT TIME IF I'M UNHAPPY
SO DO AS I ASK AND HELP ME OUT HERE. UNDERSTAND?
I UNDERSTAND . . .
I'M MAKING MYSELF SICK OVER THIS! ROLLIN'S GIVEN ME EVERYTHING-- HOW CAN I SAY NO? EVEN IF IT MEANS BETRAYING JEFF? AND NOW I CAN'T EVEN CONSULT MADAME LUCILLE-- HER PLACE WAS CLOSED DOWN!
WHAT SHE SAW IN MY TAROT CARDS YESTERDAY SCARED ME-- I KNOW I'M IN FOR BAD KARMA! BUT ROLLIN WILL PUNISH ME IF I DON'T DO AS HE SAYS . . . IF ONLY I HAD A SIGN-- AN OMEN-- TO SHOW ME WHAT TO DO . . .
SCREEECCCH-- THUD!
RAYMOND! WHAT HAPPENED?
UH, I THINK I HIT SOMEONE, MS. DEVINE . . . YOU OKAY?

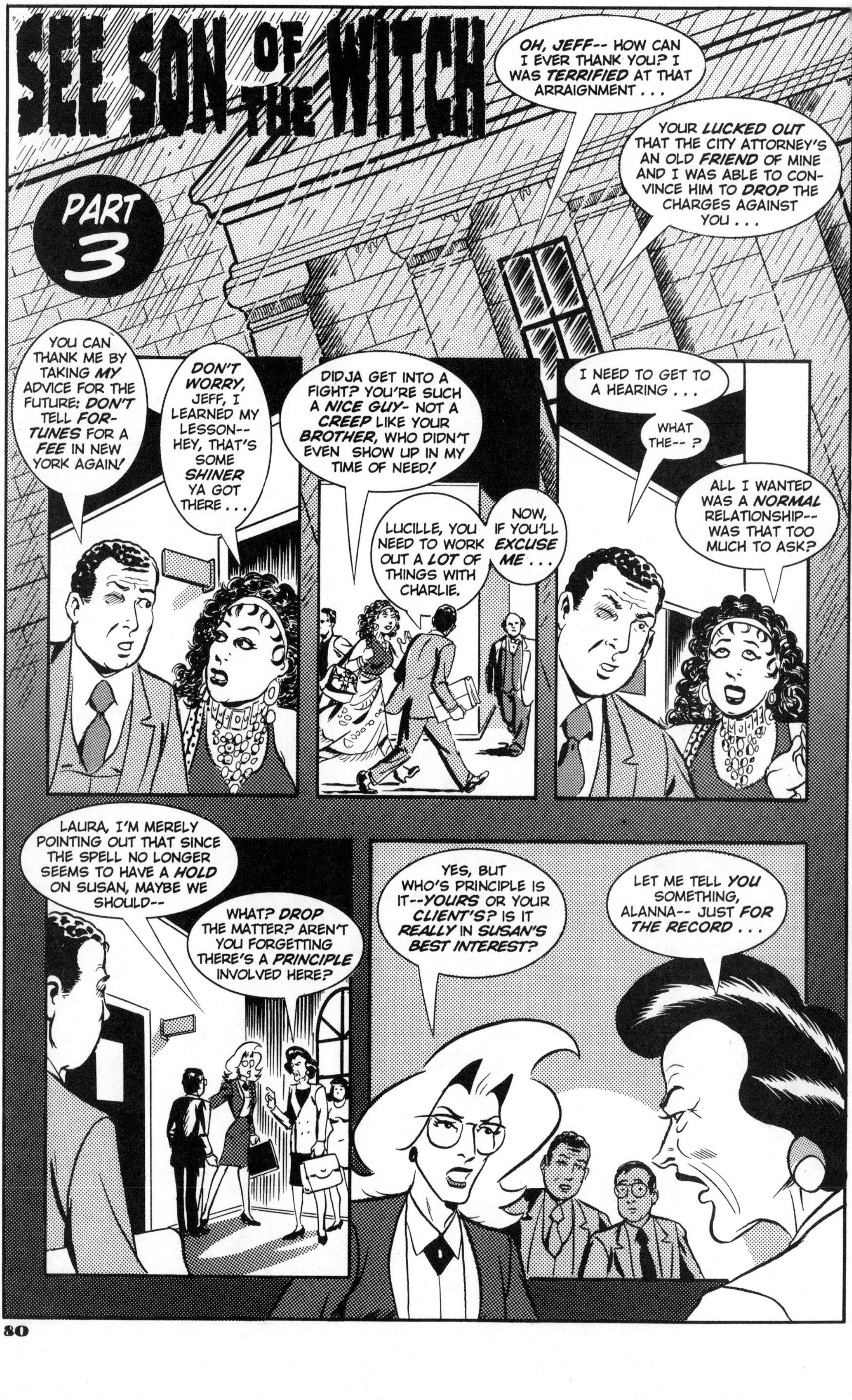
SEE SON OF THE WITCH
PART 3
OH, JEFF-- HOW CAN I EVER THANK YOU? I WAS TERRIFIED AT THAT ARRAIGNMENT . . .
YOUR LUCKED OUT THAT THE CITY ATTORNEY'S AN OLD FRIEND OF MINE AND I WAS ABLE TO CONVINCE HIM TO DROP THE CHARGES AGAINST YOU . . .
YOU CAN THANK ME BY TAKING MY ADVICE FOR THE FUTURE: DON'T TELL FORTUNES FOR A FEE IN NEW YORK AGAIN!
DON'T WORRY, JEFF, I LEARNED MY LESSON-- HEY, THAT'S SOME SHINER YA GOT THERE . . .
DIDJA GET INTO A FIGHT? YOU'RE SUCH A NICE GUY- NOT A CREEP LIKE YOUR BROTHER, WHO DIDN'T EVEN SHOW UP IN MY TIME OF NEED!
LUCILLE, YOU NEED TO WORK OUT A LOT OF THINGS WITH CHARLIE.
NOW, IF YOU'LL EXCUSE ME . . .
I NEED TO GET TO A HEARING . . .
WHAT THE-- ?
ALL I WANTED WAS A NORMAL RELATIONSHIP-- WAS THAT TOO MUCH TO ASK?
LAURA, I'M MERELY POINTING OUT THAT SINCE THE SPELL NO LONGER SEEMS TO HAVE A HOLD ON SUSAN, MAYBE WE SHOULD--
WHAT? DROP THE MATTER? AREN'T YOU FORGETTING THERE'S A PRINCIPLE INVOLVED HERE?
YES, BUT WHO'S PRINCIPLE IS IT--YOURS OR YOUR CLIENT'S? IS IT REALLY IN SUSAN'S BEST INTEREST?
LET ME TELL YOU SOMETHING, ALANNA-- JUST FOR THE RECORD . . .

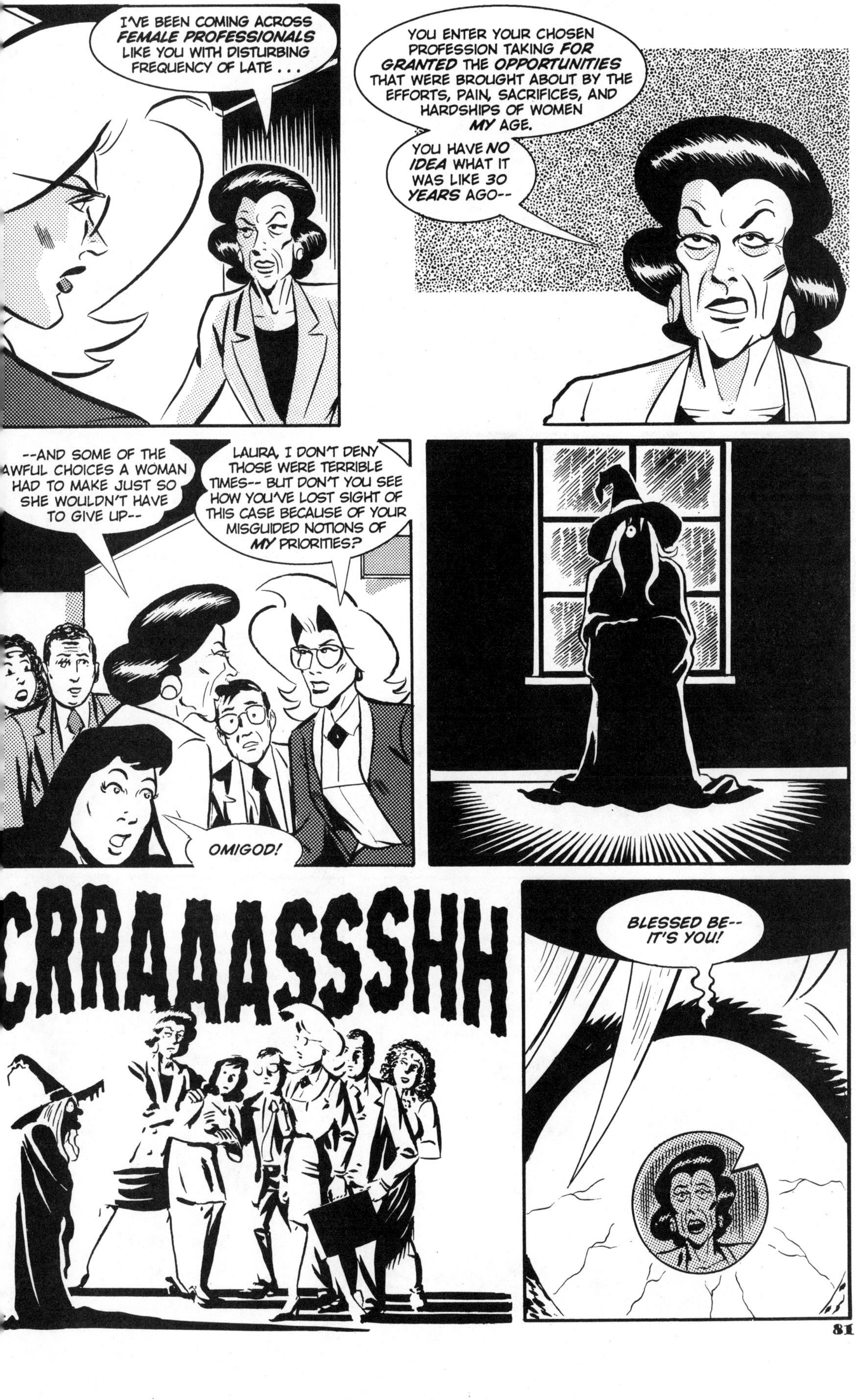
I'VE BEEN COMING ACROSS FEMALE PROFESSIONALS LIKE YOU WITH DISTURBING FREQUENCY OF LATE . . .
YOU ENTER YOUR CHOSEN PROFESSION TAKING FOR GRANTED THE OPPORTUNITIES THAT WERE BROUGHT ABOUT BY THE EFFORTS, PAIN, SACRIFICES, AND HARDSHIPS OF WOMEN MY AGE.
YOU HAVE NO IDEA WHAT IT WAS LIKE 30 YEARS AGO--
--AND SOME OF THE AWFUL CHOICES A WOMAN HAD TO MAKE JUST SO SHE WOULDN'T HAVE TO GIVE UP--
LAURA, I DON'T DENY THOSE WERE TERRIBLE TIMES-- BUT DON'T YOU SEE HOW YOU'VE LOST SIGHT OF THIS CASE BECAUSE OF YOUR MISGUIDED NOTIONS OF MY PRIORITIES?
OMIGOD!
CRRAAASSSHH
BLESSED BE-- IT'S YOU!

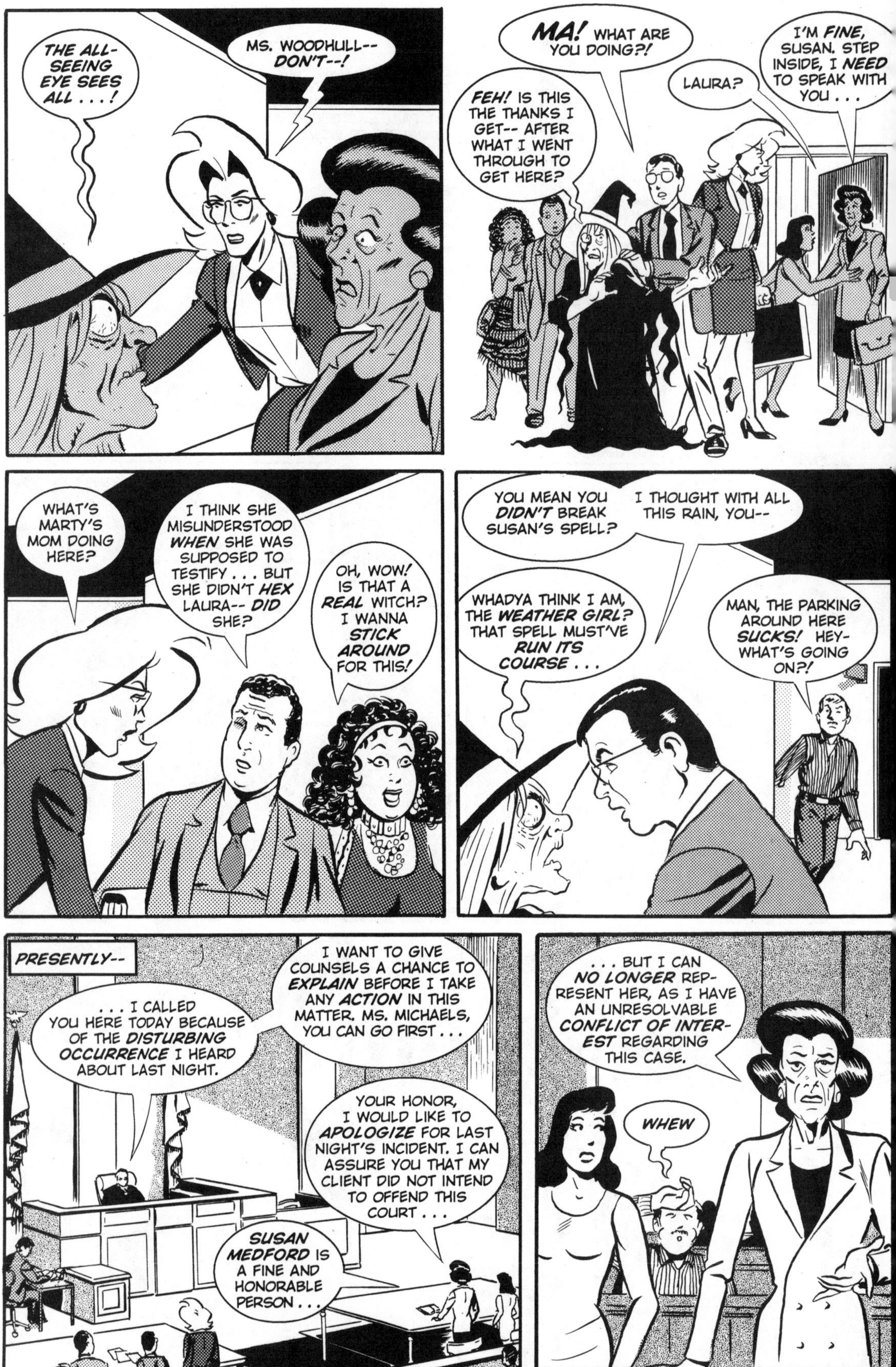
THE ALL-SEEING EYE SEES ALL . . .!
MS. WOODHULL-- DON'T--!
MA! WHAT ARE YOU DOING?!
FEH! IS THIS THE THANKS I GET-- AFTER WHAT I WENT THROUGH TO GET HERE?
LAURA?
I'M FINE, SUSAN. STEP INSIDE, I NEED TO SPEAK WITH YOU . . .
WHAT'S MARTY'S MOM DOING HERE?
I THINK SHE MISUNDERSTOOD WHEN SHE WAS SUPPOSED TO TESTIFY . . . BUT SHE DIDN'T HEX LAURA-- DID SHE?
OH, WOW! IS THAT A REAL WITCH? I WANNA STICK AROUND FOR THIS!
YOU MEAN YOU DIDN'T BREAK SUSAN'S SPELL?
I THOUGHT WITH ALL THIS RAIN, YOU--
WHADYA THINK I AM, THE WEATHER GIRL? THAT SPELL MUST'VE RUN ITS COURSE . . .
MAN, THE PARKING AROUND HERE SUCKS! HEY-WHAT'S GOING ON?!
PRESENTLY--
. . . I CALLED YOU HERE TODAY BECAUSE OF THE DISTURBING OCCURRENCE I HEARD ABOUT LAST NIGHT.
I WANT TO GIVE COUNSELS A CHANCE TO EXPLAIN BEFORE I TAKE ANY ACTION IN THIS MATTER. MS. MICHAELS, YOU CAN GO FIRST . . .
YOUR HONOR, I WOULD LIKE TO APOLOGIZE FOR LAST NIGHT'S INCIDENT. I CAN ASSURE YOU THAT MY CLIENT DID NOT INTEND TO OFFEND THIS COURT . . .
SUSAN MEDFORD IS A FINE AND HONORABLE PERSON . . .
. . . BUT I CAN NO LONGER REPRESENT HER, AS I HAVE AN UNRESOLVABLE CONFLICT OF INTEREST REGARDING THIS CASE.
WHEW

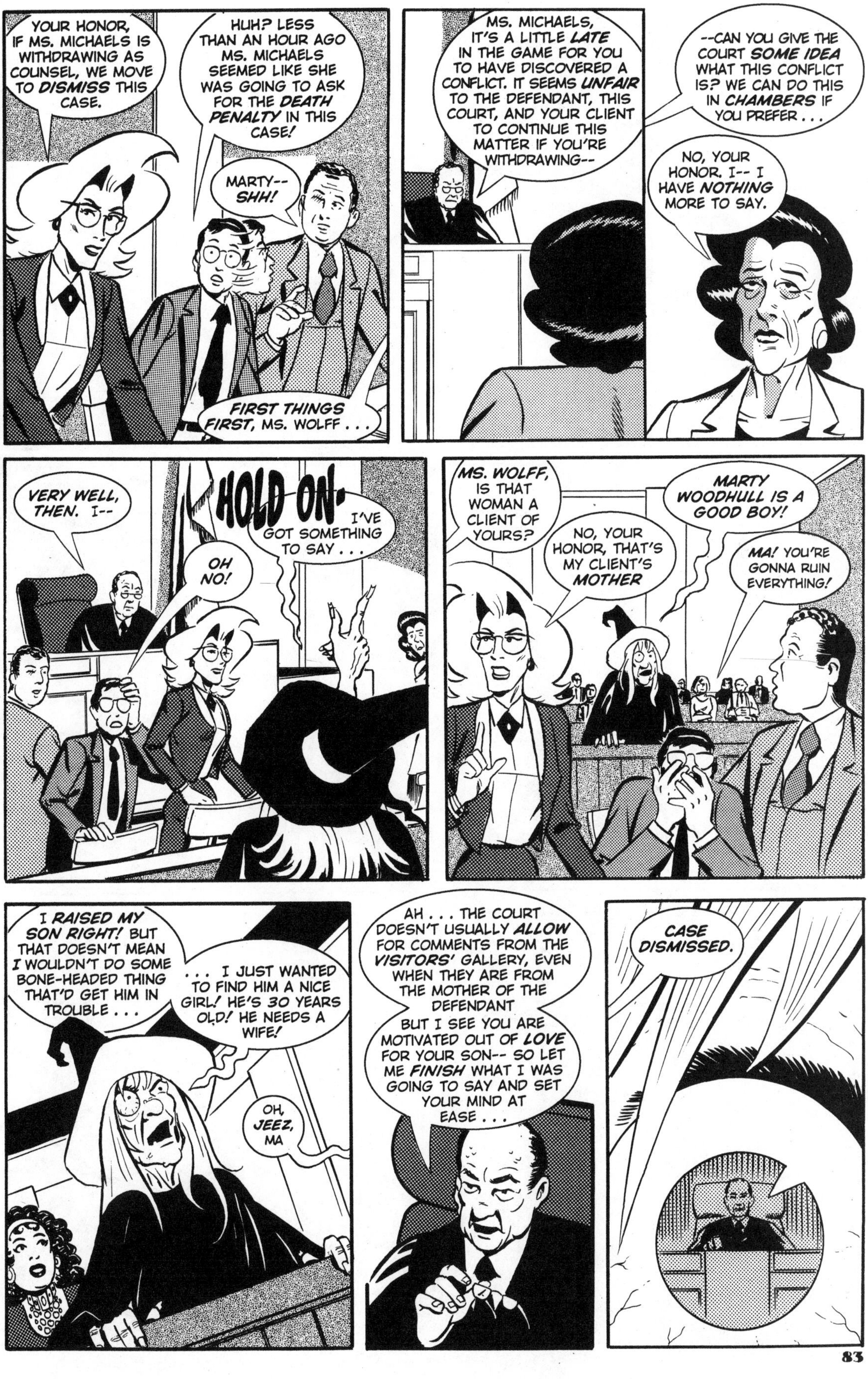
YOUR HONOR, IF MS. MICHAELS IS WITHDRAWING AS COUNSEL, WE MOVE TO DISMISS THIS CASE.
HUH? LESS THAN AN HOUR AGO MS. MICHAELS SEEMED LIKE SHE WAS GOING TO ASK FOR THE DEATH PENALTY IN THIS CASE!
MARTY-- SHH!
FIRST THINGS FIRST, MS. WOLFF . . .
MS. MICHAELS, IT'S A LITTLE LATE IN THE GAME FOR YOU TO HAVE DISCOVERED A CONFLICT. IT SEEMS UNFAIR TO THE DEFENDANT, THIS COURT, AND YOUR CLIENT TO CONTINUE THIS MATTER IF YOU'RE WITHDRAWING--
--CAN YOU GIVE THE COURT SOME IDEA WHAT THIS CONFLICT IS? WE CAN DO THIS IN CHAMBERS IF YOU PREFER . . .
NO, YOUR HONOR. I-- I HAVE NOTHING MORE TO SAY.
VERY WELL, THEN. I--
HOLD ON-
I'VE GOT SOMETHING TO SAY . . .
OH NO!
MS. WOLFF, IS THAT WOMAN A CLIENT OF YOURS?
NO, YOUR HONOR, THAT'S MY CLIENT'S MOTHER
MARTY WOODHULL IS A GOOD BOY!
MA! YOU'RE GONNA RUIN EVERYTHING!
I RAISED MY SON RIGHT! BUT THAT DOESN'T MEAN I WOULDN'T DO SOME BONE-HEADED THING THAT'D GET HIM IN TROUBLE . . .
. . . I JUST WANTED TO FIND HIM A NICE GIRL! HE'S 30 YEARS OLD! HE NEEDS A WIFE!
OH, JEEZ, MA
AH . . . THE COURT DOESN'T USUALLY ALLOW FOR COMMENTS FROM THE VISITORS' GALLERY, EVEN WHEN THEY ARE FROM THE MOTHER OF THE DEFENDANT
BUT I SEE YOU ARE MOTIVATED OUT OF LOVE FOR YOUR SON-- SO LET ME FINISH WHAT I WAS GOING TO SAY AND SET YOUR MIND AT EASE . . .
CASE DISMISSED.

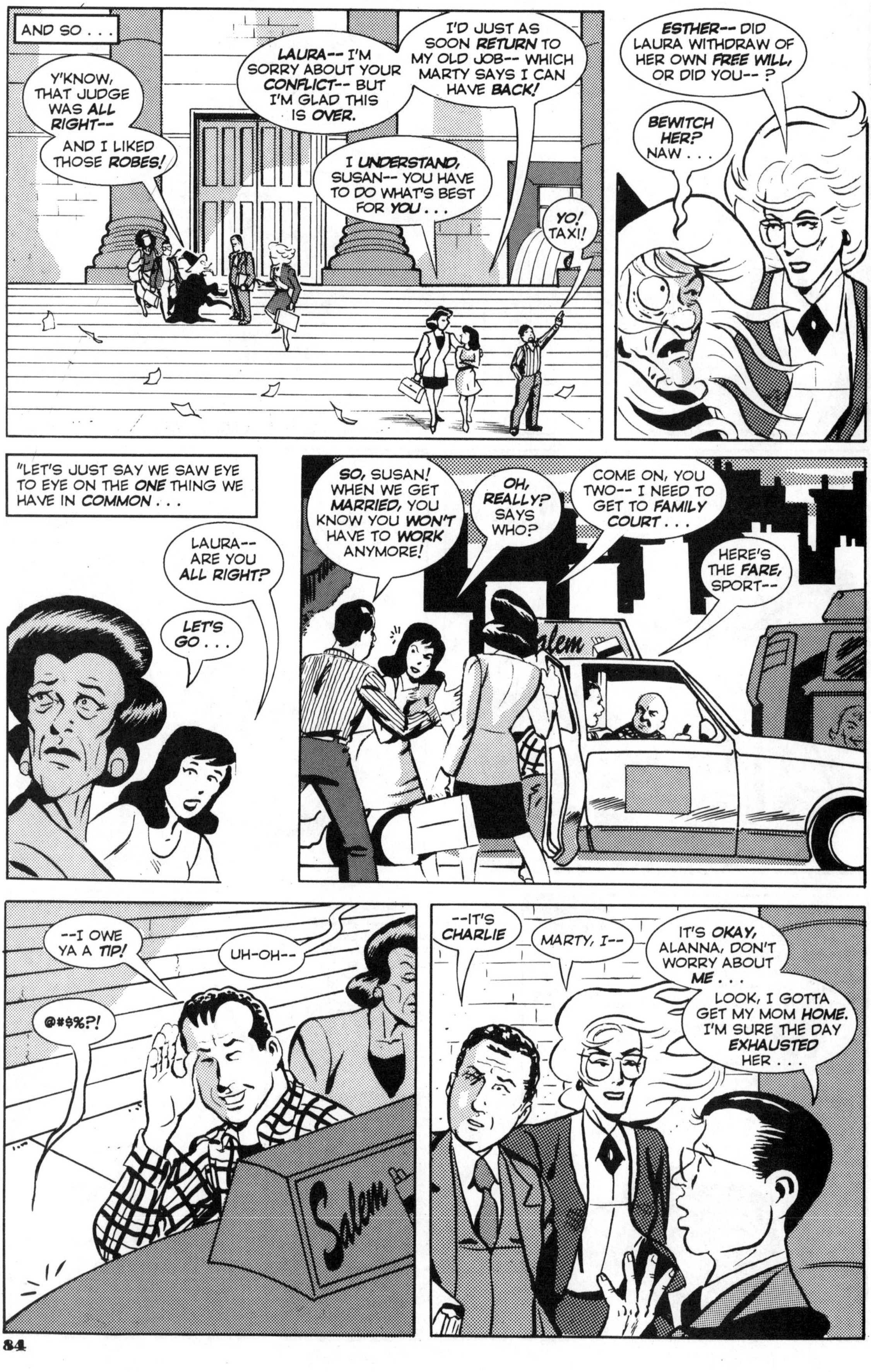

AND SO . . .
Y'KNOW, THAT JUDGE WAS ALL RIGHT--
AND I LIKED THOSE ROBES!
LAURA-- I'M SORRY ABOUT YOUR CONFLICT-- BUT I'M GLAD THIS IS OVER.
I'D JUST AS SOON RETURN TO MY OLD JOB-- WHICH MARTY SAYS I CAN HAVE BACK!
I UNDERSTAND, SUSAN-- YOU HAVE TO DO WHAT'S BEST FOR YOU . . .
YO! TAXI!
ESTHER-- DID LAURA WITHDRAW OF HER OWN FREE WILL, OR DID YOU-- ?
BEWITCH HER? NAW . . .
"LET'S JUST SAY WE SAW EYE TO EYE ON THE ONE THING WE HAVE IN COMMON . . .
LAURA-- ARE YOU ALL RIGHT?
LET'S GO . . .
SO, SUSAN! WHEN WE GET MARRIED, YOU KNOW YOU WON'T HAVE TO WORK ANYMORE!
OH, REALLY? SAYS WHO?
COME ON, YOU TWO-- I NEED TO GET TO FAMILY COURT . . .
HERE'S THE FARE, SPORT--
--I OWE YA A TIP!
UH-OH--
@#$%?!
Salem
--IT'S CHARLIE
MARTY, I--
IT'S OKAY, ALANNA, DON'T WORRY ABOUT ME . . .
LOOK, I GOTTA GET MY MOM HOME. I'M SURE THE DAY EXHAUSTED HER . . .

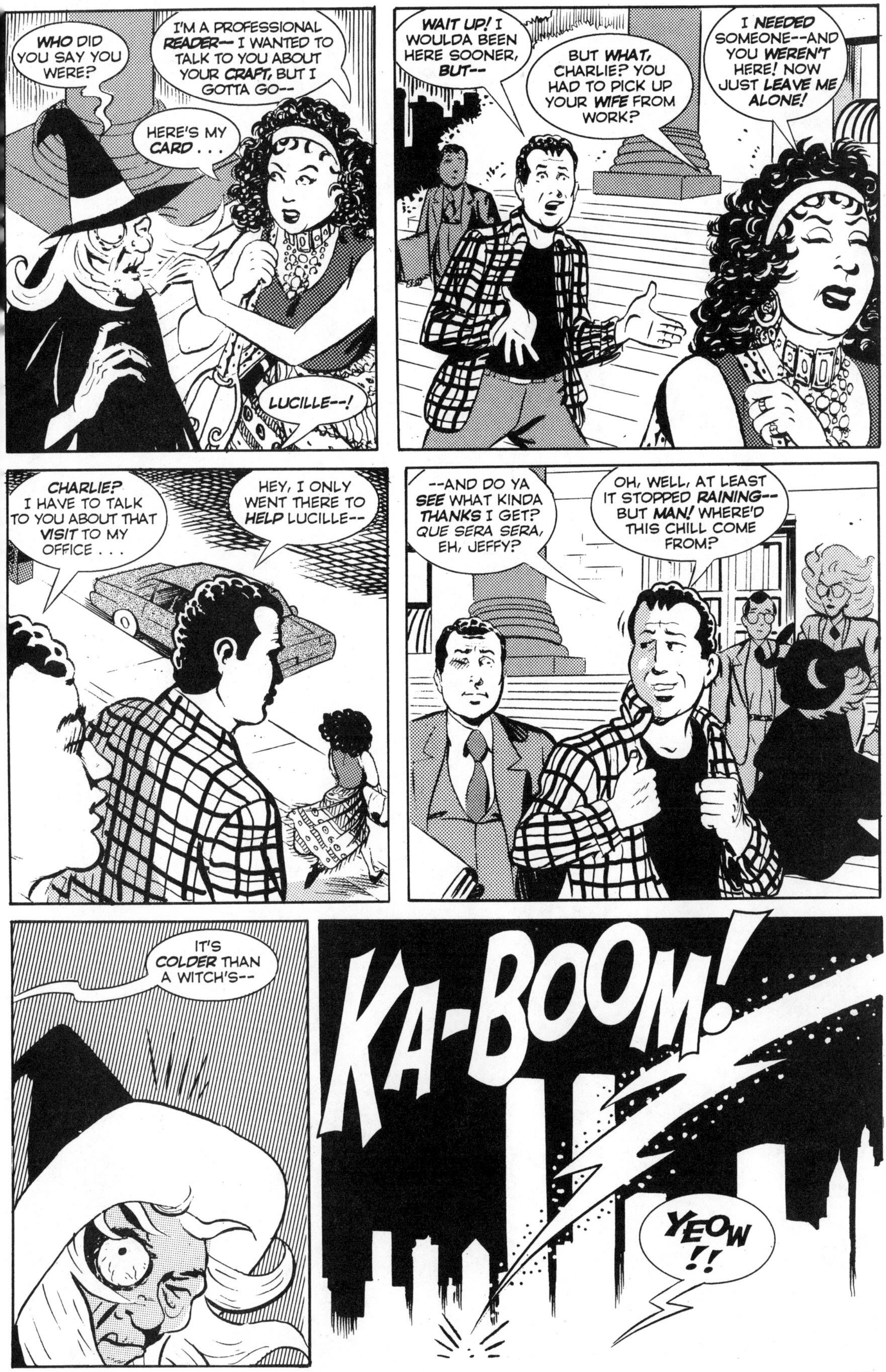
WHO DID YOU SAY YOU WERE?
I'M A PROFESSIONAL READER-- I WANTED TO TALK TO YOU ABOUT YOUR CRAFT, BUT I GOTTA GO--
HERE'S MY CARD . . .
LUCILLE--!
WAIT UP! I WOULDA BEEN HERE SOONER, BUT--
BUT WHAT, CHARLIE? YOU HAD TO PICK UP YOUR WIFE FROM WORK?
I NEEDED SOMEONE--AND YOU WEREN'T HERE! NOW JUST LEAVE ME ALONE!
CHARLIE? I HAVE TO TALK TO YOU ABOUT THAT VISIT TO MY OFFICE . . .
HEY, I ONLY WENT THERE TO HELP LUCILLE--
--AND DO YA SEE WHAT KINDA THANKS I GET? QUE SERA SERA, EH, JEFFY?
OH, WELL, AT LEAST IT STOPPED RAINING-- BUT MAN! WHERE'D THIS CHILL COME FROM?
IT'S COLDER THAN A WITCH'S--
KA-BOOM!
YEOW!!

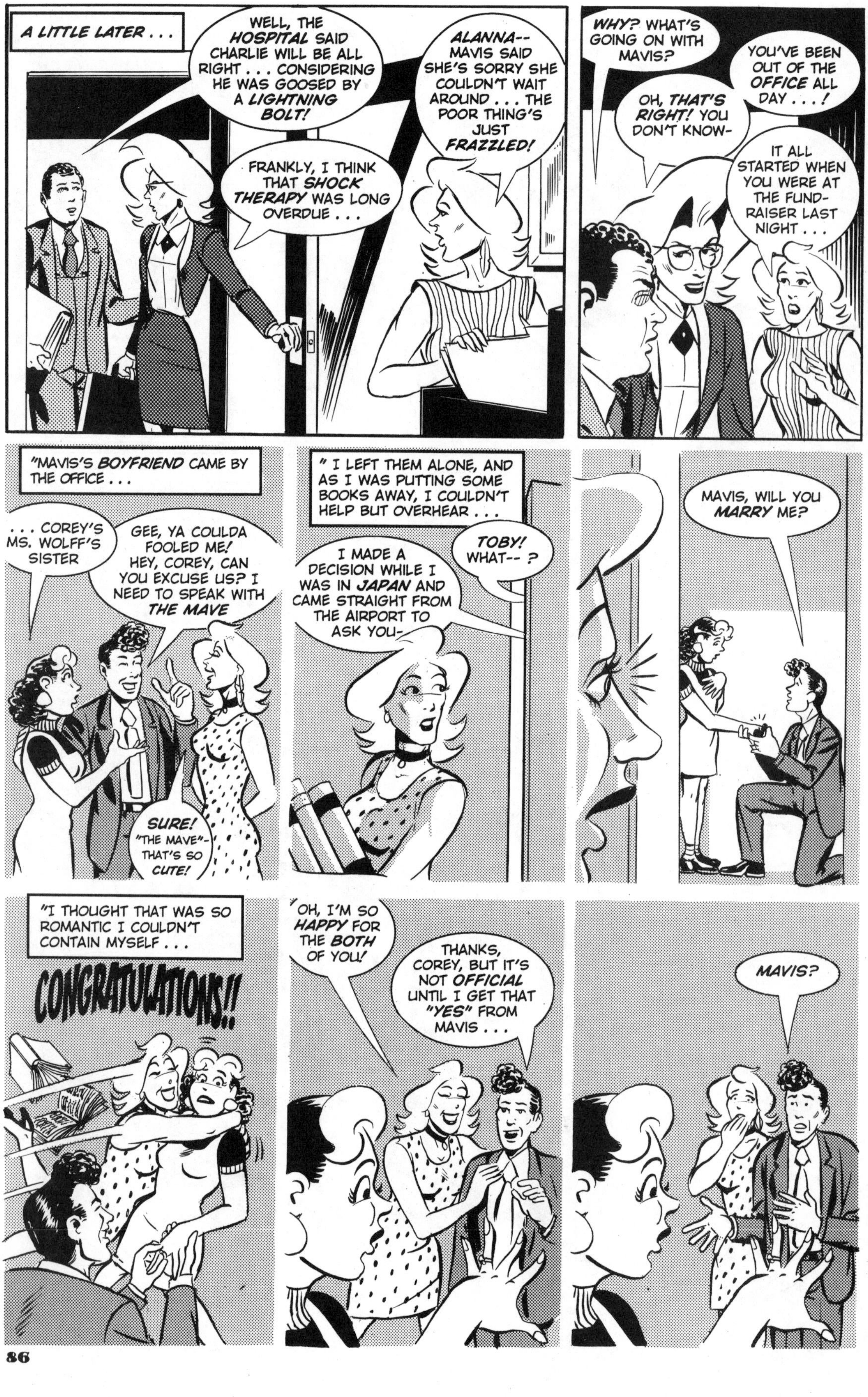
A LITTLE LATER . . .
WELL, THE HOSPITAL SAID CHARLIE WILL BE ALL RIGHT . . . CONSIDERING HE WAS GOOSED BY A LIGHTNING BOLT!
FRANKLY, I THINK THAT SHOCK THERAPY WAS LONG OVERDUE . . .
ALANNA-- MAVIS SAID SHE'S SORRY SHE COULDN'T WAIT AROUND . . . THE POOR THING'S JUST FRAZZLED!
WHY? WHAT'S GOING ON WITH MAVIS?
OH, THAT'S RIGHT! YOU DON'T KNOW-
YOU'VE BEEN OUT OF THE OFFICE ALL DAY . . . !
IT ALL STARTED WHEN YOU WERE AT THE FUND-RAISER LAST NIGHT . . .
"MAVIS'S BOYFRIEND CAME BY THE OFFICE . . .
. . . COREY'S MS. WOLFF'S SISTER
GEE, YA COULDA FOOLED ME! HEY, COREY, CAN YOU EXCUSE US? I NEED TO SPEAK WITH THE MAVE
SURE! "THE MAVE"- THAT'S SO CUTE!
" I LEFT THEM ALONE, AND AS I WAS PUTTING SOME BOOKS AWAY, I COULDN'T HELP BUT OVERHEAR . . .
I MADE A DECISION WHILE I WAS IN JAPAN AND CAME STRAIGHT FROM THE AIRPORT TO ASK YOU-
TOBY! WHAT-- ?
MAVIS, WILL YOU MARRY ME?
"I THOUGHT THAT WAS SO ROMANTIC I COULDN'T CONTAIN MYSELF . . .
CONGRATULATIONS!!
OH, I'M SO HAPPY FOR THE BOTH OF YOU!
THANKS, COREY, BUT IT'S NOT OFFICIAL UNTIL I GET THAT "YES" FROM MAVIS . . .
MAVIS?

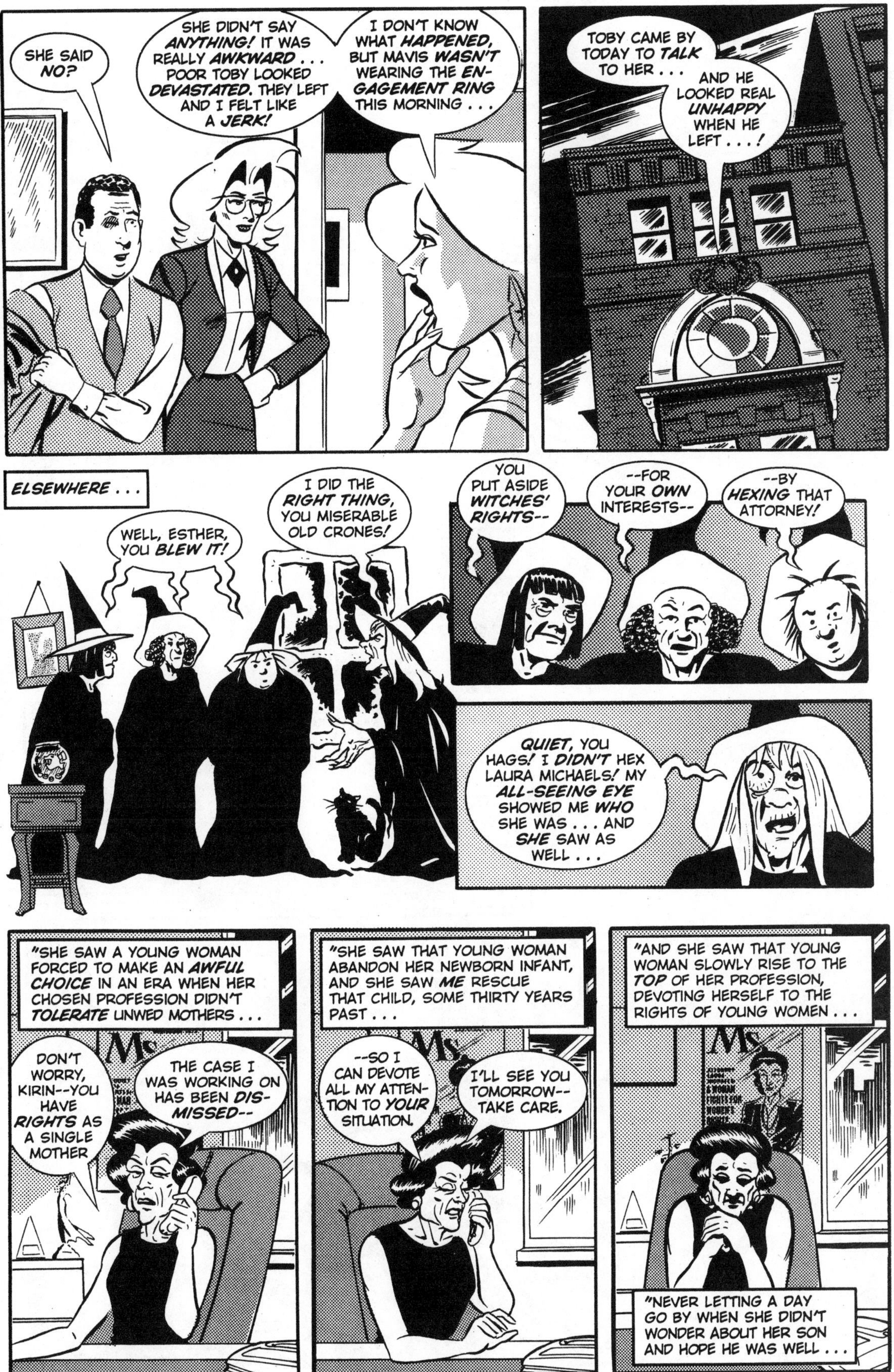

SHE SAID NO?
SHE DIDN'T SAY ANYTHING! IT WAS REALLY AWKWARD . . . POOR TOBY LOOKED DEVASTATED. THEY LEFT AND I FELT LIKE A JERK!
I DON'T KNOW WHAT HAPPENED, BUT MAVIS WASN'T WEARING THE ENGAGEMENT RING THIS MORNING . . .
TOBY CAME BY TODAY TO TALK TO HER . . .
AND HE LOOKED REAL UNHAPPY WHEN HE LEFT . . . !
ELSEWHERE . . .
WELL, ESTHER, YOU BLEW IT!
I DID THE RIGHT THING, YOU MISERABLE OLD CRONES!
YOU PUT ASIDE WITCHES' RIGHTS--
--FOR YOUR OWN INTERESTS--
--BY HEXING THAT ATTORNEY!
QUIET, YOU HAGS! I DIDN'T HEX LAURA MICHAELS! MY ALL-SEEING EYE SHOWED ME WHO SHE WAS . . . AND SHE SAW AS WELL . . .
"SHE SAW A YOUNG WOMAN FORCED TO MAKE AN AWFUL CHOICE IN AN ERA WHEN HER CHOSEN PROFESSION DIDN'T TOLERATE UNWED MOTHERS . . .
DON'T WORRY, KIRIN--YOU HAVE RIGHTS AS A SINGLE MOTHER
THE CASE I WAS WORKING ON HAS BEEN DISMISSED--
"SHE SAW THAT YOUNG WOMAN ABANDON HER NEWBORN INFANT, AND SHE SAW ME RESCUE THAT CHILD, SOME THIRTY YEARS PAST . . .
--SO I CAN DEVOTE ALL MY ATTENTION TO YOUR SITUATION.
I'LL SEE YOU TOMORROW--TAKE CARE.
"AND SHE SAW THAT YOUNG WOMAN SLOWLY RISE TO THE TOP OF HER PROFESSION, DEVOTING HERSELF TO THE RIGHTS OF YOUNG WOMEN . . .
"NEVER LETTING A DAY GO BY WHEN SHE DIDN'T WONDER ABOUT HER SON AND HOPE HE WAS WELL . . .

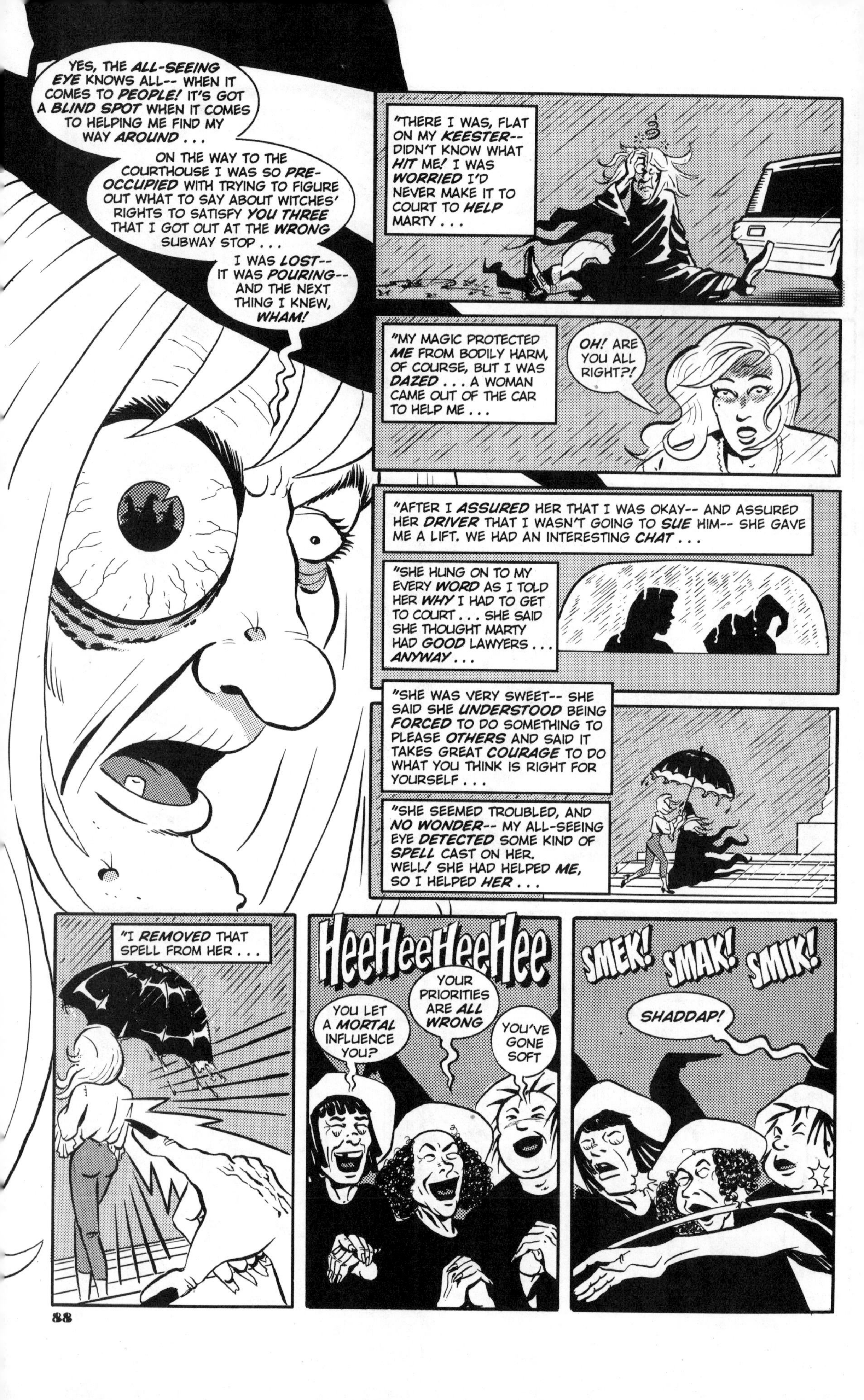
YES, THE ALL-SEEING EYE KNOWS ALL-- WHEN IT COMES TO PEOPLE! IT'S GOT A BLIND SPOT WHEN IT COMES TO HELPING ME FIND MY WAY AROUND . . .
ON THE WAY TO THE COURTHOUSE I WAS SO PRE-OCCUPIED WITH TRYING TO FIGURE OUT WHAT TO SATISFY ABOUT WITCHES' RIGHTS TO SATISFY YOU THREE THAT I GOT OUT AT THE WRONG SUBWAY STOP . . .
I WAS LOST-- IT WAS POURING-- AND THE NEXT THING I KNEW, WHAM!
"THERE I WAS, FLAT ON MY KEESTER-- DIDN'T KNOW WHAT HIT ME! I WAS WORRIED I'D NEVER MAKE IT TO COURT TO HELP MARTY . . .
"MY MAGIC PROTECTED ME FROM BODILY HARM, OF COURSE, BUT I WAS DAZED . . . A WOMAN CAME OUT OF THE CAR TO HELP ME . . .
OH! ARE YOU ALL RIGHT?!
"AFTER I ASSURED HER THAT I WAS OKAY-- AND ASSURED HER DRIVER THAT I WASN'T GOING TO SUE HIM-- SHE GAVE ME A LIFT. WE HAD AN INTERESTING CHAT . . .
"SHE HUNG ON TO MY EVERY WORD AS I TOLD HER WHY I HAD TO GET TO COURT . . . SHE SAID SHE THOUGHT MARTY HAD GOOD LAWYERS . . . ANYWAY . . .
"SHE WAS VERY SWEET-- SHE SAID SHE UNDERSTOOD BEING FORCED TO DO SOMETHING TO PLEASE OTHERS AND SAID IT TAKES GREAT COURAGE TO DO WHAT YOU THINK IS RIGHT FOR YOURSELF . . .
"SHE SEEMED TROUBLED, AND NO WONDER-- MY ALL-SEEING EYE DETECTED SOME KIND OF SPELL CAST ON HER. WELL! SHE HAD HELPED ME, SO I HELPED HER . . .
"I REMOVED THAT SPELL FROM HER . . .
HeeHeeHeeHee
YOU LET A MORTAL INFLUENCE YOU?
YOUR PRIORITIES ARE ALL WRONG
YOU'VE GONE SOFT
SMEK! SMAK! SMIK!
SHADDAP!

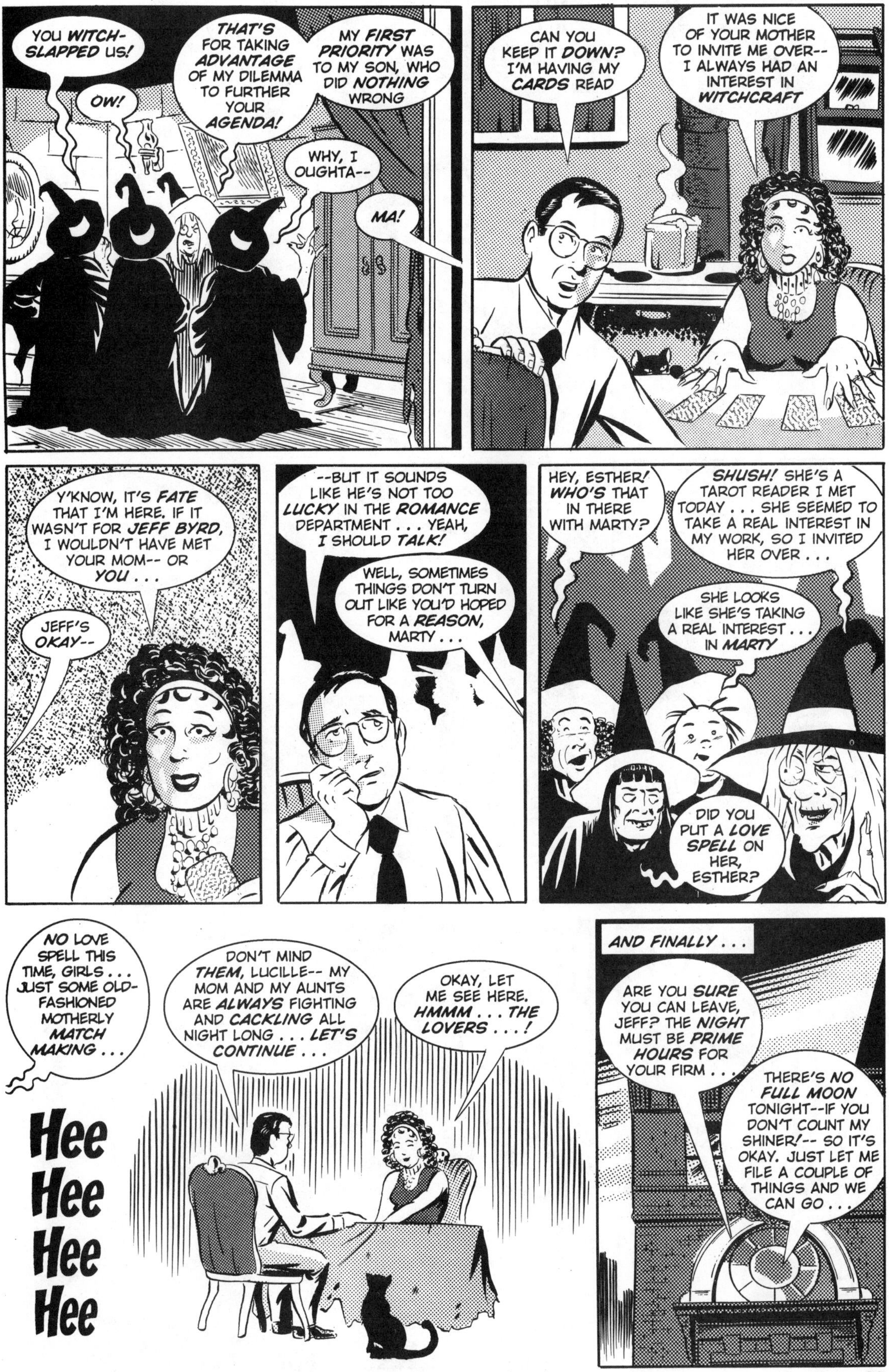
YOU WITCH-SLAPPED US!
OW!
THAT'S FOR TAKING ADVANTAGE OF MY DILEMMA TO FURTHER YOUR AGENDA!
MY FIRST PRIORITY WAS TO MY SON, WHO DID NOTHING WRONG
WHY, I OUGHTA--
MA!
CAN YOU KEEP IT DOWN? I'M HAVING MY CARDS READ
IT WAS NICE OF YOUR MOTHER TO INVITE ME OVER-- I ALWAYS HAD AN INTEREST IN WITCHCRAFT
Y'KNOW, IT'S FATE THAT I'M HERE. IF IT WASN'T FOR JEFF BYRD, I WOULDN'T HAVE MET YOUR MOM-- OR YOU . . .
JEFF'S OKAY--
--BUT IT SOUNDS LIKE HE'S NOT TOO LUCKY IN THE ROMANCE DEPARTMENT . . . YEAH, I SHOULD TALK!
WELL, SOMETIMES THINGS DON'T TURN OUT LIKE YOU'D HOPED FOR A REASON, MARTY . . .
HEY, ESTHER! WHO'S THAT IN THERE WITH MARTY?
SHUSH! SHE'S A TAROT READER I MET TODAY . . . SHE SEEMED TO TAKE A REAL INTEREST IN MY WORK, SO I INVITED HER OVER . . .
SHE LOOKS LIKE SHE'S TAKING A REAL INTEREST . . . IN MARTY
DID YOU PUT A LOVE SPELL ON HER, ESTHER?
NO LOVE SPELL THIS TIME, GIRLS . . . JUST SOME OLD-FASHIONED MOTHERLY MATCH MAKING . . .
DON'T MIND THEM, LUCILLE-- MY MOM AND MY AUNTS ARE ALWAYS FIGHTING AND CACKLING ALL NIGHT LONG . . . LET'S CONTINUE . . .
OKAY, LET ME SEE HERE. HMMM . . . THE LOVERS . . . !
Hee Hee Hee Hee
AND FINALLY . . .
ARE YOU SURE YOU CAN LEAVE, JEFF? THE NIGHT MUST BE PRIME HOURS FOR YOUR FIRM . . .
THERE'S NO FULL MOON TONIGHT--IF YOU DON'T COUNT MY SHINER!-- SO IT'S OKAY. JUST LET ME FILE A COUPLE OF THINGS AND WE CAN GO . . .

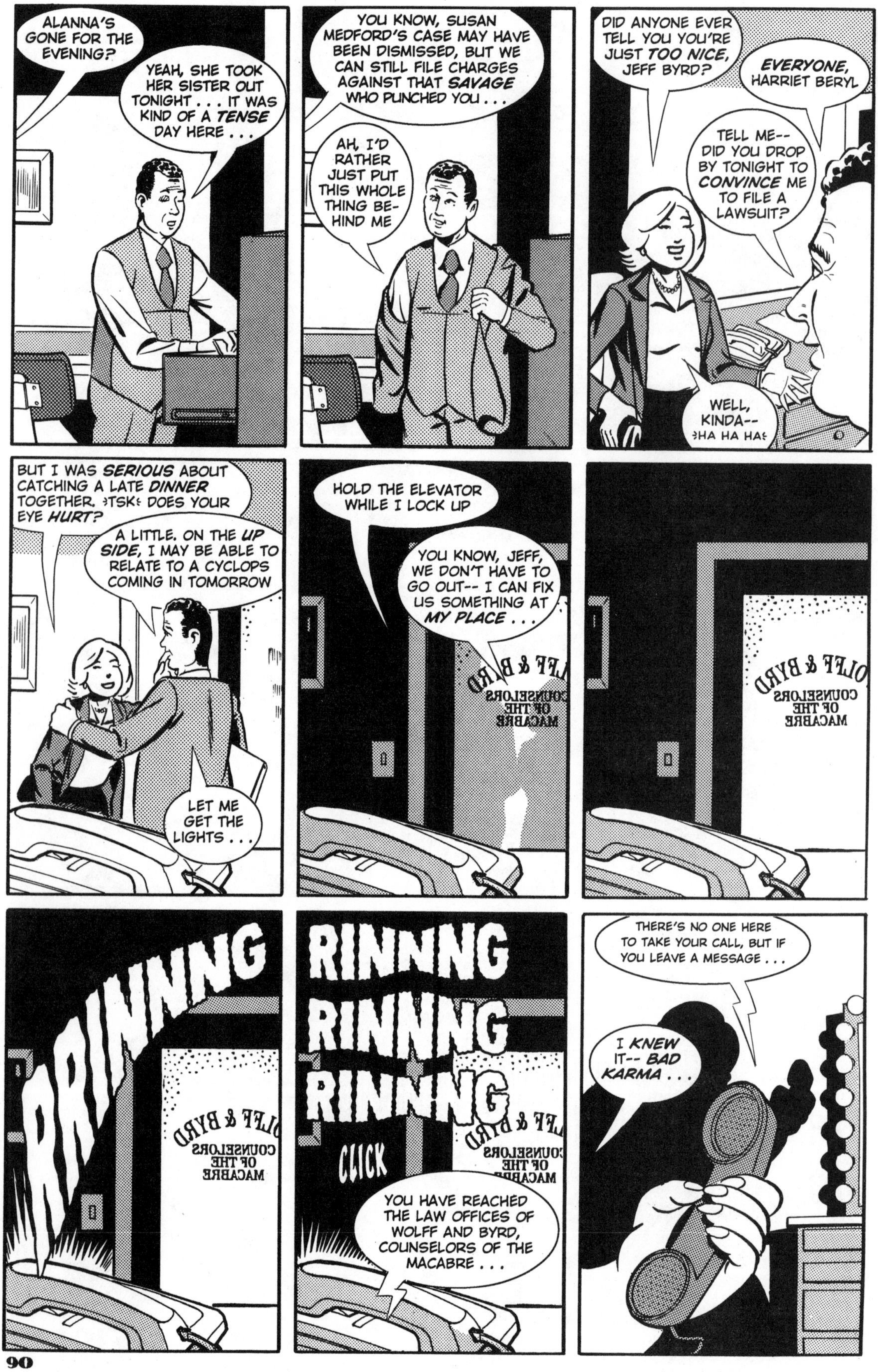
ALANNA'S GONE FOR THE EVENING?
YEAH, SHE TOOK HER SISTER OUT TONIGHT . . . IT WAS KIND OF A *TENSE* DAY HERE . . .
YOU KNOW, SUSAN MEDFORD'S CASE MAY HAVE BEEN DISMISSED, BUT WE CAN STILL FILE CHARGES AGAINST THAT *SAVAGE* WHO PUNCHED YOU . . .
AH, I'D RATHER JUST PUT THIS WHOLE THING BE-HIND ME
DID ANYONE EVER TELL YOU YOU'RE JUST *TOO NICE*, JEFF BYRD?
EVERYONE, HARRIET BERYL
TELL ME-- DID YOU DROP BY TONIGHT TO *CONVINCE* ME TO FILE A LAWSUIT?
WELL, KINDA-- ≷HA HA HA≶
BUT I WAS *SERIOUS* ABOUT CATCHING A LATE *DINNER* TOGETHER. ≷TSK≶ DOES YOUR EYE *HURT*?
A LITTLE. ON THE *UP SIDE*, I MAY BE ABLE TO RELATE TO A CYCLOPS COMING IN TOMORROW
LET ME GET THE LIGHTS . . .
HOLD THE ELEVATOR WHILE I LOCK UP
YOU KNOW, JEFF, WE DON'T HAVE TO GO OUT-- I CAN FIX US SOMETHING AT *MY PLACE* . . .
RRINNNG
RINNNG
RINNNG
RINNNG
CLICK
YOU HAVE REACHED THE LAW OFFICES OF WOLFF AND BYRD, COUNSELORS OF THE MACABRE . . .
THERE'S NO ONE HERE TO TAKE YOUR CALL, BUT IF YOU LEAVE A MESSAGE . . .
I *KNEW* IT-- *BAD KARMA* . . .

Mavis!

THE WORLD'S GREATEST SECRETARY!

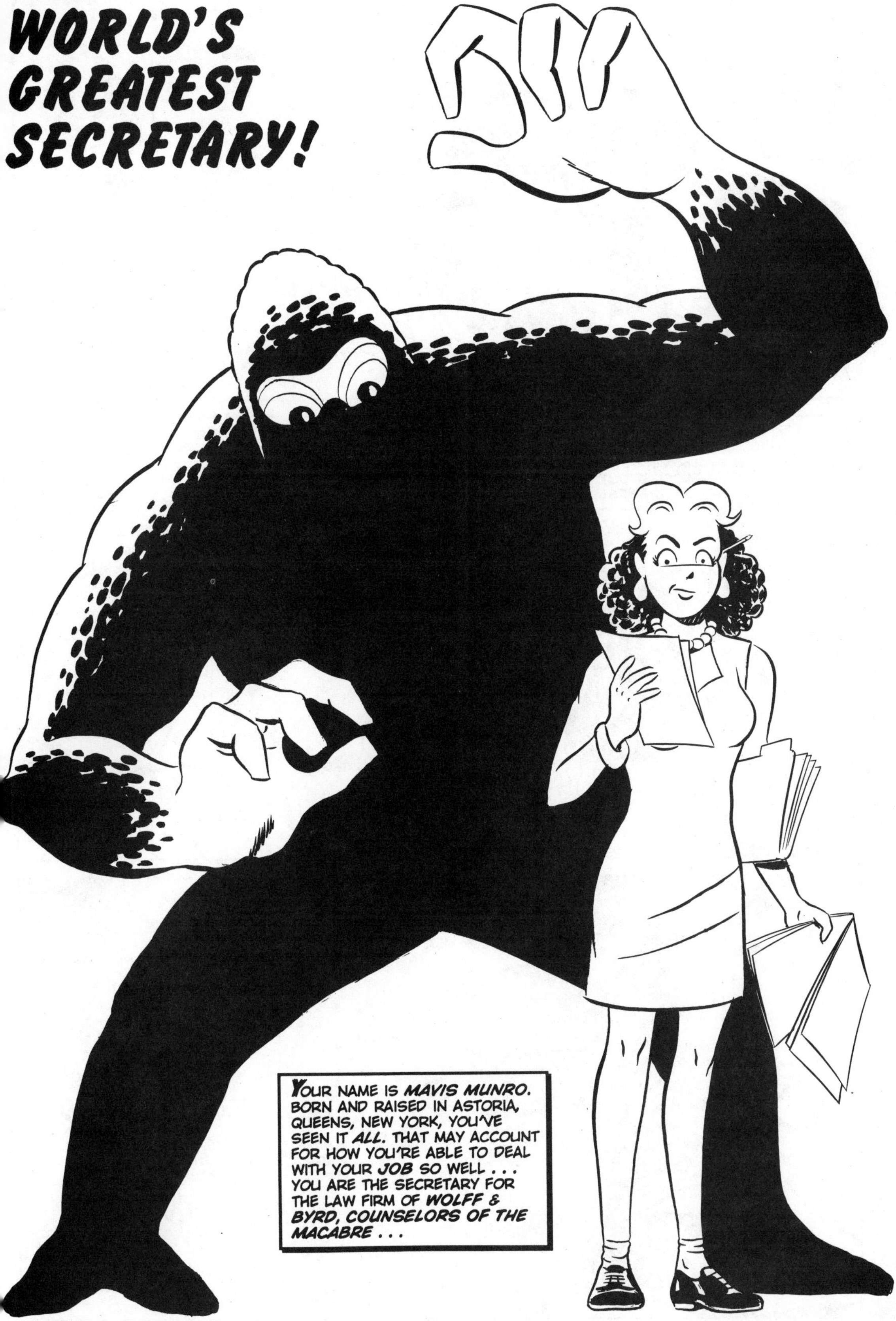
YOUR NAME IS MAVIS MUNRO. BORN AND RAISED IN ASTORIA, QUEENS, NEW YORK, YOU'VE SEEN IT ALL. THAT MAY ACCOUNT FOR HOW YOU'RE ABLE TO DEAL WITH YOUR JOB SO WELL . . . YOU ARE THE SECRETARY FOR THE LAW FIRM OF WOLFF & BYRD, COUNSELORS OF THE MACABRE . . .

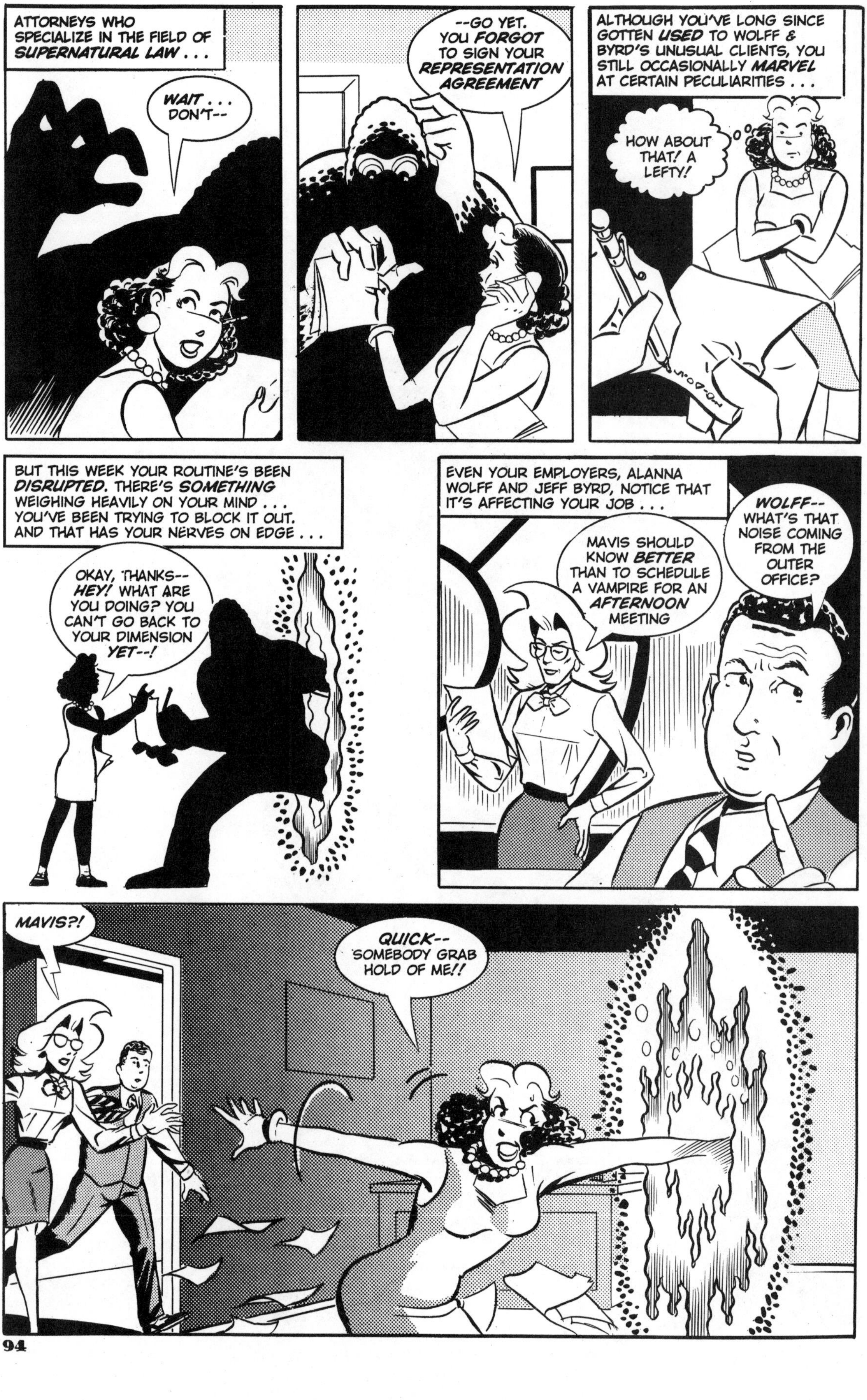
ATTORNEYS WHO SPECIALIZE IN THE FIELD OF SUPERNATURAL LAW . . .
WAIT . . . DON'T--
--GO YET. YOU FORGOT TO SIGN YOUR REPRESENTATION AGREEMENT
ALTHOUGH YOU'VE LONG SINCE GOTTEN USED TO WOLFF & BYRD'S UNUSUAL CLIENTS, YOU STILL OCCASIONALLY MARVEL AT CERTAIN PECULIARITIES . . .
HOW ABOUT THAT! A LEFTY!
BUT THIS WEEK YOUR ROUTINE'S BEEN DISRUPTED. THERE'S SOMETHING WEIGHING HEAVILY ON YOUR MIND . . . YOU'VE BEEN TRYING TO BLOCK IT OUT. AND THAT HAS YOUR NERVES ON EDGE . . .
OKAY, THANKS-- HEY! WHAT ARE YOU DOING? YOU CAN'T GO BACK TO YOUR DIMENSION YET--!
EVEN YOUR EMPLOYERS, ALANNA WOLFF AND JEFF BYRD, NOTICE THAT IT'S AFFECTING YOUR JOB . . .
MAVIS SHOULD KNOW BETTER THAN TO SCHEDULE A VAMPIRE FOR AN AFTERNOON MEETING
WOLFF-- WHAT'S THAT NOISE COMING FROM THE OUTER OFFICE?
MAVIS?!
QUICK-- SOMEBODY GRAB HOLD OF ME!!

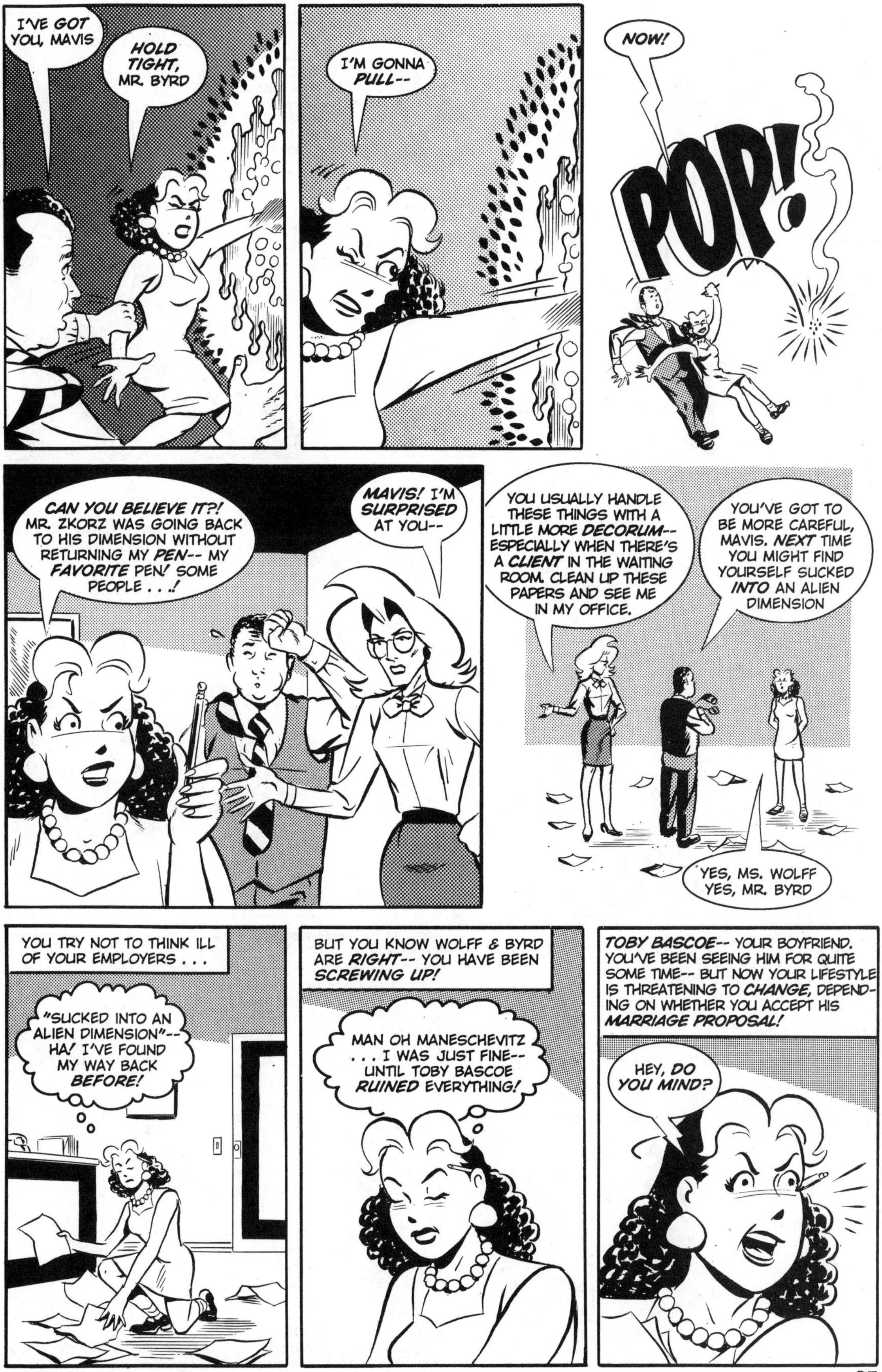
I'VE GOT YOU, MAVIS
HOLD TIGHT, MR. BYRD
I'M GONNA PULL--
NOW!
POP!
CAN YOU BELIEVE IT?! MR. ZKORZ WAS GOING BACK TO HIS DIMENSION WITHOUT RETURNING MY PEN-- MY FAVORITE PEN! SOME PEOPLE . . .!
MAVIS! I'M SURPRISED AT YOU--
YOU USUALLY HANDLE THESE THINGS WITH A LITTLE MORE DECORUM-- ESPECIALLY WHEN THERE'S A CLIENT IN THE WAITING ROOM. CLEAN UP THESE PAPERS AND SEE ME IN MY OFFICE.
YOU'VE GOT TO BE MORE CAREFUL, MAVIS. NEXT TIME YOU MIGHT FIND YOURSELF SUCKED INTO AN ALIEN DIMENSION
YES, MS. WOLFF YES, MR. BYRD
YOU TRY NOT TO THINK ILL OF YOUR EMPLOYERS . . .
"SUCKED INTO AN ALIEN DIMENSION"-- HA! I'VE FOUND MY WAY BACK BEFORE!
BUT YOU KNOW WOLFF & BYRD ARE RIGHT-- YOU HAVE BEEN SCREWING UP!
MAN OH MANESCHEVITZ . . . I WAS JUST FINE-- UNTIL TOBY BASCOE RUINED EVERYTHING!
TOBY BASCOE-- YOUR BOYFRIEND. YOU'VE BEEN SEEING HIM FOR QUITE SOME TIME-- BUT NOW YOUR LIFESTYLE IS THREATENING TO CHANGE, DEPENDING ON WHETHER YOU ACCEPT HIS MARRIAGE PROPOSAL!
HEY, DO YOU MIND?

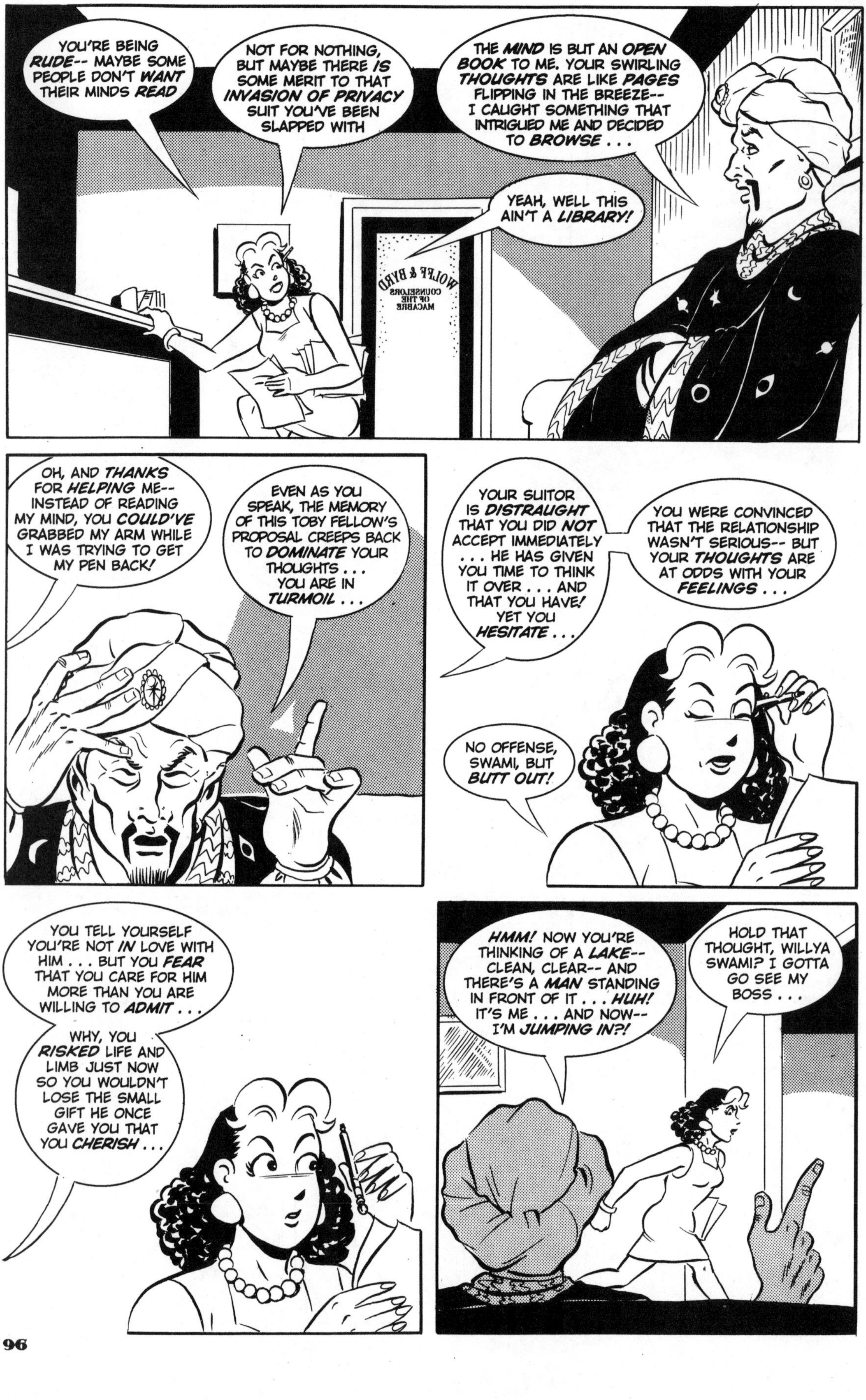
YOU'RE BEING RUDE-- MAYBE SOME PEOPLE DON'T WANT THEIR MINDS READ
NOT FOR NOTHING, BUT MAYBE THERE IS SOME MERIT TO THAT INVASION OF PRIVACY SUIT YOU'VE BEEN SLAPPED WITH
THE MIND IS BUT AN OPEN BOOK TO ME. YOUR SWIRLING THOUGHTS ARE LIKE PAGES FLIPPING IN THE BREEZE-- I CAUGHT SOMETHING THAT INTRIGUED ME AND DECIDED TO BROWSE . . .
YEAH, WELL THIS AIN'T A LIBRARY!
OH, AND THANKS FOR HELPING ME-- INSTEAD OF READING MY MIND, YOU COULD'VE GRABBED MY ARM WHILE I WAS TRYING TO GET MY PEN BACK!
EVEN AS YOU SPEAK, THE MEMORY OF THIS TOBY FELLOW'S PROPOSAL CREEPS BACK TO DOMINATE YOUR THOUGHTS . . . YOU ARE IN TURMOIL . . .
YOUR SUITOR IS DISTRAUGHT THAT YOU DID NOT ACCEPT IMMEDIATELY . . . HE HAS GIVEN YOU TIME TO THINK IT OVER . . . AND THAT YOU HAVE! YET YOU HESITATE . . .
YOU WERE CONVINCED THAT THE RELATIONSHIP WASN'T SERIOUS-- BUT YOUR THOUGHTS ARE AT ODDS WITH YOUR FEELINGS . . .
NO OFFENSE, SWAMI, BUT BUTT OUT!
YOU TELL YOURSELF YOU'RE NOT IN LOVE WITH HIM . . . BUT YOU FEAR THAT YOU CARE FOR HIM MORE THAN YOU ARE WILLING TO ADMIT . . .
WHY, YOU RISKED LIFE AND LIMB JUST NOW SO YOU WOULDN'T LOSE THE SMALL GIFT HE ONCE GAVE YOU THAT YOU CHERISH . . .
HMM! NOW YOU'RE THINKING OF A LAKE-- CLEAN, CLEAR-- AND THERE'S A MAN STANDING IN FRONT OF IT . . . HUH! IT'S ME . . . AND NOW-- I'M JUMPING IN?!
HOLD THAT THOUGHT, WILLYA SWAMI? I GOTTA GO SEE MY BOSS . . .

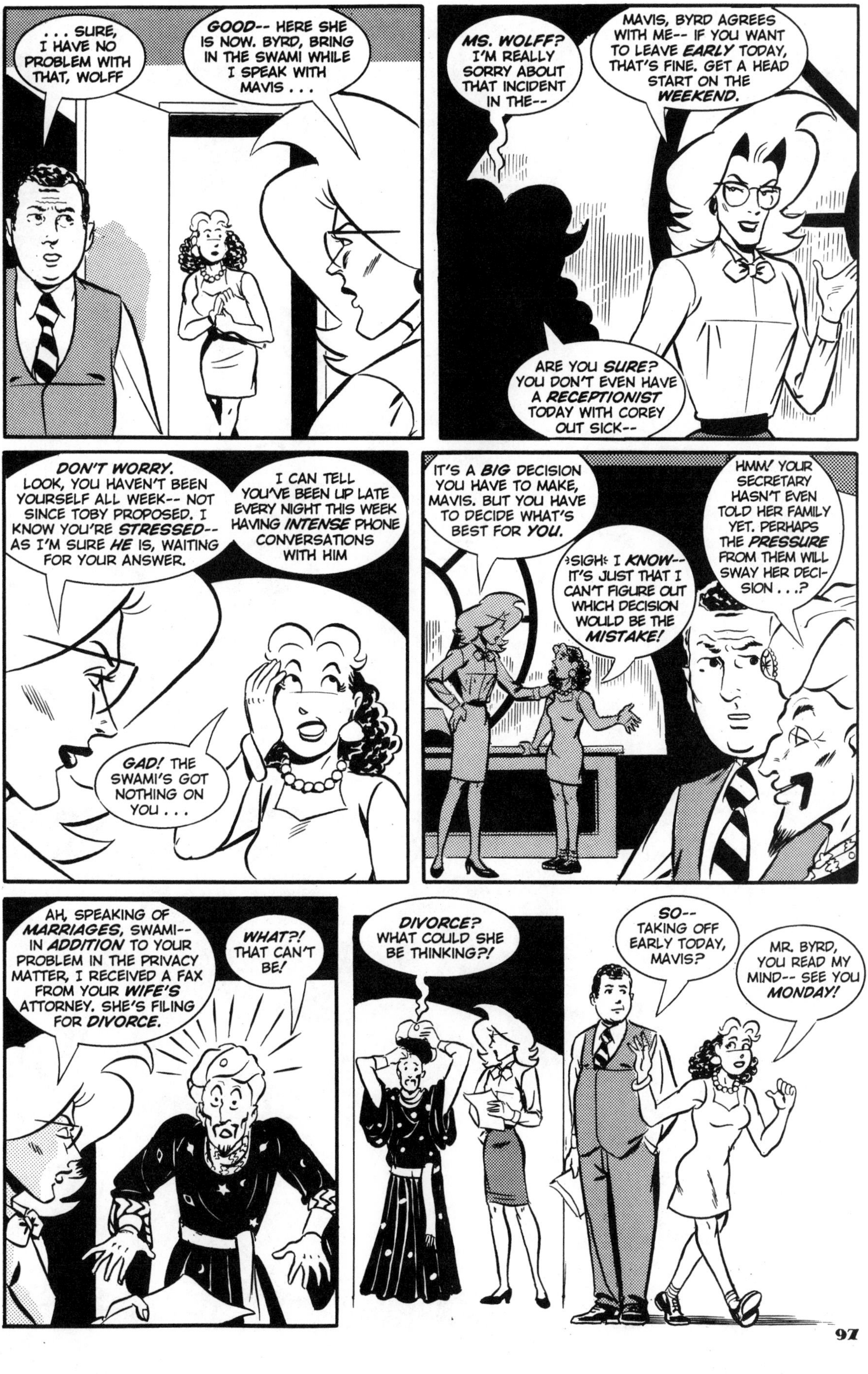

. . . SURE, I HAVE NO PROBLEM WITH THAT, WOLFF
GOOD-- HERE SHE IS NOW. BYRD, BRING IN THE SWAMI WHILE I SPEAK WITH MAVIS . . .
MS. WOLFF? I'M REALLY SORRY ABOUT THAT INCIDENT IN THE--
MAVIS, BYRD AGREES WITH ME-- IF YOU WANT TO LEAVE EARLY TODAY, THAT'S FINE. GET A HEAD START ON THE WEEKEND.
ARE YOU SURE? YOU DON'T EVEN HAVE A RECEPTIONIST TODAY WITH COREY OUT SICK--
DON'T WORRY. LOOK, YOU HAVEN'T BEEN YOURSELF ALL WEEK-- NOT SINCE TOBY PROPOSED. I KNOW YOU'RE STRESSED-- AS I'M SURE HE IS, WAITING FOR YOUR ANSWER.
I CAN TELL YOU'VE BEEN UP LATE EVERY NIGHT THIS WEEK HAVING INTENSE PHONE CONVERSATIONS WITH HIM
GAD! THE SWAMI'S GOT NOTHING ON YOU . . .
IT'S A BIG DECISION YOU HAVE TO MAKE, MAVIS. BUT YOU HAVE TO DECIDE WHAT'S BEST FOR YOU.
SIGH I KNOW-- IT'S JUST THAT I CAN'T FIGURE OUT WHICH DECISION WOULD BE THE MISTAKE!
HMM! YOUR SECRETARY HASN'T EVEN TOLD HER FAMILY YET. PERHAPS THE PRESSURE FROM THEM WILL SWAY HER DECISION . . .?
AH, SPEAKING OF MARRIAGES, SWAMI-- IN ADDITION TO YOUR PROBLEM IN THE PRIVACY MATTER, I RECEIVED A FAX FROM YOUR WIFE'S ATTORNEY. SHE'S FILING FOR DIVORCE.
WHAT?! THAT CAN'T BE!
DIVORCE? WHAT COULD SHE BE THINKING?!
SO-- TAKING OFF EARLY TODAY, MAVIS?
MR. BYRD, YOU READ MY MIND-- SEE YOU MONDAY!

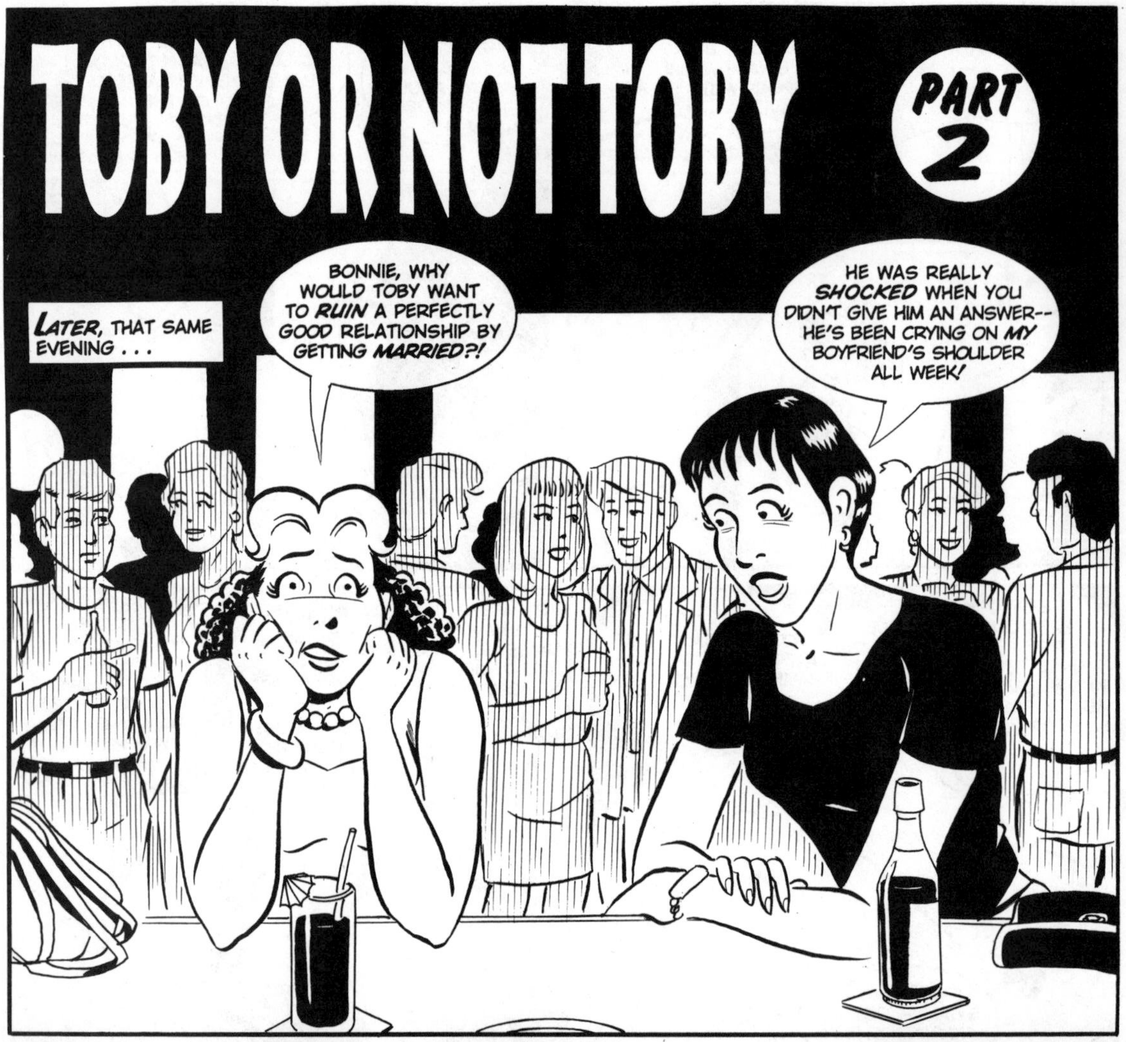
TOBY OR NOT TOBY
PART 2
LATER, THAT SAME EVENING . . .
BONNIE, WHY WOULD TOBY WANT TO RUIN A PERFECTLY GOOD RELATIONSHIP BY GETTING MARRIED?!
HE WAS REALLY SHOCKED WHEN YOU DIDN'T GIVE HIM AN ANSWER-- HE'S BEEN CRYING ON MY BOYFRIEND'S SHOULDER ALL WEEK!

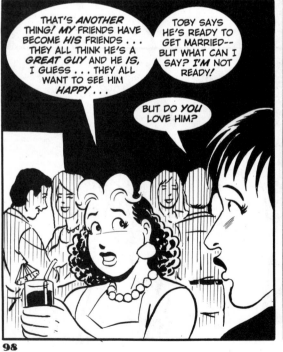

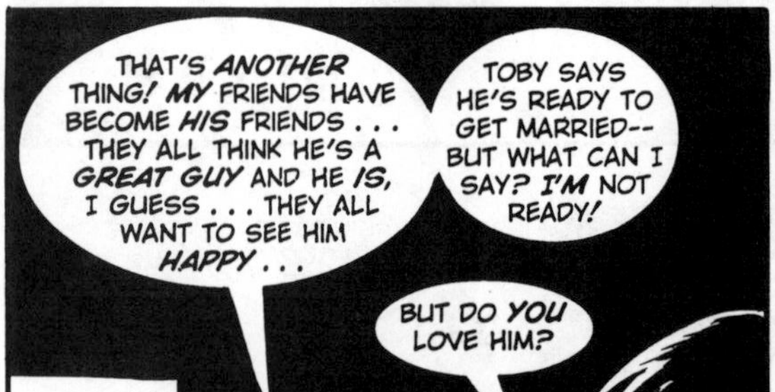
TOBY SAYS HE'S READY TO GET MARRIED-- BUT WHAT CAN I SAY? I'M NOT READY!
THAT'S ANOTHER THING! MY FRIENDS HAVE BECOME HIS FRIENDS . . . THEY ALL THINK HE'S A GREAT GUY AND HE IS, I GUESS . . . THEY ALL WANT TO SEE HIM HAPPY . . .
BUT DO YOU LOVE HIM?

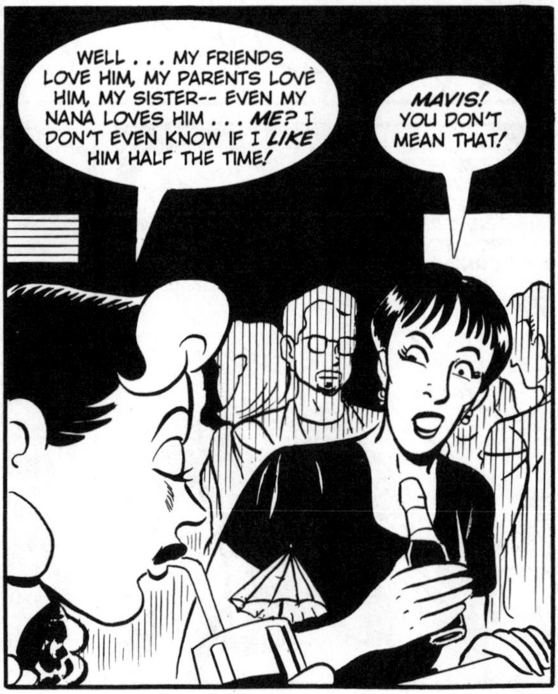
WELL . . . MY FRIENDS LOVE HIM, MY PARENTS LOVE HIM, MY SISTER-- EVEN MY NANA LOVES HIM . . . ME? I DON'T EVEN KNOW IF I LIKE HIM HALF THE TIME!
MAVIS! YOU DON'T MEAN THAT!

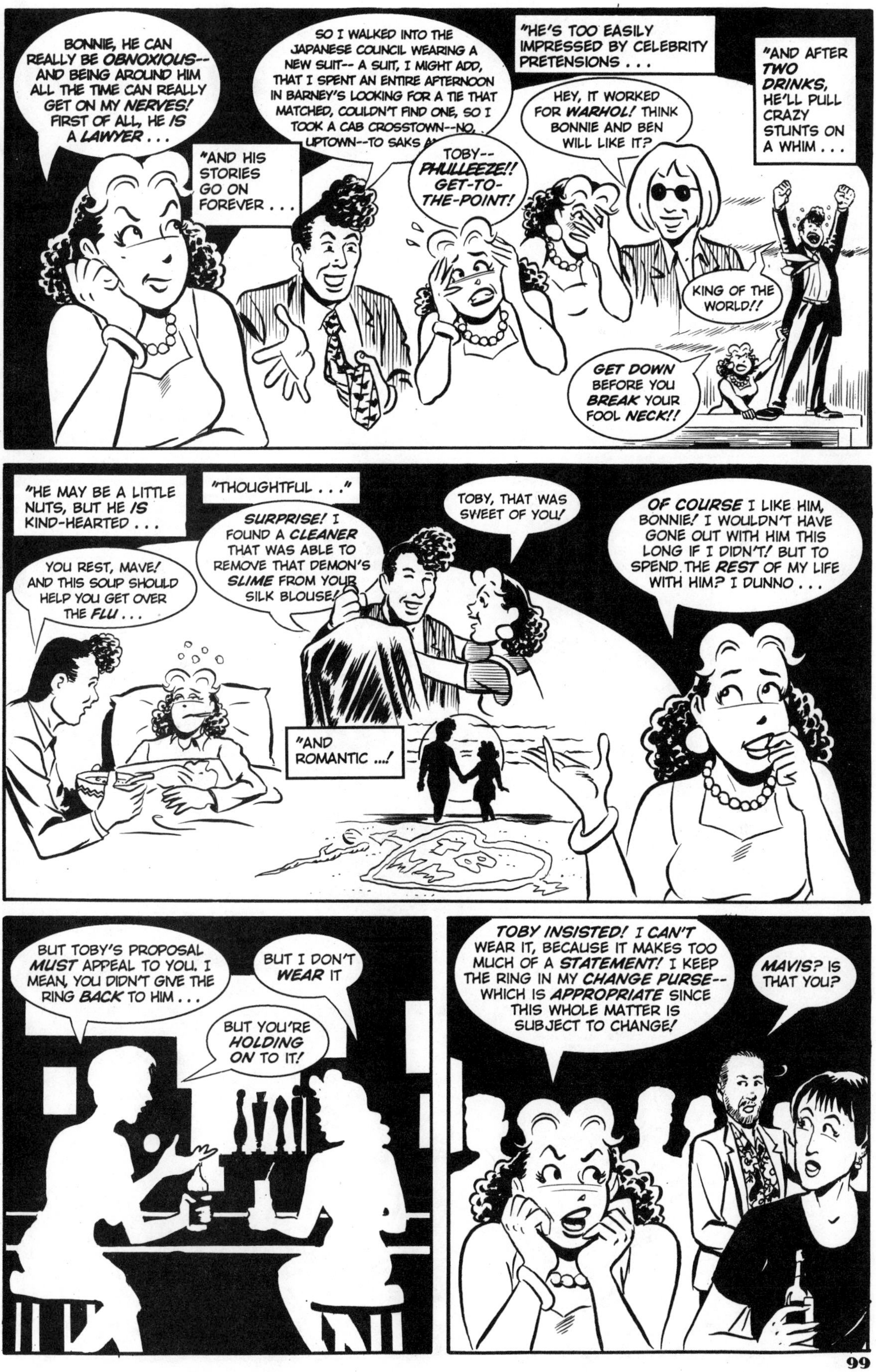
BONNIE, HE CAN REALLY BE OBNOXIOUS-- AND BEING AROUND HIM ALL THE TIME CAN REALLY GET ON MY NERVES! FIRST OF ALL, HE IS A LAWYER . . .
"AND HIS STORIES GO ON FOREVER . . .
SO I WALKED INTO THE JAPANESE COUNCIL WEARING A NEW SUIT-- A SUIT, I MIGHT ADD, THAT I SPENT AN ENTIRE AFTERNOON IN BARNEY'S LOOKING FOR A TIE THAT MATCHED, COULDN'T FIND ONE, SO I TOOK A CAB CROSSTOWN--NO, UPTOWN--TO SAKS
TOBY-- PHULLEEZE!! GET-TO-THE-POINT!
"HE'S TOO EASILY IMPRESSED BY CELEBRITY PRETENSIONS . . .
HEY, IT WORKED FOR WARHOL! THINK BONNIE AND BEN WILL LIKE IT?
"AND AFTER TWO DRINKS, HE'LL PULL CRAZY STUNTS ON A WHIM . . .
KING OF THE WORLD!!
GET DOWN BEFORE YOU BREAK YOUR FOOL NECK!!
"HE MAY BE A LITTLE NUTS, BUT HE IS KIND-HEARTED . . .
YOU REST, MAVE! AND THIS SOUP SHOULD HELP YOU GET OVER THE FLU . . .
"THOUGHTFUL . . ."
SURPRISE! I FOUND A CLEANER THAT WAS ABLE TO REMOVE THAT DEMON'S SLIME FROM YOUR SILK BLOUSE!
TOBY, THAT WAS SWEET OF YOU!
"AND ROMANTIC ...!
OF COURSE I LIKE HIM, BONNIE! I WOULDN'T HAVE GONE OUT WITH HIM THIS LONG IF I DIDN'T! BUT TO SPEND THE REST OF MY LIFE WITH HIM? I DUNNO . . .
BUT TOBY'S PROPOSAL MUST APPEAL TO YOU. I MEAN, YOU DIDN'T GIVE THE RING BACK TO HIM . . .
BUT I DON'T WEAR IT
BUT YOU'RE HOLDING ON TO IT!
TOBY INSISTED! I CAN'T WEAR IT, BECAUSE IT MAKES TOO MUCH OF A STATEMENT! I KEEP THE RING IN MY CHANGE PURSE-- WHICH IS APPROPRIATE SINCE THIS WHOLE MATTER IS SUBJECT TO CHANGE!
MAVIS? IS THAT YOU?

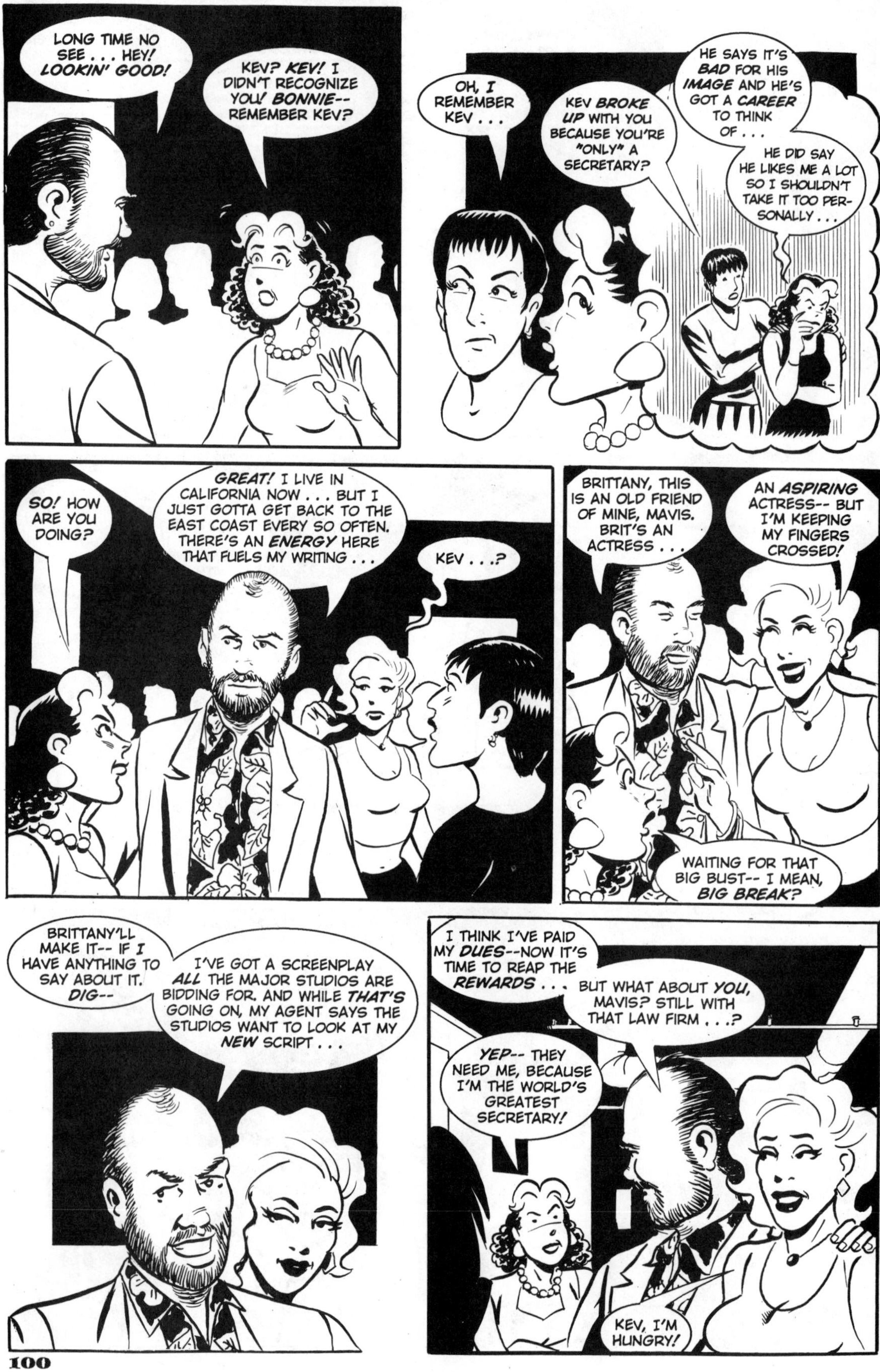
LONG TIME NO SEE . . . HEY! LOOKIN' GOOD!
KEV? KEV! I DIDN'T RECOGNIZE YOU! BONNIE-- REMEMBER KEV?
OH, I REMEMBER KEV . . .
KEV BROKE UP WITH YOU BECAUSE YOU'RE "ONLY" A SECRETARY?
HE SAYS IT'S BAD FOR HIS IMAGE AND HE'S GOT A CAREER TO THINK OF . . .
HE DID SAY HE LIKES ME A LOT SO I SHOULDN'T TAKE IT TOO PERSONALLY . . .
SO! HOW ARE YOU DOING?
GREAT! I LIVE IN CALIFORNIA NOW . . . BUT I JUST GOTTA GET BACK TO THE EAST COAST EVERY SO OFTEN. THERE'S AN ENERGY HERE THAT FUELS MY WRITING . . .
KEV . . .?
BRITTANY, THIS IS AN OLD FRIEND OF MINE, MAVIS. BRIT'S AN ACTRESS . . .
AN ASPIRING ACTRESS-- BUT I'M KEEPING MY FINGERS CROSSED!
WAITING FOR THAT BIG BUST-- I MEAN, BIG BREAK?
BRITTANY'LL MAKE IT-- IF I HAVE ANYTHING TO SAY ABOUT IT. DIG--
I'VE GOT A SCREENPLAY ALL THE MAJOR STUDIOS ARE BIDDING FOR. AND WHILE THAT'S GOING ON, MY AGENT SAYS THE STUDIOS WANT TO LOOK AT MY NEW SCRIPT . . .
I THINK I'VE PAID MY DUES--NOW IT'S TIME TO REAP THE REWARDS . . .
BUT WHAT ABOUT YOU, MAVIS? STILL WITH THAT LAW FIRM . . .?
YEP-- THEY NEED ME, BECAUSE I'M THE WORLD'S GREATEST SECRETARY!
KEV, I'M HUNGRY!

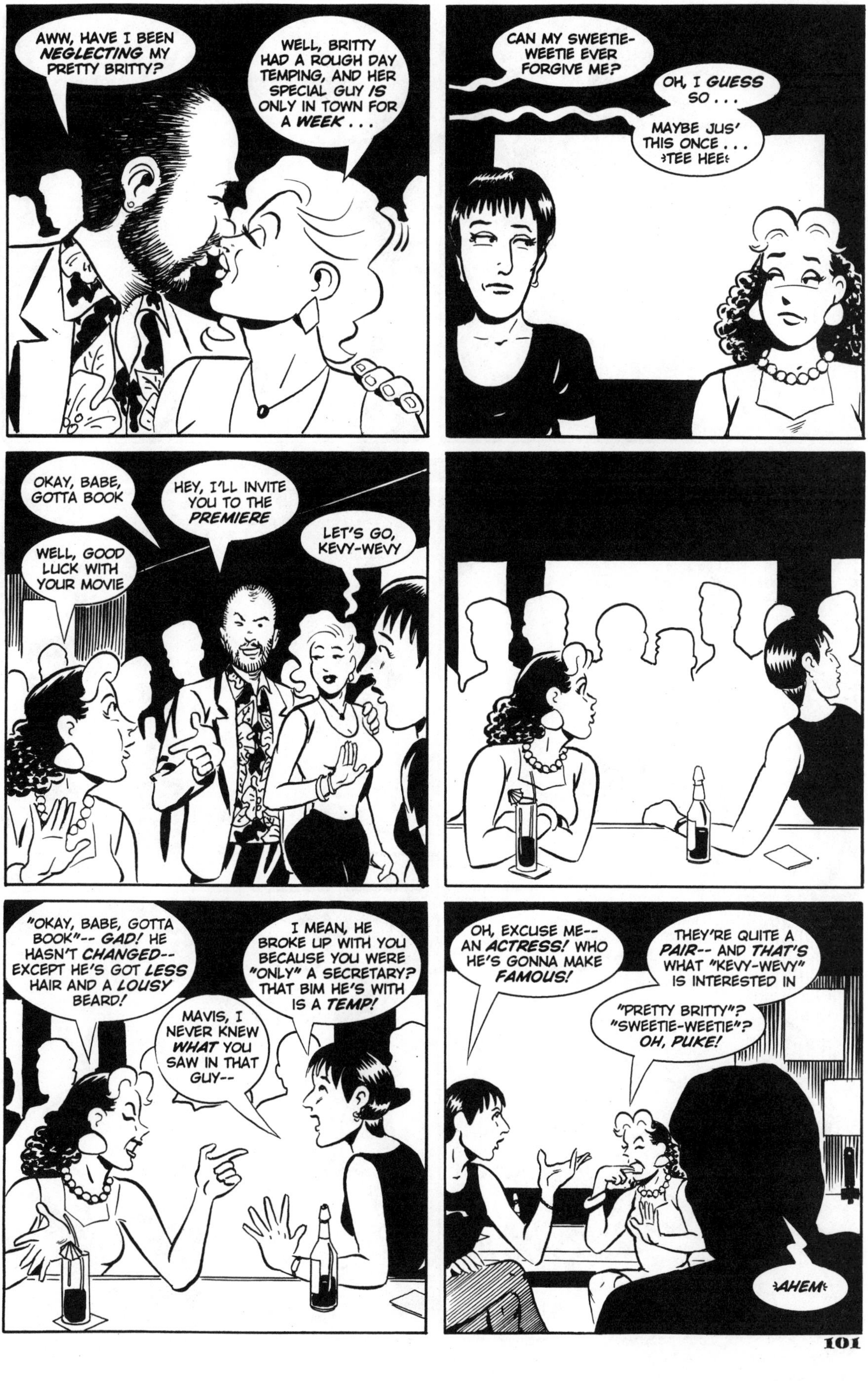
AWW, HAVE I BEEN NEGLECTING MY PRETTY BRITTY?
WELL, BRITTY HAD A ROUGH DAY TEMPING, AND HER SPECIAL GUY IS ONLY IN TOWN FOR A WEEK . . .
CAN MY SWEETIE-WEETIE EVER FORGIVE ME?
OH, I GUESS SO . . .
MAYBE JUS' THIS ONCE . . . TEE HEE
OKAY, BABE, GOTTA BOOK
WELL, GOOD LUCK WITH YOUR MOVIE
HEY, I'LL INVITE YOU TO THE PREMIERE
LET'S GO, KEVY-WEVY
"OKAY, BABE, GOTTA BOOK"-- GAD! HE HASN'T CHANGED-- EXCEPT HE'S GOT LESS HAIR AND A LOUSY BEARD!
MAVIS, I NEVER KNEW WHAT YOU SAW IN THAT GUY--
I MEAN, HE BROKE UP WITH YOU BECAUSE YOU WERE "ONLY" A SECRETARY? THAT BIM HE'S WITH IS A TEMP!
OH, EXCUSE ME-- AN ACTRESS! WHO HE'S GONNA MAKE FAMOUS!
THEY'RE QUITE A PAIR-- AND THAT'S WHAT "KEVY-WEVY" IS INTERESTED IN
"PRETTY BRITTY"? "SWEETIE-WEETIE"? OH, PUKE!
AHEM

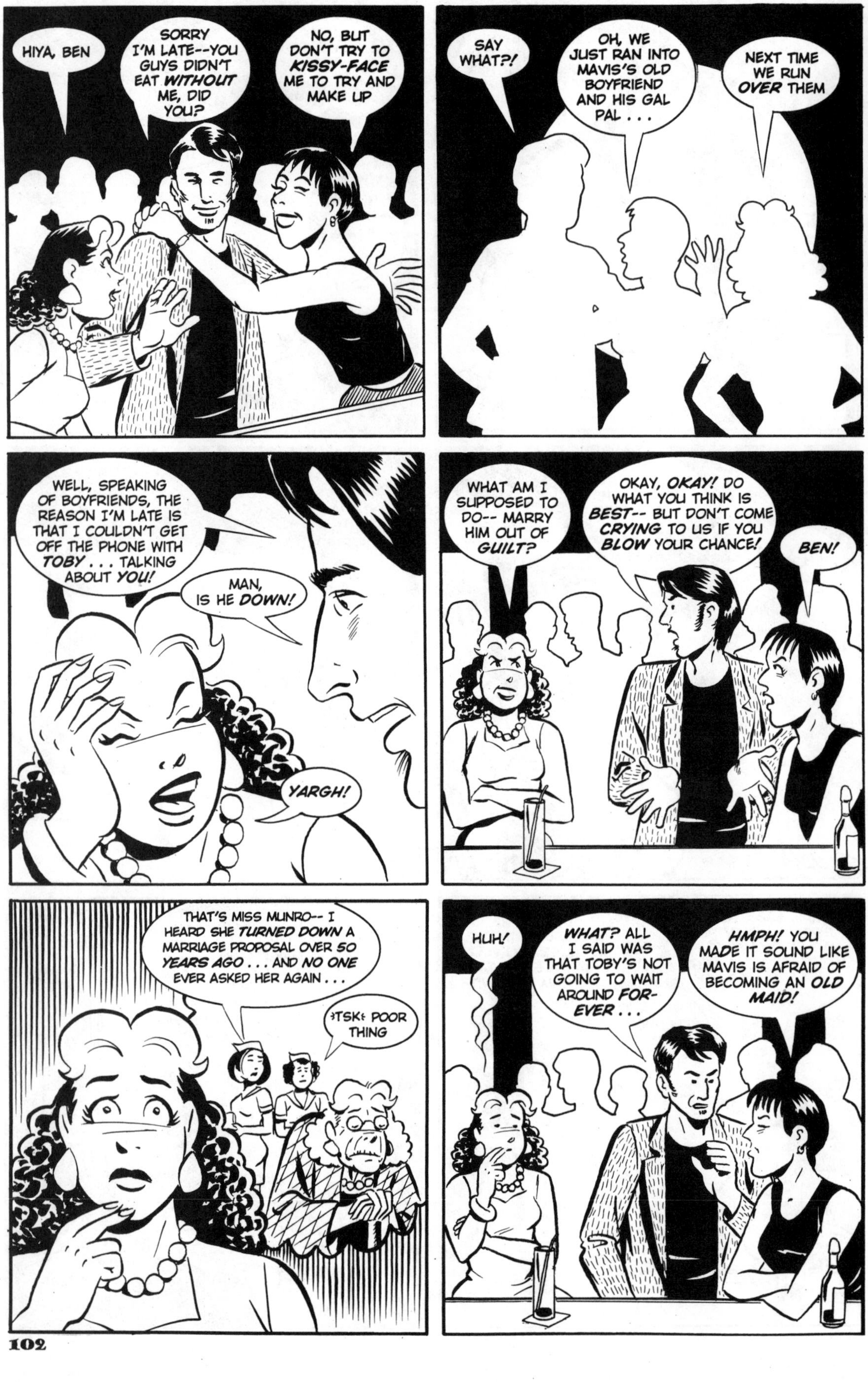
HIYA, BEN
SORRY I'M LATE--YOU GUYS DIDN'T EAT WITHOUT ME, DID YOU?
NO, BUT DON'T TRY TO KISSY-FACE ME TO TRY AND MAKE UP
SAY WHAT?!
OH, WE JUST RAN INTO MAVIS'S OLD BOYFRIEND AND HIS GAL PAL . . .
NEXT TIME WE RUN OVER THEM
WELL, SPEAKING OF BOYFRIENDS, THE REASON I'M LATE IS THAT I COULDN'T GET OFF THE PHONE WITH TOBY . . . TALKING ABOUT YOU!
MAN, IS HE DOWN!
YARGH!
WHAT AM I SUPPOSED TO DO-- MARRY HIM OUT OF GUILT?
OKAY, OKAY! DO WHAT YOU THINK IS BEST-- BUT DON'T COME CRYING TO US IF YOU BLOW YOUR CHANCE!
BEN!
THAT'S MISS MUNRO-- I HEARD SHE TURNED DOWN A MARRIAGE PROPOSAL OVER 50 YEARS AGO . . . AND NO ONE EVER ASKED HER AGAIN . . .
TSK POOR THING
HUH!
WHAT? ALL I SAID WAS THAT TOBY'S NOT GOING TO WAIT AROUND FOR-EVER . . .
HMPH! YOU MADE IT SOUND LIKE MAVIS IS AFRAID OF BECOMING AN OLD MAID!

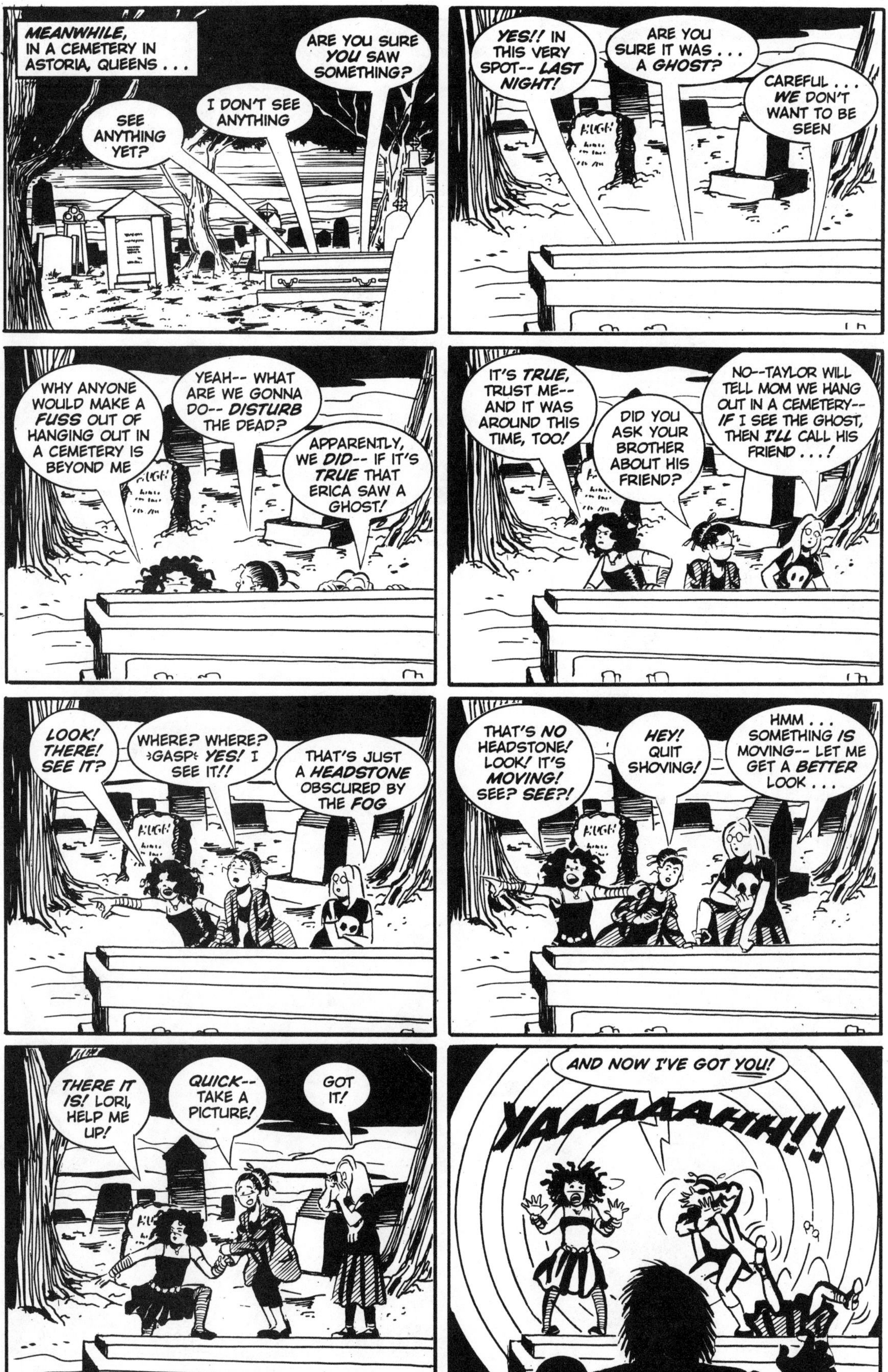
MEANWHILE, IN A CEMETERY IN ASTORIA, QUEENS . . .
SEE ANYTHING YET?
I DON'T SEE ANYTHING
ARE YOU SURE YOU SAW SOMETHING?
YES!! IN THIS VERY SPOT-- LAST NIGHT!
ARE YOU SURE IT WAS . . . A GHOST?
CAREFUL . . . WE DON'T WANT TO BE SEEN
WHY ANYONE WOULD MAKE A FUSS OUT OF HANGING OUT IN A CEMETERY IS BEYOND ME
YEAH-- WHAT ARE WE GONNA DO-- DISTURB THE DEAD?
APPARENTLY, WE DID-- IF IT'S TRUE THAT ERICA SAW A GHOST!
IT'S TRUE, TRUST ME-- AND IT WAS AROUND THIS TIME, TOO!
DID YOU ASK YOUR BROTHER ABOUT HIS FRIEND?
NO--TAYLOR WILL TELL MOM WE HANG OUT IN A CEMETERY-- IF I SEE THE GHOST, THEN I'LL CALL HIS FRIEND . . . !
LOOK! THERE! SEE IT?
WHERE? WHERE? ¿GASP¿ YES! I SEE IT!!
THAT'S JUST A HEADSTONE OBSCURED BY THE FOG
THAT'S NO HEADSTONE! LOOK! IT'S MOVING! SEE? SEE?!
HEY! QUIT SHOVING!
HMM . . . SOMETHING IS MOVING-- LET ME GET A BETTER LOOK . . .
THERE IT IS! LORI, HELP ME UP!
QUICK-- TAKE A PICTURE!
GOT IT!
AND NOW I'VE GOT YOU!
YAAAAAHH!!

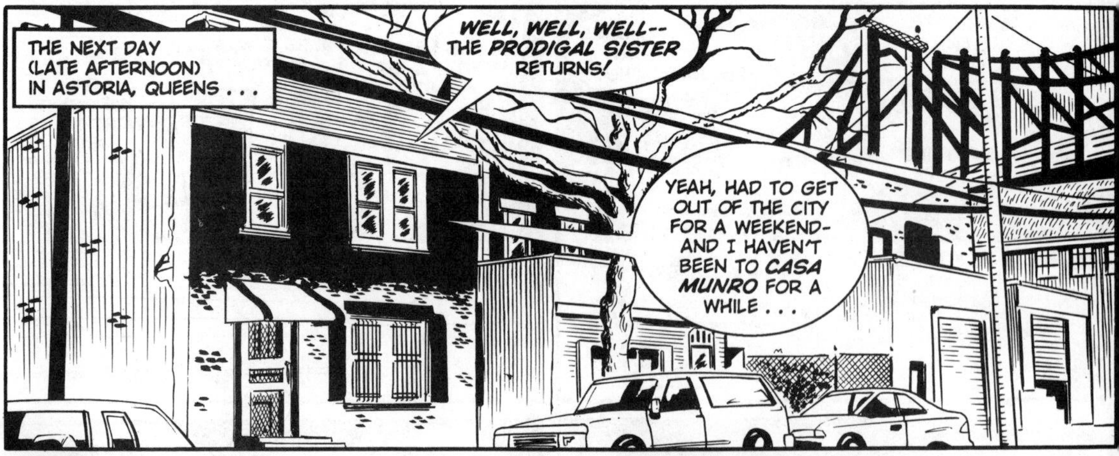
THE NEXT DAY (LATE AFTERNOON) IN ASTORIA, QUEENS . . .
WELL, WELL, WELL-- THE PRODIGAL SISTER RETURNS!
YEAH, HAD TO GET OUT OF THE CITY FOR A WEEKEND- AND I HAVEN'T BEEN TO CASA MUNRO FOR A WHILE . . .

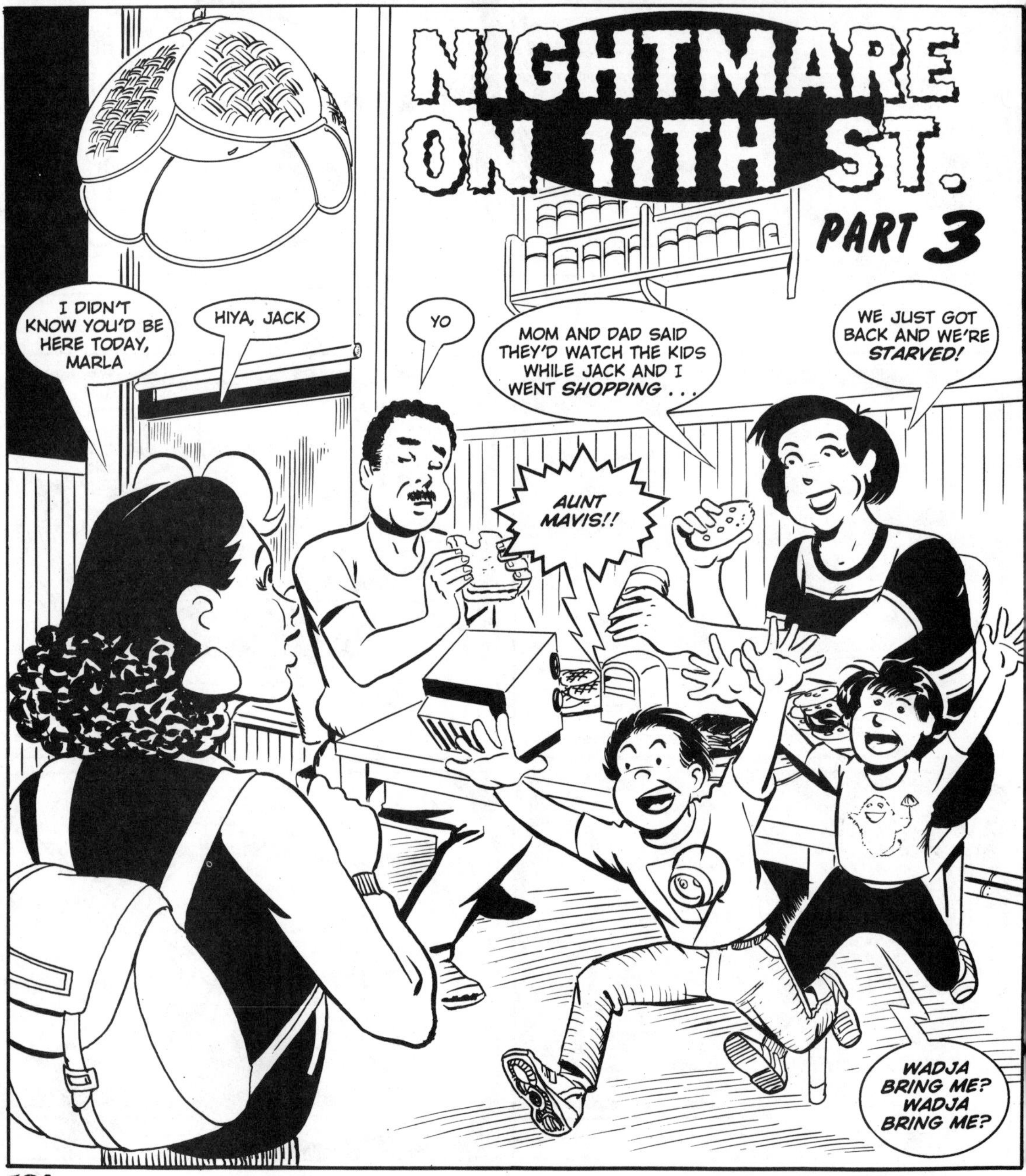
NIGHTMARE ON 11TH ST.
PART 3
I DIDN'T KNOW YOU'D BE HERE TODAY, MARLA
HIYA, JACK
YO
MOM AND DAD SAID THEY'D WATCH THE KIDS WHILE JACK AND I WENT SHOPPING . . .
WE JUST GOT BACK AND WE'RE STARVED!
AUNT MAVIS!!
WADJA BRING ME? WADJA BRING ME?

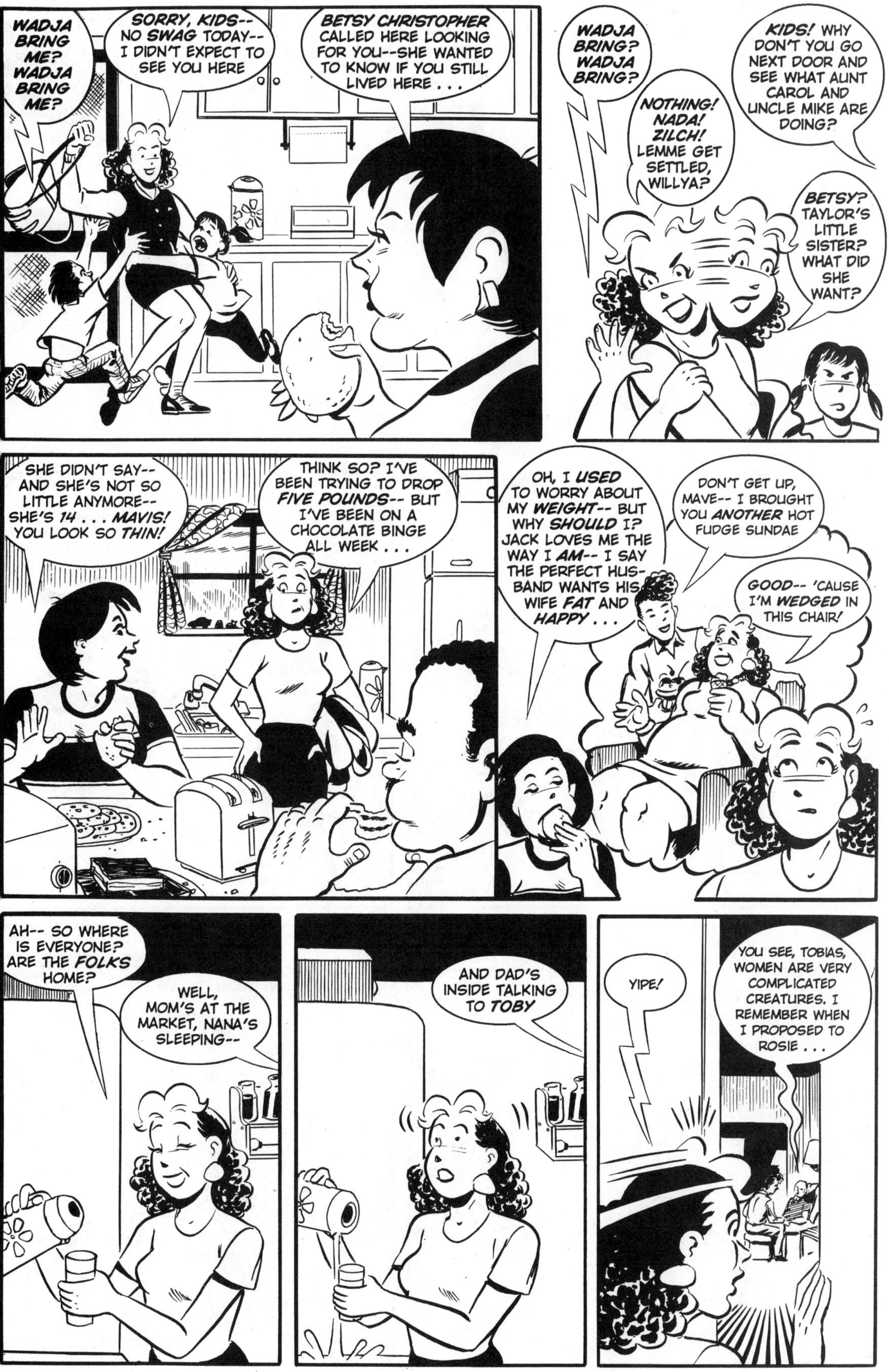
WADJA BRING ME? WADJA BRING ME?
SORRY, KIDS-- NO SWAG TODAY-- I DIDN'T EXPECT TO SEE YOU HERE
BETSY CHRISTOPHER CALLED HERE LOOKING FOR YOU--SHE WANTED TO KNOW IF YOU STILL LIVED HERE . . .
WADJA BRING? WADJA BRING?
NOTHING! NADA! ZILCH! LEMME GET SETTLED, WILLYA?
KIDS! WHY DON'T YOU GO NEXT DOOR AND SEE WHAT AUNT CAROL AND UNCLE MIKE ARE DOING?
BETSY? TAYLOR'S LITTLE SISTER? WHAT DID SHE WANT?
SHE DIDN'T SAY-- AND SHE'S NOT SO LITTLE ANYMORE-- SHE'S 14 . . . MAVIS! YOU LOOK SO THIN!
THINK SO? I'VE BEEN TRYING TO DROP FIVE POUNDS-- BUT I'VE BEEN ON A CHOCOLATE BINGE ALL WEEK . . .
OH, I USED TO WORRY ABOUT MY WEIGHT-- BUT WHY SHOULD I? JACK LOVES ME THE WAY I AM-- I SAY THE PERFECT HUSBAND WANTS HIS WIFE FAT AND HAPPY . . .
DON'T GET UP, MAVE-- I BROUGHT YOU ANOTHER HOT FUDGE SUNDAE
GOOD-- 'CAUSE I'M WEDGED IN THIS CHAIR!
AH-- SO WHERE IS EVERYONE? ARE THE FOLKS HOME?
WELL, MOM'S AT THE MARKET, NANA'S SLEEPING--
AND DAD'S INSIDE TALKING TO TOBY
YIPE!
YOU SEE, TOBIAS, WOMEN ARE VERY COMPLICATED CREATURES. I REMEMBER WHEN I PROPOSED TO ROSIE . . .

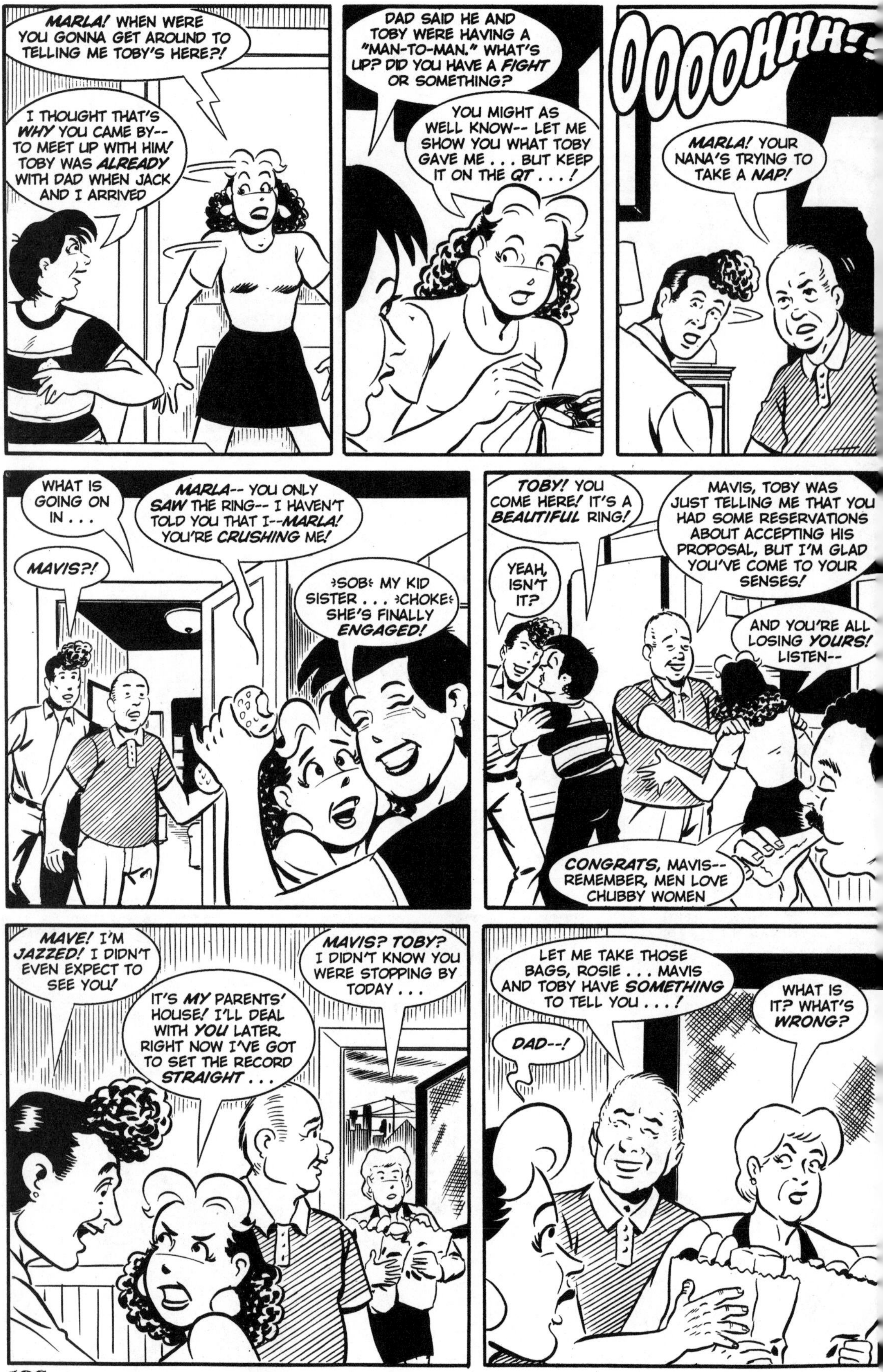
MARLA! WHEN WERE YOU GONNA GET AROUND TO TELLING ME TOBY'S HERE?!
I THOUGHT THAT'S WHY YOU CAME BY-- TO MEET UP WITH HIM! TOBY WAS ALREADY WITH DAD WHEN JACK AND I ARRIVED
DAD SAID HE AND TOBY WERE HAVING A "MAN-TO-MAN." WHAT'S UP? DID YOU HAVE A FIGHT OR SOMETHING?
YOU MIGHT AS WELL KNOW-- LET ME SHOW YOU WHAT TOBY GAVE ME . . . BUT KEEP IT ON THE QT . . . !
OOOOHHH!
MARLA! YOUR NANA'S TRYING TO TAKE A NAP!
WHAT IS GOING ON IN . . .
MAVIS?!
MARLA-- YOU ONLY SAW THE RING-- I HAVEN'T TOLD YOU THAT I--MARLA! YOU'RE CRUSHING ME!
SOB MY KID SISTER . . . CHOKE SHE'S FINALLY ENGAGED!
TOBY! YOU COME HERE! IT'S A BEAUTIFUL RING!
YEAH, ISN'T IT?
MAVIS, TOBY WAS JUST TELLING ME THAT YOU HAD SOME RESERVATIONS ABOUT ACCEPTING HIS PROPOSAL, BUT I'M GLAD YOU'VE COME TO YOUR SENSES!
AND YOU'RE ALL LOSING YOURS! LISTEN--
CONGRATS, MAVIS-- REMEMBER, MEN LOVE CHUBBY WOMEN
MAVE! I'M JAZZED! I DIDN'T EVEN EXPECT TO SEE YOU!
IT'S MY PARENTS' HOUSE! I'LL DEAL WITH YOU LATER. RIGHT NOW I'VE GOT TO SET THE RECORD STRAIGHT . . .
MAVIS? TOBY? I DIDN'T KNOW YOU WERE STOPPING BY TODAY . . .
LET ME TAKE THOSE BAGS, ROSIE . . . MAVIS AND TOBY HAVE SOMETHING TO TELL YOU . . . !
DAD--!
WHAT IS IT? WHAT'S WRONG?

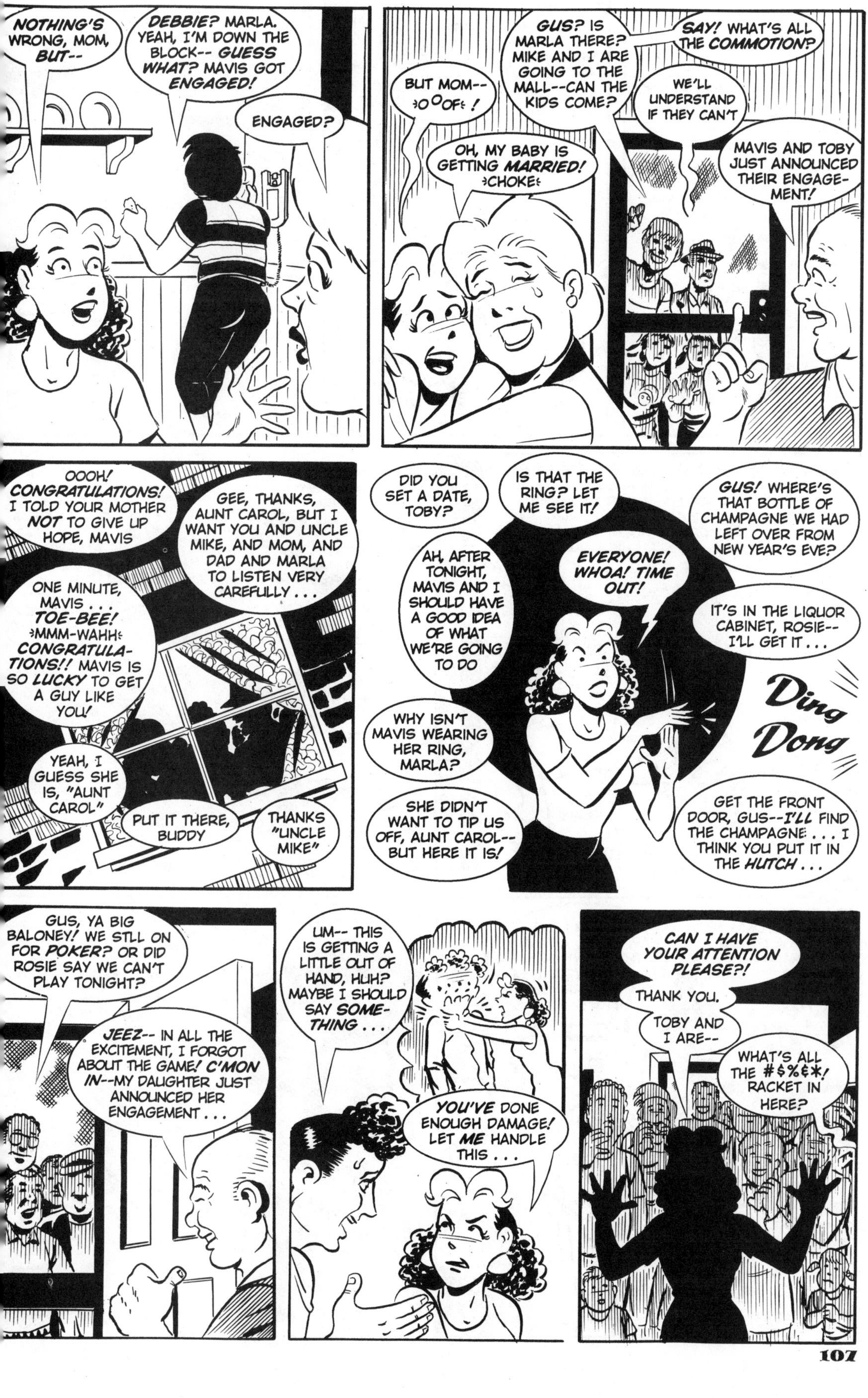
NOTHING'S WRONG, MOM, BUT--
DEBBIE? MARLA. YEAH, I'M DOWN THE BLOCK-- GUESS WHAT? MAVIS GOT ENGAGED!
ENGAGED?
BUT MOM-- OOOF !
GUS? IS MARLA THERE? MIKE AND I ARE GOING TO THE MALL--CAN THE KIDS COME?
SAY! WHAT'S ALL THE COMMOTION?
WE'LL UNDERSTAND IF THEY CAN'T
OH, MY BABY IS GETTING MARRIED! CHOKE
MAVIS AND TOBY JUST ANNOUNCED THEIR ENGAGE-MENT!
OOOH! CONGRATULATIONS! I TOLD YOUR MOTHER NOT TO GIVE UP HOPE, MAVIS
GEE, THANKS, AUNT CAROL, BUT I WANT YOU AND UNCLE MIKE, AND MOM, AND DAD AND MARLA TO LISTEN VERY CAREFULLY . . .
ONE MINUTE, MAVIS . . . TOE-BEE! MMM-WAHH CONGRATULA-TIONS!! MAVIS IS SO LUCKY TO GET A GUY LIKE YOU!
YEAH, I GUESS SHE IS, "AUNT CAROL"
PUT IT THERE, BUDDY
THANKS "UNCLE MIKE"
DID YOU SET A DATE, TOBY?
IS THAT THE RING? LET ME SEE IT!
GUS! WHERE'S THAT BOTTLE OF CHAMPAGNE WE HAD LEFT OVER FROM NEW YEAR'S EVE?
AH, AFTER TONIGHT, MAVIS AND I SHOULD HAVE A GOOD IDEA OF WHAT WE'RE GOING TO DO
EVERYONE! WHOA! TIME OUT!
IT'S IN THE LIQUOR CABINET, ROSIE-- I'LL GET IT . . .
Ding Dong
WHY ISN'T MAVIS WEARING HER RING, MARLA?
SHE DIDN'T WANT TO TIP US OFF, AUNT CAROL-- BUT HERE IT IS!
GET THE FRONT DOOR, GUS--I'LL FIND THE CHAMPAGNE . . . I THINK YOU PUT IT IN THE HUTCH . . .
GUS, YA BIG BALONEY! WE STLL ON FOR POKER? OR DID ROSIE SAY WE CAN'T PLAY TONIGHT?
JEEZ-- IN ALL THE EXCITEMENT, I FORGOT ABOUT THE GAME! C'MON IN--MY DAUGHTER JUST ANNOUNCED HER ENGAGEMENT . . .
UM-- THIS IS GETTING A LITTLE OUT OF HAND, HUH? MAYBE I SHOULD SAY SOME-THING . . .
YOU'VE DONE ENOUGH DAMAGE! LET ME HANDLE THIS . . .
CAN I HAVE YOUR ATTENTION PLEASE?!
THANK YOU.
TOBY AND I ARE--
WHAT'S ALL THE #$%&*! RACKET IN HERE?

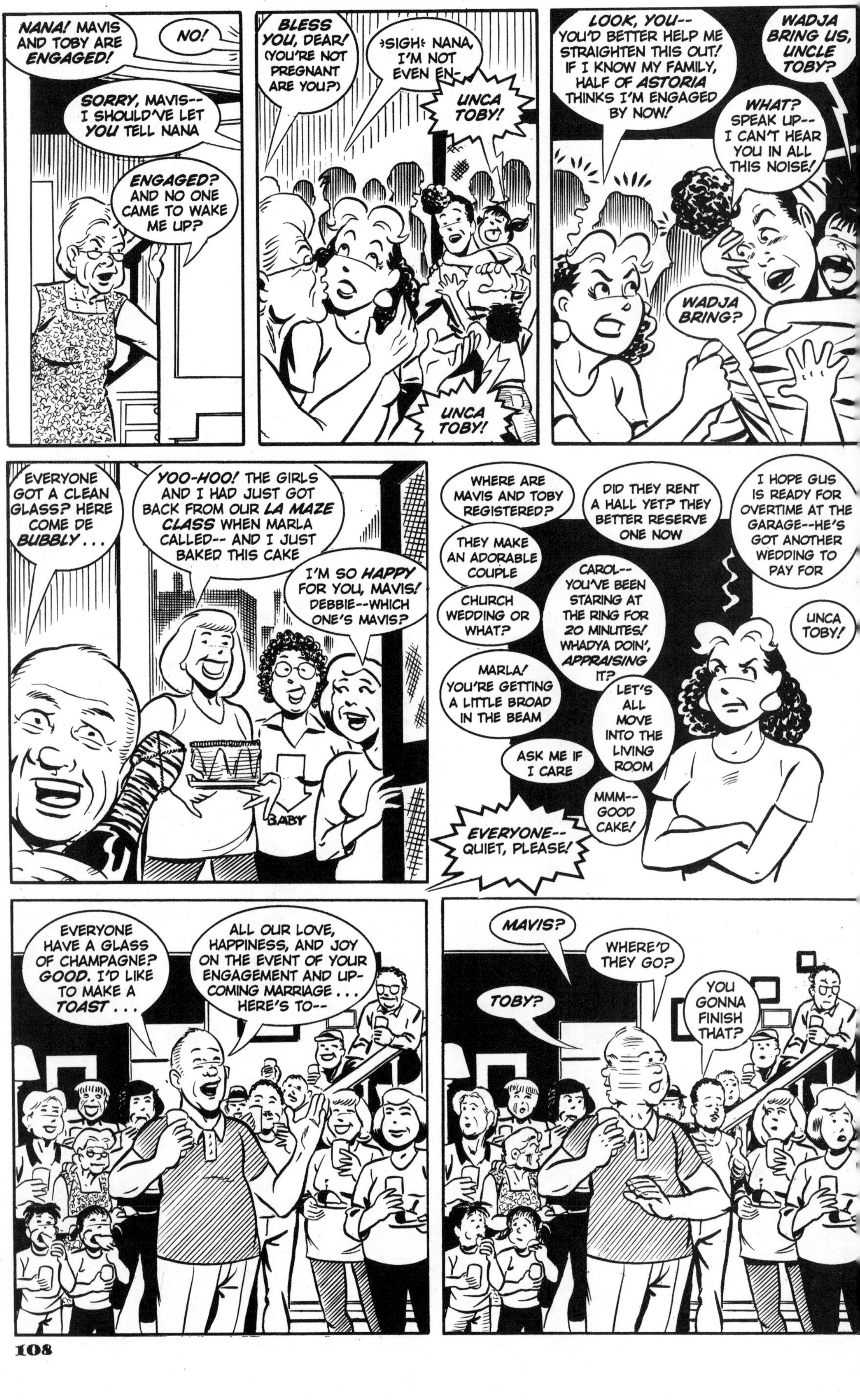
NANA! MAVIS AND TOBY ARE ENGAGED!
NO!
SORRY, MAVIS-- I SHOULD'VE LET YOU TELL NANA
ENGAGED? AND NO ONE CAME TO WAKE ME UP?
BLESS YOU, DEAR! (YOU'RE NOT PREGNANT ARE YOU?)
SIGH NANA, I'M NOT EVEN EN-
UNCA TOBY!
UNCA TOBY!
LOOK, YOU-- YOU'D BETTER HELP ME STRAIGHTEN THIS OUT! IF I KNOW MY FAMILY, HALF OF ASTORIA THINKS I'M ENGAGED BY NOW!
WADJA BRING US, UNCLE TOBY?
WHAT? SPEAK UP-- I CAN'T HEAR YOU IN ALL THIS NOISE!
WADJA BRING?
EVERYONE GOT A CLEAN GLASS? HERE COME DE BUBBLY . . .
YOO-HOO! THE GIRLS AND I HAD JUST GOT BACK FROM OUR LA MAZE CLASS WHEN MARLA CALLED-- AND I JUST BAKED THIS CAKE
I'M SO HAPPY FOR YOU, MAVIS! DEBBIE--WHICH ONE'S MAVIS?
BABY
WHERE ARE MAVIS AND TOBY REGISTERED?
DID THEY RENT A HALL YET? THEY BETTER RESERVE ONE NOW
I HOPE GUS IS READY FOR OVERTIME AT THE GARAGE--HE'S GOT ANOTHER WEDDING TO PAY FOR
THEY MAKE AN ADORABLE COUPLE
CAROL-- YOU'VE BEEN STARING AT THE RING FOR 20 MINUTES! WHADYA DOIN', APPRAISING IT?
UNCA TOBY!
CHURCH WEDDING OR WHAT?
MARLA! YOU'RE GETTING A LITTLE BROAD IN THE BEAM
LET'S ALL MOVE INTO THE LIVING ROOM
ASK ME IF I CARE
MMM-- GOOD CAKE!
EVERYONE-- QUIET, PLEASE!
EVERYONE HAVE A GLASS OF CHAMPAGNE? GOOD. I'D LIKE TO MAKE A TOAST . . .
ALL OUR LOVE, HAPPINESS, AND JOY ON THE EVENT OF YOUR ENGAGEMENT AND UP-COMING MARRIAGE . . . HERE'S TO--
MAVIS?
WHERE'D THEY GO?
TOBY?
YOU GONNA FINISH THAT?

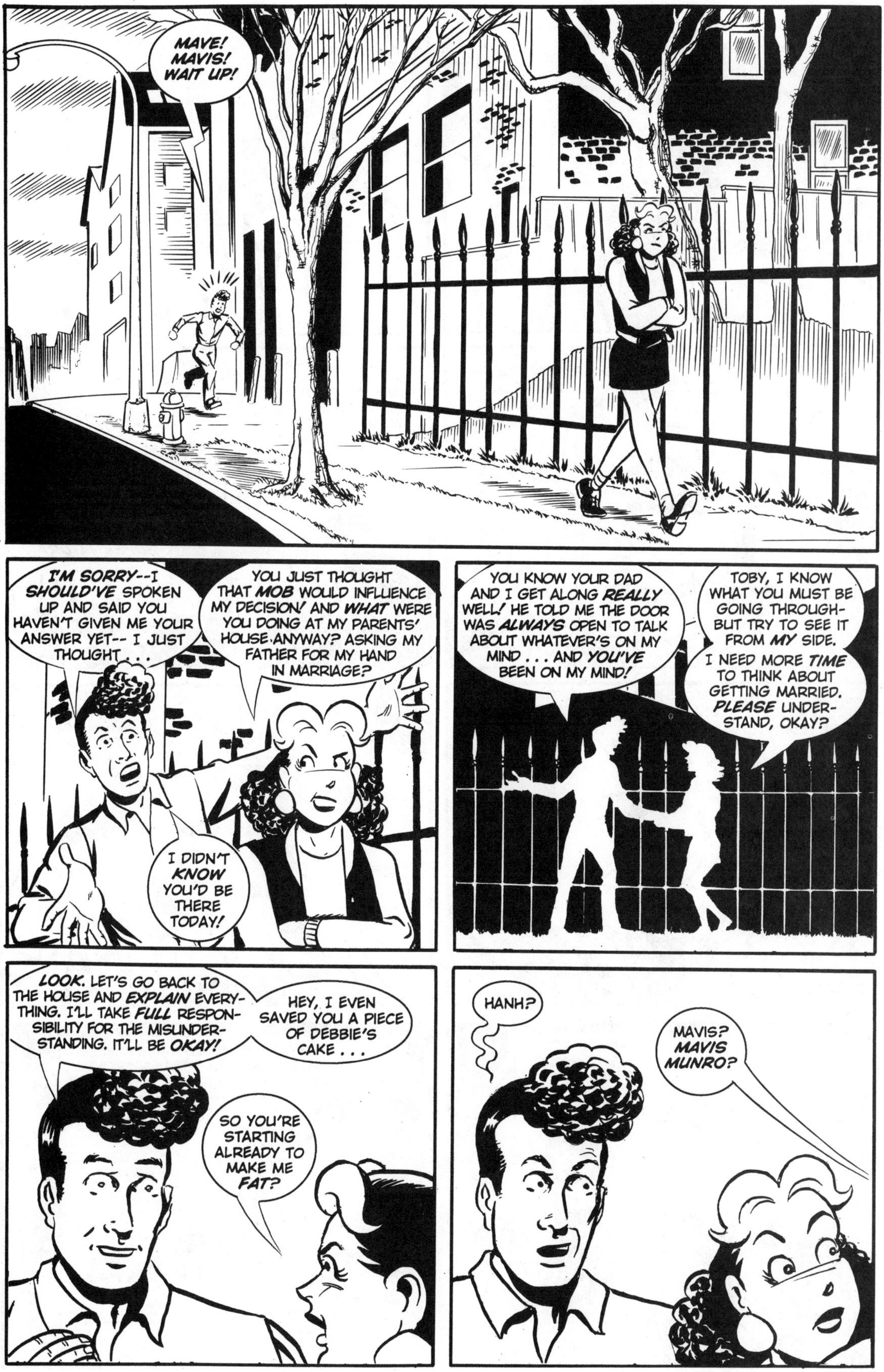
MAVE! MAVIS! WAIT UP!
I'M SORRY--I SHOULD'VE SPOKEN UP AND SAID YOU HAVEN'T GIVEN ME YOUR ANSWER YET-- I JUST THOUGHT . . .
YOU JUST THOUGHT THAT MOB WOULD INFLUENCE MY DECISION! AND WHAT WERE YOU DOING AT MY PARENTS' HOUSE ANYWAY? ASKING MY FATHER FOR MY HAND IN MARRIAGE?
I DIDN'T KNOW YOU'D BE THERE TODAY!
YOU KNOW YOUR DAD AND I GET ALONG REALLY WELL! HE TOLD ME THE DOOR WAS ALWAYS OPEN TO TALK ABOUT WHATEVER'S ON MY MIND . . . AND YOU'VE BEEN ON MY MIND!
TOBY, I KNOW WHAT YOU MUST BE GOING THROUGH- BUT TRY TO SEE IT FROM MY SIDE.
I NEED MORE TIME TO THINK ABOUT GETTING MARRIED. PLEASE UNDER-STAND, OKAY?
LOOK. LET'S GO BACK TO THE HOUSE AND EXPLAIN EVERY-THING. I'LL TAKE FULL RESPON-SIBILITY FOR THE MISUNDER-STANDING. IT'LL BE OKAY!
HEY, I EVEN SAVED YOU A PIECE OF DEBBIE'S CAKE . . .
SO YOU'RE STARTING ALREADY TO MAKE ME FAT?
HANH?
MAVIS? MAVIS MUNRO?

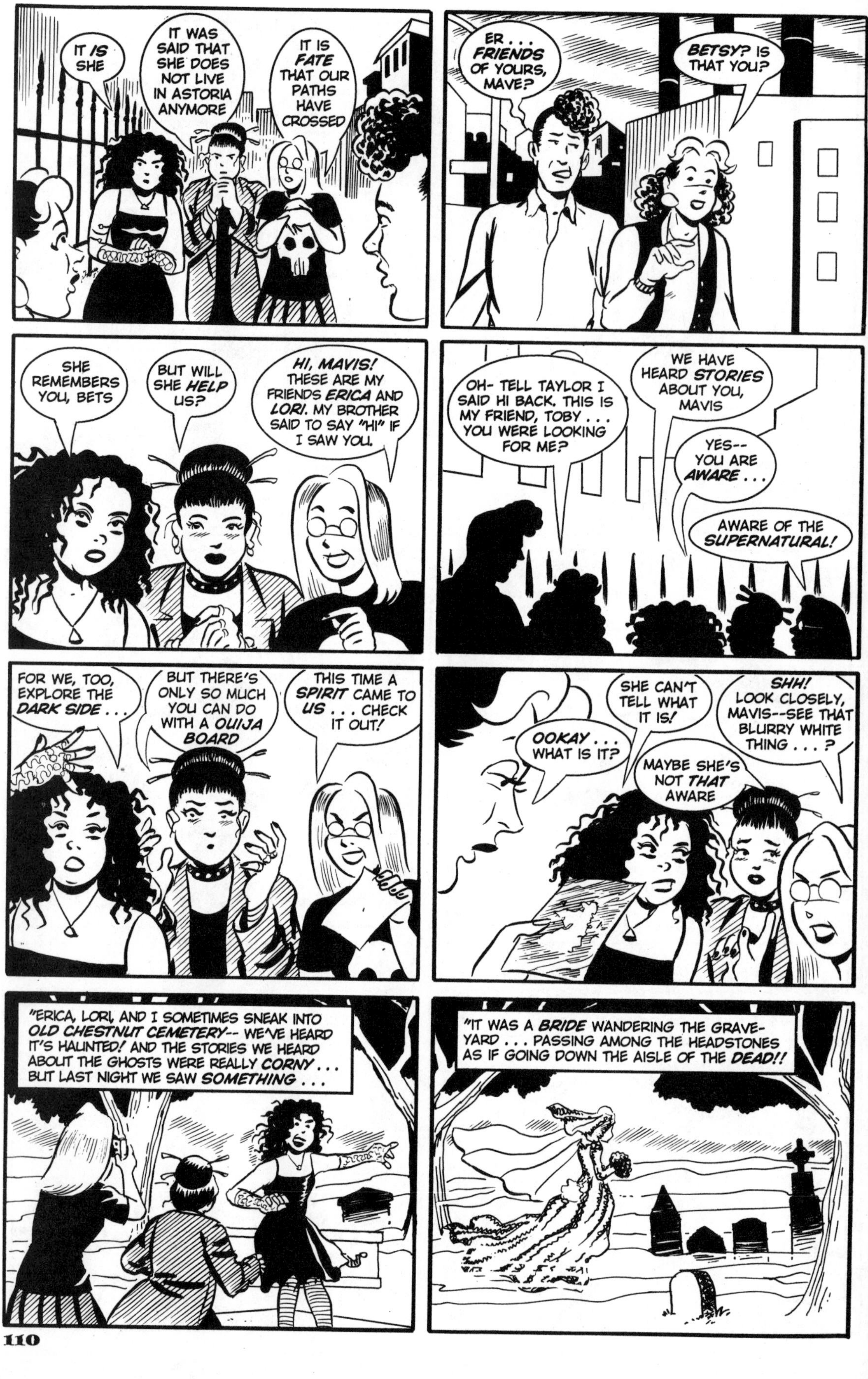

IT IS SHE
IT WAS SAID THAT SHE DOES NOT LIVE IN ASTORIA ANYMORE
IT IS FATE THAT OUR PATHS HAVE CROSSED
ER . . . FRIENDS OF YOURS, MAVE?
BETSY? IS THAT YOU?
SHE REMEMBERS YOU, BETS
BUT WILL SHE HELP US?
HI, MAVIS! THESE ARE MY FRIENDS ERICA AND LORI. MY BROTHER SAID TO SAY "HI" IF I SAW YOU.
OH- TELL TAYLOR I SAID HI BACK. THIS IS MY FRIEND, TOBY . . . YOU WERE LOOKING FOR ME?
WE HAVE HEARD STORIES ABOUT YOU, MAVIS
YES-- YOU ARE AWARE . . .
AWARE OF THE SUPERNATURAL!
FOR WE, TOO, EXPLORE THE DARK SIDE . . .
BUT THERE'S ONLY SO MUCH YOU CAN DO WITH A OUIJA BOARD
THIS TIME A SPIRIT CAME TO US . . . CHECK IT OUT!
OOKAY . . . WHAT IS IT?
SHE CAN'T TELL WHAT IT IS!
SHH! LOOK CLOSELY, MAVIS--SEE THAT BLURRY WHITE THING . . . ?
MAYBE SHE'S NOT THAT AWARE
"ERICA, LORI, AND I SOMETIMES SNEAK INTO OLD CHESTNUT CEMETERY-- WE'VE HEARD IT'S HAUNTED! AND THE STORIES WE HEARD ABOUT THE GHOSTS WERE REALLY CORNY . . . BUT LAST NIGHT WE SAW SOMETHING . . .
"IT WAS A BRIDE WANDERING THE GRAVEYARD . . . PASSING AMONG THE HEADSTONES AS IF GOING DOWN THE AISLE OF THE DEAD!!

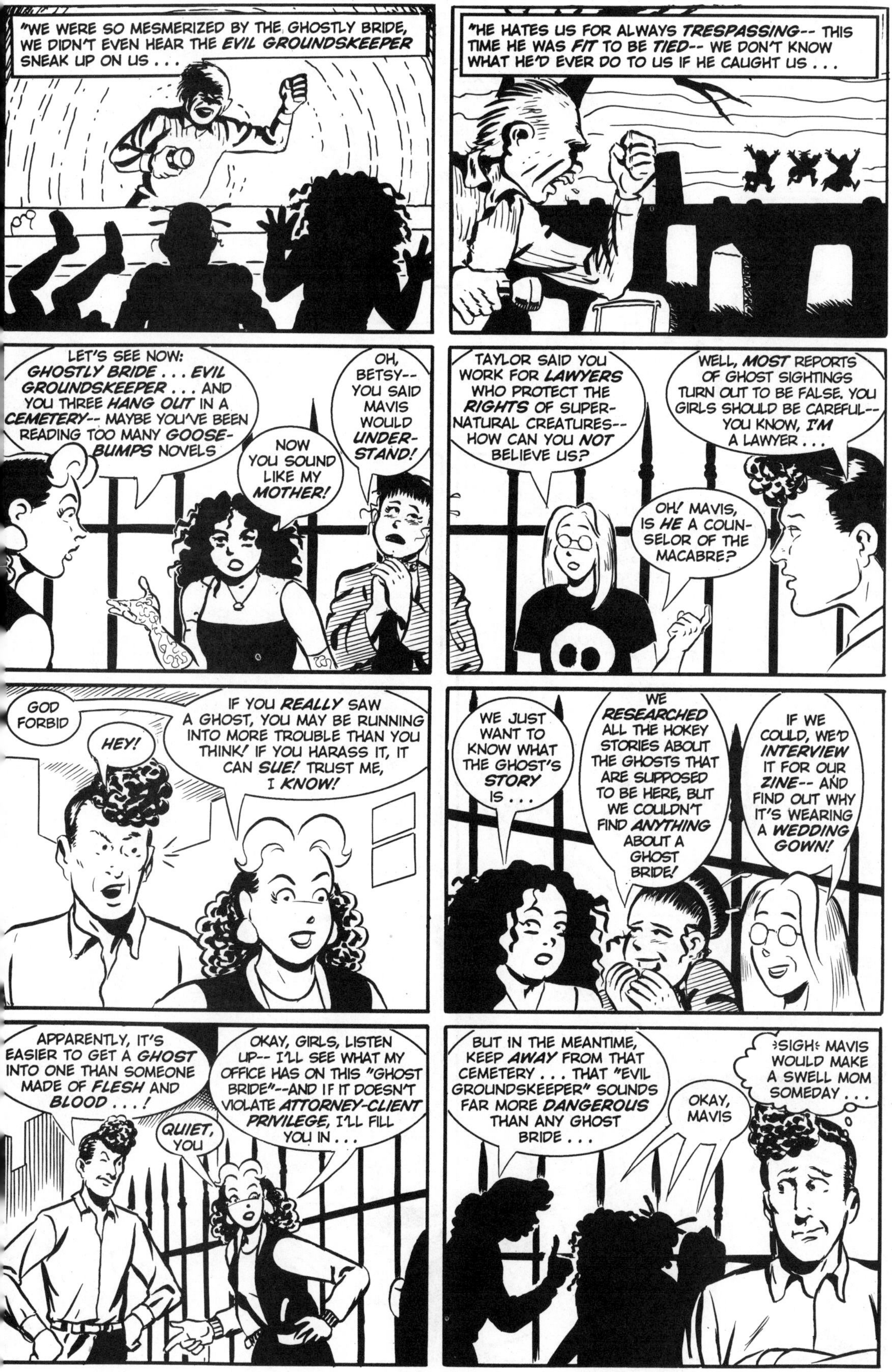

"WE WERE SO MESMERIZED BY THE GHOSTLY BRIDE, WE DIDN'T EVEN HEAR THE EVIL GROUNDSKEEPER SNEAK UP ON US . . .
"HE HATES US FOR ALWAYS TRESPASSING-- THIS TIME HE WAS FIT TO BE TIED-- WE DON'T KNOW WHAT HE'D EVER DO TO US IF HE CAUGHT US . . .
LET'S SEE NOW: GHOSTLY BRIDE . . . EVIL GROUNDSKEEPER . . . AND YOU THREE HANG OUT IN A CEMETERY-- MAYBE YOU'VE BEEN READING TOO MANY GOOSE-BUMPS NOVELS
NOW YOU SOUND LIKE MY MOTHER!
OH, BETSY-- YOU SAID MAVIS WOULD UNDER-STAND!
TAYLOR SAID YOU WORK FOR LAWYERS WHO PROTECT THE RIGHTS OF SUPER-NATURAL CREATURES-- HOW CAN YOU NOT BELIEVE US?
WELL, MOST REPORTS OF GHOST SIGHTINGS TURN OUT TO BE FALSE. YOU GIRLS SHOULD BE CAREFUL-- YOU KNOW, I'M A LAWYER . . .
OH! MAVIS, IS HE A COUN-SELOR OF THE MACABRE?
GOD FORBID
HEY!
IF YOU REALLY SAW A GHOST, YOU MAY BE RUNNING INTO MORE TROUBLE THAN YOU THINK! IF YOU HARASS IT, IT CAN SUE! TRUST ME, I KNOW!
WE JUST WANT TO KNOW WHAT THE GHOST'S STORY IS . . .
WE RESEARCHED ALL THE HOKEY STORIES ABOUT THE GHOSTS THAT ARE SUPPOSED TO BE HERE, BUT WE COULDN'T FIND ANYTHING ABOUT A GHOST BRIDE!
IF WE COULD, WE'D INTERVIEW IT FOR OUR ZINE-- AND FIND OUT WHY IT'S WEARING A WEDDING GOWN!
APPARENTLY, IT'S EASIER TO GET A GHOST INTO ONE THAN SOMEONE MADE OF FLESH AND BLOOD . . . !
QUIET, YOU
OKAY, GIRLS, LISTEN UP-- I'LL SEE WHAT MY OFFICE HAS ON THIS "GHOST BRIDE"--AND IF IT DOESN'T VIOLATE ATTORNEY-CLIENT PRIVILEGE, I'LL FILL YOU IN . . .
BUT IN THE MEANTIME, KEEP AWAY FROM THAT CEMETERY . . . THAT "EVIL GROUNDSKEEPER" SOUNDS FAR MORE DANGEROUS THAN ANY GHOST BRIDE . . .
OKAY, MAVIS
SIGH MAVIS WOULD MAKE A SWELL MOM SOMEDAY . . .

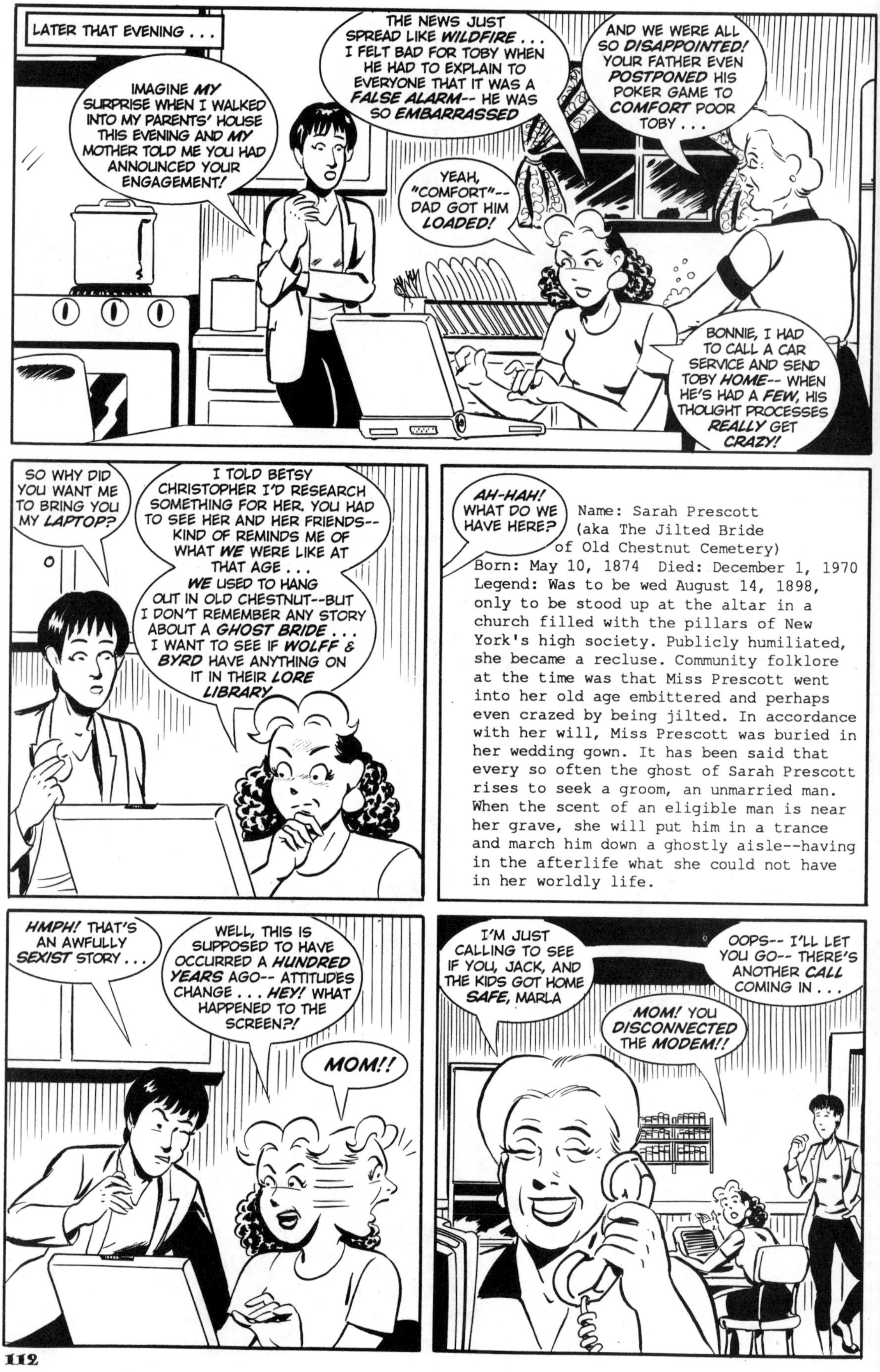
LATER THAT EVENING . . .
IMAGINE MY SURPRISE WHEN I WALKED INTO MY PARENTS' HOUSE THIS EVENING AND MY MOTHER TOLD ME YOU HAD ANNOUNCED YOUR ENGAGEMENT!
THE NEWS JUST SPREAD LIKE WILDFIRE . . . I FELT BAD FOR TOBY WHEN HE HAD TO EXPLAIN TO EVERYONE THAT IT WAS A FALSE ALARM-- HE WAS SO EMBARRASSED
AND WE WERE ALL SO DISAPPOINTED! YOUR FATHER EVEN POSTPONED HIS POKER GAME TO COMFORT POOR TOBY . . .
YEAH, "COMFORT"-- DAD GOT HIM LOADED!
BONNIE, I HAD TO CALL A CAR SERVICE AND SEND TOBY HOME-- WHEN HE'S HAD A FEW, HIS THOUGHT PROCESSES REALLY GET CRAZY!
SO WHY DID YOU WANT ME TO BRING YOU MY LAPTOP?
I TOLD BETSY CHRISTOPHER I'D RESEARCH SOMETHING FOR HER. YOU HAD TO SEE HER AND HER FRIENDS-- KIND OF REMINDS ME OF WHAT WE WERE LIKE AT THAT AGE . . . WE USED TO HANG OUT IN OLD CHESTNUT--BUT I DON'T REMEMBER ANY STORY ABOUT A GHOST BRIDE . . . I WANT TO SEE IF WOLFF & BYRD HAVE ANYTHING ON IT IN THEIR LORE LIBRARY.
AH-HAH! WHAT DO WE HAVE HERE?
Name: Sarah Prescott (aka The Jilted Bride of Old Chestnut Cemetery)
Born: May 10, 1874 Died: December 1, 1970
Legend: Was to be wed August 14, 1898, only to be stood up at the altar in a church filled with the pillars of New York's high society. Publicly humiliated, she became a recluse. Community folklore at the time was that Miss Prescott went into her old age embittered and perhaps even crazed by being jilted. In accordance with her will, Miss Prescott was buried in her wedding gown. It has been said that every so often the ghost of Sarah Prescott rises to seek a groom, an unmarried man. When the scent of an eligible man is near her grave, she will put him in a trance and march him down a ghostly aisle--having in the afterlife what she could not have in her worldly life.
HMPH! THAT'S AN AWFULLY SEXIST STORY . . .
WELL, THIS IS SUPPOSED TO HAVE OCCURRED A HUNDRED YEARS AGO-- ATTITUDES CHANGE . . . HEY! WHAT HAPPENED TO THE SCREEN?!
MOM!!
I'M JUST CALLING TO SEE IF YOU, JACK, AND THE KIDS GOT HOME SAFE, MARLA
OOPS-- I'LL LET YOU GO-- THERE'S ANOTHER CALL COMING IN . . .
MOM! YOU DISCONNECTED THE MODEM!!

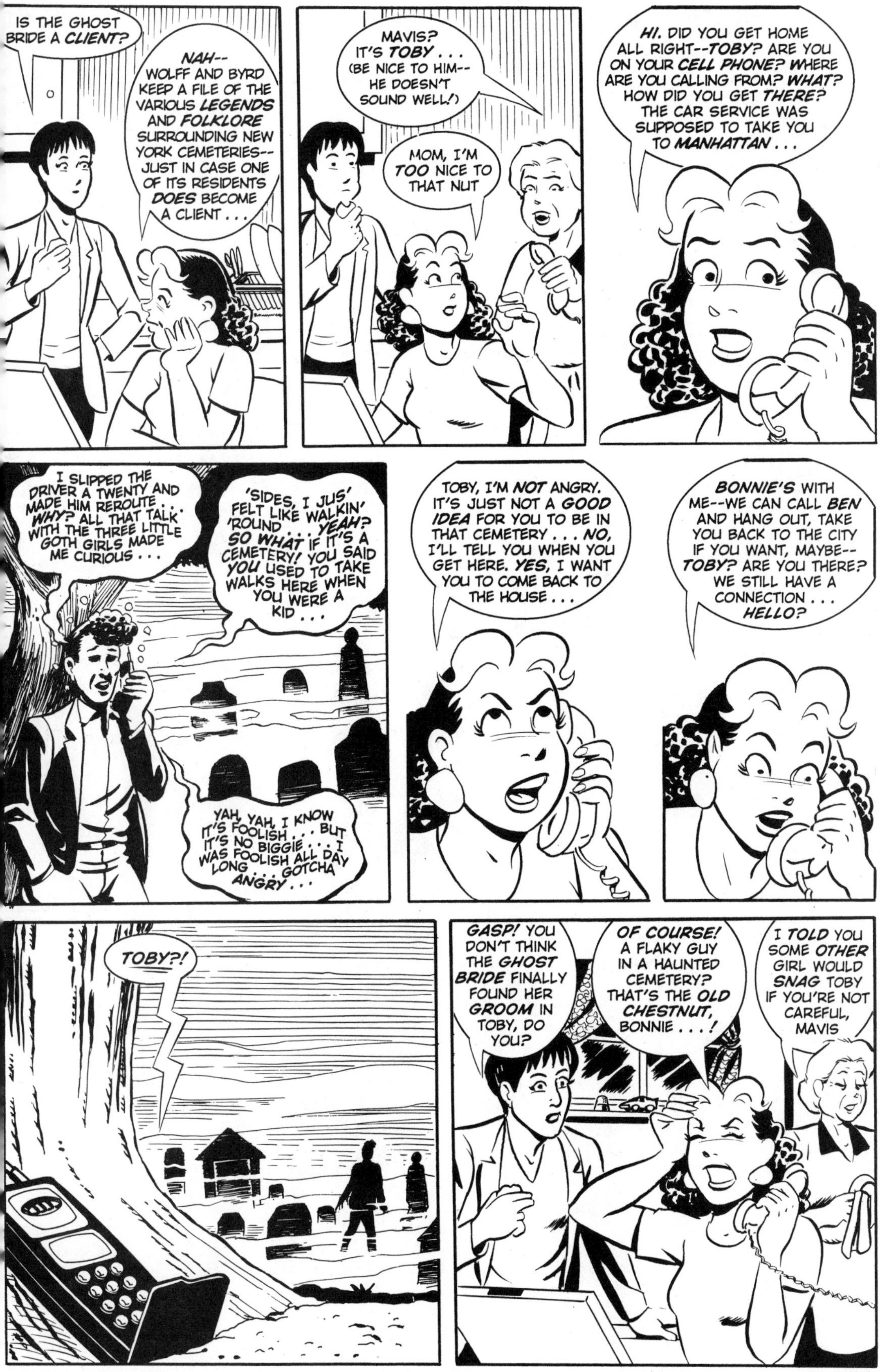

IS THE GHOST BRIDE A CLIENT?
NAH-- WOLFF AND BYRD KEEP A FILE OF THE VARIOUS LEGENDS AND FOLKLORE SURROUNDING NEW YORK CEMETERIES-- JUST IN CASE ONE OF ITS RESIDENTS DOES BECOME A CLIENT . . .
MAVIS? IT'S TOBY . . . (BE NICE TO HIM-- HE DOESN'T SOUND WELL!)
MOM, I'M TOO NICE TO THAT NUT
HI. DID YOU GET HOME ALL RIGHT--TOBY? ARE YOU ON YOUR CELL PHONE? WHERE ARE YOU CALLING FROM? WHAT? HOW DID YOU GET THERE? THE CAR SERVICE WAS SUPPOSED TO TAKE YOU TO MANHATTAN . . .
I SLIPPED THE DRIVER A TWENTY AND MADE HIM REROUTE . . . WHY? ALL THAT TALK WITH THE THREE LITTLE GOTH GIRLS MADE ME CURIOUS . . .
'SIDES, I JUS' FELT LIKE WALKIN' 'ROUND . . . YEAH? SO WHAT IF IT'S A CEMETERY! YOU SAID YOU USED TO TAKE WALKS HERE WHEN YOU WERE A KID . . .
YAH, YAH, I KNOW IT'S FOOLISH . . . BUT IT'S NO BIGGIE . . . I WAS FOOLISH ALL DAY LONG . . . GOTCHA ANGRY . . .
TOBY, I'M NOT ANGRY. IT'S JUST NOT A GOOD IDEA FOR YOU TO BE IN THAT CEMETERY . . . NO, I'LL TELL YOU WHEN YOU GET HERE. YES, I WANT YOU TO COME BACK TO THE HOUSE . . .
BONNIE'S WITH ME--WE CAN CALL BEN AND HANG OUT, TAKE YOU BACK TO THE CITY IF YOU WANT, MAYBE-- TOBY? ARE YOU THERE? WE STILL HAVE A CONNECTION . . . HELLO?
TOBY?!
GASP! YOU DON'T THINK THE GHOST BRIDE FINALLY FOUND HER GROOM IN TOBY, DO YOU?
OF COURSE! A FLAKY GUY IN A HAUNTED CEMETERY? THAT'S THE OLD CHESTNUT, BONNIE . . . !
I TOLD YOU SOME OTHER GIRL WOULD SNAG TOBY IF YOU'RE NOT CAREFUL, MAVIS

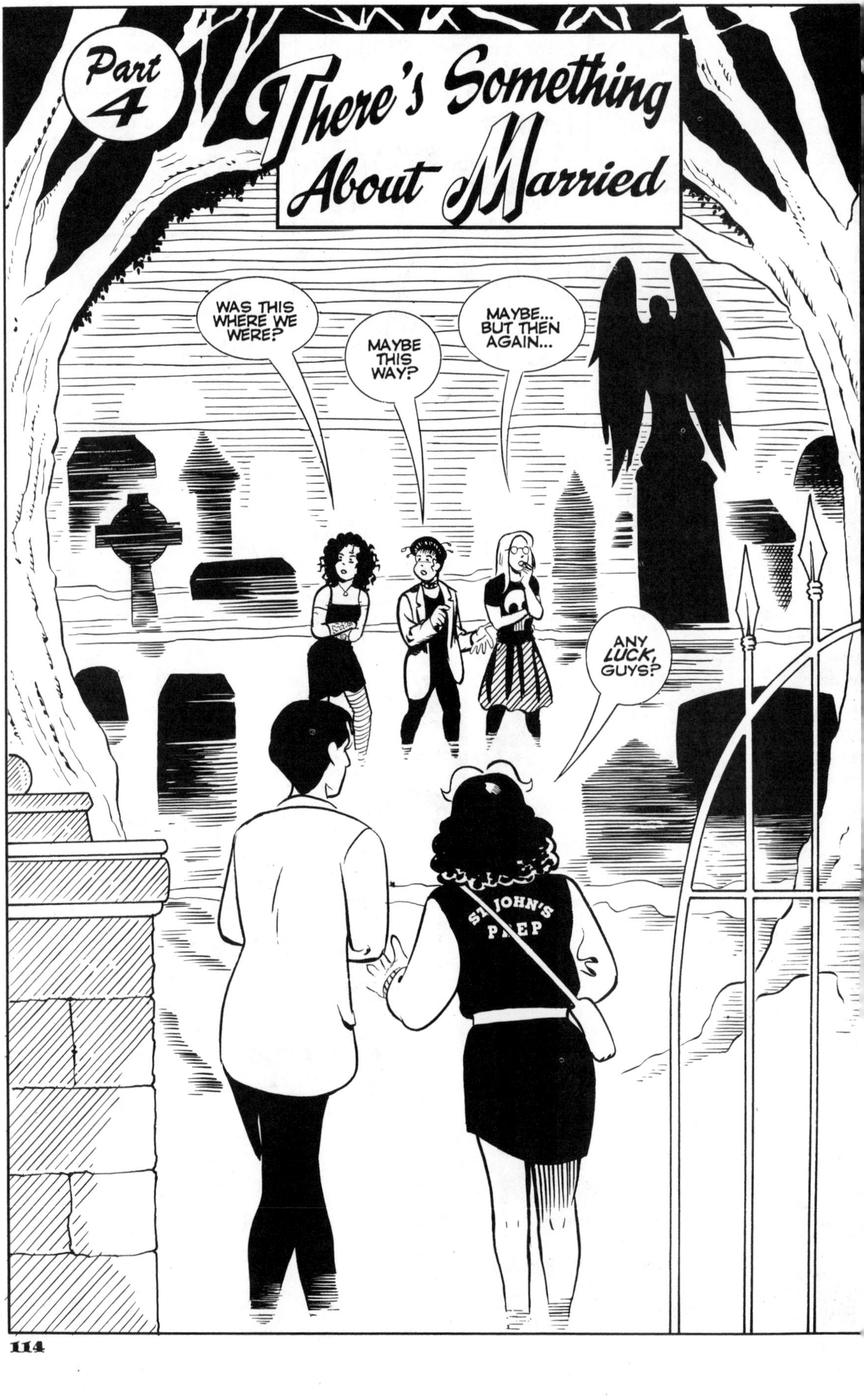
Part 4
There's Something About Married
WAS THIS WHERE WE WERE?
MAYBE THIS WAY?
MAYBE... BUT THEN AGAIN...
ANY LUCK, GUYS?
ST. JOHN'S PREP

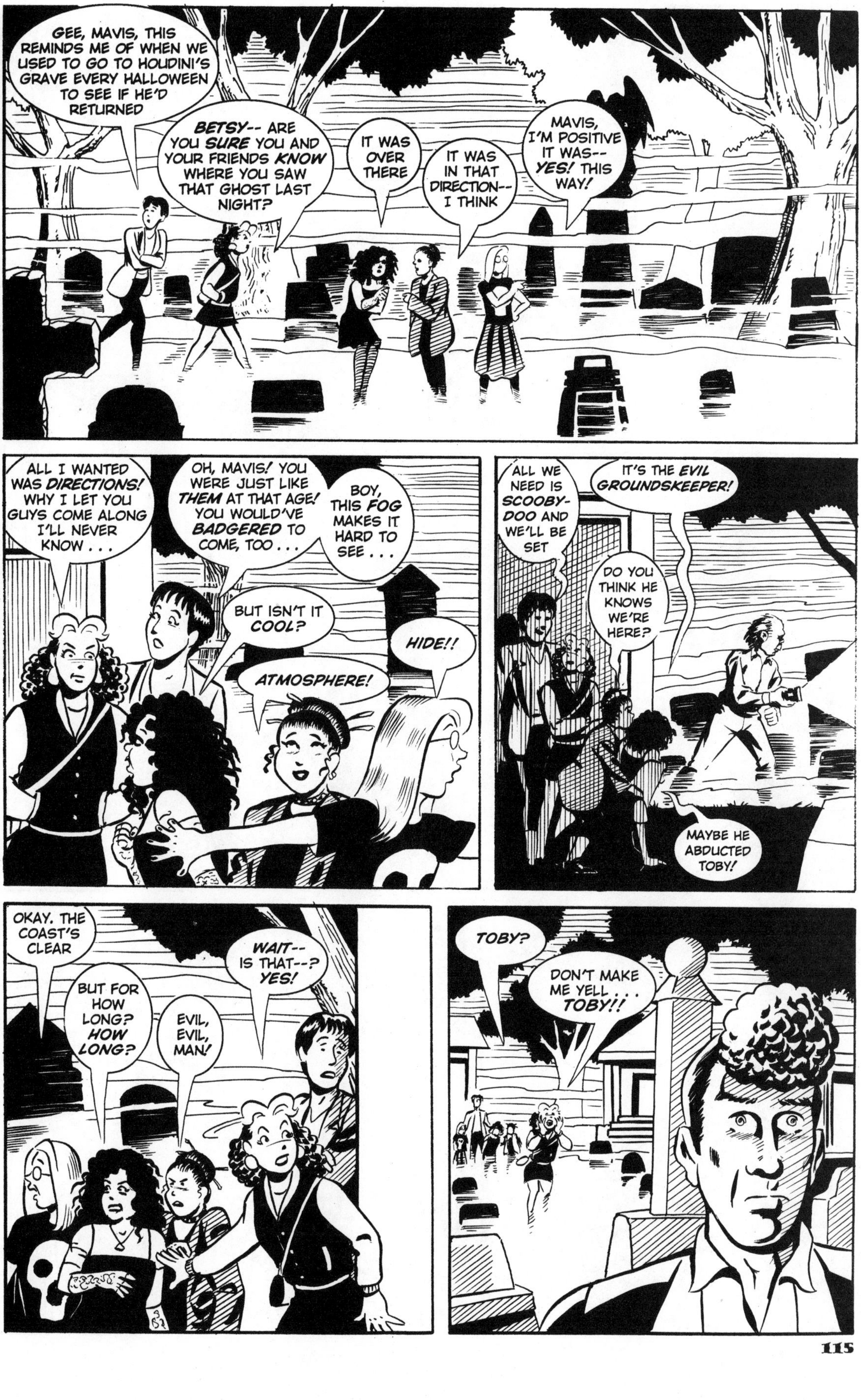
GEE, MAVIS, THIS REMINDS ME OF WHEN WE USED TO GO TO HOUDINI'S GRAVE EVERY HALLOWEEN TO SEE IF HE'D RETURNED
BETSY-- ARE YOU SURE YOU AND YOUR FRIENDS KNOW WHERE YOU SAW THAT GHOST LAST NIGHT?
IT WAS OVER THERE
IT WAS IN THAT DIRECTION-- I THINK
MAVIS, I'M POSITIVE IT WAS-- YES! THIS WAY!
ALL I WANTED WAS DIRECTIONS! WHY I LET YOU GUYS COME ALONG I'LL NEVER KNOW . . .
OH, MAVIS! YOU WERE JUST LIKE THEM AT THAT AGE! YOU WOULD'VE BADGERED TO COME, TOO . . .
BOY, THIS FOG MAKES IT HARD TO SEE . . .
BUT ISN'T IT COOL?
HIDE!!
ATMOSPHERE!
ALL WE NEED IS SCOOBY-DOO AND WE'LL BE SET
IT'S THE EVIL GROUNDSKEEPER!
DO YOU THINK HE KNOWS WE'RE HERE?
MAYBE HE ABDUCTED TOBY!
OKAY. THE COAST'S CLEAR
BUT FOR HOW LONG? HOW LONG?
EVIL, EVIL, MAN!
WAIT-- IS THAT--? YES!
TOBY?
DON'T MAKE ME YELL . . . TOBY!!

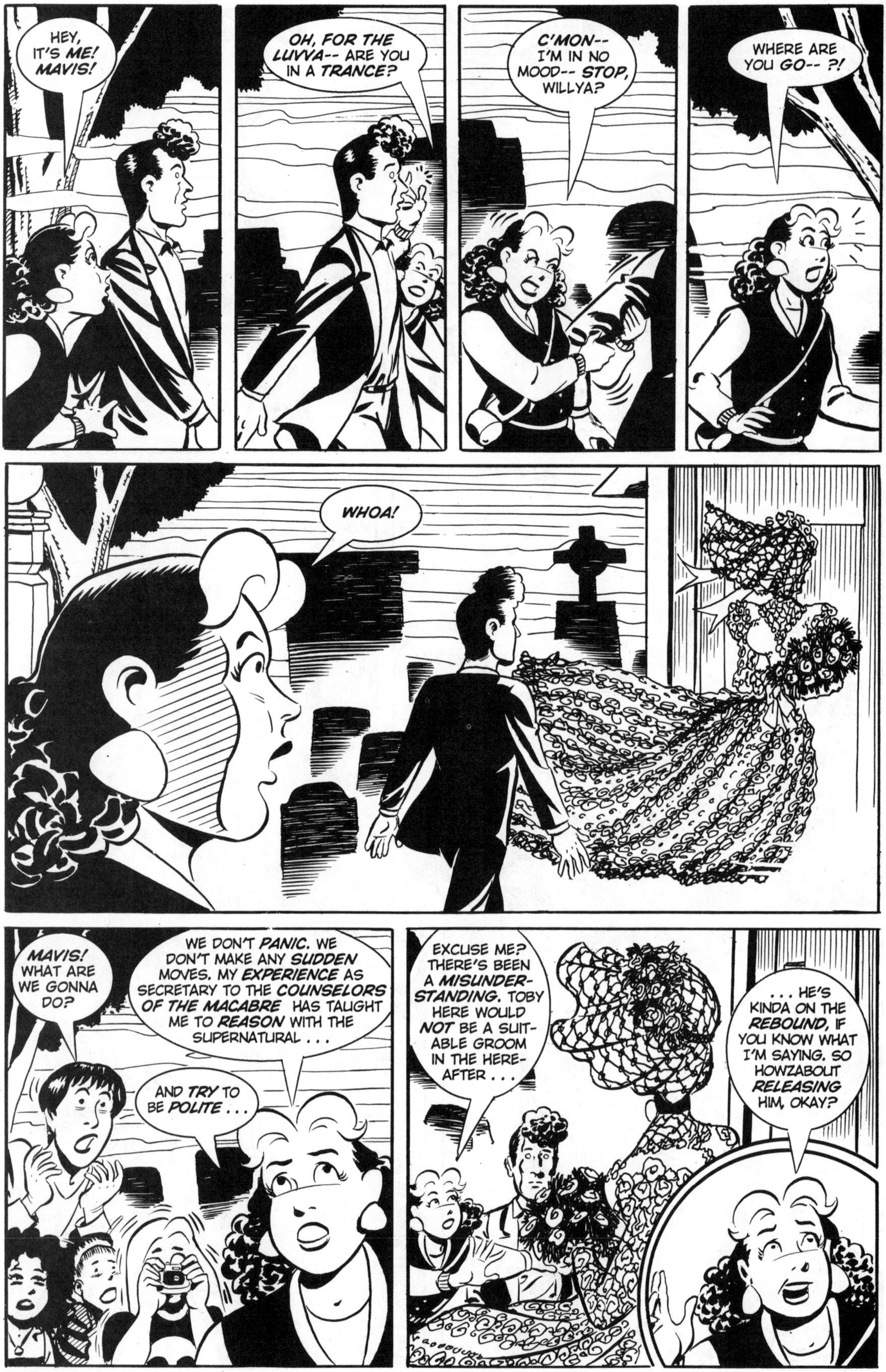
HEY, IT'S ME! MAVIS!
OH, FOR THE LUVVA-- ARE YOU IN A TRANCE?
C'MON-- I'M IN NO MOOD-- STOP, WILLYA?
WHERE ARE YOU GO-- ?!
WHOA!
MAVIS! WHAT ARE WE GONNA DO?
WE DON'T PANIC. WE DON'T MAKE ANY SUDDEN MOVES. MY EXPERIENCE AS SECRETARY TO THE COUNSELORS OF THE MACABRE HAS TAUGHT ME TO REASON WITH THE SUPERNATURAL . . .
AND TRY TO BE POLITE . . .
EXCUSE ME? THERE'S BEEN A MISUNDER-STANDING. TOBY HERE WOULD NOT BE A SUIT-ABLE GROOM IN THE HERE-AFTER . . .
. . . HE'S KINDA ON THE REBOUND, IF YOU KNOW WHAT I'M SAYING. SO HOWZABOUT RELEASING HIM, OKAY?

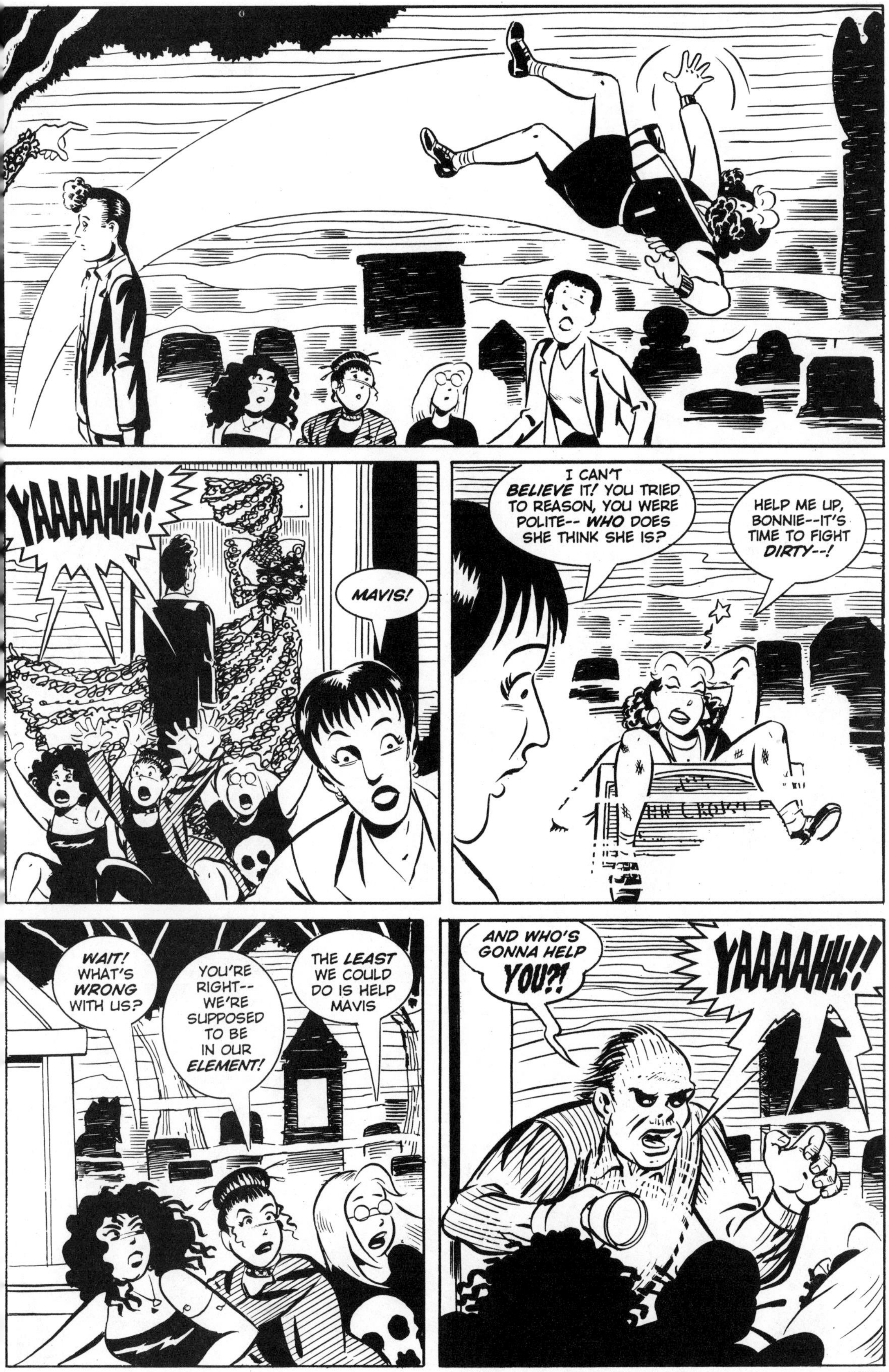
YAAAAHH!!
MAVIS!
I CAN'T BELIEVE IT! YOU TRIED TO REASON, YOU WERE POLITE-- WHO DOES SHE THINK SHE IS?
HELP ME UP, BONNIE--IT'S TIME TO FIGHT DIRTY--!
WAIT! WHAT'S WRONG WITH US?
YOU'RE RIGHT-- WE'RE SUPPOSED TO BE IN OUR ELEMENT!
THE LEAST WE COULD DO IS HELP MAVIS
AND WHO'S GONNA HELP YOU?!
YAAAAHH!!

WHAT IS THAT?!
SARAH! YOU CAN'T TAKE THAT GUY TO BE YOUR SPIRITUALLY WEDDED SPOUSE--
--HE'S ALREADY SPOKEN FOR! SEE? HE'S ENGAGED TO ME!
HUH? WHAT? I MUST BE DREAMING . . . I HEARD MAVIS TELL SOMEONE WE'RE ENGAGED-- !
MAVIS! YOU DID IT! THE TRANCE IS BROKEN!
MAVIS.. HELP!!
HEY! LEAVE THOSE KIDS ALONE!
KIDS?
WHAT KIDS--?
DON'T SAY IT . . . !
HEY, YOU'RE THE ONE WEARING MY RING!

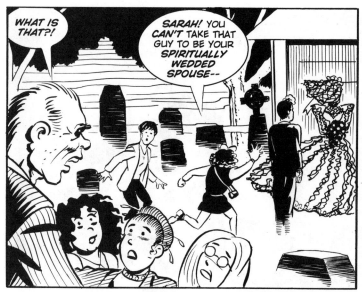

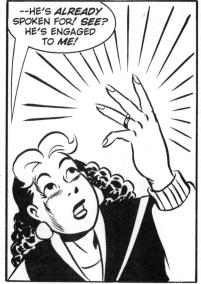

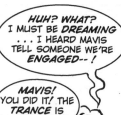

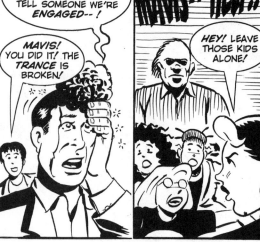

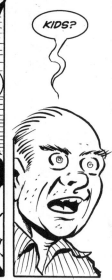

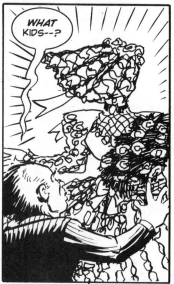

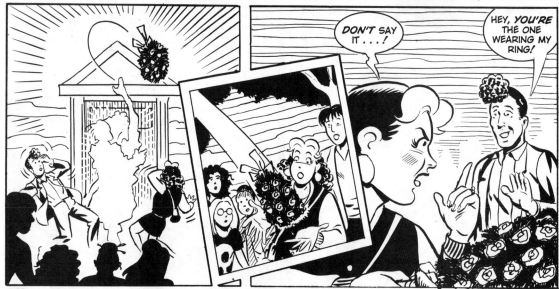

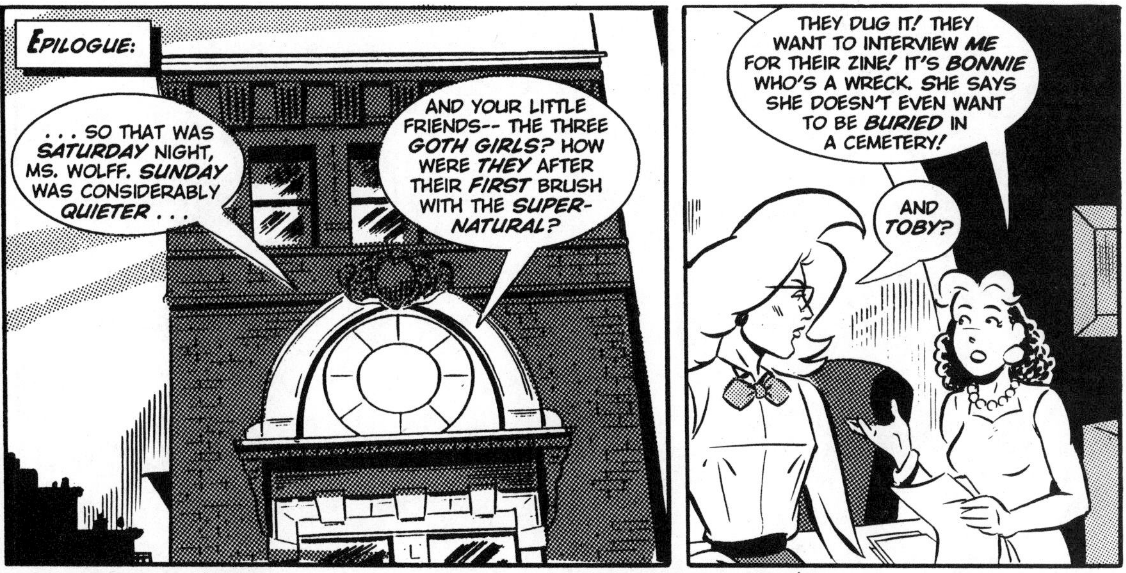
EPILOGUE:
. . . SO THAT WAS SATURDAY NIGHT, MS. WOLFF. SUNDAY WAS CONSIDERABLY QUIETER . . .
AND YOUR LITTLE FRIENDS-- THE THREE GOTH GIRLS? HOW WERE THEY AFTER THEIR FIRST BRUSH WITH THE SUPER-NATURAL?
THEY DUG IT! THEY WANT TO INTERVIEW ME FOR THEIR ZINE! IT'S BONNIE WHO'S A WRECK. SHE SAYS SHE DOESN'T EVEN WANT TO BE BURIED IN A CEMETERY!
AND TOBY?

"WELL, TOBY HAD NO ***MEMORY*** OF WHAT HAPPENED WHILE HE WAS IN THE TRANCE. BETWEEN DEALING WITH MY FAMILY, GETTING BOMBED, AND NEARLY TYING THE KNOT WITH A GHOST, THE POOR SCHNOOK HAD ***QUITE*** A DAY! I SUGGESTED HE STAY OVER WITH ME AT MY PARENTS' HOUSE (HE GOT THE SOFA). SUNDAY MORNING, WE HEADED BACK TO THE ***CITY***. WE SPENT THE ***WHOLE*** DAY WALKING AROUND, HAVING COFFEE, SWAPPING STORIES ABOUT PEOPLE WE USED TO GO OUT WITH . . . ***NO*** TALK ABOUT MARRIAGE! WE HAD A ***GREAT*** TIME. AT THE END OF THE DAY, HE ASKED FOR HIS RING BACK. IN LIGHT OF HIS ALMOST BECOMING A GHOST'S SPOUSE AGAINST HIS WILL, TOBY SAID HE DOESN'T EVER WANT TO ***FORCE*** ME TO DO ANYTHING I'M NOT ***100*** PERCENT SURE OF. BUT HE DID SAY THAT IF I EVER WANTED IT BACK--IT'S MINE ***FOREVER*** . . .

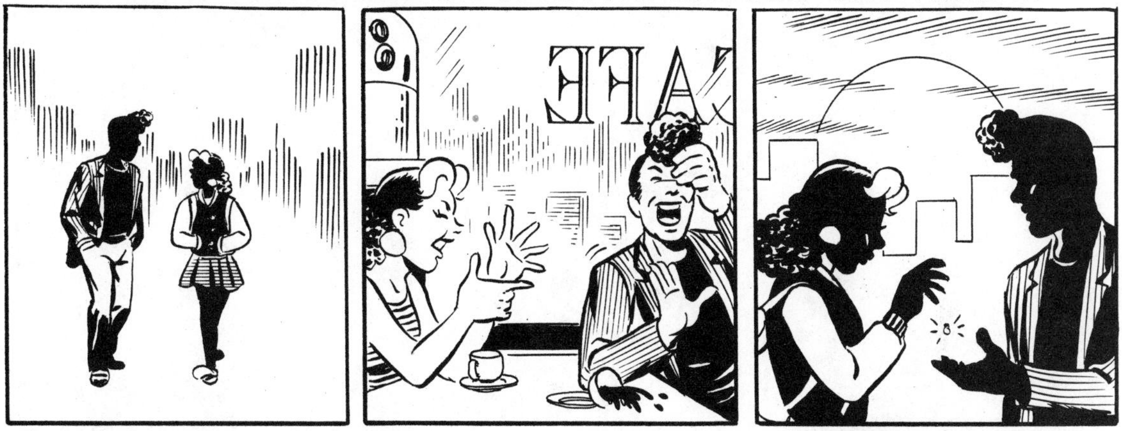

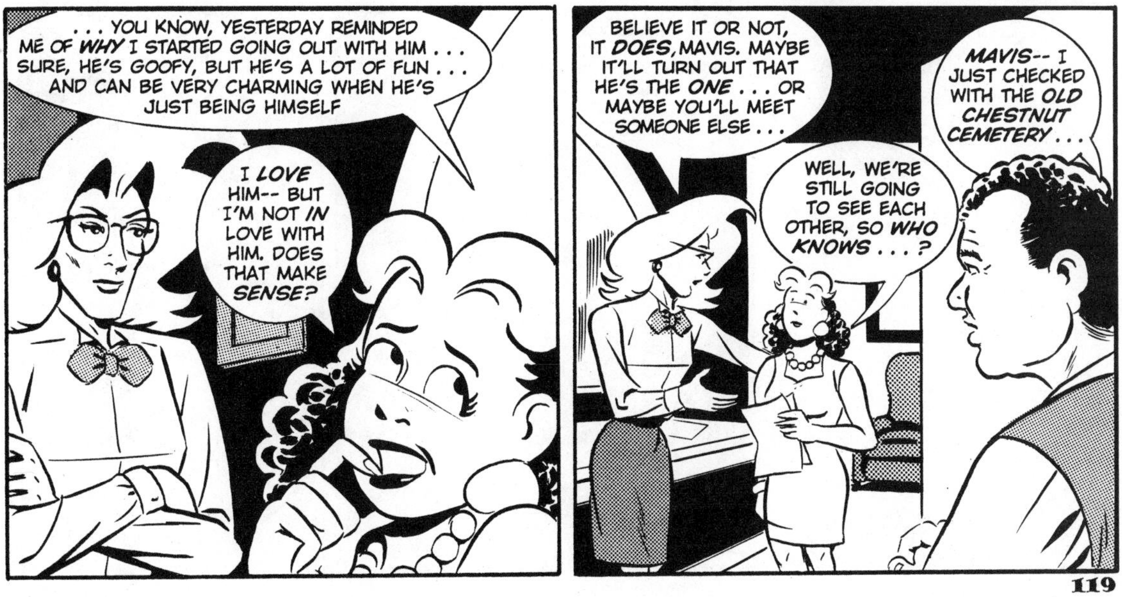
. . . YOU KNOW, YESTERDAY REMINDED ME OF WHY I STARTED GOING OUT WITH HIM . . . SURE, HE'S GOOFY, BUT HE'S A LOT OF FUN . . . AND CAN BE VERY CHARMING WHEN HE'S JUST BEING HIMSELF
I LOVE HIM-- BUT I'M NOT IN LOVE WITH HIM. DOES THAT MAKE SENSE?
BELIEVE IT OR NOT, IT DOES, MAVIS. MAYBE IT'LL TURN OUT THAT HE'S THE ONE . . . OR MAYBE YOU'LL MEET SOMEONE ELSE . . .
WELL, WE'RE STILL GOING TO SEE EACH OTHER, SO WHO KNOWS . . . ?
MAVIS-- I JUST CHECKED WITH THE OLD CHESTNUT CEMETERY . . .

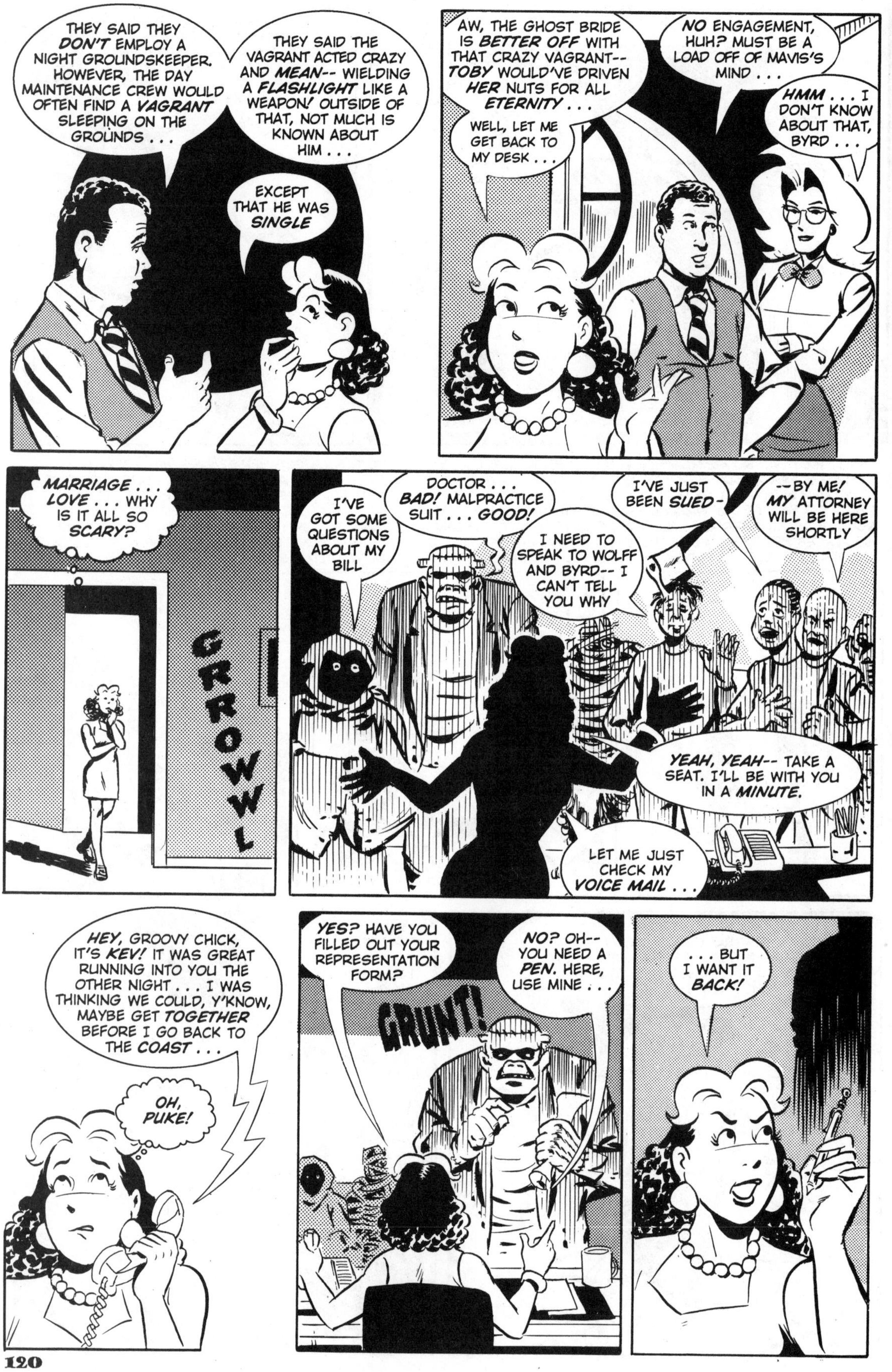
THEY SAID THEY DON'T EMPLOY A NIGHT GROUNDSKEEPER. HOWEVER, THE DAY MAINTENANCE CREW WOULD OFTEN FIND A VAGRANT SLEEPING ON THE GROUNDS . . .
THEY SAID THE VAGRANT ACTED CRAZY AND MEAN-- WIELDING A FLASHLIGHT LIKE A WEAPON! OUTSIDE OF THAT, NOT MUCH IS KNOWN ABOUT HIM . . .
EXCEPT THAT HE WAS SINGLE
AW, THE GHOST BRIDE IS BETTER OFF WITH THAT CRAZY VAGRANT-- TOBY WOULD'VE DRIVEN HER NUTS FOR ALL ETERNITY . . .
NO ENGAGEMENT, HUH? MUST BE A LOAD OFF OF MAVIS'S MIND . . .
HMM . . . I DON'T KNOW ABOUT THAT, BYRD . . .
WELL, LET ME GET BACK TO MY DESK . . .
MARRIAGE . . . LOVE . . . WHY IS IT ALL SO SCARY?
GROWWL
I'VE GOT SOME QUESTIONS ABOUT MY BILL
DOCTOR . . . BAD! MALPRACTICE SUIT . . . GOOD!
I NEED TO SPEAK TO WOLFF AND BYRD-- I CAN'T TELL YOU WHY
I'VE JUST BEEN SUED-
--BY ME! MY ATTORNEY WILL BE HERE SHORTLY
YEAH, YEAH-- TAKE A SEAT. I'LL BE WITH YOU IN A MINUTE.
LET ME JUST CHECK MY VOICE MAIL . . .
HEY, GROOVY CHICK, IT'S KEV! IT WAS GREAT RUNNING INTO YOU THE OTHER NIGHT . . . I WAS THINKING WE COULD, Y'KNOW, MAYBE GET TOGETHER BEFORE I GO BACK TO THE COAST . . .
OH, PUKE!
YES? HAVE YOU FILLED OUT YOUR REPRESENTATION FORM?
GRUNT!
NO? OH-- YOU NEED A PEN. HERE, USE MINE . . .
. . . BUT I WANT IT BACK!

Gormagon

Gormagon

The *Gormagon!* The great Saurian
monster from the depths of
the unknown! Throughout the
ages scholars have studied the
mysterious beast . . . and you
can be sure that many, many
years from now, the Gormagon
will continue to be the subject
of debate as students examine
the records, documents, and
accounts of the last known
appearance of the monster . . .

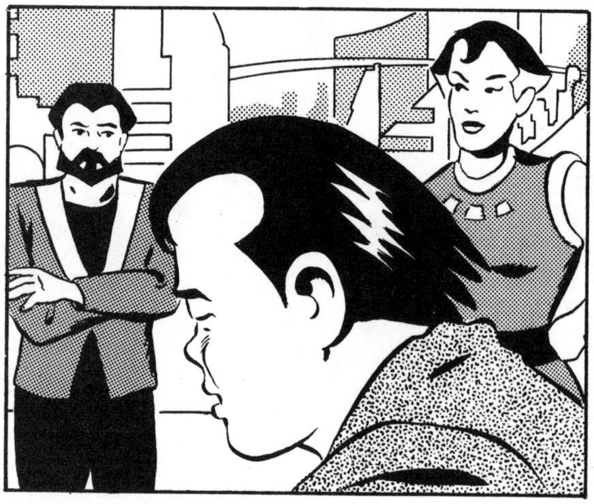

I don't understand it . . . I don't understand it at all!

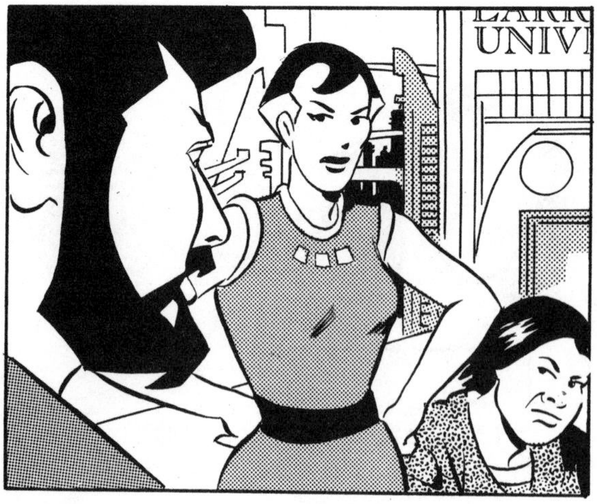

UNIV

What's wrong? What don't you understand?

Detrek had problems with the assignment . . .

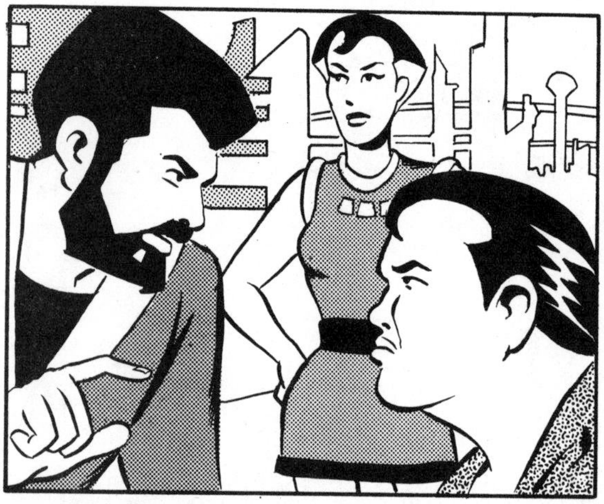

For our class in "Supernatural Phenomena in 20th Century Society"? What, you couldn't do it?

Oh, I did it, Choz--but like I told Melena, I-- I didn't like what I found!

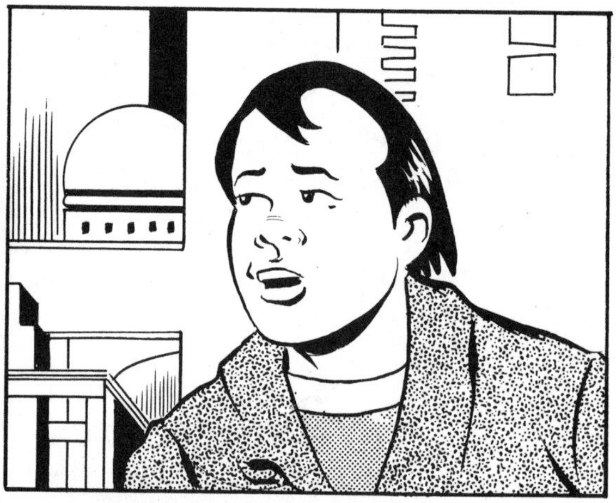

The Gormagon was released because of stupid, ***selfish*** motives . . . and history has yet to ***recognize*** the man who saved ***millions*** of lives to vanquish the monster!

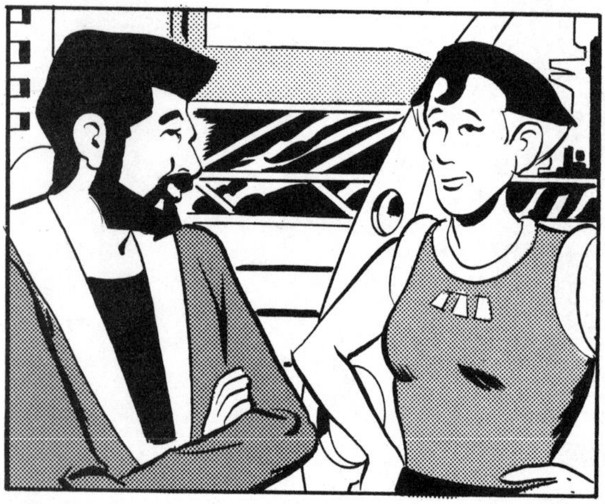

This ought to be good ⋟groan⋞!

We ***all*** had to research the same story-- but I don't know how Detrek came to *his* conclusions . . .

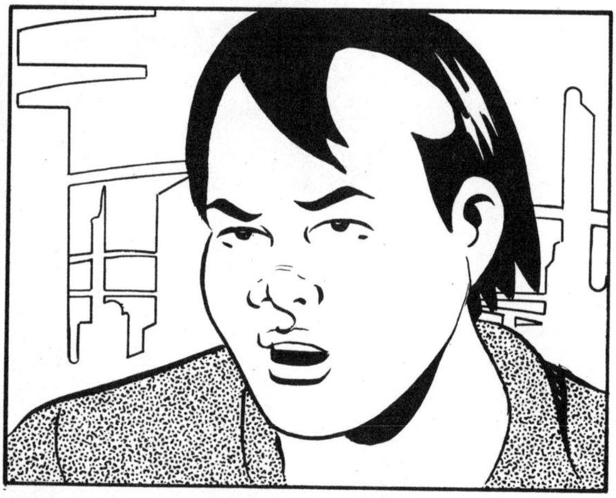

Don't be so closed-minded until you hear me out. I studied old "videotapes" and news reports from 1998. More important, I scanned everything I could find on the great man who sacrificed everything to save his fellow human beings . . .

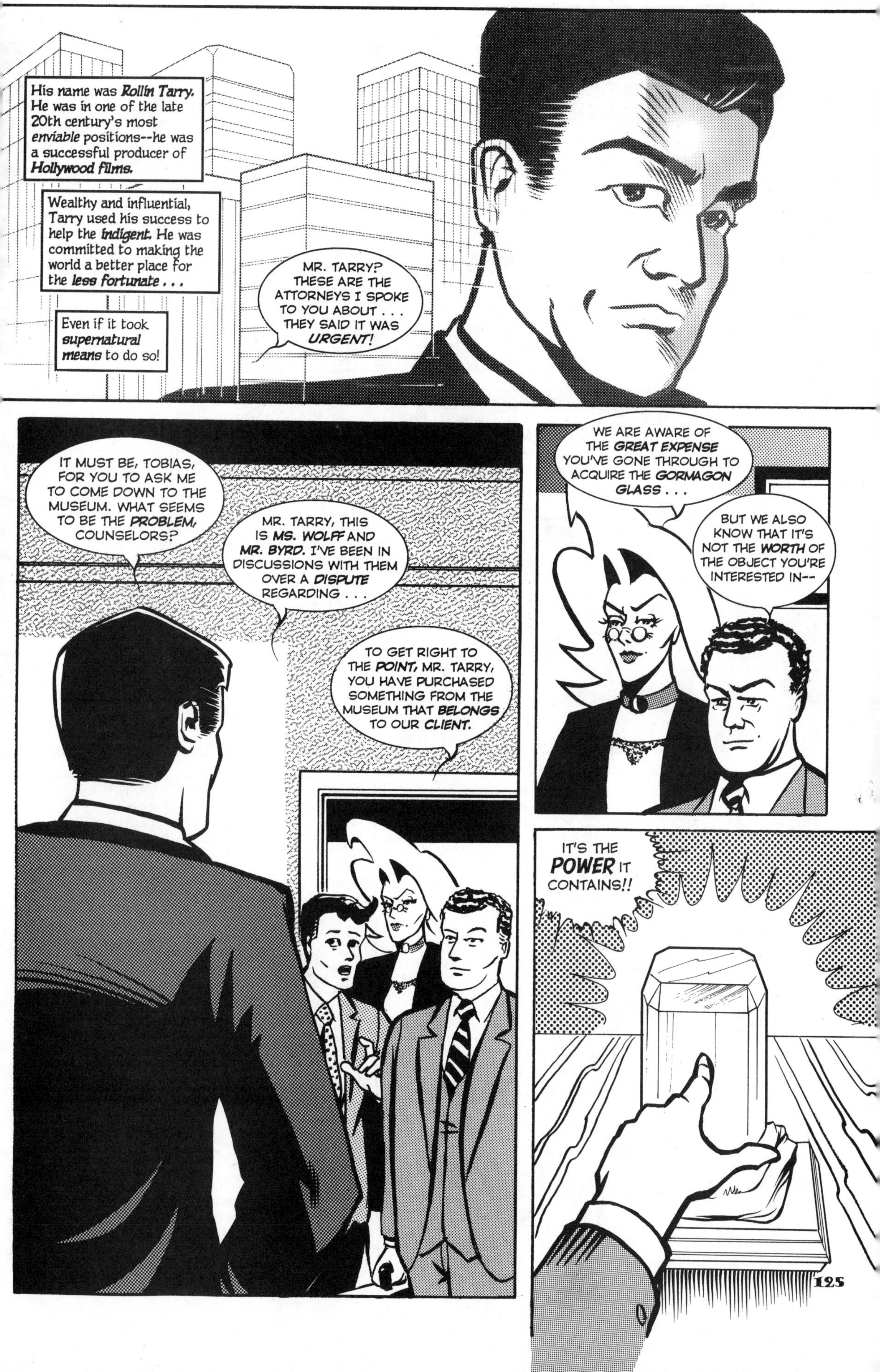

His name was Rollin Tarry. He was in one of the late 20th century's most enviable positions--he was a successful producer of Hollywood films.
Wealthy and influential, Tarry used his success to help the indigent. He was committed to making the world a better place for the less fortunate . . .
Even if it took supernatural means to do so!
MR. TARRY? THESE ARE THE ATTORNEYS I SPOKE TO YOU ABOUT . . . THEY SAID IT WAS URGENT!
IT MUST BE, TOBIAS, FOR YOU TO ASK ME TO COME DOWN TO THE MUSEUM. WHAT SEEMS TO BE THE PROBLEM, COUNSELORS?
MR. TARRY, THIS IS MS. WOLFF AND MR. BYRD. I'VE BEEN IN DISCUSSIONS WITH THEM OVER A DISPUTE REGARDING . . .
TO GET RIGHT TO THE POINT, MR. TARRY, YOU HAVE PURCHASED SOMETHING FROM THE MUSEUM THAT BELONGS TO OUR CLIENT.
WE ARE AWARE OF THE GREAT EXPENSE YOU'VE GONE THROUGH TO ACQUIRE THE GORMAGON GLASS . . .
BUT WE ALSO KNOW THAT IT'S NOT THE WORTH OF THE OBJECT YOU'RE INTERESTED IN--
IT'S THE POWER IT CONTAINS!!

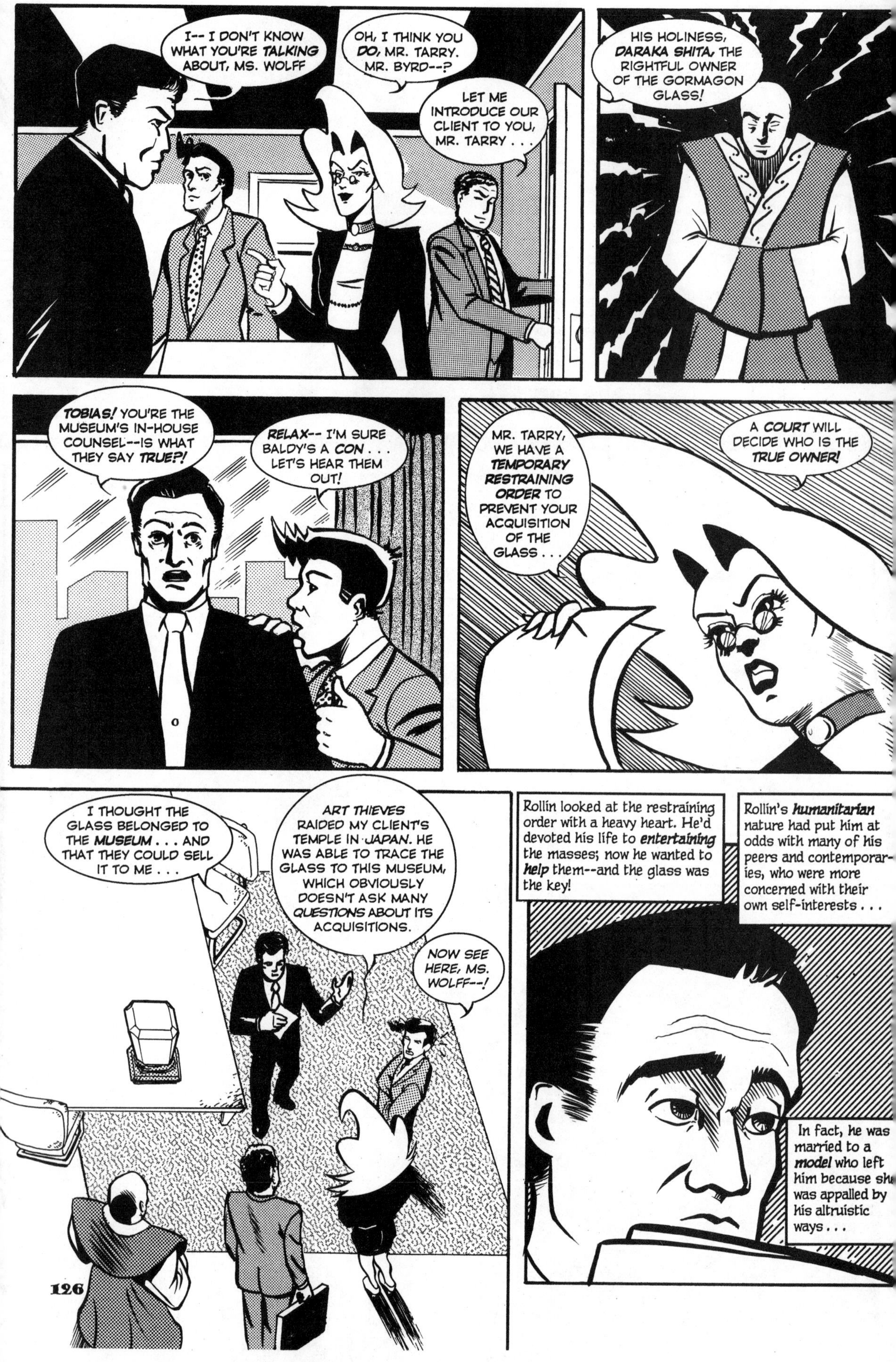
I-- I DON'T KNOW WHAT YOU'RE TALKING ABOUT, MS. WOLFF
OH, I THINK YOU DO, MR. TARRY. MR. BYRD--?
LET ME INTRODUCE OUR CLIENT TO YOU, MR. TARRY . . .
HIS HOLINESS, DARAKA SHITA, THE RIGHTFUL OWNER OF THE GORMAGON GLASS!
TOBIAS! YOU'RE THE MUSEUM'S IN-HOUSE COUNSEL--IS WHAT THEY SAY TRUE?!
RELAX-- I'M SURE BALDY'S A CON . . . LET'S HEAR THEM OUT!
MR. TARRY, WE HAVE A TEMPORARY RESTRAINING ORDER TO PREVENT YOUR ACQUISITION OF THE GLASS . . .
A COURT WILL DECIDE WHO IS THE TRUE OWNER!
I THOUGHT THE GLASS BELONGED TO THE MUSEUM . . . AND THAT THEY COULD SELL IT TO ME . . .
ART THIEVES RAIDED MY CLIENT'S TEMPLE IN JAPAN. HE WAS ABLE TO TRACE THE GLASS TO THIS MUSEUM, WHICH OBVIOUSLY DOESN'T ASK MANY QUESTIONS ABOUT ITS ACQUISITIONS.
NOW SEE HERE, MS. WOLFF--!
Rollin looked at the restraining order with a heavy heart. He'd devoted his life to entertaining the masses; now he wanted to help them--and the glass was the key!
Rollin's humanitarian nature had put him at odds with many of his peers and contemporaries, who were more concerned with their own self-interests . . .
In fact, he was married to a model who left him because she was appalled by his altruistic ways . . .

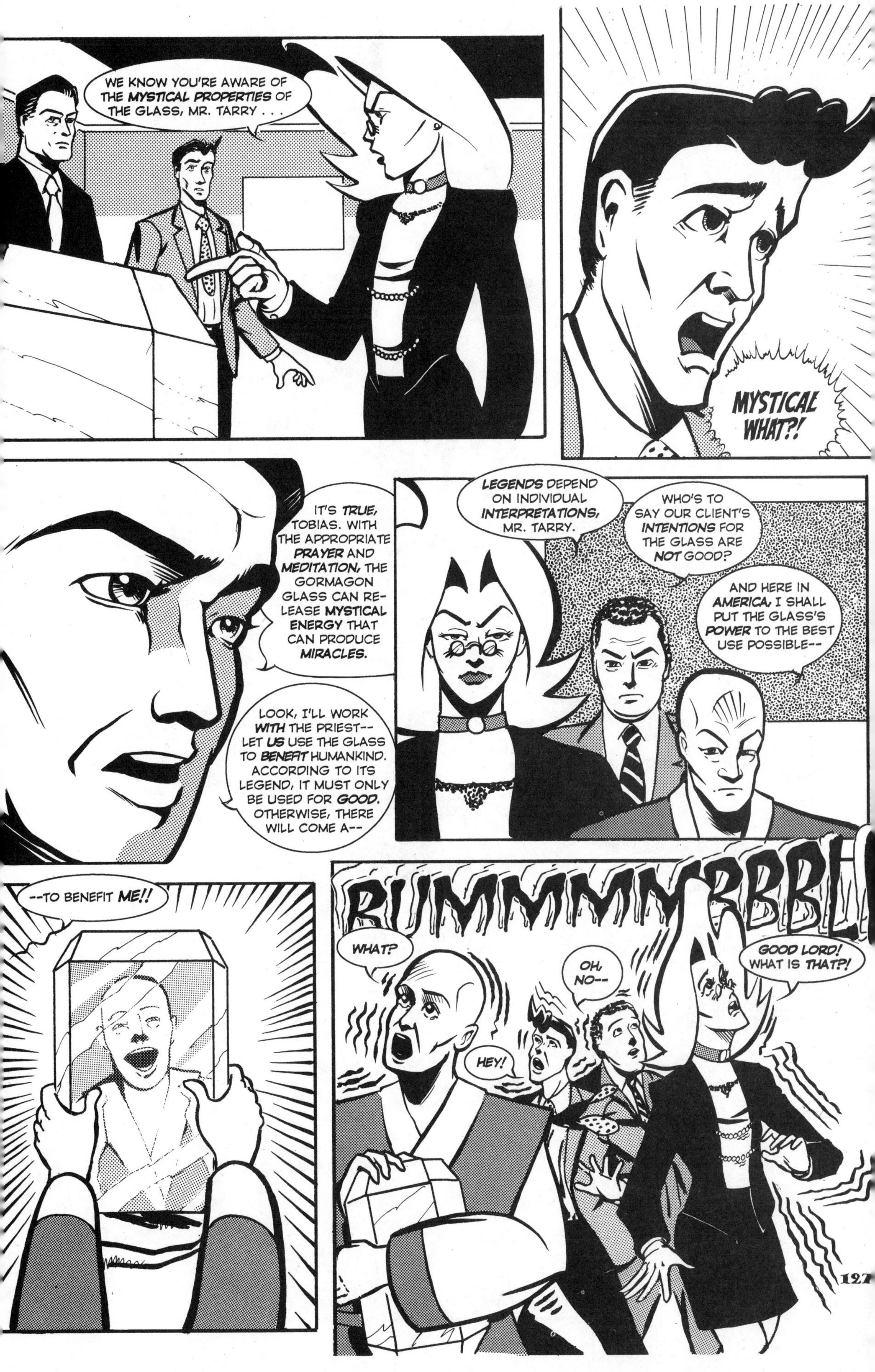

WE KNOW YOU'RE AWARE OF THE MYSTICAL PROPERTIES OF THE GLASS, MR. TARRY . . .
MYSTICAL WHAT?!
IT'S TRUE, TOBIAS. WITH THE APPROPRIATE PRAYER AND MEDITATION, THE GORMAGON GLASS CAN RE-LEASE MYSTICAL ENERGY THAT CAN PRODUCE MIRACLES.
LOOK, I'LL WORK WITH THE PRIEST-- LET US USE THE GLASS TO BENEFIT HUMANKIND. ACCORDING TO ITS LEGEND, IT MUST ONLY BE USED FOR GOOD. OTHERWISE, THERE WILL COME A--
LEGENDS DEPEND ON INDIVIDUAL INTERPRETATIONS, MR. TARRY.
WHO'S TO SAY OUR CLIENT'S INTENTIONS FOR THE GLASS ARE NOT GOOD?
AND HERE IN AMERICA, I SHALL PUT THE GLASS'S POWER TO THE BEST USE POSSIBLE--
--TO BENEFIT ME!!
RUMMMMRBBL
WHAT?
OH, NO--
GOOD LORD! WHAT IS THAT?!
HEY!

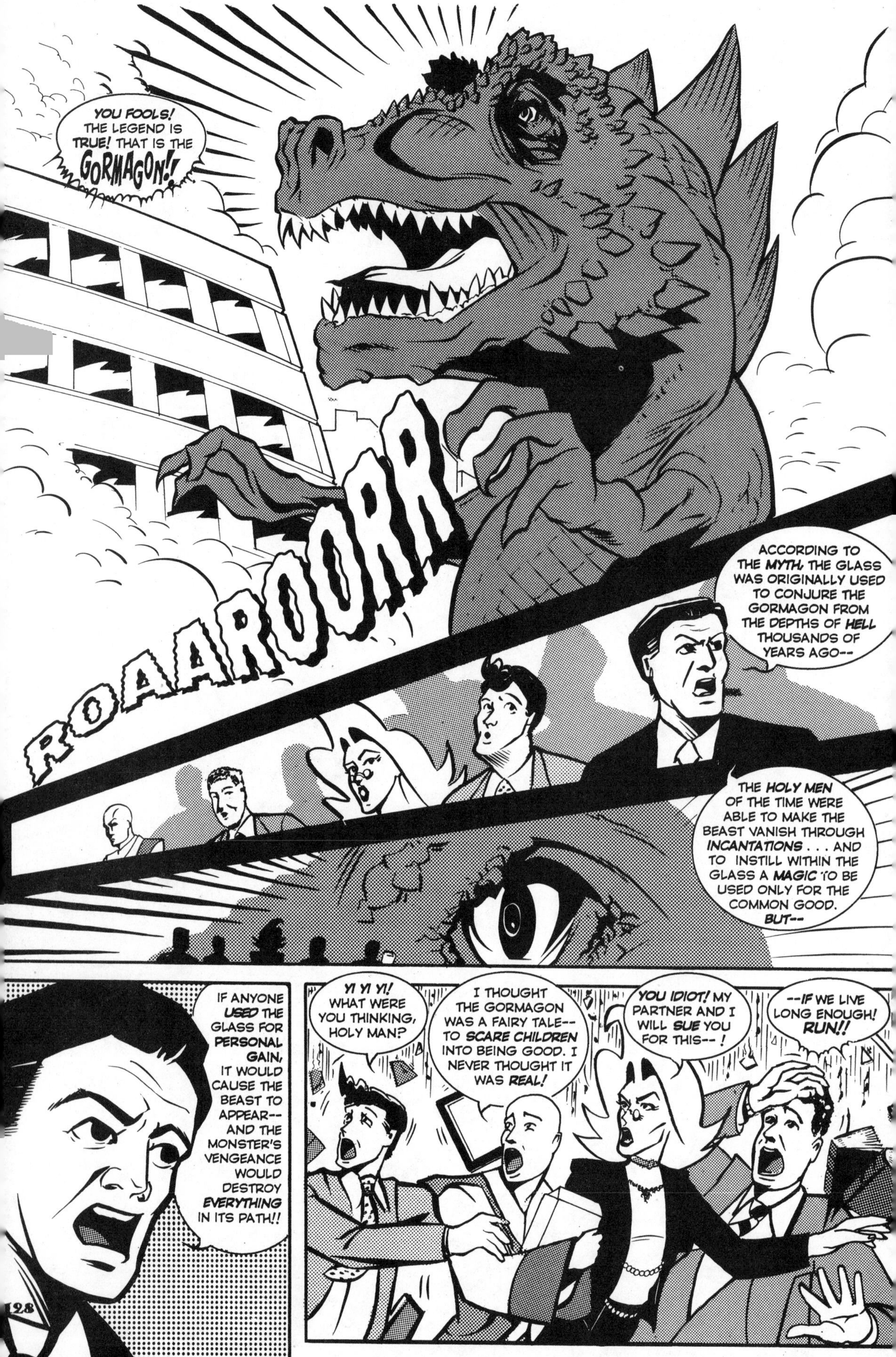
YOU FOOLS! THE LEGEND IS TRUE! THAT IS THE GORMAGON!!
ROAAROORR
ACCORDING TO THE MYTH, THE GLASS WAS ORIGINALLY USED TO CONJURE THE GORMAGON FROM THE DEPTHS OF HELL THOUSANDS OF YEARS AGO--
THE HOLY MEN OF THE TIME WERE ABLE TO MAKE THE BEAST VANISH THROUGH INCANTATIONS . . . AND TO INSTILL WITHIN THE GLASS A MAGIC TO BE USED ONLY FOR THE COMMON GOOD. BUT--
IF ANYONE USED THE GLASS FOR PERSONAL GAIN, IT WOULD CAUSE THE BEAST TO APPEAR-- AND THE MONSTER'S VENGEANCE WOULD DESTROY EVERYTHING IN ITS PATH!!
YI YI YI! WHAT WERE YOU THINKING, HOLY MAN?
I THOUGHT THE GORMAGON WAS A FAIRY TALE-- TO SCARE CHILDREN INTO BEING GOOD. I NEVER THOUGHT IT WAS REAL!
YOU IDIOT! MY PARTNER AND I WILL SUE YOU FOR THIS-- !
--IF WE LIVE LONG ENOUGH! RUN!!

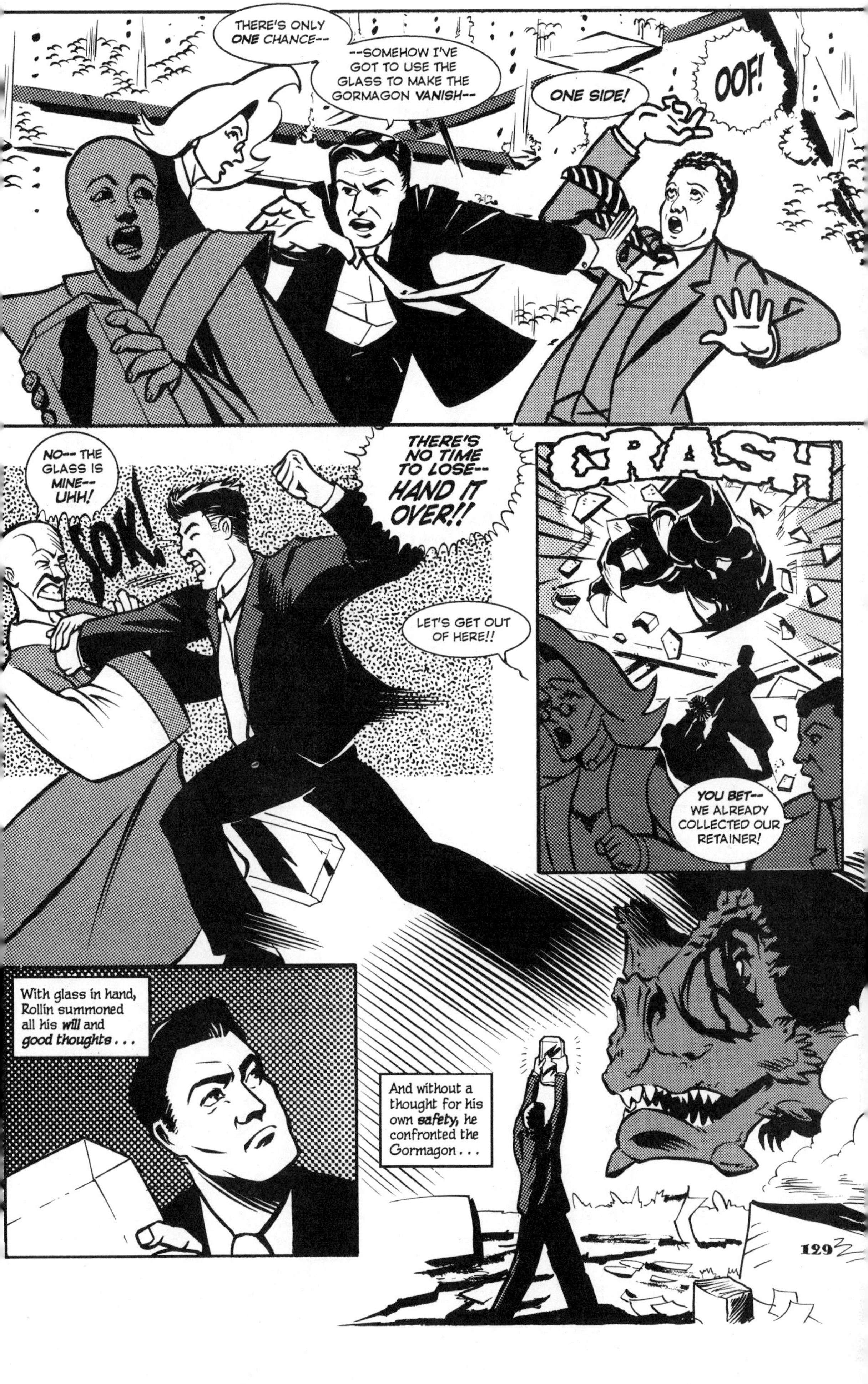

THERE'S ONLY ONE CHANCE--
--SOMEHOW I'VE GOT TO USE THE GLASS TO MAKE THE GORMAGON VANISH--
ONE SIDE!
OOF!
NO-- THE GLASS IS MINE-- UHH!
SOK!
THERE'S NO TIME TO LOSE-- HAND IT OVER!!
CRASH
LET'S GET OUT OF HERE!!
YOU BET-- WE ALREADY COLLECTED OUR RETAINER!
With glass in hand, Rollin summoned all his will and good thoughts . . .
And without a thought for his own safety, he confronted the Gormagon . . .

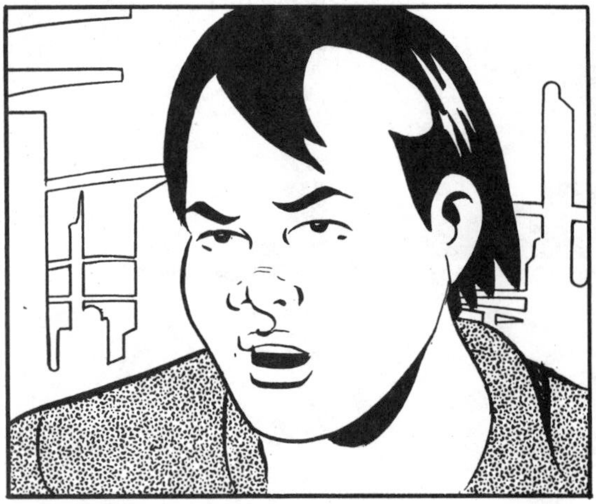

. . . and as the monster closed in on Rollin Tarry, they both disappeared--never to be seen or heard from again.

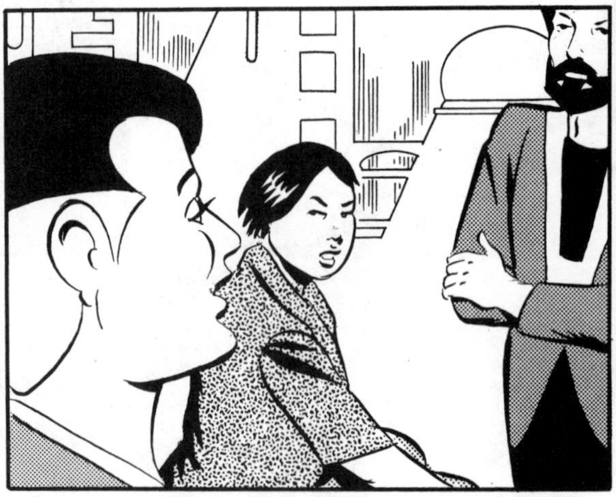

And you believe that?

Yes! I told you I researched Tarry's life thoroughly . . .

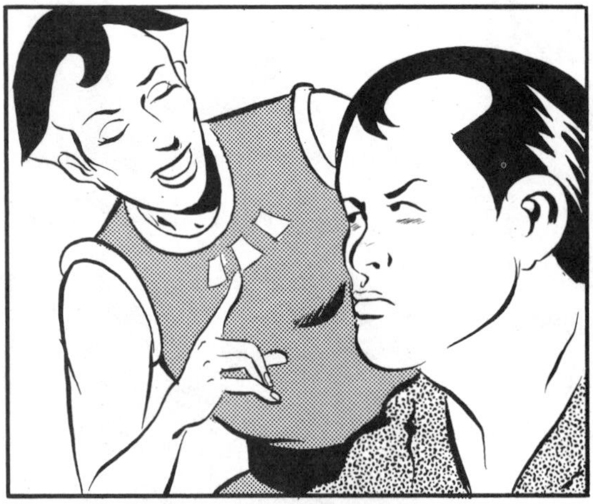

Don't tell me--you went to his official biography sites!

Hey--Rollin was a socially conscious activist in his era. I have to take what his detractors say with a grain of salt.

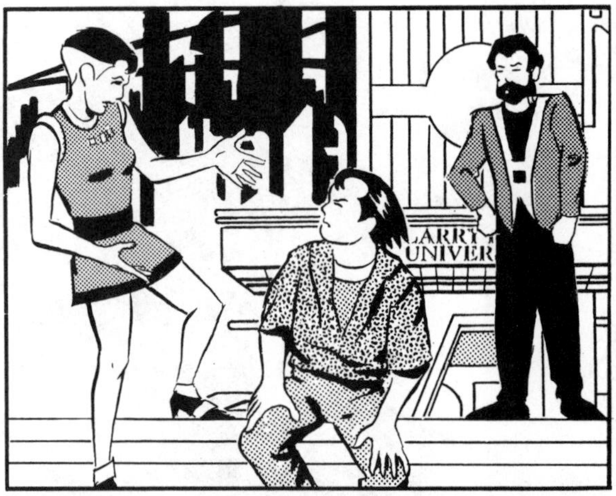
LARRY
UNIVER

Detrek, that was a crude, simplistic extrapolation of what ***really*** happened! Come on-- your hero, Rollin Tarry, lived in Hollywood in the late 20th century--how ***sincere*** could he have been?

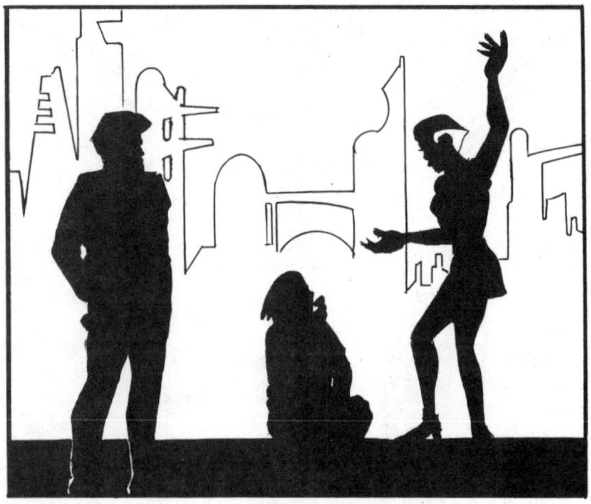

In those days when people ***had*** to pay income tax, a rich guy like Tarry would give to charities as a writeoff! But you did get ***some*** elements of what happened correct . . .

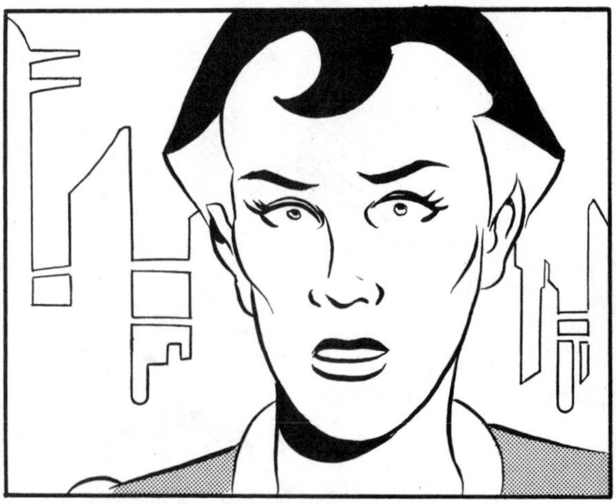

There was definitely an old gem that possessed strange mystical powers . . . and there were ***lawyers*** who took advantage of an innocent holy man who was victimized by the corrupt ways of a Western world . . .!

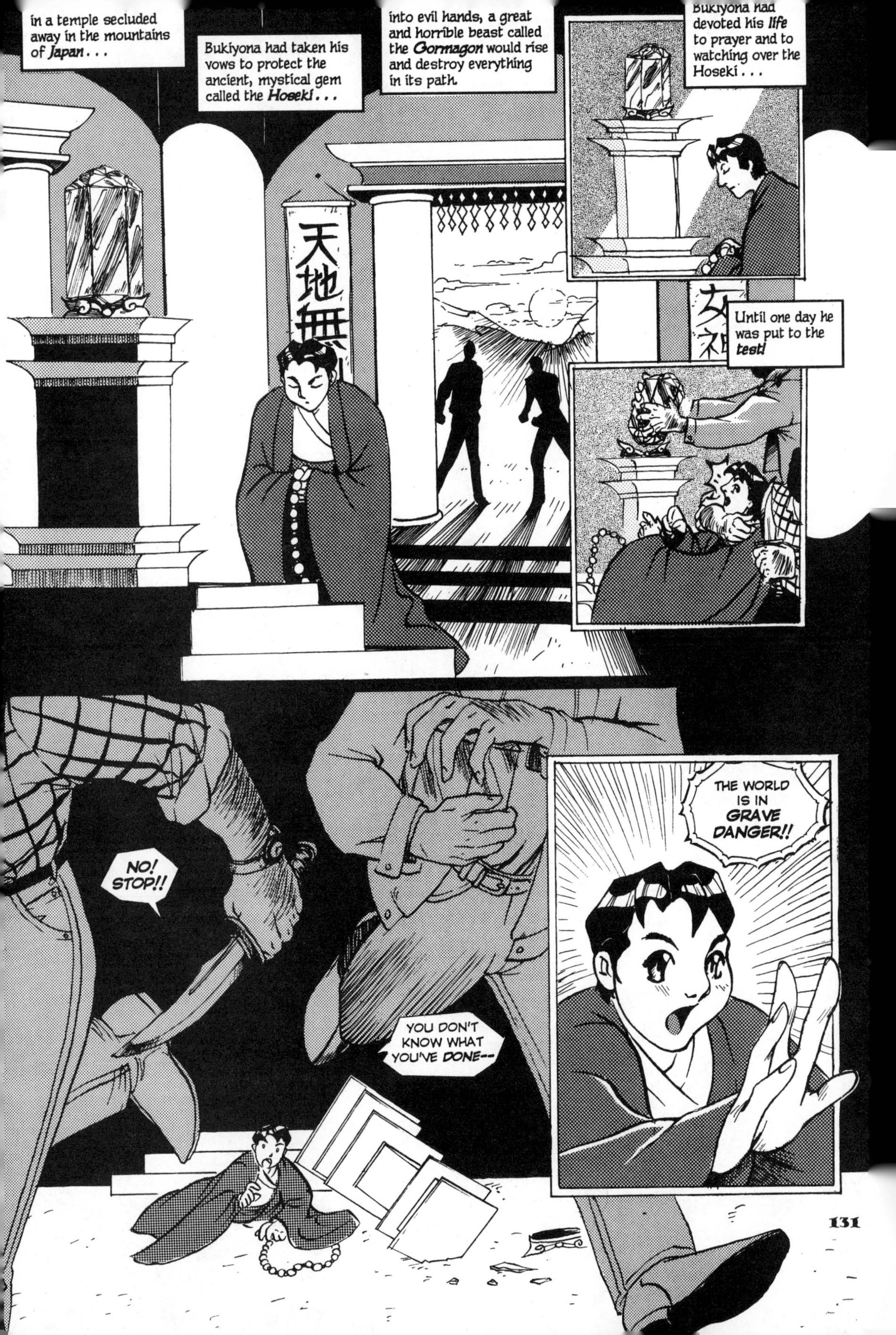
in a temple secluded away in the mountains of Japan . . .
Bukiyona had taken his vows to protect the ancient, mystical gem called the Hoseki . . .
into evil hands, a great and horrible beast called the Gormagon would rise and destroy everything in its path.
Bukiyona had devoted his life to prayer and to watching over the Hoseki . . .
Until one day he was put to the test!
NO! STOP!!
YOU DON'T KNOW WHAT YOU'VE DONE--
THE WORLD IS IN GRAVE DANGER!!

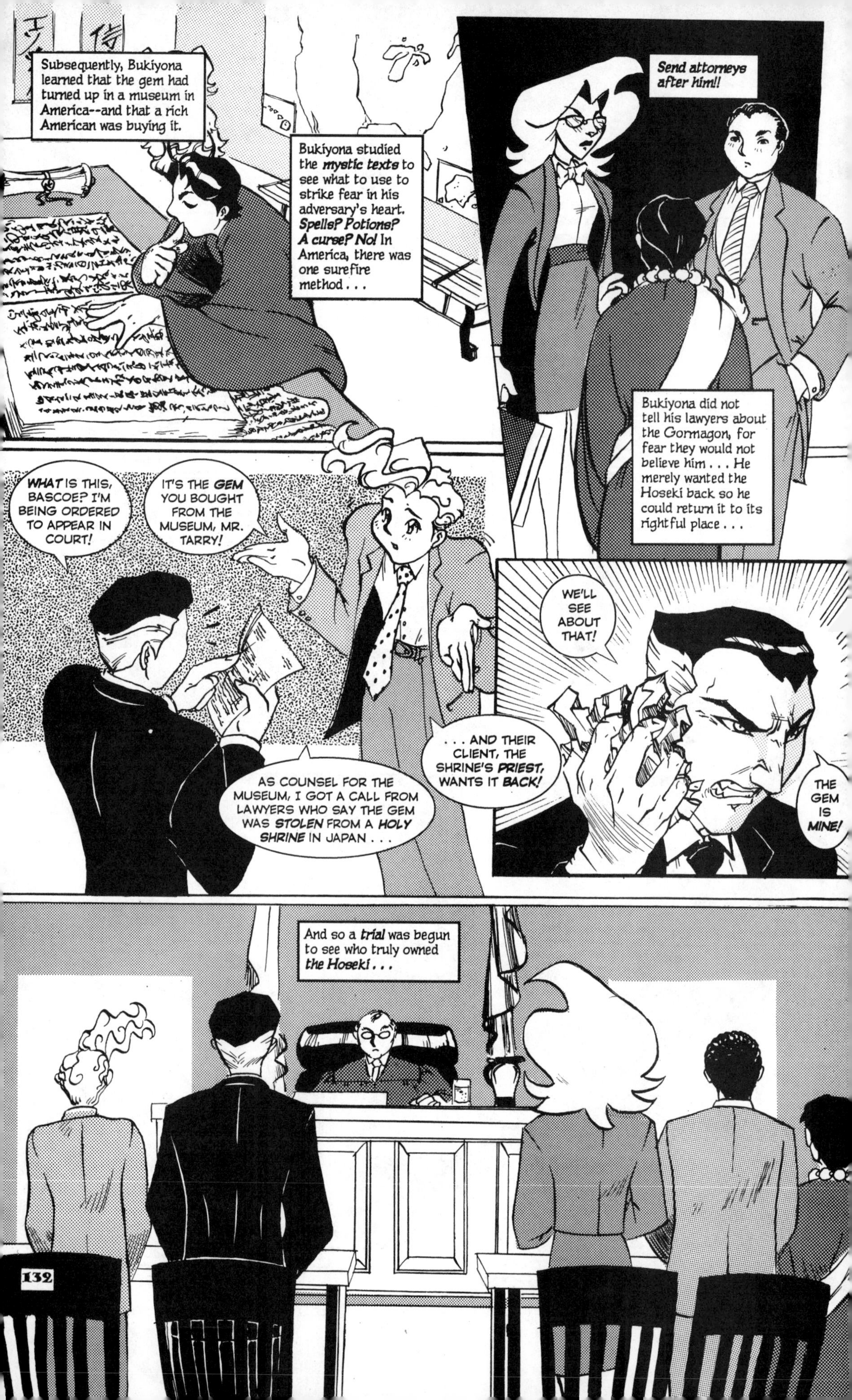

Subsequently, Bukiyona learned that the gem had turned up in a museum in America--and that a rich American was buying it.
Bukiyona studied the mystic texts to see what to use to strike fear in his adversary's heart. Spells? Potions? A curse? No! In America, there was one surefire method . . .
Send attorneys after him!!
Bukiyona did not tell his lawyers about the Gormagon, for fear they would not believe him . . . He merely wanted the Hoseki back so he could return it to its rightful place . . .
WHAT IS THIS, BASCOE? I'M BEING ORDERED TO APPEAR IN COURT!
IT'S THE GEM YOU BOUGHT FROM THE MUSEUM, MR. TARRY!
AS COUNSEL FOR THE MUSEUM, I GOT A CALL FROM LAWYERS WHO SAY THE GEM WAS STOLEN FROM A HOLY SHRINE IN JAPAN . . .
. . . AND THEIR CLIENT, THE SHRINE'S PRIEST, WANTS IT BACK!
WE'LL SEE ABOUT THAT!
THE GEM IS MINE!
And so a trial was begun to see who truly owned the Hoseki . . .

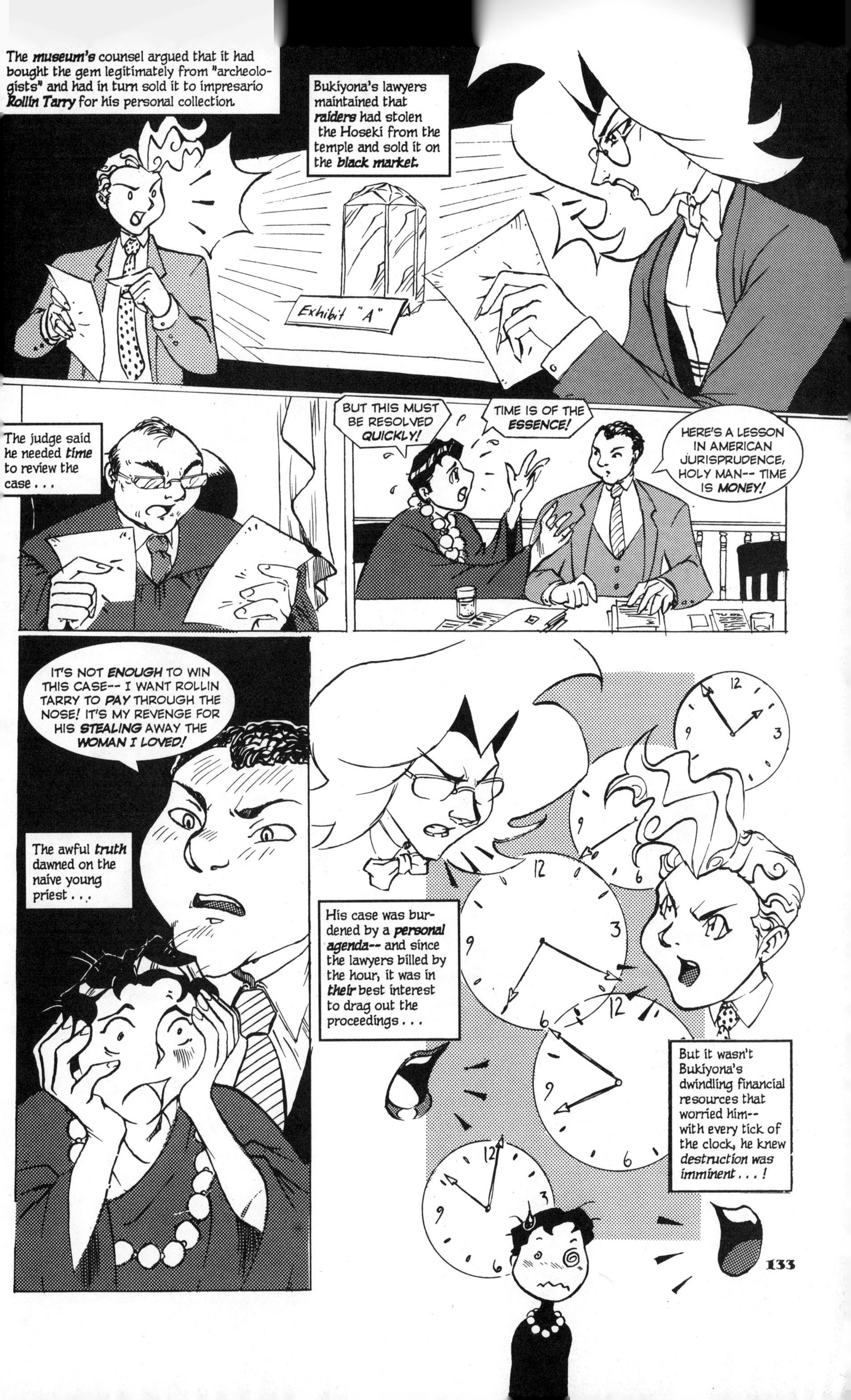

The museum's counsel argued that it had bought the gem legitimately from "archeologists" and had in turn sold it to impresario Rollin Tarry for his personal collection.
Bukiyona's lawyers maintained that raiders had stolen the Hoseki from the temple and sold it on the black market.
Exhibit "A"
The judge said he needed time to review the case . . .
BUT THIS MUST BE RESOLVED QUICKLY!
TIME IS OF THE ESSENCE!
HERE'S A LESSON IN AMERICAN JURISPRUDENCE, HOLY MAN-- TIME IS MONEY!
IT'S NOT ENOUGH TO WIN THIS CASE-- I WANT ROLLIN TARRY TO PAY THROUGH THE NOSE! IT'S MY REVENGE FOR HIS STEALING AWAY THE WOMAN I LOVED!
The awful truth dawned on the naive young priest . . .
His case was burdened by a personal agenda-- and since the lawyers billed by the hour, it was in their best interest to drag out the proceedings . . .
But it wasn't Bukiyona's dwindling financial resources that worried him-- with every tick of the clock, he knew destruction was imminent . . . !

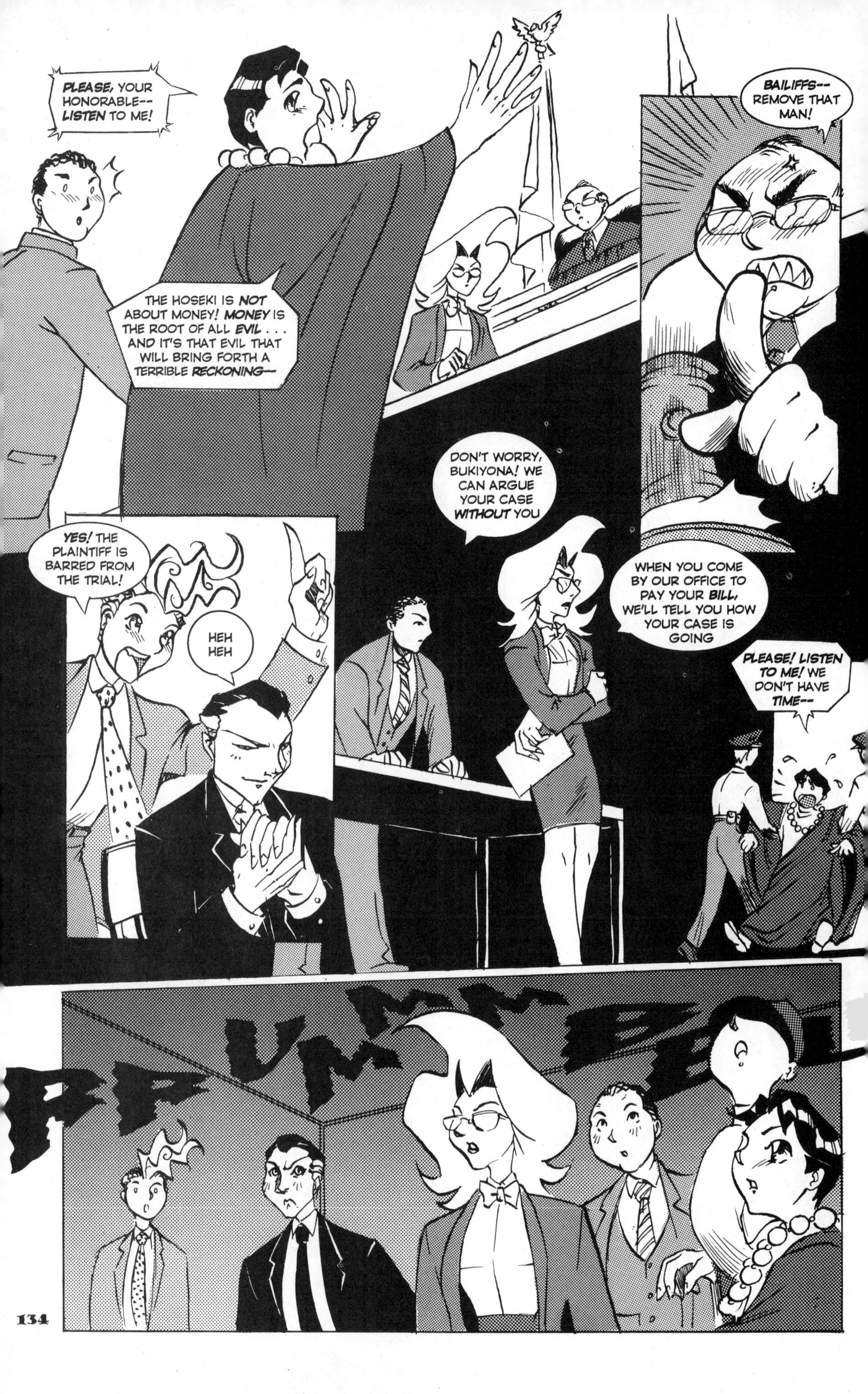
PLEASE, YOUR HONORABLE-- LISTEN TO ME!
THE HOSEKI IS NOT ABOUT MONEY! MONEY IS THE ROOT OF ALL EVIL . . . AND IT'S THAT EVIL THAT WILL BRING FORTH A TERRIBLE RECKONING--
BAILIFFS-- REMOVE THAT MAN!
YES! THE PLAINTIFF IS BARRED FROM THE TRIAL!
HEH HEH
DON'T WORRY, BUKIYONA! WE CAN ARGUE YOUR CASE WITHOUT YOU
WHEN YOU COME BY OUR OFFICE TO PAY YOUR BILL, WE'LL TELL YOU HOW YOUR CASE IS GOING
PLEASE! LISTEN TO ME! WE DON'T HAVE TIME--
PFUMMBBL

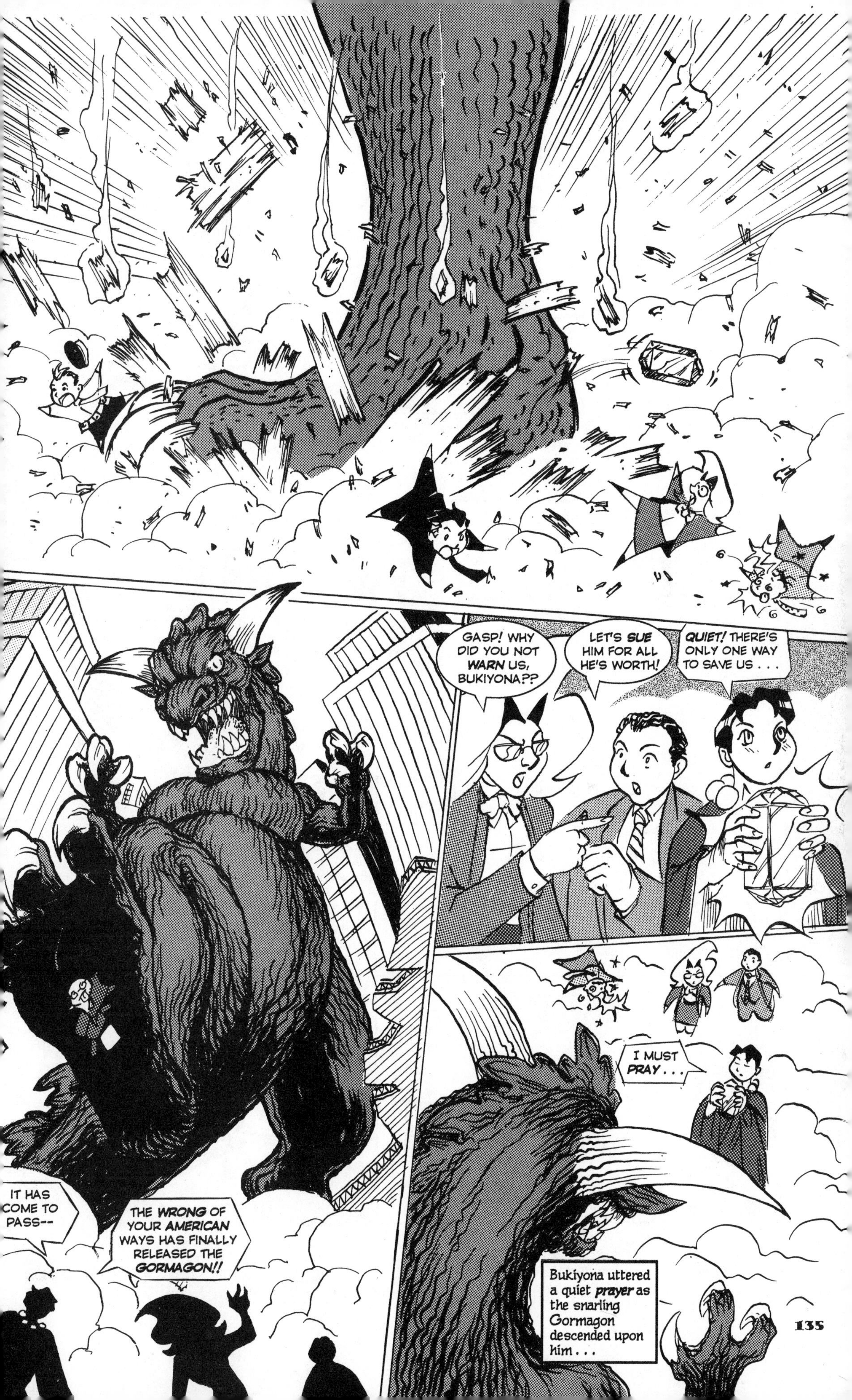
GASP! WHY DID YOU NOT WARN US, BUKIYONA??
LET'S SUE HIM FOR ALL HE'S WORTH!
QUIET! THERE'S ONLY ONE WAY TO SAVE US . . .
I MUST PRAY . . .
IT HAS COME TO PASS--
THE WRONG OF YOUR AMERICAN WAYS HAS FINALLY RELEASED THE GORMAGON!!
Bukiyona uttered a quiet prayer as the snarling Gormagon descended upon him . . .

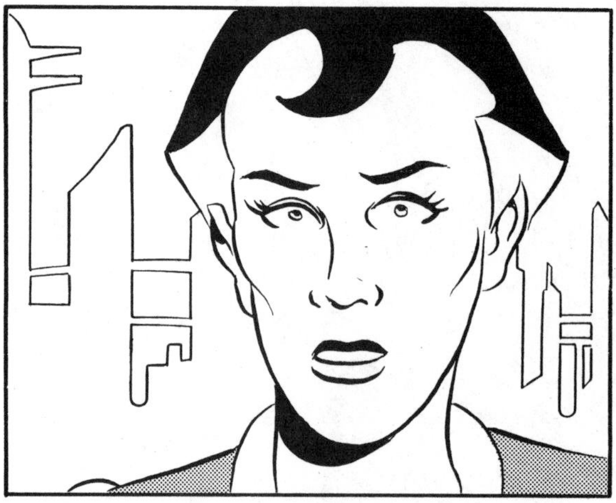

And with the power of ***prayer,*** the priest, the gem, and the monster all disappeared. Bukiyona saved the corrupt and undeserving Westerners . . . who have ever since ***discredited*** Bukiyona's noble act--since the ***truth*** exposes a depraved and decadent America.

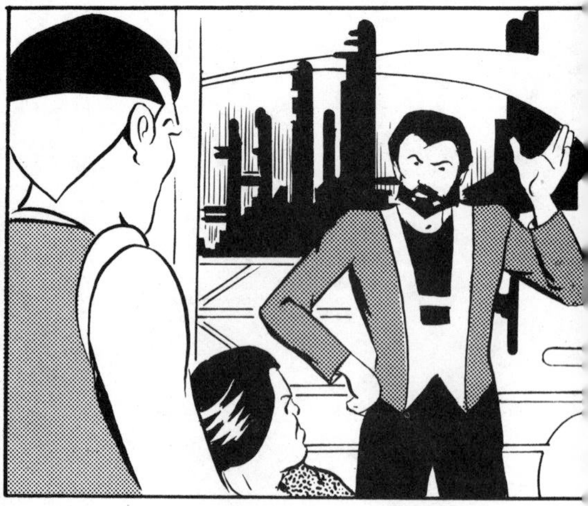

Aw, you've ***got*** to be kidding!!

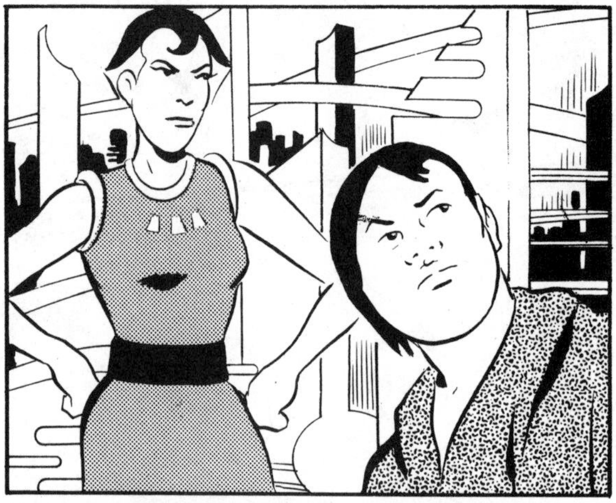

Melena, your major is divinity studies . . . and you, Detrek, are a student of pre-holo cinema--particularly Hollywood producers of the late 20th century--

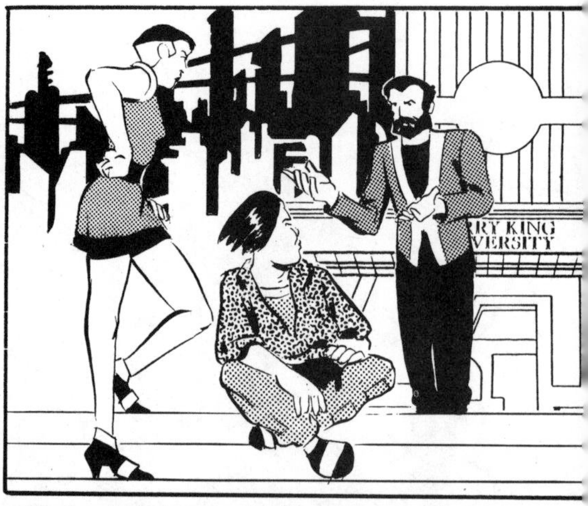
RRY KING
VERSITY

--Don't you think you each have taken a ***biased*** view and ***twisted*** the facts of what really happened? Did you ever think to go to the ***legal records*** to find the official version of the proceedings?

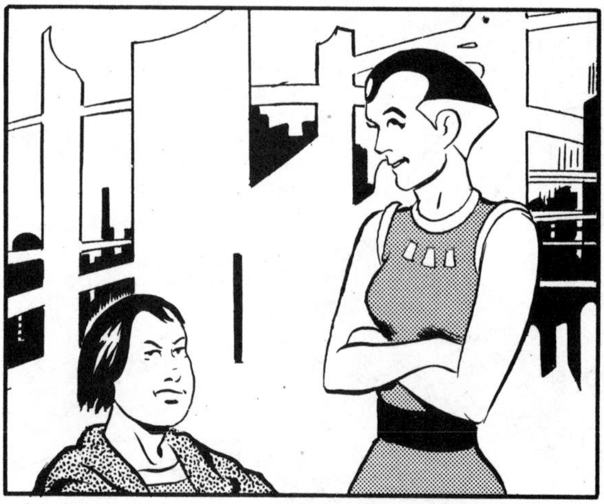

"Official" version? Ha! That's what they'd ***like*** you to believe!

Gee, Choz the law student researched the legal records--wonder whose ***side*** he's on!

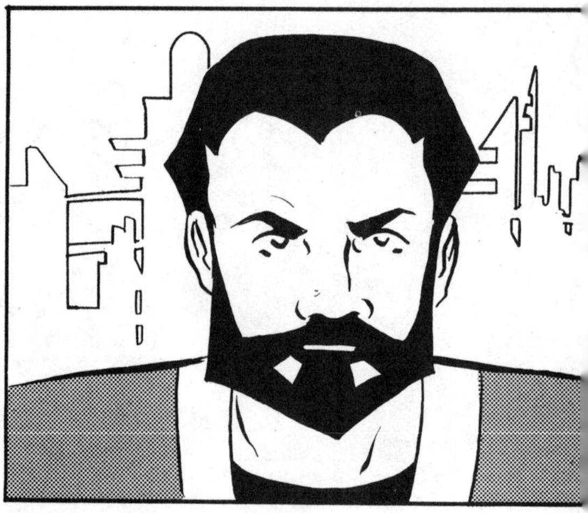

It's not a matter of taking sides, Melena! Documents, diaries, and files from that era are easily accessible. There ***was*** a legal dispute over a jewel, that is for sure. But the lawyers involved tell a very different version of the story . . .

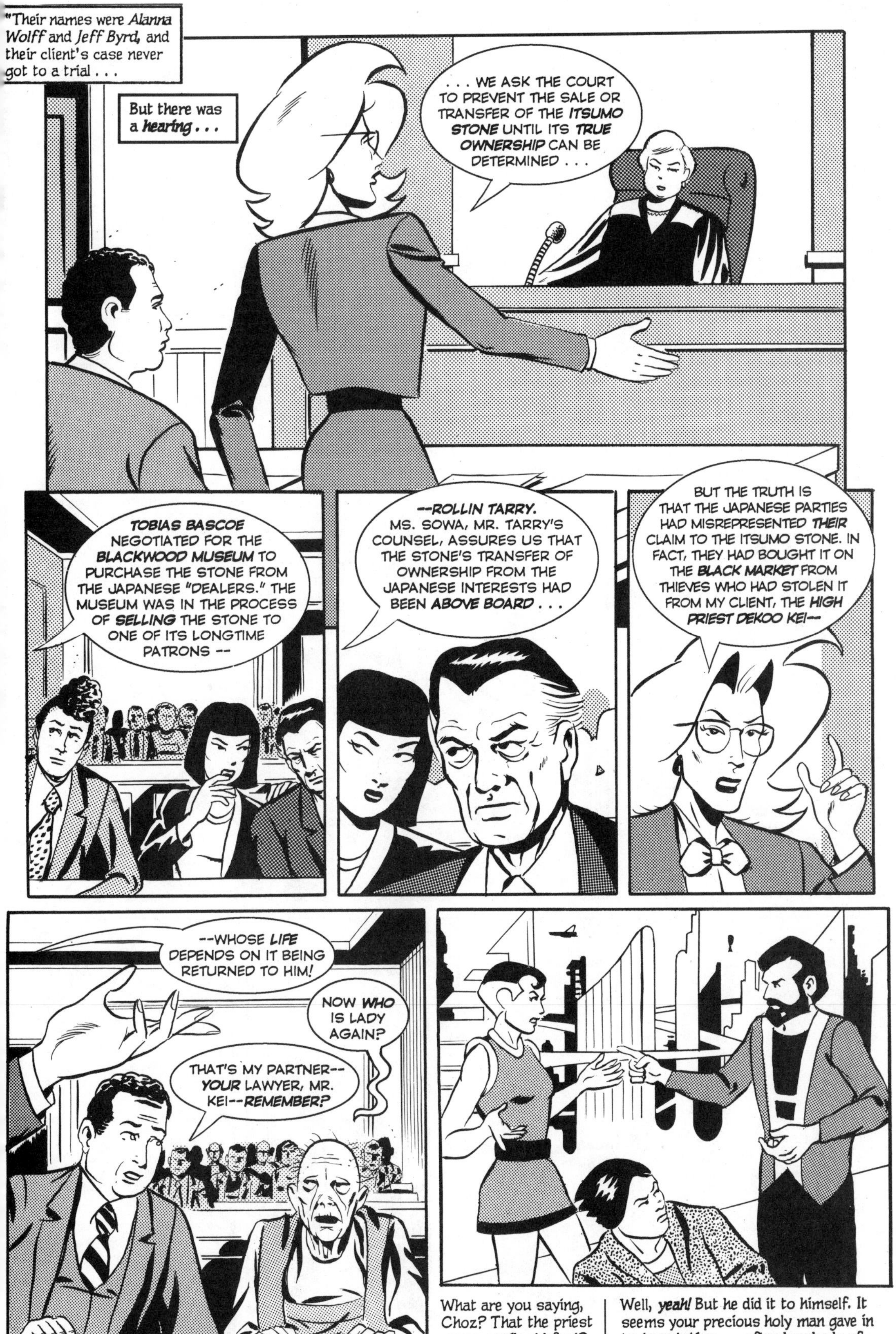
"Their names were Alanna Wolff and Jeff Byrd, and their client's case never got to a trial . . .
But there was a hearing . . .
. . . WE ASK THE COURT TO PREVENT THE SALE OR TRANSFER OF THE ITSUMO STONE UNTIL ITS TRUE OWNERSHIP CAN BE DETERMINED . . .
TOBIAS BASCOE NEGOTIATED FOR THE BLACKWOOD MUSEUM TO PURCHASE THE STONE FROM THE JAPANESE "DEALERS." THE MUSEUM WAS IN THE PROCESS OF SELLING THE STONE TO ONE OF ITS LONGTIME PATRONS --
--ROLLIN TARRY. MS. SOWA, MR. TARRY'S COUNSEL, ASSURES US THAT THE STONE'S TRANSFER OF OWNERSHIP FROM THE JAPANESE INTERESTS HAD BEEN ABOVE BOARD . . .
BUT THE TRUTH IS THAT THE JAPANESE PARTIES HAD MISREPRESENTED THEIR CLAIM TO THE ITSUMO STONE. IN FACT, THEY HAD BOUGHT IT ON THE BLACK MARKET FROM THIEVES WHO HAD STOLEN IT FROM MY CLIENT, THE HIGH PRIEST DEKOO KEI--
--WHOSE LIFE DEPENDS ON IT BEING RETURNED TO HIM!
NOW WHO IS LADY AGAIN?
THAT'S MY PARTNER-- YOUR LAWYER, MR. KEI--REMEMBER?
What are you saying, Choz? That the priest was a senile old fool?
Well, yeah! But he did it to himself. It seems your precious holy man gave in to temptation . . . after hundreds of years of piety and celibacy!

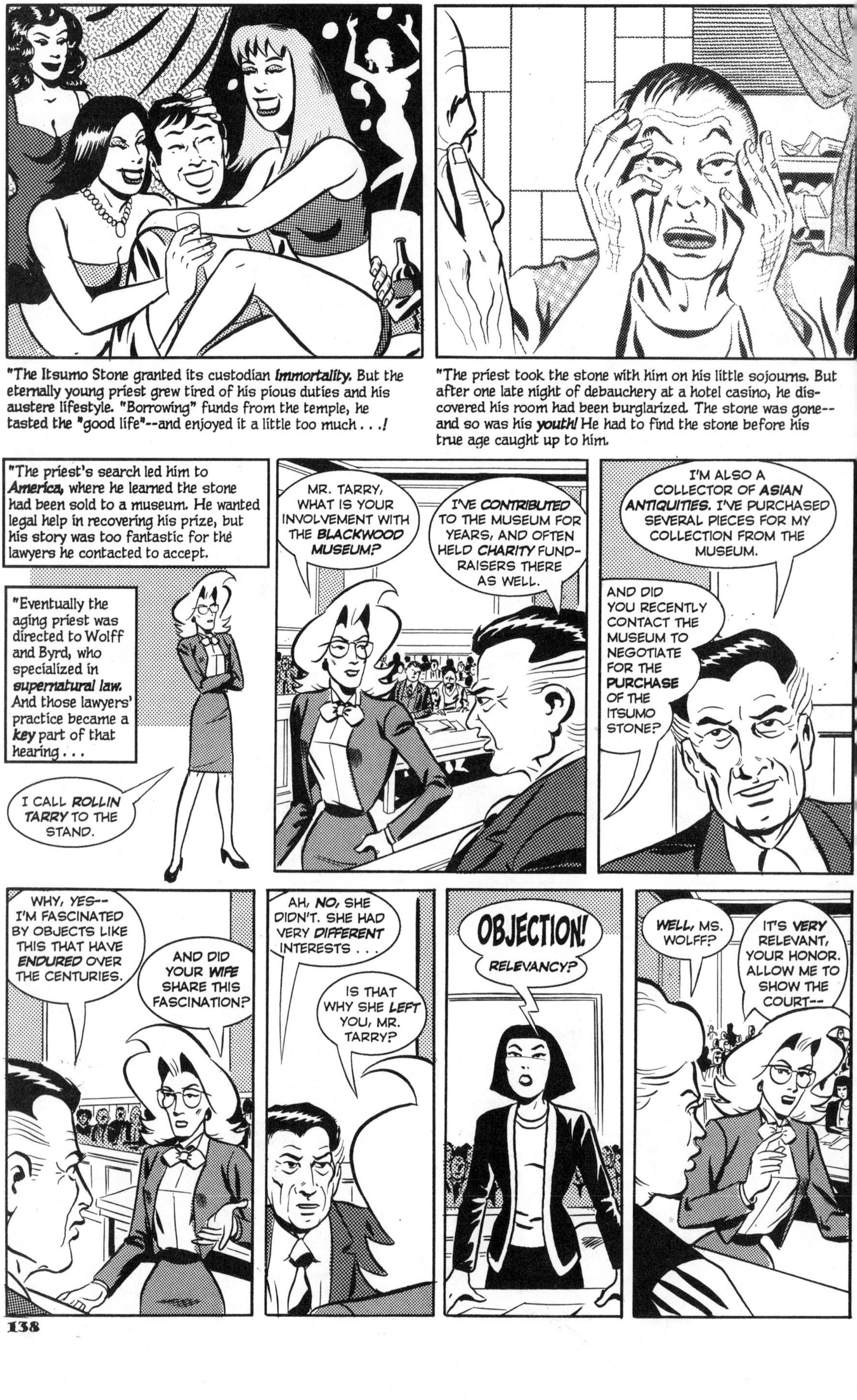
"The Itsumo Stone granted its custodian *immortality.* But the eternally young priest grew tired of his pious duties and his austere lifestyle. "Borrowing" funds from the temple, he tasted the "good life"--and enjoyed it a little too much . . .!
"The priest took the stone with him on his little sojourns. But after one late night of debauchery at a hotel casino, he discovered his room had been burglarized. The stone was gone--and so was his *youth!* He had to find the stone before his true age caught up to him.
"The priest's search led him to *America,* where he learned the stone had been sold to a museum. He wanted legal help in recovering his prize, but his story was too fantastic for the lawyers he contacted to accept.
"Eventually the aging priest was directed to Wolff and Byrd, who specialized in *supernatural law.* And those lawyers' practice became a *key* part of that hearing . . .
I CALL *ROLLIN TARRY* TO THE STAND.
MR. TARRY, WHAT IS YOUR INVOLVEMENT WITH THE *BLACKWOOD MUSEUM?*
I'VE *CONTRIBUTED* TO THE MUSEUM FOR YEARS, AND OFTEN HELD *CHARITY* FUND-RAISERS THERE AS WELL.
I'M ALSO A COLLECTOR OF *ASIAN ANTIQUITIES.* I'VE PURCHASED SEVERAL PIECES FOR MY COLLECTION FROM THE MUSEUM.
AND DID YOU RECENTLY CONTACT THE MUSEUM TO NEGOTIATE FOR THE *PURCHASE* OF THE ITSUMO STONE?
WHY, *YES*-- I'M FASCINATED BY OBJECTS LIKE THIS THAT HAVE *ENDURED* OVER THE CENTURIES.
AND DID YOUR *WIFE* SHARE THIS FASCINATION?
AH, *NO,* SHE DIDN'T. SHE HAD VERY *DIFFERENT* INTERESTS . . .
IS THAT WHY SHE *LEFT* YOU, MR. TARRY?
OBJECTION!
RELEVANCY?
WELL, MS. WOLFF?
IT'S *VERY* RELEVANT, YOUR HONOR. ALLOW ME TO SHOW THE COURT--

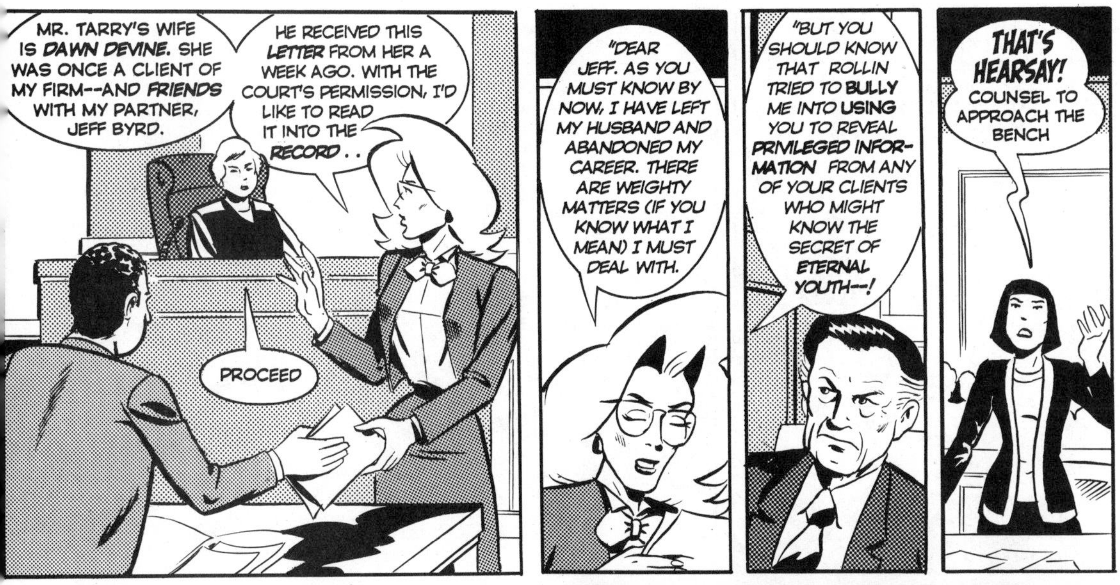
MR. TARRY'S WIFE IS DAWN DEVINE. SHE WAS ONCE A CLIENT OF MY FIRM--AND FRIENDS WITH MY PARTNER, JEFF BYRD.
HE RECEIVED THIS LETTER FROM HER A WEEK AGO. WITH THE COURT'S PERMISSION, I'D LIKE TO READ IT INTO THE RECORD . . .
PROCEED
"DEAR JEFF. AS YOU MUST KNOW BY NOW, I HAVE LEFT MY HUSBAND AND ABANDONED MY CAREER. THERE ARE WEIGHTY MATTERS (IF YOU KNOW WHAT I MEAN) I MUST DEAL WITH.
"BUT YOU SHOULD KNOW THAT ROLLIN TRIED TO BULLY ME INTO USING YOU TO REVEAL PRIVILEGED INFORMATION FROM ANY OF YOUR CLIENTS WHO MIGHT KNOW THE SECRET OF ETERNAL YOUTH--!
THAT'S HEARSAY! COUNSEL TO APPROACH THE BENCH

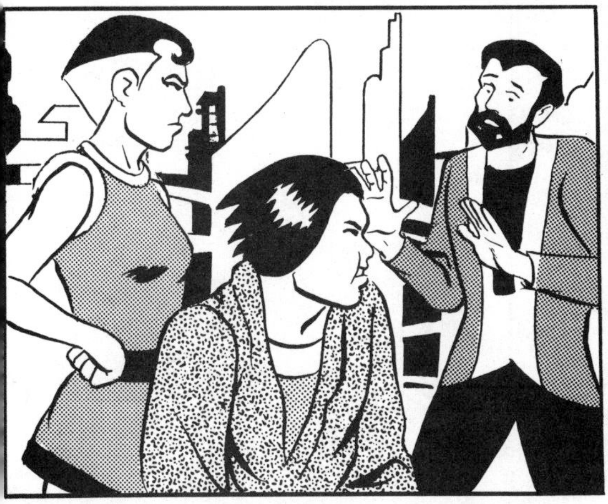

Take it *easy,* Detrek--I 'm just telling you what the public record shows. I also researched the wife, *Dawn DeVine.* She was a fashion model in the 1990s. She dropped out of sight at the end of that decade . . .

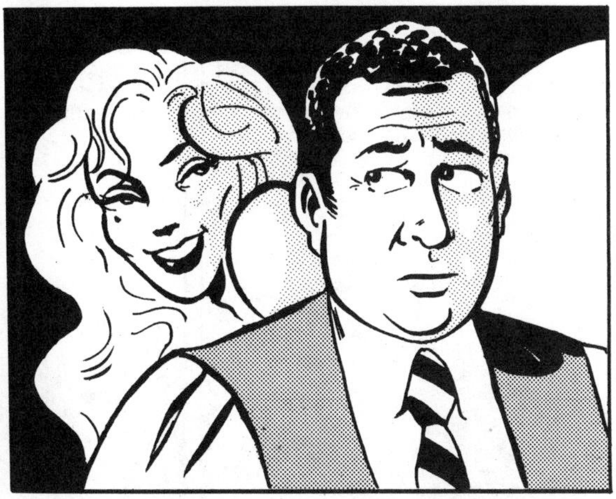

. . . and she was *pals* with her attorney, Jeff Byrd. They weren't *lovers*--at least that's what it says in Jessie Byrd's bio of her father. But they had some sort of relationship that Dawn felt strongly enough about for her to write that letter. Anyway, this came out in that hearing . . .

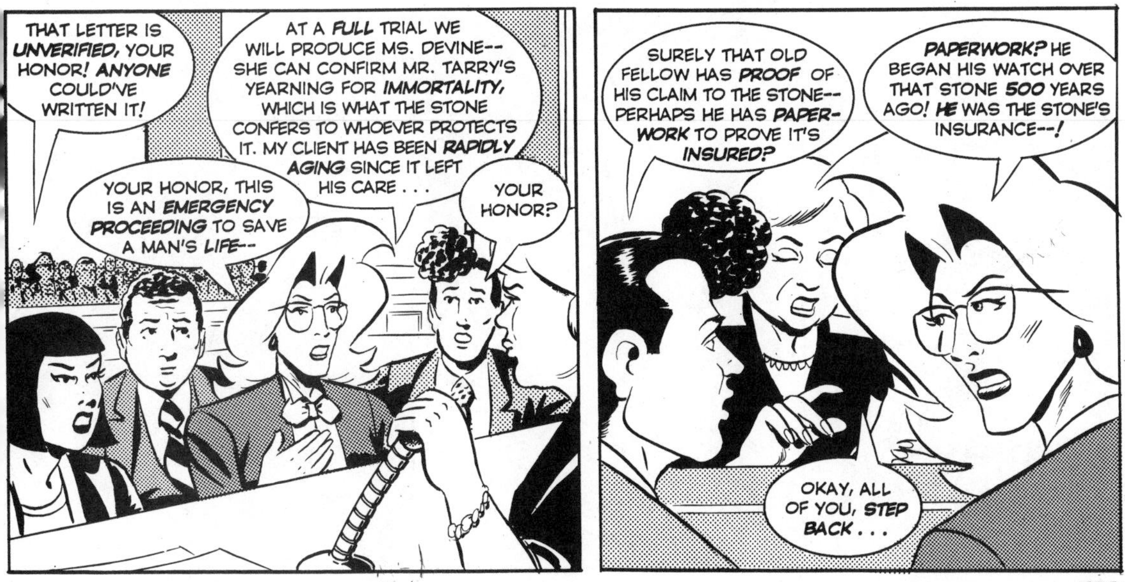
THAT LETTER IS UNVERIFIED, YOUR HONOR! ANYONE COULD'VE WRITTEN IT!
AT A FULL TRIAL WE WILL PRODUCE MS. DEVINE--SHE CAN CONFIRM MR. TARRY'S YEARNING FOR IMMORTALITY, WHICH IS WHAT THE STONE CONFERS TO WHOEVER PROTECTS IT. MY CLIENT HAS BEEN RAPIDLY AGING SINCE IT LEFT HIS CARE . . .
YOUR HONOR, THIS IS AN EMERGENCY PROCEEDING TO SAVE A MAN'S LIFE--
YOUR HONOR?
SURELY THAT OLD FELLOW HAS PROOF OF HIS CLAIM TO THE STONE--PERHAPS HE HAS PAPERWORK TO PROVE IT'S INSURED?
PAPERWORK? HE BEGAN HIS WATCH OVER THAT STONE 500 YEARS AGO! HE WAS THE STONE'S INSURANCE--!
OKAY, ALL OF YOU, STEP BACK . . .

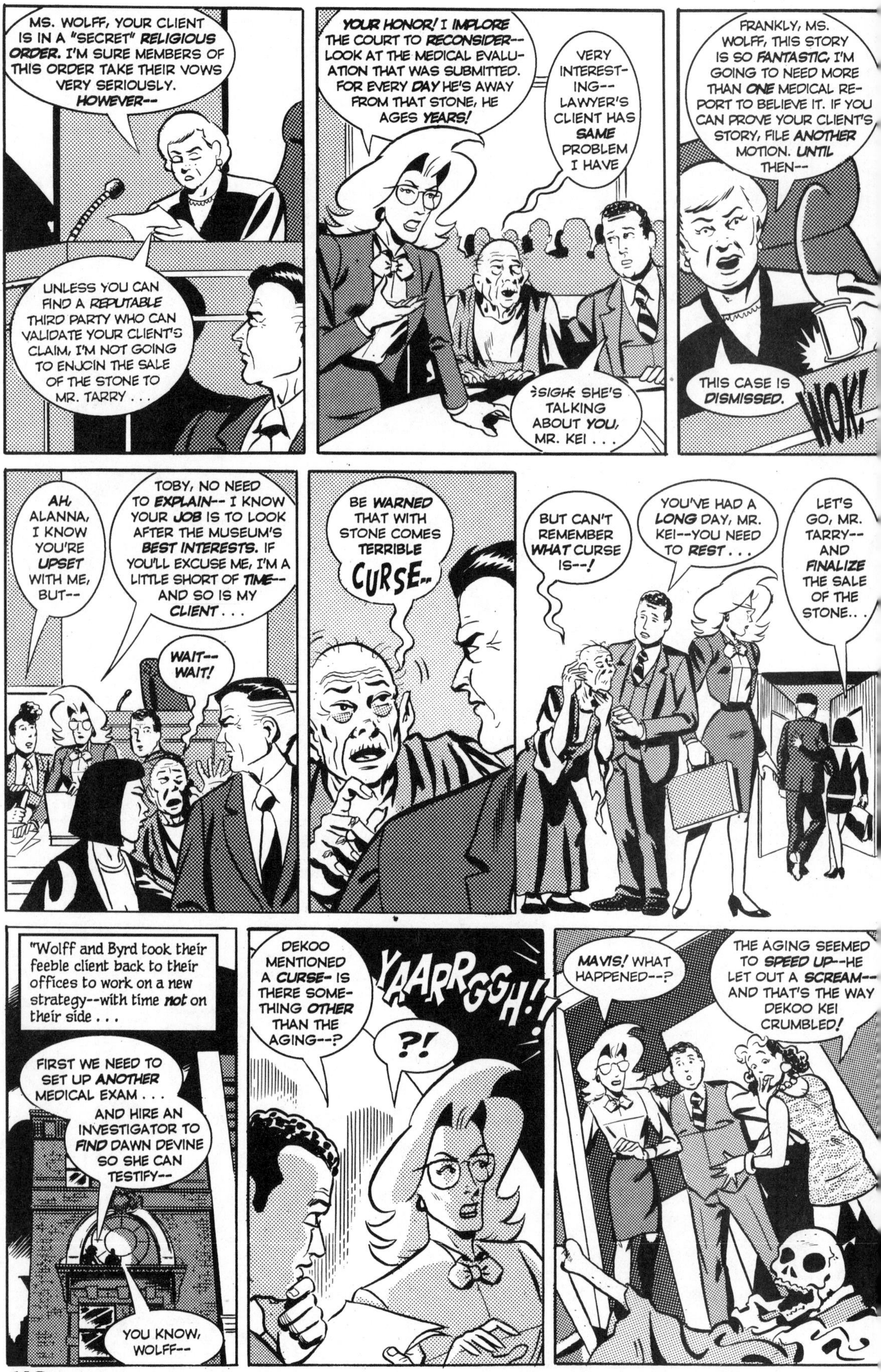
MS. WOLFF, YOUR CLIENT IS IN A "SECRET" RELIGIOUS ORDER. I'M SURE MEMBERS OF THIS ORDER TAKE THEIR VOWS VERY SERIOUSLY. HOWEVER--
UNLESS YOU CAN FIND A REPUTABLE THIRD PARTY WHO CAN VALIDATE YOUR CLIENT'S CLAIM, I'M NOT GOING TO ENJOIN THE SALE OF THE STONE TO MR. TARRY . . .
YOUR HONOR! I IMPLORE THE COURT TO RECONSIDER-- LOOK AT THE MEDICAL EVALUATION THAT WAS SUBMITTED. FOR EVERY DAY HE'S AWAY FROM THAT STONE, HE AGES YEARS!
VERY INTERESTING-- LAWYER'S CLIENT HAS SAME PROBLEM I HAVE
SIGH SHE'S TALKING ABOUT YOU, MR. KEI . . .
FRANKLY, MS. WOLFF, THIS STORY IS SO FANTASTIC, I'M GOING TO NEED MORE THAN ONE MEDICAL REPORT TO BELIEVE IT. IF YOU CAN PROVE YOUR CLIENT'S STORY, FILE ANOTHER MOTION. UNTIL THEN--
THIS CASE IS DISMISSED.
WOK!
AH, ALANNA, I KNOW YOU'RE UPSET WITH ME, BUT--
TOBY, NO NEED TO EXPLAIN-- I KNOW YOUR JOB IS TO LOOK AFTER THE MUSEUM'S BEST INTERESTS. IF YOU'LL EXCUSE ME, I'M A LITTLE SHORT OF TIME-- AND SO IS MY CLIENT . . .
WAIT-- WAIT!
BE WARNED THAT WITH STONE COMES TERRIBLE CURSE..
BUT CAN'T REMEMBER WHAT CURSE IS--!
YOU'VE HAD A LONG DAY, MR. KEI--YOU NEED TO REST . . .
LET'S GO, MR. TARRY-- AND FINALIZE THE SALE OF THE STONE. . .
"Wolff and Byrd took their feeble client back to their offices to work on a new strategy--with time not on their side . . .
FIRST WE NEED TO SET UP ANOTHER MEDICAL EXAM . . .
AND HIRE AN INVESTIGATOR TO FIND DAWN DEVINE SO SHE CAN TESTIFY--
YOU KNOW, WOLFF--
DEKOO MENTIONED A CURSE- IS THERE SOMETHING OTHER THAN THE AGING--?
YAARRGGH!!
?!
MAVIS! WHAT HAPPENED--?
THE AGING SEEMED TO SPEED UP--HE LET OUT A SCREAM-- AND THAT'S THE WAY DEKOO KEI CRUMBLED!

"Wolff and Byrd informed the museum's counsel of their client's untimely demise . . .

WHAT!?

CARA! ROLLIN! I JUST HEARD FROM WOLFF AND BYRD--

I HOPE YOU TOLD THEM ROLLIN NOW OWNS THE STONE, TOBY

YES, IT'S MINE--

FOREVER!!

RRRUMMMBBBLE

YEOW!!

OH NO- NOOOOOOOO!!

"Witnesses swore they had seen a huge monster--. but there were no footprints or any other signs of destruction besides to the Blackwood Museum . . . People assumed it had been a bomb or maybe pipes exploding . . . but a monster? *It just couldn't be . . .* It was suggested that the trauma of the explosion caused delusions . . .

"Even the testimony of Tarry's attorney and the museum's counsel was not widely believed. . . .Rollin Tarry's body was never *found*--and neither was the Itsumo stone. Was he dead-- or was the immortality the vainglorious Tarry sought more than he had bargained for?

141

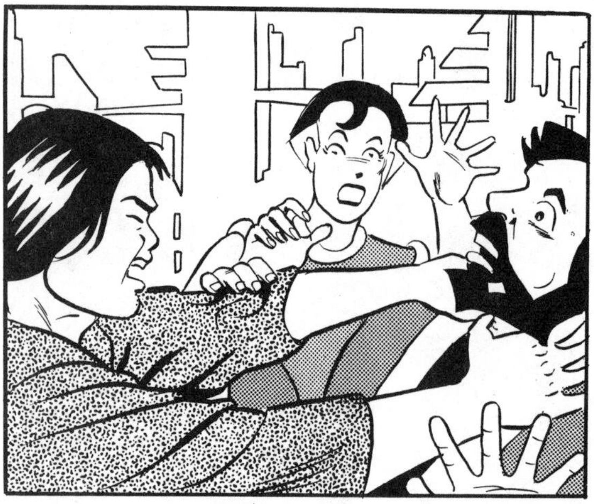

You lie! *You lie!!* | ***Detrek!*** Stop! You're hurting him! | ***Akkkk!***

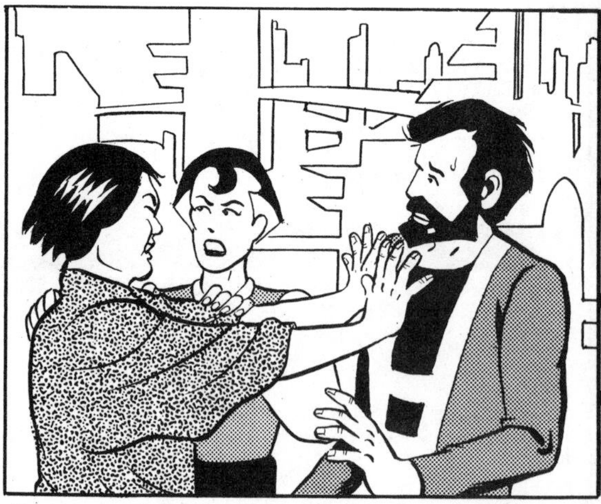

Sorry, man | ⊰tsk⊱ Get a hold of yourself, huh? | Hey, I know it's tough for you to accept. I know you thought Rolin Tarry was a ***good guy***--

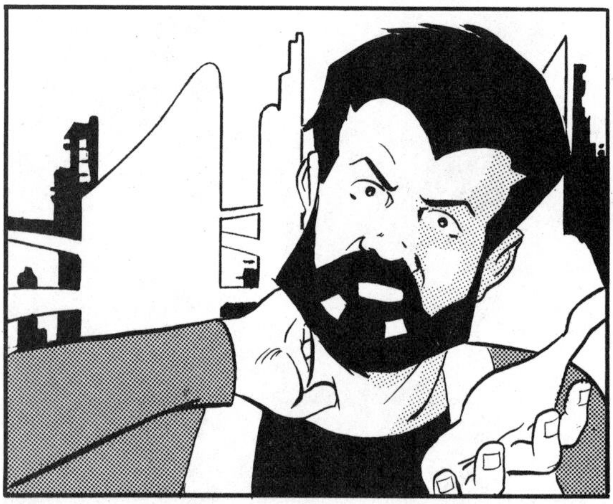

--and you researched the accounts that ***supported*** that belief. But why did Dawn DeVine leave him? You didn't even address ***that.*** Her reason would've ultimately revealed ***why*** Tarry wanted that stone. If you dig ***deep*** enough, you'll learn that there are stories within stories . . .

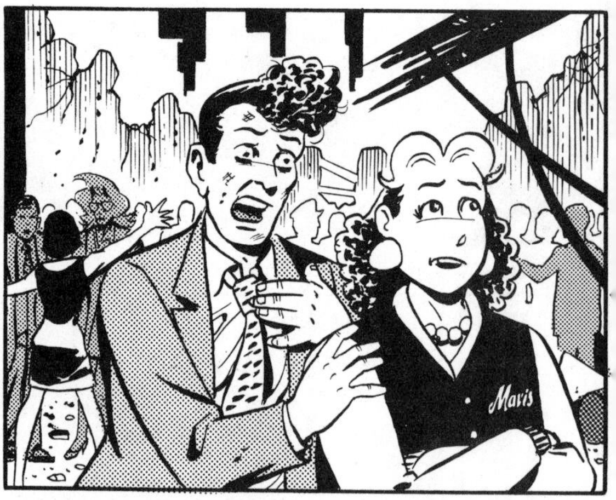
Mavis

"For instance, in ***my*** research, I learned that the museum's counsel had wanted to marry Wolff and Byrd's secretary. But ***she*** was holding him partially responsible for the ***demise*** of Mr. Kei because of his arguing at the hearing, and her feelings toward him changed--and ***that*** was the catalyst for--

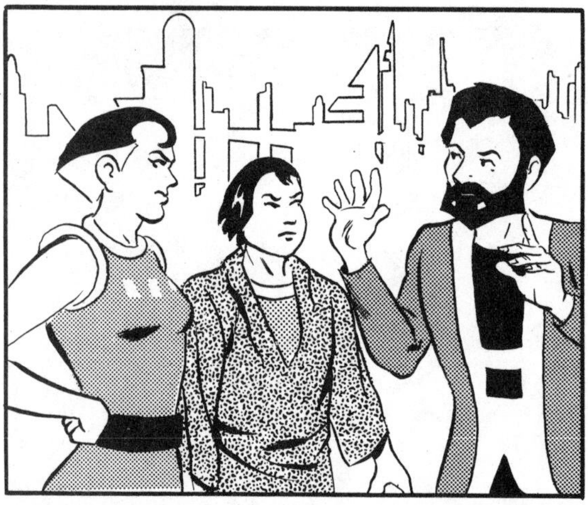

Who cares about them?! Let's get back to the priest--you're ***off base*** with him! | I understand you're upset, Melena--but he had the gift of ***immortality*** and like a ***loser,*** he blew it!

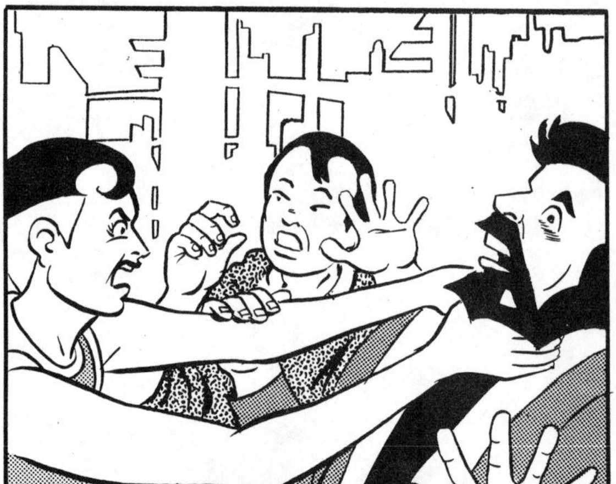

You lie! *You lie!!* | ***Melena!*** Stop! You're hurting him! | ***Akkkk!***

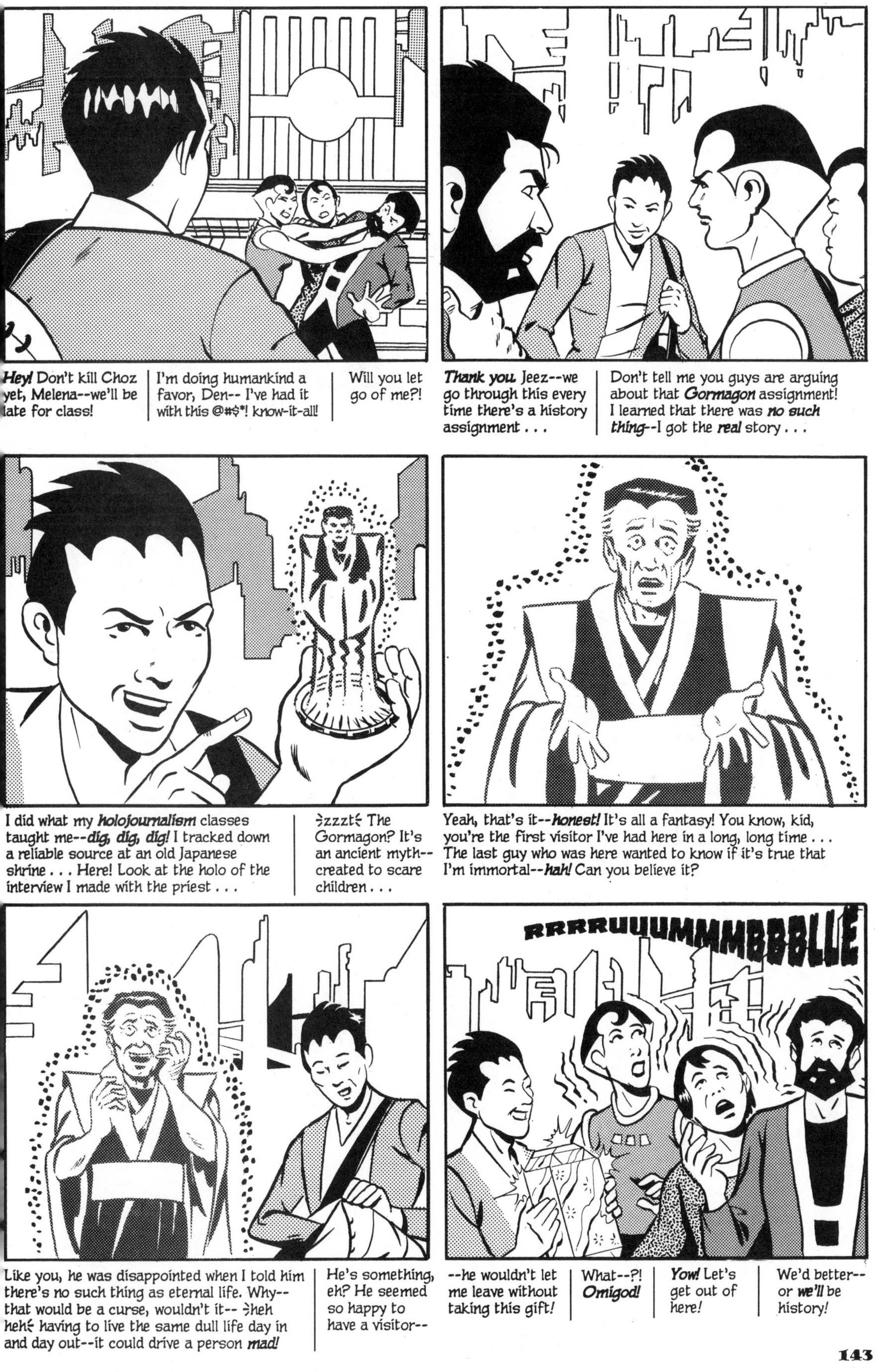
Hey! Don't kill Choz yet, Melena--we'll be late for class!
I'm doing humankind a favor, Den-- I've had it with this @#$*! know-it-all!
Will you let go of me?!
Thank you. Jeez--we go through this every time there's a history assignment . . .
Don't tell me you guys are arguing about that Gormagon assignment! I learned that there was no such thing--I got the real story . . .
I did what my holojournalism classes taught me--dig, dig, dig! I tracked down a reliable source at an old Japanese shrine . . . Here! Look at the holo of the interview I made with the priest . . .
zzzt The Gormagon? It's an ancient myth--created to scare children . . .
Yeah, that's it--honest! It's all a fantasy! You know, kid, you're the first visitor I've had here in a long, long time . . . The last guy who was here wanted to know if it's true that I'm immortal--hah! Can you believe it?
Like you, he was disappointed when I told him there's no such thing as eternal life. Why--that would be a curse, wouldn't it-- heh heh having to live the same dull life day in and day out--it could drive a person mad!
He's something, eh? He seemed so happy to have a visitor--
RRRRUUUMMMMBBBLLE
--he wouldn't let me leave without taking this gift!
What--?! Omigod!
Yow! Let's get out of here!
We'd better--or we'll be history!

The Human Within Me

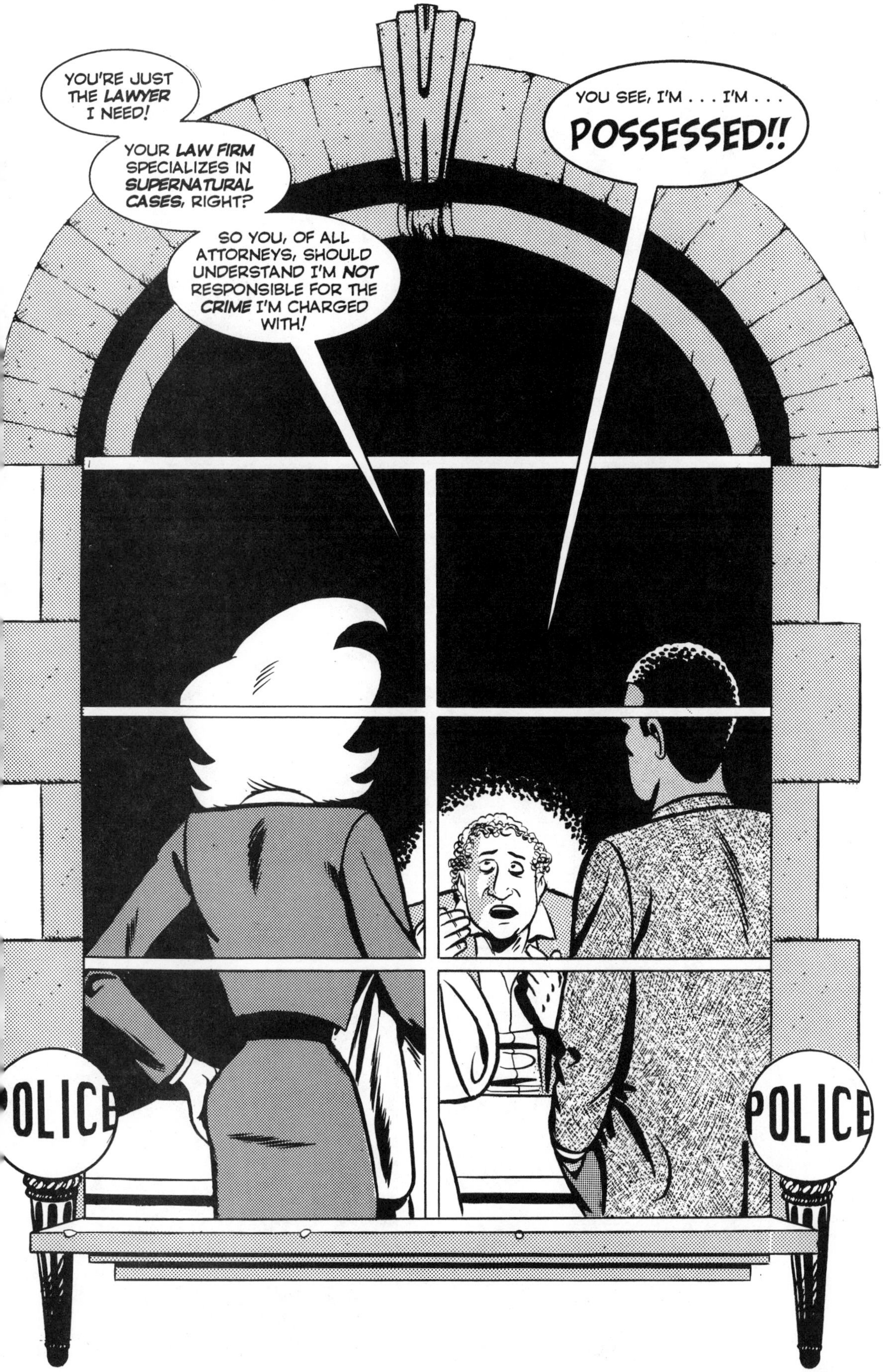
YOU'RE JUST THE LAWYER I NEED!
YOUR LAW FIRM SPECIALIZES IN SUPERNATURAL CASES, RIGHT?
SO YOU, OF ALL ATTORNEYS, SHOULD UNDERSTAND I'M NOT RESPONSIBLE FOR THE CRIME I'M CHARGED WITH!
YOU SEE, I'M . . . I'M . . . POSSESSED!!
POLICE
POLICE

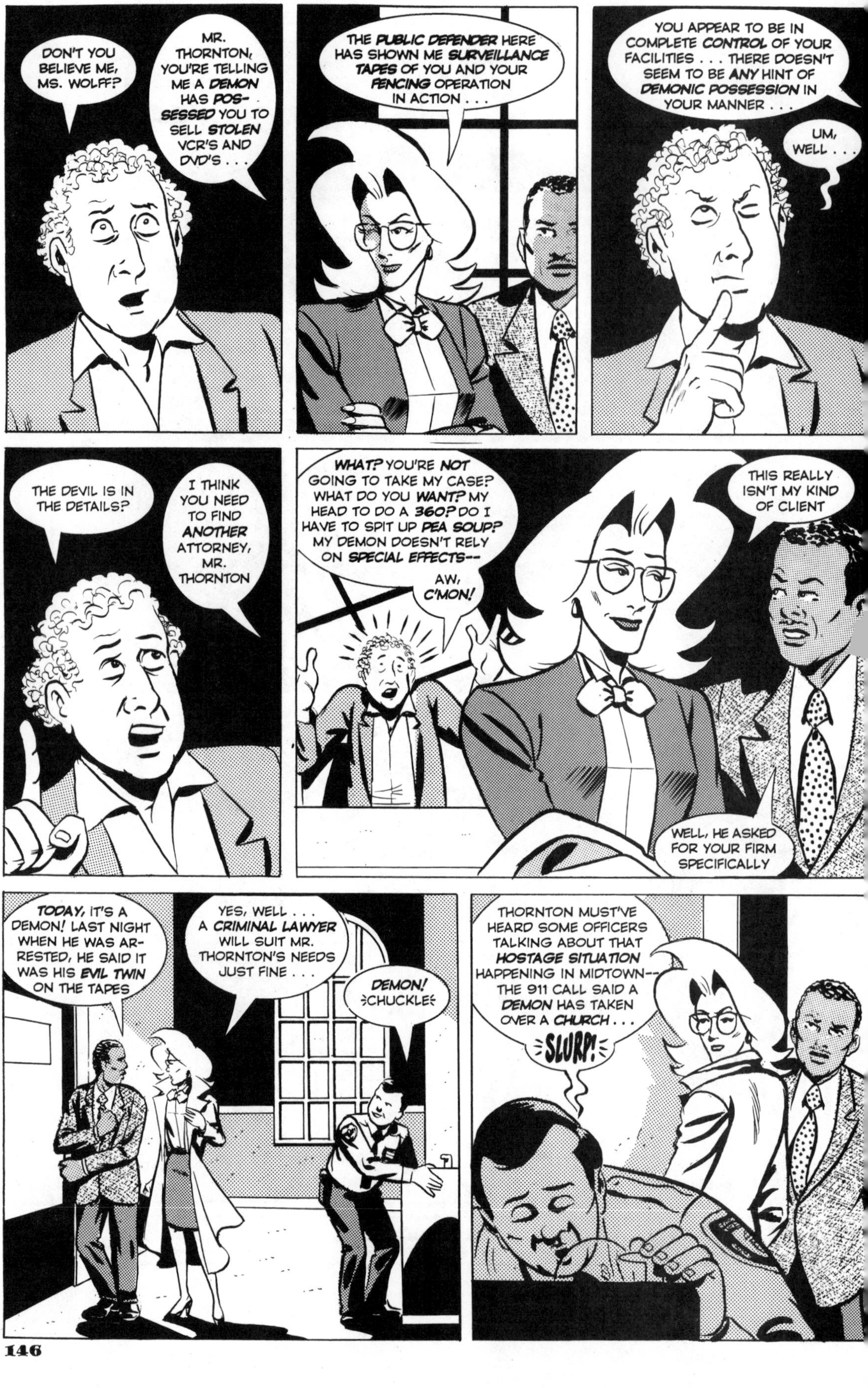

DON'T YOU BELIEVE ME, MS. WOLFF?
MR. THORNTON, YOU'RE TELLING ME A DEMON HAS POS-SESSED YOU TO SELL STOLEN VCR'S AND DVD'S . . .
THE PUBLIC DEFENDER HERE HAS SHOWN ME SURVEILLANCE TAPES OF YOU AND YOUR FENCING OPERATION IN ACTION . . .
YOU APPEAR TO BE IN COMPLETE CONTROL OF YOUR FACILITIES . . . THERE DOESN'T SEEM TO BE ANY HINT OF DEMONIC POSSESSION IN YOUR MANNER . . .
UM, WELL . . .
THE DEVIL IS IN THE DETAILS?
I THINK YOU NEED TO FIND ANOTHER ATTORNEY, MR. THORNTON
WHAT? YOU'RE NOT GOING TO TAKE MY CASE? WHAT DO YOU WANT? MY HEAD TO DO A 360? DO I HAVE TO SPIT UP PEA SOUP? MY DEMON DOESN'T RELY ON SPECIAL EFFECTS--
AW, C'MON!
THIS REALLY ISN'T MY KIND OF CLIENT
WELL, HE ASKED FOR YOUR FIRM SPECIFICALLY
TODAY, IT'S A DEMON! LAST NIGHT WHEN HE WAS AR-RESTED, HE SAID IT WAS HIS EVIL TWIN ON THE TAPES
YES, WELL . . . A CRIMINAL LAWYER WILL SUIT MR. THORNTON'S NEEDS JUST FINE . . .
DEMON! CHUCKLE
THORNTON MUST'VE HEARD SOME OFFICERS TALKING ABOUT THAT HOSTAGE SITUATION HAPPENING IN MIDTOWN-- THE 911 CALL SAID A DEMON HAS TAKEN OVER A CHURCH . . .
SLURP!

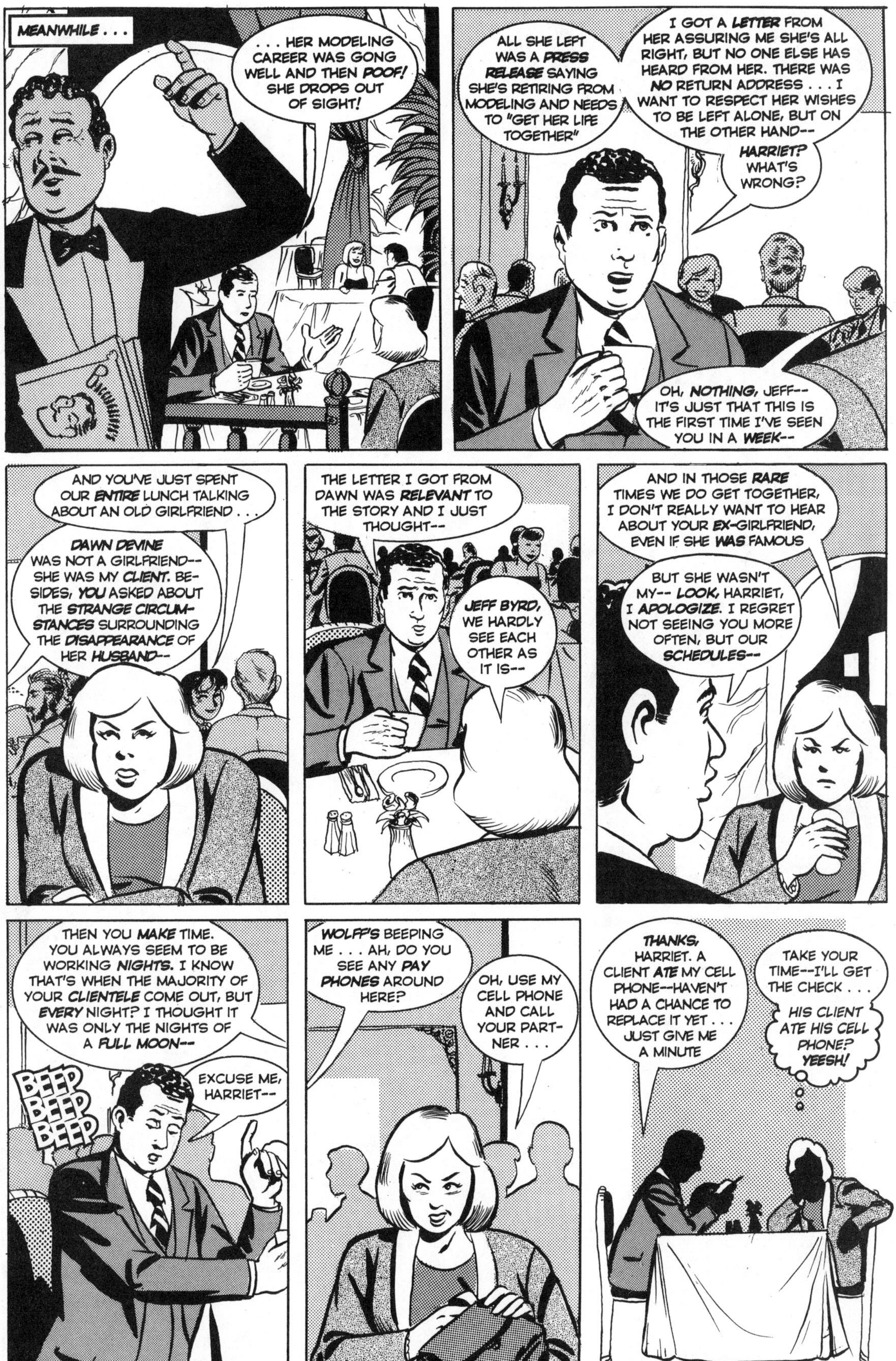
MEANWHILE . . .
. . . HER MODELING CAREER WAS GONG WELL AND THEN POOF! SHE DROPS OUT OF SIGHT!
ALL SHE LEFT WAS A PRESS RELEASE SAYING SHE'S RETIRING FROM MODELING AND NEEDS TO "GET HER LIFE TOGETHER"
I GOT A LETTER FROM HER ASSURING ME SHE'S ALL RIGHT, BUT NO ONE ELSE HAS HEARD FROM HER. THERE WAS NO RETURN ADDRESS . . . I WANT TO RESPECT HER WISHES TO BE LEFT ALONE, BUT ON THE OTHER HAND--
HARRIET? WHAT'S WRONG?
OH, NOTHING, JEFF-- IT'S JUST THAT THIS IS THE FIRST TIME I'VE SEEN YOU IN A WEEK--
AND YOU'VE JUST SPENT OUR ENTIRE LUNCH TALKING ABOUT AN OLD GIRLFRIEND . . .
DAWN DEVINE WAS NOT A GIRLFRIEND-- SHE WAS MY CLIENT. BESIDES, YOU ASKED ABOUT THE STRANGE CIRCUMSTANCES SURROUNDING THE DISAPPEARANCE OF HER HUSBAND--
THE LETTER I GOT FROM DAWN WAS RELEVANT TO THE STORY AND I JUST THOUGHT--
JEFF BYRD, WE HARDLY SEE EACH OTHER AS IT IS--
AND IN THOSE RARE TIMES WE DO GET TOGETHER, I DON'T REALLY WANT TO HEAR ABOUT YOUR EX-GIRLFRIEND, EVEN IF SHE WAS FAMOUS
BUT SHE WASN'T MY-- LOOK, HARRIET, I APOLOGIZE. I REGRET NOT SEEING YOU MORE OFTEN, BUT OUR SCHEDULES--
THEN YOU MAKE TIME. YOU ALWAYS SEEM TO BE WORKING NIGHTS. I KNOW THAT'S WHEN THE MAJORITY OF YOUR CLIENTELE COME OUT, BUT EVERY NIGHT? I THOUGHT IT WAS ONLY THE NIGHTS OF A FULL MOON--
BEEP BEEP BEEP
EXCUSE ME, HARRIET--
WOLFF'S BEEPING ME . . . AH, DO YOU SEE ANY PAY PHONES AROUND HERE?
OH, USE MY CELL PHONE AND CALL YOUR PARTNER . . .
THANKS, HARRIET. A CLIENT ATE MY CELL PHONE--HAVEN'T HAD A CHANCE TO REPLACE IT YET . . . JUST GIVE ME A MINUTE
TAKE YOUR TIME--I'LL GET THE CHECK . . .
HIS CLIENT ATE HIS CELL PHONE? YEESH!

THE *HUMAN* WITHIN ME

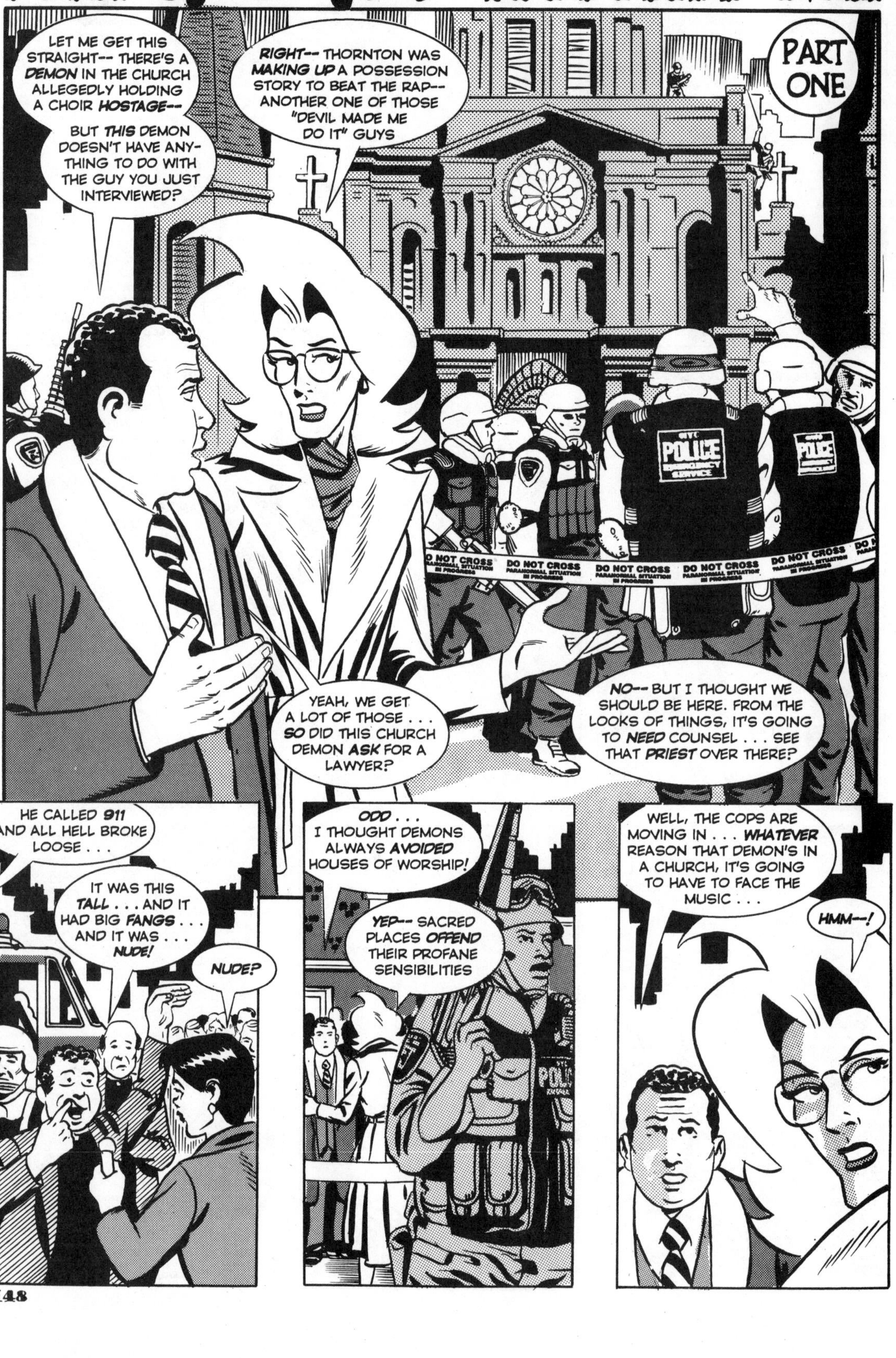

PART ONE
LET ME GET THIS STRAIGHT-- THERE'S A DEMON IN THE CHURCH ALLEGEDLY HOLDING A CHOIR HOSTAGE--
BUT THIS DEMON DOESN'T HAVE ANY-THING TO DO WITH THE GUY YOU JUST INTERVIEWED?
RIGHT-- THORNTON WAS MAKING UP A POSSESSION STORY TO BEAT THE RAP-- ANOTHER ONE OF THOSE "DEVIL MADE ME DO IT" GUYS
POLICE
DO NOT CROSS
YEAH, WE GET A LOT OF THOSE . . . SO DID THIS CHURCH DEMON ASK FOR A LAWYER?
NO-- BUT I THOUGHT WE SHOULD BE HERE. FROM THE LOOKS OF THINGS, IT'S GOING TO NEED COUNSEL . . . SEE THAT PRIEST OVER THERE?
HE CALLED 911 AND ALL HELL BROKE LOOSE . . .
IT WAS THIS TALL . . . AND IT HAD BIG FANGS . . . AND IT WAS . . . NUDE!
NUDE?
ODD . . . I THOUGHT DEMONS ALWAYS AVOIDED HOUSES OF WORSHIP!
YEP-- SACRED PLACES OFFEND THEIR PROFANE SENSIBILITIES
WELL, THE COPS ARE MOVING IN . . . WHATEVER REASON THAT DEMON'S IN A CHURCH, IT'S GOING TO HAVE TO FACE THE MUSIC . . .
HMM--!

HALLELUJAH!
HALLELUJAH!
HALLELUJAH!
HALLELUJAH!

And He Shall Reign Forever and Ever

HANDEL'S MESSIAH?

≈CRACKLE≈ OFFICER SCALING WALL TO SURVEY SITUATION--

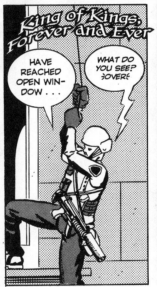

King of Kings, Forever and Ever

HAVE REACHED OPEN WINDOW . . .

WHAT DO YOU SEE? ≈OVER≈

And Lord of Lords HALLELUJAH!

HOLY--!

Forever and Ever Hallelujah Hallelujah Hallelujah

THERE WAS NO SHOOTOUT, AND THE CHORALE WAS OK WHEN POLICE STORMED A CHURCH IN MIDTOWN TODAY. THEY ARRESTED A **DEMON** WHO WAS **SINGING** WITH A BOYS' CHOIR. A **911** CALLER SAID THE HELL-SPAWNED CREATURE WAS HOLDING THE SINGERS **HOSTAGE,** BUT THAT APPEARS TO **NOT** HAVE BEEN THE CASE . . .

. . . WE WERE **SCARED** AT FIRST, ESPECIALLY WHEN FATHER WAMBAUGH **FREAKED** AND RAN OFF TO GET HELP. BUT THE DEMON SAID HE **LOVED** CHOIR MUSIC AND JUST WANTED TO LISTEN TO US **SING**. HE SEEMED LIKE A **REGULAR GUY** FOR A DEMON. WHEN HE ASKED IF HE COULD SING **WITH** US, WE JUST DIDN'T HAVE THE HEART TO TURN HIM DOWN . . .

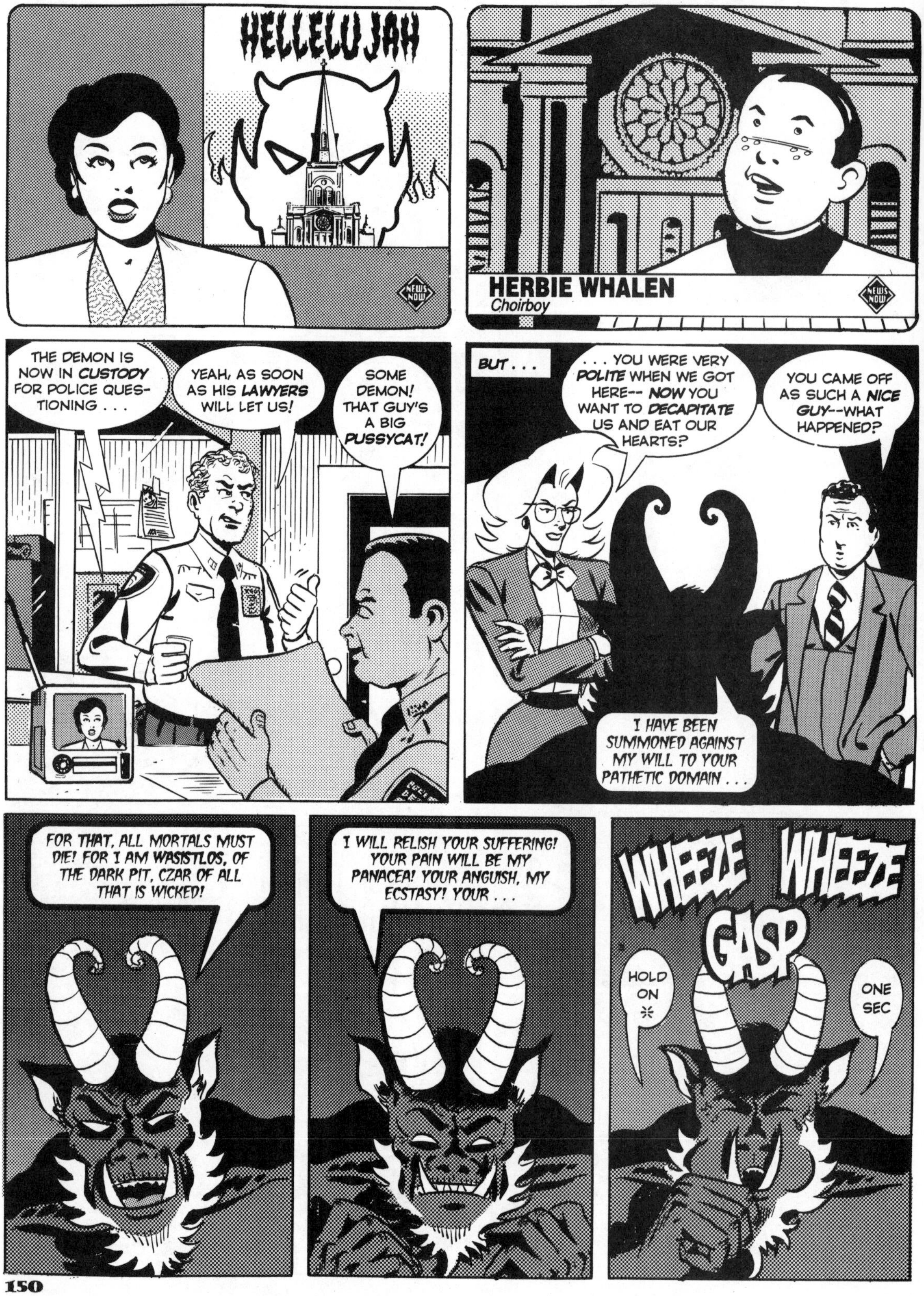
HELLELUJAH
HERBIE WHALEN
Choirboy
THE DEMON IS NOW IN CUSTODY FOR POLICE QUESTIONING . . .
YEAH, AS SOON AS HIS LAWYERS WILL LET US!
SOME DEMON! THAT GUY'S A BIG PUSSYCAT!
BUT . . .
. . . YOU WERE VERY POLITE WHEN WE GOT HERE-- NOW YOU WANT TO DECAPITATE US AND EAT OUR HEARTS?
YOU CAME OFF AS SUCH A NICE GUY--WHAT HAPPENED?
I HAVE BEEN SUMMONED AGAINST MY WILL TO YOUR PATHETIC DOMAIN . . .
FOR THAT, ALL MORTALS MUST DIE! FOR I AM WASISTLOS, OF THE DARK PIT, CZAR OF ALL THAT IS WICKED!
I WILL RELISH YOUR SUFFERING! YOUR PAIN WILL BE MY PANACEA! YOUR ANGUISH, MY ECSTASY! YOUR . . .
WHEEZE WHEEZE
GASP
HOLD ON
ONE SEC

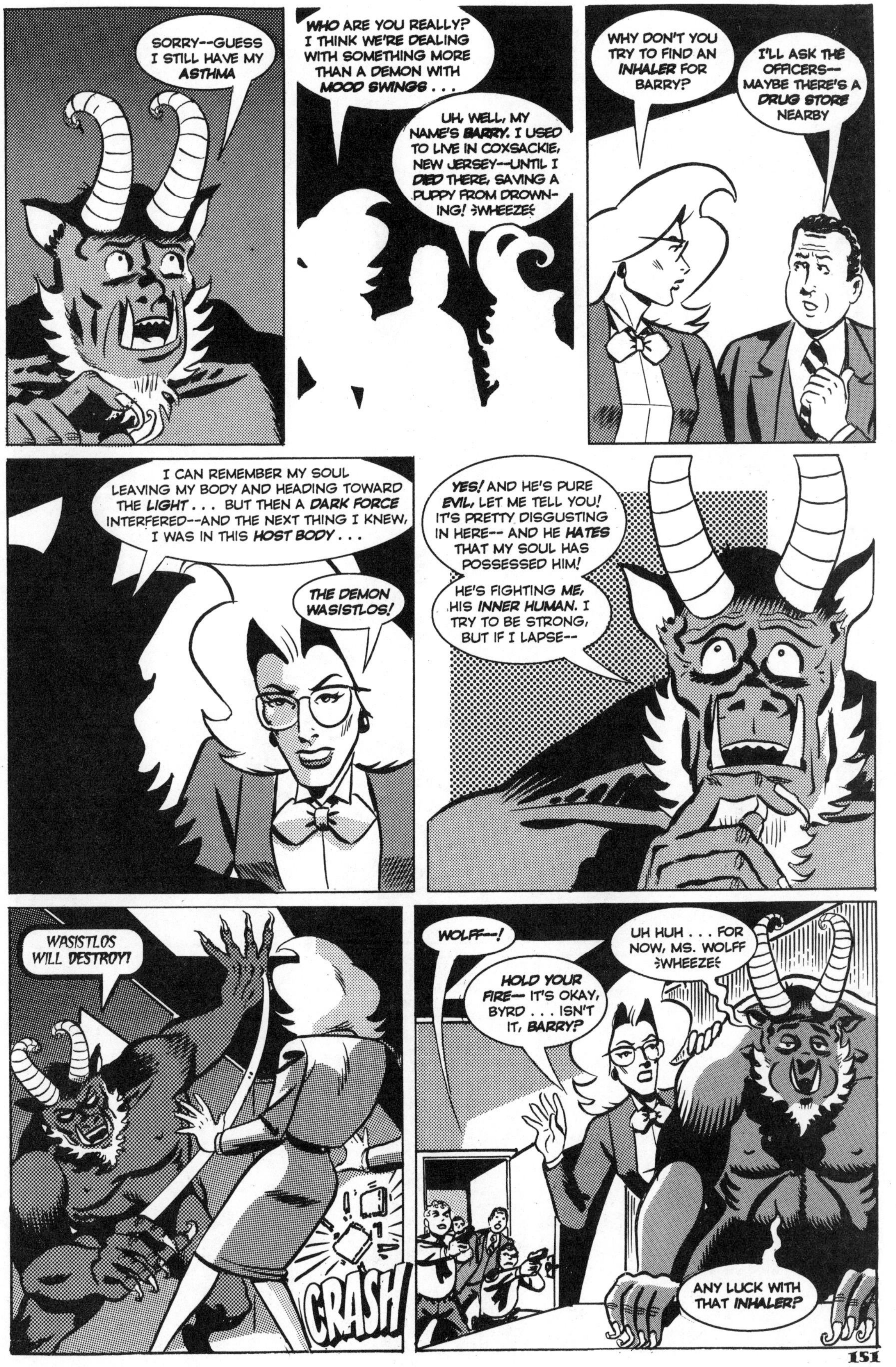
SORRY--GUESS I STILL HAVE MY ASTHMA
WHO ARE YOU REALLY? I THINK WE'RE DEALING WITH SOMETHING MORE THAN A DEMON WITH MOOD SWINGS . . .
UH, WELL, MY NAME'S BARRY. I USED TO LIVE IN COXSACKIE, NEW JERSEY--UNTIL I DIED THERE, SAVING A PUPPY FROM DROWNING! ≶WHEEZE≶
WHY DON'T YOU TRY TO FIND AN INHALER FOR BARRY?
I'LL ASK THE OFFICERS-- MAYBE THERE'S A DRUG STORE NEARBY
I CAN REMEMBER MY SOUL LEAVING MY BODY AND HEADING TOWARD THE LIGHT . . . BUT THEN A DARK FORCE INTERFERED--AND THE NEXT THING I KNEW, I WAS IN THIS HOST BODY . . .
THE DEMON WASISTLOS!
YES! AND HE'S PURE EVIL, LET ME TELL YOU! IT'S PRETTY DISGUSTING IN HERE-- AND HE HATES THAT MY SOUL HAS POSSESSED HIM!
HE'S FIGHTING ME, HIS INNER HUMAN. I TRY TO BE STRONG, BUT IF I LAPSE--
WASISTLOS WILL DESTROY!
CRASH
WOLFF--!
HOLD YOUR FIRE-- IT'S OKAY, BYRD . . . ISN'T IT, BARRY?
UH HUH . . . FOR NOW, MS. WOLFF ≶WHEEZE≶
ANY LUCK WITH THAT INHALER?

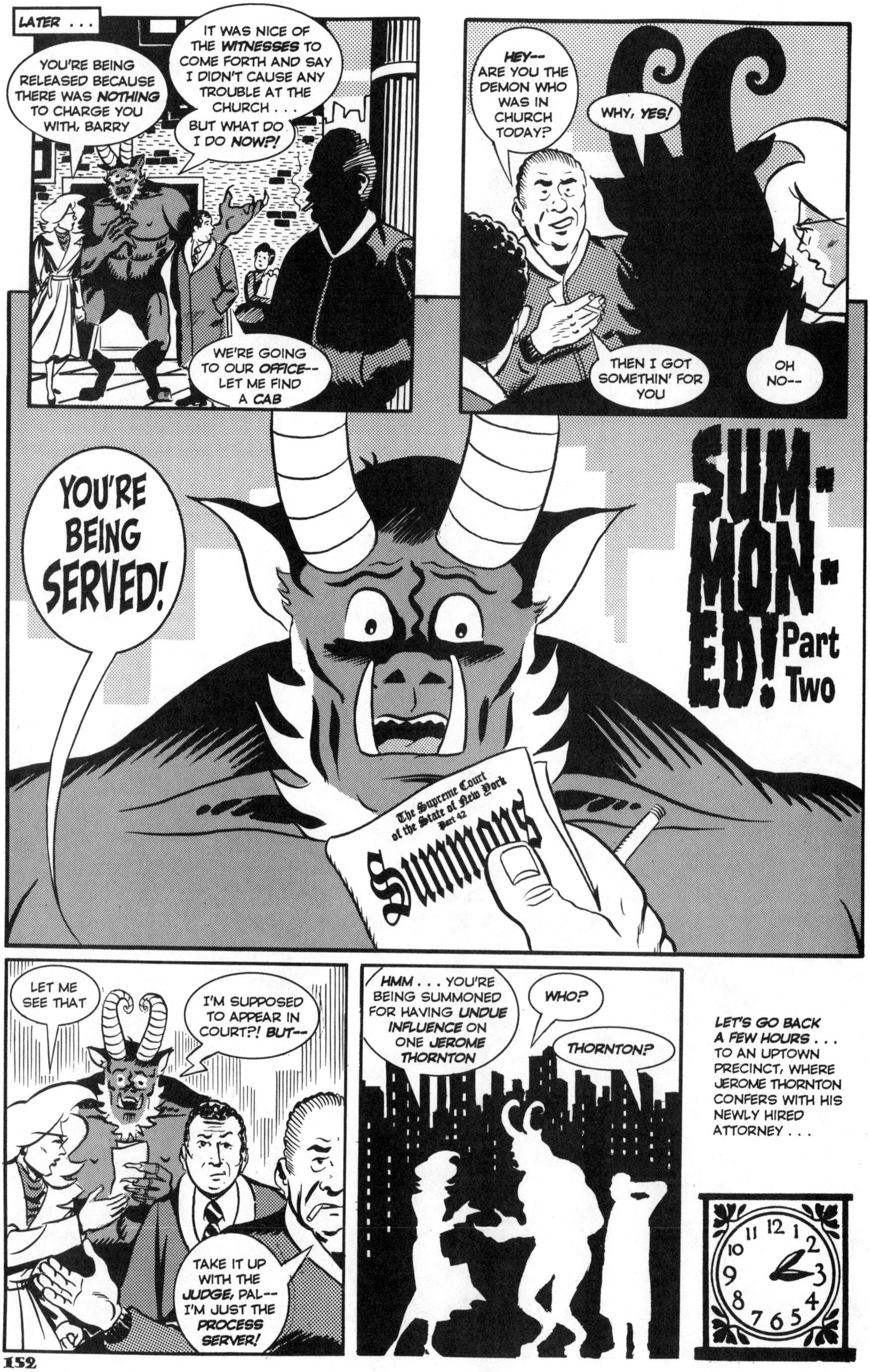
LATER . . .
YOU'RE BEING RELEASED BECAUSE THERE WAS NOTHING TO CHARGE YOU WITH, BARRY
IT WAS NICE OF THE WITNESSES TO COME FORTH AND SAY I DIDN'T CAUSE ANY TROUBLE AT THE CHURCH . . .
BUT WHAT DO I DO NOW?!
WE'RE GOING TO OUR OFFICE-- LET ME FIND A CAB
HEY-- ARE YOU THE DEMON WHO WAS IN CHURCH TODAY?
WHY, YES!
THEN I GOT SOMETHIN' FOR YOU
OH NO--
YOU'RE BEING SERVED!
SUM-MON-ED! Part Two
The Supreme Court of the State of New York Part 42
Summons
LET ME SEE THAT
I'M SUPPOSED TO APPEAR IN COURT?! BUT--
TAKE IT UP WITH THE JUDGE, PAL-- I'M JUST THE PROCESS SERVER!
HMM . . . YOU'RE BEING SUMMONED FOR HAVING UNDUE INFLUENCE ON ONE JEROME THORNTON
WHO?
THORNTON?
LET'S GO BACK A FEW HOURS . . . TO AN UPTOWN PRECINCT, WHERE JEROME THORNTON CONFERS WITH HIS NEWLY HIRED ATTORNEY . . .

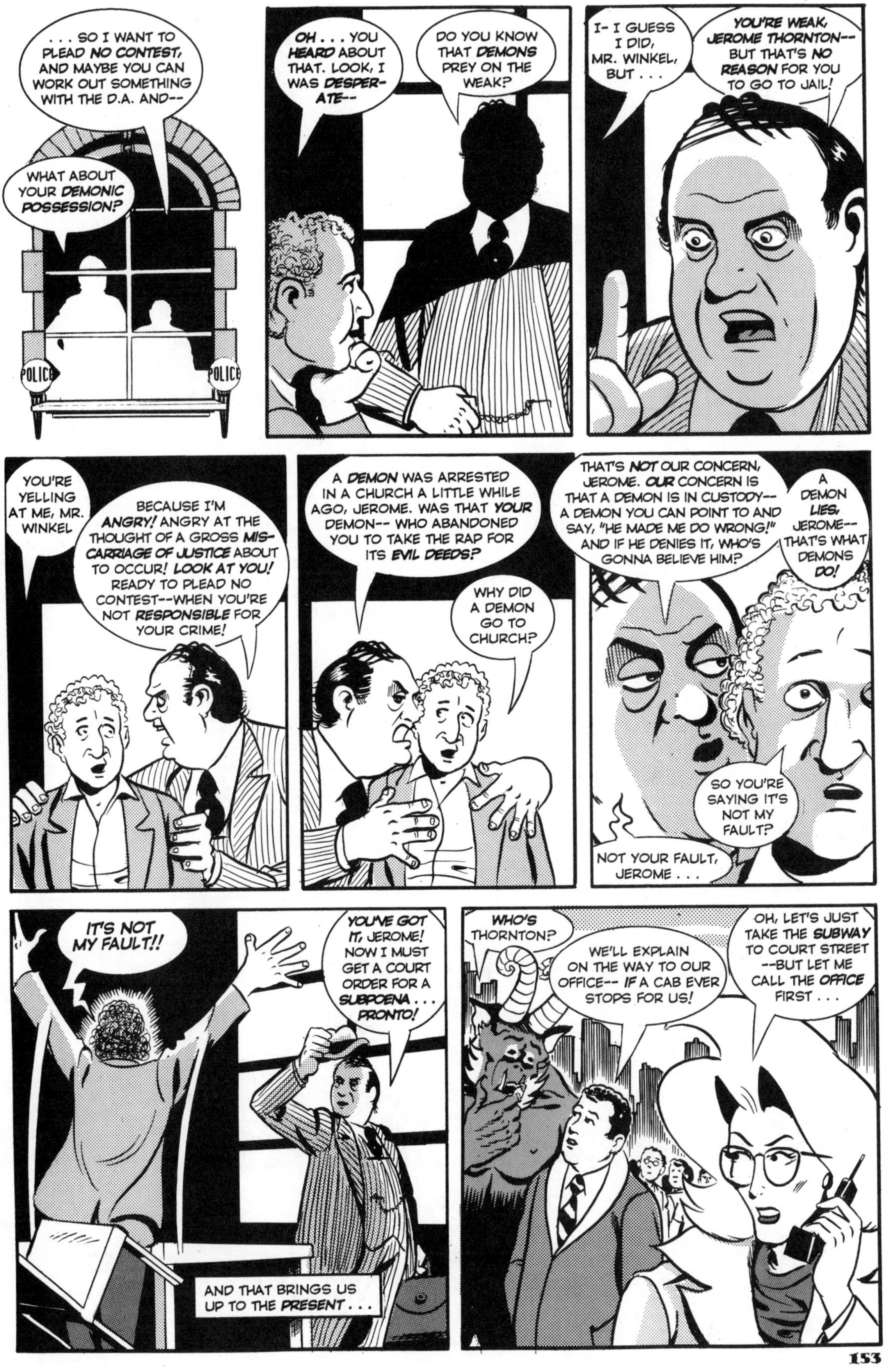
. . . SO I WANT TO PLEAD NO CONTEST, AND MAYBE YOU CAN WORK OUT SOMETHING WITH THE D.A. AND--
WHAT ABOUT YOUR DEMONIC POSSESSION?
POLICE
POLICE
OH . . . YOU HEARD ABOUT THAT. LOOK, I WAS DESPERATE--
DO YOU KNOW THAT DEMONS PREY ON THE WEAK?
I- I GUESS I DID, MR. WINKEL, BUT . . .
YOU'RE WEAK, JEROME THORNTON-- BUT THAT'S NO REASON FOR YOU TO GO TO JAIL!
YOU'RE YELLING AT ME, MR. WINKEL
BECAUSE I'M ANGRY! ANGRY AT THE THOUGHT OF A GROSS MISCARRIAGE OF JUSTICE ABOUT TO OCCUR! LOOK AT YOU! READY TO PLEAD NO CONTEST--WHEN YOU'RE NOT RESPONSIBLE FOR YOUR CRIME!
A DEMON WAS ARRESTED IN A CHURCH A LITTLE WHILE AGO, JEROME. WAS THAT YOUR DEMON-- WHO ABANDONED YOU TO TAKE THE RAP FOR ITS EVIL DEEDS?
WHY DID A DEMON GO TO CHURCH?
THAT'S NOT OUR CONCERN, JEROME. OUR CONCERN IS THAT A DEMON IS IN CUSTODY-- A DEMON YOU CAN POINT TO AND SAY, "HE MADE ME DO WRONG!" AND IF HE DENIES IT, WHO'S GONNA BELIEVE HIM?
A DEMON LIES, JEROME-- THAT'S WHAT DEMONS DO!
SO YOU'RE SAYING IT'S NOT MY FAULT?
NOT YOUR FAULT, JEROME . . .
IT'S NOT MY FAULT!!
YOU'VE GOT IT, JEROME! NOW I MUST GET A COURT ORDER FOR A SUBPOENA . . . PRONTO!
AND THAT BRINGS US UP TO THE PRESENT . . .
WHO'S THORNTON?
WE'LL EXPLAIN ON THE WAY TO OUR OFFICE-- IF A CAB EVER STOPS FOR US!
OH, LET'S JUST TAKE THE SUBWAY TO COURT STREET --BUT LET ME CALL THE OFFICE FIRST . . .

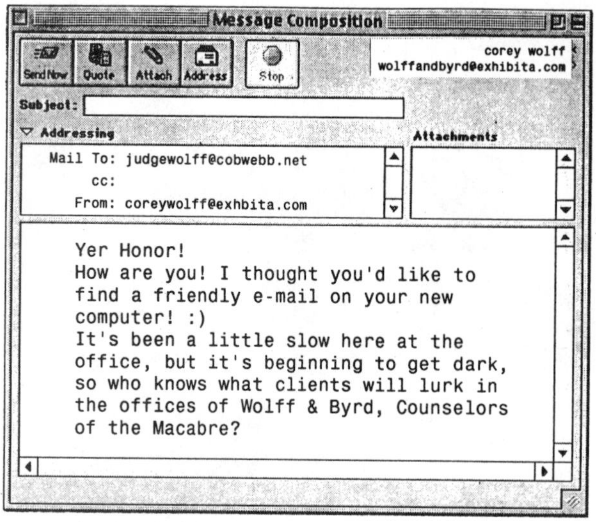
Message Composition
Send Now
Quote
Attach
Address
Stop
corey wolff
wolffandbyrd@exhibita.com
Subject:
Addressing
Attachments
Mail To: judgewolff@cobwebb.net
cc:
From: coreywolff@exhbita.com
Yer Honor!
How are you! I thought you'd like to find a friendly e-mail on your new computer! :)
It's been a little slow here at the office, but it's beginning to get dark, so who knows what clients will lurk in the offices of Wolff & Byrd, Counselors of the Macabre?

Oh, don't worry. Big sister Alanna is very protective of me. Maybe too protective--sometimes it gets on my nerves. And I seem to have a "big brother" in Jeff . . . though he's more worried about me taking the subway at night than about my receiving monsters at the front desk.

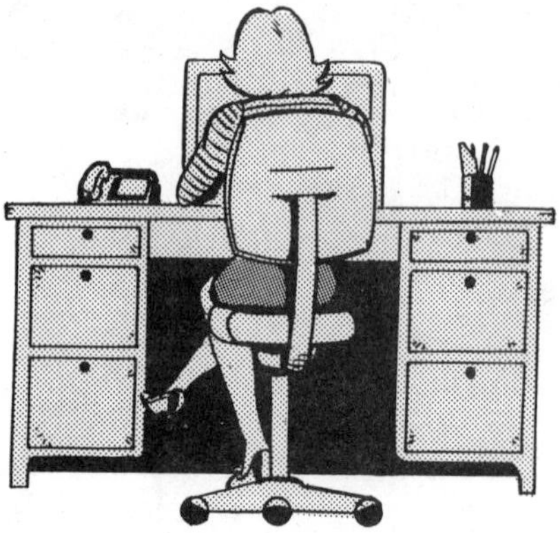

I wish I had more to do than just answer the phones. I asked Mavis why Alanna and Jeff aren't worried about her being with some of the scarier clients. Mavis said Alanna and Jeff are more worried about the clients being scared of HER! Sometimes I can't tell when Mavis is kidding or not.

I got my hair cut! I thought I was finally going to meet Alanna's beau, Chase Hawkins. The three of us were going to go this fancy restaurant. But then he had to go out of town. Alanna said she understood--she SHOULD, because she's always busy. But I think she is wondering where this relationship is going, IMHO. I wonder what Chase is like. Mavis said he's a dick

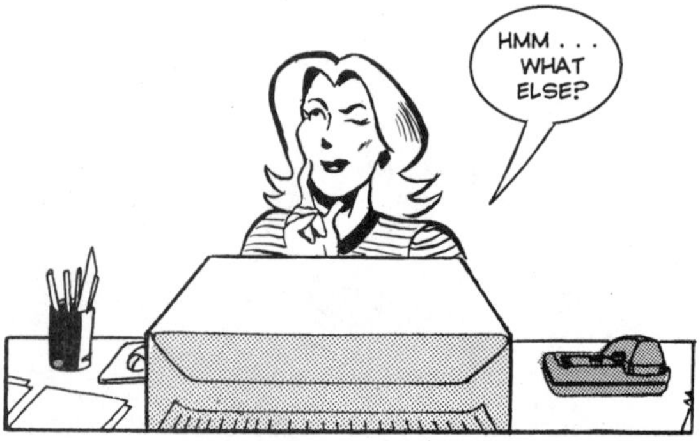
HMM . . . WHAT ELSE?

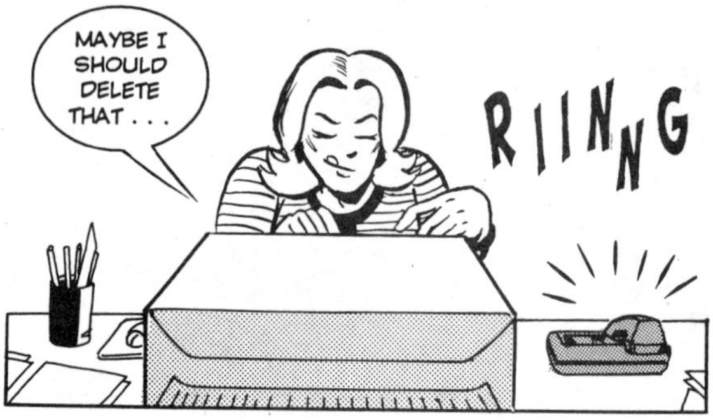
MAYBE I SHOULD DELETE THAT . . .
RIINNG

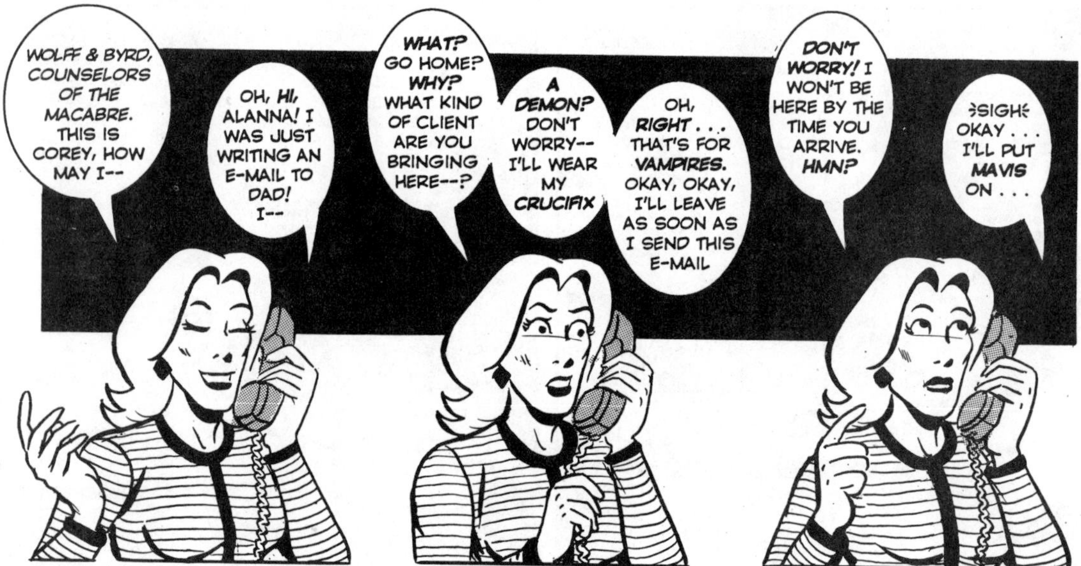
WOLFF & BYRD, COUNSELORS OF THE MACABRE. THIS IS COREY, HOW MAY I--
OH, HI, ALANNA! I WAS JUST WRITING AN E-MAIL TO DAD! I--
WHAT? GO HOME? WHY? WHAT KIND OF CLIENT ARE YOU BRINGING HERE--?
A DEMON? DON'T WORRY-- I'LL WEAR MY CRUCIFIX
OH, RIGHT . . . THAT'S FOR VAMPIRES. OKAY, OKAY, I'LL LEAVE AS SOON AS I SEND THIS E-MAIL
DON'T WORRY! I WON'T BE HERE BY THE TIME YOU ARRIVE. HMN?
SIGH OKAY . . . I'LL PUT MAVIS ON . . .

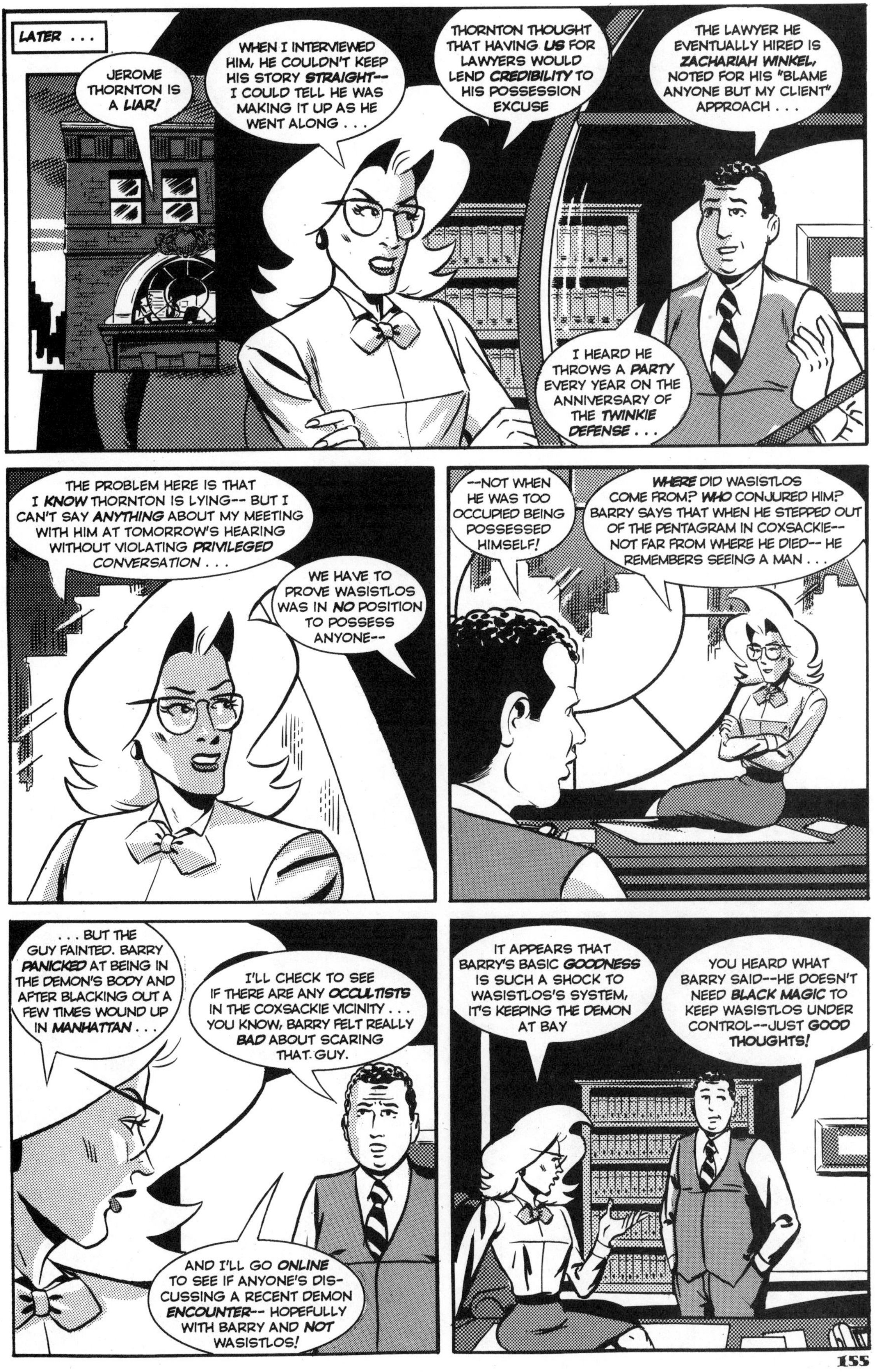
LATER . . .
JEROME THORNTON IS A LIAR!
WHEN I INTERVIEWED HIM, HE COULDN'T KEEP HIS STORY STRAIGHT-- I COULD TELL HE WAS MAKING IT UP AS HE WENT ALONG . . .
THORNTON THOUGHT THAT HAVING US FOR LAWYERS WOULD LEND CREDIBILITY TO HIS POSSESSION EXCUSE
THE LAWYER HE EVENTUALLY HIRED IS ZACHARIAH WINKEL, NOTED FOR HIS "BLAME ANYONE BUT MY CLIENT" APPROACH . . .
I HEARD HE THROWS A PARTY EVERY YEAR ON THE ANNIVERSARY OF THE TWINKIE DEFENSE . . .
THE PROBLEM HERE IS THAT I KNOW THORNTON IS LYING-- BUT I CAN'T SAY ANYTHING ABOUT MY MEETING WITH HIM AT TOMORROW'S HEARING WITHOUT VIOLATING PRIVILEGED CONVERSATION . . .
WE HAVE TO PROVE WASISTLOS WAS IN NO POSITION TO POSSESS ANYONE--
--NOT WHEN HE WAS TOO OCCUPIED BEING POSSESSED HIMSELF!
WHERE DID WASISTLOS COME FROM? WHO CONJURED HIM? BARRY SAYS THAT WHEN HE STEPPED OUT OF THE PENTAGRAM IN COXSACKIE-- NOT FAR FROM WHERE HE DIED-- HE REMEMBERS SEEING A MAN . . .
. . . BUT THE GUY FAINTED. BARRY PANICKED AT BEING IN THE DEMON'S BODY AND AFTER BLACKING OUT A FEW TIMES WOUND UP IN MANHATTAN . . .
I'LL CHECK TO SEE IF THERE ARE ANY OCCULTISTS IN THE COXSACKIE VICINITY . . . YOU KNOW, BARRY FELT REALLY BAD ABOUT SCARING THAT GUY.
AND I'LL GO ONLINE TO SEE IF ANYONE'S DISCUSSING A RECENT DEMON ENCOUNTER-- HOPEFULLY WITH BARRY AND NOT WASISTLOS!
IT APPEARS THAT BARRY'S BASIC GOODNESS IS SUCH A SHOCK TO WASISTLOS'S SYSTEM, IT'S KEEPING THE DEMON AT BAY
YOU HEARD WHAT BARRY SAID--HE DOESN'T NEED BLACK MAGIC TO KEEP WASISTLOS UNDER CONTROL--JUST GOOD THOUGHTS!

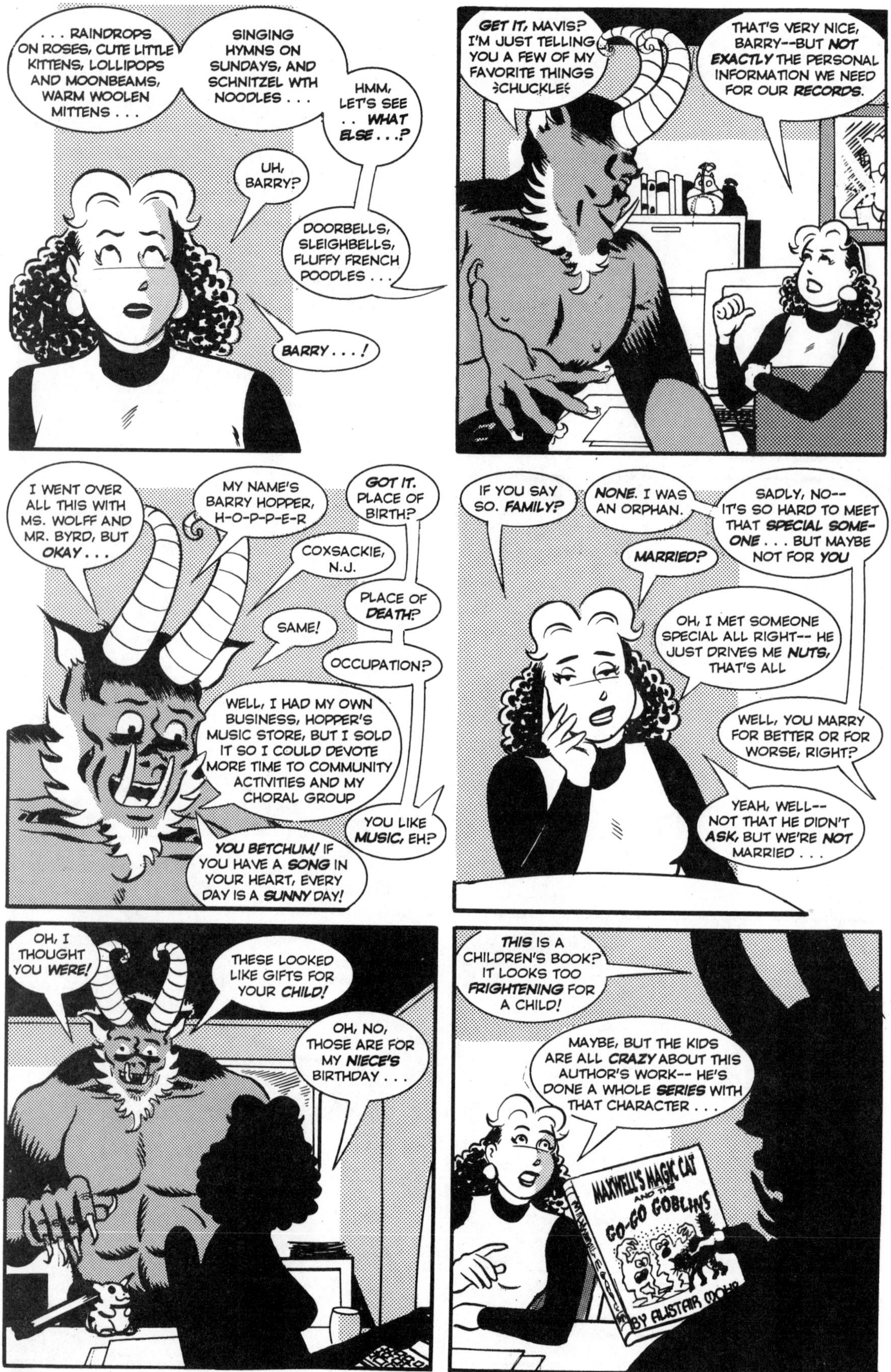

. . . RAINDROPS ON ROSES, CUTE LITTLE KITTENS, LOLLIPOPS AND MOONBEAMS, WARM WOOLEN MITTENS . . .
SINGING HYMNS ON SUNDAYS, AND SCHNITZEL WITH NOODLES . . .
HMM, LET'S SEE . . WHAT ELSE . . .?
UH, BARRY?
DOORBELLS, SLEIGHBELLS, FLUFFY FRENCH POODLES . . .
BARRY . . . !
GET IT, MAVIS? I'M JUST TELLING YOU A FEW OF MY FAVORITE THINGS ≥CHUCKLE≤
THAT'S VERY NICE, BARRY--BUT NOT EXACTLY THE PERSONAL INFORMATION WE NEED FOR OUR RECORDS.
I WENT OVER ALL THIS WITH MS. WOLFF AND MR. BYRD, BUT OKAY . . .
MY NAME'S BARRY HOPPER, H-O-P-P-E-R
GOT IT. PLACE OF BIRTH?
COXSACKIE, N.J.
PLACE OF DEATH?
SAME!
OCCUPATION?
WELL, I HAD MY OWN BUSINESS, HOPPER'S MUSIC STORE, BUT I SOLD IT SO I COULD DEVOTE MORE TIME TO COMMUNITY ACTIVITIES AND MY CHORAL GROUP
YOU LIKE MUSIC, EH?
YOU BETCHUM! IF YOU HAVE A SONG IN YOUR HEART, EVERY DAY IS A SUNNY DAY!
IF YOU SAY SO. FAMILY?
NONE. I WAS AN ORPHAN.
MARRIED?
SADLY, NO-- IT'S SO HARD TO MEET THAT SPECIAL SOME-ONE . . . BUT MAYBE NOT FOR YOU
OH, I MET SOMEONE SPECIAL ALL RIGHT-- HE JUST DRIVES ME NUTS, THAT'S ALL
WELL, YOU MARRY FOR BETTER OR FOR WORSE, RIGHT?
YEAH, WELL-- NOT THAT HE DIDN'T ASK, BUT WE'RE NOT MARRIED . . .
OH, I THOUGHT YOU WERE!
THESE LOOKED LIKE GIFTS FOR YOUR CHILD!
OH, NO, THOSE ARE FOR MY NIECE'S BIRTHDAY . . .
THIS IS A CHILDREN'S BOOK? IT LOOKS TOO FRIGHTENING FOR A CHILD!
MAYBE, BUT THE KIDS ARE ALL CRAZY ABOUT THIS AUTHOR'S WORK-- HE'S DONE A WHOLE SERIES WITH THAT CHARACTER . . .
MAXWELL'S MAGIC CAT AND THE GO-GO GOBLINS
BY ALISTAIR MOHR

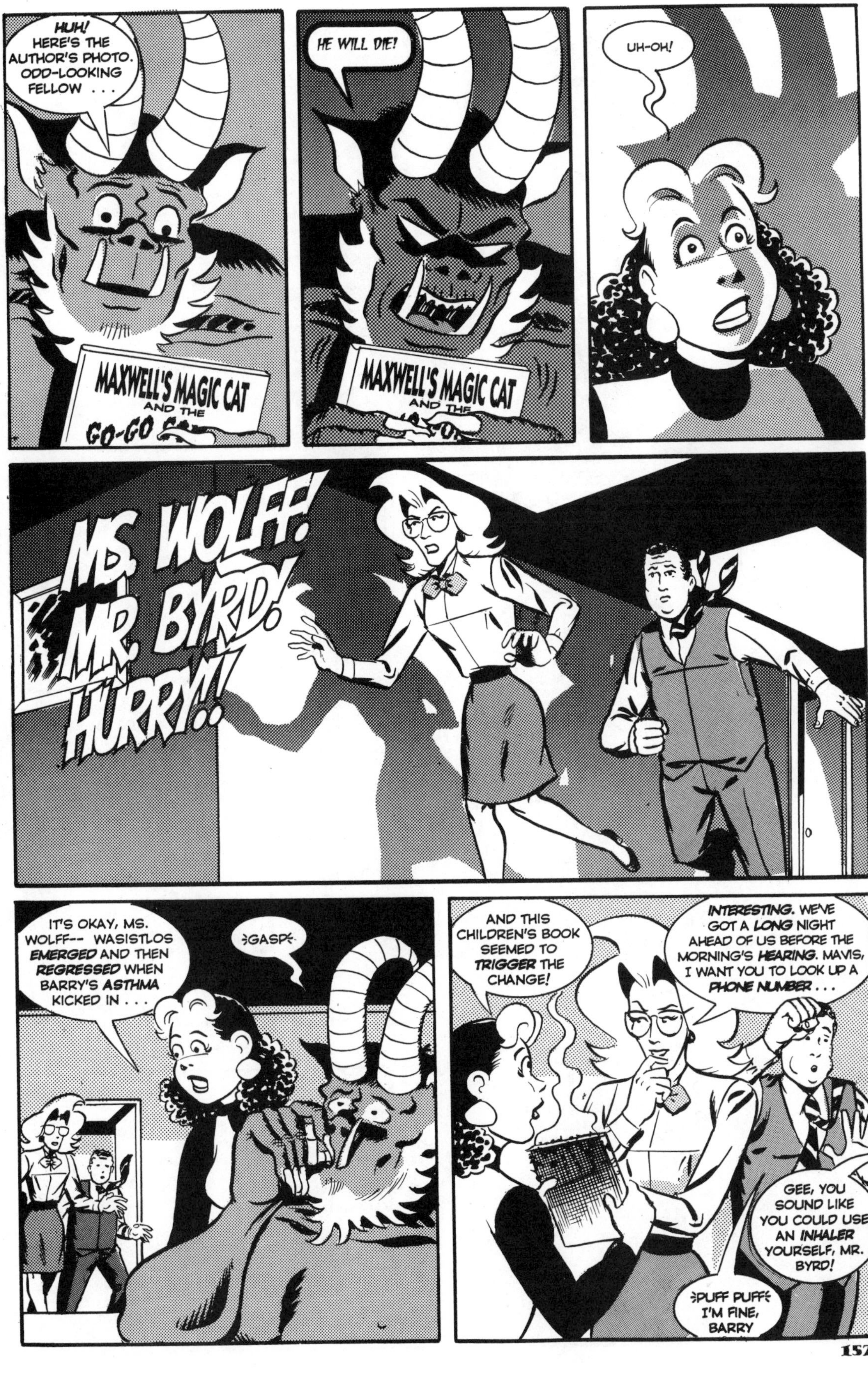
HUH! HERE'S THE AUTHOR'S PHOTO. ODD-LOOKING FELLOW . . .
MAXWELL'S MAGIC CAT AND THE GO-GO
HE WILL DIE!
MAXWELL'S MAGIC CAT AND THE
UH-OH!
MS. WOLFF! MR. BYRD! HURRY!!
IT'S OKAY, MS. WOLFF-- WASISTLOS EMERGED AND THEN REGRESSED WHEN BARRY'S ASTHMA KICKED IN . . .
GASP
AND THIS CHILDREN'S BOOK SEEMED TO TRIGGER THE CHANGE!
INTERESTING. WE'VE GOT A LONG NIGHT AHEAD OF US BEFORE THE MORNING'S HEARING. MAVIS, I WANT YOU TO LOOK UP A PHONE NUMBER . . .
GEE, YOU SOUND LIKE YOU COULD USE AN INHALER YOURSELF, MR. BYRD!
PUFF PUFF I'M FINE, BARRY

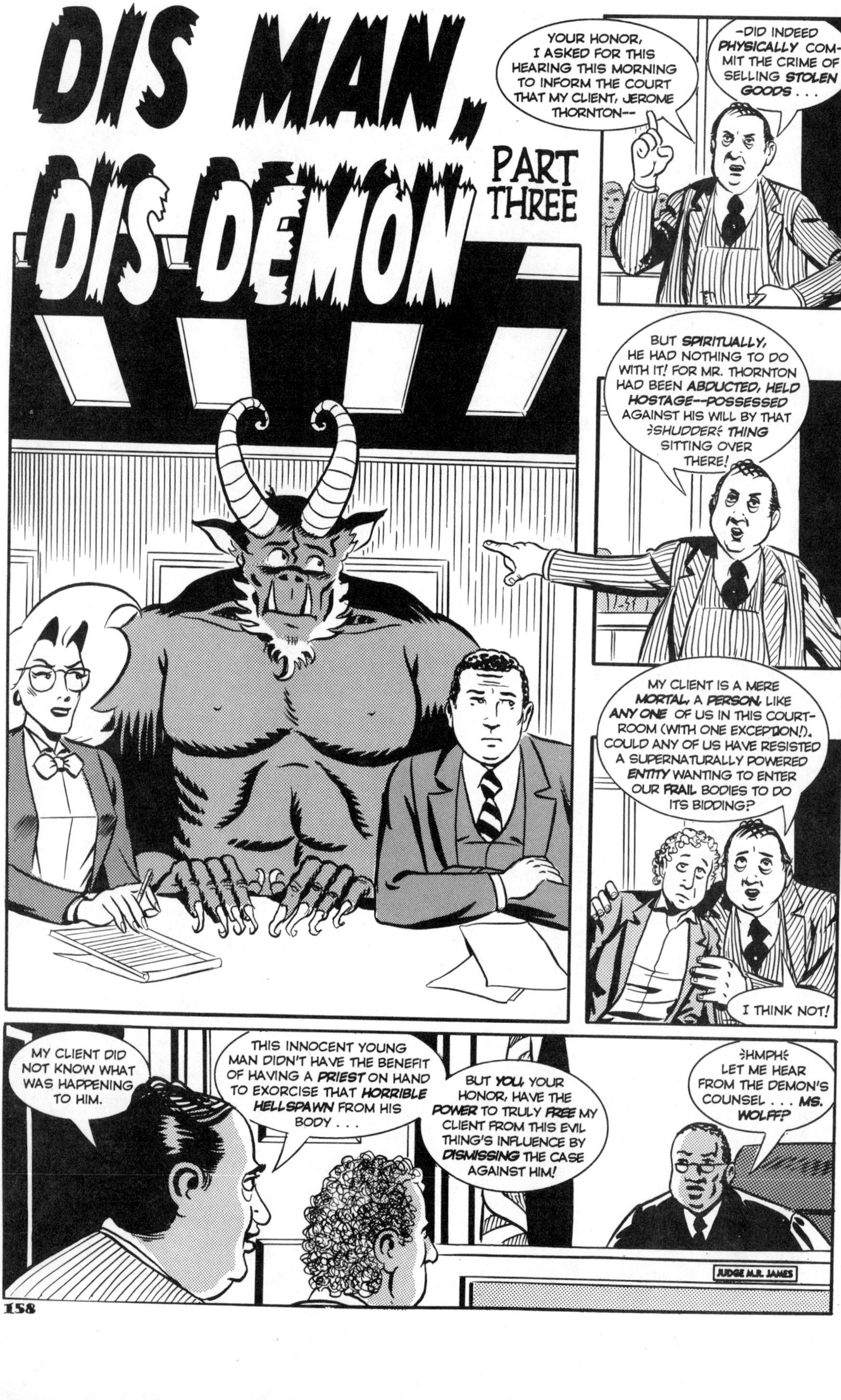
DIS MAN, DIS-DEMON
PART THREE
YOUR HONOR, I ASKED FOR THIS HEARING THIS MORNING TO INFORM THE COURT THAT MY CLIENT, JEROME THORNTON--
-DID INDEED PHYSICALLY COMMIT THE CRIME OF SELLING STOLEN GOODS . . .
BUT SPIRITUALLY, HE HAD NOTHING TO DO WITH IT! FOR MR. THORNTON HAD BEEN ABDUCTED, HELD HOSTAGE--POSSESSED AGAINST HIS WILL BY THAT ≯SHUDDER≮ THING SITTING OVER THERE!
MY CLIENT IS A MERE MORTAL, A PERSON, LIKE ANY ONE OF US IN THIS COURTROOM (WITH ONE EXCEPTION!). COULD ANY OF US HAVE RESISTED A SUPERNATURALLY POWERED ENTITY WANTING TO ENTER OUR FRAIL BODIES TO DO ITS BIDDING?
I THINK NOT!
MY CLIENT DID NOT KNOW WHAT WAS HAPPENING TO HIM.
THIS INNOCENT YOUNG MAN DIDN'T HAVE THE BENEFIT OF HAVING A PRIEST ON HAND TO EXORCISE THAT HORRIBLE HELLSPAWN FROM HIS BODY . . .
BUT YOU, YOUR HONOR, HAVE THE POWER TO TRULY FREE MY CLIENT FROM THIS EVIL THING'S INFLUENCE BY DISMISSING THE CASE AGAINST HIM!
≯HMPH≮ LET ME HEAR FROM THE DEMON'S COUNSEL . . . MS. WOLFF?
JUDGE M.R. JAMES

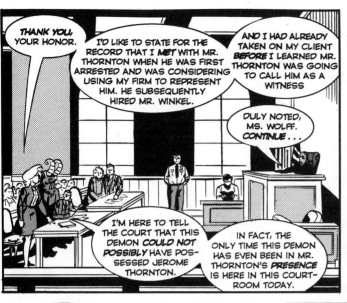

THANK YOU, YOUR HONOR. I'D LIKE TO STATE FOR THE RECORD THAT I MET WITH MR. THORNTON WHEN HE WAS FIRST ARRESTED AND WAS CONSIDERING USING MY FIRM TO REPRESENT HIM. HE SUBSEQUENTLY HIRED MR. WINKEL.

AND I HAD ALREADY TAKEN ON MY CLIENT BEFORE I LEARNED MR. THORNTON WAS GOING TO CALL HIM AS A WITNESS

DULY NOTED, MS. WOLFF. CONTINUE . . .

I'M HERE TO TELL THE COURT THAT THIS DEMON COULD NOT POSSIBLY HAVE POSSESSED JEROME THORNTON.

IN FACT, THE ONLY TIME THIS DEMON HAS EVEN BEEN IN MR. THORNTON'S PRESENCE IS HERE IN THIS COURTROOM TODAY.

ZACH! WHAT IF SHE TELLS THE COURT ABOUT MY CONVERSATION WITH HER?

THEN SHE'LL BE BETRAYING PRIVILEGED INFORMATION! THAT'S UNETHICAL--AND IF THERE'S ONE THING I CAN'T ABIDE, IT'S AN UNETHICAL LAWYER . . . !

I AM NOT HERE TO DISPUTE THAT DEMONIC POSSESSION MIGHT HAVE MOTIVATED MR. THORNTON TO COMMIT A FELONY . . .

RATHER, I SIMPLY WISH TO POINT OUT THAT THIS PARTICULAR DEMON WAS IN NO POSITION TO POSSESS ANYONE--

BECAUSE IT WAS CONJURED TO THIS REALM OF EXISTENCE AGAINST ITS WILL!

CONJURED?

CONJECTURE! WHAT EVIDENCE DOES MS. WOLFF HAVE FOR THIS SUPPOSED CONJURGATION?

IF SHE'S TAKING HER CLIENT'S WORD, LET ME REMIND THE COURT THAT DEMONS ARE NOTORIOUS FOR THEIR DECEIT AND TREACHERY . . .

WELL, MS. WOLFF?

WITH THE COURT'S PERMISSION, I'D LIKE TO CALL A WITNESS WHO CAN CLEAR MY CLIENT OF ALL INVOLVEMENT IN MR. THORNTON'S CRIMES . . .

GEE, MR. BYRD, ALL THIS COURTROOM STUFF IS REALLY MAKING MY HEAD SPIN . . .

DON'T WORRY ABOUT ANY OF THAT, BARRY-- JUST CONCENTRATE ON KEEPING WASISTLOS UNDER CONTROL WHILE ALISTAIR MOHR IS ON THE STAND . . .

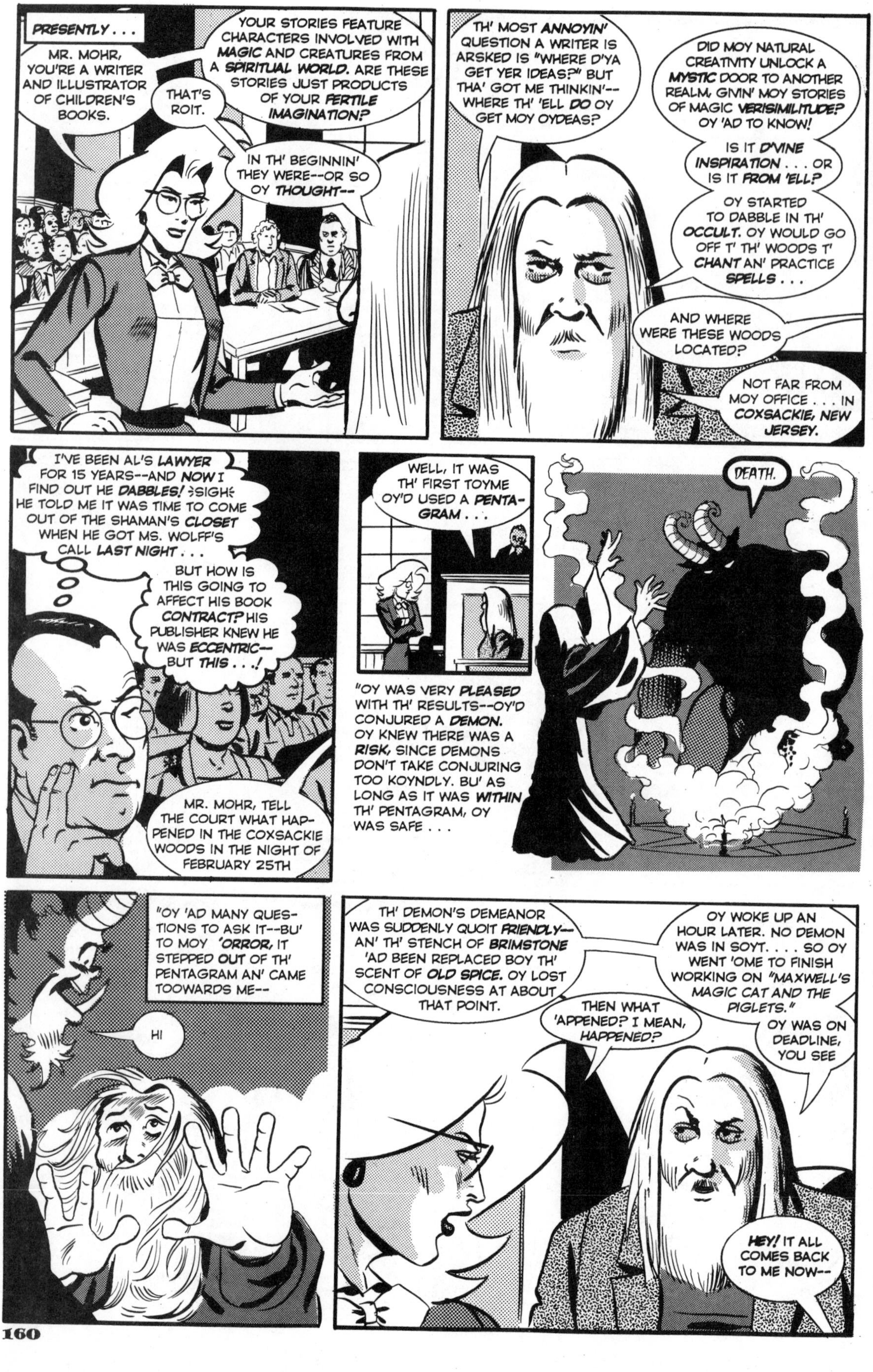
PRESENTLY . . .
MR. MOHR, YOU'RE A WRITER AND ILLUSTRATOR OF CHILDREN'S BOOKS.
THAT'S ROIT.
YOUR STORIES FEATURE CHARACTERS INVOLVED WITH MAGIC AND CREATURES FROM A SPIRITUAL WORLD. ARE THESE STORIES JUST PRODUCTS OF YOUR FERTILE IMAGINATION?
IN TH' BEGINNIN' THEY WERE--OR SO OY THOUGHT--
TH' MOST ANNOYIN' QUESTION A WRITER IS ARSKED IS "WHERE D'YA GET YER IDEAS?" BUT THA' GOT ME THINKIN'--WHERE TH' 'ELL DO OY GET MOY OYDEAS?
DID MOY NATURAL CREATIVITY UNLOCK A MYSTIC DOOR TO ANOTHER REALM, GIVIN' MOY STORIES OF MAGIC VERISIMILITUDE? OY 'AD TO KNOW!
IS IT D'VINE INSPIRATION . . . OR IS IT FROM 'ELL?
OY STARTED TO DABBLE IN TH' OCCULT. OY WOULD GO OFF T' TH' WOODS T' CHANT AN' PRACTICE SPELLS . . .
AND WHERE WERE THESE WOODS LOCATED?
NOT FAR FROM MOY OFFICE . . . IN COXSACKIE, NEW JERSEY.
I'VE BEEN AL'S LAWYER FOR 15 YEARS--AND NOW I FIND OUT HE DABBLES! SIGH HE TOLD ME IT WAS TIME TO COME OUT OF THE SHAMAN'S CLOSET WHEN HE GOT MS. WOLFF'S CALL LAST NIGHT . . .
BUT HOW IS THIS GOING TO AFFECT HIS BOOK CONTRACT? HIS PUBLISHER KNEW HE WAS ECCENTRIC--BUT THIS . . .!
MR. MOHR, TELL THE COURT WHAT HAPPENED IN THE COXSACKIE WOODS IN THE NIGHT OF FEBRUARY 25TH
WELL, IT WAS TH' FIRST TOYME OY'D USED A PENTAGRAM . . .
"OY WAS VERY PLEASED WITH TH' RESULTS--OY'D CONJURED A DEMON. OY KNEW THERE WAS A RISK, SINCE DEMONS DON'T TAKE CONJURING TOO KOYNDLY. BU' AS LONG AS IT WAS WITHIN TH' PENTAGRAM, OY WAS SAFE . . .
DEATH.
"OY 'AD MANY QUESTIONS TO ASK IT--BU' TO MOY 'ORROR, IT STEPPED OUT OF TH' PENTAGRAM AN' CAME TOOWARDS ME--
HI
TH' DEMON'S DEMEANOR WAS SUDDENLY QUOIT FRIENDLY--AN' TH' STENCH OF BRIMSTONE 'AD BEEN REPLACED BOY TH' SCENT OF OLD SPICE. OY LOST CONSCIOUSNESS AT ABOUT THAT POINT.
THEN WHAT 'APPENED? I MEAN, HAPPENED?
OY WOKE UP AN HOUR LATER. NO DEMON WAS IN SOYT. . . . SO OY WENT 'OME TO FINISH WORKING ON "MAXWELL'S MAGIC CAT AND THE PIGLETS."
OY WAS ON DEADLINE, YOU SEE
HEY! IT ALL COMES BACK TO ME NOW--

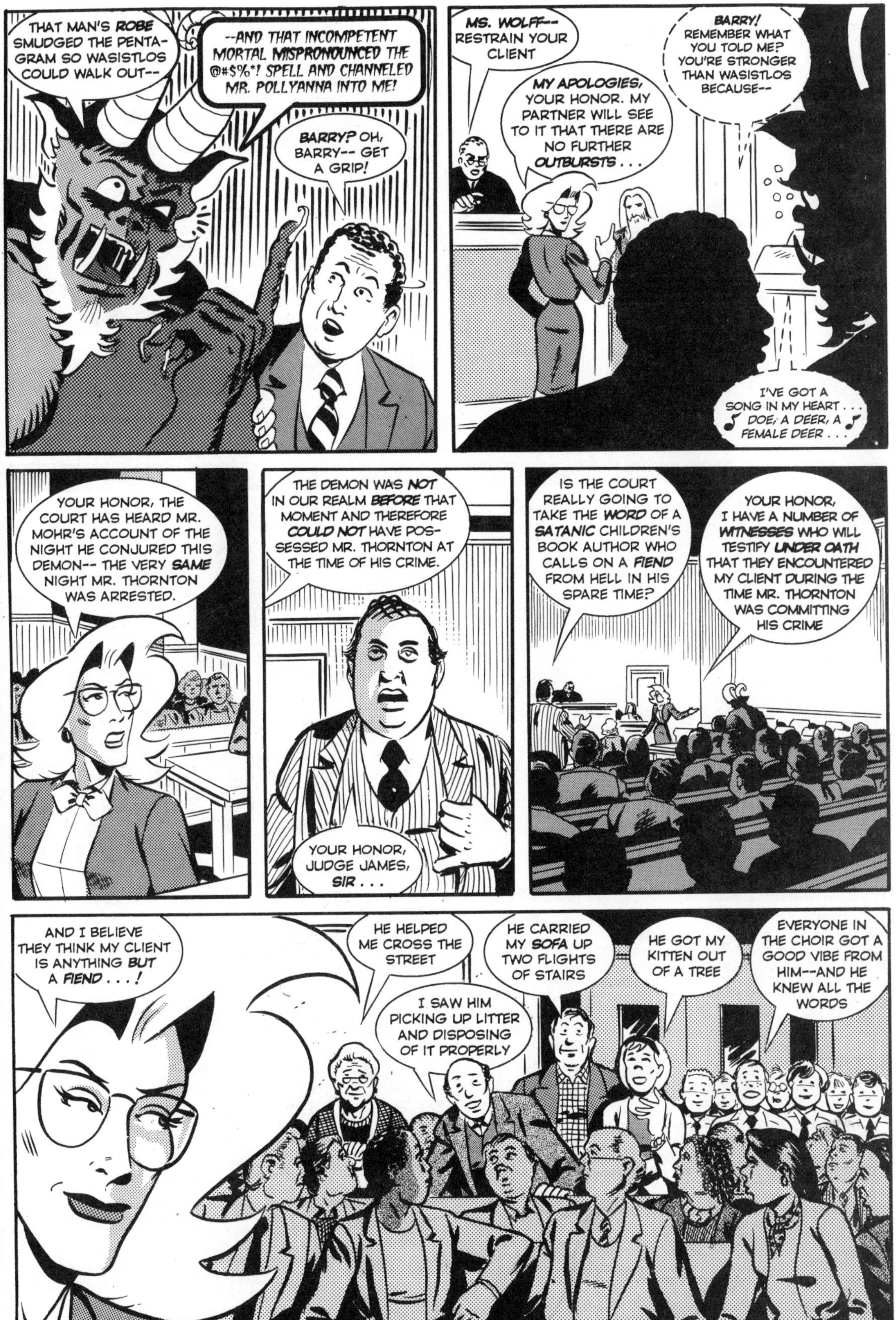
THAT MAN'S ROBE SMUDGED THE PENTAGRAM SO WASISTLOS COULD WALK OUT--
--AND THAT INCOMPETENT MORTAL MISPRONOUNCED THE @#$%*! SPELL AND CHANNELED MR. POLLYANNA INTO ME!
BARRY? OH, BARRY-- GET A GRIP!
MS. WOLFF-- RESTRAIN YOUR CLIENT
MY APOLOGIES, YOUR HONOR. MY PARTNER WILL SEE TO IT THAT THERE ARE NO FURTHER OUTBURSTS . . .
BARRY! REMEMBER WHAT YOU TOLD ME? YOU'RE STRONGER THAN WASISTLOS BECAUSE--
I'VE GOT A SONG IN MY HEART . . . DOE, A DEER, A FEMALE DEER . . .
YOUR HONOR, THE COURT HAS HEARD MR. MOHR'S ACCOUNT OF THE NIGHT HE CONJURED THIS DEMON-- THE VERY SAME NIGHT MR. THORNTON WAS ARRESTED.
THE DEMON WAS NOT IN OUR REALM BEFORE THAT MOMENT AND THEREFORE COULD NOT HAVE POSSESSED MR. THORNTON AT THE TIME OF HIS CRIME.
YOUR HONOR, JUDGE JAMES, SIR . . .
IS THE COURT REALLY GOING TO TAKE THE WORD OF A SATANIC CHILDREN'S BOOK AUTHOR WHO CALLS ON A FIEND FROM HELL IN HIS SPARE TIME?
YOUR HONOR, I HAVE A NUMBER OF WITNESSES WHO WILL TESTIFY UNDER OATH THAT THEY ENCOUNTERED MY CLIENT DURING THE TIME MR. THORNTON WAS COMMITTING HIS CRIME
AND I BELIEVE THEY THINK MY CLIENT IS ANYTHING BUT A FIEND . . . !
HE HELPED ME CROSS THE STREET
I SAW HIM PICKING UP LITTER AND DISPOSING OF IT PROPERLY
HE CARRIED MY SOFA UP TWO FLIGHTS OF STAIRS
HE GOT MY KITTEN OUT OF A TREE
EVERYONE IN THE CHOIR GOT A GOOD VIBE FROM HIM--AND HE KNEW ALL THE WORDS

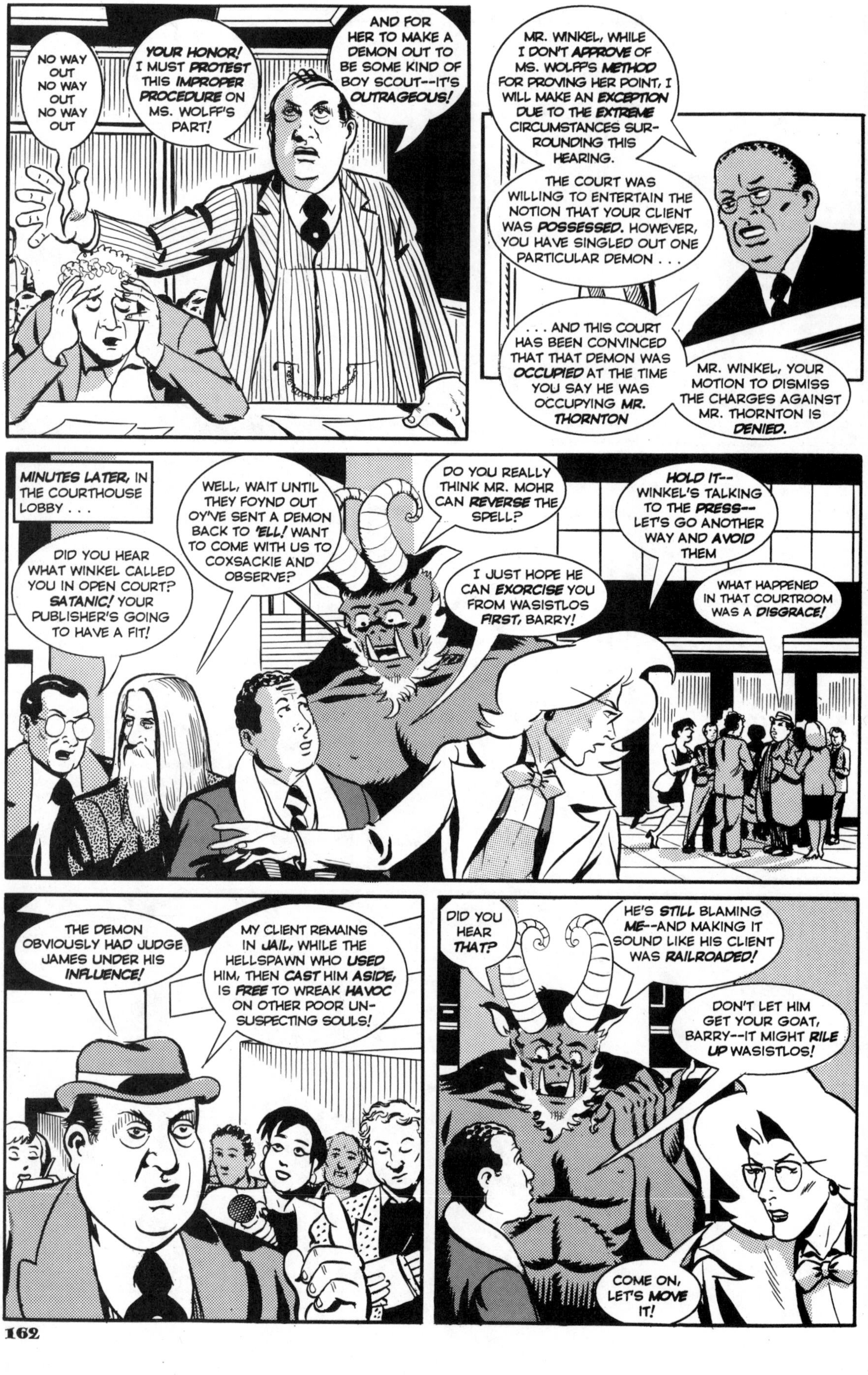
NO WAY OUT NO WAY OUT NO WAY OUT
YOUR HONOR! I MUST PROTEST THIS IMPROPER PROCEDURE ON MS. WOLFF'S PART!
AND FOR HER TO MAKE A DEMON OUT TO BE SOME KIND OF BOY SCOUT--IT'S OUTRAGEOUS!
MR. WINKEL, WHILE I DON'T APPROVE OF MS. WOLFF'S METHOD FOR PROVING HER POINT, I WILL MAKE AN EXCEPTION DUE TO THE EXTREME CIRCUMSTANCES SURROUNDING THIS HEARING.
THE COURT WAS WILLING TO ENTERTAIN THE NOTION THAT YOUR CLIENT WAS POSSESSED. HOWEVER, YOU HAVE SINGLED OUT ONE PARTICULAR DEMON . . .
. . . AND THIS COURT HAS BEEN CONVINCED THAT THAT DEMON WAS OCCUPIED AT THE TIME YOU SAY HE WAS OCCUPYING MR. THORNTON
MR. WINKEL, YOUR MOTION TO DISMISS THE CHARGES AGAINST MR. THORNTON IS DENIED.
MINUTES LATER, IN THE COURTHOUSE LOBBY . . .
DID YOU HEAR WHAT WINKEL CALLED YOU IN OPEN COURT? SATANIC! YOUR PUBLISHER'S GOING TO HAVE A FIT!
WELL, WAIT UNTIL THEY FOYND OUT OY'VE SENT A DEMON BACK TO 'ELL! WANT TO COME WITH US TO COXSACKIE AND OBSERVE?
DO YOU REALLY THINK MR. MOHR CAN REVERSE THE SPELL?
I JUST HOPE HE CAN EXORCISE YOU FROM WASISTLOS FIRST, BARRY!
HOLD IT--WINKEL'S TALKING TO THE PRESS--LET'S GO ANOTHER WAY AND AVOID THEM
WHAT HAPPENED IN THAT COURTROOM WAS A DISGRACE!
THE DEMON OBVIOUSLY HAD JUDGE JAMES UNDER HIS INFLUENCE!
MY CLIENT REMAINS IN JAIL, WHILE THE HELLSPAWN WHO USED HIM, THEN CAST HIM ASIDE, IS FREE TO WREAK HAVOC ON OTHER POOR UNSUSPECTING SOULS!
DID YOU HEAR THAT?
HE'S STILL BLAMING ME--AND MAKING IT SOUND LIKE HIS CLIENT WAS RAILROADED!
DON'T LET HIM GET YOUR GOAT, BARRY--IT MIGHT RILE UP WASISTLOS!
COME ON, LET'S MOVE IT!

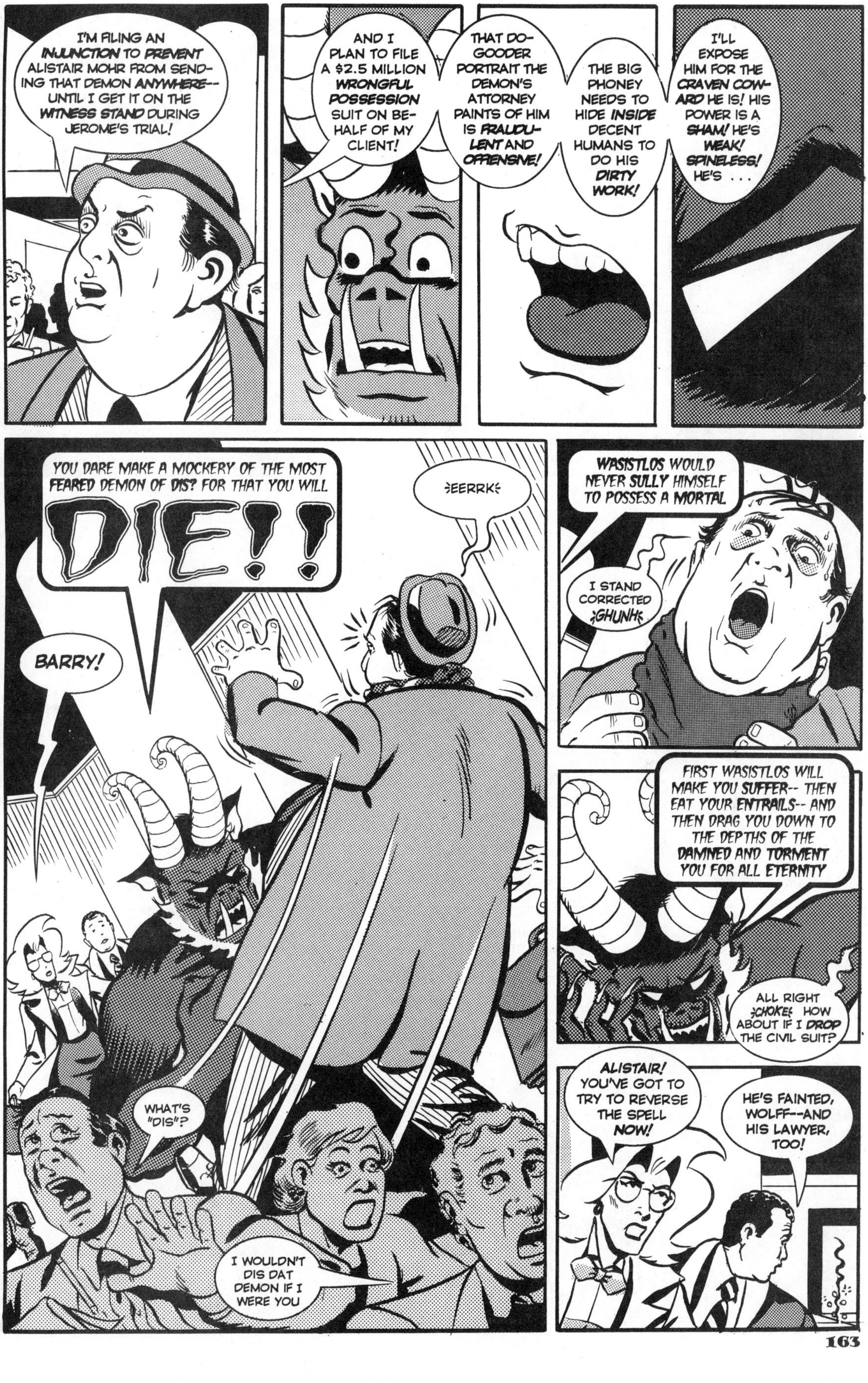
I'M FILING AN INJUNCTION TO PREVENT ALISTAIR MOHR FROM SENDING THAT DEMON ANYWHERE--UNTIL I GET IT ON THE WITNESS STAND DURING JEROME'S TRIAL!
AND I PLAN TO FILE A $2.5 MILLION WRONGFUL POSSESSION SUIT ON BEHALF OF MY CLIENT!
THAT DO-GOODER PORTRAIT THE DEMON'S ATTORNEY PAINTS OF HIM IS FRAUDULENT AND OFFENSIVE!
THE BIG PHONEY NEEDS TO HIDE INSIDE DECENT HUMANS TO DO HIS DIRTY WORK!
I'LL EXPOSE HIM FOR THE CRAVEN COWARD HE IS! HIS POWER IS A SHAM! HE'S WEAK! SPINELESS! HE'S . . .
YOU DARE MAKE A MOCKERY OF THE MOST FEARED DEMON OF DIS? FOR THAT YOU WILL DIE!!
EERRK
BARRY!
WHAT'S "DIS"?
I WOULDN'T DIS DAT DEMON IF I WERE YOU
WASISTLOS WOULD NEVER SULLY HIMSELF TO POSSESS A MORTAL
I STAND CORRECTED GHUNH
FIRST WASISTLOS WILL MAKE YOU SUFFER-- THEN EAT YOUR ENTRAILS-- AND THEN DRAG YOU DOWN TO THE DEPTHS OF THE DAMNED AND TORMENT YOU FOR ALL ETERNITY
ALL RIGHT CHOKE HOW ABOUT IF I DROP THE CIVIL SUIT?
ALISTAIR! YOU'VE GOT TO TRY TO REVERSE THE SPELL NOW!
HE'S FAINTED, WOLFF--AND HIS LAWYER, TOO!

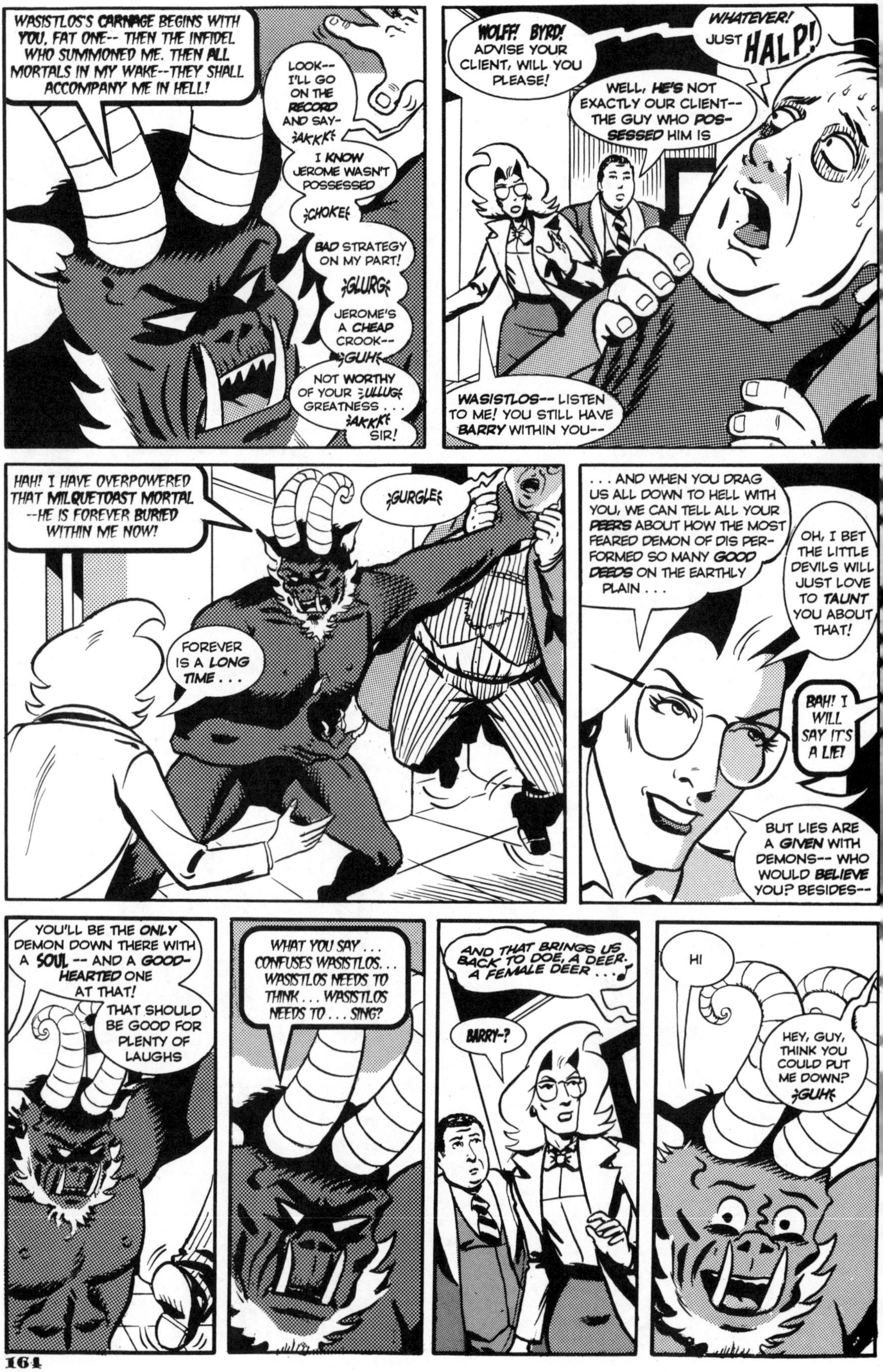
WASISTLOS'S CARNAGE BEGINS WITH YOU, FAT ONE-- THEN THE INFIDEL WHO SUMMONED ME. THEN ALL MORTALS IN MY WAKE--THEY SHALL ACCOMPANY ME IN HELL!
LOOK-- I'LL GO ON THE RECORD AND SAY- AKK
I KNOW JEROME WASN'T POSSESSED
CHOKE
BAD STRATEGY ON MY PART!
GLURG
JEROME'S A CHEAP CROOK-- GUH
NOT WORTHY OF YOUR ULLUG GREATNESS . . . AKK SIR!
WOLFF! BYRD! ADVISE YOUR CLIENT, WILL YOU PLEASE!
WHATEVER! JUST HALP!
WELL, HE'S NOT EXACTLY OUR CLIENT-- THE GUY WHO POSSESSED HIM IS
WASISTLOS-- LISTEN TO ME! YOU STILL HAVE BARRY WITHIN YOU--
HAH! I HAVE OVERPOWERED THAT MILQUETOAST MORTAL --HE IS FOREVER BURIED WITHIN ME NOW!
GURGLE
FOREVER IS A LONG TIME . . .
. . . AND WHEN YOU DRAG US ALL DOWN TO HELL WITH YOU, WE CAN TELL ALL YOUR PEERS ABOUT HOW THE MOST FEARED DEMON OF DIS PERFORMED SO MANY GOOD DEEDS ON THE EARTHLY PLAIN . . .
OH, I BET THE LITTLE DEVILS WILL JUST LOVE TO TAUNT YOU ABOUT THAT!
BAH! I WILL SAY IT'S A LIE!
BUT LIES ARE A GIVEN WITH DEMONS-- WHO WOULD BELIEVE YOU? BESIDES--
YOU'LL BE THE ONLY DEMON DOWN THERE WITH A SOUL -- AND A GOOD-HEARTED ONE AT THAT!
THAT SHOULD BE GOOD FOR PLENTY OF LAUGHS
WHAT YOU SAY . . . CONFUSES WASISTLOS . . . WASISTLOS NEEDS TO THINK . . . WASISTLOS NEEDS TO . . . SING?
AND THAT BRINGS US BACK TO DOE, A DEER. A FEMALE DEER . . .
BARRY-?
HI
HEY, GUY, THINK YOU COULD PUT ME DOWN? GUH

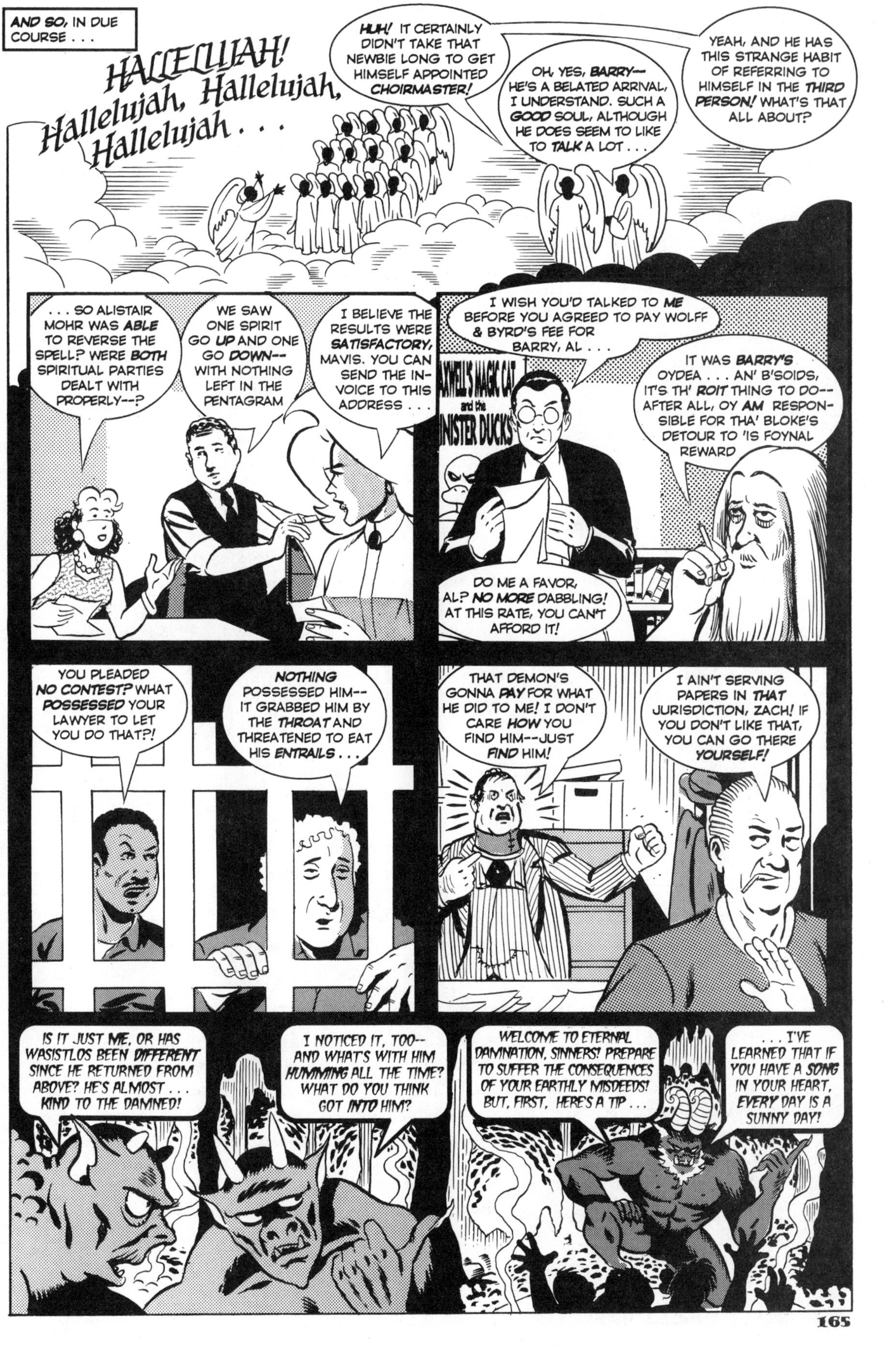
AND SO, IN DUE COURSE . . .
HALLELUJAH! Hallelujah, Hallelujah, Hallelujah . . .
HUH! IT CERTAINLY DIDN'T TAKE THAT NEWBIE LONG TO GET HIMSELF APPOINTED CHOIRMASTER!
OH, YES, BARRY-- HE'S A BELATED ARRIVAL, I UNDERSTAND. SUCH A GOOD SOUL, ALTHOUGH HE DOES SEEM TO LIKE TO TALK A LOT . . .
YEAH, AND HE HAS THIS STRANGE HABIT OF REFERRING TO HIMSELF IN THE THIRD PERSON! WHAT'S THAT ALL ABOUT?
. . . SO ALISTAIR MOHR WAS ABLE TO REVERSE THE SPELL? WERE BOTH SPIRITUAL PARTIES DEALT WITH PROPERLY--?
WE SAW ONE SPIRIT GO UP AND ONE GO DOWN-- WITH NOTHING LEFT IN THE PENTAGRAM
I BELIEVE THE RESULTS WERE SATISFACTORY, MAVIS. YOU CAN SEND THE INVOICE TO THIS ADDRESS . . .
I WISH YOU'D TALKED TO ME BEFORE YOU AGREED TO PAY WOLFF & BYRD'S FEE FOR BARRY, AL . . .
AXWELL'S MAGIC CAT and the INISTER DUCKS
IT WAS BARRY'S OYDEA . . . AN' B'SOIDS, IT'S TH' ROIT THING TO DO-- AFTER ALL, OY AM RESPONSIBLE FOR THA' BLOKE'S DETOUR TO 'IS FOYNAL REWARD
DO ME A FAVOR, AL? NO MORE DABBLING! AT THIS RATE, YOU CAN'T AFFORD IT!
YOU PLEADED NO CONTEST? WHAT POSSESSED YOUR LAWYER TO LET YOU DO THAT?!
NOTHING POSSESSED HIM-- IT GRABBED HIM BY THE THROAT AND THREATENED TO EAT HIS ENTRAILS . . .
THAT DEMON'S GONNA PAY FOR WHAT HE DID TO ME! I DON'T CARE HOW YOU FIND HIM--JUST FIND HIM!
I AIN'T SERVING PAPERS IN THAT JURISDICTION, ZACH! IF YOU DON'T LIKE THAT, YOU CAN GO THERE YOURSELF!
IS IT JUST ME, OR HAS WASISTLOS BEEN DIFFERENT SINCE HE RETURNED FROM ABOVE? HE'S ALMOST . . . KIND TO THE DAMNED!
I NOTICED IT, TOO-- AND WHAT'S WITH HIM HUMMING ALL THE TIME? WHAT DO YOU THINK GOT INTO HIM?
WELCOME TO ETERNAL DAMNATION, SINNERS! PREPARE TO SUFFER THE CONSEQUENCES OF YOUR EARTHLY MISDEEDS! BUT, FIRST, HERE'S A TIP . . .
. . . I'VE LEARNED THAT IF YOU HAVE A SONG IN YOUR HEART, EVERY DAY IS A SUNNY DAY!

About the Author

Batton Lash was born and raised in Brooklyn, New York, where he attended James Madison High School. He went on to study cartooning and graphic arts at the School of Visual Arts in Manhattan, where his instructors included the legendary cartoonists Will Eisner and Harvey Kurtzman.

After graduating he took on various art-related jobs, including doing copywriting for an ad agency and serving as comic book artist Howard Chaykin's first assistant. As a freelance illustrator, Lash did drawings for *Garbage* magazine, a children's workbook, the book *Rock 'n' Roll Confidential,* the Murder to Go participatory theater group, a reconstructive surgery firm, and other projects.

In 1979 Brooklyn Paper Publications asked him to create a comic strip. Lash came up with "Wolff & Byrd, Counselors of the Macabre," which ran in *The Brooklyn Paper* until 1996 and in *The National Law Journal* from 1983 to 1997. He also did editorial cartoons for *The Brooklyn Paper* off and on for a 12-year period, did courtroom graphics for two cases, and prepared charts for *The New York Daily News* advertising department for sales meetings and in-house presentations.

In the 1980s and early 1990s Lash drew W&B stories for such publications as TSR's *Polyhedron, American Fantasy,* and *Monster Scene.* Original Wolff & Byrd stories have also appeared in a number of comic books and anthologies, including *Satan's Six, Mr. Monster, Munden's Bar, Frankie's Frightmare,, Crack-a-Boom, The Big Bigfoot Book,* and *Murder By Crowquill.*

Lash's non-W&B work includes art for Hamilton Comics' short-lived horror line (*Grave Tales, Dread of Night,* etc.) and for *The Big Book of Death, The Big Book of Weirdos, The Big Book of Urban Legends,* and *The Big Book of Thugs* for Paradox Press. He wrote the notorious *Archie Meets The Punisher,* the 1994 crossover between Archie Comics and Marvel Comics, as well as a 4-part Archie story, "The House of Riverdale," in the fall of 1995. Most recently, he wrote a story for the annual *Bart Simpson's Treehouse of Horror* from Bongo Comics, and he drew the 1998 Foodmaker Corp. (Jack in the Box) Annual Report as a graphic story.

Since May 1994, Wolff & Byrd have held court in their own bimonthly comic book, now titled *Supernatural Law,* from Exhibit A Press, which Lash established with his wife, Jackie Estrada. Exhibit A has published four other collections of the comic book issues and two collections of the weekly comic strips, as well as two specials featuring Mavis, W&B's intrepid secretary. The comic book is currently under option at Universal, where it is being developed as a major live-action film.

Exhibit A Press co-publisher and editor **Jackie Estrada** wears many other hats, including convention organizer, book editor, and administrator of the Will Eisner Comic Industry Awards.

A San Diego resident since the 1950s, Jackie got involved in helping to put on the San Diego Comic-Con (now called Comic-Con International: San Diego) in the mid-1970s. In addition to having edited ten of the Comic-Con's souvenir program books, she helped start the annual blood drive, created (and was the first coordinator of) artists' alley at the Comic-Con, and handled guest relations. She has been administrator of the Eisner Awards (the "Oscars" of the comics industry) since 1990, and she chairs the Con's guest and awards committees. As part of her commitment to the comics artform, she also served five years as president of Friends of Lulu, a national nonprofit organization devoted to getting more women and girls involved in comics.

As a professional editor for over 30 years, Jackie has edited hundreds of books. Most recently she edited *Comics: Between the Panels,* a lavish four-color coffeetable book from Dark Horse Comics. The book features more than 100 of her photos, taken of various comics professionals over the past 20-plus years. Jackie was also one of the founders of the San Diego Professional Editors' Network (SD/PEN) and has taught editing at the University of California, San Diego.

With husband Batton Lash, Jackie co-founded Exhibit A Press in 1994. Jackie edits all of the company's comics and books, does the principal lettering for the comic book, and handles the marketing and public relations.

Want More?

If you enjoyed these cases and would like to read more Wolff & Byrd (and Mavis!) stories, you've got lots to choose from! Exhibit A Press has published four trade paperback *Case Files* collecting the first 16 issues of *Wolff & Byrd, Counselors of the Macabre,* leading up to the issues collected in this volume. Exhibit A also continues to publish the regular *Supernatural Law* comic book, as well as special *Mavis* issues.

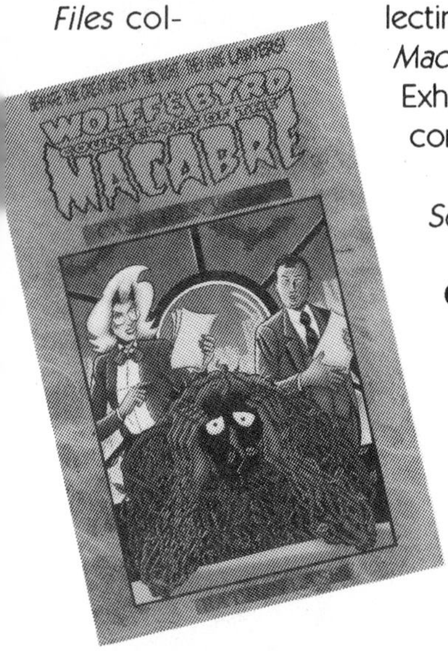
WOLFF & BYRD
MACABRE

Some highlights of the collections:

Case Files, vol. I:
Wolff & Byrd counsel a married couple who have wished unwisely on the monkey's paw; defend Sodd, the Thing Called It; help people whose house becomes haunted whenever there's a full moon; advise zombies who want to go on strike at the voodoo doll factory; deal with a client who has learned to defy the laws of gravity; and grapple with issues of free speech when it comes to horror shows on TV. 96 pages, $9.95

Case Files, vol. II:
Clients include a supermodel (Dawn DeVine) under the influence of a svengali-like agency owner; the owner of a freak show who claims to have the original Dracula and Frankenstein's monster on display; and a mobster haunted by an obsequious ghost. Plus: the origin of Sodd, the Thing Called It. 96 pages, $9.95

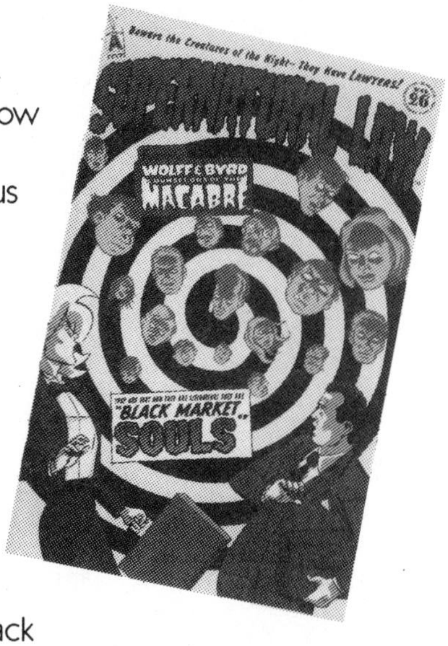
Beware the Creatures of the Night— They Have Lawyers!
WOLFF & BYRD
MACABRE
BLACK MARKET
SOULS

Case Files, vol. III:
All of these classic issues are out of print. In issue 9, "The * Files," two FBI agents investigate the alien abduction of the daughter of Wolff & Byrd's client. Issue 10 features "I'm Carrying Satan's Baby," the critically lauded story of a small-town girl's dilemma. Rounding out the collection are two stories from issue 11 ("I Married a Quivering Blob of Jelly" and "The Man with His Own Personal Laugh Track") and the Jack Benny–inspired story from issue 12: "Personal Injuries and Guardian Angels." 96 pages, $9.95

Case Files, vol. IV:
In unlucky issue 13, longtime client Sodd, The Thing Called It, finally goes to trial, with disastrous results. The whole "Soddyssey" wraps up in issue 16. In between, Wolff & Byrd encounter vampires and mysterious horror writer Ayn Wrice in her New Orleans stomping grounds (issue 14), and zombies, a loup garou, and statues that come to life (issue 15). 96 pages, $10.95

All these books are available from **Exhibit A Press,** 4657 Cajon Way, San Diego, CA 92115 (if ordering by mail, include $2 per book for postage and handling) and online from **Amazon.com**. For a full catalogue of Wolff & Byrd/Supernatural Law books and comics, check out **www.exhibitapress.com.**

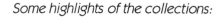